The Borrible Trilogy

Michael de Larrabeiti was brought up in Battersea, one of five children, and educated at Clapham Central Secondary School. His mother lived most of her life in the Lavender Hill area; his father was a disappearing Basque from Bilbao.

After leaving school at sixteen, he worked at many things, but mainly on camera in documentary films and as a travel guide in France and Morocco. In 1959 he fell in with a group of Provençal shepherds and went with them on the transhumance, herding three thousand sheep from their winter pasture to summer pasture in the French Alps. He then taught English in Casablanca, and in 1961 was the photographer on Oxford University's Marco Polo Expedition, travelling four months overland on a motorcycle to Afghanistan and India. He later read French and English at Trinity College Dublin, won a scholarship to the École Normale Supérieure in Paris, and began a DPhil at Oxford which he later abandoned to take up full-time writing.

The author has three grown-up daughters and lives with his wife in Oxfordshire. His other published works include *The Redwater Raid*, *A Rose Beyond the Thames*, *The Bunce*, *Igamor*, *The Provençal Tales*, *The Hollywood Takes* and *The Journal of a Sad Hermaphrodite*. He is also a regular contributor to the *Sunday Times* travel section.

'The adventures of *The Hobbit* and the rabbits of *Watership Down* are more than once called to mind . . . and de Larrabeiti has brought something of these mythologies to the street markets and the back-alleys of South London and the thronged waterways of the Thames itself'
The Times

'A strong and vivid fantasy, much recommended'
Observer

'With considerable ingenuity and finesse, de Larrabeiti has projected a grim, violent futureworld . . . he presents an alien culture with its own folkways, legends and taboos . . . *The Borribles* won't win friends among the starry-eyed or squeamish all the same they are the offspring of a singular imagination'
New York Times

'It's stuff as strong as Fagin's underworld. Dickens would have approved of this book'
Evening Standard

'May be regarded as a moral satire on the consequences of violence and cupidity or a cynical recognition of the times in which we live. Either way this *Clockwork Orange* projects a gripping story through slam-bang action'
Los Angeles Times

'A funny, moving, poetic fantasy . . . Not to be missed'
Time Out

'It is a great fantasy, and honestly one of the best books I have read this year'
Daily Mirror

'An exciting adventure with a sour twist . . . a well-written story with very subtle overtones'
Times Literary Supplement

'No one can deny that de Larrabeiti has written a modern epic. It's a brilliant invention, and no more horror-filled than, say, *Treasure Island*, *King Lear* or other great works'
Publishers Weekly

'Battersea's answer to *Watership Down*, *The Lord of the Rings* and the *Guns of Navarone* . . . It is a tale of low cunning and dubious morality . . . here is an epic with an eyeful of smut – what the Trojan Wars were really like. Try the *Borribles*, warts and all, before they become a legend'
Times Educational Supplement

MICHAEL de LARRABEITI

The Borrible Trilogy

TOR

The Borribles first published 1976 by The Bodley Head Ltd
and published by Pan Books in 1983
The Borribles Go for Broke first published 1981 by The Bodley Head Ltd
and published by Pan Books in 1984
The Borribles: Across the Dark Metropolis first published 1986 by Pan Books

First published as a combined edition 2002 by Macmillan

This edition published 2013 by Tor
an imprint of Pan Macmillan, a division of Macmillan Publishers Limited
Pan Macmillan, 20 New Wharf Road, London N1 9RR
Basingstoke and Oxford
Associated companies throughout the world
www.panmacmillan.com
www.toruk.com

ISBN 978-1-4472-5179-8

A CIP catalogue record for this book is available from
the British Library.

Typeset by SetSystems Ltd, SaffronWalden, Essex

For Celia, Aimée, Phoebe and Rose

Contents

BOOK ONE

The Borribles

I

The swirling rain-clouds rushed on revealing the bright moon, and the two Borribles dodged behind the bushes and kept as quiet as they could. There was danger in the air and they could feel it. It would pay to be cautious.

'Strewth,' said Knocker, the chief lookout of the Battersea tribe, 'what a bloody cheek, coming down here without so much as a by-your-leave.'

Lightfinger, Knocker's companion, agreed. 'Diabolical liberty I call it . . . nasty bit of work, covered in fur like nylon hearthrugs . . . snouts like traffic cones . . . like rats, aren't they?'

'There's a big one, just getting into the motor, he's shouting at the others, he's the boss all right. Tough-looking, do you see?'

'Yeah,' answered Lightfinger, 'they do what they're told, don't they? Look at them move.'

Presently the two Borribles saw the large car drive away in the moonlight, passing along the shining tarmac which led between the trees to the limits of Battersea Park. The car stopped for an instant at the gates and then turned left into Albert Bridge Road and disappeared on its way southwards into the quiet streets of the outer London suburbs.

The two Borribles stood up and looked around. They weren't too happy in parks, being much more at ease in crowded streets and broken-down houses. It was only occasionally that the Borrible lookouts checked on the green spaces, just to see they were still there and that everything was as it should be.

When Knocker was sure they were alone he said, 'We'd better see what they were up to over there. Something's going on and I don't like it.'

All at once the patch of ground at his feet began to tremble and clumps of grass began to pop up and away from their roots. There was a noise too, a scraping and a scrabbling, and a muffled voice swore and mumbled to itself. The carpet of grass rose and fell violently until a squat protruberance established itself between turf and top soil. The bump hesitated, as if it didn't know whether to continue upwards or retreat downwards. It grunted, swore again and, as if undecided, took off on a horizontal course, forcing the turf up as it wriggled along.

At the first sign of trouble Knocker and Lightfinger had taken refuge behind a bush but as the bump moved away they came from cover and followed it.

'It's got to be . . .' said Knocker. 'It can't be anything else, and down here in Battersea, it's bad, double bad.'

The mound stopped and shook and struggled and became bigger, and as it grew more clods of grass fell from it. 'Watch yourself,' whispered Knocker. 'It's coming out. Get ready to jump it.'

Lightfinger and Knocker crouched, their minds racing. The turf rose higher and higher till it was as tall as the Borribles themselves, then it burst and the grass fell away like a discarded overcoat and revealed a dark and sinister shape of about their own size.

It looked like a giant rat, a huge mole or a deformed rabbit, but it was none of these for it stood on its hind legs and had a long snout and beady red eyes, like the things that had gone away in the car.

Knocker gave a shrill whistle and at the signal both he and Lightfinger leapt forward. Knocker got an armlock round the thing's head and pulled it to the ground while Lightfinger fell onto the hairy legs and bent one over the other in a special hold that could dislocate a knee. The thing shouted so loudly that it would have woken the neighbourhood if there'd been one in Battersea Park. Knocker squeezed it round the neck and whispered, 'Shuddup, you great fool, else I'll smother yer.' The creature shuddupped.

Knocker levered the prisoner into a sitting position and got behind it so he could tie its arms back with a length of rope he took from his waist. Lightfinger moved so that he was sitting on the thing's legs, looking into the eyes, which were like marbles rolling around at the wide end of the snout.

'All right,' said Knocker when he was ready, 'give it a duffing.'

Lightfinger grabbed the beast by the scruff of its fur and pulled its snout forward. 'Name?' he asked gruffly.

The snout moved a little and they heard a voice say in a distinguished tone, 'Timbucktoo.'

'Tim who?' asked Lightfinger again, shaking the snout good and hard.

'Timbucktoo.'

'And where are you from, you moth-eaten overcoat?' asked Knocker, in spite of the fact that he knew the answer.

Timbucktoo shook himself free of the two Borribles and, though his hands were bound, he got to his feet and glared haughtily down his snout, his red eyes blazing.

'Why, I'm fwom Wumbledom of course, you dirty little tykes. You'd better welease me before you get into sewious twouble.'

'I knew it,' said Knocker turning to Lightfinger with excitement. 'A Rumble from Rumbledom. Ain't it strange as how they can't pronounce their *r*s?'

'So that's a Rumble,' said Lightfinger with interest. 'I've often wondered what they looked like – bloody ugly.'

'It's the first time I've been this close to one,' said Knocker, 'but you can't mistake them – nasty.'

'You wevolting little stweet-awabs,' the Rumble had lost his temper, 'how dare you tweat me in this fashion?'

''Cos you're on our manor, that's how, you twat,' said Knocker angrily. 'I suppose you didn't even know.'

'I only know what you are,' said Timbucktoo, 'and what I am and that I'll go where I like and do what I like without having to ask the permission of gwubby little ignawamuses like you. Untie me, Bowwible, and I'll forget about this incident.'

'He's a real pain,' said Lightfinger. 'Let's throw him in the river.'

The moon was clear of clouds again and glinted on the nearby Thames. In spite of himself the Rumble shivered. 'That will do you no good. I can swim, you know, like an otter.'

'So you should,' said Knocker, 'you look like one.' And he cuffed the Rumble once more and told him to hold his tongue.

Knocker thought deeply, then he said, 'I s'pose the river's the best idea for getting him off our manor, but maybe we ought to take him back and find out more about him, what his mob are up to. I don't like the look of it; suspicious this is, Rumbles down here in Battersea, it's wrong. We ought to give Spiff a chance to give this thing the once over.'

'You're right,' said Lightfinger, and they hauled the Rumble to its feet and pushed it towards the park gates.

When they reached the sleeping streets they kept to the dark shadows between the lamp posts and marched rapidly in the direction of Battersea High Street.

*

Borribles are generally skinny and have pointed ears which give them a slightly satanic appearance. They are pretty tough-looking and always scruffy, with their arses hanging out of their trousers. Apart from that they look just like normal children, although legions of them have been Borribles for more than a lifetime – as long as a Borrible remains at liberty he or she will never age.

Most of them have sharp faces with eyes that are burning-bright, noticing everything and missing nothing. They are proud of their quickness of wit. In fact it is impossible to be dull and a Borrible because a Borrible is bright by definition. Not that they know lots of useless facts; it's just that their minds work well and they tend to dislike anyone who is a bit slow.

The only people likely to get close to Borribles are ordinary children, because Borribles mix with them to escape detection by 'the authorities' who are always trying to catch them. Any child may have sat next to a Borrible or even talked to one and never noticed the ears for the simple reason that Borribles wear hats, woollen ones, pulled down over their heads, and they sometimes grow their hair long, hanging to their shoulders.

Normal kids are turned into Borribles very slowly, almost without being aware of it; but one day they wake up and there it is. It doesn't matter where they come from as long as they've had what is called a bad start. A child disappears and the word goes round that he was 'unmanageable'; the chances are he's off managing by himself. Sometimes it's given out that a kid down the street has been put into care: the truth is that he's been Borribled and is caring for himself someplace.

One day a shout might be heard in a supermarket and a kid with the goods on him is hoisted out by a store detective. If that kid gets away he'll become a Borrible and make sure he isn't caught again. Being caught is the end of the free life for a Borrible: once in custody his ears are clipped by the police surgeon and he begins to grow into a malevolent and adventureless adulthood, like any ordinary child.

So Borribles are outcasts, but unlike most outcasts they enjoy themselves and wouldn't be anything else. They delight in feeling independent and it is this feeling that is most important to them. Consequently they have no real leaders, though someone may rise into prominence from time to time, but on the whole they manage without authority and they get on well enough together, though like everybody, they quarrel.

They don't get on with adults at all, or anyone who isn't Borrible, and they see no reason why they should. Nobody has ever tried to get on with them, quite the contrary. They are ignored and that suits them down to the ground because that way they can do what they want to do in their own quiet and crafty way.

Knocker and Lightfinger had been on night patrol in Battersea Park when they'd stumbled across the Rumbles and the discovery had made them uneasy. Borribles like to make sure that no other Borrible tribe is encroaching on their territory, that's bad enough. They live in fear of being driven away from their markets and houses, of seeing their independence destroyed; that is why scouting round the frontiers of their borough is a regular duty.

Unearthing a Rumble was a calamity. They are the real enemies of the Borribles and the Borribles hate them for their riches, their power, their haughtiness and their possessions. If the Rumbles were coming all the way down from Rumbledom to colonize the Park, what price Battersea High Street?

*

Knocker and Lightfinger harried Timbucktoo along in front of them. They went through Battersea Church Road, by St Mary's down by the river, and then into the High Street. They saw no one and no one saw them, it being well into the early hours of the morning. They were making for an empty house standing opposite the end of Trott Street. It was tall and wide and the bottom windows were boarded up and a sheet of corrugated iron covered the main doorway. The facade of the building was painted over in grey, and in black letters was written, 'Bunham's Patent Locks Ltd. Locksmiths to the trade.'

It was a typical Borrible hideaway, derelict and decaying, and Knocker and Lightfinger lived there. Borribles live where they can in the streets of the big cities, but they like these abandoned houses best of all.

The two Borribles halted on the pavement and glanced up and down the street. Nobody. They opened a gate in the railings and Knocker pushed Timbucktoo down some stone steps that led to a basement. The two lookouts followed, opened a door and dragged the Rumble into the house by the neck. Once the door was closed Knocker switched on the light.

The Borribles had entered a large room furnished with orange boxes for use as chairs and tables. Two doors opened from it; one into an underground larder, which served as a storeroom, the other to some stairs which led to the rest of the house. The bay window was covered with scraps of old blanket to prevent light shining into the street and alerting the police that someone was squatting in a dwelling that was supposed to be empty.

'What we gonna do with him, now we've got him here?' wondered Lightfinger, and he pushed Timbucktoo down into a seat.

'Yes,' said the Rumble, looking up, his eyes glinting crimson, 'you won't get away with this you know, it's iwwesponsible. You Bowwibles must be insane. I'll see you get your ears clipped.'

'Clip me ears, will yer?' said Knocker tight-lipped, and he went into the store cupboard. A second later he was out again, carrying a roll of sticky tape. He went over to the Rumble, grasped its head and wound the tape round and round the animal's snout so that it could no longer speak.

He stood back to admire his work. Lightfinger sat and cupped his face in his hands and rested his elbows on his knees.

'There,' said Knocker, 'that's the way to deal with a talking mattress.'

'I'm glad all animals can't speak,' said Lightfinger. 'We'd have meningitis within the week, or run out of sticky tape.'

'I'll go and get Spiff,' said Knocker. He ran up to the ground floor of the house and tapped on the door of a large room that overlooked the back garden, a back garden that Knocker knew was a wilderness of weeds; a dangerous dump of rusting oil drums and broken bicycles.

The door opened a crack and another Borrible appeared. He was perhaps an inch taller than Knocker and his ears were very pointed. He was dressed in a bright orange dressing gown made from new warm towelling. His carpet slippers were comfortable.

'Who are you? Ah, Knocker, what do you want then?'

'Sorry to wake you, Spiff,' said Knocker, 'but me and Lightfinger found something in the park and think you ought to have a look at it. It's down in the basement.'

'Oh Lor',' groaned Spiff, 'can't it wait till morning? You haven't got the law on your trail, have you?'

'No,' said Knocker, 'it's nothing like that. What we've got is worse. It's a Rumble! There was a whole lot of them in a posh car and we caught this one tunnelling. Cheek, ain't it, coming down here without a by-yer-leave and digging?'

Spiff had become more and more intent on what Knocker had been saying until finally he seemed quite beside himself.

'A bloody Rumble, in the park? You get back downstairs, me lad, and I'll come right away. I'll put me hat on.'

He closed the door and Knocker darted back down the uncarpeted stairs. He understood Spiff's caution; no Borrible ever left his room without putting on a woollen hat to cover the tops of his ears. It wasn't that they were ashamed of them, quite the contrary, but they liked to be prepared for an emergency. Any unforeseen circumstance could force them into the streets and it wouldn't do to be spotted as a Borrible.

'He's coming,' said Knocker as soon as he re-entered the room. 'He's a good bloke, you know . . . short-tempered sometimes, but they don't come any craftier than Spiff.'

'You can't get anything past him and that's a fact,' said Lightfinger. 'They say he's pulled more strokes than the Oxford and Cambridge boat race put together. And they say that he won dozens of names in fights with the Rumbles, and we're only s'posed to have one. Nobody knows how many names, nobody . . . He's a mystery, but one thing's for sure, he hates Rumbles.'

'Yeah, I know,' said Knocker. 'There's millions of stories about his names and some of them not very Borrible either, but I'd rather have him for me than against me.' He sat down and looked at Timbucktoo and thought about names and the gaining of them, something that occupied his every waking hour.

A Borrible name has to be earned because that is the only way a Borrible can get one. He has to have an adventure of some sort, and the name comes out of that adventure – stealing, burglary, a journey or a trick played on someone. That was the rule and Knocker was against it; it made it difficult, if not impossible, for a Borrible to join an adventure once he was in possession of a name. The first chance was always given to those who were nameless and this infuriated Knocker for he had a secret ambition to collect more names and have more adventures than any other Borrible alive.

A noise on the stairs disturbed Knocker's reflections. He stood up and at the same moment Spiff flung open the door and strode theatrically into the room. His head was adorned with a magnificent hat of scarlet wool and he clutched the orange dressing gown tightly to his chest. Spiff had the clear face of a twelve-year-old child but his eyes were dark with wisdom: the wisdom, so it was rumoured, of a hundred years of existence. His nose was prominent; the kind of nose that smelt out trickery with ease.

He stopped short as soon as he saw the Rumble and he pushed his breath out over his teeth and made a whisper of a whistle.

'At last,' he said, like he was praying, 'at last. It's been a long while since I had my hands on one of these stinking rodents.' He turned and beamed at Knocker and Lightfinger. 'You lads have done marvellous, you've captured one alive and well, though he won't be for long, the little basket. Found him in the park, eh? With hundreds of others, digging holes! That's how it starts. Down here on our manor, taking it all for granted, think they're the lords of creation, don't they? Go anywhere, do what they like, we don't count.' He prodded and screwed the Rumble with a rigid index finger as he spoke. He turned to Knocker. 'You know what this is?'

'A Rumble.'

'Yeah, a Rumble.' Spiff was bitter. 'No better than you or me for all their la-di-da manners. Years of them I've seen, sneerin' at us down their hoity-toity snouts . . . lords of creation, moving in on our space whenever they think they will.'

Knocker and Lightfinger looked at each other. They had never seen Spiff so angry.

'Oh, come on, Spiff,' said Lightfinger, 'it can't be that bad; the Rumbles have never done me any harm.'

Spiff jumped a foot from the floor. 'You don't know you're born. You know nothing about the struggles and fights we had to win free. It weren't easy to stay alive even.'

'Oh, I know about it all right but that was your time, not mine.' And Lightfinger leaned against the wall, crossed his ankles and shoved his hands into his pockets.

'Don't care was made to care,' said Spiff sententiously, 'and history repeats itself; in fact it don't repeat itself, it just goes on being the same.'

'Well anyway, what are we going to do with this rabbit?' asked Knocker.

'Shove it in the cupboard,' said Spiff, rubbing his chin. 'I'll call a meeting tomorrow. You two can run down the street with the message right now, before you go to bed. I know Borribles don't like meetings but this is an emergency, and we will have to act and think together for once!'

Spiff took one last look at the Rumble, then he pulled his Borrible hat further on to his head, spun on his heels and left the room. Knocker got the prisoner to his feet and locked him in the store cupboard, then he and Lightfinger left by the basement door and spent the next few hours informing all High Street Borribles what was afoot. Finally the two exhausted lookouts got to their own room at the top of Spiff's house and climbed into a bundle of old blankets and sacks that formed their bed.

'Argaah,' yawned Knocker, 'what a day.'

'Goo' night,' said Lightfinger, and was immediately asleep.

*

A Borrible's main business is to stay alive. This is an occupation that takes up most of his time; getting food from wherever he can discover it, finding things before they are lost, stealing his provisions from barrows and out of superstore warehouses: stealing because the fundamental Borrible rule, the rule that is primordial to the way they live, the mainspring and motivation of their very being – rule number one – is that they must never have dealings in money. They have been brought up without it, and they must never touch it. If they do, bad luck and loss of freedom will follow as sure as night the day. That is why Borribles steal, and why they prefer to live near shopping centres and street markets like Brixton and Petticoat Lane, where food is easy to come by.

So important is that aspect of their life that they have many sayings that deal with it and they are all gathered together in the *Borrible Book of Proverbs*. Some of these maxims are very ancient, like, 'that which falls off a lorry belongs to him who follows the lorry,' and 'That which is found has never been lost.' One of their favourites is, 'It is impossible to lose that which does not belong to you,' and Borribles use that one a lot to people who complain about their thieving.

By eight o'clock on the morning following the capture of Timbucktoo Rumble, Battersea High Street market was in full swing. There were barrows and stalls along each side of the road and so little space was left for traffic that not a car dared venture down there. The barrows had been shoved very close together and it was easy for a Borrible to crawl underneath them from one end of the street to the other, picking up fruit on the way. It was a good way to get breakfast.

The costermongers shouted at each other and at prospective customers, urging them to buy. There were barrows selling fruit, ironmongery, fish and large crabs; the shops had their doors wide open and people were drinking tea in Notarianni's cafe, talking loudly, making wild gestures with their hands. Brown's, the pie and eel shop, was doing a brisk business and the inhabitants of the buildings – Archer House, Eaton House and White House – were loafing on street corners and thinking about passing bets in Ernie Swash's, the bookmaker's. The noise was so great that it rose right up the side of the house where Knocker and Lightfinger were sleeping and woke them from a deep slumber.

Knocker rolled over and woke his companion. 'Come on, breakfast.'

He stretched his arms above his head; he hadn't slept enough. The two Borribles had been out so late the night before that the costermongers had been loading their barrows as they came home; finding breakfast had been no problem and it was there beside them: one grapefruit, an orange and two large doughnuts dripping with jam.

Lightfinger rubbed his eyes and the old sacks and blankets dropped from him. He reached for the orange, bit it open and sucked hard, making a lot of noise. The orange was wonderful, fresh-tasting, chilled to ice crystals by the lorry journeys to and from Covent Garden.

'Ooaagh,' he groaned with pleasure, 'that's lovely.'

'We'd better hurry up,' said Knocker, 'or we'll miss the meeting.'

Halfway down the High Street was a disused brick-built hall. It had last been occupied by a firm of photographers called Scots of London, but they had departed long since and now the shop fell within the province of the Borribles. It was here that Spiff had asked the members of the Battersea tribe to gather; decisions had to be made and everyone was allowed a say.

Inside the hall, on a kind of podium, stood Spiff in conversation with a score of his cronies. Other Borribles, ragged, dirty and inquisitive, slipped in through broken doorways, and, talking furiously, waited in groups to see what might happen.

The moment he thought enough people were present Spiff stepped to the front of the stage and held up both arms like a politician. He shouted several times and gradually the hubbub of voices became less and less until eventually a kind of excited silence hung on the air, then Spiff began to speak, relishing the occasion, for he took a delight in speechifying.

'Brother and sister Borribles, I am pleased to see so many of you here, for today is a day of decision. Our way of life is in jeopardy and we must either act together or perish.'

The hall became quieter and the tension rose.

'Not to beat about the bush, I'll give you the facts, then anyone who wants a say can have a say. Right, the facts. Last night, our chief lookout and his assistant . . .'

All heads turned to Knocker and Lightfinger.

'. . . while on a routine inspection of the Battersea area, discovered that we had been invaded by the Rumbles.'

The crowd drew in a deep breath and then let it out again in a long explosion and Spiff looked round for effect and more silence.

'It seems that a large force came down here, all the way from Rumbledom, and occupied the park for several hours. They were digging! Now, in my opinion, this can only be a preparation for a takeover of Battersea, an attack on our freedom, a new and subtle kind of slavery and a clipping of ears. Things have been bearable as long as the Rumbles have stayed in Rumbledom, where they belong, but this is something else.'

Murmurs of assent came from the assembly but Spiff held up his hand and went on.

'In my opinion there is only one answer, my friends, pre-emptive defence. We must attack before we are attacked. We must destroy the Rumbles at the heart of their organization. However—'

Spiff broke off for a second and admonished the ceiling with a grubby finger.

'—to carry out this plan we shall need to search carefully among the ranks of the nameless. From those who have not yet had their first adventure we must select the bravest, the slyest, the craftiest and the most resourceful. It is not only the enemy we have to fear, but the enormous distance between us and him, dangerous terrain. The Rumble is confident in his stronghold, blinded by his own conceit, safe, so he thinks, in the security of his own riches and comfort, but that is where we shall strike, with a handful of chosen Borribles. We shall need dedicated volunteers, but remember, those who go may never return. Blood will be spilt.'

At this there was a terrific hush in the hall and the Borribles looked at each other with trepidation. An adventure was one thing, death another.

'We feel,' went on Spiff, 'that Battersea should not bear this brunt alone. All London Borribles are threatened. To this end messages will be sent out over the city and certain tribes will be asked to send their likeliest un-named champions to us for training and instruction. Likewise, from among the ranks of the Battersea nameless, we shall choose one who shows the greatest promise. We intend to approach the following groups: the Totters of Tooting, the Wendles of Wandsworth, the Stumpers of Stepney, the Whitechapel Wallopers, the Peckham Punch-uppers, the Neasden Nudgers and the Hoxton Humpers. Details of the raid will be worked out when all the candidates have arrived.'

Spiff stopped for breath and the hall became alive and words buzzed like bees. Who, people wondered, would be chosen as the Battersea representative on the expedition? An honour, yes, but a danger too.

Knocker swore to himself. 'Why do I have my name already? What an adventure it's going to be.'

Spiff called for quiet again. Now he prepared for his moment of high drama. He made a sign to the side of the stage and the prisoner was brought on for all to see. There was silence. The Rumble was still taped round the snout but its beady eyes glowed a fearful red and it stood upright and unmoved.

'This,' shouted Spiff, 'is the enemy, no braver than us, no more dangerous; but they are difficult of access, living underground as they do, well-protected in their burrows. They are rich and they are powerful, and think themselves superior to all Borribles by divine right. This is the enemy who wants to take Battersea into its grasp. Even now they may be digging under the streets to emerge in your very backyard, even now they may be undermining your way of life, silently; dirty and evil, moles of the underground.'

Spiff took a deep breath and shook his arms in front of his body as if he was emptying a sack of cement; the crowd stirred with emotion. Spiff raised his voice a further notch.

'This is the enemy, and we all know that they must be stopped at all costs. Yes, but more than that, they must be eliminated, and who are the Borribles to do it? Why we are!'

An enormous cheer rose from the audience. 'Throw it in the river,' came a voice from the back of the hall, 'with a bicycle round its neck.'

This suggestion was so popular that it was taken up on all sides.

'Yeah,' came the shout, 'in the river, steal a bike someone.'

Spiff smiled indulgently. 'I understand your feelings,' he looked at the Rumble, 'but I have a better plan. Let me explain. The one thing that these objects fear above all others,' he touched the Rumble lightly with a disdainful finger, 'is disclosure! They would hate to be unmasked and shown for what they really are. In their mythology the greatest possible disaster is what they call the Great Rumble Hunt – an attack on their citadel of power – and we, the Borribles of Battersea, will start that Rumble hunt. But,' Spiff had to shout across the cheering, 'this is also to be a war of nerves; we want them to know that something really nasty is on the way – us! And that is where this little rodent comes in. We propose to stick a notice on to the fur of this carpet bag, and send it back to Rumbledom, living proof that we mean business. The message will say, "The Great Rumble Hunt is on. Beware the Borribles!" All those in favour say "Aye".'

Another enormous cheer rose from the assembly; Spiff's oratory had done its work, that was what he wanted. Borribles clasped each other, jumped up and down and shouted, 'We'll show 'em, we'll teach them rabbits to come down here.'

As the cheering died away Spiff and his cronies left the building with the prisoner, and the hall gradually emptied as the Borribles went back to their squats, eager to discuss the morning meeting and to wonder who would be chosen as the Battersea 'no-name' for the Great Rumble Hunt. Those who were not known for their bravery kept very quiet and decided not to call attention to themselves, for a few Borribles manage to pass through life without ever earning themselves a name. But most are of a different stamp, and they ran to the market without delay, stole paper and wrote directly to Spiff, begging for the position.

But Knocker was disconsolate. He returned home alone, thwarted. He knew there was no chance of him being considered for the expedition to Rumbledom. He went into the basement of the deserted house and made his way upstairs. As he passed Spiff's door it was thrown open and the cunning face of the most cunning of Borribles appeared, beaming.

'Right, lad,' he said, 'in here. Just the bloke I want, look lively . . . Want a word with you.'

Knocker stepped inside the room, and removed his woollen cap; he had good pointed ears, a sign of high intelligence and alertness. Spiff smiled and settled into an armchair that must have fallen from a very expensive furniture lorry.

'Sit down, lad,' he said. 'I wanted to thank you for your good work last night, champion that was, champion . . . but now I want to ask your advice. As you know, there are eight Rumbles in the Rumble High Command. I'm sure that if we can eliminate them, the rest of the Rumble set-up will fall to pieces, they'll be too busy even to think of us any more. So that's why I thought of sending eight Borribles only, one for each High Rumble. There will be one from Tooting, Hoxton, Wandsworth . . . You heard all that already. But, Knocker, who are we going to send from Battersea? The point is, you are out and about a lot, you see a lot of Borribles in action, who do you think would be a good choice?'

Knocker thought for a while. 'It's tricky,' he said at length. 'There's quite a few who are good. There's a bunch of bright lads down by the river, some others under the railway arches at Battersea Park station, but I think the brightest of the lot, out of the whole borough, is one who lives up on Lavender Hill, bright as a button and smart as paint.'

'Whereabouts does he hang out?' asked Spiff.

'Underneath the nick,' said Knocker.

'Underneath the nick!' cried Spiff. 'He must be mad.'

Knocker laughed. 'Oh, no. Bright. There's a stack of rooms up there that are left empty every night. It's centrally heated, blankets galore, constant electricity. You name it, he's got it. In fact he's very friendly with some of the coppers – the Woollies.'

'Hmm,' said Spiff, 'and he's a no-name?'

'Yes.'

'Right,' Spiff went on, 'that's settled then. Send a runner up to Lavender Hill and get that wazzisname down here. As soon as the other seven come in from across London we shall have to begin a training session. As well as that, I want you to get some volunteers to do some spare-time thieving. We're going to need lots of things for this expedition: grub, weatherproof clothing, high-quality catapults, watches, compasses, anything that might be useful . . . so get that organized. I know you've got your own thieving to do, and so have the others, but do what you can . . . We can't afford to fail.'

Knocker nodded. His heart was bursting with pride, he was being involved in the Great Rumble Hunt, which was more than he had dared to hope.

'Is there a chance of anything else, Spiff?'

'What do you mean? You can't go on the expedition, you know, that's a rule.'

'I know that. It's, well, you said they would have to be trained. I'm a good Borrible lookout, well, I could train them . . . couldn't I?'

Spiff gave Knocker a long look, a look that went right through him and saw everything. 'Hmm,' he said, smiling a secret smile, 'you are keen, aren't you? How many names have you got?'

'Just the one,' answered Knocker feeling uncomfortable.

Spiff chuckled. 'You know what Knocker, you reminds me of me. You didn't have to ask, I'd already thought of you . . . yes, you can train the team.'

Knocker got up to go, feeling proud of himself.

'Here, take this envelope,' said Spiff, 'it's instructions about the Rumble; he's downstairs in the cupboard. Send him packing. Try not to let anyone see him, they might still chuck him in the river.'

Knocker ran downstairs and opened the cupboard. Sure enough the Rumble was there, his paws tied behind him and a notice glued on to his fur. Two other lookouts came into the room and leant against the wall to watch as Knocker read his instructions. When he had finished he removed the tape from the animal's snout and sat it on a grape barrel.

'You are being sent home, Rumble, alive. Take that message to your leaders and tell them what you have seen and heard.'

Knocker turned to the lookouts. 'You two can escort him on the first stage of the journey. This envelope has instructions from Spiff. Take him to Clapham Junction and hand him over to the next Borrible tribe. Then he can be taken to the Honeywell Borribles, and they can take him up to the Wendles beyond Wandsworth Common; from there the Wendles will take him to Merton Road. This letter goes with him and explains what should be done at each stage. Finally, he should be released as near Rumbledom High Street as possible and allowed to find his way home. Any questions?'

The two lookouts shook their heads.

'Right,' said Knocker, 'as soon as you've got rid of him report back to me. It is very important that he gets home in one piece, though it doesn't matter what he looks like; the rougher the better. We've got to frighten the fur off every Rumble in existence.'

Timbucktoo jumped to his feet at this. 'You don't fwighten me, Bowwible, nor your fwiends. You don't know what you're taking on. We'll be keeping a watch out for you; you'll be skewered on our Wumble-sticks before you get a sight of Wumbledom Hill. You may be safe down here in your gwimy stweets and stinking back-alleys, but Wumbledom is a wilderness with twackless paths that only we can follow. This means war.'

Knocker swiped the Rumble round the ear, almost affectionately. 'Go on,' he said, 'you old doormat, before I knock that snout of yours through the back of your bonce.'

At a sign from Knocker his two assistants hauled the Rumble from the room on the first stage of his long and perilous journey, a journey on which he would be passed from hand to hand like a registered packet in the London post.

2

During the fortnight that followed the capture of Timbucktoo, the lookouts' room in Spiff's house became the centre for the collection of all gear that might turn out to be useful on the Great Rumble Hunt. Under the watchful eye of Knocker it was stacked and sorted: there were rucksacks and life jackets from the sports section of Arding and Hobbs, thick warm coats, sleeping bags, unbreakable nylon rope for climbing trees and the sides of houses, stout boots, oilskins, woollen underwear, sharp knives, sou'westers and ski goggles.

Looking at the spoils Knocker felt pleased; his job was finished and every eventuality had been foreseen. The store cupboard was full and the lookouts' room was piled high with valuable items. The only space left clear was a small area round the desk and a kind of corridor to each of the doors. Knocker rubbed his hands together in contentment and at that moment Lightfinger appeared, sidling between the goods towering above his head.

'You look tired,' he said.

'I am that,' answered Knocker. 'But I think I've got everything now, though I suppose I'm bound to have forgotten something.'

'Well, you haven't finished yet, mate,' said Lightfinger. 'Spiff wants to see you right away, upstairs.'

Knocker ran up to the ground floor landing and knocked on Spiff's door. It was opened immediately.

'Ah, there you are Knocker, come in, sit down. Good news, they're here.'

'Who?' asked Knocker, whose mind was tired and preoccupied.

'Oh, come on,' said Spiff. 'The Brightest of the Borribles, the Magnificent Eight, call 'em what you like, they're here.'

'Where?' asked Knocker.

'In the old storeroom under the gym in Rowena Crescent, other side of Prince's Head. I want you to put them through a complete lookout training. Make sure they are first-class thieves, good at shoplifting and Woollie-dodging; and see they know the Borrible proverbs by heart. Then take them on a few runs in Battersea Park; I know they don't like the countryside, but they've got to get used to it; Rumbledom's rough . . . I know, I've been there. I'll give you two weeks, that's all. There'll be another bloke to help you, he's from the Northcote Road tribe, was brought up in a paratrooper's family before he was Borribled, he could be useful. By the way—' Spiff threw over some books and Knocker caught them in his lap '—you'd better read those from cover to cover, they're the Rumble manuals, their whole history from the word go, gives the layout of their place, the structure of their command and the way they fight with their Rumble-sticks. Nasty long lances they are, with a four-inch nail at the end.'

Knocker was caught off-balance. 'Rumble manuals, Spiff, how did you get your hands on those? No Borrible's meant to have seen 'em.'

Spiff tapped his nose with a finger. 'Never you mind, young feller me lad. Everything you need is there. Just get on with it. I'll come and see you in two weeks. If there's anything you need, send a runner.'

Knocker gathered up the books and rose to leave, but Spiff raised a hand to stop him.

'Oh, yes, in the first volume I've made a list of the Eight High Rumbles of Rumbledom, their names. I thought it would be a good idea if you gave each of your Borribles one of those names to win, so if they ever get that far, each of your blokes will know exactly which Rumble he's got to do for. All right?'

'How shall I give them out? Did you decide that?'

Spiff laughed to himself mysteriously. 'You'd better put the names into a hat and your guys can draw for them, then there can be no arguments about the targets they are given.' Spiff hesitated, and then laughed again. 'That is except for two of them, those you'll have to put into a separate hat. You'll see them marked on the list. Go on, buzz off, Knocker.'

As he went down the stairs Knocker let out a long low whistle. He would have loved to have gone on the expedition, to have earned a new name and a new story to tell, but fancy going through life with a Rumble title; that would be strange. Then he reflected that it was not the name after all, but the story it carried with it that mattered. He could think of some fine Borribles with the most extraordinary monikers, but when you saw them or heard their names you didn't think of the word alone or its sound, you thought of the life and the deeds that lay beyond it – the story.

But then stories are very important to Borribles. Most of the time they can't have a real adventure because they are too busy making sure they get enough to eat, so to compensate they read tales like westerns or spy stories or science fiction. For a Borrible the next best thing to an adventure of his own is hearing other Borribles tell how they won their names; and it doesn't matter if they exaggerate their deeds in the telling, exaggeration is accepted as long as it makes a good story.

So in Knocker's mind, as he made his way up the High Street, there was no doubt that the eight Borribles who were going on this adventure would have wonderful stories to tell. The Rumble names they were going to win would remind them of their targets during the expedition and, in years to come, if they were successful, everyone who heard the names would know how they had been won. 'Yes,' concluded Knocker as he turned into Rowena Crescent, Spiff had come up with a good idea, but then Spiff was as sharp as a cut-throat razor.

Outside the gym Knocker stopped to make sure his hat was on firmly, his ears covered. The building was long and low, looking like an empty pub and faced with green tiles. Above the door and three long windows was a sign. Knocker looked up at it, though he knew what it said: 'Rowena Gym. Tough Guys for Stage and Screen and TV. Stunt Men. Kung Fu. Laetitia Martin, prop.'

Knocker could hear grunts and groans coming from inside: adult males trying to break into show business. In the pavement he saw the telltale grilles revealing where the basement was, where the Borribles would be. Tightening his grip on the Rumble books, Knocker went through the gym's main entrance and down a corridor that was tiled in the same dirty colour as the front of the building. As he went forward a security guard threw open the door of his office and came to stand in Knocker's way. He was huge, with his legs spread and his hands on his hips. He had a cauliflower ear and his breath smelt sickly-sweet of brown ale.

'And where d'you think you're going, mush?'

'It's all right,' lied Knocker, 'my big brother's here and I got to give him these books. I'm late already.'

The man thought slowly, then: 'Okay, but don't hang about. Kids ain't allowed in here, 'specially little squirts like you.' With that he retreated into his office and slammed the door.

At the end of the corridor Knocker ignored the up staircase and descended a flight of dank cement steps until he was in a darkness so deep that he had to feel his way. He groped along a wall until he came up against a rough wooden door which did not give when he pushed it. He tried the Borrible knock, gently at first and then, when nothing happened, a little louder – one long, two shorts, then a long – Dah . . . di-di . . . dah.

There was a slight noise behind the door, a bolt clanged, a lock clashed and an eye peered through a slit.

'Borrible?' asked the person behind the door.

'Borrible,' answered Knocker.

The door was opened, just wide enough for Knocker to pass through, and then it was closed and bolted behind him. He found himself in a long dusty space with exercise bars covering each wall from floor to ceiling. From central beams hung thick ropes for climbing; jute mats were piled in the corners and here and there various bits of machinery, designed to improve the efficiency of the human body, had been abandoned. The light in the room was grey and faltering; indeed it was so weak that Knocker could hardly make out the eight shapes sitting quietly on a bench at the far end of the gym.

The chief lookout turned to the Borrible next to him. 'Northcote Road?' he asked, and his companion nodded.

'Name is Dodger,' he said, and smiled.

'That sounds like a good name,' said Knocker, 'you must have had a good adventure getting it. Perhaps you'll tell me one day.'

'Everyone knows how you got your name, Knocker, that's one of the best Borrible stories ever told.'

Knocker was pleased by this tribute to his celebrity and he felt sure that he and Dodger would get on. It is usual for Borribles meeting for the first time to exchange compliments on their respective names and the winning of them. Until they have a name Borribles are known simply as 'You', 'Oi' or 'Mush', sometimes as 'Fingy', or even 'Wazzisname'. But to call a named Borrible by one of the foregoing is an unforgivable insult and will lead to fighting.

An even greater insult for a named Borrible is for him to be told that he acquired his name only because he'd found it, or someone had thrown it away. And for an un-named one it is very galling to have it suggested that he is nameless because no one has yet had the devious ingenuity to invent an epithet bad enough for him.

Knocker glanced at the beret Dodger was wearing; it was dark red in colour, and bore the badge of the Parachute Regiment, shining bright.

'Army?' observed Knocker.

'Oh yes,' said Dodger proudly. 'My family was Parachute Regiment and SAS until I became a Borrible. I wouldn't have run away at all if they hadn't wanted to pack me off to some school. Up until then I'd spent all my time watching the soldiers doing their training. That was the life.'

Knocker laughed. 'Well, we'd better get a shift on, we've only got two weeks.' They turned from the door and made their way down the long hall, their feet kicking into piles of rubbish and releasing stale smells from old cardboard cartons.

'How did you get in here?' asked Knocker.

Dodger pointed to the ceiling. 'I had the bolts off a couple of those grilles in the pavement. Easy. That way we won't have to go past "Punchie the porter" every day.'

Knocker nodded. 'I'll remember next time.'

The Eight Adventurers sat motionless on their bench. Some were leaning back against the wall with their eyes closed; some held their heads in their hands and others sat looking straight in front of them, staring at nothing.

At a sign from Knocker, Dodger switched on some electric lights and the Borribles blinked their eyes.

'Stand up. Get your hats off.'

When they had done what Knocker asked he walked down the line and inspected their ears to see if they showed signs of the intelligence he was expecting. It was a manoeuvre that gave him time to think. He would have admitted to no one, apart from Spiff perhaps, that he was flabbergasted; one of the champions was black. Of course he knew that many Borribles were black, more and more all the time. There were legions of them in Battersea and Tooting, and an even greater number in Brixton; he just hadn't thought of one on this expedition. He had no one to blame but himself for this oversight. He was, after all, a chief lookout and his mind should have been open to all possibilities, not drifting around in preconceptions and prejudices.

Mentally he kicked himself for being a fool, but he hadn't finished kicking himself. When he stopped at the end of the row he found that the last two Borribles were females. Here his surprise nearly got the better of him, but he pursed his lips and pretended to be thinking. One of the girls smiled and to cover his embarrassment Knocker looked closely at her ears. They indicated a high degree of intelligence and great individuality, and that could mean trouble. Now Knocker knew why Spiff had laughed and why he'd said he'd have to put the names into two different hats.

Knocker went back to where Dodger stood, handed over the Rumble books, and took the list of names from his pocket. He looked at it, making the eight champions wait. Finally he said, 'You will be here for two weeks. We are going to see how good you really are. When Dodger and I have satisfied ourselves about your basic knowledge we will move on to more specialist skills, but before that I want to be convinced that you are good: good with a catapult, good with your hands, good with your feet. I want you to be the best runners, the best fighters, and I want to see how you deal with tricky situations. You'll have to be the best if you want to go on this trip, because if I don't think you are, you ain't going.'

Knocker looked along the faces, scrutinizing them one after the other. 'Anyone hears an order from me or Dodger, jump. That's against the grain for a Borrible, I know it, but there hasn't been an adventure like this in years and if you want to be in on it you've got to do what I say. Any questions?'

There were no questions.

'Good, now to the names. It was decided to give you your names now – provisionally.'

There was a stir in the line and eyes flashed.

'This is to make it more convenient for me during training and for you all when you're out on the adventure. These names will not be confirmed until your return – if you ever make it. These names have been lent to you on trust. One false step at any time and your name will be withdrawn, and you will never be given another adventure.'

There was silence; the eight faces looked at him and waited. They were tense and excited, but these Borribles were too canny to give much away. He went on.

'These are fine names, names that have a good ring to them and will remind you, and others in the future, of this adventure; but more important, the name that each of you will be given is also the name of the Rumble that is your individual target. While you remember your own name you cannot forget the name of your enemy.'

Knocker paused. He knew that each Borrible standing before him could hardly wait for the moment when he would carry a name, the one word which would symbolize a whole life. 'All right,' went on the chief lookout, 'the names will be distributed by drawing lots, six names in one hat, and two names in another. Dodger.'

Dodger and Knocker removed their hats and Knocker tore each name separately from the sheet that Spiff had given him. He put six names into his own woollen cap and two into the red beret of the paratroops. Dodger held the beret while Knocker shook his own hat vigorously to mix the names fairly and squarely. 'I'll start at one end and move along,' he said. 'It's all the luck of the draw.'

He studied the face of the first person in line. By chance it was the one he had recommended to Spiff, the Battersea Borrible from Lavender Hill. Knocker had always liked the look of him, although they didn't know each other very well. He was slightly built, even for a Borrible; his skin was clear and his hair was dark and tightly curled, like wire wool. His eyes were sharp and blue and they moved quickly, but were never furtive. He smiled a lot and Knocker could see that it would take a lot to get him down. He glanced at Knocker, winked, then plunged his hand into the hat and pulled out a scrap of paper. He opened it, read it to himself and then smiled at the chief lookout. He rolled his tongue once or twice, getting the feel of his name for the very first time.

'Bingo,' he said, 'the name's Bingo.'

'That's a good name,' said Knocker, and stepped sideways. He stood in front of the black Borrible. 'Where you from?' asked Knocker.

'Tooting, man, Tooting, and you?'

Knocker raised his head sharply. 'I'm from here.'

The Tooting Borrible, or Totter, had hair standing out in a solid uncut mass all round his head like a black halo. His teeth protruded and he seemed to be smiling all the time, an expression of cheerful slyness. Knocker liked that. He shook the hat again and the Totter took a piece of paper.

'My name is going to be O-ro-coc-co,' he said, splitting the word into separate syllables and pronouncing them with care.

The next person was smaller than Bingo even. He had a triangular face with a pointed chin and his mousy hair lay flat across the top of his head. He had a way of wagging his head that said there wasn't a trick in the book he didn't know.

Knocker stopped in front of him with the hat and the Borrible said, 'I'm from Stepney, the best place in the world.'

Knocker nodded only and offered the hat. The Stepney Borrible looked at the name on the paper he had drawn and whistled, then he said, 'Good, I've got Vulgarian, I've heard he's the chief Rumble. Don't reckon his chances when I catch up with him.'

'I see, so you know why you're here?'

'Course, to get a name, and because they said that this was going to be the best adventure ever.' And the Borrible glanced up and down the line and the others nodded in agreement.

'You've got to convince me that you're good enough first. Then you go,' said Knocker.

'Perhaps you ought to start by showing that you're good enough to train us,' said a brittle voice to Knocker's right, but Knocker ignored it and moved on a step.

'I'm from Peckham,' said the next adventurer without being asked, and he thrust his hand into the hat and pulled out his name. Knocker watched him closely as he read the paper. He seemed strong and resourceful. He had dark heavy eyebrows and a red face with a firm jaw and enormous shoulders and arms. The kind of bloke who would not mince his words; not very witty perhaps, but dogged and persistent.

'Well,' said Knocker, 'which one have you got?'

The Peckham Borrible did not even show pleasure as he said, 'I've got the name I wanted, Stonks. Someone in Peckham said he was the keeper of the Great Door of Rumbledom – the strongest one. He'll need to be when I hit him.'

When Knocker came face to face with the next person he wrinkled his nose. There was an unmistakable smell about him and Knocker guessed immediately where he came from.

'You're from Wandsworth, aren't you? A Wendle?'

'So what, the finest Borribles in the world come from Wandsworth.'

Knocker recognized at once the brittle voice that had spoken out of turn a little earlier. 'Is that a fact?' he retorted, smiling a smile that had no warmth in it.

In common with most other Borribles he wasn't over fond of the aloof Wandsworth Brotherhood. They dwelt along the banks of the River Wandle in disused sewers and in the smelly holes they had scooped out below the streets. But no one knew exactly how they lived, for they were the most suspicious and warlike of all Borribles; they did not encourage visitors and rarely spoke to anyone outside their own tribe. Most repulsive of all, their skin had a green tinge to it which came from living so much underground, and being so often in and out of the filthy Wandle water.

Once the Wandle had been a pleasant stream, but years of industrialization had turned it into a treacherous ooze of green and muddy slime, a mixture of poison waste, decomposed rubbish and undigested lumps of plastic which rolled slowly along the river's surface as it slid like a thick jelly down to the Thames. The Wandle mud would entrap any stranger who was foolhardy enough to wade across it without guidance; no one but the Wendles knew its secret paths, and only rarely could they be prevailed upon to guide travellers through their territory.

Every Wendle carried the smell of the Wandsworth marshes with him, and that smell was the smell of treachery and decay. Knocker had seen but few Wendles; none of them had been this close and he didn't like what he saw: the green glow to the flesh, the dark eyes of an indeterminate colour, and the cold proud bearing of the born scrapper. There seemed to be no spontaneous warmth in the Wendle and warmth was normally the first thing that was noticed in a Borrible.

'Take your name, anyway,' said Knocker flatly, and he held out his hat.

The Wendle narrowed his eyes and screwed up his mouth to prove that he didn't care a damn about Knocker, or anyone else, and he pulled out his name. He nodded, then he laughed loud, pleased and hostile.

'Out with it,' said Knocker impatiently. 'What is it?'

'What a name I have,' cried the Wendle. 'I shall cover it in glory.'

'Or mud.'

The Wendle ignored Knocker and looked up and down the line of adventurers. 'Napoleon Boot,' he said loudly. 'Call me Napoleon Boot.'

'And I suppose you know why you're going to Rumbledom?' asked Knocker.

'Why am I going?' The other was angry. 'What's wrong with you? Because I hate them, that's why. I always have hated them, and if you'd always had 'em leering down at yer from Rumbledom, like I have, you'd hate 'em as much as I do. I don't need these others to come with me. I'll tear Rumbledom apart on me tod.'

Knocker shrugged. He was glad to move on to the last of the male Borribles. He looked at the face and liked it. It was square and flat, and the eyes were optimistic under the spiky brown hair. This Borrible looked like he could take a lot of knocks and still come up smiling.

'Well,' said Knocker, 'you're the last so I know the name; it's Torreycanyon.'

'Yes,' said Torreycanyon, 'that'll do nicely.'

Knocker gave the empty hat to Dodger and took the beret with the two names only in it. He stood in front of the two Borrible girls, and felt embarrassed. He was used to girls of course but he'd never heard of any being trained as lookouts. He didn't like the idea of girls on this adventure and wondered how it had happened. He looked from one to the other of them; he was forced to admit that they were tough-looking, and certainly their ears were amongst the most beautifully shaped he had ever seen, denoting strong character, unbendable wills and great slyness and cunning. He couldn't fault them there. But, he wondered, would they be able to support the rigours of the trek, the dangers, the rough living out of doors, every night a different bivouac. And what effect would they have on the team as a whole? That was a worry. Borribles could quarrel and fight just as well as they could steal.

Knocker glanced back down the line and found the others watching him closely. Orococco was smiling, his white teeth shining against his black skin; even the Wendle, Napoleon Boot, was smirking.

'Where are you girls from?' asked Knocker.

'Whitechapel,' said the first.

'Neasden,' said the second. Knocker held out the hat to the girl from Whitechapel.

'Take one of these,' he said. The girl chose a piece of paper and read her name simply, with no comment.

'Chalotte,' she said, her voice cool and relaxed. Her green eyes flickered over Knocker's face and she smiled. Knocker didn't like to admit it but over and above her other attributes she was beautiful too; her fair hair fell to her shoulders, her skin shone and her legs were strong and full of running, an asset to any Borrible.

He gave the last piece of paper to the girl from Neasden.

'Sydney,' she said when she'd looked at it. Knocker glanced at her. Another good-looking girl; her hair was dark and shiny and her eyes were grey, her face kind.

'Why did Whitechapel and Neasden send you two?' he asked, disguising his shyness behind a sarcastic tone. 'Haven't they got any male Borribles out there?'

Chalotte said, 'The message that came to Whitechapel specified a female Borrible.'

'And the Neasden message?'

Sydney nodded. 'We were told that two of the High Command are female. That's why we were asked, I should think.'

'Hm,' said Knocker. He went to move away from the girls, but then turned on them suddenly, raising his voice. 'There will be no favouritism, you will be treated just like the others, you will train like the others and sleep on the ground like the others, and you will wear the same combat clothes. When you leave you must expect the same conditions, exactly. You will march as long, eat as little and fight as much as every other member of the expeditionary force. No favours, so ask for none. You will take the same risks as the others, and maybe perish with them. Do you understand?'

If Knocker had hoped to frighten Chalotte and Sydney with this outburst he failed.

'That is why we came,' said Chalotte, and quoted a Borrible proverb: '"No name earns itself."'

'Yes,' said Sydney, 'and there's another proverb: "Every way forward has a way back."'

Knocker turned again and retraced his steps to the centre of the line.

'Right,' he began, 'now you have your names, training will be all day and every day. I'll give details tomorrow. First thing you must do is learn your enemy. We have Rumble books here and we have something that is better, Spiff's notes and studies of 'em. We will start reading right away. In his notes you will find a detailed description of each of the Rumbles of the High Command. Now you know your names you know which one is yours and you must know exactly what he or she looks like. You will have to distinguish between him and a thousand others right in the middle of a punch-up. Another thing, we shall be training with the Rumble-stick or sticker, the enemy's weapon. For those of you who don't know it's a four-inch nail stuck into the end of a lance of wood. They use it like a spear, or as a quarterstaff and dagger combined. The Rumble is good with it, cuts his teeth on it; you've got to be better. From now on we work hard. Your survival will depend on this training.'

The next two weeks were weeks of exhausting activity. The eight members of the expeditionary force never stopped working. Every morning at five Knocker had them on their feet for half an hour's physical jerks, just to get the blood circulating properly through their brains. After breakfast they had a morning training session inside the gym, the subject chosen by Dodger or Knocker. They perfected their skills with the Rumble-stick and practised stealing in pairs and in fours. Before lunch they slipped out for a quick run, just a mile or so to improve their wind – all Borribles need to be speedy runners – and to keep them in trim Knocker made them responsible for purloining their own midday meal – a meal which they ate all together in some uncomfortable spot along by the river, or in some draughty house with no windows. And all the time Knocker watched the girls closely, but they never complained and they did everything just as well as anyone else.

After the midday meal they went back to the gym for a short rest of half an hour or so and then Knocker would test them on Borrible knowledge and Rumble studies; every one of them had to have a mind as sharp and as hard and as useful as a brand new tin-opener. They learned practical information too: how to avoid capture, how to escape when caught and how to aid other Borribles when in trouble. Knocker insisted that the eight of them should have all this knowledge ready in their minds. There was no telling what they might come across on the long and dangerous journey to Rumbledom; they would have to be prepared for anything and everything.

After the session with the books there was always more physical training. Dodger taught them how to jump from a great height and fall without hurting themselves; how to take punches rolling with the blow, how to duck and weave. He taught them the vulnerable spots of the Rumble anatomy and again how to use the Rumble-stick. Then, in the latter part of the afternoon, Knocker, who'd had a great deal of experience, more than any other known Borrible, taught them field tactics: how to climb trees, how to cross commons and parks without being seen.

Like other Borribles Knocker much preferred crowded streets, alive with markets and shops, but unlike the others he'd been obliged, because of his calling, to do an enormous amount of country work. Somehow he had made himself overcome the basic fear that Borribles have when faced with woods and fields. They hate such things.

'Fields,' they say, 'are always windy and there is nowhere to hide, no crowds to get lost in, and there is nothing to pick up, no lorries for things to fall off . . . Fields are a pain and your Borrible is only really happy when he's up to something in the street.'

But there was one thing that was more important than everything else put together: Knocker made the Eight train hour after hour with the Borribles' traditional and preferred weapon. It had been used by them for generations, and had been chosen for its simplicity, its range, its power and its deadliness. It was an ancient weapon but was as efficient as any modern invention. It could be made anywhere and, back in the days of the nineteenth century when Borribles had endured great hardships and had been hounded from place to place, it had become their favourite method of defence because of the cheapness of its manufacture. The weapon was a very dangerous one – the catapult.

Every Borrible was an expert with the catapult, but the Eight would have to surpass the usual standards and become boringly accurate, able to hit a Rumble on the snout each time they fired.

'You must never miss,' Knocker told them. 'You will have a great deal of provisions to carry, but if you each have forty stones on you that will account for three hundred and twenty of the enemy between you. If you are besieged, always choose somewhere where you can find plenty of ammunition lying about, then you will be invincible.' And so each of the Eight became a crack shot; every one of them could take a fly off a park keeper's nose at a hundred yards and he'd never even notice.

That was how the days were filled. And every evening the Eight returned to the gym to find that the High Street Borribles had provided them with a supper of food stolen from the market. They ate with huge appetites and, after talking to each other for a little while, they rolled into their sleeping bags and slept on the floor of the long dusty room. The next day they would have to wake early and do the same things again – run a little faster, shoot a little straighter.

Knocker gave them no rest. He made them rehearse the expedition route on the street map of London until they knew it by heart; and he insisted they play war games that placed them in impossible situations, obliging them to think their way clear as quickly as they could, and if Knocker wasn't satisfied with their efforts they would have to do their tasks again, and then again. The Eight were tired all the time.

*

About one o'clock on a grey afternoon towards the end of the fortnight, Spiff, with two of his cronies from the High Street, made an appearance in the storeroom of the Rowena Crescent Gym. It was the beginning of the rest period and Spiff walked around the room talking to the Borribles who were stretched out on their sleeping bags, dozing with their eyes only half open. When he'd had a short word with each, he came over to speak to Knocker and Dodger.

'Knocker,' said Spiff, nodding his head abruptly at the two Borribles by his side. 'This is Rasher and this is Ziggy.'

Knocker stood and said, 'Those are fine names, certainly, I would like to hear the stories one day.'

The two nodded but did not smile. They looked out of humour.

'Yes,' said Spiff, 'that will have to wait of course. Now, Knocker, you've reached the end of the two weeks. How have you got on?'

Knocker reached for a large notebook on his desk. It contained a detailed description of each Borrible's training, together with various comments.

Spiff waved it aside. 'No, I can look at that later, just a verbal report will do.'

'Keep it general, too,' said Rasher.

'Well,' said Knocker, looking sideways at Dodger, 'they are very good, all of them. Some are better at one thing than another, but they are all naturals with the catapult. They could knock a running cat over with their eyes closed, girls as well. In fact Chalotte is better than all of the others, except perhaps Orococco. Hand-to-hand fighting is good, climbing good, running very fast. With the Rumble-stick they vary, but Bingo is fantastic. They aren't so good at scouting work in the countryside, but that takes years of practice and it's unnatural, but they're first-class in the streets and markets, you hardly see their hands come up from beneath a barrow when they takes their dinner. Marvellous. And all of them are dead keen.'

Knocker hesitated and lowered his voice. 'I'm only worried about one of them, although he's worked as hard as anyone, harder. But I dunno, there's something that worries me about Napoleon Boot. He always seems to be thinking about something else, there's a slimy feel to him, it's . . . well, to tell the truth, Spiff, I dunno, it's just a feeling.'

Dodger nodded to substantiate what Knocker had said.

Spiff looked back down the hall to where the Borribles were resting. Some were reading the Rumble books, others were just relaxing and looking at the ceiling. Napoleon Boot was scrutinizing the road map of Greater London and memorizing street names.

'He never stops,' said Knocker. 'They all know the *Borrible Book of Proverbs* by heart, but Napoleon knows it backwards and sideways as well. He's too good to be true.'

Spiff creased his face. 'Well, son, there's nothing to be done now. They have to have a Wendle with 'em because they've got to cross the Wandle. You know how suspicious Wendles are of anybody who wants to cross their bloody river.' He sniffed. 'Wendles are so crooked they find it hard to stand up straight . . . but it'll work out, you'll see.'

There was silence as if nobody agreed with him, not even Spiff himself. He changed the subject.

'Well, your blokes must leave soon anyway; the longer they wait the more dangerous it is. There was a psychological advantage in letting the Rumbles know we were on to them, but the longer we take getting up there, the more time they will have to prepare their defences. Our Eight might not be able to get into the Rumble burrows. Imagine, all that way for nothing!'

Ziggy, who had been trying to interrupt Spiff's flow, at last got a word in. 'I've never liked this idea, you know, Spiff. I think we should have gone up there in force, taken them on, given them a thumping, duffed 'em up.'

'Out of your mind,' said Spiff impatiently; he was always right and knew it. 'We'd have been outnumbered ten to one and they'd have been fighting on their own ground. We stand a much better chance by sending in eight professionals like this, and eliminating their leaders, mark my words.'

'Oh, it sounds all right,' said Ziggy, 'but I don't think those Eight over there can manage it. They haven't done anything yet. Anyone can fire a catapult at a Woollie and run, but what if it's a Rumble with a Rumble-stick at your throat, eh?'

'Look,' said Knocker, 'I've trained this lot. If anyone can get inside the Rumble burrows they can.'

'Rubbish,' said Rasher, joining in the argument, 'they don't stand a monkey's.'

'They do,' said Knocker.

'They don't,' said Ziggy.

Spiff sniffed once more. 'I've been looking at the map, Knocker. I think the Eight ought to go up the Thames, from St Mary's to Wandsworth Reach. I know it's dangerous, but it will save days on the journey, and it means the Eight will be going in from a direction that the Rumbles won't dream of. Even if they've got lookouts deployed as far as Wandsworth Common station and Earlsfield, we'll outflank them. What do you say?'

Knocker was angry all over again. 'But, Spiff,' he cried, grabbing his arm, 'the river is a death trap, all those barges and tugs and police launches, they'd be run down or run in without a chance. They've had no training for water. I don't even know if they can row. I thought they were going to march overland, and now you want to throw 'em in the oggin. It's not on, Spiff.'

'How far do you think they'd get then if they went overland,' asked Ziggy, 'with a solid line of Rumbles from Merton to East Hill?'

Rasher shoved his face up to Knocker's and tilted it sideways. 'If your blokes are as good as you say they are, why are you making excuses? Can't they do it?'

'It's a question of time, training,' spluttered Knocker.

Spiff nodded. 'Just so, you'll get an extra day for boat training and rowing.'

'But we haven't got a boat,' said Knocker, looking at Spiff as if he were mad.

'Oh, you'll need a boat,' said Spiff, 'to row up the river. You'll need one before then to train in, won't yer?'

'Where can we get one?' asked Dodger, looking distraught.

Spiff turned on him, venom in his voice. 'You're a Borrible, ain't yer? Steal one, this afternoon, instead of kipping. Try Battersea Park.'

'Yes,' said Ziggy. 'Let's see how good this team is, or can't they do it?'

Spiff laughed. 'Don't take any notice of him, Knocker. I'm sure your blokes have more tricks up their sleeves than a conjuror's overcoat.' And with that, Spiff, Ziggy and Rasher climbed up the wall on the exercise bars and, one by one, disappeared through the narrow windows that led to Rowena Crescent.

Knocker was shaking with temper as he watched them go. He saw this criticism of his team as a personal insult.

'Just like that, eh?' he said to Dodger. 'Steal a boat, launch it, learn to row, just like that!'

'And only today and tomorrow to do it in,' said Dodger. Knocker walked over to where the Eight were waiting, propped up on their elbows, their interest aroused by the discussion. 'Get yer hats on,' he said. 'I'm taking you to the lake in Battersea Park. We're going to steal a boat.'

Only one person among the Eight registered enthusiasm. Napoleon's dark face became brilliant in anticipation. He stood up and said, 'A boat, eh? That's good, know about boats we do, up the Wandle.'

Knocker breathed a sigh of relief. Nasty as he was, Napoleon could make all the difference.

'We're going to have to steal a boat that can make the river trip along the Thames as far as the mouth of the Wandle. And you, Napoleon, can you teach this team to row in a day?'

'Why, of course, Knocker,' said Napoleon, a sneer in his voice. 'It'll be a pleasure.'

One by one the Borribles slipped from the gym and went their separate ways to the park. They reassembled by the huge iron gates, then walked along the roadway till they arrived at the boating lake. Each Borrible had his hat well down over his ears, a catapult under his jumper and a few stones ready in a pocket, just in case.

Napoleon led the way forward until the Adventurers came in sight of a jetty on which stood a small wooden hut where boat tickets were sold. The high summer season was nearly over, and most of the boats were chained to tree stumps on one of the islands in the middle of the lake, out of harm's way; a dozen others were moored at the jetty itself.

Inside the ticket office sat a park keeper wearing a brown suit and a dark brown hat. He was licking a pencil then writing with it slowly in a ledger; beyond him nothing moved on the surface of the water. Napoleon took cover behind some bushes and the others did likewise. 'Well, Napoleon,' said Knocker after a while, 'what do you think of the boats?'

'We're a bit too far away to judge,' said the Wendle. 'They've got some metal ones there, by the jetty—' His voice changed when he talked about boats; its tone lightened and lost its menace. On the other hand his companions were terrified; Borribles dislike water even more than woods and fields. '—but they aren't really any good for a river trip, too short and wide, unstable, and not big enough anyway to take eight of us. Those over there are the ones we want.' He pointed out to the islands and the others could see that among the flotilla of metal dinghies were a few wooden pleasure boats – with seats and cushions, and rudders that were worked by two pieces of rope – perfect for the Eight.

'Lovely, graceful things they are,' said Napoleon enthusiastically, 'low in the water, they will float over any wave or wash cast up by barges and such. Four rowlocks, two to an oar . . . if the girls are up to it.' He looked behind him at Chalotte and Sydney.

Chalotte said, 'First get your boat, Wendle.'

'Take it easy,' said Knocker, stopping any quarrel before it started. 'How do we get it?'

'I ain't swimming out there,' said Vulgarian, whom they all called Vulge now.

'And the keeper won't hire us one because we're not adults,' said Sydney, 'even if we had money, which we don't.'

'So we'll have to pinch a metal boat to get out there,' added Stonks.

'Yeah,' said Torreycanyon, 'but they keep the oars separate, locked in the shed; they only hand 'em out with the boats.'

Suddenly Napoleon Boot stood up. 'Boats,' he said, 'is my business, I'll do it.'

'All right,' said Knocker, 'who do you want to take with you?'

'I don't need anyone. I do this on my own.'

'Oh yeah!' Knocker said. 'I'd like to see it.'

'You will, mush,' answered Napoleon. 'You will.'

'Well, it better be good,' said Knocker. 'We haven't got time to waste, and don't mush me, faceache.'

'Just wait till the park closes and it's dark,' said Napoleon scornfully, 'then you'll have your boat, and you'll be able to row this lot of matelots up and down till their arms drop off.'

'That'll do me fine, Napoleon Boot,' said Knocker, but his expression was grim and his dislike of the Wendle gleamed through his words.

Dusk crept through the trees and the flower beds. The park keeper closed his ledger, locked the door to his hut, mounted his bicycle and slowly pedalled away. A bell sounded and the paths emptied; now the park was deserted and the Borribles had it to themselves.

Napoleon left his companions and went towards the ticket office. He swaggered as he walked and the others peered through the twilight and wondered about the Wendle.

'He's as friendly as a frozen mitt,' said Stonks.

'Too right,' agreed Orococco, 'but there's not a single fly or bluebottle on him.'

When he arrived at the door of the hut Napoleon put his hands on his hips and squinted at it.

'What's the little bleeder up to now?' asked Dodger of no one in particular, and he got no answer.

After a second or two of staring Napoleon drew a piece of wire from his trouser pocket, bent it into the shape of the letter L and inserted one end of it into the lock. It didn't take long; suddenly the door sprang open and Napoleon turned to face the bushes where the Borribles were concealed. He gave a shrill whistle and waved them down to the water's edge.

'You see,' he said as soon as they got there, 'picking locks, picking noses – all the same to a Wendle.'

In no time at all the Eight had taken the oars they needed and were crowded together in one of the small metal craft. Napoleon rowed them to the island in the centre of the lake and there they waited while he inspected the larger boats. They were fine comfortable things, possessing four wide seats with cushions, two pairs of rowlocks and lots of space for stowing gear fore and aft. But they were solid and heavy and would need scientific rowing.

Napoleon chose the best one: 'Number Seventeen,' he said. 'Been well looked after . . . Climb aboard everyone.' As the group moved to embark Napoleon pulled Knocker aside. 'That boat's bloody heavy,' he said. 'It won't be a piece of cake, out on the river. I hope they can do it.'

But the Adventurers had no time to worry about the future, the task in hand was far too important, and Napoleon worked them hard, for they had only one night in which to learn the art of rowing. The Wendle sat in the stern and steered the boat by pulling on the lengths of rope which were attached to each side of the rudder behind him. And Dodger stood lookout in the bow to make sure they didn't crash into anything, though by now the moon had risen and it was possible to see from one end of the lake to the other.

The crew sat two to an oar as Napoleon had suggested, for they would need a great deal of power when they were out on the River Thames. Not only would they have to contend with the tide but there would be waves washing outwards from passing barges and tugs, and there would always be the danger of a collision. Napoleon gave them their positions in the boat and told them that they weren't to be changed, except that he would take Knocker's place on the journey because, as Knocker knew only too well, he wouldn't be going.

'When we're on the river,' Napoleon said, 'there'll be only eight of us so there'll be no one on the rudder. That means we will have to steer by rowing; listen very carefully to my commands and act on them immediately. Anyone being a bit slow could get us run down, capsized. We could lose all our equipment and worse we could drown.'

And so the instructions went on, and Napoleon taught his companions the basic rowing commands: how to begin rowing, how to stop, how to feather the oars, and how to pull steadily and hard without wasting too much energy. Next time they got into the boat they would be on the wide and thronged waterway of the Thames itself.

All through the night they rowed and listened to Napoleon Boot, navigator. As the hours wore on they realized what a serious thing the river trip was and they looked at each other with concern. Their minds grew numb with the physical effort, blisters rose on their hands, but Napoleon kept them rowing till they could row as well as any Wendle and could change course at the slightest order from the stern. Only when the sky had paled and dawn climbed over the blocks of flats along Battersea Park Road did Napoleon direct them to the lake-side.

Once there the Borribles were happy to obey the command to ship oars, and they sighed with relief when they heard the prow of their boat grate on the gravel of the shore. They sat motionless for a while, their heads bowed, their muscles tight. Dodger, who had done little all this time, stood up, stretched, then jumped ashore.

'Come on, you lot,' he said. 'We've got to hide this boat before it's spotted by the keepers.'

Nearby was a dense clump of bushes and the Borribles manhandled the heavy boat right into the middle of them. They stumbled and tripped over their own feet so tired were they, having been awake for twenty-four hours without a break. They tore foliage from the bushes and grass from the ground and camouflaged the boat so well that it couldn't be seen, even from a distance of a yard or two. When he was quite satisfied, Knocker ordered the team of Borribles back to base.

It was full daylight by the time they reached the Prince's Head, and the early morning office cleaners were already chatting at the bus stops as the Borribles turned into Rowena Crescent. Wearily they climbed into the basement gym and crawled under the sleeping bags and blankets which were laid out on the exercise mats. There were loud groans as they closed their eyes and stretched their burning limbs but Knocker could not sleep; he kept asking himself the same question over and over again: 'Now we've got a boat, how do we get it from Battersea Park to Battersea Reach?'

3

Knocker need not have worried. By the time he awoke later the same day the problem had been solved.

It was not easy waking up; his body felt as stiff as a wire coat hanger and he thought he'd never be able to move again. Even to open his eyelids and look at the ceiling took a concentration of all his effort into the necessary muscles. He turned his head and saw that Dodger was coming in through one of the windows with Napoleon. They were carrying steaming jugs and fruit and bread rolls. They had been to the market for breakfast.

Knocker staggered to his feet, moving like a wooden doll with swollen joints. Napoleon landed gracefully on the floor, his limbs supple, and he laughed.

'Just as well you aren't coming on the trip, ain't it, Knocker? You ain't fit enough.'

Dodger laughed then and that got through to Knocker.

'Okay, okay, you two. If that's breakfast, hand it over and wake the others.' Knocker sat down on a bench and poured himself a cup of tea and drank it.

It hit the right spot. He poured another and tore at a roll with his teeth. Dodger came and sat next to him and helped himself to some food.

'Bingo's not here,' he said conversationally. 'He must have gone out.'

'Of course he has, if he's not here,' said Knocker irritably. 'You're not very bright this morning.'

'I mean out on a job,' said Dodger, and he stood up and looked down at Knocker unpleasantly. No Borrible likes to be told that he isn't bright.

'Anyway, it's not the morning. It's the afternoon.'

Knocker returned Dodger's gaze. 'I'm sorry, Dodger, I didn't mean that. Forget it.'

'All right, then.' Dodger wasn't frightened of a quarrel, no Borrible is. 'Chalotte and Sydney and Stonks and Torreycanyon are out, too,' he said, looking straight in front of him.

Knocker jumped up, spilling his tea. 'What?' he cried. 'Gone off without permission, without saying where?'

'What's wrong, Knocker?' asked Dodger, genuinely surprised. 'You can't expect Borribles to act like regular troops. They're not Rumbles . . . That's why we're Borribles. I think you've been lucky to keep them together this far; most Borribles would have chucked it last night on the lake, but ours didn't, they stuck together.'

Knocker sat down again. 'Damn it all,' he said.

'I think,' said Dodger wisely, 'that you're jealous. You wish you were going on this adventure; you'd like to have a second name, even before others have got their first. That's not right, you know.'

Knocker looked at his friend and sucked his cheeks in between his teeth to avoid showing emotion, but he showed it all the same. He didn't admit it to Dodger but he felt guilty for having overslept so badly and he was ashamed of having aches and pains when he should have been fitter than any of his companions.

'I'm worried about the adventure,' he insisted. 'Will the Wendles let them through Wandsworth without trouble? How will Napoleon behave? It's all a worry.'

'They'll be fine,' said Dodger, 'and Napoleon will turn out all right, even though he is a Wendle.'

'He may be all right now, but what will he be like when he's back in Wandsworth?'

'"Remember today and forget tomorrow,"' said Dodger, quoting a Borrible proverb.

The conversation was interrupted by the arrival of Chalotte, who came in through one of the windows. She crossed the gym and stood in front of Knocker, breathless. Her cheeks bright with running, she shook the hair out of her eyes.

'Bingo said could we all meet him at St Mary's. He's had a plan.' She tossed her head again and laughed.

'What kind of a plan?' asked Knocker sternly.

'I couldn't tell you that; it's not Borrible.'

'I order you,' said Knocker.

'Oh yeah. You said yourself yesterday that the adventure had virtually begun. You're not going on the expedition, so you can hardly give orders any more.' She turned and marched over to where Napoleon, Vulge and Orococco were eating their breakfast, her cheeks no longer shining with exertion but with anger.

'You ought to remember,' said Dodger, 'that they are feeling just as tense as you are. They know they're leaving tomorrow night, and they know that they may not be coming back.'

When Knocker had finished his breakfast and regained his temper a little he set off with Napoleon, Vulge and Orococco to follow Chalotte and Dodger through the streets to Battersea churchyard. There, concealed in the long grass which grew between the big square tombs, they found Number Seventeen. Bingo and his fellow conspirators, dressed as members of the Battersea Sea Scouts, were loafing by the embankment wall.

'How did you manage it?' asked Knocker, unable to keep the admiration from his voice.

'Simple,' said Bingo, with pride. 'Rescued the uniforms from the Sea Scouts, shoved the boat on to a set of old pram wheels that I also liberated, and pushed the boat through the park and down the street as bold as brass. Got stopped by the Woollie on point duty in Parkgate Road but we told him that we were fund-raising for the Sea Scouts and would be taking the boat back this very night; had the head keeper's permission, didn't we? Decent copper, held the traffic up for us to cross the road.'

The church itself was locked and the churchyard deserted. It was the quiet, dusty part of the afternoon and the lunch time boozers were long gone from the Old Swan pub. The great factories and towering flats loomed around the tiny octagonal steeple of St Mary's like idiots surprised by beauty, and no one watched from the lofty isolation of their smoky windows.

Two sailing barges were moored against the river wall which skirted the graveyard, sturdy boats constructed in polished wood. They had rigging climbing their solid masts and their gangplanks creaked and shifted backwards and forwards when the waves from midstream reached the bank. Napoleon's green face became greener with envy.

'I'd love to live on a boat,' he said. 'Look at them names, *The Raven* from Chester, *The Ethel Ada*, Ipswich, marvellous.'

''Ere,' said Bingo, 'that's a point, we ain't got a name for our boat . . . I mean we can't call it *Number Seventeen*, can we? Not on an adventure.'

Chalotte, who had been staring about her, suddenly pointed into the sky. 'There's your name,' she cried. 'Look up there!'

Right behind the church, and dominating it completely, was a huge factory built from the pallid bricks of a dead and unlovely clay. Written across the blank wall in huge white letters they read, 'Silver Belle Flour, Mayhew.'

'We could call it *The Silver Belle Flower*,' said Chalotte. 'You know, it sounds just right.'

'It don't matter what we call it,' said Knocker. 'I name this boat *The Silver Belle Flower*.' And he kicked it by way of ceremony.

The Adventurers adopted the name, then leant against the embankment wall and looked across the broad sweep of the river to the gasometers and the Chelsea Flour Mills opposite. The surface of the Thames here was an alarming greeny-grey colour, and only the floating rainbow whorls of diesel oil and petrol brightened the dullness of it. Far away the horizon was cut out in dirty brown and black against a sky of diluted yellow ochre, and the sun had not shone all day.

They should have been disheartened by such a prospect but somehow it inspired them all with pride and determination. The shift of the waves nudging clumps of flotsam downstream; the hooting of tugs and barges as they passed; the unmoving blocks of black smoke from Lots Road Power Station; the smell, like varnish, of the Thames in London, all these things combined to make their hearts swell and they looked at each other and smiled modestly, knowing that whatever was before them, they would be equal to it.

But Knocker could not partake of this emotion. All he could think of was that he would soon be left behind, and he felt a great surge of self-pity, so he broke the spell, shouting harshly at his companions, 'Well, stop this daydreaming, let's get this boat launched.'

The task was none too easy, for the boat, out of its element, was cumbersome. It took all their strength to mandhandle one end of *The Silver Belle Flower* on to the river wall, and then they swung her round so that they could use ropes to lower her on to the scum-covered rectangle of water that lay imprisoned between *The Ethel Ada* and the embankment.

'She'll be safe there,' said Knocker. 'We'll tie her up midway between the two boats. *The Ethel Ada* will think she belongs to *The Raven* and *The Raven* will think she belongs to *The Ethel Ada*.'

And so *The Silver Belle Flower* was firmly tied to a mooring ring and, with one last look at the gloomy river, the Borribles turned and went back to the gym for a celebratory meal and an early night. Only twenty-four hours to go and the expedition would be under way.

*

The last day was a day of rest for the eight but not for Dodger and Knocker. They went first to tell Spiff about the boat, and they found him sitting at his desk in his orange dressing gown, flicking through a huge book of Borrible rules.

'That Ziggy was always a pessimist,' he said. 'I knew you could do it. A piece of pudding stealing a boat.'

The visit to Spiff was brief in the extreme for there was still plenty for Knocker to do in the storeroom: eight rucksacks had to be packed with a selection of the gear that the High Street Borribles had collected from the shops of Battersea. Each Adventurer had a pair of sturdy boots, waterproof khaki trousers and a combat jacket to keep warm at night when most of the travelling would be done. There were Borrible hats – brown camouflage on one side and a luminous reddy-orange on the other; a life jacket each for the river trip and sharp long-bladed knives. There were catapults too, with spare rubbers and pouches.

Knocker and Dodger fingered the catapults lovingly. They were the best, as used by professional poachers, made out of polished steel, strong and springy. They had a long range and fired stones, marbles or ball bearings with great power. To carry a supply of ammunition Spiff had acquired some old army money belts which had little pockets stuck on them; each pocket would carry a rounded stone, and the belts could be slung across the shoulders like bandoliers. Every Adventurer would have two of them, giving forty shots per person.

Spiff had also seen to it that every Borrible on the expedition had a waterproof watch on one wrist and a compass on the other, and in each rucksack was the *A to Z* map of the London streets. There were matches for lighting fires and a basic ration of food in case anyone got lost or separated from the others.

Knocker was pleased with the work that had been done.

'Everything,' he said, 'except money.'

At dinner time Spiff came into the room with some food and he sat with the two trainers while they ate. He inspected the haversacks and asked what was in each one, making sure that nothing had been overlooked. He asked about the route, made suggestions, chuckled one moment, was grave the next. He stayed about an hour before he got up to leave.

'Well, life is all a chance anyway,' he said. 'Our Eight have got a hard time in front of them but they couldn't have been better prepared. I'd like to thank you, Dodger, for helping . . . so here's a little memento.' He pulled from his pocket one of the waterproof watches that the expedition had been equipped with. 'The lads got a bit enthusiastic and got too many of them,' he added by way of explanation. 'It's engraved on the back.'

Dodger turned the watch over and read out loud: 'The Great Rumble Hunt. Dodger Borrible, Trainer. Good luck.' He was delighted, Knocker could see that. The watch was one of those big army timepieces with an assortment of different faces and knobs on it. 'It's luminous, too,' said Spiff. He looked at Knocker. 'Don't you worry, there'll be something for you later on.'

Knocker nodded without enthusiasm. 'Thanks, Spiff,' he said.

Still Spiff didn't pass through the door. There was something complicated going on behind that crafty face.

'I want you to bring the Eight here on the way to the boat,' he said at last. 'I want to say a last word to them, good luck and all that.'

Knocker felt tired and empty. Everything was beginning for the others; for him all was ending. Why, oh why, he thought, do I have a name already!

Spiff continued to linger by the door. 'Look, Dodger,' he said, 'I'm not trying to get rid of you, but if you'd like to start back home now, you can . . . You'd make it before dark. Drop into the gym on your way, say goodbye to the team and tell them to come here tonight, about elevenish.'

Dodger stood up and strapped on his watch. 'Good idea,' he said. 'That's just what I'll do.'

'Right,' said Spiff. 'That's settled.' And he left the room whistling.

Knocker had a miserable afternoon and evening. He checked the haversacks over and over again just to give himself something to do. He meandered and mooched about the storeroom until at last he went upstairs and rested on his bed in the room which he shared with Lightfinger. He hadn't seen Lightfinger for ages. How long ago it seemed, that night when they had found the Rumbles in Battersea Park and had captured one. How much had happened since then; now everything was ready for the attack. He gazed at the ceiling until he dozed and the noises of the street drifted further away, and his sleep became deeper and deeper.

It was dark when he awoke and he felt very cold, having neglected to creep under his blankets. He sat up and shook himself and rubbed his body vigorously to get the blood running. Getting to his feet he groped for the light switch. What time could it be? Not that the others needed him any more but he would have liked to have seen them off. He made for the stairs and ran down them, two at a time.

On the landing he bumped into Spiff who was coming from his room with some papers in his hand. 'Aha, there you are, Knocker,' he said and beamed at the chief lookout. 'Got your lads downstairs, just going to give them a word or too, can you come down?'

'Course,' answered Knocker, and followed Spiff to the basement.

The Eight were all present and correct. They too had spent a restless time, though they had tried their hardest to sleep to ready themselves for the rigours of the night.

They looked very soldier-like, thought Knocker as he examined them. Warmly dressed, their hats cocked jauntily over their ears, they stood tense and straight, glancing occasionally at their watches or compasses. Most impressive and warlike of all were the double bandoliers of stones they wore and the shiny, lethal catapults stuck into their pockets. The Adventurers shone with health, their skins glowing, but they could not conceal their impatience. They wanted Spiff to say what he had to say and then let them get on the road.

Spiff rustled his papers. 'You'll be off in a minute, so I won't keep you long. I just want to remind you of the object of your expedition. Whatever happens you must not forget it. It is to knock out the Rumble High Command, eliminate them. We want no more of them in our part of London. They must be shown that they can't come down here whenever they think they will and move on to our manor. Whatever happens to you, and we all know the dangers you face, if you eliminate your target, your name will be confirmed and remembered. You have the luck to be going on the greatest adventure anyone has ever heard of.'

Knocker shuffled his feet and wished Spiff would stop making a meal of it. He was feeling sorry for himself and wanted the Eight out of sight, out of mind.

But Spiff hadn't quite finished. 'You've a long way to travel, a dangerous way, and a difficult, perhaps impossible task to accomplish, and I'm sure I speak for all Borribles when I wish you the best of luck. And don't get caught.'

The speech was over and Knocker and Spiff watched as the Adventurers stepped forward to pick up their rucksacks. With a nod for Spiff and a nervous smile for Knocker they left the room one by one. The last to leave was Napoleon. He stood by the open door, looking trim and dangerous; his eyes were bright and excited. His face broke into a cocky and unpleasant smile.

'Sorry you ain't coming, Knocker,' he said triumphantly, 'but I'll tell you all about it when I get back.' And he slid silently out into the darkness.

Knocker swore and rushed across the room and shoved the door hard with his foot so that it slammed and shook the house.

Spiff sat down at the table and looked at Knocker's back while he opened the enormous rule book he'd been reading that morning. 'Over here, Knocker,' he said. 'You've got a farewell present too.'

'Stuff the present,' said Knocker ungraciously, but none the less he crossed the room to sit down opposite Spiff.

Spiff ignored Knocker's remark. 'Well, here it is,' he said. 'I'm going to read it to you, only once, so you'd better listen . . . This is from the *Borrible Book of Rules*, paragraph thirty-four, subsection three a. I quote, "No Borrible who is already named may go on any name adventure whatsoever, he may not even go on a non-name adventure if a Borrible who has no name wishes to take precedence. This rule is unalterable and no exceptions may be made at all, ever." '

Spiff drew a breath and ran his finger to a note at the bottom of the page.

' "Except for the following exceptions." ' He pursed his lips to stop from smiling as Knocker looked up sharply.

' "One. A named Borrible may take part in a name adventure when no other un-named Borrible is available. The choosing of the named Borrible in such a case will be by drawing lots." '

Knocker looked down at the table again.

Spiff went on. ' "A named Borrible may take part in a name adventure when a vacancy occurs through accident or injury at the last moment and there is no time to draw lots." ' Spiff looked up. 'That's a very useful one that is, very useful, I've nobbled a dozen or so in my time, I can tell you . . . Do you know, I've got more'n a few names myself, maybe a score . . . Never believe it to look at me, would you? Oh yes, you have to know yer way round the old rule book, can't break the rules until you know the rules, but let's get down to exception seven two. It's one I haven't used before.'

Spiff coughed and put on a special voice. ' "When an expedition is deemed to be exceptional and outstanding, a named Historian may accompany the expedition to record its deeds for later inclusion in the *Borrible Book of Proverbs*. He may act in an advisory capacity only, taking no part in the actual adventure, be it fighting or stealing, etc., etc. . . ." ' He paused for effect. ' ". . . until such time as all members of the adventure have won their names by performing the tasks allotted to them. At that time the Historian becomes equal with the expedition and may join entirely in the expedition." '

Spiff closed the book with a bang and looked at Knocker, who was dying to smile and laugh and shout all at the same time but didn't want to in case he'd misunderstood.

Spiff winked and jerked his head. 'How would you like to be an Historian, Knocker? Never been one of those, have you?'

'No,' said Knocker, his heart thumping.

Spiff rose to his feet. 'Right, Knocker, clothes are in the cupboard, and a knapsack; everything's there, I did it myself this afternoon. Get changed. Don't want to miss the boat, eh? Ho, ho!'

Knocker dashed into the cupboard and threw off his everyday clothes and got into the set of expedition gear that was hanging ready behind the door. As he changed Spiff talked to him, for he had much to say before Knocker left.

'Don't worry,' he began, suddenly serious, 'they don't know you're coming but they won't go without you. I sent Lightfinger down there with some cock and bull story. He won't let them away till you arrive.' Spiff was silent for a minute or two, watching Knocker's preparation with more attention than the event deserved.

'Do you want to know the real reason you're going?' he asked at last.

Something in Spiff's voice made Knocker stop tying his bootlaces and he listened intently.

'Real reason?' he queried.

'Yes, the real reason. Look, you will have to be Historian, write it all down when you get back and all that cobblers, but it don't really matter, see, long as it looks like you are obeying the rules, but as soon as the Eight have won their names or look like winning their names, brother, you move.'

'Move?'

'Double fast,' Spiff said, his sharp expression getting sharper. 'I've had reasons for setting this adventure up . . . and now I'm telling you. In those Rumble manuals they hint about a treasure they've got hidden, tons of it. We need that treasure down here, Knocker, and you're the Borrible to get it.'

'But Spiff!' Knocker was appalled. 'Money ain't Borrible, we're not supposed to touch it, or have anything to do with it.'

'And look how we live, Knocker, nicking grub, abandoned houses . . . That money could make a difference. I know what I'm talking about; I've been around since the days of the old queen, Victoria I mean. We suffered then, really suffered . . . Now I know you want a second name more than anything on earth, and I'll see you get it, but only if you do what I say. I've been waiting years for this chance, and

I've wangled it so you can sort things out, Knocker. You get the Rumble treasure and I'll see you get another name, maybe two, the sky's the limit . . . But whatever you do, don't tell anyone what you're up to, especially Wazzisname Boot. I know the Wendles, inside out, back and front, up and down. They're trouble, real trouble. Above all, watch out for one called Flinthead; he'd kill you for the fun of it. Believe you me, if you get on the wrong side of him your life won't be worth a fiddler's fart.'

Knocker's face paled. 'But this is an adventure within an adventure,' he said, coming closer to Spiff.

'That's right, Knocker, it is. I'll see you get your second name all right, but it's going to be bleedin' dangerous and don't think it isn't.'

Spiff closed an eye to indicate that he'd said his say; Knocker pushed his arms into his haversack straps and went to the door. 'A second name, bloody hell. I'd best be off then.'

'That's about the size and shape of it,' said Spiff.

Knocker opened the door and felt the coolness of the night on his face. He looked round the room one last time. 'Goodnight, Spiff, and thanks. Don't get caught.'

'You're the one who needs to remember that,' said Spiff. 'There's ten million dangers in that city out there . . . Now go, son, and say nothing to no one.'

Once in the open Knocker looked up through a fine rain to the few stars in the sky and hoped they were his lucky ones. Then he took a deep breath and ran with a loping stride down the High Street towards Battersea church, the knapsack bumping on his back. The pavements were empty and shone damply in the reflected light of the street lamps; his footsteps echoed from the wet walls of the black buildings and his heart sang and bubbled within him. He still could not believe it. He was going – going on the best expedition he'd ever heard of – the Great Rumble Hunt.

Twenty yards from St Mary's church he halted and listened carefully. Lightfinger rose from behind a dustbin.

'Knocker,' he whispered.

'Knocker.'

'It's OK, over here.'

Knocker went forward and patted Lightfinger on the shoulder. 'I'm going,' he said.

'I know,' answered Lightfinger. 'You must have lost your marbles. This expedition is madness . . . It's all down to Spiff, I bet. I'm not even sure it's Borrible.'

Knocker crossed the churchyard and climbed on to the embankment wall. *The Silver Belle Flower* lay just below him, rocking gently in the slight swell that came from midstream. The oars were out and Napoleon was giving whispered commands to keep the boat from banging against *The Raven*. Seven white faces and one black one looked up as Knocker jumped down to join them. He saw amazement in their expressions; how would they take it? But then did he care? It was his adventure, too, now. Whatever they said, whatever they thought, he was going.

Knocker had boarded at the stern, by the rudder, and he sat down and faced Napoleon, who was in the stroke seat.

'I'll row, you steer,' said Knocker putting his face close to the Wendle's.

'What do you mean?' asked Napoleon, half rising, the question full of suspicion, his face tight with anger.

'I mean,' said Knocker, 'that I'm coming with you.'

4

There was no one to see them off but Lightfinger, and he watched the boat edge slowly round the stern of *The Ethel Ada* like a huge insect with only four legs. Darkness covered the craft and soon Lightfinger could only hear the voice of Napoleon giving orders: 'Paddle, stroke side, ease up, bow. Hands on the gunwale, number five. Forward all.' When Lightfinger could hear no more he turned and walked quickly away, glad that he had no part in the Great Rumble Hunt, glad that he was to have nothing to do with the murky and perilous Thames.

The Silver Belle Flower crept out from the shelter of the barges moored along the southern side of the river, but not too far out. Napoleon wanted to be within easy reach of the bank and its complicated blackness; should a police launch appear the Borribles would need to take cover in the shortest possible time.

Napoleon let the boat drift until the bow was pointing westwards, then he tensed his muscles and gripped the two rudder strings tightly.

'Come forward,' he whispered. The crew leant towards him in their seats. 'Paddle,' said the navigator, and the boat sprang upriver like a live thing, eager to be under way.

Nobody spoke except Napoleon, there was too much work to be done. Every rower was concentrating his whole body, every bit of his brain, on handling his oar as cleanly as possible. The water surged below the boat and lifted it regularly, trying to bear it backwards and down to the sea. Occasionally a dark mass of barges, lashed together into one rigid floating city, slid by them, towed or pushed by a small tug. Mysterious lights gleamed and men with deep voices called to one another, and from either shore came the distant groan of traffic, trapped in the streets. It was nearly midnight, and small and fearful on the

Thames the Borribles soon lost the sense of time and place. No matter; as the rowers' technique improved, a feeling of exhilaration passed from one to the other and Napoleon, who had never been out on the great river before, let alone in command of his own ship, was bursting with pride. He could have sailed for ever.

But the swift tide was against them and it took most of their effort to stay in the same place. There was no ornamental pleasure lake beneath them now, instead a sinuous monster had them in its vigorous grip, with rolling ropes of muscle that could shatter a boat like a walnut caught in the crook of a navvy's arm.

They clawed every inch of the way, leaving Battersea Church and moving up to Ransome's Dock, where Eaton House and Archer House stood at the end of Battersea High Street. Underneath the grey girders of Battersea Railway Bridge it was blacker than black, but Napoleon kept them rowing, exerting their arms and legs to the uttermost. To the north was Chelsea Creek and Lots Road LTE Generating Station. Far ahead, glowing crimson in the night sky, at the end of Battersea Reach, was Fulham Power Station, a beacon for the night's work.

Napoleon watched his crew carefully, determined not to overtire them, and before long he decided to take cover and let the Borribles rest and eat. His instructions came clearly and the boat slipped into the southern shore and came to a halt between two enormous barges.

'Ship your oars,' commanded Napoleon, and he went bounding over the benches to tie the boat's painter to a cable which ran from one of the barges to a huge buoy. That done he returned to the stern of the boat and shoved his face up against Knocker's.

'Well,' said Napoleon, and there was hatred in his voice, 'how did you fiddle this then?'

The attention of the others was caught by the question. How had Knocker managed to get himself included in the expedition?

'I'm not here as an Adventurer,' said Knocker. He didn't sound too sure of his argument. 'It was Spiff's idea. In the rules there's a provision for exceptional adventures . . . It allows an Historian to go along and write it all down . . . for the story . . . Spiff asked me to come, at the very last moment, that's all. I couldn't refuse really, not that I wanted to.'

Orococco beamed. 'I'm glad, pleased to see you with us.'

'Well I ain't,' said Napoleon, speaking through his teeth. 'There's something dodgy going down here. I don't trust Spiff and I don't trust you, Knocker; you're as crooked as a pair of concertinas.'

'Oh it's all right,' said Vulge. 'After all, he knows all about parks and countryside and stuff . . . useful in Rumbledom.'

Napoleon narrowed his eyes. 'Useful is as useful does,' he said. 'Let's get one thing clear, Knocker-two-face, your status as instructor is over, you don't give any orders. All decisions will be arrived at jointly, and you're included out.'

'Well of course.' Knocker tried to sound reassuring. 'I won't even give my opinion unless you ask for it. You see, I can't take part in the adventure until you've all got your names, though I can use my catapult in self-defence.'

Napoleon thought for a while. 'I'll be watching you, Knocker,' he said, 'awake and asleep. You step out of line and I'll rattle your skull.' He pursed his lips and when the others were not listening he leant close to Knocker and whispered in his ear, 'I don't believe that's all you've come for – just to be an Historian.'

Knocker pulled his head back. 'I've come for the adventure, that's all. What other reason could there be?'

'I dunno,' said Napoleon, 'but there's something in the wind and I can smell it.' And he scowled and shoved a sandwich into his mouth, munching the bread with hatred.

The Adventurers stayed in the shadows by the barges for two hours, then, rested and fed, they took up the oars once more. There was not much of the night left to them, and they would need to be well under cover before the slightest hint of dawn should appear in the sky.

'We ain't going much further,' said Napoleon. 'We'll hide along by Fulham Power Station.'

They rowed on. Several large tugs passed dangerously close to *The Silver Belle Flower*, causing it to ship a little water, but the Borribles passed unseen and there was no sign of police launches. Napoleon peered into the darkness, his eyes keen, like some mariner of the high seas eager for a landfall. Just before dawn he spied what he had been searching for, a cluster of four or five moored barges, and in the middle of them, he hoped, a space of calm water, large enough to lie low in during the coming day. Another night and a little more rowing would put them at the mouth of the Wandle. There they could conceal the boat and begin their long trek overland.

'One last good pull,' said Napoleon, 'and then we can rest.'

The Borribles worked with a will and they shot across the river, the greasy waves striking *The Silver Belle Flower* on the beam, making her lurch and shudder.

'Keep pulling,' shouted Napoleon. 'One two, one two.' He gave a sharp tug on the rudder strings, the boat changed direction, and his eyes found the gap he sought between the barges.

'Ship yer oars.'

The rowers obeyed with relief, their craft sailed into a little haven of steady water and Napoleon secured the boat fore and aft.

'How do you think we've done then?' asked Stonks, massaging his biceps.

'Good,' said Napoleon. 'We'll stay here all day, and when it's dark we'll go on to Wandsworth Bridge, then it's only a spit and a jump to the River Wandle.'

It was decided to leave two Borribles standing guard while the others slept. Knocker volunteered for the first two hours, and Orococco stood with him. The remainder of the crew unrolled their sleeping bags and curled up as best they might in the bottom of the boat. Knocker kept his watch looking down the grey dawn of the river, while Orococco stared upstream and hummed a Borrible song as a kind of lullaby for his companions, a lullaby they did not need, so exhausted were they.

'River, river, the dawn is breakin'
On shadow and wave and wharf and wall
And the sun'll soon be appearin', river,
Like a big red ball.

'River, river, stop fer a minute;
I know yer journey never ends,
But the city is comin' ter life, river,
All of yer friends!

'River, river, listen, the yawnin'!
Good and bad dreams are nearly gone,

Bottles are clinkin' on doorsteps, river;
The world's movin' on.

'River, river, windin' ferever,
I reckon you've seen it all before.
Wot's night's endin' ter you, river?
Just one daybreak more.'

The Thames was busy now. The two lookouts could hear the sound of hooting tugs and the swish and the slap of the waves thrown up by passing barges, low in the water, nearly sinking under the weight of tons and tons of cargo: coal for the power stations and containers bound for the London Docks.

The first hour of the watch soon passed and Knocker was beginning to feel sleepy when he heard a very slight noise above him on the deck of the nearest barge. He tensed his muscles, slid his catapult from his back pocket and loaded it with a stone from his bandolier. Slowly he stood up and pulled the chunky elastic back so that it was half ready. He glanced quickly up the boat but Orococco was facing the other way, his head nodding. He looked asleep; Knocker waited.

The boat rocked and the Borribles slept on. A scrabbling sound, very cautious, came from above. It seemed to Knocker that someone was trying to find a way out from underneath the tarpaulin that covered the lighter which gave them protection on the shore side. Knocker ran his gaze along the iron wall of the barge, along the criss-cross of ropes that held the tarpaulin down. He could see nothing. Again he looked towards the other end of the boat. Orococco's head still nodded.

The scrabbling noises stopped. Then Knocker heard the noise of a knife cutting through canvas. He pulled the rubber of his catapult tighter, but as yet he had nothing to aim at. Suddenly a small figure dressed in green and brown burst into view on the very edge of the barge right above *The Silver Belle Flower*. Whoever it was had his back towards Knocker, who, aiming for the kidneys, pulled his catapult to its full extent and let fly. He heard a pained intake of breath and the intruder teetered back and forth as if he could not decide which way to fall.

At that moment Orococco turned, his catapult in his hand. He had been feigning sleep, only waiting for the unseen enemy to appear. He took in the situation, saw the enemy and fired, but luckily, as it proved, he missed. As Orococco's stone sped from his catapult the newcomer lost his balance and fell headlong and heavily into the boatload of Borribles, landing in a crumpled heap between Knocker and the first seat. Knocker let fall his catapult and leapt on the interloper, holding him down while Orococco stumbled over the sleeping forms of his companions to give assistance.

In spite of the blow from the stone and the fall from the barge the new arrival put up a spirited struggle. He shouted in some strange language and twice managed to get to his feet, before finally he was pinioned to the deck by the two guards. By this time Stonks and Torreycanyon were awake and the combined weight of the four Borribles was too much for the foreigner. With a sigh and a curse he stopped struggling.

'All right, all right, I give no more trouble,' he said, his English heavily accented.

'Give us a bit of rope,' said Knocker to Napoleon, who had also come awake. 'We'll tie him up and see what we've caught.'

Bingo, too, was out of his sleeping bag and he climbed up the side of the barge to make sure there was no one else who might give them trouble. Vulge followed him but they returned in less than a minute; it was all clear. No one else on the barges, nothing suspicious on the river.

The Borribles looked down at their prisoner.

'Is it a normal, a child?' asked Chalotte.

Napoleon bent over and pulled off the balaclava hat in leather that the captive was wearing. The ears were pointed, very much so. The Adventurers had captured a Borrible, and moreover a foreign Borrible.

'Could you please rub me here, on the back?' said the foreigner in his strange voice. 'That stone you catapulted hit me hard.'

Stonks, who was kind as well as very strong, lifted the prisoner on to a seat and massaged him for a while.

'Oh, thank you, thank you. I feel better now.'

'You're a Borrible,' said Knocker.

'Borrible,' affirmed the other.

'All right, Knocker,' said Napoleon. 'I'll ask the questions. You ain't on this expedition, remember, and anyhow I'm captain of this ship.' He crouched down before the captive. 'If you're a Borrible, where do you come from? Not from London, not with that accent.'

'No,' said the foreigner, and he laughed. 'I'm from Hamburg.'

'Blimey,' said Orococco, 'an immigrant.'

'Cut that out, 'Rococco,' said Napoleon angrily. 'We haven't got time for joking.'

'Who's joking?' said the black Borrible.

'What's your name?'

'My name,' said the prisoner, trying to draw himself up proudly even though he was bound hand and foot, 'is Adolf Wolfgang Amadeus.'

'Swipe me,' said Torreycanyon in disbelief. 'Three names! Don't they have the same rules in Hamburg?'

'Yes,' said Knocker. 'Borribles have the same set-up everywhere.'

'That means he's had three adventures, and successful ones,' said Sydney, and she looked at Adolf with a new interest.

'That's all very well, but he's a nuisance,' said Napoleon. 'He's in the way. He'll have to swim ashore, and then make his own way back to Hamburg.'

Adolf laughed again. 'You have got it all wrong, my friends. I am not superfluous, I am extra. I have come along to join you. I am a great fighter, an experienced general, a marvellous shot with the catapult and I have a high rate of survival. My three names prove that, *verdammt*.'

'What do you mean, join us?' asked Napoleon. 'We're not going anywhere, this is just a kind of outing.'

'Outing,' scoffed Adolf. 'You are the Eight . . . the Magnificent Eight – though I see nine of you – and you are going to Rumbledom to teach those rabbits a lesson.'

Now the captors looked more uncomfortable than the captive. 'How do you know all that?' asked Knocker, breaking his silence. He grasped the German by the collar and shook him. 'How do you know? Come on, spill the beans, you stinking kraut.'

Adolf didn't look at all perturbed. 'Hamburg is a port; often we get English Borribles stowing away on ships for their name adventure. In Hamburg we are hospitable to foreign Borribles. We do not tie them up and beat their heads in.'

'Get on with it,' Knocker urged.

'Not so long ago, we had a Battersea Borrible arrive, very tired, very hungry. I took him into my house, gave him food and beer. We became good friends; he lived under the arches by Battersea Park railway station, he said. Perhaps you know him, no? Anyway, he had been at the meeting when Knocker, that's you—' Adolf Wolfgang Amadeus laughed at Knocker's surprise, '—you had captured a Rumble and it was decided to send an expedition to Rumbledom. My friend, the name he won by the way is Steamer, good, isn't it? Anyway Steamer told me all about it, and I said, *verdammt*, what an adventure, what a chance for me to get a fourth name, and in England, too, with English Borribles! What a name I shall have then: Adolf Wolfgang Amadeus Winston.' He looked round proudly, pleased with himself. 'What do you think, is that not a name and another half?'

'No, not a bit.' said Napoleon.

'So I came to Battersea High Street to see what you did, but, I thought, they will never let me on the boat there, they will just leave me behind, but I must get on the boat, and to get on the boat I have to get on the river, so at high tide I waited on Battersea Bridge and when there is a barge going under with a nice soft load in it, I jump and here I am. I meant to watch for you going by and swim out so you couldn't put me ashore, but the barge men covered me over with canvas. Luckily for me you have come here instead.'

'We can throw you ashore from here, too,' said Napoleon, 'quite easy.'

'I wouldn't do that,' said Adolf, leaning back in his bonds quite relaxed.

'And why not?'

'Oh, you wouldn't want anyone to know which way you were coming, and if you let me go I might go around chatting about what I saw on the river and it might get to the ears of the Rumbles, and the element of surprise . . . lost. A pity? *Stimmt*?'

'We might throw you into the river,' said Napoleon, 'tied to a convenient lump of cement.'

Adolf hooted. 'Anyone else, maybe, but not a friendly Borrible.'

There was a silence then, and as no one could think what to do all eyes turned to Knocker.

'It seems to me,' he said, 'that his story is true. I mean he looks the kind who would want a fourth adventure; I mean mad enough. But however you look at it we can't let him go in case he does give us away. We'll have to take him along, and we'll have to watch him all the time; see if he's a spy, if he leaves messages, things like that. If he isn't, then he's an extra catapult and a bloody good punch-up artist, I bet. We'll have to keep our eyes peeled, that's all.'

'We'll have to watch him like I'm watching you.' Napoleon sneered as he said it.

'Leave it out, Wendle,' said Knocker.

'Let's vote on it,' suggested Bingo, 'all except Knocker. Shall we keep Adolf or throw him in the river? Who's for keeping him?'

Seven hands went up; Napoleon abstained.

'You're making a big mistake,' he said sourly. 'See if I ain't right. Make sure you take his catapult away, and keep his hands tied.'

Bingo went down the boat to the prisoner and untied his feet. Adolf was searched and a catapult and knife were found in his pockets.

'You can stay for the time being,' said Napoleon, 'but I'm not keen on it. If you give any trouble on this boat I'll send you to the bottom of the river so fast the fish will think you're an anchor.'

'I love your English understatement,' said Adolf, and after flashing a mad grin at his new companions he curled up under a seat and was soon snoring. Everyone else, save Torreycanyon and Stonks, who had volunteered to stand second guard, followed the German's example, wriggling into their sleeping bags and falling sound asleep. So through the morning, afternoon and evening, the boat rose and fell softly on the waves, and the slumbers of the Borribles remained unbroken, and their dreams untroubled.

*

The fog-ridden sun had long since fallen below the red horizon when the boat came alive again. Napoleon roused everyone with a rough shove and told them to eat. He wanted to be rowing again as soon as possible. The Wandle wasn't far away but there would be much to do before the dawn of the next day.

The Borribles stretched and rubbed each other's backs; they shared the food from their haversacks and poured the last of the tea from their Thermos flasks. Knocker took his rations and sat by the German.

'There you go, Adolf, me old china,' he said. 'We might have thrown you in the river quite happily but seeing as you're still here, you'd better have some grub.'

Adolf sat up and ate with an appetite. '*Danke*,' he said between mouthfuls. 'Excellent.'

'How come you got three names, then?' asked Knocker enviously.

'Aha,' said Adolf, 'it's a question of knowing the rules. You must know a few, otherwise you wouldn't be here, would you?'

'Oh, that was Spiff, not me,' said Knocker. 'He's as sly as a saveloy. So where'd you get the names? Wolfgang, Amadeus, and Adolf, of course.'

'Adolf I got at home, Wolfgang I got in Denmark, Amadeus in Salzburg of course, burgling. Now I want to get an English name: Winston.'

'They are good names,' said Knocker, 'very good names, and I bet there are good stories behind them.'

'Every name has a story,' said Adolf philosophically, 'but I am glad you like them, and Winston will add something special. But, please, tell me the names of all the others.'

'They haven't got them yet,' said Knocker, 'but I can tell you what they will be when this adventure is over.' And he explained the reason for the Rumble names and what they were, but the conversation was cut short by the arrival of Napoleon, pushing his body between them. 'Less of this nattering,' he ordered. 'This ain't a holiday, you know.'

The rowers went to their seats and Napoleon slipped the moorings and *The Silver Belle Flower* drifted from its hiding place. Once more they crossed the Thames rapidly and, still heading westwards, they skirted the southern shore on the last leg of their river journey. At dawn, if Napoleon's navigation was correct, they would land at the mouth of the Wandle, the muddy stream where only Napoleon Boot's people knew a way through the treacherous swamps which stretched for miles under the hard streets of Wandsworth.

5

The wide curve of the river was empty and still, and the ripples of its heavy green water were frozen and dirty. On the Fulham shore squatted the oil depots, faceless places waiting on faceless roads that led nowhere and where nobody lived. Just before dawn Wandsworth Bridge passed over the Battersea boat, casting a darker shadow than the night, and all that the rowers saw were the powerful and unmoving waves that stood and gnawed at the stone piers on which the bridge was built.

They were now into Wandsworth Reach. Along the southern side of the Thames stretched a great wasteland, and although the Adventurers saw nothing, they could sense the existence of a wild space from the shapeless whistling of the wind. On the northern bank stood a cement factory and beside it the great bulk of the Trinidad Asphalt Company, but the Borribles could not see where the buildings touched the sky because the sky was as black as roof-slate.

It was so murky that Napoleon was convinced he would never find the mouth of the Wandle and his companions began to despair. After several fruitless attempts he went to the front of the boat and knelt down to peer into the blackness. There were dozens of barges here, deeply laden with the old lumber of all Wandsworth, for the land around the estuary was a vast rubbish dump and somewhere amongst the hillocks of refuse meandered the slimy river.

An overpowering stench was brewing by the bank, a mixture compounded of rancid sewage, mouldering waste paper and the rotting flesh of dead seabirds. The water dripping from the raised and expectant oars of the rowers made no sound, so thick and oily was it. The Borribles coughed and retched, drooping on their benches, only just able to obey Napoleon's commands as he made the boat nose this way and that, his torch stabbing at the night.

At last he turned and in a whispered shout, sharp with a weary excitement, said, 'I've got it.'

The boat faltered. The rowers twisted on their seats to look and their hearts shrank to the size of peanuts. In the flat wall of the Thames embankment, hidden behind a flotilla of barges, a gap had appeared.

'This must be Wandle Creek,' said Napoleon. 'Anyway, there's only one way to find out, and that's go up the thing.' It was obvious to the others that he was tense, that he didn't really know.

The boat swung slowly until it was knocking against the solid current of the Wandle, and as soon as he was on course Napoleon ordered his crew to paddle upstream. He ran quickly down the middle of the boat, freed Adolf's hands and told him to lift out the rudder. 'If you try to escape I'll catapult you right up the back of the bonce.'

Adolf looked surprised. 'Escape? This is what I came for, I'm not leaving you now.'

Napoleon ran back to the bow to direct the progress of the boat and the Borribles pulled steadily, only too glad they couldn't see where they were in the foetid gloom.

They had gone only a short distance when the creek forked and after a moment's hesitation Napoleon steered them to the left and they rowed on, levering their oars with difficulty out of water that seemed as tenacious as treacle. After ten minutes they heard Napoleon swear loudly and then call out urgently for them to stop. He struck the gunwale of the boat in anger.

'Dammit! I forgot the weirs.'

The boatload of Borribles was utterly dismayed. Across the quiet of the night came a sound from beyond their experience, a rushing and a roaring of the elements. Swivelling again in their seats they saw a foaming slope of water slanting towards them in the torch light; racing yellow suds forced themselves up through a black and shiny surface which slid, unstoppable, towards them, like the most precipitous moving staircase in the London Underground. Polythene containers, empty paint cans and plastic bottles surged and danced around the boat, buffeting against its sides, like evil spirits on the river to hell.

'W-what is it?' asked Bingo, trying to keep his lips steady.

'It's an effin' weir, that's what, too high to get round. We'll have to take the other fork. There's another weir but it's not so steep.' Napoleon's voice was dispirited and exhausted. He felt at the end of his tether, worn out by the responsibilities of the river trip and now this at the end of it. 'If we're caught out here in the daylight, we'll be sussed by the rubbish men and caught by the Woollies for sure.' He thought for an instant and the others waited, the boat still staggering under the onslaught of the swirling water. 'Ship yer oars,' he said at length, and as soon as the oars were on board he took one of them and began to punt the boat back the way they had come, while his crew sat uselessly on the benches of *The Silver Belle Flower*, squinting hard to right and left but seeing little. It was all too silent and ugly.

'Keep your eyes peeled for that fork in the creek,' growled Napoleon, 'otherwise I'll miss it and we'll be out on the Thames again. We must be hidden by dawn. This place is lousy with adults in daytime.'

His fear was shared by the others. Already the high banks of the Wandle, held in place by slimy green sleepers and sheets of pitted iron, were taking on a shape and the black sky was not so black as it had been.

Then suddenly, 'The fork, the fork!' It was Adolf's voice.

Napoleon let the boat drift round into the other branch of the Wandle.

'Get those oars going quick,' he commanded, wrenching his own from a mudbank that was reluctant to let it go. There was a nasty squelch as the oar came away and large dollops of sludge rolled down the wood and slunk back into the river.

Napoleon urged his crew on. The flow of the tide was less strong here and they soon went under a railway bridge, the boat bashing through floating atolls of muck like a trawler in pack ice. Another fork came up before them but Napoleon did not hesitate this time.

'Bow side paddle,' he called, 'stroke side rest. One, three, paddle.' And the boat veered to the left.

'We went left last time and it was wrong,' said Torreycanyon, loudly, with some edge to his voice.

'Yeah,' said someone else.

Napoleon's face became so white with anger that it glowed phosphorescent in the dark dawn. 'Well, we're going left this time and it's right.'

At that moment there was a clang and a boom and Napoleon was knocked forward and thrown down in the scuppers. The boat stopped moving with a jolt and a scraping was heard as the bow slid against metal. Napoleon jumped to his feet rubbing his head.

'Damn you, don't talk to me when I'm navigating,' he shouted. 'We've gone and run into a conduit; could have drowned us.'

Slung low over the water a huge pipeline spanned the Wandle near a footbridge and it was this that had flung Napoleon to the deck.

'You at the stern, row hard,' he cried. 'This pipe's so low over the water that we'll have to force the boat under it. Don't fall in any of yer, there's eels in here will have yer leg off.'

Those at the rear of the boat leant on their oars while those at the front got down on their backs and tugged and shoved *The Silver Belle Flower* under the pipeline. When they emerged on the far side it was easy enough for them to push the boat through, while those in the stern ducked under in their turn.

'It's not finished yet,' said Napoleon. 'There's a real waterfall here, ten foot high, right under The Causeway. To get round it we've got to beach the boat and pull it overland.'

Above their heads was a high fence that had been made by the rubbish men, using old bed frames, bedsteads and strips of metal. Napoleon took a pair of wire cutters from his pocket and got Bingo to give him a leg-up. He clung to the bankside and cut all the springs out of one of the bed frames, making a gap large enough to get himself and the boat through.

'Throw up the painter,' he ordered next, and when he had the rope in his hands he told the crew to jam their belongings firmly under the seats and then scramble up to join him.

'We've got to get this bleeder up here,' explained Napoleon, whose weariness had momentarily dropped from him under the excitement of leadership. 'Then drag it across this island we're on, then we'll be above both weirs, but we've got to hurry.'

The Adventurers gathered around the painter and hauled with every ounce of strength they possessed. Slowly *The Silver Belle Flower* came up from the water to hang vertically above the Wandle. Napoleon looped a turn of the rope around a notice board while the others seized the bow of the boat and manhandled her on to The Causeway until she rested flat on the ground.

'Right, four each side,' said Napoleon. 'I'll pull, the Jerry can push.'

'Not half,' said Adolf.

They dragged and pushed the boat across a littered roadway where splintered glass and the debris from long abandoned houses made a crunching sound under the keel. Fifty yards they had to go; it was hard work and they slipped and stumbled and cursed, but at last they came to the main branch of the Wandle, well beyond the two dangerous weirs.

It was pale daylight now and the danger of being spotted in this open and desolate country was increasing every minute. Hurriedly they balanced their boat on the river bank and Napoleon grouped them together.

'When I give the word, push like hell. She has to land flat on the water. If she don't, she'll sink.'

On his command they all heaved together, and *The Silver Belle Flower* flew out into the air and bellyflopped on to the water, making a sound that reverberated like a gunshot across the no-man's land of the empty estuary. Before she could float away Napoleon dived down into the boat, sprawling between the benches. He rolled over, grasped the painter and threw it up into the hands of Torreycanyon.

'All back in,' yelled the Wendle, 'quick as yer like.'

As the others embarked, Knocker looked back the way they had come, and now in the weak light he could see.

Two black steam cranes guarded the mouth of the Wandle, square and ugly, covered in sheets of flimsy metal, and they had iron wheels which ran on iron rails. These machines it was that loaded the barges with rubbish, scratching patiently every day into mountains of garbage that were always replenished, never diminishing. Scattered lorries waited to go scouring across Wandsworth in search of more waste; huge tipper trucks and skip carriers stood idle between piles of discarded stoves and gutted refrigerators. Far off, between the Wandle and Wandsworth Bridge, was a mile of undulating mud-coloured barrenness, relieved only by the blobs of white that were seagulls, big as swans, tearing at offal with beaks like baling hooks.

Knocker shivered at the awesome beauty of it.

'Strike a light,' he said. 'What a place.'

'It's home to me!' Napoleon's voice was harsh. 'Get a move on.'

Knocker jumped down into the boat and took up his oar.

'Row on,' called Napoleon. 'This 'ere Wandle's the steepest river in London, like rowing up Lavender Hill it is, with the traffic against yer.'

The adventurers bent forward. Their hands were sore, their backs ached and the tensions of the night had exhausted them. With their eyes closing and their muscles burning they rowed on and on, across a windswept landscape with no trees or buildings, until, after Armoury Way, they came by the backyards of factories to Young's Brewery and at last they heard Napoleon's soft command: 'Hold it steady now, ship yer oars.'

They relaxed and the boat came to rest. In the distance dawn was lying along the streets of Wandsworth like a dead dog, and the straight sides of the buildings, raised up in smoky yellow bricks, towered into a dusty sky. And very high, one bright window of light showed where an early morning bus driver grumbled his way from a warm bed into a cold kitchen.

Napoleon did not allow the crew to rest for long.

'Right, you lot, we're here!' he said, a certain amount of satisfaction in his voice, and the Borribles turned and not one of them didn't gasp in horror. In a cliff-like factory wall a deep hole was visible: a brick culvert, barely large enough to allow the passage of the boat, hardly high enough to clear the heads of the rowers. It dripped with green slime and Napoleon's voice echoed feebly around it, fading, sucked into nothing. The stench was disgusting and solid, rolling out on to the river in misty clouds, like the foul breath of a dying dragon.

'Swipe me, man,' said Orococco, his eyes and teeth all green in the queer light that floated up from the water, 'we ain't going in there.'

Napoleon stood up in the prow, his legs spread, his hands on his hips like a ruffian pirate captain. 'This is the River Wandle,' he said, 'an ordinary little river that flows under houses.'

'It stinks,' said Bingo.

'You've had it too easy,' retorted Napoleon. 'This is Wandsworth where the best Borribles come from.'

Knocker grinned to himself in spite of the trepidation he felt in common with his companions. Whatever else he thought about Napoleon Boot he had to admit that the Wendle had guts and style.

'Now we're taking this boat in,' said the navigator, 'and anyone who don't like it can swim home in this.' He bent and scooped up a handful of the river water and cast it into the bottom of the boat. The eyes of the Borribles were mesmerized by the evil-looking liquid while their bodies were repelled by it. The water hardly disintegrated as it hit the deck, but green globules of it rolled into the crevices of the woodwork to lie there glowing.

'Right,' went on Napoleon, crouching in the prow. 'Gently does it . . . Keep your heads down and I'll fend off with my hands.'

Under the cautious power of the rowers the boat shoved its nose into the steaming dankness of the sewer and Napoleon shone his torch this way and that, but it did little good, for the rolling clouds of fog swallowed and digested the tiny beam before it could travel a yard.

The rowers leant back in their seats, digging their oars through the surface of the water. Adolf sat in the stern, shining his torch over the way they had come, and in its light the Adventurers could see the dripping roof of the cavern and sometimes the gaping holes of side tunnels where thick water slid slowly out to fasten itself to the main stream. The German hummed gently to keep up their spirits: 'Ho, ho, heave ho. Ho, ho, heave ho. Come, my brothers, ho, ho, heave ho.'

Napoleon's commands came regularly in a quiet voice. 'Slowly bow side, two strokes. Easy stroke side.' And so they groped forward, hesitating at times before tunnels that forked to right and left, Napoleon sometimes knowing where he was going, sometimes guessing.

After what seemed hours of paddling, the oars began to strike against the tunnel walls. 'Bring 'em in,' said Napoleon. 'It's too narrow for rowing now, someone will have to get into the water and pull the boat along.'

There was silence among the Borrible crew. Napoleon bent under a seat and pulled out a pair of rubber waders. He was laughing to himself, as the others could see in the light of his torch.

'I knew I'd have to do it,' he said. 'The best Borribles come from Wandsworth all right.'

Adolf chuckled. 'Ho, I don't know about that; we've got a lot of dirty water in Hamburg, my friend. Give me the waders; I will pull you. I haven't done any of the rowing.' The German bustled down the boat. He took the waders from Napoleon, slipped them on and jumped into the stream with no hesitation. The rowers swivelled in their seats, amazed.

Bingo knelt and shone his torch ahead so the German could see where he was going, but Adolf had his own torch hooked on to a button of his jacket. He grabbed the painter in both hands and with a 'Ho, ho, heave ho' he pulled the boat smartly along as if it weighed nothing.

'Well I never,' said Sydney.

Napoleon shook his head. 'There'll be a kind of path by the side of the sewer a little further on,' he called. 'You'll be able to walk on that.'

This information turned out to be true and soon Adolf was striding along a brick walkway that had been built originally for the sewer men of Wandsworth. 'This is more like it,' he yelled, and began to sing his song even louder than before.

Suddenly the singing stopped. The rope went slack and *The Silver Belle Flower* bumped into the bank. Those in the boat looked up to discover what had stopped the German and saw, crouching aggressively against the curving wall of the sewer, an armed Wendle.

He was a wiry figure and was wearing the same kind of rubber waders that Napoleon had lent to Adolf. Instead of the normal woollen Borrible cap this Wendle, like other warriors of his tribe, wore a metal helmet made from an old beer can; it covered his ears and guarded his head, and in the light of the torches it glowed a coppery green. To keep himself warm he wore a chunky jacket of wool covered with plastic to keep out the water, and the plastic shone orange and luminous like the coats worn by the men who work on motorways. The Wendle's face was hard and tough, much tougher than Napoleon's even, and his eyes moved quickly. He was not afraid even though he was one against ten. With a shout he thrust forward with the Rumble-stick he bore in his hands.

It was then that Adolf showed what a redoubtable fighter he was. Although unarmed, he was not one to avoid a good fight; as he had said, he liked fighting. The spear jabbed towards him and he slid gracefully to one side, his body folding into the water. The Adventurers, all excepting Napoleon, had come to admire the German, and they sprang to their feet in dismay. But Adolf was down not out, for as he fell he stooped under the vicious weapon and caught hold of the

Wendle's right foot. As soon as Adolf's feet touched the river bottom he yanked as hard as he could and the Wendle lost balance and landed flat on his back on the edge of the pathway, the spear shaken from his grasp. In that same moment the German grabbed his opponent's head and pulled it brusquely into the water, shoving it under the filthy surface.

'Ho, ho, ho,' he roared, his face bright with triumph and his blue eyes flashing like police beacons revolving.

There was a clatter further along the tunnel and three more Wendles appeared, armed with powerful catapults, raised and ready, aimed at Adolf.

Napoleon waved his arms and his torch. 'A Wendle, a Wendle!' he shouted at the top of his voice. 'Don't fire! We're Borrible! Adolf, let him up. Quick or you're as kaput as a kipper.'

The German kept his eyes on the strung catapults and cautiously raised the limp body of his assailant from the black water. He held it in front of him like a shield and without being noticed, save for Knocker who was now in the prow of the boat with Napoleon, he slid a catapult from the unconscious Wendle's pocket and secreted it in his own.

'Good work,' said Knocker to himself, 'that kraut's a real find.'

'You, put that Wendle back on the path,' said one of the new arrivals. 'The rest of you keep dead still. There's another fifty of us up round the next bend.'

Adolf carried his burden to the bank and unceremoniously dumped it. Napoleon shouted, 'I'm a Wendle myself, on the Great Rumble Hunt. Flinthead knows about it, hasn't he told you?'

'He told us,' came the answer, 'but if you've killed Halfabar then you're in serious trouble.' Two of the Wendles came forward and knelt beside the half drowned warrior. They turned the sodden body over and pummelled the water out of it, then, reassured, they installed Halfabar in *The Silver Belle Flower* so that he might recover; meanwhile Adolf was ordered to continue pulling the boat.

'Walk in the river, you,' said the Wendle in charge, 'the rest of you do everything we say. If anyone so much as makes a move towards a catapult, there'll be more stones on your head than an avalanche. There's fifty of us following you now, as well as fifty in front.'

Knocker glanced over his shoulder, as did his friends, and there they were, a crowd of figures wading through the water behind them, perhaps more than fifty, all bearing Rumble-sticks. It was obvious that all the Adventurers could do was obey.

'Who's the Borrible who's been doing all the talking?' Knocker whispered into Napoleon's ear.

'He's a two-name Borrible,' said Napoleon, 'but he's just called Tron. If he had a name for all the things he's done he'd be a hundred-name Borrible, I can tell you. Hard as nails he is, and Flinthead, our chief, why, he's just the same. Nobody comes in or out of here without their say-so.'

'But you're a Wendle yourself . . .'

'Don't matter. I've been out, away; they've got to be careful. Only right isn't it, when you think about it? I mean you jumped on the Rumbles quick enough when they came into your patch.'

The tunnel widened out a little now. There were paths on either side and both of them were crowded with warriors who gazed without friendliness at their brother Borribles in the boat below. Adolf they prodded with their spears and the Adventurers sat quietly in the boat, hoping that the German would not lose his temper.

They were apprehensive. Borribles, although inclined to argue among themselves, were on the whole congenial people. The Adventurers had been told that Wendles were the fiercest of all the tribes, but hadn't realized that they were quite so military, quite so suspicious. Napoleon tried to explain the situation to his companions as they went along.

The Wendles, he argued, lived in constant fear of the Rumbles; their territory was the nearest to Rumbledom and had a long frontier with it. Along that frontier the Rumbles outnumbered the Wendles by at least five to one and the Borribles of Wandsworth had only kept their freedom by maintaining a warlike stance. Over the years this had made them warriors, mistrustful, cunning and hard.

'I dunno about that,' said Vulge. 'They certainly look like a gross of top quality villains to me, and I should know, we've got a few over in Stepney.'

This conversation was brought to a halt by the loud voice of Tron shouting at the exhausted Adolf, tapping him on the head with a Rumble-stick.

'Stop there, you, mush!'

'I've got a name, you know, Wendle,' said Adolf, looking up, his face covered in mud and sweat. 'In fact, I've got three names, Adolf Wolfgang Amadeus, and I would never tell you the story of how I got them.' And with that insult Adolf swore his favourite oath, '*Verdammt*.'

'You probably got the names second hand,' said Tron, bringing out the first in a series of Borrible sarcasms.

'Even that is better than finding your name in a dustbin,' said Adolf with spirit. 'Fingy is the name that would suit you well if it were not too flattering.'

'Cut it out,' yelled Knocker. 'This can only lead to trouble. Remember we are after the Rumbles, not each other.'

The Adventurers were next ordered to stand on the bank while the boat was made fast and Halfabar lifted out. He had recovered enough to stand now, although he looked a little groggy and his face was greener than usual because of the quantities of stinking water he had swallowed. He peered round until he saw Adolf, a wet and muddy figure who was being hauled ashore by Stonks and Torreycanyon. Halfabar staggered away from the two Wendles who held him upright and pushed roughly through the little knot of Adventurers who waited on the towpath. He halted in front of Adolf and shoved his green face up to the slime and sweat-covered one of the German.

'It is not over between you and me,' he hissed, his angry and smelly breath enveloping Adolf's head and making him wince. 'One day we'll meet again, where you can play no tricks, and I'll kill you.'

'A Borrible who has no tricks is no Borrible,' said Adolf pleasantly, reciting an old German proverb. 'You'd better go and have a good rest; you need more strength, my little girl. Right now you could probably hit me a hundred times before I noticed you were there.' And the German turned and followed his companions along a narrow but dry sewer tunnel that led upwards and away from the main river.

The Adventurers were escorted by an armed guard of Wendles, and the noise of their squelching tread echoed everywhere. On river patrols the Wendles wear waders, and the sound they make when they walk is a strange one; when a hundred march together that sound is the sound of a wet centipede on the move.

'Where's Napoleon?' Knocker asked Bingo, who was beside him.

'They took him off ahead, on his own,' answered Bingo. 'I hope he sticks by us.'

Knocker was made uneasy by the information, but he comforted himself with the thought that however suspicious the Wendles might be of outsiders, it was in their interest that the Great Rumble Hunt should take place. The chances of it succeeding were small, but if it did the Wendles would be safe for years to come. After all, they had sent one of their own men to be trained for the mission; that must mean something.

'It'll be all right,' said Knocker, loud enough for all his companions to hear. 'They've probably just taken Napoleon off to check that we are who we say we are. He'll be back.'

They marched on and the tunnel rose and twisted and they shone their torches at the floor which was uneven and broken.

'Keep close,' said Knocker. 'If there's any trouble we'll form two lines, back to back.'

A few minutes later the Adventurers came into a vast underground cavern with a floor that sloped steeply away from them. It must have been the central chamber for the Wandsworth sewage system back in the nineteenth century. Now it was dry and its elegant brick arches were beginning to crumble.

Scores of Wendles were already present, and latecomers were emerging from the corridors that led from all parts of the huge borough. Each Wendle held a torch and together they spread an eerie light over the scene. Tron's voice sounded from behind: 'Keep going, straight in front of you, over there, where you see that platform. You're going to meet Flinthead.'

On the far side of the hall stood a small podium and on it was one chair and in that chair sat Flinthead himself; by his side stood Napoleon Boot, talking rapidly.

Flinthead gazed down at the Adventurers as they came before him. His eyes didn't move and though Knocker watched very carefully the chief Wendle didn't seem to blink either. Knocker assumed that this was because he always lived in the dark and never saw the sun, though it was said that he knew exactly what happened everywhere. As Spiff had intimated, Flinthead was the most cunning, the most merciless and the most unpredictable of all the Wendles. Every Wendle went in deadly fear of him, yet he commanded a strange loyalty, a loyalty born out of the threat that surrounded the whole community.

Knocker looked across at Napoleon for some hint of what was going to happen but Napoleon ignored the glance; they would all have to wait and see what Flinthead had in mind.

Still the chief of the Wendles said nothing, and everything that had been in the boat was now brought forward and exhibited in front of the line of captives. While he waited, Knocker continued his scrutiny of Flinthead's face. The eyes were indeed strange, frosted over like lavatory windows, impenetrable; they didn't gleam or glint and still they didn't move. It was uncanny. His face was rubbery, streaked with grey and dark green. His nose was like a false plastic one that had been too near the fire and had melted. It was an evil nose, a dangerous nose, a nose that could smell out treachery and deceit even when there was none. On his head he wore a helmet of copper riveted together in sections, and it had an extra piece that came between his eyes and attempted to protect, or hide, the nose, but the nose was too big for concealment. His body was small and sinewy, like that of most Borribles, and he was clothed in warm wool-lined waders and a plastic jacket painted with bright golden paint. And, in a way that Knocker could not define, in a way that puzzled him, Flinthead looked like someone Knocker knew.

The chieftain's head moved at last and his eyes moved in the same axis, as if they had no independent life. He looked along the line of adventurers and at their belongings, then his head became immobile again. Napoleon continued to pour his story into Flinthead's ear, pointing out his companions in turn, giving their names and telling what equipment they had brought. Flinthead nodded as the tale went on.

What power he has, thought Knocker, looking round the great hall. There must have been hundreds of Wandsworth Borribles in the cavern now, and although they talked among themselves there was none of that cheerful anarchy that Knocker associated with the meetings of any of the Borrible tribes he knew.

'Is your lot like this?' he asked. Chalotte was standing next to him.

'No,' she replied. 'Creepy, I call it.'

It was amazing to Knocker how Flinthead had acquired this power.

Normally a Borrible community has little organization above that of the Borrible house, or at the most and in emergencies only, the street.

At this point Knocker's thoughts were interrupted; Flinthead slowly raised his left hand, and conversation in the great hall ceased immediately. Every Borrible there must have had at least one eye on the chieftain, every Borrible that is except Bingo and Adolf, who had been deeply engrossed in cheering each other with tales of what they were going to do to the Wendles when they got half a chance.

'*Ja*,' Adolf's voice boomed over the silent hall. 'Starting with Halfabar, I'll obliterate them.'

'And I'll see to Flintbonce there, just for starters,' yelled Bingo, and then stopped as he realized that maybe two hundred ears had heard him, that one hundred torches now beamed on him and two hundred eyes had seen him and would remember his face. Worst of all, the blank eyes of Flinthead himself now came to rest upon Bingo like the heavy hand of death.

Flinthead waited and the hall became quieter and quieter, every increase in the tension making the atmosphere more difficult to breathe. Then he spoke, and when his voice came it came as a shock. It was a friendly voice, warm and solicitous, like a kind uncle asking after a favourite nephew's health. His mouth smiled, but no other part of his face shared in that smile. He addressed the line of Adventurers.

'Welcome, my friends,' he said, looking as if he wished Adolf and Bingo six feet deep in Wandle mud. 'Welcome to Wandsworth. You must forgive us, fellow Borribles, if we seem so defensive. You live far from these rugged frontiers, whereas we exist under the constant threat of Rumbledom and its rapacious denizens. It would be so easy for them, you understand, to come pouring down the hillsides, across Southfields and into this Borough where we . . . pick up a poor living. Heaven knows why they covet what is ours, but then greed is a terrible thing, and although the Rumbles seem to us to be rich beyond the dreams of avarice, we find them everywhere, taking more and more. You captured only one Rumble on your frontier and yet you immediately gathered an elite force from all over London to punish them. Think how much more we feel the need to protect ourselves when we have thousands of warrior Rumbles on our very doorstep. But let us forget your awkward welcome. Now that we know exactly who you are, and where you are going, we join in common cause with you. Your enemy is our enemy, your fight our fight.'

He coughed, thought for a moment and then went on. 'Napoleon Boot, a warrior whom we trust, has told me of you and what you intend to do when once you reach Rumbledom. It is a good plan, though hazardous, and we hope you succeed. For the present our warriors will look after you. Sleep well and tomorrow Tron will set you on your way; we shall see that your every need is satisfied. We shall give of our best.'

Knocker stepped forward and looked straight into the cold eyes.

'What,' he asked, making his voice sound even and mature, 'will happen to our boat? We shall need it for the return journey.'

A smile lived for a second on Flinthead's face and then died for want of sustenance. 'We shall guard your boat as carefully as if it were our own. After all, you will need it to carry your spoils.'

'We do not go for spoils,' replied Knocker. 'But there is another thing: will you, on our return, guarantee us a passage down the Wandle, till we are safe on the Thames?'

'My own personal bodyguard shall be with you as you leave here and shall be at your disposition when you return. That shows how important it is to us that your mission succeeds, and will be a measure of our gratitude if it does. Next time we shall know you and our welcome will be more . . . amiable. For the present Tron will take you all to a comfortable room that has been prepared.'

Flinthead gestured and Tron and Halfabar came forward and indicated that the Adventurers should follow them. After a last glance in the direction of the podium, they turned about and walked across the huge hall in the footsteps of their Wendle guides.

Knocker did not follow the others immediately. He moved closer to the platform and looked up at Flinthead once again.

'Does Napoleon come with us, or does he stay here with you?' he asked the chieftain.

The chief Wendle smiled like a tombstone. 'He had best stay with you, I think, then you can leave together in the morning. He has told me all I want to know, especially about you, Knocker. I think the adventure might succeed with you at its head.'

'I am not its leader, Flinthead,' protested Knocker, looking angrily at Napoleon.

'I know,' said Flinthead dismissively. 'You are a . . . What is it? An Historian? We all know how to bend the rules, especially the one called Spiff. I know of him and he knows of me. Well, whatever you are, I hope you win through. I ask only one thing, and this I want you to promise: that you come back to us and recount in every detail the dangers of your expedition. One of the few pleasures I have is listening to the stories of those who make a journey to earn their names. I want to hear how you fare, including Napoleon here; a fine name he will have.'

'It will be the least we can do by way of thanks for the hospitality we have received at your hands,' said Knocker politely, though he was deeply troubled in his mind by Flinthead's behaviour. But at that moment all Knocker could do was to pretend he believed everything he was told. Knocker looked at Napoleon. He was a Wendle too, and in a crisis would stand and fight with the Wendles, that was only natural. It wouldn't do to trust him with any secrets; secrets would only get to the ear of Flinthead and if the secrets were valuable then Knocker's life, and the lives of the others, wouldn't be worth a handful of Wandle mud.

Flinthead stood, ready to leave. 'You are too kind,' he said, and then without another word he raised his hand and the Wendles in the hall began to leave. Flinthead's bodyguard assembled at the rear of the platform and the chief went down the steps and was lost in the middle of his men. Knocker watched them march away, an elite corps of well armed and experienced fighting Wendles, about fifty of them. It would, he reflected, be almost impossible to harm the chieftain without their connivance, and they were, without doubt, loyal to a man.

As they disappeared, Napoleon came to the front of the platform and jumped down to stand beside Knocker.

'I tell yer,' he said scornfully, 'that is a great Borrible; no little Spiff in a dressing gown, but a warrior who plans ahead and knows things. He sees what you are thinking even as it comes to your mind.'

'Spiff is just as crafty and just as clever,' answered Knocker.

Napoleon shrugged his shoulders and turned to lead the way across the hall which was emptying now of Wendles. 'They should have sent half a dozen of my tribe on this expedition,' he said. 'We'd have done it easy.'

Knocker did not bother to answer the jibe, and the two Borribles hastened to catch up with their companions. After marching for half a mile or so the Adventurers were led into a well furnished and comfortable room, which by Borrible standards was luxurious indeed, with carpets on the floor, a few armchairs and an abundance of cushions and blankets for relaxation and sleep. The haversacks were brought in and the Wendle escorts hurried away. When they'd gone, Tron and Halfabar stood at the door for a moment, then they too departed and there was the sound of a key turning and bolts being rammed home.

Orococco stood up quickly. 'They've locked the door,' he said angrily, looking at Napoleon.

'Yeah,' said Bingo. 'What's that about, eh? Answer me that.'

'It's all right,' said Napoleon, 'I . . . asked Flinthead to do it, so we could sleep and eat without being disturbed.'

'We could get drowned in here if the tide rose,' said Vulge. 'I don't like it. Us Borribles hate being locked in anywhere.'

'You've got a cheek.' Napoleon defended himself. 'Why, this is part of Flinthead's own apartments that he's gone and let us use.'

'He don't exactly trust us, do he?' said Vulge, striding up and down the room. 'Don't let us go anywhere on our own, and locks us in for the night. I hates being locked up at all. It's worse than the nick, underground, gives me the creeps.'

'It's not natural,' continued Bingo, 'all this bowing and scraping to Flinthead. Shouldn't bow an' scrape to anyone, a Borrible. I don't think your lot are very Borrible, come to that.'

'Are you saying I'm not a Borrible?' cried Napoleon, livid, and he pulled off his hat and pointed to his ears.

'We don't know about you, yet,' put in Knocker, quietly.

'And we don't know about you, yet,' retorted Napoleon.

'How does a bloke like Flinthead get all that power, eh?' asked Chalotte. 'That's what I should like to know.'

'Because he saw what needed doing and he did it, because he's tougher and brighter than anyone else,' answered Napoleon furiously. 'Look. We came on this trip to get the Rumbles, not for a holiday.

Why don't you all just have a good meal and a good night's sleep? That's what I'm going to do.' And with that the Wendle began to help himself to the food that had been provided, and refused to be drawn into any further conversation that night.

The others grumbled for a while among themselves, but then, being just as hungry and as tired as Napoleon, they ate their fill, stretched their limbs, chose a few cushions, spread the blankets and were all soon fast asleep.

*

They slept long and deep and woke late. Fresh food and drink was brought to them, and when they were ready to march there was a loud knocking at the door and it was thrown open. In the doorway and in the high corridor beyond, stood a crowd of about thirty Wendles, part of the elite guard, armed and dressed for a foray beyond the limits of the underground caverns. Each one carried a Rumble-stick as well as a catapult, and bandoliers were slung over their shoulders. The detachment was again led by Tron and Halfabar.

'Come,' called Tron into the room. 'We are to take you to King George's Park, then you have only a little way to go before you cross Merton Road and so leave our territory.'

The Adventurers checked their catapults and stones, stepped out into the corridor and stood together. The Wendles formed up tightly, and the whole group made off down the tunnel, guiding their steps with circles of light from their torches.

After a brisk march they entered the huge hall where they had met Flinthead. The small stage was still there but now no one sat on it nor was there one Wendle, apart from their escort, to be seen. They crossed the hall and entered a tunnel which dropped down to the Wandle and once there they followed the towpath along its edge.

'The tunnels look deserted,' explained Tron, 'but don't forget that it is four in the morning. The night-stealers have not returned from their work and the day-stealers are still sleeping. Then we have permanent lookouts everywhere along Merton Road; that is the beginning of no-man's land.'

The Adventurers had to admit that the Wendles were more friendly than they had been the previous day. Even Halfabar seemed to regret the misunderstanding that had occurred between him and Adolf on their first meeting.

'Come back safely so that you can tell me the story of your adventures,' he admonished the German in warm tones.

'So I will, Halfabar,' hooted Adolf, 'so I will.'

Suddenly, on a command from Tron, the column halted. They had come to the end of the underground section of the River Wandle. All torches were extinguished and the warriors stood motionless in the obscurity, waiting patiently until their eyes had become completely accustomed to the darkness of the night. Only then did Tron make a sign and one of his scouts slipped soundlessly from the tunnel, wading slowly through the mud and water.

After a second or two the scout gave a low whistle which was answered immediately by a guard stationed on the river bank. Tron lifted his hand again and two more Wendles disappeared outside, and so he continued until half his command had gone. Then the first Wendle reappeared. All was well; the guards had advanced along the Wandle and had seen no suspicious activity. It was not quite dawn and they could get the Adventurers to King George's Park and be back underground before it was full daylight.

Tron waved the Adventurers forward and one by one they slithered down from the towpath until they were waist deep in clinging sludge. They strode away stiffly, well protected in borrowed waders, but they could not escape the terrible stench of the mud where it bubbled up in steamy clouds as they pushed their legs and feet forward. Fortunately they did not have far to go. As soon as they were clear of the tunnel entrance the guards hauled them on to a small path lying on the east side of the river and there the escort awaited them.

'And how do you like Wandsworth, my friend Adolf?' asked Halfabar, as he pulled the German to the bank.

Adolf spat down into the muddy stream. 'Why, it is just as smelly as Hamburg; I feel quite at home.' He grinned.

The column formed up once more, half the bodyguard in front with a torch or two to show the way, the Adventurers in the middle, and the rest of the bodyguard behind. Tron gave the word and they stepped out in good order. The Wendles sang heartily as they marched, a stirring fighting song which was their favourite.

'We are the Wendles of Wandsworth Town,
We're always up and the others are down.
We're rough and we're tough and we don't give a damn,
We are the elite of the Borrible clan.
Reach for your Rumble-sticks!
Try all your dirty tricks!
Nothing can beat us
And none shall defeat us.
Say a wrong word and we'll hammer you down,
We are the Wendles of Wandsworth Town!

'We are the geezers who live below
The shoppers and coppers and the traffic flow.
We revel in muck and we rollick in mud,
The slime of the sewers enriches our blood.
Call yourself Borribles!
We are the Horribles!
Cruel black-as-inkers,
Cut-throating stinkers!
Say a wrong word and we'll hammer you down,
We are the Wendles of Wandsworth Town!'

Tron led the group along at a fast pace. The sky became lighter and the torches were extinguished. After a ten-minute march the green fields of King George's Park came into view, and Tron raised his right hand and the column halted.

'What's going on?' Bingo asked Napoleon, who was standing just in front of him.

'Wait and see,' said Napoleon. 'They know what they're doing.'

'I'll be glad when we're away on our own,' whispered Vulge. 'Wendles is creepy.'

As if in answer to Vulge's impatience, Tron came back down the line and spoke to them. 'We have to cross the river here,' he said, 'but there are some secret stepping stones, just under the surface of the water, so you shouldn't even get wet. Halfabar will go over first and show you where they are. I must get back underground before it gets much lighter. We're too conspicuous along here, not like the streets.'

Halfabar stepped down from the towpath and, prodding with a

Rumble-stick to find his way, he indicated the exact position of the stepping stones. Once the Wendle was across, each Adventurer in turn was lent a spear by a member of the bodyguard, and they followed Halfabar through the wide quagmire of sucking mud until they came up against the railings of the park. Not one person slipped from the sunken stones and soon Tron joined them to give directions for the next stage of their journey. The bodyguard remained on the east bank, squatting on their haunches, obediently waiting for their leaders to return.

'Right,' said Tron. 'Now we must leave you. The next part of your trip will be easy. We have sent messages out during the night and our lookouts know of your passage. You won't see them but they will see you, and as they know what you look like and how many you are, they won't bother you as long as you keep to the route. If you stray from it, we won't be responsible for the consequences.

'Follow the river through the park until you come to the end of the fields. There the river goes under a bridge. Above you is a road, Mapleton Road. That will take you westward, across another bit of the park, past the bandstand, and at the end of Mapleton turn into Longstaff, right at the end, then left, then right. That's Merton Road, where our influence and power to help you ends.

'Head south along Merton until you reach Replingham Road. We have our last outpost in a school there. Take that road westward until you reach Southfields, which lies under the great hill you will have to climb to reach Rumbledom. Once you have left our last outpost the dangers that wait for you are many. Beyond Southfields there will be a Rumble scout in every tree. You will have to devise some way of passing their lines unnoticed, or you will never reach Rumbledom alive, let alone achieve your aim. I wish you success and the gaining of a good name and . . . don't get caught.'

With this Tron and Halfabar left the Adventurers, taking the spare Rumble-sticks and waders with them. They bounded over the Wandle without hesitation, flitting across the mud of the river as if it had been as solid as the pavement on Wandsworth High Street. On the other side they gathered their bodyguard together and with a wave they ran off at a trot, back to the safety of their underground citadel.

When they had gone, Vulge patted Napoleon on the back with a friendly hand. 'Lost your playmates, now. Have to put up with us again, won't yer?'

Napoleon knocked Vulge's hand away. 'He is a fine Borrible, that Tron,' he said, 'and he has given us good advice.'

Torreycanyon shouldered his haversack and looked out over the deserted park. 'Well, me chinas, I think we'd better get a move on and get as far away from this park as we can. It's cold and nasty.' And without a further word the Adventurers set off into the green silence, bearing their burdens with them.

The journey to Merton Road was not difficult and Napoleon led them there at a steady pace. It was a busy and noisy road, with cars roaring by and adults waiting in long bus queues, shifting from foot to foot or staring helplessly into the middle distance, hating the idea of yet another day at work.

When the Borribles came to Replingham Road they gathered together and crossed in a bunch, avoiding the heavy traffic. On a corner they could see a large secondary school of five storeys, with groups of pupils waiting by the main gates for the whistle blast that would announce the start of lessons. Just to one side of the group stood two Wendles disguised in the uniform of the school.

'Wendles?' asked Napoleon.

They nodded and waited for the rest of the band to approach, moving away from the school children before they spoke.

'We are the last outpost. When you leave us you're on your own. You go straight up there. See the twist in the road? Follow it. It's a long walk, they say, lonely, a kind of no-man's land; no Borribles, no Rumbles . . . as far as we know. Things will change when you get to Southfields and cross into Augustus Road. It will start to climb rapidly; steep, very. Then more trees and lots of posh houses. Some Wendles have won their names up there. The stories say there are no shops, so you won't be able to live off the land, and there will be Rumble patrols in every garden, I should think. I don't know how you'll get through without being sussed, but then that's your problem, isn't it?'

The two Wendle scouts looked at each other as if to say that nobody would get them on such a foolhardy mission. They were being brave enough just guarding this place and likely to get caught at any minute.

The Adventurers strode on, realizing that their adventure was perhaps a lot more forlorn than they had at first imagined, and that many perils still lay between them and the achievement of their goal.

Now, thought Knocker, the adventure begins in earnest, with dangers everywhere, and it will be a long, long while before we return to the safety of Wandsworth and the comforts of Battersea.

6

As the two Wendle scouts had indicated, the journey up the rising slope of Replingham Road was long and tiring. The houses in that part of Wandsworth wore a desolate air and there was hardly any movement in the streets, but then it was past nine thirty in the morning; children were at their lessons, their parents at work.

The Borribles kept close together, eyes flickering to left and right. It was the first daytime trek of the expedition and they had to be ready to run, hide or give battle; their catapults were grasped in their hands, stones ready for firing.

They were trudging towards the lower slopes of Rumbledom, haversacks becoming heavier with every step. Occasionally a door opened in the dead front of a house and a woman shook a doormat or came out to sweep a step. A man hastened by, late for work, and he turned briefly to scrutinize this strange band of earnest children who carried catapults and wore woollen hats; but he was too preoccupied by his own problems to think much about the bizarre nature of the sight and he hurried on.

Then things began to happen. The steady progress of the Borribles' advance was interrupted when a car passed them, close to the pavement, and screeched to a halt fifty yards further up the road. A policeman, burly in his blue uniform, leapt from the car and stood in the middle of the pavement with his arms and legs spread wide as if he owned the road, the front gardens, the houses and all the world. His face was red and glowing with pleasure.

'Blimey! A Woollie in a nondescript,' said Bingo. 'There'll be another one behind us.'

Bingo was only too right; glancing over their shoulders the Borribles saw another car parked a hundred yards behind them. A second brawny policeman was getting out of it, a grin on his face.

'*Verdammt*,' swore Adolf. 'We'd better get out of here.'

The Adventurers had stopped on the corner of a side road leading out of Replingham; it was called Engadine Street and the Borribles were never to forget that name. Slowly, having loaded their catapults, they backed into it, and then took to their heels, putting on a burst of speed for twenty or thirty yards before skidding to a standstill.

'Bingo,' shouted Knocker, 'you know the Woollies. Take over.'

The two policemen appeared on the corner and stood together for a moment, looking along the street. They waved the first car back to them, the other flashed on up the hill.

Bingo said, 'That second nondescript will have gone round the block to seal off the other end of the road. They know we're Borribles. We're going to have to fight this one, and even then there's a good chance of getting caught.'

'Oh, I'm glad this has happened.' Stonks grinned, flexing the elastic on his catapult. 'Walking gets boring on its own.'

'Right,' said Bingo, 'here they come. Pretend to be scared . . . like we're running away. Spread across the road. When I give the word, turn and fire. I'll be in the middle. Those of you on my left take the copper on the left, those on the right the copper on the right. Aim for their knees.'

The Borribles retreated, slowly at first, then more quickly until they were running as hard as they could. But the policemen could also run and were gaining on the fugitives when Bingo yelled at the top of his voice, 'Now!' and the Adventurers turned, springing into the air and landing with their catapults ready. They fired their volley together and both policemen fell as if their legs had been scythed from underneath them. Five stones arriving like bullets on a kneecap are as effective as amputation.

The police driver, at the near end of the street, had been watching the skirmish from the open window of his car, but when he saw his two colleagues rolling on the ground, clasping their knees in pain, he slipped his motor into gear and drove it down the middle of Engadine to come to their rescue.

Chalotte ran to the cover of a front garden. As the car came by, she let it have a stone, glancing along the bonnet. It was beautifully done; the windscreen veined suddenly with a million lines of cold silver and the driver could see nothing. He was going too fast and swerved to be sure of avoiding his crippled colleagues who still lay in the road. The car went out of control, bounced across the pavement and sent Adolf spinning into the gutter. There was the sound of tearing metal and shattering glass as the car buried its nose in the brick coping that protected one of the house fronts. The driver, who had earlier unfastened his seat belt, went through the frail windscreen like a locomotive and concussed himself on what was left of the wall.

'Yippee!' yelled Bingo and 'Yippee!' yelled the others, but Vulge called a warning. 'There's one on his radio. There'll be a squad of coppers up here in less time than it takes to wink an eye.'

Sure enough, one of the lamed policemen had pulled out his pocket transmitter and was about to speak into it.

Perhaps the quickest loader and firer of the team was Chalotte. A stone had flown from her catapult almost before Vulge had finished shouting. It smashed into the hand radio and knocked it to the ground, broken and useless.

'We'll have to get out of here quick,' said Bingo, looking down to the far end of the street. 'The other car will be coming round this way soon.'

'I don't mind staying here and taking them on,' said Torreycannon. 'I enjoyed that. I hope the Rumbles fall over as easily.'

'We need somewhere to disappear,' said Sydney. 'The roads will be crawling with John Law in ten minutes' time.'

The group went silent. What Sydney had said was true, but concealment would not be easy. There were no abandoned houses in Engadine and the police would soon be knocking at every door asking if the Borribles had been seen.

It was then that their luck changed.

They were standing on the pavement near the wrecked car, watching the injured policemen crawl away, when at their feet they heard a slight noise – a grating and a scratching. They half turned and looked at the metal coal-hole cover set into the pavement just behind them. They glanced along the street. Every house they could see had a similar cover in front of it, circular and made from heavy iron, put there so that coalmen could lift them out of the way and empty their hundredweight sacks directly into the cellars, and so avoid tramping dirt and dust into people's hallways. But this cover was special; it was revolving on its own.

'Aye, aye,' said Vulge. 'What's this then, undercover coppers?'

Suddenly the coal-hole cover floated up an inch, balanced on a human head. It hesitated, then up it came another inch, warily. A long moment went by and it tilted to one side and a nose appeared, a large nose and crooked, with coal dust on it as well as a heavy dewdrop which looked as if it might leave the nose at any moment, but which didn't.

Vulge bent down quickly. 'What's your game, Sunshine, eh?'

A voice came out of the hole; it was cracked and petulant but the words it used were friendly enough. 'Borribles, ain't yer? He! He! Only Borribles could do that to the Woollies. I was watching from my front room. I'm a good friend to the Borribles, always have been. They help me and I help them. Was one myself once, ain't it, till I got caught. Nasty business growing old. You don't ever want to get caught, do you?'

Vulge looked at the others. 'I don't know what we've got here,' he said, 'but he might be able to get us out of this pickle.'

'We'd better hurry,' said Bingo. 'I can see the other car at the far end of the road, getting ready.'

'You come down here, mateys,' said the voice from the coal-hole and the dewdrop quivered ecstatically, threatening to lose its passionate hold on the nose. 'You come down here, ain't it? I won't tell where you are, and in a couple of days you can carry on to wherever you're going.'

'We haven't got a lot of choice,' said Torreycanyon. 'None of us wants to get caught, at least not before we gets to Rumbledom and does what we came to do.'

'Okay, down here,' called Vulge. 'Move over, we're coming in.' He pushed the coal-hole cover till it slid over to rest on the pavement and saw a narrow head, covered with a wisp of grey hair, duck back into the darkness.

'Well,' asked Vulge, 'who's first?'

'Man, if we stands round here nattering all day, we'll spend tonight in the nick with our ears clipped,' said Orococco, and he struggled out of his haversack, threw it into the hole and then wriggled through the narrow opening.

The others followed quickly one by one until Knocker was left alone. He looked about him. The driver was still unconscious and the two injured policemen had crawled into Replingham out of sight. The street was empty and no one had seen the disappearance of the Borrible Adventurers. The whole battle had taken no longer than two or three minutes and the crash had not yet attracted attention. However, at the far end of Engadine, Knocker could see the other police car in position. Its occupants were still too far away to see what had happened, but shortly those policemen would be driving towards him. He must get underground.

Knocker lowered himself through the pavement until his feet touched a shifting pile of coal. The light from above got smaller as he pulled the iron lid into its grooves. Finally it dropped into place and there was a clang like the top half of a sarcophagus shutting a corpse off from the living world, and a suffocating darkness enfolded Knocker and his nine companions in its close and clammy embrace, safe below the long stretches of Engadine Street, Southfields.

*

Knocker slipped and slithered on the knobs of coal. He stumbled, regained his balance for a moment, then fell forward. He was caught and the breath was crushed out of him by two wiry adult arms. He struggled but the arms were strong. He kicked and squirmed but he couldn't free himself. Hot breath scalded his face as his assailant carried him along; the breath was foul and Knocker twisted away from it.

The breath became words. 'Don't you struggle, my little beauty. We're on your side, ain't it? Oh, me little deario, you are in safe hands now, ain't you though?'

Knocker stopped kicking and waited. The voice he heard close to his ear was the voice that had invited the Adventurers into the coal-hole; it was a sickly whining voice with a creaking edge to it. Knocker was carried into another part of the cellar and not for one second did the strong and stringy hands that clutched him relax their hold. Knocker didn't like this at all. He slid his hand behind him to reach for his catapult but his hand encountered a large adult one in the act of pulling the weapon away, yet he was still held firmly by two other hands. Was there then another adult in the dark cellar, or did the beast that was carrying him have three hands? Knocker shivered; where on earth were the others?

Suddenly his captor shifted his grip and Knocker was grasped by the scruff of the neck and thrown roughly into space. He landed against another body and he heard Torreycanyon shout, 'Swipe me, what's occurring?' At that moment there was a clashing sound as someone slammed a steel door; then a moment's silence and a light was switched on, revealing the most dismal of scenes.

Knocker on his hands and knees blinked his eyes, the brightness coming after the dark almost blinding him. He shook his head. He could not believe what he saw. He and the others were imprisoned in a large cage such as one might see at a circus, only this cage had its bars placed very close together, so close that even a Borrible could not get through. In fact, the cage might well have been made especially for Borribles.

Outside the cage, in a large cellar room, stood two men, one middle-aged, the other old. The old man, a bony creature, was rubbing his hands, grinning and sniffing with glee at his dewdrop. The younger man, Dewdrop's son, stood nodding his head stupidly and smiling an uneasy smile, as if he had made a mess in his trousers and was not quite sure what to do about it. He was an idiot, squarely built, a monster of great strength.

Knocker got to his feet and looked at his companions. They were motionless, staring at the evil old man. Their faces were white and hard with fear.

'Shit a brick,' cried Napoleon, his expression bitter with anger. 'A Borrible-snatcher.'

Stonks grabbed at the bars and tried to shake them with all his power. 'You dirty old sod,' he yelled at the top of his voice. 'Let us out of here. I'll kill you, I'll kill you.'

The old man only rubbed his hands harder and sniffed more happily. He elbowed his son and nodded his head so vigorously that it seemed that the dewdrop must leave his nose for ever, but it stuck like gum, swinging backwards and forwards clanging against his nostrils.

'Look at the dearios,' he chortled. 'Ten lovely little Borribles. I've never had such a haul in me own whole life. We'll be rich, Erbie, so rich that the horse and cart won't be able to carry all our goodies. Strike me pink, ain't it beautiful? A little bit of persuasion and they'll be workin' day and night, ain't it? Best little deario burglars in the whole wide world, ain't it, Erbie?'

On Erbie's vegetable visage there was not the slightest glimmer of thought, but he nodded slowly and said, 'Yeah, Dad, yeah,' and dead ideas sunk sightless through his muddy brain, like poisoned fish in the Wandle.

'Blimey, we're in serious trouble now,' said Bingo. 'Dewdrop and Son. We'll be lucky to get out of this alive, sure as eggs is fried.'

'Keep your heads,' said Knocker quietly, though he felt as scared as the others. 'Anyone here got a catapult?'

Dewdrop cackled and slapped his son on the shoulder so heartily that the moron staggered forward a step or two and lost his inane smile, though it returned in a second or two, as gormless as before.

'Oh no, me deario, we got all the catapults; dangerous things as can hurt blokes, like those poor constables outside, rolling on the ground with their knees cracked, ain't it? And my boy Erbie, he took all the stones too. We're going to keep them for you, don't you worry your little heads . . . and your haversacks, too. I'll look after you real well while you're here. And you're going to be here a nice long while, me dearios, and we're going to be real good friends, ain't it?'

Napoleon's face was white with anger. He raised his fist and shook it at Dewdrop. 'You can't keep us for ever, you stinkin' old goat.'

'Not for ever, no,' agreed Dewdrop, 'but for as long as I or you live, or until you get caught, eh, me deario.' And he smirked and slapped his legs in glee.

His mirth was interrupted by a loud knocking on the street door. Dewdrop glanced towards the ceiling. 'Right, Erbie,' he said, 'we'd better go and tell those nice peelers that we haven't seen a thing. Wouldn't know a Borrible from an ordinary child, would we?' And he twisted his head on his neck and gloated over the caged Adventurers who could do nothing but hang their heads in despair.

'Come on, Erbie.' Dewdrop seized his son by the collar and pulled him away. 'We'll see to these pretty children in a minute and you can persuade 'em about a bit if they don't agree to our little plan, me deario, ain't that just it?'

Erbie's smile intensified and his eyes probed the Borribles' bodies like damp fingers. He followed his father out of the door, which Dewdrop locked and bolted with care, the sound of its closing echoing through the cellar like the sound of forever.

The Adventurers fell silent; no one said anything because no one could think of anything to say. There was no way out. The cage was solid, not one bar in it would budge. The floor was made of iron and so was its ceiling. The situation seemed hopeless; it was hopeless.

'Well, damn me,' said Orococco at last, 'we're supposed to be the best in the world, and we get ambushed first time out by a snatcher. That's the end, man, the very end.'

'What will he do to us?' asked Sydney.

'What they always do,' answered Napoleon, angry with himself and everyone else. 'He'll keep us prisoner, beat us, hand us over to that crazy son of his, and then he'll divide us into two teams, and he'll let one team out while the other stays here as hostages; and we'll have to steal for him, day after day, night after night. Steal not for grub or things that he needs, but for things he can sell, for money, so he can get richer and richer.'

'We'll have to do shops, houses, post offices, banks, anything he can think of,' added Bingo. 'And if one of the team out thieving doesn't come back, why he just beats the others near to death and makes them carry on stealing, and when we're no good any more he'll hand us over to the Woollies.'

'So you've had it every way,' said Knocker, finishing off the explanation. 'You stay here for ever thieving till you get caught, or your mates get handed over or Dewdrop kills 'em for fun. That's it, no way out.'

The group fell silent again. Borrible-snatchers were a rare phenomenon but they were the most dangerous enemy that a Borrible could encounter. Snatchers had infested London in the nineteenth century, abducting Borribles off the streets, even from their beds, and then forcing them to steal. Snatchers sometimes kidnapped ordinary children but they preferred Borribles because they ran faster, were brighter and, above all, Borribles did not grow up and could be used for ever to wriggle through small windows. In modern times only a handful of snatchers were known of and their descriptions and whereabouts were common knowledge to all Borribles.

But in this strange and unknown part of London, below Rumbledom, Dewdrop had made his lair. He had waited patiently and now he had captured more Borribles in one swoop than he could ever have hoped for in his wildest dreams. Soon he would be rich.

'This looks like the end of our adventure,' said Torreycanyon eventually. 'We'll never get to Rumbledom now and no one will ever know what happened to us.'

'Don't give up hope,' said Adolf, but he didn't hoot and he didn't sound as if he meant it.

'There's one way out,' said Knocker, 'a way that will save the expedition, but it means a sacrifice.'

'You get us out of here,' said Napoleon bitterly, 'and I'll sacrifice anything, anybody.'

'It's like this,' said Knocker, and he spoke slowly as if words were hard to come by. 'Half of us will be left here always, and five will be out stealing, turn and turn about. When things get too bad we could draw lots and the five who are out, well, they just don't come back, but get away. That's all we can do.'

The Adventurers looked at each other. It was a solution but a drastic one. Five to go and face the dangers of Rumbledom even more outnumbered than before; five to be torn apart by Erbie, or handed over to the authorities, never to be Borribles again. The thought was horrid. Being caught was an extinguishing of identity, it was death. Worse than death, it was the loss of beauty, of freedom, a descent into ugliness. Look what had happened to Dewdrop; he had been a Borrible and then he had been caught and turned into something normal.

'That's not much of an option,' said Stonks. 'Two chances we got, a dog's chance and no chance.'

'Let us wait,' suggested Adolf. 'Let us wait a while before we decide on such a dreadful step.' He tried to smile. 'They will beat us and not give us much food, so snatchers behave, it says in the old books, but they must let us out to steal. Let us promise always to come back, for the time being at least. Maybe we will find a way.'

With heavy hearts they agreed that for the present they would do what Dewdrop ordered. They would bide their time as well they might and hope against hope that their luck would one day turn.

*

Dewdrop and his son Erbie pretended to earn their living by going from street to street with a horse and cart collecting rags and bones and old iron. On the side of the cart was painted, in deep red paint, 'D. Bunyan and Son, Breakers and Merchants'. The poor old horse who did all the work, pulling the cart up the steepest hills with the two men aboard, was called Sam.

Dewdrop and Erbie did collect rubbish and old iron when it was positively thrust on them, but they never went out of their way to find it. They had a reason for riding round the streets: they were looking for things to steal and houses to burgle. Everything they found or stole they sold for money which they concealed in a secret hiding place in the old house in Engadine.

Dewdrop Bunyan had snatched Borribles in the past for burgling purposes but he'd only captured them in ones and twos. Now here he was with ten and he decided to work them to within an inch of their lives so that he would become richer, quicker. He would force them to burgle the big houses on the other side of Southfields and even some on the hill leading towards Rumbledom. He would become the richest man in the whole world.

As for the policemen who had knocked on Dewdrop's door, they had been easily satisfied by the rag-and-bone man's explanation.

'I saw them,' he told an inspector. 'They ran round the corner, down Merton way; miles off by now, I should think, vicious little bleeders.'

Several days after the policemen had given up their search and as soon as the rag-and-bone man felt secure, he began to starve the Borribles and encouraged his imbecile son to prod them with a sharp stick through the bars of the cage. And, what was worse, Erbie delighted in choosing a prisoner to drag through the house on a dog lead, tormenting the Borrible until he or she could stand the pain no longer and would strike out in despair.

But Erbie was so strong that the blows delivered by a tiny Borrible just made him snigger; but sniggering or not he would still beat his prisoner till the blood flowed and the bruises blossomed. Then, when he had tired of the amusement, he would haul the semi-conscious captive back to the cellar and the cage, and his imbecile smile would explode into a strange and sinister exultation.

Dewdrop always joined in these manifestations of joy, rubbing his hands and rocking his head sideways on his shoulders so that his dewdrop wagged this way and that in the light of the single bulb that lit the underground prison. Every one of the Adventurers endured these torments and everyone of them lost weight, and all of them sported cuts and contusions and black eyes.

'I'm going to kill Erbie before I'm much older,' Napoleon would mutter under his breath. 'I'm going to kill that great stupid loon, and then I'll kill his father, and if I don't, I hope as how the Wendles hear about them and come up here and take these two and stake them out on the mud flats of the Wandle, and sit around and sing songs while these two maniacs slowly slip below the surface and suffocate . . . bloody lovely.'

And so the days crawled by and it was not long before Dewdrop began to take the Borribles stealing. Sometimes they went at night to burgle the houses of the rich; at other times they sallied out during working hours to steal from supermarkets and department stores.

By way of insurance, to make sure the captives did his every bidding, the rag-and-bone man always kept at least five of them locked in the cellar under the demented eye of his son; and so sadistic were this oaf's pleasures that it was more of a hardship for the Borribles to be kept in the cage than to be taken out to rob and steal. For stealing comes naturally to Borribles, although it is not usual for them to purloin things they do not need. On the other hand they knew that Dewdrop would let Erbie beat them into unconsciousness if they did not do well as burglars and shoplifters. Furthermore, he was eminently capable of turning them over to the police just for the pleasure of seeing them get their ears clipped.

And Dewdrop took no chances: the key to the cage was kept in his pocket and it was attached by a long chain to his braces and he never let it out of his sight or gave it to his son for one minute, for Dewdrop trusted no one. He was sly and he was cunning.

Weeks went by and still the Adventurers were no nearer escape. They stole and they burgled, returning to Dewdrop after each sortie to find him waiting by his horse, with Sam munching in the nosebag, shaking his head at the sky to get to the hay. Wearily they would load their booty on to the back of the cart and clamber in after it, hiding under a piece of canvas so they would not be seen by prying eyes. Then Dewdrop would settle back in his seat, flap the reins and Sam would lean into the traces and take them home. Back to the dreary house in Engadine and the dreadful cold cellar with a cage in it, and in the cage ten desperate and forlorn Borribles.

During this period of time they became cheerless and moved without minds. There was not one glimmer of hope anywhere and they hardly talked to each other. Their spirits sank lower and lower until there came a day when they spoke no more. The ten companions lost count of the weeks spent in the cage, and back in Wandsworth the Wendles forgot about the expedition; even the Borribles of Battersea gave the Adventurers up for dead.

The imprisonment seemed eternal, and Knocker's original suggestion – that they should draw lots and allow one team of Borribles to escape – became more and more attractive. Each Adventurer was convinced in his own heart and mind that this was the only way. All that stopped them taking up the subject again was the bleak thought of being left behind, alone with Dewdrop and Erbie. But then, just when they needed it, luck took a hand. Something happened.

Very late one evening, about eleven o'clock, Knocker and Adolf, Chalotte, Bingo and Torreycanyon were taken out by Dewdrop and driven in the cart to a spot halfway up the hill beyond Southfields. The five Borribles sat silent beneath the tarpaulin on the back of the cart and listened to the tread of Sam's hooves on the tarmac. It was a cold evening, for winter was coming on, and they shivered all the more because they were hungry. Sam pulled slowly; the hill was long and steep.

Occasionally they could hear Dewdrop call out, 'Come along you, Sam, me old deario,' and then there was the crack of the whip as the rag-and-bone man hit the old horse as hard as he could. Once the Borribles would have said, 'Poor old Sam,' because Borribles are mighty fond of horses, but now they had no sympathy to spare for Borrible or beast.

Sam tugged the cart far up the steep hill, past many silent mansions standing in great gardens, until Dewdrop stopped in front of the largest house of all, hidden behind high hedges and surrounded by acres of lawns and flower beds. The Borribles heard the brake being wound on and then the tarpaulin was jerked back and the cold air came rushing in. Dewdrop's dewdrop was a frozen jelly of snot, green in the pale light of the stars.

'Well, me little dearios,' creaked the evil voice, 'we're going to have a fine time tonight. Here's a nice big house, what we have here, family gorn away for a second holiday, ain't it? Skiing and somesuch; I hopes they breaks their legs. But that's not why we're here, is it, to look into their health? We're here because they're there, ain't it? This is a family with a lot of money; no doubt they've taken it with them, but you can't take everything, oh no, too cumbersome and heavy. Can't have a skiing holiday with a grand piano stuck up your jumper, eh? Now, I'm going to wait here with Sam, me horse. You three . . .' He suddenly jabbed his bony finger into Chalotte, Bingo and Torreycanyon one after the other. 'You three will concentrate on the downstairs; should be some lovely silver in there, knives and forks, Georgian flower bowls and such. Oh, me dearios, I do like a beautiful thing, it was beauty that put me on this road, ain't it?'

He turned and jabbed Adolf and Knocker. 'And you two will go upstairs, look into the studies and bedrooms. Nice antique stuff they'll have up there, Ming vases I should think, and if that don't work out you get into the children's playroom. Rich family, ain't it, spends a fortune on their little brats, I shouldn't wonder. Well, stealing's a great leveller, I say. Beats income tax. We'll take some of those rich toys, me dearios, and I'll give 'em to someone else, make 'em happy. Now go on, and don't forget to come back, else you won't see your friends no more . . . not alive.'

The Borribles leapt from the cart, each of them taking a sack to carry booty in, and they ran across the grounds of the house to the back garden, out of sight of the road. It was dark everywhere and not a thing moved in the whole world. Knocker soon had a window open and the Adventurers lost no time in getting inside. Leaving the other three to work the ground floor, Knocker and Adolf raced for the stairs and in the light of their torches they rifled the bedrooms, snatching up anything they considered worthwhile.

When their sacks were nearly full, they went into a long wide room that was obviously the nursery; there were models and games everywhere. Without a word Adolf and Knocker began to collect some of the smaller and more expensive items.

After a while Adolf said, 'I think we've got all we can carry.' His voice was flat and depressed. 'We'd better get back to Dewdrop now, or he'll be beating us again for being too slow.'

'And if we don't get enough stuff he'll beat us for that, too,' said Knocker. He went to the last of the toy cupboards and said, 'I'll just have a look in here.'

Adolf was at the other side of the room when Knocker opened the cupboard. He couldn't see what Knocker saw but he heard a gasp and a chuckle, and then a whistle of pleasure and happiness with a note of hope in it too. It had been so long since Adolf had heard anything so uplifting that he took notice immediately and scuttled across the room shouting, 'What is it, what is it?' and then he saw and he swore his favourite oath. '*Verdammt*,' he said and then again, '*verdammt*,' and finally, 'A million *verdammt*s.'

In front of the two Borribles, on the second shelf, level with their eyes, were two of the finest steel catapults they had ever seen. The elastic was black and square and powerful, new and full of resilience. Adolf and Knocker looked at each other, their eyes gleaming and shining with a bright spark such as had not glowed there for many weeks.

'How on earth can we get them back to the cage?' asked Adolf. 'Dewdrop and Erbie search us every night.'

'They do,' said Knocker. 'They do, but they never look under our feet.'

'You're right,' shouted Adolf. 'You're right. I saw some Sellotape over there, just the thing, but we must be quick, or he'll think something fishy is going on.'

Both Borribles, their hearts thumping, hastily fixed a catapult to the sole of a boot. With a minimum of luck, their plan might be successful.

'Where can we get some stones?' asked Knocker. 'And how could we smuggle them in if we had them?'

Adolf struck his forehead with the flat of his hand.

'I saw some large marbles in that cupboard over there. I tell you, the kids in this house have everything.'

It was true enough. In a large cake tin was a fine collection of coloured marbles, all of them as big as a good-sized stone and all of them heavy.

'We can't take more than five,' said Knocker, counting them out. 'We'll have to carry them in our mouths and just hope that Dewdrop doesn't make us speak when we get back to Engadine.'

They left the house and ran across the starlit lawns to where Dewdrop sat on the cart, his shoulders hunched and his head swivelling at the slightest sound.

'Where've you been?' he snapped. 'The others got here hours ago. You're trying to get me caught, ain't it? Well, you remember, me dearios, if I gets caught I'll make damn sure you lot does, so hop in the cart with them sacks and make sure no one sees you.' And Dewdrop cracked the whip and old Sam leant into the traces, turned the cart round and set off, his bones aching.

Half an hour later the cart rattled into the backyard of the house in Engadine, the place where the rag-and-bone man kept his scrap metal and where he stabled the horse. That night Sam was shut away as usual and Dewdrop shoved the Borribles into the house, staggering as they were under the sacks of booty.

'Come along, my beauties, my little stealing wonders,' he muttered. 'I want to see how well you have been working for my early retirement. Ho yes, this is my redundancy pay, ain't it, me dearios? Hurry along, you brats, 'fore I flattens yer.'

The five Borribles said nothing. Each was holding a precious marble in his mouth and dared not speak. Inside the house they dumped the sacks in the hallway and then filed down the narrow steps to the cellar. Erbie was waiting, snorting like a brainless ape, drooling and smiling and nodding as they went into the room and stood in line.

'Hurry up, Erbie, me ol' darlin',' said Dewdrop as he came into the room. 'There's such a lot of stuff tonight we'll be up till morning just looking at it. Get those little dearios locked up safe and sound and give 'em a little bit more bread, just so they knows how much I appreciates 'em.'

Erbie came along the line and under the watchful eye of his father he ran his hot and heavy hands over the frail forms of the Borribles. He felt everywhere, making sure they had stolen nothing from the sacks to keep for themselves. The Borribles stood with their mouths firmly closed, the marbles feeling as big as footballs. When Erbie had finished his searching and fondling, Dewdrop went over to the cage and stood there with a truncheon in his hand. He opened the gate and quickly pushed the Borribles inside. The door clanged, Erbie threw some stale bread through the bars and then both he and his father sped from the room, to spend avaricious hours with their swag.

As soon as Dewdrop and Erbie were upstairs the marbles were brought from their hiding places and aroused a certain amount of interest: but when the catapults appeared, why then there was rejoicing and hope.

'Oh, my,' chortled Vulge, as he fingered one of the weapons, 'I know who's going to get a clout round the ear with this little beauty. Knock his bloody brains out, if he had some. Ain't it, me deario?' he added in impersonation of his jailer.

'Man, oh man,' cried Orococco, jumping up and down and smashing his right fist into his left hand, 'this is it. I'll pulverize them, I'll feed 'em to the sparrows.'

'How'd it happen?' asked Napoleon. 'How'd you do it?'

'Knocker found them,' said Chalotte, her eyes alight, 'at the house we were turning over, and Adolf found the marbles; there's only five, but that'll be enough.' She blushed and added, 'Knocker told us all about it in the cart on the way home.' Then she smiled at Knocker, apologizing in a way for telling his story but showing that she was proud of him.

'Look,' said Knocker. 'Tomorrow it's you others who go out. When you get back, me and Adolf will have our catapults ready. We're out of practice but we should be all right, and we've got five good heavy marbles. This is how we'll do it. When you're lined up and Erbie's waiting for his old man to come and supervise the searching, that's when we strike . . . We shoot to kill.'

'After what we've put up with nothing else will do,' said Napoleon, and his face had murder in it.

'We must get Dewdrop,' Knocker went on. 'He's got the keys. You lot will unlock the cage. Then we'll get into the backyard, take the horse and cart, and anything else we want. Agreed?' Everyone nodded. For the first time in weeks they were happy and hopeful.

The next day was a long day and there was a longer evening to follow it as Knocker and Adolf waited for the return of Dewdrop. Two catapults and five marbles were all they had to help them reach freedom. Knocker walked up and down the cage, flexing his muscles, watched by his four companions.

'They won't be long now,' said Chalotte, trying to calm him. 'It will be all right, you'll see.'

'Adolf,' said Knocker at one point, 'you have had more adventures than me. We have five stones only; you take three, I will take two. You aim at Dewdrop, I will take Erbie. We fire, without words, as soon as Dewdrop steps into the room.'

Adolf said, 'You do me a great honour, Knocker my friend, for you are a good shot with the catapult.'

'I saw you fire at the policemen,' said Knocker. 'You did it well.'

'Listen,' said Bingo, in a whisper. 'Here they come.'

Sure enough there were footsteps upstairs and Erbie came creeping sideways into the cellar like a white crab. He slithered over to the cage and prodded the captives with his pointed stick, a glimmer of pleasure showing on his vacant face.

'Better get an aspirin, Sonny,' murmured Bingo, 'because you're going to have an awful headache. You think you're dopey now, but wait till you've had a little bash round the bonce.'

There was a slamming of doors above and some heavy thumps as sacks of loot were dropped onto the floor.

'You lazy little fools,' shouted Dewdrop. 'Nothing, nothing you brought me. How can I make a living like this? Monsters, ungrateful monsters, I'll be working until I'm a failing old man at this rate, never able to retire.'

He rushed into the cellar, his face an angry red, purple in the tight skin near his mouth. 'None of you shall eat tonight, none of you,' he snarled.

Adolf and Knocker had their backs to the door, crouching in the cage, catapults firmly gripped, spare marbles in the ready hand of a colleague. They glanced at each other and on the nod they turned unhurriedly, stretching the catapult rubbers as far as they would go, a murderous extent, and let fly, each at his target.

Knocker's marble hit Erbie on the left temple hard. He swayed, his smile petrified, stiff as blancmange, but he did not fall; unconscious, some trick of gravity kept him upright.

Adolf did not have the same luck. As he released his missile Dewdrop moved forward, intending to thrash the Borribles, for he was in a foul temper, and the marble only clipped him on the back of the head, serving but to increase his anger and his vigilance.

He looked towards the cage and reached for the truncheon that always stood just inside the cellar door; the moisture at the end of his nose glowed blue, green and mauve.

'Throwing stones, ain't it?' he roared, then he saw the catapults and was terrified.

'Erbie, we'll have to lock the doors on these guttersnipes until they comes to their senses.'

But it was too late. Napoleon kicked the truncheon out of Dewdrop's reach. Adolf reloaded and he didn't miss a second time. The projectile crashed and splintered into the middle of the rag-and-bone man's forehead and he staggered back against the wall, sorely hurt, and his dewdrop, that globe of multicoloured mucus, finally broke its infatuation with the nose and fell to the floor.

'Oh, Erbie,' Dewdrop cried piteously. 'Oh, Erbie, help me, my boy, my son, my joy.'

But Erbie was in no state to help anyone. Chalotte had thrust a second marble into Knocker's hand as soon as he had fired the first. He reloaded and shot at Dewdrop's crazed offspring, still rocking on his heels. The heavy glass bullet struck Erbie a fatal blow above the heart and he fell backwards, demolished, like an old factory chimney.

Dewdrop could not believe what he saw. He raised a bewildered hand to his bleeding forehead; the blood trickled down into his eyes and confused him. Napoleon picked up the truncheon and stood ready, but he waited for Adolf to fire his last shot.

The German, veteran of many a battle and survivor from a multitude of tight corners, took his time.

'Oh, my son, my poor little Erbie, what have they done to you, you little darling what wouldn't hurt a fly? Oh, what a cruel world it is, my boy. Erbie, speak up and chat to your father.'

Adolf's marble flew straight as an arrow, and as fatally, to the temple of the Borrible-snatcher, who lurched and pressed both hands to his head. Then, lifeless himself, he fell forward with a mighty crash across the lifeless body of his son.

'So perish all Borrible-snatchers,' said Knocker grandly, and the others looked at each other with a wild delight. They were free.

It was the work of only a few minutes to find the keys and open the door of the cage. The expedition haversacks were discovered in the adjacent cellar room; the catapults and bandoliers were there too. Soon the adventurers were re-equipped and in marching order. They found food upstairs in the well stocked kitchen and they ate as they had not eaten for many a week. Then, smiling and almost crying with happiness, they went out into the yard.

Knocker moved towards the cart and threw his haversack into it; Napoleon, keeping close behind him, did the same. The others hesitated.

'Where,' asked Sydney, 'are you going with that cart?'

'What do you mean?' said Knocker, his eyes widening, taken aback. 'Rumbledom, of course.'

'We think,' said Chalotte, 'that escaping from a Borrible-snatcher is an adventure in itself, let alone killing one. We've earned our names already, twice over.'

'But that is not what we came for.' Knocker looked at the ring of faces that surrounded him, searching for some support. The support came immediately, from an unexpected source.

'No,' said Napoleon Boot stepping forward, 'that is not what we came for. I'm with Knocker.'

'I think I have earned my English name,' said Adolf. 'I understand Chalotte, she is right, we have done enough, but I go with Knocker. That is because I am round the loop. I have a thing about adventures.'

'We all want to go really,' said Bingo, sitting on his haversack, 'but . . . I mean, we've been so knocked about by Erbie, and we haven't eaten properly for ages.'

'We aren't fit for the job now, are we?' said Torreycanyon. 'Perhaps we should rest up for a bit, eh?'

'What are you on about?' snapped Knocker. 'We can't go back now; what would we look like?'

Seven Borribles looked self-conscious and shifted their feet.

'However rotten we feel,' insisted Knocker, 'we've got to go on. We're free now, that's a tonic in itself. Anyway, you lot can do what you like. The three of us are going. Get the horse, Adolf.'

Bingo shrugged his shoulders, threw his haversack into the cart and quoted a proverb at no one in particular: 'If you're my friend, follow me round the bend.'

Chalotte said, 'If Knocker and Nap can agree for once then something very dodgy is happening. Perhaps we ought to go along, if only to see what they're up to.' And she gave Knocker and Napoleon a long and piercing look.

The others picked up their rucksacks and exchanged grim smiles with Knocker. The horse was brought from the stable and Sydney went over and spoke to him: 'So we're all going to Rumbledom, Sam, after all, and you will come with us. Rumbles don't like horses, they say, but we do, so you will be our mascot and mate and we will protect you.' With that sentiment everyone agreed; they stroked the horse and fed him lumps of sugar stolen from the house, then they put him between the shafts and made ready.

They also stole a long raincoat, a good one that Dewdrop had always worn on wet nights, and Bingo who was the lightest sat on Stonks's shoulders, for he was the strongest, and Stonks sat on the driving seat of the cart and they put the raincoat round Bingo's shoulders and it looked for all the world as if an adult was driving. The rest of the Adventurers hid under the tarpaulin, and with a crack of the whip and with a 'Giddy-up, old Sam, me deario, ain't it?' Bingo drove them out of the yard and they began the last lap of their journey to the borders of Rumbledom.

'There's one thing,' said Knocker, as they all sat warm and content under the canvas. 'We were in Engadine Street so long that the Rumbles have probably given us up for dead. And if they don't like horses, so much the better. Sam can take us right up to their front door and kick it down.'

7

It was dark.

It was the darkest part of the night but Sam knew the way to Rumbledom and he pulled the cartload of Borribles joyfully, knowing in his heart that he would be beaten and cursed no more. He carried his friends away from the hateful memories of Engadine, and Bingo, secure on the shoulders of Stonks, sang a rousing Borrible song to himself, a song that told of the dangers past and the dangers to come.

'Sound the fife and beat the drum,
We're riding, we're riding to Rumbledom!
Dewdrop's dead, and Erbie too,
We're going to do what we must do.
Onwards we ride to glorious fame,
To rout the Rumbles and earn a name!
With a fee and a fo and a fie and a fum,
We're riding, we're riding to Rumbledom!

'From Peckham, and Stepney, and Tooting we come!
We're riding, we're riding to Rumbledom!
Wandsworth, Whitechapel and Neasden too,
We're going to do what we must do.
Ahead lies battle and maybe death,
We'll soldier on as long as we've breath
To rid the world of that snouted scum,
We're riding, we're riding to Rumbledom!

'Armoured in courage from bonce to bum,
We're riding, we're riding to Rumbledom!

Though they are many and we are few,
We're going to do what we must do.
So, giddy-up Sam, and spare no speed!
Forward to war, O noble steed!
To triumph, or hell, or kingdom come,
We're riding, we're riding to Rumbledom!'

Bingo's companions joined in the song, their hearts full of a divine excitement, a feeling which mingled strangely with the serene joy they felt at being Borribles, at being alive and together on an adventure of their own, an adventure that would be sung about again and again in the years to come.

Sam took them through many deserted roads and gardens and strange silent streets, hauling the old cart across the steep hills which guarded the borders of Rumbledom. The horse strode out purposefully, head high and legs thrusting hard, the colour of his coat alternating between deep purple and gold as he entered and left the quiet pools of light which fell gracefully from the tall white swan-necks of the concrete street lamps.

Sam trudged on, from Brookwood Road to Elsenham Street, and into Augustus where the slope began in earnest. Up Albert Drive and Albyn Road, through Thursley Gardens and along Seymour Road and Bathgate Road, up Somerset Road at last and the slope flattened and the sky lightened and turned blotchy, like yesterday's porridge. And a cold dark wind came across a boundless space and numbed the intent of the Adventurers as they peered from beneath the warm canvas. The crisp air lined their lungs with ice, chilling their blood at the heart. Sam hesitated. One last road to cross – Parkside. He shook his head and neighed valiantly, and went out into the green and black stillness that was Rumbledom.

Bingo guided the horse and cart to a large clump of trees not far into the wilderness. The wintry light of morning glinted without friendliness on a sheet of water nearby. 'Bluegate Gravel Pit, Disused', said the map.

'We'll camp by the water's edge,' said Knocker to Bingo, 'then at least we can't be attacked from the rear, and we can post lookouts along the line of trees.'

'It doesn't look like we've been spotted,' said Bingo. 'If we make it to those trees, we'll be safe.'

Sam pulled them towards a copse. The cart lurched and jolted and the Borribles, who were standing now, had to hang on with all their strength to avoid being thrown to the ground. They looked keenly about them to see if there was any sign of the Rumbles, but not a bird flew overhead and nary a dog hunted through the clumps of grass, not even on the horizon where the grey sky was brightening.

'Come on, Sam, me old deario,' cried Bingo in a tired voice. 'Nearly there, ain't it? Then we'll rest and eat all day, my little darling.'

Sam came to a halt. His coat was steaming and his legs were trembling after the long uphill flight from Engadine. Bingo yanked on the brake lever and the Adventurers leapt to the ground. They spread out in all directions to search through the undergrowth, making certain that there were no Rumbles in hiding or, even more dangerous, that there was no entrance here to a burrow, one of those large underground warrens where Rumbles live in security and comfort.

They found no trace of the enemy and so Napoleon and Vulge prised Bingo up and away from the shoulders of Stonks and stood him on the ground. Bingo stretched and rubbed his legs. 'What a gloomy old dump Rumbledom is,' he said. 'What's on the other side?'

'Not much,' said Knocker. 'There's no more London, just countryside with separate houses, funny.'

'And they lives down below,' whispered Torreycanyon, pointing downwards, 'right under our very feet, eh?'

'That's right,' said Orococco. 'They lives in burrows and we lives in boroughs. That's the difference!'

'Hey, you lot,' called out Napoleon, 'come over here and help me with Stonks. He's gone all stiff-solid, carrying Bingo all this way; he's got cramp in all his muscles. Poor sod can't move.'

The Borribles gathered round the cart and stared up at their companion.

'Oh, don't worry,' he said, hardly able to move his mouth. 'I'm all right, honest. Keep your eyes open 'stead of fussing about me; they might creep up on you.'

'Chalotte and me will go on guard,' said Sydney, and the two girls went to the edge of the copse. The others lifted Stonks gently from his seat and laid him on the grass, though his body remained in a sitting position, quite rigid.

'He looks like a bloody armchair,' said Bingo.

'Just give me a rub-down.' Stonks tried to laugh. 'I'll soon be as good as new.'

They took turns in rubbing Stonks hard on his legs, and when his muscles had loosened a little they covered him with sleeping bags to keep him warm. Then they settled down for a council of war.

No noise came across the open spaces of Rumbledom but traffic whined along Parkside now as people began to make their way to work. Only one thing was moving near them in the dreary landscape, the cool black steam that rose from the surface of the gravel pit.

It was easy to decide what they needed at that moment – food and rest. They opened their haversacks and made a feast of the food they had brought from Dewdrop's house. There were tins of beans, loaves of sliced bread, packets of biscuits, tins of steak-and-kidney pie, rice pudding, slabs of chocolate both milk and plain, nuts and raisins. There was cheese and liver sausage and bottles of Guinness and cans of ale. It was a complete banquet, coming as it did after the weeks of privation in the cellars of Engadine.

Then, with two of their number constantly on watch, they slept all morning. In the afternoon they just dozed or chatted lazily to one another, firing their catapults at the water as they talked. Some fell asleep again, to wake up later and join in the conversation. They discussed the Rumbles, their adventures so far and the training that Knocker and Dodger had given them, and if they would ever, all of them, get home safe and sound.

'They like staying in the warm,' said Knocker of the Rumbles. 'It is well into winter now, so they'll spend most of their time in the burrows. We've been so long in coming that they've probably forgotten all about us and won't have many lookout patrols on the go. On the other hand they are no fools. They may have seen us already; they may be on the other side of the horizon gathering their forces.'

'Has anyone, apart from a Rumble that is, ever seen the inside of a burrow?' asked Chalotte.

'No,' said Knocker, 'but according to Spiff, who knows more about them than any other Borrible, you want to forget the idea of it being a cosy little burrow; it's really a defensive bunker, very luxurious though – carpeted, pictures on the wall, beds, blankets and bathrooms, centrally heated of course, workshops. They want for nothing and they eat well. The bunker is complicated, designed like a spider's web, strong, lots of cement. Rumbles, they know every inch of it. Some of you will get lost, be set on in a cul-de-sac. But remember the place in the middle to which all the tunnels lead, it's called the Central. Once you get in the bunker you'll be on your own, each one of you has got to do for your namesake and then hop it. You know what they look like, you did that in training.'

'We get in, get our target, and then get out,' said Sydney.

'That's it,' answered Knocker. 'We'll rendezvous back here. If anyone is captured or wounded or killed, the others do not wait. The survivors take the horse and cart and they go, night or day. There'll be thousands of Rumbles after us and they can fight too, overrun us by sheer weight of numbers.'

'I wish I knew what they were up to,' said Vulge, standing up and firing his catapult at a plastic ice cream cup floating on the gravel pit and sinking it with his first stone. 'It's too damn quiet!'

Just then Orococco pushed his head through the trees. 'There's a Rumble comin' this way, sniffin' with his snout and pokin' about in the grass with a nail on the end of a long stick! I could exterminate him from about fifty yards.'

'Oh, boy,' said Vulge, slipping his bandolier over his shoulder. 'If he's alone let's nobble him and ask him a few questions, see what his mates are up to.'

Napoleon, who had been catnapping, rolled over and said lazily, 'Yeah, someone go and bring the bastard in.'

'Don't harm him,' said Knocker to Orococco. 'We want him alive. If he doesn't suss you as a Borrible, tell him you've got something you want him to see, right here.'

'That might make him run a mile,' joked Orococco, flashing his teeth.

'Well, in that case, clout him across the head and drag him in by his snout,' said Napoleon, and went back to sleep.

Those who were awake sprang to their feet and slipped through the bushes till they reached the perimeter of the copse. Across the windswept grass, picking his way slowly through the gorse bushes, they saw the

Rumble. He was sniffing the air cautiously and peering to right and left as if fearing attack or discovery.

Orococco kept the gorse bushes between himself and the Rumble for as long as he could but eventually he was noticed. The Rumble sank behind a small bush till only his snout protruded. Orococco pretended he'd seen nothing and made as if to pass by, but then he stopped and the watchers saw him wave at the Rumble, who came out into the open and stepped hesitantly towards the black Borrible.

For a while Orococco engaged the enemy in conversation; he pointed towards the copse where his companions were hidden, then he waved again at the Rumble and moved on.

'Wonder if it'll work,' said Vulge.

'Depends what he told him,' said Chalotte.

The Rumble remained where he was for several minutes waiting for Orococco to disappear, but the second he thought he was alone he turned and began to run towards the Borribles.

'*Verdammt*, it has worked,' cried Adolf, rubbing his hands.

'Spread out,' said Knocker. 'Get behind a tree and when the little bleeder comes by, jump him.'

From their hiding places the Borribles watched the approach of the solitary Rumble. The animal's snout pulsated with suspicion, the small red eyes probed everywhere, trying to see through the undergrowth, beyond the bushes. His padded feet brought him nearer and nearer. At the edge of the trees he halted and turned to look over the wild downs. Nothing moved on the surface of the countryside. The Rumble took a deep breath through his snout and plunged into the copse. He did not plunge very far. As he passed between two trees Vulge and Torreycanyon rose from the matted undergrowth like two fast-growing man-eating plants, one before and one behind the surprised Rumble.

'Aaaaagh,' he squealed, the sound beginning loudly but fading away to a weak and disjointed whimper.

'Aaaaagh,' imitated Vulge. Then he grabbed the Rumble by the scruff of its neck and shook him, as if trying to dislocate every bone in his body. 'You mouldy old eiderdown, we've come a long way to have a chat with you. Gone through endless dangers to engage you in fruitful converse, and all you can do is go "Aaaaagh".'

'Yeah,' joined in Torreycanyon, slapping the animal gently across the snout, 'you're a rat.' He did not have the same inventive vocabulary that Vulge was blessed with.

The animal drew himself up. 'I'm not a wat,' he said, 'I'm a Wumble.'

'And I'm Towweycanyon, a howwible Bowwible,' said Torreycanyon and he seized the Rumble-stick. 'Look at this,' he said to Vulge, 'a very nasty tool.'

'Yeah,' agreed the Stepney Borrible. 'And there's thousands of Rumbles out there and they've all got one. Come on, let's get back to the clearing.'

They held the prisoner by his arms and dragged him back to the middle of the trees where the others soon gathered. They sat the Rumble down by the cart and tied him to one of the wheels.

'Oh, my goodness,' said the Rumble, looking nervously around. 'I weally can smell a horse. You can't wealize how dweadful they are.'

'Isn't it marvellous how they can't talk properly?' said Vulge, giving the ropes a really good pull and a tug to make sure the prisoner couldn't escape.

The Borribles sat round the prisoner in a semicircle and even those who had been dozing woke up and approached the captive; for most of them it was their first close look at the enemy.

'Right,' said Bingo cheerfully to the Rumble, 'we're going to ask you some interesting questions, and you're going to give us some interesting answers. If you don't keep us amused, if we should get in the slightest bit bored, I shall give you to Sam to eat. He likes hay.'

'Sam's the horse,' said Chalotte.

'Aaaaagh,' groaned the Rumble.

'Well that's bloody boring for a start,' said Vulge. 'If he's going to say nothing but "Aaaaagh" all the time, we might as well give him to Sam straight away.'

Sam the horse, hearing his name mentioned so often, ambled across to the group of Borribles and stood contentedly looking over their shoulders, munching. He looked at the furred creature with a certain amount of appetite, for it is a fact that horses enjoy eating Rumbles, finding that they taste like well matured hay, good and sweet and nourishing. The Rumble shrank back in his bonds. Though normally as brave as anyone, understandably enough neither he nor any of his kind could bear the sight or smell of a horse.

'Don't let him near me,' he shrieked. 'I'll talk, I'll tell you evewything, only don't let him touch me.'

Vulge looked round the half circle of his friends. 'Well,' he said, 'at least that's better than "Aaaaagh".'

'How many Rumbles in your bunker?' asked Torreycanyon.

A thin yellow tongue appeared briefly along the slit in the Rumble's snout. 'There's hundweds, certainly, maybe more, but we're only one bunker, the main one, but there are others too, all interconnected.'

'And the High Command, the eight top names, they're in your bunker, aren't they?' asked Sydney, her voice cool.

'You know about the Eight?' asked the Rumble, seized by a sudden terror. 'Then you're not ordinawy childwen, you're—'

'That's wight, my old china,' scoffed Vulge, 'we're howwible Bowwibles. You ought to listen when we talk to you.'

And the Rumble did listen, for the questioning went on all through the afternoon, with the prisoner gradually coming to realize that this was indeed the Great Rumble Hunt that had been promised, and dreaded, for so many years.

As the hours went by the Borribles found out many things. The Rumble that Knocker and Lightfinger had captured all that time ago had returned alive to Rumbledom country. His story had struck fear and dismay into the hearts of all Rumbles, young and old, male and female. But that fear had hardened into anger, and the dismay had crystallized into resolution, and the Rumbles had looked about them.

At first the High Command, following the general mood, had overreacted, conscripting all their able-bodied animals into the Warrior Corps. Training had been intensive and Rumble scouts had been sent out regularly as far as Southfields and even to Wandsworth Common, for the Rumbles had expected a mass invasion. This impression had been conveyed to them by Timbucktoo. He had led his compatriots to believe that a vast horde of Borribles was on the march and that all of Borrible London was in a state of war.

But the weeks had gone by and there had been no sign of the enemy. The Borrible threat receded in the mind of the ordinary Rumble. The scouts deserted their posts and returned to the life of comfort and ease to which, to tell the truth, they were well used. Patrols still went out to Southfields and such, but Rumbles dislike the streets as much as

Borribles hate the countryside and so the patrols had become less frequent and more inefficient.

Most Rumbles completely forgot the menace of the Great Rumble Hunt, others suggested that it had only been a vain threat made in anger, one that the Borribles could never sustain. Anyway, thought the average Rumble, if he thought about it at all, those Borribles are mean snivelling little dirty things, they could never make the long and perilous journey to Rumbledom, they don't possess the wherewithal, the knowledge, the brains. They couldn't mount such an expedition with their resources. They live in rotten little streets and barely scrape a living. They have enough to do to stay alive. No, they argued, the vast domain of Rumbledom, on top of the great hill, on top of the world, is safe.

But the Rumble High Command did not see the problem in quite the same way. They had been threatened, and though the threat might only be an idea as yet, it was an idea of their overthrow and a great danger lurked in it. It was a concept that could lead only to disaster if nothing was done. Furthermore, they felt, they had a perfect right to go wherever they wished, beholden to no one, and that right must be defended.

So the High Command had made a plan, emanating from their chief and dictator, Vulgarian. They must strike before they were struck; destroy the Borribles of Battersea before their idea could take root and spread. A large force of crack warriors could be equipped for a night attack on Battersea High Street, to seek out and destroy any Borribles they found and obliterate the Borrible war machine that Timbucktoo had assured them was being prepared.

Warriors had been put into special training and were ready to undertake the long journey. They had not the slightest intention of marching those many miles; they already had one motor car and only awaited the delivery of others before setting out. They intended to strike with speed and in several places at once, causing as much panic and destruction among the Borrible population as possible.

In addition to such offensive measures, the Rumbles had seen to their own defences and reviewed the whole situation. There were only two entrances to the main bunker, and both were guarded day and night. Rumbles, it was said, never let go of anything, and they would hang on to Rumbledom like grim death. What had never occurred to them was that a tiny force of chosen Borribles would infiltrate their territory and attempt to assassinate the High Command and so leave the Rumbles leaderless and ineffective. Thus the Adventurers found that the element of surprise was with them; no one knew of their arrival. That was the good news; the bad news they already knew: they were hopelessly outnumbered and retreat, even if they succeeded in their task, would be impossible.

When the Borribles were satisfied with their interrogation they moved away from their prisoner so they could talk without being overheard. They leant against the trees and discussed matters, scanning the horizon at the same time.

'Well,' said Bingo, 'how are we going to play it?'

'What our friend forgot to mention,' said Knocker, 'is that although there are only two entrances to the bunker, there is in fact a ventilation shaft that comes out above the kitchens. It's in Spiff's notes. I think that's the way we – I mean you – should go in.'

'Wait a minute,' interrupted Stonks. 'My target is the doorkeeper. I'll have to go in through the door, otherwise I might not find him.'

'I've got an idea,' cried Torreycanyon. 'We can make a diversionary attack on both doors, just a couple of us, and the main body can get in through the ventilator.'

'Here comes 'Rococco,' said Stonks. 'Running.'

'I hope,' said Sydney, 'it's not bad news.'

Orococco stopped a few yards from the copse, turning to make sure no one was watching before he slipped into the trees.

'Hello,' he panted, 'everything okay?'

'We're just talking about how to attack,' said Napoleon. 'Any trouble?'

'Nah,' answered the Tooting Borrible. 'I've just been for a little runaround, see what I could see.'

'And what did you see?' said the Wendle.

'Well, I don't think they know we're here. I saw a couple of them wandering about with their Rumble-sticks, but they didn't look worried, just stooging up and down. I found the two entrances to the place, and I found out where the ventilation comes out, on top of a hill. It will be a piece of duff.'

Napoleon turned from listening to the Totter and looked at Knocker, suspicious again. 'And what will you be up to during the attack, eh?'

'Adolf and me will help cause as much confusion as possible,' answered Knocker, avoiding eye contact with the Wendle.

'Not half, *verdammt*,' agreed the German. 'Alarm and confusion and mayhem . . . that I am good at.'

Napoleon scowled, unconvinced. 'Just don't interfere, Knocker,' he said. 'I still don't trust you.' He took out his catapult and affected to examine the thick rubber on it. 'Well, what about Torrey's plan?'

The discussion continued and during the next half an hour several ideas were weighed in the balance until at last Torreycanyon's plan was adopted unanimously. Then, feeling that they had accomplished something, the Adventurers returned to the clearing. There a surprise awaited them. The Rumble had disappeared, even the ropes that had bound him were gone.

'Who tied him up then?' Napoleon shouted at Vulge, anger tightening his face. 'Now we're in trouble. He'll tell 'em everything; they'll be waiting for us.'

Vulge looked guilty. 'I made sure he couldn't get free.' He glanced at the others. 'Really I did.'

'Bloody well looks like it, don't it?' said Napoleon. 'Idiot. If he gets back to his bunker we've had it.'

'Don't panic,' said Sydney, and she giggled. 'Look at Sam.'

The horse was lying on the ground at the edge of the clearing with a stupidly contented expression on his long face. From his mouth dangled a frayed bit of rope, swinging gently with the movement of his champing jaws.

'Well, strike me pink,' cried Adolf. 'Sam's eaten him.' And he hooted.

'Would you Adam-and-Eve it?' said Stonks. 'So he has, the sly old rogue.'

'That makes one Rumble less,' said Napoleon. 'I was wondering what we were going to do with him.'

Sam shook his head and snickered, then he gave a neigh of pleasure, rolled over, stuck out his legs and promptly closed his eyes. It was an excellent idea, and while most of the Adventurers followed suit, Knocker, Adolf and Chalotte volunteered for the first two hours of guard duty: two hours for them to gaze across the chill expanses of inhospitable Rumbledom, two hours for them to think of the coming battle.

It was cold now and high up on the hill the air was sharp-edged and brittle. No wonder those Rumbles have fur coats, thought Knocker, as he watched and shivered. Nothing moved in the vastness.

Chalotte came and leant against a tree nearby. She didn't look at Knocker at first, but kept watch over the green land where the advancing mist of dusk was making it difficult to distinguish between trees and gorse bushes, pathways and grass.

'It's going to be dangerous, isn't it?' she said. It wasn't a question.

'We always knew some of us wouldn't survive,' answered Knocker.

'I sometimes think,' said Chalotte, 'that we're not really meant to go in for this kind of adventure. It would be nice to go back to being just a Borrible, living in our broken-down houses. You know the proverb, "Fruit of the barrow is enough for a Borrible." I mean this adventure has turned out to be far beyond what we normally do. It's suicide.'

'Wait a minute,' protested Knocker, surprised. 'This is the greatest adventure we're ever likely to hear of, let alone go on.'

'Hmmmm.' She sounded unconvinced. 'You ought to make it clear to the others that by this time tomorrow they're likely to be dead. Who wants to die for a name? That was never Borrible.'

'Fruit of the barrow may be all right, but we've got to have adventures, too. Look, if you hadn't come on this one you wouldn't have seen Dewdrop and Erbie and learned what happens to us when we get caught. We'd have heard about it, but now we've seen it, we know.'

'Yes, but supposing Spiff got it all wrong; supposing those Rumbles just came down on a spree, just to visit the park, not take over all of Battersea, like he said. What then, eh? It would be silly, just them scared of us and us scared of them.'

'Oh, that's rubbish,' said Knocker. 'Old Spiff don't make cock-ups like that, he just don't. He has studied the Rumbles for years, he knows them inside out. I mean, do you think the Wendles don't know what they're up against? Flinthead is like he is because of the Rumbles. They'd take Wandsworth over if they had a chance, Battersea too.'

'You admire Spiff too much,' said Chalotte. 'You believe everything he says. He might have set us up for this . . . had his own reasons . . . He's a mystery, he is, and I don't like mysteries. After all, how important is a name? You've got one and yet you're going on a suicide mission for another.' She shook her head, glanced at Knocker, and then said what was really on her mind. 'There's something else, isn't there? Something secret, that you know and Spiff knows. Ordinary expeditions are fine adventures, a bit of a laugh, but this one is making us like the Wendles, and that can't be good, can it? The things we are doing might look right now but they could turn out wrong in the end.'

Knocker turned nasty. 'You and Sydney have really pulled your weight all along. I didn't believe you could at the beginning, but you have. Are you going to spoil it all now by being scared?'

Chalotte didn't pick up on the insult, in fact she smiled. 'I told you at the start we'd be as good as anyone else. As for scared, well, we're all scared of something. You're scared that you won't get another name, and another after that . . . All I'm scared of is getting in too deep, too deep into something that isn't really Borrible. That's all.' And she placed her hand ever so lightly on Knocker's and took it away again.

Knocker blushed and turned his head to look at her but she was gone through the bushes, back to her lookout post. Over the sunless fields of Rumbledom the mist lay in pools and there was not a soul to be seen. Soon it would be dark.

And as the dusk deepened in the trees the Borribles watched and slept by turns, but by midnight they could rest no longer, so they roused themselves for one last meal together. They crowded under the cart and held their feast by the light of torches tied to the spokes of the wheels. They were subdued, but Adolf cheered them with tales of his travels and the stories of his names, telling them how this was the best adventure he had ever known, and how happy he was to be with such a band. He slapped Napoleon on the back and said he 'wasn't bad for a Wendle' and even Napoleon had to laugh at that, and he gave the German another can of Dewdrop's Guinness.

In the blackest part of the night the Adventurers prepared themselves. They reloaded their double bandoliers with the choicest stones, and Adolf and Knocker even took with them the spare catapults they had used for their escape from Dewdrop's house. They removed all shiny things from their jackets, and they tucked their trousers into their socks, tying the laces of their combat boots as tightly as they could. They put Sam back between the shafts and loaded their haversacks on to the cart so they would be ready to run for it if they ever managed to get clear of the bunker.

When all was done they shovelled up a huge pile of stones from the gravelly shore of the lake and threw them into the cart as well. If they had to make a running retreat it would be an advantage to have a good supply of ammunition with them.

At the very last, Knocker took a tin from his pocket, opened it, and began smearing his face with the contents. It was black greasepaint, so that his white skin would not be spied by the enemy in the frosty starlight. Orococco laughed as the others followed suit.

'Man, oh man, I knew my colour would come in useful one day. If we have a daylight attack, will you fellas get me some white paint so my face don't stick out so much?'

Then the Adventurers were ready – tough and determined. One by one they went to the horse and patted him and asked him to be patient, standing in the traces like that, and Sam neighed like a charger and stamped a hoof. Then the Borribles synchronized their watches and took a compass bearing on the copse and finally, without a light to guide them, they moved off in single file. Orococco led them out, for as he said, not only did he know the way, but he was still the blackest of them all.

8

It was a clear night and a ground frost made the Adventurers' footsteps crunch loudly as they advanced over the stiff white grass. They said nothing, each one nursing his or her own private thoughts, each one yearning for the crowded and friendly streets that they called home, but there was no turning back now.

They walked on for about a mile, then Orococco stopped and his companions gathered around him. Even then the Borrible from Tooting could not resist a joke: 'Why, friends,' he laughed, 'we looks like a Black and White Minstrel Show.'

'Get on with it,' snapped Stonks, who like everybody else was very tense and eager to begin.

'Okay, Mr Bones,' said Orococco. 'You see that mound beginning to rise a little, over there against the sky? That's the bunker, only it looks like a hill. There's a couple of saplings and a few bushes to the right; they screen the Great Door. If we climb the hill and walk over it in a straight line, we'll come to the exit hole of the ventilation network, and going on from that, 'bout half a mile, is the back door, smaller, not so well made. Don't stamp your feet when you're on the hill; you'll wake up all the rats in Rumbledom if you do.'

'Right then,' said Stonks, 'I'll get off here. My target's just the other side of that door.'

'With a hundred thousand unfriendly friends,' added Napoleon.

'Kind of odds that keep a Borrible alert,' answered Stonks, not to be put down by a Wendle.

'Who do you want to go with you?' asked Knocker. 'We must get a move on, we've got to be out before dawn.'

'Torreycanyon, if he'll come,' said Stonks, turning to his friend.

'Course I will,' said Torreycanyon. 'We'll give you guys ten minutes, then we'll go in.'

The others went on, moving at a trot up the side of the hill, and sure enough, at the top, hidden by thick gorse bushes, was the main outlet for the air conditioning system of the whole bunker city. It was covered by a large iron grille, solid and heavy, painted green to camouflage its appearance. Orococco said, 'There she is. Now, who's coming with me to the other door? I can recommend it, very frail and only five hundred and fifty Rumbles guarding it. Any offers?'

Bingo gave a nod. 'Battersea and Tooting together,' he cried. 'What a team! I'll pick you up by the legs, you old Totter, and bash them to smithereens with your head bone.'

Orococco turned to Knocker. 'Give us five minutes,' he said, 'and by the time you've got the kettle boiled for tea we'll be in there with you.' And he and Bingo began the descent that led to the Small Door of Rumbledom.

There were six of them left standing at the vent now: Chalotte, Sydney, Adolf, Napoleon, Vulge and Knocker himself. They squatted and waited.

'Friends,' said Vulge after a while, 'those five minutes have gone into eternity. Shall we begin the dance?'

Napoleon forced his knife under the edge of the ventilation grille and pushed it in as far as it would go, Then he exerted all his strength and levered and twisted; the grille shifted, just a little.

'It's coming,' said Sydney, and shoved a stone into the gap so that the grille could not fall back into its grooves. Adolf and Knocker seized the edge of it and pulled together to upend the square of heavy iron before lowering it to the ground. Chalotte bent over the dark aperture and peered in. 'It looks a long way down,' she said.

Napoleon risked a quick beam of light from his torch. The ventilation shaft dropped vertically for about ten feet then turned a right-angled corner.

'There's only one way to find out where it goes,' said Vulge, 'and that's to go.'

They had all brought a length of strong rope with them, tied around their waists, and Vulge took his and attached it to the foot of a nearby growth of gorse.

'I'll go first,' he said. 'I'll give you the whistle if it looks all right.' He looked closely at the faces of his fellow Adventurers. 'This is it, then, so 'ere we go.' And he slipped over the edge of the air vent and was gone. One moment he had been standing there smiling and wagging his head, the next nothing was to be seen but a section of tightened rope. A minute later the rope became slack and they heard the familiar Borrible whistle.

'I'll go next,' whispered Chalotte excitedly, and she took the cord firmly between her hands and stepped backwards into space, walking casually down the side of the shaft.

'*Verdammt*,' said Adolf, nudging Knocker, 'no mug that girl.'

Napoleon decided that Sydney should follow Chalotte and then he himself would go down. To Knocker and Adolf he simply said, 'You two come after, and remember it's our adventure, not yours. I don't want you interfering, 'specially not you, Knocker. I wouldn't trust you further than I could throw Nelson's Column.'

Adolf watched the Wendle slither down the rope.

'He doesn't like you very much, you know,' he said to Knocker. 'He thinks you are up to something.'

Knocker grinned. 'I am up to something, mate, and you're going to be up to it with me. As for Napoleon, it's in his nature to be suspicious; Wendles always are.'

'Ho ho,' hooted Adolf. 'Never mind all that. Something is what I like to be up to. Let us hurry.'

*

Stonks and Torreycanyon sneaked through the gorse bushes on their bellies and approached the Great Door with caution. A premature alarm would alert the Rumble defences and make the difficult task of the Borribles into an impossible one. The grass and bushes were damp with the threat of the coming dew and soon the two attackers were drenched.

'We'll soon dry off when we get inside,' said Torreycanyon. 'I'll use my Rumble as a towel.'

'It's funny in a way, isn't it?' said Stonks. He stopped crawling and faced his companion. 'Going after a bloke with the same name. It's like going after yourself. I mean, the names we've got aren't our names, they're really theirs; but when we've eliminated them, the names will be ours for ever, and the adventure we've had, even if we've been killed, can never be taken away.'

'It'll be taken away if we're all killed and nobody gets back to tell the story. If it's never written down, then it's gone for ever. The story's the thing; have you thought of that?'

'Yeah, maybe Knocker shouldn't have come this far. He can't be Historian if he's captured or killed . . . You know, I hadn't realized Historians were so important.'

Torreycanyon held Stonks by the arm for a moment.

'Ah,' he said, 'but if he hadn't come this far he would have had no story to tell. Historians have to go where the history is, I s'pose.'

They crept on until they were about ten yards from the door; there they stopped and checked their watches.

'Another five minutes.'

'Look at that door,' said Stonks, with respect in his voice. 'Im-bloody-pregnable.' It was true. Although not large, for Rumbles are about the same size as Borribles, it was stoutly built in oak, with iron bars reinforcing it. Its hinges were massive and heavy, designed to withstand a great deal of battering. By the time it was vanquished, that door, all the Rumbles in Rumbledom could be behind it.

'This is the time for guile,' said Torreycanyon wisely, 'but what kind of guile, I do not know.'

Stonks looked at his watch. 'Come on,' he said. 'I have an idea. Let's unwind our ropes.'

Stonks joined the two pieces of cord together, then, crouching, he made for the trees that grew a short distance from the bunker door. Torreycanyon followed. At the foot of a stout sapling Stonks said, 'You're going to climb this, so it'll bend under your weight. Here's the rope, tie the middle of it round the top of the trunk and drop both ends down to me. Got it?'

'Yeah,' said Torreycanyon. 'Course I got it.' And he scrambled up the tree making it droop more and more as he climbed higher, and making it sway from side to side as he secured the rope and threw the loose ends of it to Stonks. Then Torreycanyon felt himself drawn nearer and nearer to the ground, as the strongest of the Borribles pulled on the rope until the topmost twigs of the sapling touched the grass.

'Stay where you are, Torrey,' said Stonks breathlessly. 'Keep your weight on while I tie it down to this root over here.'

It took Stonks but a moment to fasten the sapling, and when he had finished he allowed Torreycanyon to step from his perch.

'Whatever it is you're going to do, Stonksie, you'd better do it now, because the others are going in at this very moment.'

As Torreycanyon spoke someone stirred behind the door. Stonks winked at his companion and took up the spare piece of rope that dangled from the tree top. He went over to the Great Door, knocked and then spoke up firmly in a Rumble voice: 'Sowwy to twouble you, Stonks, but I've found something mighty suspicious here. You'd better check it over. Open up.'

There was a second's hesitation on the far side of the door and then Stonks and Torreycanyon heard the bolts being slid and a key being turned in the massive lock.

'Torrey,' whispered Stonks, 'when I tip you the wink, cut that rope.'

Torreycanyon crouched and Stonks stood behind the door as it swung slowly open.

'I wealize you're vewy stwong,' said the Borrible, 'but I don't think that even you can keep hold of this.' He put the rope's end around the door and thrust it into the hand of the Rumble. 'Hang on tight,' he insisted. 'Wemember we Wumbles never let go.' And he made the sign to Torreycanyon, who, with one slash of his knife, severed the cord that held the tree top to the ground. The sapling was immediately released from constraint and it sprang upright with an irresistible power, dragging the short end of rope with it. The Rumble doorkeeper at the end of the rope, true to his upbringing, held on tightly and shot through the doorway like the first Rumble rocket to the moon, knocking the Great Door open with such force that it would have killed Stonks had he not jumped clear of it.

The Rumble whizzed over the Borrible's head at escape velocity and was swung away in a wide arc. Still he held on, and could he have strengthened his grip he might have lived for ever, but when the sapling reached its apogee it suddenly and treacherously reversed its direction. So there came a moment when the Rumble was travelling away from the door at a speed that was much faster than safe, and the top of the sapling was travelling at the same speed but back towards the door. The rope became taut and even the remarkable strength of Stonks the Rumble could not hold on to it, and it was torn from his grasp. He disappeared into the black night, a fast-moving silhouette against the starry sky.

'He'll be burned to a frazzle on re-entry,' said Stonks with a sniff and a spit. They waited a long while in silence.

'He's been ages up there,' ventured Torreycanyon.

Just then there came a scream and a crashing of branches from about three hundred yards away. Then there was a dull crump and the ground where the Borribles stood shook and shivered.

'Ah, that sounds like a satisfactory abort,' said Torreycanyon, rising from his crouching position and sheathing his knife at last. He stepped over to Stonks and took his hand and shook it. 'I'd like to be the first,' he said, 'to congratulate you on being the first of us to win a name. Well done, Stonks, no other's name but yours now.'

The door to the bunker now stood open and undefended. The two Borribles tiptoed towards it and peered in. An electric light showed an entrance hall furnished with a comfortable armchair for the duty guard to rest in; there were some blankets and nearby a little table with food and books on it. On the other side of the hall a lighted tunnel led off to the heart of the bunker. Both the hallway and the tunnel were built in brick and there was carpet on the floor and pictures on the walls. It looked warm and comfortable.

'Nobody about,' said Stonks, and they entered the hall and pulled the massive door shut behind them.

'What a smashing place,' said Torreycanyon. 'Don't stint themselves, do they?'

'They have no need to, mate, no need,' said Stonks, and he shot the bolts and turned the key in the lock. 'Look,' he went on, 'I've done my bloke so I'll stay here and watch the exit, that way we've got a line of retreat.' He picked up the Rumble-stick which had belonged to the guard who had left his post so precipitately, and hefted it in his hand. 'Any Rumble who tries to get the door from me will have four inches of nail in him. You can tell the others when you see them. I'll also pull some bricks from the wall and make a couple of barricades across the tunnel. If you come back this way you'll have to give the whistle and I'll let you over.'

'Good idea,' said Torreycanyon. 'I'll tell anybody I see.' Then he said, 'I'd better get going. Goodbye, Stonks. Don't get caught, eh?' And there was a catch to his voice as he spoke.

Stonks caught hold of his friend and embraced him. 'Take care, me old china. Win your name well. Don't you get caught now, I'd miss you.'

And Torreycanyon turned abruptly, a tear in his eye, and he ran down the lighted, twisting, dangerous tunnel as fast as he could go, eager for his name.

*

Orococco and Bingo slid down the bumpy hillside, getting wet where they sat and slithered on the soaking grass. The slope ended in a small cliff and they fell together, all of a heap, into a little open space at the bottom of the hill.

'Careful, Bingo,' whispered Orococco. 'We've landed right on their doorstep.'

They crept on all fours till they came up against the Small Door. As its name indicated it was less important than the Great Door on the other side of the hill – even a Borrible would have to crawl through this one – and in the middle of it there was a judas hole so that whoever was on guard could open a flap and see outside without having to put himself in danger.

'Time for a bit of the old crafty,' said Bingo.

'That's all we got, man,' said Orococco. He knocked at the door. There was no answer.

'The fools are sleeping,' said Bingo. 'You see, they don't know we're here.' This time he knocked, with the butt of his catapult, very loudly indeed.

There was a sudden and muffled snort from inside the bunker and Orococco put his face close to the judas. The flap in the door flew open and a sleepy voice said, 'Who goes there, Wumble or foe?'

'A Wumble,' said Orococco, flashing his teeth.

'No such thing as a black Wumble,' said the guard, his snout coming close to the opening and quivering distrustfully. 'What's your name?'

'Owococco,' said Orococco, nodding at Bingo, who was close to the door but out of sight of the person within.

There was a shocked silence from the Rumble, then he said, 'Wait a minute, that can't be your name, it's my name.'

'Sowwy,' said Orococco, 'you're mistaken. Owococco is my name, always has been, Honky.'

'Idiot,' said the voice behind the door, 'Do you think I don't know my own name? I'm Owococco.' The snout pulsated and sniffed. 'You don't even smell like a Wumble.'

'Well,' said the Totter from Tooting, 'all I can say is open the door and have a look.'

'I can't do that,' said the guardian. 'It's against the wules, and according to my list evewyone is in tonight.'

'All wight then,' said the black Borrible. 'Stick your nose out and take a weally good sniff and let me in. I'm exhausted. I have important news for the High Command.'

'I'm one of the High Command,' said the Rumble, suddenly intrigued. 'You may tell me all.'

'I'll tell you nothing until you let me in,' insisted Orococco.

The snout pushed through the judas in an attempt to sniff the Borrible's face, but Orococco fell back half a step and the protuberance was obliged to push itself a little further and again a little further, still snuffling and vibrating. It was then that Bingo rose and seized it in both hands and held on with all his might.

Quickly, Orococco slipped the length of strong cord from his waist and wound it several times round the Rumble's snout. Tying it very tightly, he secured the free end to the root of a gorse bush. The Rumble could hardly breathe but Bingo did not let go, nor did the rope slacken for all the animal's struggles behind the door.

'Shuddup Rumble,' whispered Orococco. 'If you don't stop that wriggling I'll beat your nose till it looks like a limp wind sock.'

The struggling abated, then ceased altogether.

'Now, listen,' went on the black Totter. 'You can reach the bolts, and you can reach the lock, so open up. We have an ultimatum for your mates, and they're going to get it one way or the other, whether you have a snout left or not.'

Orococco Rumble hesitated. There was a little more kicking of padded feet and a flailing of arms, but the snout did not move an inch from its imprisonment. Then the two Borribles heard the bolts slide and the key grate in the lock, and Orococco threw his body at the door with such force that the cord holding the snout broke with a loud twang and nearly pulled the Rumble's head through the judas. This fierce assault slammed the body of the guardian back against the wall of the passage and there was a sickening thud.

Bingo vaulted into the corridor, rolled over and came up holding his catapult at the ready, but he did not fire for this was Orococco's game. Orococco seized a Rumble-stick, one of many that stood in a rack; he drew back his arm, ready to thrust the deadly sticker into the furry body of his namesake, but before he could act the Rumble fell forward on to the floor, the weight of his body banging the Small Door shut.

Bingo turned the body over with a foot. 'Strewth,' he said, 'you must've broke his neck when you opened the door.'

'Never stand behind a door when there's a Totter coming through the other side,' said Orococco. 'That's an old Tooting proverb which ain't in the book but ought to be.'

'Hey,' said Bingo, 'you've got your name already. That's great, congratulations.' He slapped his friend on the shoulder.

'Thanks, man,' said Orococco. 'Now we'd better see about getting yours.' And he turned and locked and bolted the door before slipping the key into his pocket. 'Remember I got the key, Bingo, just in case I don't make it. Now let's go see if the others got the kettle on yet.' And holding his Rumble-stick across his body he ran as fast as he could down the tunnel, and Bingo ran with him.

*

Vulge lay full length in the narrow ventilation shaft and inched his body along with his elbows. Behind him he could hear the others, breathing hard as they followed. After a few yards, which seemed like miles, he came to a grating set in the floor. He reached behind him with an effort and pulled his torch from a pocket of his combat jacket. He masked the beam with his hand and saw that he was at the end of the tunnel. Someone bumped against his feet.

He shone his torch on the grating and saw that it was held in place by four screws. He reached for his knife and slowly began to undo them.

'What's up?' asked Chalotte.

Vulge twisted his head as far as he was able.

'A grating, four screws.' He whispered the words and went back to the task; it wasn't easy but finally the barrier came free and he slid it below his body. Now he could see into the kitchens.

They were enormous – an expensive modern installation kitted out with long stainless steel ranges and endless working surfaces – for this equipment had to cater for the hundreds of Rumbles who lived in the bunker, and on its smooth running would depend their health and well-being. The management and ordering of such a place demanded complex skills and the Rumble commissariat was in fact controlled and directed by the two female members of the High Command – Chalotte and Sydney Rumble.

At that moment only three Rumbles of any importance were visible to Vulge, two females and one male still in his dressing gown. They had not been in the kitchens long for they were rubbing their eyes and yawning. As Vulge watched, the two female Rumbles began bellowing orders, and skivvies and scullions, about a dozen of them, rushed to their duties. Huge saucepans were sent clanging and spinning on to the stoves, the hotplates glowed red and vegetables were washed and shredded. The morning porridge simmered in the pots.

With a start that nearly gave him away, Vulge recognized the male Rumble; it was the chief, the main one, his very own target. Vulge quickly withdrew his head and scrambled over the opening into the end section of the shaft, allowing Chalotte to move up a little. He shone his torch behind her and saw Sydney; he gave them a thumbs up then popped his head down through the hole again, wondering what he should do.

The High Rumbles had taken up a position in the middle of the kitchen urging their minions on, supervising the baking of the Rumble bread. Vulge pulled out his catapult and was easing a stone from his bandolier when the chief Rumble, Vulgarian himself, spoke to the women. He sounded irritable and short-tempered.

'I wish you'd huwwy, you two. When I say an early bweakfast, I mean an early bweakfast. I've got a nasty feeling something's afoot. Last night, one of our sentwies didn't weturn, and I'm wowwied. Come on, huwwy it up.'

'It's no good,' snapped Chalotte Rumble. 'It won't be weady for another half-hour at least.' And she jerked her snout up an inch to indicate that the discussion was at an end.

'Vewy well,' said Vulgarian. 'Then I'll take a bath. Send me my bweakfast on a tway as soon as it's weady.' He pulled his dressing gown tight to his body and stalked off without another word.

'What an awwogant swine he is,' said Chalotte Rumble to her companion. 'Who does he think he is? We wun this department.'

'Ignore him,' said Sydney Rumble. 'He's due for a nasty shock one day.'

'Yeah, and today's the day,' said Vulge to himself grimly. 'I missed a chance there.' He pulled his head back into the darkness of the tunnel where Chalotte waited.

'Mine's gone to have a bath,' said Vulge, 'but yours is right below you, and Sydney's. You're lucky, all you got to do is thump 'em.'

Chalotte twisted and spoke to Sydney, then she crouched over the hole and looked down. Below her was a good ten-foot drop to the top of a wide kitchen table, white with scrubbing. She took her catapult from her back pocket, wrapped the elastic carefully round the butt and clenched the weapon between her teeth, then with a nod at Vulge, she let herself fall from his sight.

Immediately Chalotte had gone, Sydney wriggled forward, her catapult already prepared, and sprang, eager as a cat, through the opening. Napoleon was still some distance away but inching nearer. Vulge did not wait for him. He sat on the edge of the hatch, lowered himself by his arms till his body was at full extent, and then let go.

His feet hit the wooden surface and, following the precepts of Dodger's paratroop training, he allowed his legs to crumble and he rolled over, curving his shoulder to take the force of the fall. He came off the edge of the table and fell easily into a crouching position on the kitchen floor. From there he witnessed a fight that he knew he would never forget, a story that he would tell until the end of his days.

Chalotte and Sydney had arrived in the kitchen perhaps ten seconds before Vulge, but they had wasted no time. The two Rumbles of the High Command had been caught flat-footed by Chalotte's inexplicable appearance but they had soon rallied. They each seized a Rumble-stick from a rack which stood against the wall and shouted to the kitchen hands to arm themselves and give the alarm. But Chalotte was a magician with the catapult. She had loaded and fired her weapon twice before the two Rumbles could cast their spears, and they retreated down the kitchen towards the hot stoves and steaming ranges. The sound of Chalotte's stones as they sliced through the air unnerved the Rumbles, and their lances, when they were thrown, skeetered harmlessly along the tiled floor.

Now Sydney's catapult was ready, and, ignoring the shouts of the scullions and the possibility of being wounded by a flying Rumble-stick, she stood and drew the heavy-duty elastic right back to her ear, and a well aimed stone flew to strike her foe in the centre of the forehead. Sydney Rumble fell lifeless to the floor, bringing down a pile of soup bowls with her.

Chalotte's namesake was to meet a more grisly fate. At the noise of the crashing crockery the High Rumble took fright, for she was now outnumbered three to one, and pushing and kicking the terrified menials from her path she ran quickly to the far end of the kitchen where huge cauldrons boiled quietly on deep square stoves, warming the day's broth.

Against the largest of the containers leant a stepladder, placed there so that ingredients could be added without difficulty and so that the soup could be inspected from time to time by the cooks. None of that mattered now, for Chalotte Rumble wanted only to get away. If she were to climb that ladder and take one step across the cauldron she could squeeze through a large vent that led into a different part of the bunker, escaping to raise the alarm and fight another day.

But Chalotte Borrible, her blood pounding with the heat of battle, was a fast and nimble runner and she pursued her namesake closely. As the Rumble reached the top of the stepladder, Chalotte reached the bottom; she grabbed it and lifted it up with all her energy. There was the briefest of silences as the Rumble spun in space, weightless for a second, then a scream split the steamy air and the scream wailed on long and loud until, with a splash, it was submerged deep in the hot and lumpy soup. But even then the scream went on, freighted up to the surface of the stew in rippling bubbles, like a fart in bath water.

Vulge yelled in triumph and ran across the room to cover the saucepan with a huge heavy lid.

'Blimey,' he crowed, 'she's really in the soup now, ain't she?'

Just then Napoleon's legs appeared through the opening in the ceiling, and he dropped to the table and jumped to the floor. He ran to a corner and grabbed a Rumble-stick. He felt the weight of it and looked at the group of kitchen hands who cowered together in a corner.

'Okay, you bunch of bunnies,' he snarled. 'You move and I'll tear yer ears off.'

Sydney pulled her target's body into a broom cupboard, closed the door and locked it. 'Cripes,' she gasped, 'that was over so fast it don't seem right.'

'Getting in was easy,' agreed Chalotte. 'It's the getting out that might prove tricky.'

'What are we going to do with the skivvies?' asked Vulge.

'Lock 'em in the pantry,' suggested Sydney. 'They won't give us any trouble.'

'You do that,' said Napoleon, making for the door. 'Me and Vulge better get going, we've still got work to do. Before you leave here turn the electrics up; let it all burn dry so it'll smoke and fuse and catch fire. Roast Rumbles can't fight.'

Vulge crossed the room to leave with Napoleon. 'And when you've done that you'd better try to make your way to the Great Door and see if you can meet up with Stonks and Torrey.'

'We might see you again at the Central,' said Napoleon, 'and then again we might not. Don't wait for anybody. From now we each takes our chance.' With this, he and Vulge slipped through the door and were gone.

'Well, goodbye,' said Chalotte, 'and if I don't see you again, have a good life.' She and Sydney herded the kitchen hands into the larder, using the sharp spears to encourage them. Once the Rumbles had been disposed of the two girls ran around the kitchen switching all the stoves and ovens to full on, and then, propped against their lances, they looked at each other and a slow smile crept from their eyes to their lips and became a grin.

'Here, we've got our names,' said Sydney. 'Fancy that.'

*

Torreycanyon made his way down the main tunnel. It felt strange to be alone after so long in the company of the others, but there was no stopping now. Somewhere ahead of him would be the main hall, the Central, with corridors running out from it like a spider's web. For now the bunker was deserted, the Rumbles still sleeping, but in a very short while they would be coming from their dormitories and making for the refectory, ready to eat breakfast.

Occasionally Torreycanyon saw a signpost which, he supposed, was to direct the younger Rumbles until they had learnt their way around. There weren't enough indications for his taste and he realized what a task the Borrible team had taken on. He understood suddenly that he was going to need a lot of luck to find his target, and a lot more to get out of this labyrinth alive. He gripped his catapult tightly, a stone ready for firing, and he stepped bravely forward. Best to press on and meet the dangers as they came, no point in worrying about them prematurely. Good old Stonks was behind, guarding a way of escape, and it would take an avalanche of Rumbles to move him.

Torreycanyon crept past several doorways leading from the corridor. He listened at each of them but heard no noises coming from within. So far so good. He went on, halting and listening at every branch corridor, peeping around every corner before advancing and then peering behind him to make sure he was not being followed.

'Cripes,' he said, at least half a dozen times. 'I wish I could find my target and then get out of here; it's spooky being on your own.'

At last luck was with him. He was on the point of passing by the entrance of a passage, broader than the rest, when his foot slipped and he nearly lost his balance. Looking down he saw a patch of oil on the floor. He moved into the passage and in the light of his torch he saw that at eye level words had been daubed on the wall in blue paint, and although faded and difficult to decipher, they were still legible. 'Garage and Workshops. Keep Out. Signed Torreycanyon Rumble.'

'Oh boy, oh boy,' said Torreycanyon, 'I've done it right. I'll wait for him in the garage.' He knew from his reading of the Rumble books that the workshops were a nerve centre of this underground complex, and it was part of the Borrible plan, once they had eliminated their targets, to cause as much confusion as possible. Torreycanyon hoped that possession of the workshops would enable him to wreak great damage throughout the bunker, merely by pulling a few switches. If he could break in before the Rumbles awoke, he would be in a strong position.

The corridor sloped downwards beneath the Rumbledom hillside. It was greasy underfoot because over the years so much machinery had passed that way. Torreycanyon stepped carefully until he came up against a heavy wooden door, sagging on its hinges. It was scarred and battered where sharp metal edges had bashed against it. To Torreycanyon's amazement the door was open and a light shone inside.

He pushed his torch into his pocket and flexed the rubber on his catapult. He was ready. However many Rumbles were in the workshops he would take them on and then destroy their equipment before they destroyed him. But he must be sure to get his target; not one of the Rumble High Command must be left to organize pursuit or retaliation.

Torreycanyon took a deep breath, thought briefly of the others and wondered where they were, then shoved the door with a vigorous thrust of his foot and jumped into the room in the style of the adventure stories he had read and the spy films he had seen. The door swung back and banged into the wall. Torreycanyon burst through the doorway and landed in the crouched position. His eyes raced over the workshops, his head turned this way and that, searching, but there was not one enemy to fire at.

Torreycanyon had come into a large rectangular room. It was lined with shelves on which was stowed every tool that might be needed in the underground stronghold, and in addition there was row upon row of spare parts for the machinery that kept the bunker ticking over. There were workbenches and power points, electric drills and lathes, winches and a conveyor belt. It was an extremely well equipped functional workshop and Torreycanyon liked it.

'Blimey,' he said, looking around in wonder and respect, 'what couldn't we do with this little lot?' But then he thought of why he was there and he shook the feelings of respect and admiration from his mind. He bolted the door and made a tour of inspection, making certain that no unseen Rumble lurked behind the shelves or between the workbenches.

The more he saw of the place the more impressed he became. He had a practical turn of mind himself, and all those shining tools laid out in perfect order, and those handy workbenches, the carpentry, the work in progress, every bit of it made him regret that he was about to destroy such order. Why, oh why, did he not have such a workshop back in Hoxton? He knew he could have done it justice.

He sighed and came to a corner where he thought the shop ended, but he had simply discovered another section of it and he could see at a glance that this was the garage. He remembered then that the Rumbles had built a car and had in fact used it for their trip to Battersea, that time when Knocker had captured one of their number. And here it was, the very car. He lowered his catapult; this place seemed empty too.

The car itself was long and sleek and powerful, but what struck Torreycanyon were the changes being made to it. Someone was converting the vehicle into an armoured troop carrier, a weapon of war. Narrow gun ports had been made in the bodywork so that weapons could be fired from inside while the occupants remained protected from attack. And on the steel panelling, not yet painted, was scrawled in chalk, 'Death to all Borribles'. Torreycanyon glanced about him once more; these workshops did not look beautiful now, they looked sinister, and compassion drained from his heart.

These reflections were interrupted by the clink of a spanner falling to the concrete floor, and the sound of a Rumble oath. Torreycanyon raised his catapult. Protruding from underneath the car's rear axle were two padded feet. It was obvious that a Rumble was doing an early morning stint on the mechanics, and that was the reason the vehicle had been jacked up high at the back, so as to enable the fitter to move comfortably about his business.

Torreycanyon thought quickly. If that Rumble was the only one present, then all well and good, but was there another entrance and were there more Rumbles to come? He stepped towards the car.

'I say,' he said, 'any twouble?'

'Who's that? What are you doing here? Hand me that fourteen Whitworth,' said the mechanic, rapidly and without waiting for answers.

'It's Bingo,' said Torreycanyon, using the first Rumble name that came into his head.

'Bingo,' cried the voice attached to the two feet. 'Look, if you give me a hand for a couple of hours, we can do the test wun tonight. This car will be invincible; it'll take us down to Battersea High Stweet in half an hour, give those Bowwibles a beating and bwing us back in time for bweakfast.'

The Borrible tensed his muscles and was just about to drag the

Rumble out from underneath the car when he had a thought. ‘Who is that, anyway?’ he asked. ‘I can’t wecognize you by your feet, they’re not vewy distinctive.’

‘Towweycanyon, of course. Who else would be here at thwee in the morning when evewy other Wumble is still in bed? We of the High Command have got a sense of wesponsibility, a devotion to duty.’

Torreycanyon smiled to himself. What a stroke of luck. Unbelievably his target was right there with him, and they were all alone. The voice continued, ‘Go wound the back and pass me the working light, it’s wolled out of my weach. Time is of the essence. The sooner we can exterminate those Bowwibles the better.’

‘All wight,’ said Torreycanyon, and he began to walk round the car hoping Torreycanyon Rumble wouldn’t notice that his feet were not padded as they should be. But the Rumble said nothing and he continued to talk as he struggled with the job in hand.

‘Now, when you get wound the back, be vewy careful, the handle of the jack is sticking out, just don’t touch it at all, do you hear that, Bingo? They’re dangewous, cars and jacks and that, specially if you’re underneath them.’

Torreycanyon moved stealthily to the rear of the garage. Here was the enormous jack, here tools littered the floor, and there was the working light, up against the second entrance to the workshop, a sliding door of steel large enough to allow the passage of the armoured car. No doubt, thought Torreycanyon, the door was concealed on the other side, camouflaged to look like a grassy bank behind gorse bushes or trees.

‘If I stwetch out my hand you can put the working light underneath, there, just by the nearside fwont wheel and then I . . .’ The voice trailed off, and then, falteringly, it started again. ‘Bingo . . . you’ve got shoes and feet, weal feet. You can’t be Bingo. You’re human . . . or . . .’

‘A Borrible,’ cried Torreycanyon. And with those words he leapt for the car jack, knocked off the safety catch and triggered the mechanism that released its power. The mighty machine, the great car, the massive tool of destruction, sank slowly, relentlessly, to the oily floor and crushed the small life out of the Rumble who had tended it with such love. There was a scream, then quiet, and Torreycanyon slipped his catapult into his pocket. He spoke out loud to himself and his voice echoed round the hard walls of the garage. ‘Congratulations to you,

Torreycanyon,' he said, 'on achieving your name. Now you may construct a little mayhem out of the materials that lie about you.'

*

Knocker dropped down into the kitchen as the others had done. Adolf followed him and they both seized Rumble-sticks from the corner of the room.

'Aha,' said Adolf, 'good weapons for close work.' The door opened and they stiffened, but it was Chalotte and Sydney returning from the corridor.

'It's all quiet outside,' said Chalotte, 'but we don't know for how long.'

'What's all this nasty steam and stink?' asked Knocker, peering round the room. Sydney gestured to the huge pots still boiling and bubbling on the stoves.

'Chalotte shoved her namesake into the porridge,' she said.

Adolf hooted. 'So we have to felicitate you on your first name. I'm sure you will have many in the future.'

'I got mine as well,' said Sydney, 'in the cupboard.'

'You certainly wasted no time,' said Knocker. 'What about the others?'

The two girls told them what Napoleon and Vulge had suggested: a rendezvous, if possible, in the heart of the bunker, the Central, where most of the tunnels met.

'That sounds all right,' agreed Knocker. 'Adolf and I will try to stir things up a bit; some alarm and despondency is what is called for. Meanwhile, you girls could start preparing a line of retreat. Guard one of the tunnels.'

The moment Chalotte and Sydney had gone on their way, Adolf leant on his Rumble-stick and looked at Knocker from under his eyebrows.

'Well, my Battersea friend,' he asked with the bright light burning in his blue eyes, 'what is it we are up to?'

Knocker laughed with a happy excitement. 'I'm going to get a second name out of this, and you can help, Adolf. Somewhere in this maze of corridors is a chest of treasure. My job is to get it back to Battersea High Street, so that it can be shared among all Borribles.'

'A fine Historian you are,' said Adolf. 'Where is this treasure . . . and is it Borrible?'

'I don't know, and right now I don't care,' said Knocker, making his catapult ready and inspecting the nail on the end of his lance, 'but I'm going to the head Rumble's quarters; it seems a likely enough place.'

'Excuse.' Adolf held up his hand. 'That is where we are going. You're going to need someone to look after you.'

*

Vulge came to a halt at a place where the corridor he was following divided. A notice showed him which way to go: 'Headquarters'. He turned to Napoleon.

'See you back at the Central, or at the Great Door.'

'Or not at all,' said the Wendle, his smile a smile of granite.

'It is sad to pass through life without one good adventure,' said Vulge, quoting one of the oldest of Borrible proverbs, and with a reassuring jerk of his head he slapped the palm of his right hand against Napoleon's and marched on.

'And remember,' said the Wendle as he watched the small figure recede, 'it is foolish to run faster than what you run after.' Then he settled his bandoliers across his shoulders and made his way into the other corridor, desirous of only one thing, a meeting with his namesake.

Vulge had not far to go. He rounded a bend in the tunnel and came upon a well lit and commodious hall. It was more luxuriously carpeted than any other part of the bunker. Rows of armchairs had been placed there for lesser Rumbles who might wait to see their chieftain, and opposite Vulge was a stout oaken door guarded by two warriors, armed with lances.

Vulge gave no warning. His catapult was loaded and the first shot slammed one of the guards on the forehead and he fell to the floor, his body making no sound on the carpet. Vulge reloaded quickly but not before the second guard had thrown his Rumble-stick with all his force. It struck the Borrible in his left shoulder and he fell back, staggering against the wall. He could feel blood running down his arm and the pain made him blink his eyes.

'Dammit,' he said, but pulled back the elastic of his catapult as far as his wound and the pain would let him.

His antagonist reached for another spear and lifted it above his shoulder; he was a mighty thrower but he was not to throw again. The second stone from Vulge's catapult hit him fairly on the temple. He fell forward, the lance dropping from his hand.

Vulge stuck his catapult into his belt and, with an effort, pulled the four-inch barb from his shoulder and threw the lance to the ground.

'I hope the bleeder weren't rusty,' he said to himself, crossing the room, 'and I hope there aren't too many guards inside.' He rapped on the oak door with the butt of a lance.

'Who's there?' asked a rich and plummy voice from the other side.

'I've come with the bweakfast,' said Vulge, whose imitation of a Rumble was perfect.

The door swung open and Vulge saw the chieftain's major-domo standing before him. A haughty sneer was stretched along his snout and his rich beige fur was decorated with a green, white and gold sash, the colours of Rumbledom.

'Here's your bweakfast,' said Vulge, and prodded the regal domestic in the solar plexus with the sharp end of his lance. The butler doubled up, clutching at his chest, and Vulge clouted him hard across the head with the back of his hand. The Rumble collapsed and rolled over on his back, his snout crashing open like an unhinged drawbridge.

'That's sorted you out, weasel-chops,' said Vulge.

He stepped over the body and entered a magnificent and luxurious sitting room. The carpet was a spotless white and a huge sofa in cream leather was matched with armchairs of the same material; on the misty green walls were original paintings in oils and watercolours. There was a colour television set, telephones in brass with ivory mouthpieces, and copies of the national newspapers rested aristocratically on small leather-covered tables.

Vulge jerked a linen runner from one of the tables, spilling a majolica vase to the floor, where it broke. He folded the material and shoved it inside his combat jacket to pad his wound and stop the bleeding.

'The sooner I get this over with, the better,' he muttered, 'otherwise this arm will go as stiff as a Rumble's snout.'

He opened another door and saw that he had come to the chief Rumble's office. Here he found a huge desk meant to impress visitors with its top of dark green morocco, a map of the world on the wall, bookshelves, computers and copying machines. Once more, everything was furnished in white and misty green. It was an expensive and oppressive room, but what Vulge wanted was not there.

Next he entered a circular bedroom, furnished as if for some great pop star. A huge round bed stood in the centre of white goat-skin carpets, its coverlet made from green silk, the colour of gorse bushes at dawn. The lighting was concealed and gentle.

'Blimey,' said Vulge between his teeth. 'I'd like to put a match to this lot.' He winced with pain, for his wound troubled him. He walked round the bed and spots of blood stained the floor. On the far side of the room a door stood open and perfume-laden steam floated through it. The bathroom, thought Vulge, and he stepped inside.

Through the clouds of sweet-smelling vapour Vulge saw his namesake and enemy, Vulgarian Rumble. The chieftain reclined in an oval bath of green marble big enough to swim in. The taps were gold and shaped like Rumble snouts, and scented water poured through them to wash across the furred body and out through an overflow grating, also of gold. The floor, where it was not overlaid with absorbent carpets, was covered with Italian tiles of a warm southern tint. Near the bath were several telephones on articulated arms that could be pulled in any direction. Two enormous electric fires faced the marble steps that led down from the magnificent pool so that Vulgarian could warm himself the moment he emerged from the water. Right by the two fires stood a hot air blower on a stand, ready to dry the chieftain's magnificent coat.

Vulge stepped across the room, trailing the bloody lance point behind him. The Rumble's snout turned; there was a flurry in his bath water.

'I twust you've got my bweakfast at last,' he began angrily, and then he saw not the obsequious butler or even one of his guards; he saw a Borrible.

Vulge was no reassuring sight at that moment. His face was still smeared black from Knocker's greasepaint. His combat jacket was filthy and torn from scuffling through the ventilation shaft. Even more dramatically, blood was spreading out to stain his shoulder. The Borrible hat was jaunty on his head, however, and there was a gleam of triumph in his eye. Vulgarian Rumble slid down into the water until only his snout was visible. His small red eyes, intelligent and cunning, fluttered over the room, but he saw no escape. For a while the only sound was the gurgling of the bath water.

'A Bowwible?' asked the Rumble at last.

'A Borrible,' said Vulge, 'all the way from Stepney, bloody miles.'

'There's no sweawing here,' said the Rumble.

'Knickers,' answered Vulge, and gobbed into the bath. 'This is the Great Rumble Hunt, mate. You've got everything you need up here, you should have stayed out of Battersea.'

Vulgarian raised himself a little. 'As if we would want your stinking markets and wubbishy old houses, but I'll tell you this, you hooligan, we'll go where we like and—'

'Don't want it, eh? What about all that digging down there in Battersea Park? What about that, then? You started this, Rumble.'

'Started it! I know Timbucktoo is over-enthusiastic at times, always wants to be pwospecting, but he's harmless. No, it won't do. This twouble is all your fault, Bowwible.'

'Cobblers,' said Vulge, moving nearer the bath.

'How many of you are there?' asked the chieftain.

'Only eight of us, but that's enough to wreck the place.' Vulge stood between the two electric fires and let them warm the pain in his shoulder. He was getting weaker and stiffer by the minute. He knew he must finish the task quickly; he felt in no state to defend himself if reinforcements arrived on the scene.

Vulgarian suddenly rose up and the water cascaded from his fur. He was the tallest of all the Rumbles, impressive and commanding. He looked down his snout at the grimy little Borrible.

'Eight of you!' he cried. 'Why, you impudent little whippersnappers, you insignificant hobbledehoys. I tell you Wumbles will go whewever I say, fwom Hampton Wick to Amos Park, and fwom Ealing golf course to Bexley Heath. We won't be stopped by a handful of ignowant street urchins – thieves who live in slimy slums and damp cellars – who cannot afford a bar of soap and would eat it if they could, who smell, whose ears are pointed by the effect of cheap peasant cunning and who are fit only to be our slaves. You Bowwible bwat, I have only to press that alarm bell and my bodyguard will make a pincushion of you with their Wumble-sticks. Hand me that towel, you scwubby little serf. Hand me that towel I say, barbawian!'

Vulge smiled and did not move for a moment. Then he pushed the end of his Rumble-stick through the handle of one of the electric fires and he raised the sticker and the fire pivoted on the end of it. He slid his feet up the steps, his eyes remaining steady on Vulgarian's face, and he held his spear forward so that the fire was above the water and near to the chief Rumble's fur. There was a smell of singeing and Vulgarian took a step backwards, horror replacing the expression of disdain on his snout.

Vulge smiled ironically at the Rumble. 'Don't worry about the towel,' he said pleasantly, 'I'll soon have your fur dry.' And he allowed the lance to slant down to the water and the fire plopped into the bath and hissed. In less than a millisecond the electric current had sprung from its cable and arced across the water, and from the water it raced through the flesh of the Rumble chieftain, destroying muscle and sinew. It burnt into his heart and demolished it like an old fuse box, and Vulgarian Rumble's voice cried out, but he never heard the sound. His body jerked upright, his dead eyes stared in amazement. Then, as stiff as a scaffolding plank, he fell forward with a gigantic splash, and a tidal wave washed over the rim of the beautiful bath and gushed down the veined green of the marble steps.

Vulge sniffed and prodded the body with the point of his spear. It bobbed lifelessly in the tinted foam.

'Well, there you are, me ol' Rumble,' said Vulge reflectively. 'That's 'ow you singe your fur at both ends. Kilowatts will kill a weasel any day. So,' he added, 'I've got my name. Mind you, the way I feel, I shan't have it long . . . alive.'

He descended the steps and unplugged the second of the electric fires and cut the cable that led to it. That done he trailed the flex across the room to the door, which he closed, scraped the wires bare and then wound them round the metal door handle. He looked at his work and continued talking to himself. 'I don't think I could fight my way out with this wound, so I might as well have a scrap here; saves walking.'

He crossed the room once more, reconnected the mains supply and pressed the red alarm bell by the bath. 'That should bring the bodyguard at a run,' he said, and he pulled a couple of chairs and cushions across the bottom of the bath steps to form a rough barricade and squatted behind it. The dead Vulgarian floated behind him.

Vulge next removed his bandoliers and placed them near to hand; his knife and lance also. He leant back then on a cushion, waiting, favouring his injured shoulder, which was very stiff now though it pained him less. He wagged his head and thought of a few old Borrible proverbs to while away the time.

'It is better to die young than to be caught,' he quoted from memory, and he smiled and hoped the others were getting on all right.

*

Knocker and Adolf ran together from the end of the tunnel and into the hall that led to the head Rumble's apartments. Alarm bells were ringing and lights were flashing in the ceiling. In the distance a siren howled and a recorded voice called all Rumbles to their battle stations. Knocker and Adolf loaded their catapults but they need not have bothered. The bodies of the two Rumble guards lying in the doorway did not move. Knocker put his catapult away and picked up a lance.

'Look,' he said, showing it to Adolf. 'Blood.'

'Vulge?' said Adolf. 'I hope he is still alive.'

Inside the doorway they found the body of the major-domo. Blood stained the whiteness of the carpet, blood turning brown.

'Wait a minute,' Knocker whistled through his teeth and pointed. 'Can you beat that?'

In the sitting room lay several Rumbles in a line, one behind the other, their bodies contorted, their fur singed. Both Borribles sniffed the air.

'Electrics,' said Adolf. 'Dangerous stuff.'

'They must have been the elite guard,' said Knocker. 'Look at their uniforms, their weapons.'

'The bodies lead to that door over there,' said Adolf, gesturing with his catapult.

'And do you notice how they are all touching each other?' said Knocker, and with the butt end of his lance he bashed the door free from the charred paw of the first in the line of electrocuted bodyguards.

He stepped over the corpse, and eased himself into the bathroom where the wires attached to the doorknob told their own story.

The first warrior to arrive on the scene had grasped the handle and died. The second had attempted to pull his comrade away from danger and he too had died. Many had perished in this manner, their bodies soldered together, their fur crisp. Then the door had been broken down, but there were dozens more bodies in the bathroom, electrocuted on the threshold, slain by stones as they crossed the room, or stabbed as they had attempted to storm Vulge's little barricade. The room was a shambles.

'Oh, *verdammt*,' said Adolf reverently. 'What a scrapper, that Vulge. Who would have guessed that such a little Borrible had so much courage in him?'

The trail of bodies led across the room and up to the very edge of the bath. At the bottom of the steps half a dozen of the bodyguard lay in a heap. There had been a terrific battle waged in this bathroom but there was no sign of the Stepney Borrible.

Knocker scrambled over the bodies and the barricade and discovered the half-submerged form of the Rumble chieftain.

'He got him,' he shouted. 'Vulge got his name.'

'Posthumously, I should think,' said the German.

'Wait,' said Knocker. 'I can see him.' And it was true. Sticking out from under the pile of Rumble bodies was a human foot. Knocker and Adolf pulled the corpses aside and underneath everything lay a pathetically frail Borrible holding a knife in one hand and the broken barb of a lance in the other. They knelt beside him.

'Look at his leg,' said Knocker. 'Has he gone?'

Adolf put his head to Vulge's chest. 'No,' he said. 'I can hear his heart.'

Tenderly they raised the Stepney Borrible into a sitting position and rubbed his hands and his cheeks. Vulge's eyes flickered and then opened weakly. He was covered in blood, though most of it was not his own. He licked his lips.

'Trust you to get here when it was all over,' he said, and he tried to grin. 'Get me something to drink.'

Adolf returned in an instant with a jade tooth-mug full of cold water, and Vulge drank it greedily.

'That's better,' he said, looking round the room. 'Pretty good fight it was,' he added, 'but you'd better get out of here. With those bells and alarms going the tunnels will be solid with Rumbles.'

'Okay,' said Knocker. 'We're going. I've just got something to do first. Adolf, watch the door.'

Vulge grabbed Knocker's arm. 'Give me one of your bandoliers,' he said. 'I feel lonely without a few stones.'

Knocker slipped a bandolier over his head, retrieved a catapult from the floor and handed them to Vulge.

'Leave some Rumbles for us,' he said, then left the bathroom and passed into a large study. It was an inner sanctum, different from the main office, more private and intimate. Here there was just a bare desk, some books and a watercolour of the Rumbledom countryside on the wall. Knocker flung the picture to the floor and found what he had been hoping to find, a large safe. He looked at it, baffled. The safe was firmly closed and there was a complicated combination lock keeping it that way. He fiddled with it, listened to it, pulled the large brass handle, but the safe door would not budge. He ran back to the bathroom and shouted desperately to Adolf, 'Damn it, I can't get the safe open. We're snookered.'

The German bobbed his head round the door he was guarding. 'A safe,' he cried, 'is that all? Did I not tell you how I got my third name, Amadeus? By stealing from the most renowned burglar in all of Austria. You come and watch. I will persuade your safe to be friendly.'

In a moment Adolf had his ear pressed against the door of the safe and his nimble fingers were twiddling with the lock. There was a click, then another and another until there was a click that sounded more definite than all the rest and Adolf's eyes glowed like the jackpot lights on a fruit machine. He pulled the handle with both hands and the massive steel door swung open.

'Bullseye,' he cried. 'You see, I haven't lost my touch.'

Knocker gazed into the safe and saw a large brass-bound box. 'You must be the best safe cracker in the whole world,' he said, 'Adolf Wolfgang Amadeus Winston!'

'*Danke*,' said the German. 'I am proud of my new name and will enjoy telling how I earned it, if we ever get out of here.'

They pulled the box from the safe and it thumped to the floor.

Knocker flung back the lid and squatted on his heels in amazement. It was full to the top with bright coins and crisp notes of the realm.

'I'll be jiggered,' he said. 'There's a fortune here.'

'No good if you can't get it out,' said Adolf.

'Wait,' said Knocker, seizing the German's shoulder. 'It will need two of us to carry this. We'll have to leave Vulge behind.'

Adolf stood up, his face angry. 'You may do what you wish,' he said. 'I am taking Vulge . . . and I remind you, Knocker, money isn't Borrible.'

Knocker faced his friend, his mouth tight. 'Spiff wanted me to steal this treasure . . . I'll get a second name. Vulge has taken his chances like the rest of us. Why, he's half dead already.'

'And half of him is worth all of you, Knocker, and the money too,' cried Adolf. 'Remember the great proverb, "Money maketh mad."' He kicked the lid of the box so that it closed with a crash.

'This money,' said Knocker, lowering his voice, 'could change life for thousands of Borribles. It's important, more important than any one of us; that's why Spiff wanted me to get it home, no matter what.'

'Who cares about your Spiff? I don't want my life changed,' cried Adolf with passion. 'Nor do other Borribles. The lives I care about at this moment are my life and Vulge's life, and yours if you will stop being stupid.'

Knocker hesitated. He knew that what the German said made sense, but there were other considerations.

'Vulge got his name by a valiant battle,' he argued. 'You were destined to open the safe. My part is to take this money out of here and win my name that way. Can't you see that?'

'I see it,' said Adolf, 'but it doesn't mean I have to look at it. You carry the money if you can, I will carry Vulge if I can; the rest is chance. Let us remain friends though we differ. I like stealing too you know, but sometimes other things come first.'

Just then there was a yell from Vulge in the bathroom. Both Borribles grasped their catapults, and loading them as they moved, dashed through the door.

Two Rumbles armed with stickers were coming into the room, a third lay stunned in the entrance. Vulge was reloading his catapult. A Rumble threw his sticker at Adolf who sidestepped it with ease; the spear thudded into the wall. Knocker fired, Adolf fired and both Rumbles fell. It became quiet and Adolf went to the door to look out.

'Only those three,' he said, 'but others will be coming. Let's go.' He crossed the room and knelt beside Vulge. 'You're coming with me, my friend,' he said. 'I will give you a fireman's lift. It will be painful but safer than staying here.'

'You can't take me.' The wounded Borrible grimaced. 'Leave me another bandolier, and I'll do for a few more.'

'Rubbish,' laughed the German. 'Are you content to die with only one name?'

Vulge wagged his head in that way of his. 'Go on then, idiot. "It is madness to quarrel with a madman." '

Adolf ignored the proverb, hoisted his wounded comrade up and carried him towards the door. Knocker meanwhile ran back into the inner sanctum and lifted the box on to his shoulders with a supreme effort. With both of us laden like this, thought Knocker, there is very little chance of us getting out alive. Adolf is right, of course, but then I'm not wrong.

The three Borribles made slow progress. They stopped frequently to rest and Vulge was in great pain, though he said nothing. The electrical system had obviously suffered serious damage, for the lights flickered and often went out. Bells and sirens clanged and wailed as the general alarm spread through the maze of corridors, and shouts and calls could be heard echoing from side tunnels. Something somewhere was burning and smoke was beginning to drift by, sucked along by the ventilation fans. Soup from the cauldrons left boiling in the kitchens lent an acrid smell to the atmosphere, and the temperature in the bunker was rising fast.

The fugitives encountered several dazed and panic-stricken bands of Rumbles but they were not trained warriors and a show of belligerence was enough to make them sheer off. But every time they passed a branch corridor Rumbles issued from it noiselessly on their padded feet and followed at a safe distance, waiting for the right moment to pounce and bear down upon the Adventurers.

'I must rest,' said Knocker for the fifth time. 'Money weighs you down.'

'I too could rest,' said Adolf, panting, and he lowered Vulge to the floor, asking him how he did.

Vulge was near to fainting with pain but he said, 'Mustn't grumble. Got to keep going till you can't go any more, ain't it?'

They had stopped by the entrance to a dark branch corridor and suddenly two figures leapt out with a cry, brandishing lances. Adolf and Knocker stepped back and reached for their weapons but then held their hands. Before them stood Bingo and Orococco, fresh and alert.

'Well, hello sailor,' said Orococco. 'What's a nice Borrible like you doing in a place like this?'

Knocker smiled with relief. He gestured towards Vulge and the box. 'We're trying to get Vulge out. He's done for the chief, but the bodyguard nearly did for him.'

'He knocked them about beautifully,' Adolf laughed. 'He deserves twenty names.'

'He doesn't look too good,' said Bingo, 'that's for sure.'

'How did you get on?' asked Knocker, sitting on the box of money.

Bingo knelt by Vulge and felt his pulse. ''Rococco got his, at the door. He came along to keep me company. I've been running all over the place but I'm damned if I can find mine anywhere. I hope someone else hasn't done him. I'll be stuck without a name if they have.'

The lights in the corridor flickered off and the Borribles grasped their lances and stood back to back. They heard the shuffling sound of Rumbles moving nearer, but then the lights snapped on again and the Adventurers saw their foes scrambling to get beyond the range of the Borrible catapults.

Knocker came to a decision. 'You could come along with us . . . give me a hand with this box and help carry Vulge.'

'I don't mind that,' agreed Bingo, 'as long as I am free to take off after my bloke at any time. I gotta get him.'

Bingo's proposition was agreed and the five Borribles moved on, pausing at every intersection. They were followed and sniffed and snuffled at but not attacked. The hazards would increase when they reached the open space of the Central. There, hosts of angry Rumbles might trample them down, no matter how well they defended themselves.

At length, Bingo, who was leading, stopped and held up a hand. 'It's the Central,' he whispered.

They gathered at the end of the corridor and looked out into the wide cavern from which radiated the main arteries of the bunker. A fearful sight met their eyes. Hundreds of Rumbles ran backwards and forwards across the immense hall. Blue lights flashed in the ceiling and alarm bells rang. The roadway leading to the Great Door was crammed with warrior Rumbles, struggling to enter the tunnel and do battle with whoever was at the other end. Thick smoke issued from a corridor above which was written 'Kitchens', and stretcher bearers were disappearing into a tunnel marked 'Infirmary' carrying their wounded comrades to safety.

Bingo took stock of the scene and turned to the others.

'I've got an idea,' he said. 'There's a tunnel over there with no one in it, or so it seems, the one that says "Library". I'll run across the hall, throw a few spears, and it's more'n likely that a good few of those warriors will chase after me. You'll have to fight the rest, but then you would anyway. Not much of an idea but it's Hobson's, isn't it?'

It was the only way. Bingo took extra stickers from his companions and with no goodbyes he ran light-footed into the hall. So sudden was his appearance that he got three quarters of the way across before he was noticed; then there were shouts from the non-combatant Rumbles, and the warriors who were crowded round the Great Door tunnel looked up and shouted in their turn.

Bingo planted his feet firmly on the floor and threw sticker after sticker at the enemy. He threw well and he threw hard. Each of his lances struck a mark and half a dozen Rumbles fell dead or sorely wounded. The others fell back and hesitated, so Bingo drew his catapult and two more Rumbles fell stunned before he took to his heels and, with a remarkable burst of speed, vanished into the library tunnel yelling defiantly, 'I'm a Borrible, I'm a Borrible.' Scores of warrior Rumbles raced after Bingo, shaking their lances above their heads, and in a few seconds the entrance to the Great Door corridor was left deserted.

'Vulge,' said Knocker, kneeling, 'Can you make it across the Central? We'll need all hands to fight our way over.'

'Get me to my feet,' said Vulge, sitting up, 'and give me a sticker to lean on. I'll waltz it over there.'

His companions pulled him upright and thrust a lance into his hand. He tucked the butt of it under his good armpit and used it like a crutch. 'There you go,' he wheezed. 'Nice as ninepence.'

'Go for it, then,' said Knocker, heaving the treasure box on to his back once more, and Orococco and Adolf formed up on either side of him. They had only a few Rumble-sticks left but here in the Central there would be room for catapult work.

'You lead the way, Vulge,' said Knocker. 'We'll take your pace.'

Because of the confusion that had followed Bingo's exit the Borribles managed to advance well into the Central before being seen, and when they were the Rumbles were at a loss, for they had no troops of their own on hand to deal with the situation. They knew that Borribles were loose in the tunnels, but they had no idea how large the invading force was. Above all they had not expected a band of Borrible fighters to appear without warning in their midst.

They shouted and squealed and their stomachs turned to water. They ran in every direction, except towards their enemies; they knocked each other down and exchanged blows, anything to get away from the deadly stones that flew so rapidly from the Borrible catapults. They called for their warriors, but they were deep in the tunnels chasing phantoms or other Rumbles in the belief that they were the enemy. Smoke made pursuit and identification difficult and a great turmoil was spreading into the very outposts of the Rumble bunker.

Slowly the Borribles moved over the open area. Vulge hobbled and stumbled manfully, gritting his teeth to keep back the pain, willing himself not to fall and ruin the escape. As for the Rumbles they kept their distance, making no attempt to attack, but all that changed in a second when a party of their warriors burst from a tunnel on the Borrible flank.

'We've been rumbled,' said Orococco.

'This is no time for bad jokes,' panted Knocker, sweating under the weight of his box and wishing he had his hands free.

'The proverb says,' hissed Orococco as he fired and reloaded his catapult, '"Bad times need jokes though never so bad."'

A flight of lances whistled over from the Rumbles, but the catapult fire, rapid and sustained, detracted from their aim and the stickers missed their targets and fell harmlessly to the floor; all save one, which struck the box that Knocker carried and pierced the lid and stayed there quivering. The force of the blow staggered Knocker and he went down on one knee. Adolf helped him back to his feet.

The Rumbles searched round for more lances but the flying Borrible stones still hampered them and one by one they were hit and retreated to the safety of the tunnels. But there was one Rumble, braver and quicker than the rest, who exhorted his comrades to come out again and began to organize the non-combatants into a compact mass, ready to charge the tiny band of Borribles. If he could get his men to act together, all would be over with the retreating Adventurers, but Orococco had other ideas.

Snatching a lance from the floor, he ran forward, one Borrible charging a hundred of his foes. About twenty yards from the brave but offending Rumble, Orococco threw his lance like a javelin. It left his hand with the power of a bullet and the four-inch nail buried itself deep in the warrior's thick fur. A groan went up from the enemy ranks and scores of stickers clattered about the head of Orococco, but he bobbed and ducked and returned to his friends unscathed, and together they gained the temporary safety of the Great Door tunnel.

Vulge fell to the floor in a dead faint. Knocker flung down his box, tugged the lance free of the lid and threw the weapon back into the hall.

Adolf knelt to inspect Vulge's injury, lifting the jacket aside to reveal the blood-soaked bandage.

'Our Vulge has lost lots of his strength,' he said, 'but the wound has stopped bleeding. He may be all right, if he can rest.' He refolded the cloth and replaced it.

Orococco, watching from the mouth of the corridor, called a warning: 'There's a lot of those warrior boys out there, and all coming our way.'

Knocker looked at the others and said, 'Rest, just a minute or two. We're not finished yet. I can hear fighting up ahead; we ain't out of this holiday camp yet.'

'It's a lovely place,' said Vulge, who was becoming delirious. 'Lots and lots of Rumbles in it.'

9

Bingo ran like the wind along the corridor. As far as he could see it was empty of Rumbles ahead, but from behind came the noise of shouting as the warriors from the Central gave chase.

Bingo ran easily, keeping plenty of strength in reserve. Wherever the library was it seemed a long way. He ran on, outdistancing his pursuers until at length he could hear them no more. He slowed his pace to a jog, a sticker swinging loosely in his right hand, his catapult in his belt. He was in the furthest reaches of the bunker here; it was strangely quiet and the air was free of smoke and acrid steam.

After what seemed miles, Bingo came to a green baize-covered door hanging crazily on one hinge. Several stickers stood embedded in it and two Rumble warriors, with their throats slit, lay dead across the threshold.

'Wendle work,' said Bingo, and he went past the bodies and slipped into the room that lay beyond. It was indeed the library but it had been badly mauled. It was a long high chamber, with massively tall bookcases soaring up to an embossed ceiling that had been painted in bright colours with the coats of arms of the richest and most ancient Rumble families. Diminutive wooden balconies ran round the walls and cunningly carved spiral staircases led up to them.

Quiet alcoves with comfortable desks were situated between the bookshelves, and green-shaded lamps gave a friendly and academic glow. It was a place for rest and study, richly decorated, and it had obviously cost a great deal of money and labour to establish and build up over long years. Here was assembled all the knowledge, wisdom and power that the Rumbles had amassed over many centuries, and now it was being dismantled by a very busy Borrible. Napoleon Boot was hard at work with the cool ferocity of a Wendle with a grudge.

Bingo glanced round the room to check that there was no enemy, and there wasn't, alive. The bodies of a dozen or so vanquished Rumble warriors littered the dark green carpet, all but covered in mounds of heavy books. Napoleon carried on with his work, unperturbed by Bingo's arrival, which he acknowledged with a curt nod.

The Wendle had already pushed or levered over two or three of the huge bookcases, and spilled their contents out across the floor. At the far end of the room one of the long library ladders was propped up to a grating of the ventilation system. Napoleon had prepared his retreat, but was not going to leave before he had caused the maximum amount of damage. The Wendle was nobody's fool.

Bingo watched as Napoleon pushed over a few more bookcases and the volumes cascaded down, covering more of the Rumble dead. He advanced, climbing across the treacherous surface of jumbled books.

'How are you getting on?' he asked.

'Nicely, thanks,' said the Wendle, preoccupied, 'and you?'

'I can't find mine anywhere. Where's yours?'

'Under that pile of encyclopaedias. Polite little fellow, didn't cause any trouble.'

'How?' asked Bingo, adopting the same terse speech as the Wendle.

'He was at the top of a long ladder,' explained Napoleon, pleased to tell the story of his name for the very first time. 'I came to the bottom of it and said, well-mannered like, "Excuse me, are you Napoleon Boot Rumble?" and he said, "Yes, I am." So I says, "Could you come down please, I have a word to say to you." Bloke didn't even look at me, toffee-nosed little twit. "Oh, no," he said, "I'm too busy. You'll have to wait. I'm looking for a book on Bowwible fighting methods for the High Command, of which I am a member, I'll have you know. So be off." So I says, "You're coming down one way or the other, mate. Gravity is stronger than you are." That was a remark that caught his fancy, must have, 'cos he looked at me then. "Aaaaaagh," he says, like they do, and drops his book, nearly hit me on the head, bloody dangerous, and he grabs hold of the top of the bookcase. At the same time I kicked the ladder away, so he's got nothing to stand on, has he? Well, the sudden increase of weight at the top of the bookcase made it wobble violently, so that gave me an idea. I runs round the back, up another ladder on the next bookcase and pushes with me sticker, and over went the whole lot, bookcase, books, Rumble and all. Goodnight, Napoleon Rumble. Splat!'

Bingo shook his head. 'What a way to go.'

'Overcome by the weight of his studies, you might say,' said Napoleon, and he smirked like a cold draught. 'Got any matches on you?' he asked suddenly.

'What for?' asked Bingo.

'Don't be slow,' said Napoleon, sighing. 'Start a fire, of course, bit of mayhem, cover our retreat. Seen the others?'

Bingo told him what he knew.

'Ah,' crowed the Wendle, nodding his head. 'I knew Knocker was up to something, and that Spiff as well, he's as crooked as a mangle handle. Got a box, eh? That's treasure, that is. Well, we'll have to see about that, won't we?'

'We haven't got away yet,' pointed out Bingo reasonably.

'I'm getting out, mate,' said Napoleon, indicating the ladder. 'I'm getting into that ventilation shaft and no Rumble in the world is going to stop me leaving for home. Only two Rumbles can get at you at once up there, one in front, one behind, and any Borrible is a match for a score of Rumbles . . . and a Wendle can deal with twice that number.'

'You do for these?' asked Bingo, indicating the prone Rumble warriors.

'Well, they didn't commit suicide,' said Napoleon. 'Mind you, they only came into the place in fives and sixes. It was easy really, like falling off a . . . bookcase.'

Bingo took a box of matches from his pocket and handed them to Napoleon. 'It's a shame about the books. Are there any good adventure stories there?'

Napoleon gave him an old-fashioned look. 'I haven't had a lot of time for reading in the last half-hour,' he said, and he went over to a pile of dusty tomes, put a match to them and stood back as they burst into flames on the instant.

'What I mean,' persisted Bingo, 'is that it's a shame; they're good things, books.'

'Good things! You sound like a bloody Rumble. Can't have no half measures in an attack like this, Bingo. Got to go the whole hog or it don't work. What would happen if we left these books up here untouched? I'll tell you what, there'd be another Rumble High Command on the go in five minutes. This is what it's all about, Sonny – books is power! The whole world knows that.' And Napoleon threw another volume into the blaze.

'I suppose you're right,' said Bingo. 'I never thought of it like that.'

'Course I'm right,' said Napoleon. 'Now then, it's time for me to go home. Can't stand fires, water's my element. Are you coming?'

'Can't,' said Bingo miserably. 'I told you, I haven't found my bloke.'

'Tough, but I'm off. I want to see that Knocker; that treasure's got to be looked into.' Napoleon winked mysteriously, made his way from the fire, which was now burning well, and began to climb his ladder. 'You could come with me, Bingo, and drop down through the ventilation system somewhere else. It's going to get very hot in this library very shortly.'

'It's going to be hotter than you think,' said Bingo. 'There were two million Rumble warriors chasing me down the corridor out there. They don't run very fast, but they ought to be here at any moment.'

Napoleon stopped dead on about the eighth rung and looked down. 'How many? You can't have that lot to yourself, that's greedy.' He dropped back to the floor and threw more books on the fire.

They waited and the flames crept along the mounds of books and began to rise towards the high ceiling. Soon there was a noise of shouting from the tunnel beyond the green baize door and Bingo and Napoleon placed themselves within sticker-throwing range of the entrance.

'We'll let the first ones have it with these stickers,' said Napoleon, 'then we'll get behind that pile of books, there beyond the fire, and let them have it with the catapults as they try to get in. When we're out of ammo, we'll scarper up the ladder, okay?'

'Right,' said Bingo. He picked up a couple of lances from the floor and hefted one in his right hand; it was then that two breathless warriors burst into the room, and Bingo and Napoleon threw their weapons as one man and the two Rumbles fell.

Other Rumbles crowded into the room in a compact mass, pushed on from behind by their impetuous companions. The two Borribles continued to throw spears until they had exhausted their meagre supply.

Several Rumbles had been accounted for, but so great were their numbers it was impossible to prevent them from spilling into the library and taking cover behind desks and bookcases.

Napoleon and Bingo fell back and crouched behind an enormous pile of books, their catapult rubbers stretched.

'I've hardly fired a stone yet,' said Bingo. 'It's all been lance work.'

Napoleon peered through the fumes that were beginning to fill the room. 'This smoke is going to help them to creep up on us,' he said to Bingo. 'That's not good.' He broke off and fired a shot towards the door. 'Look,' he said, 'there's scores of them coming.'

Bingo could see for himself that many more of the enemy were rushing into the room. They were led by a slim but powerful Rumble covered in sleek brown fur and with a hard expression on his dangerous snout. He carried three or four lances and wore a sash of gold, green and white to denote his position as commander of the warriors. He looked proud and impatient, and Bingo knew that at last he had found his target.

The commander ran this way and that at the far end of the library, gathering his forces and making them emerge from their hiding places between the fallen bookshelves. He shouted and waved his arms and slowly the Rumbles came forward, throwing lances at the two Borribles who, crouched behind their barricade, stood up every now and then to loose off a stone.

In this manner the battle continued and things would have gone very badly for Napoleon and Bingo if the Rumbles had been in possession of any reasonable number of lances. Fortunately most of their missiles had been thrown in a panicky fashion at the beginning of the skirmish. Now there was a great pile of spears on the Borribles' side of the room and there soon came a moment when the two of them could stand up in full view of the Rumbles because the Rumbles had no stickers left to fight with.

With a sign, the commander sent some of his troops off into the corridor to bring more weapons; the rest of his warriors took up defensive positions among the bookcases and the piles of burning books. It was hard to breathe in the room now as the conflagration gradually gained a firmer hold and the smoke grew thicker. Some Rumbles tried to stamp or beat out the flames, but more often than not their fur was singed or caught fire and their friends had to come to their rescue and save them from being scorched to death.

Napoleon checked his bandoliers. 'Not many stones left,' he said. 'How about you?'

'I've got a lot still, but they won't last for ever,' said Bingo, and he fired a stone at a Rumble who was trying to creep along the side of the room to get at a stray lance. 'But I can't leave now, I've got to have a crack at my target, and I'd better do it before his mates get back with a new load of stickers.'

Bingo reached behind and picked up two sharp Rumble lances. He put his catapult carefully into his back pocket and went slowly down the long slope of books. The commander was standing by the library door, waiting for his men to return with more lances, for even he was weaponless.

Bingo leant backwards, arcing his body, and threw one of his spears with all his might. His name would have been won there and then had the High Rumble not chosen that moment to step into the corridor to see if his men were returning.

The sticker plunged deep into the green baize of the library door and hung there, humming. Bingo swore and grasped his second lance securely, but did not throw it, for there are two ways of fighting with the Rumble-stick. The first is simply to throw it from a distance; the second is to wield it like a quarterstaff, until the fighter finds a moment to use the point and slay his stunned or unconscious foe.

Bingo moved nearer to the door and the Rumbles fell back. He glanced over his shoulder to see that Napoleon had followed him, his catapult eager to dissuade anyone who thought they could intervene in the fight between Bingo the Borrible and Bingo the Rumble.

The High Rumble leapt back into the room, saw the advance of the two Borribles and saw the sticker still singing in the door. He pulled it free with both hands and moved towards Bingo. Neither of them said a word, and no Rumble attempted to interfere; they watched from the safety of their hiding places, their snouts and eyes only just visible through the red smoke.

Bingo held his lance with a hand at each end, using the long haft to ward off blows from his adversary who began the contest by working his weapon like a two-handed sword, hoping to stun the Borrible and then spear him. But Bingo had learned his Rumble-stick fighting well all that time ago in the Rowena Crescent Gym, and he protected his head and shoulders, and was content to defend himself while he measured the style of his enemy, conserving his strength.

It was treacherous underfoot; the books slipped and tripped and burnt the feet. Whoever fell first during this fight would be hard put to it to rise again. Suddenly the Rumble changed his tactics and began jabbing consistently and forcefully, making Bingo avoid the blows like a fencer. The Rumble was an expert, perhaps the best lancer of his tribe.

Just my luck, thought Bingo, and redoubled his efforts, but backwards and backwards his opponent forced him. The Rumble troops emerged from their hiding places, exulting, and some climbed on to bookcases and, hanging on with one arm, waved the other and jeered at the two Borribles, so lonely and outnumbered.

Sweat was pouring down Bingo's face and into his eyes, and his arms were aching and his hands were bruised and bleeding from the many blows that had clouted them. He dodged, he weaved, he ducked. He tried to remember all he had ever learnt about fighting with the Rumble-stick, but it didn't seem to be enough. He had managed to ward off most swipes and stabs so far, but he himself had not yet struck a blow. His antagonist looked fresh and powerful, smiling grimly, his red eyes shining with triumph as he bore down on the Borrible from Lavender Hill.

The battle passed far beyond Napoleon but the Wendle kept his position, holding the main contingent of warriors at bay with his catapult, though he realized that if the Rumble did for Bingo he himself would have little chance of escape. Bingo too was aware of that possibility and he strove all the harder. He thought of his other friends and their long quest and all they had been through together. He had a brief mental picture of them being torn to death by the sharp teeth of the Rumbles; the notion angered him and he stopped retreating. He stooped suddenly and allowed the Rumble's sticker to whistle over his head. He jabbed at his foe and at last wounded him in the knee.

The Rumble staggered and it was his turn to go on the defensive. Bingo thrust and fenced and fought, holding the lance now one-handed, now two-handed. He circled and struggled, and still the fight went on and still Bingo found it impossible to get through his adversary's guard. But Bingo had had time to think; only cunning would win him this battle. So, pressing his namesake slowly back down the hill of books, Bingo tried a stratagem. He pretended to stumble. He slithered a step, and, keeping a wary eye on his opponent, allowed himself to fall backwards, crying in pain for an imagined twisted foot.

The watching Rumbles cheered anew and Napoleon cursed his luck and moved nearer the ladder. He only had one chance, to climb out of the library as quickly as possible while the Rumbles celebrated their victory. But Napoleon was sure of one thing: if that Rumble did for Bingo, he wouldn't live long to brag about it. He, Napoleon Boot, would make certain that a stone was rattling round the inside of the commander's skull before his brain had time to register his conquest.

Bingo lay on the books, groaning and writhing, but his eyes kept still, watching the Rumble who, in his excitement, had not noticed that the Borrible, in spite of all his supposed pain, had not let go his lance.

The commander stepped forward. Quickly he raised his spear, ready to pierce Bingo's breast. He plunged it down hard, leaning on it like a man pushing a shovel. At that moment Bingo rolled over with a thrust from legs and hands. He came to his knees, and as the point of the Rumble's weapon embedded itself in the closed pages of some solid volume, he swung the shaft of his sticker and smote his enemy behind the ear.

The animal swayed, his legs buckling. He half turned, as if to run, but Bingo's lance, still twirling in a circle above his head, struck the Rumble again and he fell into a crouching position. Then Bingo, slipping his grasp along the haft of his spear so that he could hold it like a sword, leapt upon the swaying figure of his enemy and bore him to the ground, and four inches of steel found the commander's heart.

The fire crackled in the room and a hopeless groan came from the Rumbles; their greatest warrior was slain. The smoke swirled crimson in the draught between door and ventilation vent. Napoleon twisted his head and saw that his comrade, who he had imagined dead, was in fact rising from the prostrate body of the Rumble. His face was grimy and his clothes were torn. Blood was pouring down his left arm and down the side of his face where the Rumble spear had grazed his head, taken off his hat and cut his pointed ear. He was a sorry sight, blackened by soot, smoke and sweat.

'Are you all right?' called the Wendle, not taking his eyes from the Rumbles, who stood motionless in despair.

'Yes,' lied Bingo. 'Ace, but I think we've outstayed our welcome.'

Napoleon did not reply but went over to the body of the Rumble, removed the sash and placed it over Bingo's shoulders.

'There, Bingo,' he said with a smile. 'When you get home you can hang it on the wall and write underneath, "Souvenir of Happy Holidays in Rumbledom".'

Bingo looked down at the trophy. 'Here,' he said proudly, 'I've got my name. I hope everyone else has.'

They backed slowly up the mountainous pile of books, and the Rumbles made no attempt to stop them; they were leaderless and weaponless for the time being. The danger would come when the two Borribles mounted the ladder and the Rumbles could charge forward and repossess the lances they had thrown earlier. They would be able to pick the Borribles off as they climbed, or, more likely, would overturn the ladder and spike their falling enemies on the raised barbs of their spears.

At the bottom of the ladder Napoleon and Bingo weighed their chances. 'Best thing would be to have one of us at the top first,' said Bingo, 'then he can cover the other while he climbs.'

The Battersea Borrible had been greatly weakened by his battle, and Napoleon could see that he was in no condition to sustain another fight should the need arise, so he sent Bingo to the top of the ladder first.

Bingo climbed slowly, like an injured snail. His head ached and there was only a faint strength left in his hands. The hole in the ceiling seemed to get no nearer but he went on, taking care all the way. A fall from that height would be fatal. Looking down on the library he saw a scene of chaos. The great bookcases were cast down, and the once carefully classified books were strewn everywhere, or had been built into redoubts by the Rumbles. The smoke was dense and lay across the floor in dirty wraiths and had crept up the walls towards the ventilation shaft. From his high vantage point Bingo could see scores of Rumbles looking at him from their barricades and from under tables. Their snouts were pointed upwards, greedily twitching for his blood. All that held them in check was the steady gaze of Napoleon Boot.

When Bingo neared the opening in the ceiling he stopped climbing and shoved his left arm under and over a rung. He took his catapult from his back pocket with his right hand, loaded a stone and stretched the thick black rubber, ready to fire at any Rumble that moved.

'All right, Nap,' he called, and the Wendle, with a last threatening look around the room, began to climb, fast, his catapult between his teeth. He had climbed barely a dozen rungs when there was a commotion in the corridor leading to the library. Rumble warriors, sent on the errand by the commander, were returning, their arms loaded with lances. Their companions in the library shook themselves free of their fear, emerged from their hiding places and surged towards the ladder, calling loudly for vengeance.

Bingo shot his catapult as rapidly as he could, but hanging by one arm made it tedious work, and he was becoming terribly feeble. Rumbles were near to Napoleon now and lances struck the ladder by the Wendle's hands, one took a chunk of flesh from his leg. He slipped and almost fell. The Rumbles shouted but Napoleon gritted his teeth and pulled his body upwards even faster, and Bingo fired his catapult past his friend's head and broke many a Rumble's skull with stones from the banks of the Bluegate Gravel Pit.

But at last Bingo was forced to retreat into the ventilation shaft in order to give Napoleon a clear run through the trapdoor. No longer threatened by missiles from above, the Rumbles swarmed forward and seized the ladder, keen to tear it down. The ladder shook and trembled and began to tilt, and it seemed that Napoleon was destined to fall on to the deadly spearheads below. Bingo seized the top rung and pulled against the dozen or so Rumbles who were tugging with might and main from the library floor, but, as Napoleon had said earlier, gravity was a force to be reckoned with and now it was on the side of the Rumbles.

Inside the shaft Bingo struggled and swore, bumping his head and knocking his wounds till the blood ran. Napoleon scurried upwards, hand over hand, not looking at the shining spears beneath him.

When the Wendle was a few rungs only from safety, the exhausted

Bingo was almost lugged out of the shaft by a violent heave on the part of the Rumbles. Bingo managed to hold fast but he was now protruding, half in and half out of the trapdoor. He wrestled resolutely with the ladder which was threatening to shake Napoleon into space. A great shout went up from the Rumbles and the Wendle only stuck to the ladder by clinging with legs and arms together, but he still found time to spit directly downwards.

'You cross-eyed bunch of weasels,' he yelled. 'You swivel-eyed moles.'

The Rumbles only pulled the harder, determined to drag the wretched Bingo back into the library. The top rung was torn from his bleeding hands and Napoleon seemed about to sway away from his friend for ever. But Bingo held his arms out to Napoleon and, as the Rumbles threw the ladder down with a fearsome roar, the Wendle thrust his feet into space, floated on air for a split second and then grabbed Bingo's right arm with both his hands. He swung there, lances falling about him, and he looked up into the pained and desperate face of his fellow Adventurer.

'Don't faint now, Bingo,' he cried. 'I'll be skewered like a pork joint if you do.'

Bingo slipped and slithered in the narrow space, lucky that it was so tight. Had the shaft been wider, the weight of Napoleon dangling and trying to work his way up to the lip would have pulled them both down. As it was, Bingo wedged himself across the opening, and although the pain seared into his shoulder like an axe, he kept still as Napoleon climbed up his arm. When the Wendle had one hand on the edge Bingo shifted his grip a fraction and hauled Napoleon in and they fell together in a heap.

It took a long while for them to recover. They gulped deep breaths, though each lungful had more smoke than air in it, and they coughed and retched in dreadful spasms. At last Napoleon got to his hands and knees and peered cautiously from the hole. A dozen or so of the Rumbles were grappling with the ladder, attempting to get it upright. Others raced from the fiercely burning library, instructing their comrades to run from room to room and along the corridors to guard against the escape of the two Borribles.

Napoleon roused the flagging Bingo. 'Come on,' he said tenderly, the first time that Bingo, or anyone else, had heard him talk in such a manner. 'We've got to get you out of here.'

'You'd better leave me,' said Bingo, raising his head with an effort. 'I can knock them off the top of the ladder as they come up. Give you time to get away.'

'I'm not leaving you,' said Napoleon firmly, 'not after you saving my life. Anyway, all you've got to do is crawl.'

Bingo got to his hands and knees. 'All right, I'll have a go. Which way?'

That was a problem. The shaft stretched away darkly on either side of the opening. In which direction lay safety, if at all, they could only guess.

'Let's go the way the smoke is going,' suggested Napoleon. 'It might lead us out. If it don't, it won't.'

So, coughing and spitting, their eyes smarting and running with tears, they moved along the metal tunnel, banging their heads from side to side, like ping-pong balls in a drainpipe.

*

Torreycanyon leant back against the armoured car and felt pleased with himself. He had caused enough mayhem to account for three adventures. The engine of the armoured car lay smashed to smithereens by the blows of an iron bar he had found among the tools. He had emptied dozens of petrol cans all over the workshops, saturating the workbenches and the shelves where the spare parts were kept. Into the petrol tank of the car he had lowered a long length of rag and the petrol had soaked its way up and out. All he needed was a match and the whole place would go up like a bonfire and retard the Rumble war effort by a dozen years. But a match he did not have, his box must have fallen from his pocket somewhere.

During his work he had been interrupted by the Rumbles many times. The warriors had forced the door and chivvied him back along the workshop with their lances, but Torreycanyon had taken a lid from a dustbin and used it as a shield. Not one lance had really hurt him, though he was cut in several places from near misses.

He had defended himself like a lion in the garage area, just in front of the armoured car, and had beaten off many attacks. Scores of dead and unconscious Rumbles littered the battleground, others had crawled away to lick their wounds. Torreycanyon was almost content; all he wanted was one match so that he could add to the smoke that had drifted to him from the fires in the kitchens and library.

He leant against the car, liking the solidity of it behind him. He was tired. Twenty yards away stood a group of Rumble warriors, waiting for help and more spears. It was only a question of time before they wore him down and captured or killed him, but all he could think of was his match; he wanted to go out in a blaze of glory, like a firework. One match to that rag in the car and a touch of it to the floor and fire would spurt round the workshops quicker than a Borrible could run.

He wouldn't care what happened to him then; perhaps he would be able to escape through the garage door. Set in the wall he had seen a red control button marked 'Exit – Push once' but there might be more Rumbles on the outside, waiting. It would be dawn over Rumbledom, he reckoned; time to be going.

'One of you Rumbles nip off and get a match, will you? I want to pick my teeth.' He leant on his iron bar and shifted the grip on the dustbin lid. He laughed aloud at his own stupidity. He hoped the others were safe out of it by now and not wasting time joking with the enemy.

A sudden noise above his head made him spring into action. So that was why the Rumbles had been so quiet, they'd found a way to outflank him through the roof. If they came at him from two directions at once he wouldn't last long. He clambered on to the car and looked closely at the ceiling. A square flap was being lifted away. Torreycanyon glanced at the Rumbles standing by the workshop entrance. They hadn't moved. He swung the iron bar over his shoulder; if any Rumble put so much as a snout through that trapdoor, he would swipe it flatter than a dead cat on a motorway.

The trapdoor lifted and a hand appeared, took a grip on the underside and pulled it open to reveal a black hole from which thick smoke drifted. There was coughing and spitting from the shaft and somebody was taking in large gulps of air. Torreycanyon prepared to strike.

'I'll give you cough and spit, you myxomatosed rabbit,' he said, 'you snouty old stoat.'

The hand came out again and Torreycanyon lowered the bar. It was a small human hand, not a paw at all. On the other end of that hand must be a Borrible.

A begrimed and bloody face appeared. Its red-rimmed eyes blinked and the mouth was open, taking in as much air as it could. And then, very nearly suffocated and lifeless, the small body of Bingo flopped out like a filleted fish, and fell into Torreycanyon's arms.

Torreycanyon placed his comrade on one of the seats of the car and looked again at the enemy. They were sliding nearer, so with a mighty and blood-curdling bellow he threw his iron bar and it skeetered and bounced across the concrete, sweeping the Rumbles' legs from underneath them. They retreated; they'd had enough of this mad Borrible, and they did not want to take him on again until he was dropping with fatigue.

Bingo opened his eyes. 'Oh, Torrey,' he groaned, 'I'm so glad it's you. I couldn't go a step further. My knees are worn raw and my lungs feel like two smoked haddocks.' And Bingo started coughing again.

At the same time there was another scrabbling noise above Torreycanyon's head, and he drew his catapult and seized a stone from Bingo's bandolier. But he saw another hand and the head of Napoleon Boot soon followed it. He was in no better state than Bingo. His eyes were streaming and cuts from a dozen lance wounds had covered him in blood which in turn was covered in grime and grease and soot. His clothes were torn and his scuffed knees stuck out through large holes in his trousers. Torreycanyon helped him down and rested him on a seat alongside Bingo.

'Looks like you done all the fighting yourselves,' said Torreycanyon, 'and you're going to have some more to do, soon as you get your breath back.'

Napoleon said nothing but lay gasping. Bingo, breathing a little more easily, raised himself to a sitting position and looked over the twenty yards of body-strewn no man's land to where the Rumbles stood.

'What are they waiting for, Torrey?' he asked.

'More ammo and more friends,' answered Torreycanyon. 'They've gone right off me.'

'Have you any kind of a plan?' asked Bingo, a little dazed.

'Not half,' said Torreycanyon. 'Get out!' And in answer to Bingo's puzzled shake of the head he said, 'There's a garage door here, but the trouble is I don't know what's on the other side. More Rumbles most like. It must be daylight – very dodgy.'

'It's the only chance we've got,' said Napoleon, coming to himself and standing up, although he staggered violently. 'There's no point in going back into the shaft, that would be certain death.'

'Well, in that case,' said Torreycanyon, 'watch the bunnies while I get down and try the door. If they move, let them have it with your catapults. You're lucky to have a stone or two left; I haven't.'

He jumped down on to the floor of the garage near the huge sliding door. He approached the red button, licked his lips and looked at it as if trying to cast a spell. As his hand hovered in the air he turned suddenly to look up at Bingo and Napoleon.

'Here,' he said sharply, 'either of you Borribles got a match?'

*

Knocker stumbled on down the Great Door corridor, the weight of the treasure boring deep into his back. His muscles ached, the sweat poured from underneath his Borrible hat and down into his eyes, and the pungent smoke chafed at his lungs. Orococco led the way, scouting round every bend and corner and beckoning the others on. Vulge limped and staggered behind, supported by Adolf when the German was not fighting a rearguard action against the Rumbles who followed along the tunnel.

When the lights flickered out they could feel their enemies come nearer and strike at them in the dark with the sharp points of their lances. Furry bodies brushed past and tried to separate them and bring them down, but they kept together and counter-attacked with such ferocity that the Rumbles suffered many casualties.

They pushed on as best they could until, without warning, Orococco stopped at a sharp bend in the tunnel and called to Knocker. What Knocker saw made him drop his precious box and bound forward. About twenty yards from him Sydney and Chalotte stood ringed by enemy warriors. They were backed into a kind of alcove and a circle of steel-pointed lances held them in check. Their bandoliers were empty, they were fighting with captured Rumble-sticks against ten of their enemies and were obviously on their last legs. Their hats were gone and their hair was grimy with soot, hanging in stiffened strands over their lined faces. Chalotte's lance was broken and she used it like a dagger, wielding it with a desperate fury.

Orococco and Knocker arrived together on the scene and struck the Rumbles from behind with lances they had scooped from the floor. They yelled and they shouted and the Rumbles fled into a side tunnel, thinking that the whole Borrible nation was at their heels. Three of their number lay on the ground and would fight no more.

Chalotte and Sydney leant against the wall and wiped the sweat from their eyes.

'One minute later would have been one minute too late,' said Chalotte. Her body was shaking.

'I thought I'd never see the sky again,' said Sydney. 'How many of us left?'

'What you see,' said Knocker, 'and we aren't in good shape. The others have probably had it.'

'Let's get on,' said Adolf. 'There's a couple of hundred Rumbles behind me.'

It was decided that Sydney should join the German in the rearguard, while Chalotte marched up front with Orococco. Their progress was slow. They were obliged to fight every inch of the way towards the Great Door, and Rumbles came thick and fast from the side tunnels the moment the Borribles had gone by, crowding close, just waiting for a favourable moment to attack.

What lay ahead, the Borribles dared not imagine. Even if Stonks was still guarding the way out there would be hundreds of Rumbles, all well armed, lying in ambush for them in the cold green grass of Rumbledom.

At last they came to the remains of one of the brick barricades that Stonks had built just inside the Great Door when he had captured it. Not much of the barrier could be seen now, trampled down in some great fight, and what was visible was covered with the bodies of fallen Rumbles, piled one upon the other and reaching halfway to the roof of the tunnel. It was strangely quiet too and the Borribles halted. Nothing moved before them and they looked at each other, puzzled.

'I wonder if Stonksie is under that lot?' said Chalotte.

'He couldn't possibly have survived,' said Knocker, dropping his box again. 'He must have seen off hundreds of Rumbles, though. What an artist!'

'I should cocoa,' said Chalotte. 'Perhaps there isn't anyone between us and the way out.'

At that moment an enormous Rumble bounded over the broken barricade and scrambled towards them. He had a spear in each hand and hallooed and shouted in a muffled way.

'Anyone got any stones?' asked Knocker urgently, but there was no answer. For the time being their catapults were useless.

'Those with spears up front,' said Knocker, throwing the lance he held at the oncoming monster. He grabbed another spear from the floor and formed a line with Orococco and Chalotte. The great shambling figure advanced on them with a strange and lolloping gait. He was the largest Rumble they had ever seen and probably the strongest. Perhaps, thought Knocker, Stonks had been fighting the Rumbles that now littered the battlefield when this powerful creature had pitched into him from behind. But whatever had happened the mighty shape still bore down on them, fearlessly, gleefully.

At some distance from the line of Borribles, the giant Rumble stopped and waved the spears in his hands and danced from one foot to the other, then turned in a circle and shouted happily. The muffled voice became a little clearer.

'A Borrible, a Borrible,' shouted the Rumble. 'Don't worry, it's me, Stonks. Stonks, you fools. I've kept the Great Door safe for you, oh, come on.'

'Careful,' said Knocker. 'It must be a trick.'

'It's no trick, Knocker,' said the shaggy animal. 'Look.' The great Rumble threw down his spears and, lifting two hands – and they were hands – reached behind his neck and fiddled with something. Then the hands got hold of the snout and pulled hard and the whole furry cloak fell away to reveal none other than Stonks, the Borrible. 'There,' he cried, dancing some more, 'it's only me.'

Astonished, the Borribles lowered their weapons and crowded up to their friend, all of them asking questions at once.

'Take it easy,' said Stonks, delighted by their amazement. 'I'll explain.'

And he told them how he had captured the door with the sapling trick, and how Torreycanyon had gone off into the tunnels alone while he, Stonks, thought it a good idea to stay and guard the door to secure a line of retreat. But before building the barricades he'd gone to find the Rumble doorkeeper, to make sure that he didn't recover and return to the fray. And Stonks had not been obliged to search for long; he had indeed found the doorkeeper, though all that remained of him was his skin.

'Just a big coat with nothing inside,' he said. 'Can't imagine what happened to his guts and innards . . . All splatted out of him on impact, I suppose.'

In any event it had seemed to Stonks that it might help his defence of the Great Door, at least for a while, if he pretended to be a Rumble, and so he had donned the skin and it had worked very well, as they could see by the number of dead Rumbles lying everywhere.

'I got so used to wearing the skin,' continued Stonks, 'that I forgot I had it on when you lot appeared. It was only when Knocker threw a sticker at me that I remembered. Anyway, the door's in our possession now, but I should think there's twenty Rumble brigades on the other side of it.'

Weary as they were, the Borribles congratulated Stonks and patted him on the back and laughed again and again at his tale. Though their position was hopeless, it certainly helped to be told a cheerful story. Even Vulge limped forward, leant against the wall and wagged his head till it nearly fell off.

'Take the skin home and use it as a mat,' he said. 'It will look like one of those tiger rugs they have in posh houses sometimes.'

They marched on then, over the barricades that Stonks had defended so valiantly and with so much cunning, and came at last to the Great Door. Here they rested for a while and took stock of their situation. Behind them were gathering the hordes of Rumbles who had followed them through the tunnels. They did not attack for they did not have to. Sooner or later the Borribles would have to leave the bunker, they would have to open the door, and the Rumbles knew that waiting on the other side of it were hundreds more of their warriors, brought in from other bunkers, fresh and eager to fight. The Borribles would be caught between two fires and one by one they would perish. Then would the Rumbles take their revenge.

Knocker looked at his sorry and exhausted band. All of them were wounded to some degree, and all of them had dried blood mixed into the dirt of their faces. There was no ammunition left for their catapults, so there was no chance of them carving their way through the Rumble ranks with well-aimed stones. They had as many lances as they could carry, for lances lay discarded all around the Great Door where Stonks had fought. But a lance could be thrown but once, and at close quarters they would be swamped by sheer weight of numbers and taken alive. Knocker shuddered to think of it. Furthermore, they had no food and nothing to drink. The longer they stayed where they were the weaker they would become. Their plight was grim.

The red eyes of the Rumbles watched from the nearest of the barricades, glowing, burning into the Borribles, hating them and yearning for their deaths. They began a low chant which rose louder and louder and was taken up by hundreds more beyond them, pouring down the tunnels, united and organized now for the final battle.

'Bite up the Bowwibles,' they chorused. 'Bite up the Bowwibles.' And there came a beating on the door and it trembled in its frame and the same chant was taken up outside and the door was smashed regularly now with some kind of battering ram, probably an old tree trunk rolled in from the fields of Rumbledom.

'Rest until they batter down the door,' said Knocker. 'Then we'll have to fight.'

'Well,' said Vulge, whose wound had been re-bandaged by Adolf, 'at least we did it. We've taken five of their names, probably the whole eight if we could hear the others tell their stories.'

'Torreycanyon, Bingo and Napoleon,' said Stonks. 'I wonder . . .'

'Well, man,' said Orococco, 'we never expected to get right through the adventure without losing someone.'

The thumping on the door continued.

'It looks like we might lose everyone,' said Vulge, leaning against the wall and feeling his shoulder.

'Isn't it funny?' said Chalotte. She was sitting on the floor with her legs stretched out in front of her. 'Isn't it funny, only a little while ago we were doing our best to get into this place? Now we're inside and they are bashing the door down to get at us. Things do change round, don't they?'

The Great Door was beginning to loosen on its massive hinges; it wouldn't be long now before the door fell open, and Rumbles mustered around the entrance to throw in their lances. The Borribles had no option; they would have to fight back to back until they fell.

The strategy was simple: Stonks, Knocker and Chalotte took up a position facing the door; Adolf, Sydney and Orococco would man the barricade, while Vulge kept them supplied with weapons – lances or bricks. They swore not to be taken alive, to endure the ignominy of capture, to be beaten, tortured and worked to death as slaves, their ears clipped.

At length, when the door could stand no more attacks, Stonks quickly slid the bolts and undid the lock. The next blow from the battering ram encountered no resistance and the door toppled to the ground and six Rumbles and a tree trunk fell through the opening. Three Borribles sprang upon them with lances and dispatched them before they could rise. So far so good, but looking beyond the doorway they saw a sight to shrink the heart of the bravest Borrible.

Dawn, grey and bleak, had spread across the dark green wetness of Rumbledom. The trees were black and leafless and their branches stirred roughly in the gusts of a damp wind. Rain fell heavily and swirled in the stormy air like shreds of cloud come down to earth, but it was not the weather that caught Knocker's eye as he looked out. As far as he could see, across the foul morning, stood rank upon serried rank of Rumbles, the steel of their lances reflecting the cold light. They stood there, compact and unmoving, their fur plastered to their bodies by the rain, their snouts raised to a warlike angle. They neither shouted nor shook their weapons. They waited patiently for the Borribles to emerge and meet their end.

The Rumble troops were formed into sections, and as the battering ram detail was conquered, another section detached itself from the mass of the army and moved forward to attack the Great Door. Beyond them every Rumble was ready to advance, determined to win this battle, however pluckily the Borribles fought and however long it might take.

Knocker swallowed hard, the biggest lump he'd ever swallowed. 'Swipe me,' he said to Stonks. 'Rumbles for ever, and all armed.'

'Tonight's goodnight, all right,' replied Stonks. 'They've brought all their aunts and uncles this time.'

The first Rumble section was within range now and it threw its missiles and retired. A second section ran forward immediately and threw their stickers. Knocker, Stonks and Chalotte pressed their bodies up against the side of the door and waited until the lances fell, then ran out and cast two spears each at the departing warriors. Many of the enemy perished, but the Rumbles could ignore these reverses, the next platoon was already speeding forward, their lances poised. With their advantage in numbers, the Rumbles could fight in this fashion for days, if need be. Eventually the spears would take their toll and the defenders would be wounded and weakened. Then would the Rumbles sweep over them.

The Borribles retreated and took cover. Behind him Knocker could hear Adolf and Orococco and Sydney fighting for their lives; he saw the injured Vulge hobbling backwards and forwards between the two groups, gathering as many lances as he could. On and on the battle raged, and more and more exhausted the Borribles became and still the Rumbles attacked. Before long all the defenders had been wounded at least superficially and Stonks had received a lance thrust full in his thigh. He could no longer run in and out of the door, but threw his spears from the shelter of the hallway.

'Oh, for some stones,' he kept muttering. 'Oh, for a pile of stones as big as a house. I'd have my catapult twanging away like a banjo.'

The Rumbles were nearer now. Their warriors did not even bother to charge section by section but stood their ground, throwing lances until they were wounded. Then another Rumble would step forward to take his fallen comrade's place. They fought with a silent hatred, and they did not lack courage. Knocker's arm was weary; he knew at last that he could not lift another spear, let alone throw it with any force.

'Knives out, lads,' he said, and he and Stonks and Chalotte retreated into the hallway and found themselves back to back with Adolf, Sydney and Orococco. Beyond them Knocker saw hundreds of Rumbles, pushed along the corridor from behind by their bloodthirsty mates.

Vulge wedged himself into a little corner and wiped the long blade of his knife across his sleeve. 'I like close work,' he said, and winced as the pain surged through his shoulder.

Then the Rumbles were all among them and there was a dreadful scrimmage in the hallway, but the attackers were not used to the kind of frenzied resistance put up by the desperate Borribles, and under the cut and thrust of the knives they fell back momentarily.

'Oh, ho,' yelled Adolf at the top of his voice. 'This is cold steel and too close for comfort, eh? Adolf Wolfgang Amadeus Winston will account for at least a hundred of you. Come on! Come on!' And he shouted and hooted and the others shouted and hooted with him, although their muscles ached and their eyelids smarted and the blood ran down their arms and legs from a thousand cuts.

But the Rumbles did not come again. Outside, where there had been a calm dedication, was now all panic and shouts for help. Simultaneously, from the corridors came a surging waft of heavy air, followed by the muffled crump of a great explosion deep in the bunker. A sheet of flame licked out of the tunnel, killing all that stood in its way. It touched but did not burn the battle-weary Borribles, but the blast of a solid wave of gas raised them from their feet and tossed them violently to the floor. The Rumbles in the bunker had been silenced, and the smell of singed fur and flesh floated over everything.

Stonks recovered first, and getting to his hands and knees, he crawled to the door. The Rumbles were still outside but a mighty swathe had been cut right through their ranks and the thing that had cut that swathe was a horse and cart. Sam was charging right through the massed Rumbles, and their fear of horses, their loathing of being munched up like a succulent truss of hay, had overcome their hatred of the Borribles and they had fallen back in panic.

'It's Sam,' shouted Stonks to the others. 'It's good old Sam.'

Who knows what goes through the mind of a horse when he is left alone and is not working? Sam had spent the night dozing between the shafts of his cart and, when he had woken in the morning, he had missed the company and affection of the Borribles who had befriended him. There had not been a great deal of love in his life, none at all with Dewdrop, and he did not want to lose his new friends. He had munched a little grass but had found it dull and boring after the delicate flavour of the Rumble he had eaten, so he had pulled his cart to the edge of the copse and there he had gazed wistfully over the dank fields and sniffed. He hadn't smelt Borrible or even adult human but he had smelt Rumble. Sam had been tempted and had set off – he couldn't resist it. The smell had been so strong that he had imagined a whole meadow full of Rumbles and his imagination had been right. He saw the Rumbles, thousands of them, and with a snort and a stamp he had charged; the cart behind him had felt as nothing and the Rumbles melted away on his right and left. Then he heard a voice he recognized calling his name, calling it with thankfulness and love. Then more voices called out, and looking before him he saw his friends, penned into some kind of a hole set in the hillside, and all that lay between him and those friends were a few hundred Rumbles, so he charged again.

Knocker and the others crawled and dragged themselves to the edge of the Great Door and they saw a great clear road leading to the horizon. Sam came galloping down the slope and swung the cart round so it skidded to a halt alongside the doorway in a cloud of rain-spray.

'Oh,' cried Sydney, tears of relief standing in her eyes. She ran to the horse and kissed him. 'Good old Sam, you've saved us, all of us. Oh, Sam.'

As quickly as they could the Borribles clambered into the cart. Vulge was pushed from below and pulled from above because his wounds had stiffened so much that he could not climb the cartwheels unaided. Everyone was eager to get Sam on the move and escape to the streets; everyone that was except Knocker who, with unbelievable single-mindedness, returned through the Great Door to retrieve the Rumble treasure box.

It was a foolhardy move. Smoke poured from the opening and the huge door jambs were wilting and twisting under the effect of an immense heat. Once inside, Knocker found that the hallway was an inferno of flaming and falling timber; charred bricks expanded and exploded from the walls like cannon shot. The bunker ceiling drooped more every second as the whole Rumble edifice began to collapse, but Knocker heeded none of that and ran on, risking his life to get at the money.

Adolf and Orococco, against their better judgement, followed, not for the treasure but to help Knocker if they could for, in spite of his faults, they loved the chief lookout and were willing to risk their lives to save him.

Knocker came to the box all right but found it almost buried in fiery rafters and white-hot bricks. When he had kicked the box clear of debris, he discovered that it was incandescent, defiantly red and pulsating with a dangerous light. Every part of the box would scorch the skin of whoever tried to carry it, but Knocker didn't hesitate and hauled the dreadful burden to his shoulders. The handle seared deep into the flesh of his palms and the brass-bound corners of the box smouldered through his clothing and down into his back. He staggered and slipped, but Adolf bore him up and shoved him on towards the doorway that Knocker could not see in his pain.

Orococco yelled, 'Over here, Knocker, damn you!' Then, 'Watch out, Adolf!'

The warning came too late. A dying Rumble had risen to his knees unnoticed, and with a sticker in his grasp he fell against Adolf and brought him down. The German scrambled to his feet immediately, though the spear had snapped off in his right thigh. '*Verdammt*,' he cried in agony, and he pulled the broken shaft from his leg, kicked the Rumble in the head and killed him once and for all.

Orococco hurled Knocker from his path and ran towards the German who, blinded by the billowing smoke, was limping away into the heart of the fire.

'Adolf,' he shouted, his heart breaking, 'this way.'

It was then that the ceiling of the hallway collapsed. With a roar like an avalanche the great red-hot timbers fell, bringing with them a lethal barrage of blazing stone. A molten wall reared up between Orococco and Adolf and the brave Totter was forced out of the smoking Rumble hall, his clothes aflame, his hair burning like a torch. Adolf was gone; lost in the heart of a volcano.

Once outside Orococco threw himself down and rolled over and over. Sydney jumped to the ground and beat him about the head to extinguish the flames that might have killed him. She helped him to his feet and he saw that Knocker, with the strength of a madman, was pushing the box up and into the cart while Chalotte leant over him, bashing at his smoking shoulders with the flat of her hand. An angry shout went up from the Rumbles. They had seen the treasure chest, and a shower of lances came over, some wounding the horse and making him lurch in the traces. Sydney and Orococco ran forward and, catching hold of the pain-crazed Knocker, they propelled him angrily aboard. Then Stonks stretched out a hand and helped them as they climbed up the spokes of a wheel.

'Where's Adolf?' screamed Chalotte. 'Where's Adolf?'

'He's had it,' said Orococco, his face tight with anguish. 'The roof came down. I couldn't get to him. There's nothing we can do; we'll have to go. Nothing could live in there, nothing.'

'You mean Adolf's been killed all because of a bloody box?' said Stonks. 'What the hell's in it, anyway?'

Knocker jumped to his feet. 'It's the Rumble treasure,' he shouted, his eyes sunk in greed. 'It's money.'

The others looked at him in horror and they knew then that Knocker had been on a secret mission all along; that Spiff had sent him to steal this treasure and take it home, and that for Knocker nothing else mattered.

'It's evil, that box,' cried Chalotte. 'It has killed Adolf and will kill more of us. It's bad luck; throw it out.'

'Yes,' said Orococco, 'that's enough. The Rumbles might let us go easier if they see us leave the money. We've done what we came to do. Let's get it off while we still have a chance.'

'No,' roared Knocker, his hand falling to the bloody knife at his belt. He looked wild, his hat was gone and his hair swung over his eyes. 'You've all won your names, but I will get a second one if I can take this treasure back to Battersea. It's going with me, I tell you, and I'll kill anyone who tries to stop me.' And to put an end to the argument he picked up a stone from the bottom of the cart and threw it hard at Sam's hindquarters and, with no need for guidance, the brave horse bore the Adventurers away from the shattered remains of the Great Door.

The Rumbles had been terrified by the precipitate arrival of Sam and his cart and had retreated in panic, but when they saw the treasure carried from the bunker they were roused to action and advanced en masse to prevent, even now, the escape of the Borribles.

They were wary of approaching the horse from the front, but they did not scruple to run at the cart from an angle and throw their lances with all the strength they could muster. The bravest of them ran alongside and tried desperately to climb on board, and some threw lances at Sam, hoping to wound him, to injure a leg or a hoof. But things had changed in favour of the Borribles. Inside the cart were the hundreds of stones they had loaded earlier, and this godsend was as important as the arrival of Sam himself. Now the Borribles took out their catapults to fire broadsides of sharp projectiles with telling effect, and the Rumbles, though attacking constantly, were forced to retreat to a respectful distance.

Nothing could stop Sam. He pulled the cart along by the side of the hill that covered the bunker. The ground pitched and rolled beneath his hooves, as explosions and fires continued to devastate the Rumble stronghold. A hundred plumes of yellow smoke were hanging foul against the sky, misshapen and forlorn, like the clouds of burning dust above a hundred London crematoria. The heart of the Rumbledom empire had been consumed by a mysterious detonation and it would be many years before it could be repaired and rebuilt.

Sam headed into the dense mass of warriors and they brandished their spears in fury. One slip from the horse under the salvos of those flying lances and the escape would be over.

'Keep going, Sam,' prayed Knocker, 'as fast as you can.'

But Sam veered suddenly, so violently as almost to tip the Borribles overboard.

'Hey, what's going on?' shouted Stonks.

'I don't know,' cried Knocker. 'It's Sam—' He broke off and stood up in the driver's seat. 'Look, look,' he yelled, 'over there.'

Over there was back towards the hill they had just left with such difficulty and danger, and Sam, for good reasons of his own, had decided to charge in that direction.

'Now, we're really in the cart,' said Orococco.

Seeing Sam turn, the Rumbles also looked across to the bunker and, when they did, gave a mighty shout and ran to intercept the Borribles. Here perhaps was a chance of victory. On the edge of the steep slope, in the centre of an embattled gateway, at the very core of the explosions, three figures had appeared, silhouetted against high flames that leapt and danced behind them. Unless they were rescued within a minute or two, Torreycanyon, Bingo and Napoleon would be forced to retreat into the fire, or die on the spears of the enraged Rumbles.

Knocker urged Sam to a gallop 'Oh, come on, Sam,' he pleaded. 'Oh, Sam, run, run, run, or we'll be too late. No more to die, not now, not now!'

The horse galloped on and the Borribles crowded to the front of the lurching cart, firing forwards and sideways to keep their enemies beyond lance range of the horse. Sam neighed as loudly as he could and the

Rumbles fell back in dismay under his second onslaught, robbed yet again of the Borrible blood they had hoped to spill. When Sam skidded and slid to a halt before the burning garage only Torreycanyon was able to get into the cart without help. Bingo and Napoleon, weakened by the wounds they had sustained in the library, and their insides demolished by the near-suffocation of their trip along the ventilation shaft, had to be manhandled aboard. They fell into senseless heaps over the unconscious form of Vulge, and they knew nothing more until several hours later.

Knocker wheeled the fearless horse about once more to face the enemy troops, but courage was deserting the Rumbles. They knew now that their High Command had gone and there was no real cohesion in their ranks. Their principal bunker had been completely ruined and was in flames about their ears. The workshops, the armoured car, the laboratories, the library, the kitchens, the dormitories – the whole structure had been dismantled and their best warriors killed, slain in single combat or vanquished by stealth and cunning.

They had tried everything and they had fought well, but they had perished beneath wheels and hooves or they had been struck down by the unerring aim of the Borrible catapults. Demoralized, they fell back, and though they kept pace with the cart they kept well out of range and their numbers thinned as Sam cantered to the very confines of Rumbledom, and to the main road that bounded it.

Sam halted. It was rush hour on a cold, wintry morning. The cars and buses zipped along the wet road, sending up a fine spray, hastening into the centre of the city. Not one adult could be seen walking anywhere; it was too early, the weather too inclement. The Battle of Rumbledom, fought mainly underground, seemed to have passed unnoticed.

The Borribles gathered at the back of the cart and held on to the tailboard; even Knocker left his seat and came to look. There in the falling mist and swirling rain stood several hundred Rumbles, leaning despondently on their spears. They could come no further; in the streets they would be recognized and caught. The Borribles had eluded them, sorely wounded it was true, but still they had escaped. Now the Rumbles would have to return to their shattered bunker and salvage what they could.

The Borribles did not cheer, did not wave their catapults aloft, they simply watched as the Rumbles turned slowly and melted away between gorse bushes and trees, or went down into the hollows or up over the hillsides, until there was nothing to be seen but the blue-grey rain blurring the outlines of the black and green of Rumbledom. There might never have been a Rumble on the face of the earth and sadness filled the hearts of the victorious Adventurers.

'Oh,' sighed Chalotte, blinking, 'I wish there'd been some other way.'

'Maybe there was, maybe there wasn't,' said Torreycanyon. 'One thing is sure, once we got in there, we had to fight like the clappers to get out. They ain't soft.'

The moment of reflection was ended by Sam, who saw a gap in the traffic and set off across Parkside and passed into Queensmere. The Borribles were heading into the broad calm of the residential area where Dewdrop had taken them stealing. They were safe from Rumbles now, but if the bodies of Dewdrop and his son had been found, the police would be looking for them and, of course, Sam.

10

Knocker sat on the driving seat of the cart wrapped in Dewdrop's mackintosh. To the adult eye he looked a little small to be in charge of a horse but there was hardly anyone to be seen anywhere, and what further aided the Borribles was that it was raining heavily, and those few people who were moving in the streets ran by with their heads down, intent only on their own thoughts.

As for the other Adventurers they had strung the canvas over the back of the cart like a tent, and in its shelter they were bandaging each other's wounds and eating what was left of their provisions. They needed rest badly and it was comforting for them to lie down and ease the pain in their limbs, allowing a friend to tend to their cuts and bruises. Each of them took a turn at delivering first aid and eventually Knocker left his seat to be replaced by Stonks, and he lay back while Chalotte bound the gashes in his arms and legs, and rubbed ointment into the burns on his shoulders and hands.

'These are bad wounds,' she said. 'You are a fool. You worried about the money when you could have escaped, and worse, Adolf is dead because of it.'

Knocker did not answer. It was warm and dry under the canvas, and the steady sound of the horse's hooves and the drumming of the rain on the canvas was lulling him to sleep. Napoleon, Bingo and Vulge had been cleaned up and fed but had hardly opened their eyes during the process and were once again in a deep slumber. Sydney was keeping watch over the tailboard but she too was tired, and Knocker could see her head nodding forward as if it were going to fall off at any moment.

Torreycanyon was the only one who had any energy left. 'I'm as fresh as a Rumbledom daisy,' he kept saying, and insisted on recounting his adventures to Orococco, who simply closed his eyes and began to snore.

'Well, Torrey,' said Sydney, 'if you're so daisy-fresh, you come and keep watch for me. I can't keep awake.'

Knocker waited. When it was silent inside the cart he turned his attention to the Rumble treasure chest and touched it with an injured hand. It was sooty and still warm. Quietly, taking care not to awaken anyone, he shoved the box behind him and disguised its appearance with a piece of old canvas and some discarded clothing. Then he leant back against it so that no one could move it without his knowing.

He tried to keep awake, to guard the treasure and to relive the events of the past hours, but his head fell forward and Sam the horse plodded calmly along the edge of the traffic, across Augustus Road and over by Southfields Underground station, down Replingham Road and past the opening to Engadine where they had been attacked and forced into the clutches of Dewdrop and Erbie.

And all the Borribles slept, even Torreycanyon who should have been on watch, and even Stonks who should have been guiding Sam, but Sam paced on without need of command. He had heard talk of the Wandle and of King George's Park so that was where he went. He stepped out evenly, realizing the Borribles were exhausted, halting gently by traffic lights and paying particular attention when changing lanes and navigating roundabouts.

He trudged on and Stonks snored in the driving seat and the others dreamt behind, at the mercy of chance. But luck stayed with the Adventurers, the rain continued to fall in heavy drops and no adult had time to observe the horse and cart or think them out of place as they went slowly along the streets, bearing the Borribles away from Rumbledom and towards the dubious safety of Wendle territory.

*

It was dusk when they awoke. Sam stood in a deserted side street by King George's Park, sleeping between the shafts, all energy drained from him.

When the Borribles came to move their limbs they found it almost impossible. Stiffness and fatigue seemed to have fixed them in one position for ever. Stonks had fallen sideways on to the driver's seat and lay curled up in Dewdrop's raincoat. It was Torreycanyon who was the first to stick his head out into the evening air.

It had stopped raining and the street lamps shimmered gold on the wet roadway and made it dark, shiny and deep. Torreycanyon looked at his watch. Five o'clock. He glanced at the name of the road and ducked under the canvas to check it on his street map in the light of his torch.

'Longstaff,' he said. 'Good old Sam, we're right near to King George's.'

The others sat up one by one, groaning as they realized how battered their bodies were. They huddled together for warmth and made a cold meal before continuing their journey. As they ate they argued among themselves about which route they should take for the return trip to Battersea. The easiest way was by boat through Wendle country to the Thames, the way they had come, but some of the Adventurers had their doubts.

'I think we should go overland,' said Chalotte, 'not by boat.'

'What do you mean?' Napoleon looked up sharply.

'I didn't mean anything personal to you, Nap,' Chalotte answered. 'It's just that Flinthead gives me the creeps.'

'Any other way must be safer,' said Knocker. 'Must be.'

Napoleon laughed. 'It's too late, friends, you should have kept awake. Sam has brought us right to King George's.'

There was an uneasy silence under the canvas.

'Don't let's go bonkers,' said Sydney at length. 'The Wendles are Borribles, after all; they'll be pleased our expedition was a success.'

'Anyway, we are in too bad a shape to go by any but the shortest and easiest way,' said Napoleon. 'Just think, you'll be home in two or three days.'

'Remains to be seen,' said Knocker.

Napoleon laughed again. 'You're being ridiculous,' he said.

It was decided after a little more discussion that all they could do was to walk on as far as the banks of the Wandle and camp there. Napoleon would make contact with a lookout, and ask for the Adventurers to be taken back to *The Silver Belle Flower*. After that everything would depend on the Wendles.

When they were ready, they clambered down the cartwheels to the gleaming pavement and struggled into the straps of their haversacks. They were a sorry sight, limping and shuffling as they got into marching order, with improvised bandages round their heads and limbs. Vulge and Stonks had made themselves crutches from Rumble-sticks and could manage to get along only with help from the others. All of them moved badly and every step they took was torture.

Knocker, in spite of his serious wounds and the feelings of his companions, went to the rear of the cart and threw aside the coverings that hid the treasure box from view. He dragged it towards him and hoisted it on to his injured back, and though he stumbled and nearly fell under the weight, nothing in the world would have induced him to leave it behind.

'You are a fool, Knocker,' said Chalotte. 'How can you take that box after what has happened?'

'You would if it was your name, wouldn't you?' retorted Knocker, guilt making his temper short.

'Well, I don't like it,' said Torreycanyon, 'but I know Adolf would have understood about your second name.' And he took one of the handles and helped Knocker lower the box from his shoulder so that they could carry it between them.

'So!' cried Napoleon Boot, shoving forward, pushing his comrades aside. 'So that's what it's all about. That's what you've been after all along, you two-timer. You'd never have got it out of Rumbledom without us. Spiff and you had it planned all along, didn't you? Well, it's ours as well, you know . . . it's gotta be shared out.'

'It's not Borrible,' said Sydney. 'Throw it away.'

'That's not very bright, now we've got it this far,' butted in Torreycanyon. 'Look at the way those Rumbles lived. They had everything up there. You didn't see that workshop of theirs, wonderful it was . . . I'd like one, back in Hoxton.'

'Well, whatever happens, we can't share it out here,' said Knocker, turning towards Napoleon and thrusting his face up against the Wendle's. 'Spiff wants to share it equally between the tribes who sent members on the expedition. Each one of you will take a share back with him when he goes.'

'Ha! Do you expect me to believe that load of old cobblers?' asked

Napoleon, his face green in the light of the street lamp. 'You may trust Spiff, but I wouldn't give him the bogeys out of my left nostril.'

There was a dreadful silence under that lamp post, and some hearts sickened to think they had been so far and had done so much together and could now quarrel over a box of money. Stonks said as much and he was backed up by Chalotte and Sydney, Bingo, Vulge and Orococco.

'Sod the money,' shouted Stonks. 'Here we are, dying on our feet, and you two argue. Let's get into the park before that damn treasure kills us all. We need a good night's kip. We can talk about the money tomorrow.'

His voice woke Sam, who tottered on his four feet. He neighed and turned his head. Sydney ran to him and the others followed, the money forgotten for the moment. They shone their torches over the horse and saw that his hide was caked with blood and covered with scratches and stab wounds.

'Here you are yammering on about money,' cried Sydney angrily, pointing her finger at Napoleon and Knocker, 'and the horse that saved us all is neglected by the lot of you.'

They freed Sam from the traces, patted him and expressed their sorrow at having ignored him for so long. Then they led him towards the park, and as Sam stepped out they noticed that he was limping badly because of an injury in one of his back legs.

'Look at that,' shouted Sydney at them all, as if they'd each and severally been responsible for the damage. 'Wounded like he is and brought us all the way down here. You ought to be ashamed of yourselves. Sam ought to be retired on that money.'

The gates to the park had been closed at dusk but Napoleon soon picked the lock and the Borribles, Sam first, went into King George's. The park was black and silent and the grass wet, but they had brought the cart canvas with them, and when they reached the banks of the Wandle they spread the tarpaulin on the ground and sat on it to keep dry. Soon the sky cleared of clouds, the stars appeared and the night turned cold, but the Adventurers wrapped themselves in their combat jackets and sleeping bags, and sat round in a circle, except for Sydney who stood by Sam, stroking and speaking to him.

Then began the story telling, the moment that Borribles love above all others. They wanted to know who had done what and how, and in what order, and to whom. Bingo wanted to know what had happened to Vulge; Vulge wanted to hear Torreycanyon's tale, and Torreycanyon wanted to know how Chalotte and Sydney had fared. Napoleon told his story to Orococco and Orococco recounted his Adventure to Knocker, and Knocker's voice trembled as he recounted, almost as a penance, how Adolf had opened the safe.

And there were tears in the Adventurers' eyes and lumps in their throats as they remembered the German and his mad, jolly voice and the way he had hooted at them. No one said anything to Knocker directly but there were looks and silences during the story of the safe, and Knocker looked at the ground between his feet.

But the stories went on and past quarrels began to be forgotten because the Borribles looked at each other and realized how lucky they were to be alive. Never had Borribles had such an adventure.

They were still talking when Napoleon suddenly stood up. 'There's a Wendle scouting us from the other side of the river,' he said. 'Switch off your torches.' He went silently to the railings that bordered the river and whistled softly – a slight variation on the normal Borrible whistle – and he was answered within two seconds. Then the others heard him talking.

'I'm going across,' he announced when he returned. 'Got to see Flinthead. You're to wait here; better get some sleep. You're quite safe, there's Wendle night patrols all around. I'll be back before dawn. Be ready to leave, and don't try to go anywhere. You know they, we, don't like strangers on our territory.' Then without a word of goodbye he turned his back and disappeared into the night.

'He's a funny bloke,' said Bingo. 'You never know where you are with him; nice and friendly one minute, saving your life and fighting with you, and then all of a sudden he's as cold as yesterday's cabbage.'

'I think,' said Knocker, looking at the treasure chest, 'that he's just remembering he's a Wendle after all.'

*

Napoleon came back as promised just before dawn. The others rolled over in their sleeping bags and, without getting up, looked at him. The tall shapes of the buildings on the far side of the Wandle were dark against the sky. Napoleon was just a darker shape. They couldn't see his eyes or his expression; only his voice told them that he was tense and tired.

'We're to stay here until it is nearly light,' he began, 'then I am to lead you across the Wandle, along the bank and then underground. We can rest, as we did before, for as long as we like, Flinthead said. Later they'll take us to where they've hidden the boat. After that we can go – you can go – as long as we tell our stories, all of them.'

'What,' said Knocker, asking the question that was in everybody's mind, 'about the treasure?'

Napoleon hesitated. 'Flinthead didn't mention it, nor did I.' He went over to his sleeping bag, unrolled it and slipped inside.

There was quiet. Knocker got up and went and sat by Napoleon. After a while he touched the Wendle gently on the shoulder. He could see Napoleon's eyes now; they were open and staring at the sky.

'So Flinthead said nothing about the money,' he said.

Napoleon blinked and said, 'That's right. I didn't tell him about it, did I?' He tried to roll over on his shoulder but Knocker stopped him.

Bingo came over and joined them. Since the Battersea Borrible had saved Napoleon's life and escaped with him from the library he had got closer to the Wendle than any of the others, and he wanted to get between Knocker and Napoleon if trouble started. Knocker spoke again, and everyone listened. 'I don't believe you. I think we ought to go home some other way.'

The silence deepened a notch or two. Napoleon sat up brusquely and grasped Knocker's arm.

'I've told you – you've got no bloody option,' he said between his teeth. 'You're stuck, all of you. There's Wendles all round. There's only one way out, and that's down the Wandle, the way we came.'

Knocker was not put off. The others waited for the outcome, holding their breath.

'When you say we're stuck,' he said to Napoleon, 'does that include you in or out?'

Napoleon did not answer. A great struggle was going on in his mind and he could not speak while it continued. Lights came on in the building opposite and the sky was grey now. Soon they would have to make a move, one way or the other.

'Tell us what really happened,' insisted Knocker. 'Come on, straight up.'

'You owe us the truth,' said Bingo.

Napoleon got up and stepped over to the railings and looked at the surface of the Wandle as it floated by under its quilt of rubbish. Bingo thought for a second that the Wendle was going to run away.

At last Napoleon turned and spoke to them all, in a low voice so he wouldn't be overheard beyond the group. His words came all in a rush.

'I am telling the truth. I know you do not trust Flinthead, Halfabar or Tron, or even me,' he began. 'I know you do not like the Wendles, even though they are Borribles like yourselves, but remember the threat we have always lived under. I swear that Flinthead will ask only to hear your stories, will see that you get rest and food. He will take nothing from you; he is proud of us. After all, he's out of danger from the Rumbles for years to come. He told me how . . . how grateful he was . . . really.'

There was silence and the others watched as Bingo walked over to the box and said, 'Wish we'd never set eyes on the thing. Been a good adventure apart from that.'

Knocker spat. 'My job is to take the box back and I'll do it even if I die.'

'Even if we all die,' said Chalotte.

'The trick,' said Torreycanyon, 'is to get it back without dying.'

'They won't take it from us,' insisted Napoleon. 'They will wait to get their share. I'll be coming back to Battersea with you so that I can bring the Wendle share back to Wandsworth.'

'We shouldn't touch it at all,' said Chalotte. 'It's money, and money isn't Borrible.'

'Yes,' agreed Vulge. 'Chalotte's right, but any road they won't attack us. It would be Borrible against Borrible.'

'It's happened before,' said Orococco. 'Money brings trouble.'

Napoleon raised his head. The blood had gone from his face and there were mauve patches under his eyes. He shook his head sadly at his companions. 'If they wanted to take it, they would have taken it already . . . but you won't listen. They don't want it. Everything will be all right.'

'Come on,' said Chalotte. 'Have we journeyed so far and survived so much that we are now going to jump at our own shadows?'

No one answered the question and Knocker shook his head, quoting a dark proverb, '"The shadow cast by a Wendle is twice as long as his body."' He stared hard at Napoleon and tried to read the truth in the Wendle's eyes, but Napoleon's eyes wandered and looked elsewhere.

'We shall have to move soon,' he said. 'I can hear the early buses in the streets and it is nearly daylight.'

Within a few minutes the Adventurers were ready to set out once more, and they filed past Sam to give him a last stroke and a word of farewell. The uncertainty that stretched before and the sadness that lay behind had made them despondent. There was something else too: they hated themselves for deserting the horse who had helped them through so many dangers, who had risked his own life, time and time again, to save theirs. Sydney was distraught, weeping with grief, and was the last to squeeze through the gap in the railings that led to the river. She had lingered to gather a handful of fresh grass for Sam; she wanted to wish him farewell alone.

'Goodbye, old Sam,' she said. 'I'll never forget you, never. We can't take you any further because of the river, because we have to go underground, but I tell you, Sam, if I ever get out of this adventure alive I'll find out where you are and I'll come back for you, however far it is . . . and that's a promise. And I'll steal you away one night and you'll come back to Neasden with me and you won't work again, Sam, ever.' And Sydney put her arms around the horse's neck and kissed the side of his face.

When she had gone Sam ambled over to the railings and stuck his head over them to watch the tiny figures of his friends marching along the towpath, towards the dark semicircular hole where the Wandle disappeared under the streets of Wandsworth; and Sam shed bitter tears.

*

Napoleon led the way but his step was not springy or light. He looked unhappy, not at all like a Borrible returning home covered in glory. Knocker and Torreycanyon followed along with the treasure chest, and the others came behind, all of them still weary despite their night's rest.

The silence along the towpath was uncanny and the adventurers saw not a soul, at least to begin with. It was only when they glanced over their shoulders that they saw how the path had become crowded with heavily armed warriors who had materialized from the very bankside. Across the river they could see more Wendles rising mysteriously from the mud to stand watching as the Borribles marched by.

Bingo, who felt that his companions were allowing themselves to be overawed by the Wendles, raised his voice in song, and that London voice, bright and defiant, rang out over the river:

'Hurrah! Hurrah! The Battle's won!
The victors are marching from Rumbledom!
We smashed the evil furry crew,
We finished the job we went to do.
Let our great deeds and high renown
Spread to the ends of London Town.
Brave though bloody, here we come!
The victors returning from Rumbledom!

'Rejoice! The foe is overcome!
The victors are marching from Rumbledom!
We trounced the enemy through and through,
We finished the job we went to do.
Nothing can frighten us again,
We fear no monsters, fear no men.
Brave though bloody, here we come!
The victors returning from Rumbledom!'

With Bingo's example before them, the Adventurers determined to show the Wendles that they were not downcast, and each of them sang loudly of his London borough: songs that told of fine abandoned houses and good days of thieving and food.

Knocker laughed at the songs. He felt happier now they had committed themselves to a course of action. There was no going back, so they might as well make the best of it.

All too soon the Adventurers came up with Halfabar at the mouth of the sewer where the Wandle went underground. He smiled and inclined his head; the light of winter gleamed on his helmet.

'Welcome, brother Borribles,' he said. 'Napoleon has told us a little of your great adventure. Your names were well won. Flinthead is impatient to hear your stories from your own lips. A great feast awaits you.'

'There,' said Napoleon to Knocker. 'What did I tell you?'

They followed Halfabar and his men underground, and found their way by the light of torches as they had done on their previous visit. Again the Adventurers smelt the smell of the River Wandle, penned and confined in its narrow tunnels, and the stench of it rose and stung their nostrils. Even Napoleon wrinkled his nose in disgust, so many months had he spent in the fresh air.

After walking a few hundred yards they left the river and Halfabar led them directly to the great hall. There, as before, sat Flinthead, his eyes opaque. The hall was not crowded this time; only the bodyguard stood by, heavily armed and numerous, their faces unsmiling beneath their helmets. In a line before Flinthead's stage were nine armchairs, and in front of them was a long table loaded with all kinds of food from the Wendles' store.

The Adventurers filed across the hall, members of the bodyguard at their side. They were directed to the armchairs and their knapsacks taken and stacked behind them. Torreycanyon and Knocker dropped the burnt and valuable box in front of their seats, and when, on a gesture from Flinthead, they sat, they each put a foot on the Rumble treasure. Flinthead saw the movement and smiled indulgently. When all was quiet he spoke, and his voice was the same as ever: kind, warm and solicitous.

'Welcome back,' he said, and smiled again. 'Your adventure has been successful and we are proud, and not a little envious of it, though we grieve at your loss. If you are not too weary, I would like to hear of your exploits, in detail, for all we Borribles love a story of the winning of a name, and I think that there have never been names won like yours. Napoleon Boot has told me something, but I wish to hear it all from your own lips. There is food before you. Tell me your stories one by one, the rest may eat until it is their turn to tell.' He pointed a finger at the end of the line away from Knocker. 'You,' he ordered, 'begin.'

So, Stonks it was, began. He told how he and Torreycanyon took the Great Door, how he defended it and how later he took the Rumble skin, and what a fright it caused. The others ate, or aided the story with comments, correcting and enlarging the thread of the tale as it went along. Then it was the turn of Vulge, and Flinthead leant forward in his chair with great interest as he heard how the chief Rumble had met his end. Sydney and Chalotte told of the assault on the kitchens and the subsequent retreat; then came Orococco, followed by Bingo, who told how he met Napoleon in the great library and how he had fought in single combat with the greatest warrior in Rumbledom. Napoleon took up the story and told how he had shaken his namesake from the ladder and how Bingo had saved his life, and how, sorely wounded, they had squirmed and crawled their way to safety, to find Torreycanyon, who then must tell of his lonely fight in the garage and how he caused the great explosion which had put paid to the whole bunker.

After that, Flinthead asked of Adolf and what he had done, so Knocker related how the German and he had found Vulge, surrounded by the bodies of his enemies, and how the safe had been opened and the box discovered. And the Wendle bodyguard leant on their spears and everyone relaxed, except Knocker; and Torreycanyon whispered that everyone seemed friendly and happy and that things would turn out fine in the end. But Knocker scowled and whispered back that things that happened could only be judged after they had happened, and then not always correctly.

But Flinthead turned his bland face to Knocker again and said, 'And now you must speak further and tell us your own story – one full of colour, I am sure, and one for which I have been waiting with great interest – for are you not the writer, the Historian, and will you not have seen and known things that the others did not know?'

Knocker looked along the line of his companions. They were sprawling in the comfortable armchairs, their faces flushed with food and drink. They were too relaxed, too easeful, unable to defend themselves if the need arose. Knocker himself sat nervously on the edge of his seat, his feet tucked under him, ready to leap at the slightest hint of danger.

'My part was, in fact, small,' he heard himself saying. 'Adolf and I followed the others and discovered Vulge only after he had fought his great battle alone. Later it was a question of retreating slowly, grouping together and fighting our way along the tunnels to the Great Door where Adolf was killed, but if it hadn't been for Sam, the horse, none of us would be sitting here now.' And Knocker went on to praise the horse and tell of their imprisonment by Dewdrop and his son, how they had escaped and taken Sam with them.

Flinthead cupped his chin in his right hand and rested the elbow on his knee. He swayed forward, listening with an attention that did not waver for a second. He was fixing every detail of the story in his mind. When the tale was finished he leant back in his chair, clasped his hands in his lap and beamed a cold smile at everybody, a brittle smile that was simply a movement of facial muscle with no breath of warmth in it.

'I hope, Knocker,' he said, 'that you will write down this adventure as soon as you have time. There are so few good stories left. I look forward to reading it.' He paused and looked round the hall at the bodyguard, then looked at Knocker and flicked his finger against his thumb, just once. There was a clash of armour and members of the bodyguard moved behind the Adventurers to hold them fast, deep in the soft armchairs, knives at their throats. Held all that is save Knocker; he had been ready, perched on the edge of his chair. He jumped forward, butted a warrior in the stomach and snatched his lance.

But there was another Adventurer who had not been made captive, Napoleon Boot. He too sprang from his armchair as if expecting trouble but he did not need to seize a lance; one was thrust into his hands and he was joined by a band of Wendles who rushed from the side of Flinthead's stage.

Knocker crouched, his spear held low. He was convulsed with a bitter wrath. To come so far, to do so much, and then to lose everything through the treachery of a fellow Adventurer.

Napoleon stood opposite him, haughty, confident, 'Drop that spear, Knocker, you have no chance. If you resist we will kill you.'

'You thing of no name!' screamed Knocker at the top of his voice. 'Traitor! May you be un-named and cursed and your story for ever told with a curse.' Knocker drew back his arm and cast the spear at the Wendle with all the strength at his command, for he hated Napoleon with every fibre of his being. But Napoleon was ready; he knew that Knocker would throw the lance. He stooped and it struck a Wendle behind him with such force that the lance pierced the warrior's breast, and the blade stood out a handsbreadth behind his back.

The Wendle shrieked and fell lifeless to the floor, but his fellows leapt upon Knocker and bore him to the ground. He was cuffed and beaten, his hands were tied and at last he was hoisted to his feet. Blood trickled down his face and a bruise rose, purple, on his forehead.

'You'd better kill me, you no-name-bastard-Wendle,' he said, hissing the words, 'for if I live, I'll kill you. I'll train a race of Borribles who will seek you out and put you through a mincer.'

Napoleon ignored him and gave a sign. The other Adventurers were hauled to their feet and their hands bound fast. Flinthead rose from his chair and came to the edge of the stage.

'Well, there we are, nice and tidy.' Again he clicked his fingers and the treasure chest was prised open to reveal banknotes and coin. 'Hmm,' said Flinthead. 'Superb! Napoleon, you have done well. You shall be promoted to the bodyguard, co-captain with Tron, and choose yourself a second name while you are at it. I want you to see that your . . . friends are safely locked up. As for the box, that must be guarded day and night by members of the bodyguard, but you will be responsible for it . . . with your life, of course. Take as many Wendles as you need.'

Flinthead looked down at the captives and smiled his smile of death once more, but they did not see his face. They stood staring at the ground, their shame too great to bear, tears of anger in their eyes. Only Knocker held his head up and shouted after the Wendle chieftain as he left, 'Guard yourself well, Flinthead. I'll ram that money down your throat before I'm finished. I'll skin you alive, you and your bodyguard of un-named, slow-witted, snot-gobblin' morons.'

But Flinthead just waved a bored hand, and went from the hall surrounded, as always, by the pick of his men.

When Flinthead had gone, Halfabar stepped up to Napoleon and gave him a warrior's helmet and a special jacket. Napoleon put them on, tugged the lance from the corpse on the floor and rapped the bloody tip of it against Knocker's chest. 'You shuddup, sonny,' he said. 'You're a nobody and nobody wants to hear you.'

By way of reply Knocker spat directly into Napoleon's face and the saliva trickled down his nose. Angered, Napoleon twirled the lance expertly in one hand and caught Knocker a stinging blow across the head. Knocker fell to his knees.

Although bound and outnumbered by the bodyguard, Knocker's

companions stepped forward and stood fearlessly between Napoleon and his victim.

'Leave him alone,' said Stonks, in an untroubled voice. 'Leave him alone, you skinny fart, or I'll kill you.'

'Yes,' said Sydney. 'Aren't you satisfied with your day's work yet, Wendle?'

Napoleon's face clouded over for an instant, then he shook himself and said to Halfabar, 'Right, let's get them out of here.'

The Adventurers were taken only a short way into the corridors before Napoleon halted them and opened a heavy iron door. With blows raining on their heads they were forced to enter a small damp dungeon, where green slime dripped and oozed from the walls. It was lit by one weak electric bulb and there were no seats or beds, only some dirty and mildewed sacks piled in one corner.

Once they were in the cell, Halfabar entered and, protected by others of the bodyguard, he cut the bonds from the Borribles' hands.

'Ain't that cosy,' he said when he'd finished. And leering into Orococco's face he added, 'Safe and sound, the lot of you.'

Orococco bared his teeth at the Wendle, making him jump backwards.

'*I'm* going to hold you under the water next time, friend, but I will not let up until you have stopped breathing that stinking breath of yours. Couldn't you sprinkle a little deodorant on your cornflakes and make a few friends?'

Halfabar raised his hand to strike Orococco, but he remembered in time that the Totter now had his hands free and so contented himself with a sneer, backing to the door and slamming it, the noise echoing up and down the tunnels, and still echoing long after the last Wendle footsteps had faded into the distance.

The Borribles stood disconsolate in their prison. They could not even look at one another and a mixture of shame, rage and hatred, despair and disbelief, held them tongue-tied. Speech was impossible. A quarter of an hour went by, then half an hour, and the silence became hard and solid.

Finally Knocker broke into a stream of swearing that lasted for minutes on end. He thought of every Borrible curse he could remember and enlarged and embroidered on it. He went backwards and forwards through the *Borrible Book of Proverbs*, and turned each adage into a malediction on the head of Napoleon Boot. He wove garlands of evil words around that Wendle's name, and when he had finished and was breathless and his memory and mind were empty, he felt better, and so did those who had listened to him and had joined in his song of hate with imprecations of their own.

'I still can't believe it,' said Chalotte. 'What made him do it?'

'Once a Wendle always a Wendle,' said Knocker, and that was enough explanation for him and he said no more.

'I don't think we ought to be too downhearted,' said Stonks in his flat, straightforward manner. 'After all, we got there and back again and did what we said we'd do.'

'I'm not blaming anyone, 'cept maybe Spiff,' said Chalotte, 'but if it hadn't been for that money, we'd have been on our way home by now.'

'Well, as the proverb says,' said Vulge, '"It ain't fault, it's happenstance." After all, we're still alive.'

Orococco laughed harshly. 'Not for long, we ain't.' And again the adventurers lapsed into a long and moody silence.

*

The prisoners were kept incommunicado, and though food was brought to them it was the meanest of cold scraps, flung through a barely opened door. They became weak through lack of sustenance and more and more depressed as the days went by. Escape was impossible. Even if they managed to open the heavy iron door of their dungeon, they were certain to become lost in the tangle of culverts and corridors that was Wendle country. On their heels would be warriors from the toughest of all the London tribes, hard and dedicated Wendles who knew every inch of their territory, every fathom of the river and every yard of underground sewer within a radius of miles. The idea of freedom receded further and further from the captives' minds, and their hatred of Napoleon Boot dulled to a slow burning ache.

*

One day, or night, some weeks later, the door to the cell opened quietly and, after a moment's pause, clicked shut. The Borribles did not look up; it would only be some inedible Wendle meal delivered in a dirty bucket. But when Vulge rolled over in his blanket, which was green with damp mould like all the others, he saw to his surprise the slight figure of Napoleon Boot.

Napoleon looked splendid. His helmet of tin was burnished and his orange jacket gleamed in the light of the electric bulb. His waders were new and shone blackly and they fitted tightly to his calves and thighs. He had two steel catapults in his belt and a double bandolier of the choicest stones. He looked proud and well fed, though his face had once more taken on the green tinge that touched the complexion of all Wendles.

Napoleon raised a finger to his lips. The Stepney Borrible couldn't believe his eyes.

'What's going on?' he asked.

'We're getting out,' said Napoleon, his voice tense.

Hearing this conversation the others looked up and rolled out of their damp couches.

'Be dead quiet,' said Napoleon, whispering, 'or you'll be quite dead.'

The captives rose to their feet, gazing at each other with puzzlement.

'Is this some new trick?' asked Sydney. She had liked Napoleon since the day he had stolen the boat in Battersea Park, and she had taken his deception very hard.

'I haven't got time to explain now,' said Napoleon. 'You'll have to trust me.'

Knocker laughed quietly. 'Trust the honest Wendle and end up in prison?'

'We could kill him,' said Torreycanyon.

Napoleon's face creased with anguish. 'There isn't much time, don't be stupid.'

'What are you going to do this time?' said Knocker. 'Let us loose in the tunnels so the bodyguard can kill us? Hunt us down one by one and shove us under the Wandle mud when they catch us? I've heard that's one of your favourite sports.'

'Oh, listen,' said Napoleon quickly, 'and listen well, because every minute we waste is precious. Flinthead knew about the Rumble treasure even before the expedition started. He sent me on the Adventure in the first place to keep an eye on you all.'

'I could see that,' said Knocker with a sneer. 'That much was obvious.'

'On the way back,' continued Napoleon, 'my job was to lead you into the Wandle and see that you suspected nothing, so that Flinthead could capture you and the money.'

'You did that all right, didn't you?' said Bingo. 'You fooled me completely, but then I only fought side by side with you in the library. I thought we were mates.'

'Oh, shuddup,' said Napoleon. 'When we got back to King George's, I didn't know what to do. I was in a state. There was you lot on the one hand, my tribe on the other. I fretted about it all the time. Anyway, we couldn't have got away at that stage, Flinthead had patrols everywhere. He doesn't mess about, you know. So there was only one thing I could do: go ahead with Flinthead's plan. It wasn't easy being hated by all of you . . . and now, if I help you escape, I shall be hated by everyone in my own tribe. I'd like to see you lot in the same position. What would you make of it?'

'If all this is true,' asked Torreycanyon, 'why has it taken you so long to make up your mind?'

'I've been waiting for the right opportunity,' said Napoleon. 'It won't be easy getting out of here, and today's a good day.'

'What's so special about today?' asked Chalotte.

'There was a big stealing expedition yesterday,' said Napoleon, speaking more easily. 'Most of us were out in the streets, hard at it. Now they're sleeping. There's to be a big celebration soon, and as Knocker said, it's likely that you will be released into the tunnels one by one for the bodyguard to hunt down – Flinthead's favourite sport. I . . . I . . . would be one of the hunters. I couldn't stand that . . . so . . . well, there you are.'

'Well,' said Orococco, 'I don't care whether he's telling the truth or a lie. I'm for getting out of here. Anything's better than staying in this hole, even a scrap with the bodyguard and a muddy grave in the Wandle.'

'Would Flinthead really do that, just for a box of money?' asked Chalotte.

'Strange things have happened to these Wandsworth Borribles,' said Stonks. 'We don't know what they'd do.'

'You've got to believe me,' pleaded Napoleon. 'This is your only chance to get out. You know what they'll do to me if they catch me alive?'

They looked at him without speaking.

'They'll stake me out on the mudflats, just below high-water mark, and let me drown a little each day, until one day the water and muck will come a little higher, and the eels will eat the flesh from my bones . . . piecemeal. You know, in the end I am being more loyal to the Adventure than anyone.'

The eight captives looked at each other and pondered, until at length Bingo sniffed, stepped forward and threw his arms round Napoleon and hugged him tight. One by one the others did the same, even Knocker, who came last, saying, 'Well, whatever was in your mind when you betrayed us to Flinthead, let us hope that now you have come to a final decision. Tell us what to do, Napoleon. I for one am longing to see the sky again and walk through a market.'

The moment Knocker finished speaking Napoleon explained his plan. There were normally two sentries outside the door but he had sent them off to a guardroom, where they were resting. They would have to be dealt with first. In the guardroom would be found Wendle clothes and waders, arms and ammunition. The Adventurers would steal what they needed and, as soon as they were disguised and armed, he would take them to *The Silver Belle Flower*. If they ran into Wendle warriors they would have to fight. Even if they got the boat under way, they still wouldn't be safe, but they would have a good chance. Once they emerged on to the River Thames they would be out of immediate danger, though still a long journey from Battersea Reach.

The Borribles agreed to the plan and gathered by the door; Napoleon unlocked it and looked into the tunnel. After a moment he stepped out and motioned the others to follow, and in single file they crept towards the guardroom.

In no time at all they overpowered the two off-duty sentries and they were soon dressed as fierce Wendle bodyguards, wearing black rubber waders and orange jackets. They armed themselves with steel catapults and double bandoliers; there were Rumble-sticks in the room too and each Borrible took one.

'All we have to do now,' said Napoleon, 'is march along in an orderly fashion, and all being well we'll march straight on to the boat and no one will give us a second glance. It will just seem as if I am taking a fresh guard to one of the outlets.'

Knocker jammed his tin-can helmet on to his head and said, 'I want the treasure,' just like that, calm, toneless.

Napoleon looked at him in amazement. 'Don't be mad,' he protested. 'It's kept right next to Flinthead's apartments. There's a squad of the bodyguard sitting on it all the time, day and night.'

'That's right,' said Knocker, 'and you're the keeper of the box, and you're in charge of the bodyguard. I'm sure you can order them to stand aside for five minutes.'

'Straight up,' said Stonks. 'I never cared about the money from the word go – in fact I hate it – but I don't like being shoved into prison, half starved, and then used like some stuffed hare at a greyhound track to be chased about in tunnels by a lot of tin-helmeted twits. It's the principle of the thing.'

'I agree, man,' said Orococco. 'If we leave the money behind, old Flintbonce will be sitting pretty and laughing away all over his flat face. We gotta put one over on him.'

'Yes,' said Sydney, 'he ought to be shown that Borribles should treat Borribles fair and square, if nothing else.'

'It's so dangerous,' said Napoleon.

Knocker said, 'Anyone against the idea?'

'Nobody takes my catapult away and tells me to piss off,' said Bingo. 'Nobody.'

'Me neither,' said Torreycanyon.

Vulge said, 'Let's just say this one's for Adolf.'

It was this last remark that brooked no argument, only Chalotte had something to add. She shrugged her shoulders and her smile was wan. 'I think you're all mad,' she said, 'but how can I stay behind now?'

Napoleon sighed, shook his head, and gave in.

The Adventurers formed up in pairs and tramped out of the guardroom and through the long sloping tunnels. They hummed the Wendle marching song as they went, and any non-warriors they met hastily squeezed out of their way, or stepped into a side tunnel to let them pass.

'This is the way to escape,' said Bingo to Knocker, who marched beside him and behind Napoleon, 'with verve and bravado. I shall compose a song about this when I get back to Battersea.'

They marched for a long while, Napoleon leading them with confidence this way and that in a maze of criss-crossing corridors. Not once were they questioned, not once were they given more than a brief uninterested glance. The power of the warrior class had been built up over a long period by Flinthead and now it was working against him. Warrior spoke only to warrior; ordinary Wendles kept their distance.

Eventually the tunnels became more spacious and were gracefully arched and dry underfoot. This was the Victorian part of the sewers and no longer used except by Wendles. It was warm and comfortable, that was why Flinthead had established his quarters here, and the room where the treasure box was held was getting nearer at every step. So in a deserted part of the tunnel Napoleon halted his company to explain what he had in mind.

'It is nearly time for the guard to be changed,' he said, looking at his watch. 'You will pretend to be the new guard. You will march in, follow my orders exactly, and then I will march off with the old guard. I'll get back as soon as I can, on some pretext. We'll only have a few minutes before the real guard turns up, looking for me. They will discover the chest gone and will raise the alarm. We'll have to run like a train to get to the boat. If anyone tries to interfere, hit him hard and run on. Remember these ain't Rumbles you'll be fighting, but Wendles, and the best of them.'

The Adventurers formed up again and marched another fifty yards, and then wheeled smartly into a spacious guardroom, very comfortably furnished. At the far end of the room was an iron door, rather like the one that had held them in prison, but this door was larger and heavier and studded with huge rivets.

Napoleon yelled his orders: 'Guard, halt!' The Eight brought their rubber-heeled waders together as one man. 'Oh, yes, very smart,' said Napoleon, his face giving nothing away, and he went over to the door that led to the strongroom.

He rapped on the door with the butt of his lance: a special knock. A flap in the iron door swung open immediately and a helmeted Wendle's face could be seen through the opening.

'I've brought the relief guard,' said Napoleon, and before the other could ask the question forming in his mind, Napoleon added, 'I know I'm early but I'm on special business for Flinthead.'

The Wendle guard nodded, closed the flap and the door swung open. He marched his men out and formed them up in a line opposite the new arrivals. He handed the keys to Napoleon and observed, 'You're one man short.'

'Yes,' said Napoleon casually, 'he'll be along in a minute. He wasn't ready in time. I couldn't wait.'

The sergeant of the guard stood to attention at the head of his men and waited for orders, but first Napoleon led his command into the strongroom and gave Knocker the keys. 'Lock the door immediately, Wendle,' he said in his sternest voice. 'Let no one through but me.' Without another look at the Adventurers he did an about-turn and marched off with the sergeant and his eight men.

As soon as Napoleon had gone, Knocker closed and locked the door and leant against it, the sweat trickling in his armpits.

The strongroom was small and the box stood on a table in the centre of it. Round the walls were armchairs for the guards and a couple of tables with food and drink. Wendle warriors wanted for nothing.

'Help yourselves to some grub,' said Knocker. 'It may be a while before we eat again.'

The Adventurers needed no second bidding to fill their stomachs, but all too quickly came the special knock at the door and Knocker opened the flap. His heart missed a beat; he saw not Napoleon but Halfabar. Luckily he was alone and did not recognize Knocker under the Wendle helmet.

'Yes,' said Knocker.

'You mean, "Yes, sir",' said Halfabar.

'Yes, sir,' said Knocker.

'Open up,' sneered Halfabar. 'I saw you marching up here and I want to know why there's only eight of you instead of the normal nine. That cocky little Napoleon has slipped up on the job this time. Promoted over my head, he was. I'll screw him for that.'

During this conversation Orococco had flattened himself against the wall and now he nodded to Knocker, who unlocked the door, opened it and stepped back respectfully to allow the Wendle to enter. As Halfabar came across the threshold Orococco seized him by the throat and shoved him tight against the wall.

'My friend Adolf ain't here,' he said between his teeth, 'but I know he'd want me to look after you before we leave.'

He shifted his grip and grabbed the Wendle by his scruff and seat, holding him like a limp bolster. 'Remember, Halfabar,' hissed Orococco, 'you cannot live by bread alone.' And he threw the Wendle into the room like a sack of spuds. 'Leave him to me,' he cried, his black face intoxicated with pleasure and his eyes rolling as they hadn't done since the Battle of Rumbledom. But Halfabar did not rise. Orococco had thrown him into the room with such gusto that the Wendle had broken his head against the box of money. His tin helmet had split open like a rotten orange. It was wedged over his face and his ginger hair sprouted through the crest like rusty springs from a ruined sofa. Blood dripped from the box to the floor.

'There,' said Orococco, breathing deeply. 'Did you hear his brains rattle like dried lentils when I shook him?'

Five minutes later Napoleon arrived and Knocker let him into the room. When he saw Halfabar's body he swore.

'It's all right,' explained Knocker. 'He was alone and we made no noise. He didn't have time to cry out; Orococco got him.'

Napoleon nodded. 'It's time to go,' he said. 'Most of the warriors are still sleeping. It's about one o'clock in the morning in the streets, but they'll be waking soon for work. There's patrols coming and going too. It's all a question of luck now. As soon as they see that box they will know what we're up to.'

The Adventurers left the strongroom at a trot, Stonks and Torrey-canyon carrying the money. They followed Napoleon at a sustained and speedy run down a wide brick tunnel that led to the River Wandle, the boat and safety. They ran and they ran, making little noise on the rubber soles of their stolen waders. They brushed past one or two ordinary Wendles but moved so quickly that the box was not seen and no alarm raised. Indeed, they were halfway to the river before they ran into trouble. Rounding a bend at full tilt they came upon a small night patrol of warriors returning from the outside world.

'Stay where you are,' shouted Napoleon. So used were the warriors to obeying, they stopped at once and for a minute did nothing. That minute was enough and the Adventurers sprang upon them and brought them down. But the noise of the scuffle attracted the attention of another patrol in one of the side tunnels and they saw in a flash what was happening, and worse, they saw the box.

They fired their catapults and hit Stonks in the kidneys and Orococco in the arm, paralysing both Borribles for a few moments. The Adventurers returned the fire and the Wendles ran off, but the clamour they raised made the very walls shake.

'That's it, now,' shouted Napoleon. 'They'll be on us in less time that it takes to nick a spud. Run for your lives.'

Knocker and Bingo took up the box and the convoy raced on. The smell of the Wandle got stronger and the floor of the tunnel sloped more and more steeply.

'We're getting there,' panted Napoleon. 'Come on.'

The clash of weapons came from behind and all around them in the hundreds of side tunnels. Wendles slept all over the vast sewer complex and could be out of bed and dressed for an emergency faster than a crew of London firemen.

'If we don't get to the river first,' said Napoleon, 'we'll be up to our necks in mud before the night's out.'

They redoubled their efforts, and though their lungs were bursting, they ran faster. Now Chalotte and Orococco took the box, not even breaking their stride as they snatched up the burden.

At last, with a cry of relief, they burst out on to the underground bank of the river, as dark green as ever, the tenacious mud bubbling just below the surface of the water. The towpath was wide at this point and there rode their boat, *The Silver Belle Flower*, tied to a post. Napoleon drew his knife and slashed the painter.

'In with the box. Stonks, round to the front, you've got to pull real fast till the river's wide and deep enough to row; then we've got to go like Oxford and Cambridge gone bonkers.'

He glanced up the tunnel. The noise of pursuit was getting nearer; any minute now they would be overtaken. Napoleon took Knocker by the arm.

'Knocker,' he whispered urgently, not wasting a word, 'see that tunnel over there? It goes straight to the Thames but the Wandle meanders. If we all get in the boat the Wendles will run straight down that tunnel and be at the outlet before us; we'll have no chance. Two of us have got to stay here and stop them getting into that tunnel, give the others ten minutes', quarter of an hour's grace, then they'll get away. Otherwise they won't. You and me?'

Knocker glanced at the tunnel from which the pursuers would issue. 'Not you,' he said. 'You are the Navigator, you know the Wandle and you know the Thames. I will stay.'

'Not alone,' Torreycanyon said, and pushed in between them. 'Knocker is right; you must go. Two of us will be enough. Straight down that tunnel, you say? When we have dealt with the Wendles, we will catch up with you.'

'But take care,' said Napoleon. 'There's a guardroom halfway along. I'd better stay, all the same, three is better than two.'

'Then I will do it,' said Orococco, who had leapt back out of the boat, worried by the delay. 'Just make sure that Tooting's share of the money gets to Tooting.'

Napoleon took off his bandoliers and gave them to Knocker. The others, when they realized what was happening, each removed one of their bandoliers and threw it to the bank, their faces sad, staring at the three comrades who had elected to remain behind for their sakes.

'Oh, go on, Stonks, go on,' shouted Knocker, and the boat jolted away and Napoleon leapt aboard as it left the shore. Knocker watched the boat spurt out of sight round the first bend, pulled steadily by the never-tiring Stonks. There had been no time for farewells and no time for pity.

'We'll never see them again,' said Knocker.

'Well, we still got each other,' said Orococco, and he picked up the bandoliers.

'Let us go out with a fight,' cried Torreycanyon excitedly.

'Yes,' said Knocker, 'whatever happens we've won and Flinthead, with his pointed skull and his petrified grin, will not laugh like we will laugh after this battle.'

'Then we'd better get into the mouth of the short cut,' said Orococco. 'We can't possibly hold them here, out in the open.'

The Totter's tactics were simple and obvious: the three friends crossed the Wandle, up to their waists in the slime of the river, and adopted defensive positions. As they took cover an advance party of Wendles came careering out of the main corridor, and a shower of well directed, high-velocity stones rattled round the Borribles' hiding place.

'Man,' said Orococco, 'I'll go white with the shock.'

'This is no time . . .' began Knocker, and then he and the others smiled instead, and they knelt in the gloom and laid their bandoliers and lances beside them.

Within a few seconds the open area by the landing stage had become crowded with Wendle warriors, and Tron appeared in the midst of them, his face flushed with anger.

He instantly ordered a large detachment of his men to follow the course of the Wandle in pursuit of *The Silver Belle Flower*. Into the branch tunnels he dispatched smaller patrols to make sure that the fugitives were not lurking there, but the main body of his troops he directed towards the short cut so that he could block the mouth of the Wandle with a considerable force before the boat could ever get there.

'They can't get away,' he shouted. 'We'll have them yet, suffocating in Wandle mud.'

'Let us hold our fire till they get halfway across the river,' whispered Knocker, 'and we'll soon see who is in the mud first.'

Already the Wendles, ardent and fanatical fighters, had plunged into the filthy water. Tron himself was carried shoulder high by two of his personal guard. The three adventurers loaded their catapults in the darkness and waited until Knocker hissed his command: 'All right, now!'

Three well aimed stones struck their targets and three Wendles disappeared under the mud. The adventurers fired again and again, and the rate of their fire was phenomenal, but the Wendles came on in spite of their losses, for they did not lack bravery.

'Aim for Tron,' cried Orococco, 'or his guards.'

Knocker shifted his aim to one of Tron's porters, and his stone struck the bodyguard solidly on his helmet. He staggered, lost his footing on the river bottom and Tron was pitched face foremost into the Wandle.

'Swallow that!' said Knocker with relish.

This small victory gave the three defenders a breathing space, but Tron was not the Wendle to allow his enemy to relax for long. He was pulled to the bank by his followers and the mud wiped from him. He shouted more orders and wave after wave of warriors leapt into the river. Although the Adventurers fired till their arms were aching, they could not stop the Wendles crossing in force and spreading out to right and left of their tunnel.

When satisfied with his bridgehead, Tron ordered his men to attack. Fortunately only three warriors at a time could enter the short cut and deadly work was done with knife and lance in the gloom, as Torreycanyon, Knocker and Orococco fought side by side for their lives and the lives of their companions.

Suddenly Tron's voice was heard calling on his soldiers to cease fighting for a moment, and the attackers fell back. The three Borribles leant against the wall at the tunnel entrance, exhausted and nearly done for.

'How long has it been now?' asked Knocker. 'My watch is smashed.'

'Quarter of an hour,' said Orococco triumphantly. 'We've done it.'

Tron called again. 'You Borribles in there, you might as well come out, you're surrounded. The boat has been captured, we've got the treasure. You are fighting for nothing, I tell you. Save your lives while you can.'

'Don't believe him,' said Knocker. 'It must be a trick; our mates've got clean away.'

'Keep them talking, anyway,' said Orococco. 'It's not so dangerous as fighting.'

'Show us the treasure chest,' shouted Knocker, 'then we might believe you, Tron.'

Tron laughed. 'Your friends will be here soon, in chains, then you will see the box. Surrender, cause no more trouble, and we might be lenient with you. You have fought well, that is enough.'

'We would rather fight here than go back to your dungeons,' shouted Knocker.

'There'll be no dungeons for you, Knocker,' called Tron, his voice hardening.

'I can believe that all right,' said Orococco.

At that moment a runner bounded up and spoke to Tron. The crowd of warriors fell back and the three Adventurers saw Flinthead himself arrive, surrounded by his guard. His face was pitiless and he was dressed for war.

Flinthead took in the situation at a glance. He spoke quietly and his guards looked at the roof of the cavern where they stood, then they ran forward and climbed one upon the shoulders of another until the last man reached the ceiling and disappeared. A rope ladder was thrown down to the ground and half a hundred warriors scrambled up it and went out of sight.

'What does that mean?' asked Knocker.

'It means trouble,' said a voice behind him, and the Adventurers spun round, weapons at the ready.

There stood Napoleon Boot, covered in mud and gashed in the head, his helmet gone and his jacket torn.

'What happened?' cried Knocker.

'It's all right,' said Napoleon, breathing heavily. 'They got away, I saw to it. They'll be out on the Thames by now, I shouldn't wonder.'

He sank to the floor and his leant back against the wall.

'How did you get back here, man?' asked Orococco, kneeling beside the Wendle and inspecting his head wound. 'My, that sure is a beauty!'

'When the boat was safely away,' explained Napoleon, 'I made for the short cut. The guard had been alerted but they didn't know I was part of the getaway. As we were talking, some warriors appeared along the Wandle and shouted to the guard to hold me. I had to fight my way out. They can't be far behind, not a lot of them but enough.'

'What's Flinthead playing at?' asked Knocker.

'He's sending warriors up to the surface. They'll come down through a manhole behind us. When he's got us surrounded, he'll come and talk to us, or just starve us out. He can wait. He can't know yet that the boat is clean away.'

'Well, it's nice to hear such things,' said Orococco, 'but why risk your life to come back to tell us?'

Napoleon hesitated and then went on. 'I haven't told you all the story, yet. There is bad news. Halfway down to the mouth of the Wandle we were jumped by a large night patrol coming back from outside. They saw the box, guessed something was up and didn't wait to ask questions. Stonks went under the water with five of them on him, but he came back up again, alone. There was about twenty of them around the boat. They dragged the box out and we dragged it back in. We fought like double our number. Honest, Knocker, we fought like tigers.'

'Oh no! They got the box,' cried Knocker.

'No, they didn't,' said Napoleon, emphatically. 'I'd have died, rather . . . after everything.'

'Then you got it away?'

'Not that, either. We were fighting across the mudflats, they had it halfway to the shore, we came back at them, we did for every last one of them, and when we looked for the box, to get it back into the boat, there it was, sinking in the mud. We couldn't even get hold of a handle, it went down so quick. You know what that mud is like, like a live thing with the grip of a python. The mud is deep there, deeper than anywhere else along the Wandle. The old stories say it goes down to the centre of the earth.'

There was a long silence. Then Napoleon spoke again. 'I had to come back to tell you. I wanted you to know before anything happened that I'd done my best. The money's gone for ever, and even Flinthead can't get it where it's gone. But the others got away, Knocker, don't forget that. We done the Rumbles, and our Adventure was surely the best ever. That's what counts, isn't it?'

Knocker knelt by the wounded and mud-splattered Wendle and took his hand gently in his own. 'You are right, sod the money! What does that matter against friendship? We have done great things and it has been a great adventure. They will sing songs about us, all of us. For ever.'

'Flinthead's going to sing one to us right now,' said Orococco, who had been watching the enemy. 'Here he comes, to tell us no doubt what lovely treats he has in store.'

'He'll go raving lunatic when he finds out about the money,' said Napoleon, and the four of them inched over to the tunnel opening, knowing, but not saying, that they were doomed to an early and unpleasant death.

11

'We'll have to go. We'll be picked up by the Woollies if we wait any longer.' Bingo spoke reluctantly.

The others twisted in their seats and looked over the bows of *The Silver Belle Flower* to the distant bank. The far side of the River Thames was clearly visible and the silhouettes of the factories and gasometers stood sharp against the morning sky. From time to time the rowers clipped the water with the blades of their oars so as to stay on station opposite the Wandle. Boats and barges were passing by in increasing numbers and at any moment a police launch might appear, checking that all was well on Wandsworth Reach. The city was awake; from high above, on the Wandsworth Bridge roadway, came the unbroken hum of traffic on its way to work.

The survivors shifted their attention and gazed dejectedly at the wasteland that spread out on either side of the Wandle's mouth. Their eyes sought for some sign of their companions, but they saw no movement. Even the Wendle patrols had returned underground, shaking their fists at the five Borribles who sat offshore waiting and hoping, their hearts heavy with a great sorrow.

'They didn't stand a chance of getting away,' sighed Vulge, 'but I bet they gave a good scrap at the end.'

'I hope Napoleon got back,' said Bingo. 'I hope they were all together when . . .' His voice trailed off and there were tears in his eyes. 'Come on, we must go. There's no point in us getting caught as well.'

Sydney, Chalotte, Stonks and Bingo leant forward to row. Vulge sat in the stern and navigated, searching for a group of two or three barges where they could hide through the daylight hours. The tide, strong as a waterfall, bore them through the cathedral arches of Wandsworth Bridge and Vulge saw what he was looking for almost immediately. He directed *The Silver Belle Flower* into a tiny haven of motionless water and, hardly bothering to scrape the caked slime from their clothing, the Borribles huddled together in the bottom of the boat in an attempt to keep a spark of warmth glowing among them.

It was deep winter; they had neither food nor blankets and the damp river wind gnawed at their bodies. All day they tried to sleep but the pangs of hunger and the hateful cold kept them restless, and their wounds throbbed without respite.

Night rescued them. They watched the sun go down – blurred crimson on black smoke – and they took up their oars once more and warmed themselves by rowing. Though they were but four to power the strokes, the swift current of the Thames carried them homewards, and though they were clumsy and stupid with fatigue they brought *The Silver Belle Flower* safely downriver. Just before dawn the next day the boat slid between the high-masted sailing barges – *The Ethel Ada* and *The Raven* – and ended its journey on the solid wedge of floating rubbish that had been marooned from the main stream for so long. They were in Battersea at last – spent, bedraggled, filthy.

'Battersea,' said Bingo. 'I can hardly believe it, oh Battersea.'

They helped each other over the high embankment wall and stood in the quiet churchyard looking up at the green steeple. 'It's a good feeling,' said Vulge, 'being back where you belong, with a good adventure behind you and friends to remember.'

'It must be one of the best feelings there is,' agreed Chalotte.

They went from the churchyard and out into Church Road. There was not much traffic about and not many people, which was just as the Borribles wanted for they could not have passed as ordinary children. They had lost their helmets in their many fights and their pointed ears were plainly visible. They were covered in the dried mud of the Wandle swamps and most strange-looking of all were the Wendle waders and the orange road jackets they wore.

'We'd better get off the street,' said Bingo, 'before we're spotted.'

Opposite the Old Swan pub, near the church, were a couple of Borrible houses, derelict and falling apart, their window spaces boarded up with rough planks and corrugated iron. 'They'll lend us some clothes and hats,' said Bingo, pointing over the road, 'just to get us as far as Spiff's.'

Now it happened to be true that every London Borrible had heard of the expedition against the Rumbles, but it was also true that every London Borrible had, long before this time, given the Adventurers up for dead. Thus it was that it took Bingo and the others half an hour to convince this Battersea household that they weren't attempting to perpetrate a subterfuge for stealing clothes. However, once they had been convinced, the Church Road Borribles lent the clothes eagerly, and were delighted to be the first to greet the survivors of the Adventure to end all Adventures, and proud to hear the first snippets of their stories.

The Adventurers waited until eight o'clock before returning to the streets. It was safer that way, for with the pavements crowded they could mingle with children on their way to school and remain inconspicuous. Traffic was building up, busy and dangerous, but to the Borribles it was friendly and welcoming. It was home.

They walked on until they came to the fork of Vicarage Crescent and Battersea High Street. They went past Sinjen's School, and they came up to Trott Street and Spiff's house, where Knocker had lived as chief Battersea lookout all that time ago. But before they went in, with one accord they walked on. They needed to see the market, to prove to themselves that they were back where they belonged.

The stallholders were putting out their merchandise, the shops were open and there was a bustle and a friendliness that made each Adventurer feel glad to be alive. The pie and eel shop was preparing for its lunch-time trade and the smell of sauce and liquor was strong. The fish and chip shop was being swabbed out by an Indian who sang as he worked – a strange spicy song – and the second-hand shop looked reassuringly the same: a cross between a pawnshop and a junkyard.

The Battersea costers whistled and shouted at each other across the street. They manhandled their barrows into position or stacked goods on them from the vans parked sideways and awkward across the road. Even when the stallholders bawled at the Borribles and told them to clear off to school, the Borribles only smiled at each other, self-consciously indulging their nostalgia.

'Knocker loved it down here,' said Chalotte, and they turned away from the market at last, bringing with them a few things for their breakfast for they were ravenous. It was time to report to Spiff.

He was waiting for them. Their arrival had been reported and their story was eagerly awaited. Crowds of Borribles were in the house and more crowded in by the minute. The Adventurers had to push their way into the basement and struggle through an excited throng to arrive at Spiff's room. He was there, just the same in his orange dressing gown, with a cup of tea held in front of his sharp face.

He bade the Adventurers sit down and eat the food they had brought with them. He noted the absences from their ranks, but his expression gave little away and he said nothing. Like the rest of the house his room was filled to overflowing, his cronies sitting on the floor or leaning against the walls. Everyone was waiting until Spiff gave the word for the stories to be told. They would listen intently and, that very day, each Borrible present would repeat those stories to those who had not heard them, and they would be told again and again from Borrible to Borrible, and so the Adventurers would become part of a legend.

And new proverbs and sayings would be added to the *Borrible Book of Proverbs*. New ambitions would be born in the hearts of Borribles as yet un-named, and some would yearn to have such an Adventure too. But many would find the Adventure unbelievable – no Borrible could have done such things – the whole expedition was a fiction and a fabrication, that was all. 'Had anyone ever talked to those who had been on the trip?' the sceptics would ask. 'Who's ever spoken to Knocker and Napoleon? Has anyone ever seen Orococco and Vulge? Oh, you heard of people who knew somebody who had met someone who had talked to Chalotte or Sydney or Torreycanyon, but in truth nobody had really met them.'

But in Spiff's room that day were the hearers and the tellers of a great Adventure; and the tellers still had the marks of their Adventure on them. Their scars were still soft and their muscles still ached, the hearers could see this, and they knew the stories were true, and they would tell them as true and they would be believed. Only in the years to come would the stories grow in the telling and lose their firm outline to be transformed into a glorious Borrible saga: the Great Rumble Hunt.

So Spiff waited patiently until the Adventurers had finished their breakfast, then he gave a sign and Bingo started the story at the beginning, from the moment they had rowed away from Battersea churchyard. His companions listened and added to the tale if they thought he had forgotten anything, and sometimes they went on with it themselves and the story was thrown backwards and forwards among them, and it grew and grew. And each one told of his own part in the destruction of the bunker under Rumbledom, and the tale of the great explosion and Adolf's death brought forth deferential whistles from the audience, and they looked at the Adventurers with a measureless respect.

Then, sombrely, the Adventurers told of their imprisonment by the Wendles, and of the great dilemma of Napoleon Boot and how finally his cleverness had saved them. They told of the loss of the four friends who had stayed behind so that their companions might survive to thwart Flinthead's greed and escape with the chest of Rumble treasure and how, after all, they had been lucky to escape with their lives alone.

When the great story was ended a heavy silence came over the room and the Adventurers looked at the floor, remembering the five who had not returned. The Borribles in the room were deeply impressed by the Adventure and indicated to Spiff, by signs and nods of the head, that they thought he ought to mark the occasion with a few well-chosen phrases.

Spiff pondered. He took his teapot from the paraffin stove, filled a cup, spooned in some sugar and stirred it well. At last he stood and cleared his throat.

'A great Adventure!' he began. 'The threat of the Rumbles gone; their power destroyed. It will be many a year, if ever, before they come down here again. Today is a day of great rejoicing, and one of sadness, also. Four of you did not return, and one German person, who joined with you for the glory of the Adventure, has also perished. What can we do except try to remember them always, tell their stories and say their names, good names – Torreycanyon, Napoleon Boot, Orococco, Adolf Wolfgang Amadeus Winston – and of course our own chief lookout, Knocker. What second name is there worthy of his adventure?'

Chalotte looked up and interrupted; there were tears in her eyes. 'He went back into the hallway of the Great Door to get the treasure when he should have been escaping, and though it was blazing with flames and the rafters were falling in cascades of sparks, he picked it up and carried it out. I tell you, I tell you all, it was red-hot that box, and the handle burnt into his hand – down to the bone – and he bore the pain. His clothes were alight and I thought he was completely on fire. You should call him Knocker Burnthand. It is a good name.'

There was a murmur of assent from everybody present and many repeated the name to themselves to see how it sounded.

'Burnthand it shall be,' said Spiff, 'and it shall be written in the book.'

He looked at the five survivors in the chairs before him. 'Your names, too, are confirmed. You have more than won them. You left here with empty words for your titles but you return with names that are full of meaning, and every time they are heard now, great and generous deeds will be thought of. Great names they are, which will make every Borrible think of courage and cunning, loyalty and stealth, individualism and affection, every time they hear them.' And Spiff, overacting a little, recited the names like a litany: 'Chalotte, Sydney, Vulge, Stonks and Bingo from Lavender Hill.'

Spiff gave a sign and every member of the audience began to leave the room, quitting the house and running through the busy High Street, back to their own dwellings so they could begin retelling the tale immediately, and soon Spiff's house was quiet. He gulped his dark brown tea and looked at the Adventurers, still slumped in their seats.

'You must all be tired,' he said. 'Why don't you go to the room upstairs and rest? I'll see that there's some grub for you when you wake.'

The five Adventurers rose and left the room. The elation they had felt at arriving home and telling their stories had gone, and in its place was a feeling of melancholia mixed with self-pity. They felt too a yearning love for the companions they had left to perish on the River Wandle, and the immensity of the loss made a black gap in their minds.

They climbed the stairs like old cripples. On the second landing Chalotte, who was leading, turned and stopped the others; her eyes were wet.

'Oh,' she said, only just holding back her sobs, 'it all seems so useless now. We've won our names but lost our friends. Isn't it all so stupid?'

'Shuddup,' said Bingo. 'Don't make things worse.'

They went on upstairs without saying another word.

*

Alone, Spiff topped up his cup of tea and mused over what he had heard and he thought about the loss of Knocker and the others.

'I hate to think of what Flinthead did to 'em when he got his hands on 'em,' he said to himself. 'What a swine he is . . . there's no one more cruel. Good at torture . . . still, they wouldn't have lived long.' He stirred in the sugar. 'Shame about the treasure. I was never worried about the Rumbles, really . . . they probably only came down to Battersea on a little jaunt. It was the money I was after . . . what I could have done with that. I'd have changed things round here. Money . . . your average Borrible don't know the value of the stuff, they don't know what it's about, what power it has. I don't suppose I'll ever see any real money down here. Bloody shame! Ah well, there'll be another time, some time. It ain't over yet.'

BOOK TWO

The Borribles Go for Broke

I

It was the hottest Sunday in the hottest July for a hundred years and Chalotte Borrible crouched in the cool shade beneath a green-grocer's barrow in Petticoat Lane market and munched a stolen apple. It was just about noon and all over London the pub doors were opening, even though the streets were as yet silent and empty. Nearly all the inhabitants of the great metropolis were hiding away from the heat, lying undressed on their beds, turning their eyes into the dark because it was too hot to get up and they were too idle to know what to do.

But in Petticoat Lane it was different. That was the busiest place in the world. Chalotte peered between the wooden wheels of the barrow and watched the feet trudging by, feet which belonged to thousands of Londoners, come from all over the capital on a Sunday morning jaunt, up early so they could push and jostle against each other in sweat and swelter as they struggled to examine the goods on every stall. They shouted and shoved and wrestled and the costermongers shouted too, opening their loose mouths to show stained and broken teeth.

Chalotte loved Petticoat Lane, it was such a marvellous place for a Borrible to live; a place where you could steal enough food on market day to last the rest of the week. She pushed her hand up and, unseen, took another apple. The fruit was warm to her touch as her fingers closed about it; the sweet flesh was warm in her mouth as she began to chew.

She ate the apple, right down to the core and the pips, then she ducked out into the open and stood poised, ready to run, but no one had noticed her. On the opposite pavement a group of men stood outside a green-tiled pub holding large glasses of bitter in their hands.

Their eyes glinted with pleasure as they upended the amber jugs and poured the liquid into their throats. When the ale reached their stomachs they made loud sighs of happiness and looked at each other with surprise, as if beer had only been invented that very morning.

Not far from the apple barrow a man was selling stolen watches out of a suitcase, in a doorway. Just beyond him Chalotte saw a pickpocket take a wallet from a lady's shoulder bag. Above the noise of people talking and walking came the sound of a man breaking crockery, whole dinner sets. It was his way of making the passers-by notice him. Chalotte smiled to herself, stole one last apple and moved on.

As she took her first step a rough hand wound itself into her long fair hair and seized her. A voice shouted into her ear. 'You thieving little bleeder,' it said, 'got you, haven't I?'

Chalotte twisted her head and looked up at the adult who had caught her. What she saw made her heart jump. She'd been captured by a plain-clothes policeman, of that she was certain. She didn't need a uniform to tell her who was a copper and who wasn't. She fought against the hand, cursing herself for carelessness, but its grasp did not slacken. One short moment of inattention and now her whole existence was in danger.

'Ow, leggo, you're hurting me,' she said, allowing the tears to come to her eyes in the hope that this would encourage the officer of the law to let her go. All round the barrow the busy street became blocked as the curious stopped to gloat and goggle; they looked down at the slender girl with her second-hand clothes and her dirty face, and they grinned.

'Go on, kid, run,' said a man, but the others in the crowd only grinned again and waited to see what the policeman would do. But he did nothing and shouts were heard in the side streets, coming from people who could not see what was happening and who were growing impatient at being hindered in their progress.

'Get a move on, can't yer?' said some and the shoving became fiercer.

The policeman took Chalotte to the end of the barrow. 'What's your name?' he asked, and Chalotte, like a true Borrible, had her answer ready.

'Chalotte Jenkins,' she said, 'and my mum's waiting down the end of the street and she'll worry if I'm late . . . I'm sorry about the apple, honest, she'll pay for it. I'm sorry, mister, I was thirsty.' This she said to the costermonger, who wasn't particularly concerned about the theft of an apple anyway.

'Oh, let her go,' he said. 'She can have another one if she likes.'

'Yeah,' said somebody else, 'an apple a day keeps the coppers at bay.'

The policeman hesitated and Chalotte felt his hand relax in her hair; he was going to release her. She sniffed and tried to look as miserable as possible, but then, on a sudden thought, the policeman tightened his grip. He raised his free hand and, with a confident movement, swept back Chalotte's hair so that he and the crowd could see her ears. There was a gasp of surprise from the bystanders; Chalotte's ears were long and pointed – they were ears that showed great intelligence and daring – *Borrible* ears.

The policeman hooted with delight. 'Look at that,' he shouted. 'I've caught one, a Borrible, a real live Borrible,' and from the back pocket of Chalotte's trousers he pulled a catapult. 'And look at that,' he added, his face red and beaming with satisfaction, 'the Borrible weapon.'

'A Borrible,' said those in the front of the crowd, and they passed the word to the people behind them. 'A Borrible.'

'I ain't letting this one go,' shouted the policeman. 'I ain't letting her go! Quick, clear the road, you're causing an obstruction, move along there,' and he thrust the gawping spectators from his path, shouldered himself between two barrows and up on to the pavement.

Chalotte howled. She struggled and flailed her fists at the policeman, but he was too strong for her. He strode onward, clearing all before him, dragging his prisoner by his side.

'Back off, out of the way,' he bawled, 'police, police, stand back, out of my way!'

Chalotte continued to yell at the top of her voice but there was no one to help her. The policeman barged on through the shoppers and strollers, bursting open the groups of men who lounged outside the pubs, making them spill beer over their fingers and down their shirt fronts. And as policeman and prisoner went along the pavements and crossed the alleys of Petticoat Lane the hubbub quietened as they passed and men and women turned to look and laugh. Why shouldn't they?

Not one of them knew how serious the matter was; they did not realize that Chalotte was a Borrible and that for a Borrible to be caught is the very end.

*

Borribles are thin as a rule and their ears are always pointed; apart from that they look like normal children although they may have been Borribles for years and years. They are tough-looking and scruffy but are renowned for their quickness of wit and their speedy running; a life lived on the streets sees to that.

Normal children become Borribles very slowly, without being aware of it. One day they wake up and there it is, the transformation has taken place. It doesn't matter in the slightest where they come from as long as they have had what other people call a bad start. A child disappears from school and the chances are that he's run away to become a Borrible. Sometimes it is said that a child has been put into care. It's more likely that he has been Borribled and is off caring for himself. One day a shout is heard in a supermarket and a child with stolen goods on him is arrested by a store detective. If that child manages to get away he'll join the Borribles and make sure that he isn't caught again, ever.

So Borribles are outcasts and runaways and they value their independence more than anything else because they take a deep delight in being what they are. They avoid adults; they don't like them and make no effort to. In fact the only people to get close to Borribles are ordinary children and that is because Borribles mix with them in order to escape detection by the authorities. Any child may have sat next to a Borrible or even talked to one, never noticing the ears on account of their long hair or the hats they wear, woollen ones, pulled well down.

Their greatest enemies are policemen – the Woollies. Woollies represent the authorities and the authorities cannot abide a Borrible. They don't like the free and easy way the Borribles choose to live. Running away from home, squatting in derelict houses and taking orders from no one is not neat, nor is it tidy.

For a policeman the capture of a Borrible is a rare and great achievement, it is also the end of freedom for the captive. That is why

Chalotte struggled with all her strength. Once that Woollie got her inside the police station it would be curtains.

*

The policeman came to the end of Brick Lane and stopped on the edge of the Whitechapel Road, waiting for the traffic lights to change colour. He maintained his tight hold on Chalotte's hair and she continued to yell in pain. A small group of men, staggering gently from one pub to another, gathered on the corner and stared.

'Stop that bloody row,' said the Woollie, and he crouched so that he could push his big face into Chalotte's; she jerked her head backwards, the policeman's breath was damp and offensive, like mouldy bread. He laughed, spraying the girl with his saliva.

'Struggle all yer like, Borrible,' he said, 'it won't do you no good. I'll get promotion for this, I will.'

'What are you going to do with me?' asked Chalotte.

'Oh,' said the policeman, 'that's easy, got special orders for Borribles, we have. You see, about six months ago there was a rag-and-bone man killed over in Southfields, and his son, slaughtered in their own home, murdered with catapults, and we all know who uses catapults, don't we?' The policeman shoved Chalotte's weapon under her nose and tugged at her hair so fiercely that she wept, her tears making furrows down the dirt of her cheeks. The policeman smiled. 'Three of our men were injured, nearly killed one of them was, and ever since then Borribles have become top priority . . . Make no mistake, me girl, we'll be taking good care of you. You'll be going to see Inspector Sussworth, you will.'

The lights switched from red to green and the policeman stood upright and charged towards the traffic island in the middle of the wide road, pulling Chalotte along so quickly that her feet barely touched the tarmac.

'Who's Inspector Sussworth?' asked Chalotte, and she wiped her tears away with the back of her hand.

The policeman stopped on the island and looked down at her. 'Sussworth,' he said, 'he's a wonderful man, and since those Southfields murders he's formed a group of specially trained officers, all dedicated to the elimination of Borribles. They investigate Borribles, they study Borribles, they know more about Borribles than Borribles know about Borribles. You'll be sent to him, you will, and when he's asked you every question he can think of and made you answer them, why then he'll clip your ears and that'll be another Borrible less for us to worry about, won't it?'

The policeman laughed with profound enjoyment and spying a gap in the stream of cars he pulled Chalotte forward once more, hauling her to the far side of the road.

'You sod,' said Chalotte, 'you sod.' But the bravery of her words belied the fear she felt. She dreaded being sent to this Inspector Sussworth. If he clipped her ears she would revert to being an ordinary child; she would grow up. Left to themselves Borribles do not become adults and their small size is their pride and the source of their freedom. It means that they can always pass themselves off as children and yet they are often as experienced as the oldest person alive.

'Don't you swear at me,' said the policeman, 'you little savage. I've got strict orders; you're going to the SBG and that's it and all about it.'

'The SBG,' said Chalotte, 'what's that?'

'The SBG,' said the policeman, 'that's the Special Borrible Group, Sussworth's outfit, over Fulham way. That's where you'll be going, all in your own van. If you're lucky I'll come with you.' Laughing at his own joke he strode along all the faster with Chalotte trotting by his side, her mind spinning.

What the Woollie did not know was that this small female Borrible, accidentally captured, knew all about the Southfields murders and what she feared most of all was a severe interrogation. She might, under pressure, divulge valuable Borrible secrets; it would be disaster for her, disaster for her friends. She had seen Dewdrop Bunyan and his idiot son done to death, she knew those responsible, but even if she told her captors that the killings had been richly deserved it would make no difference. They would never believe her.

Chalotte and nine other Borribles had been kidnapped and held in slavery for months by this loathsome Borrible-snatcher. They had been beaten and starved and had only got away by luck. It had been her friends Knocker and Adolf the German who had killed Dewdrop and Erbie, slain them with catapults and well aimed marbles, so as to escape from torture and slow death themselves. Now Knocker and Adolf were dead too, killed during the Adventure of the Great Rumble Hunt, and so were Orococco, Torreycanyon and Napoleon; good Borribles gone for good, and soon she would be gone too. Was every Borrible who had been involved in the Great Rumble Hunt doomed to die? It certainly seemed so.

Despair welled up in Chalotte's heart and her mind misted over with it. She stumbled and the Woollie caught her with his rough hand.

'Come on, chummy,' he said, and then Chalotte heard herself shouting, as if from a great way off, shouting for help, knowing that only one of her own kind could save her now.

'A Borrible,' she screamed, 'a Borrible.' And away on the other side of Whitechapel another Borrible heard her; it was Twilight, the black-haired Bangladeshi from Folgate Street, up near Spitalfields.

*

Twilight was thin and fragile but he could run like a train. His clothes were ragged and his hair was cut unevenly, long and thick and so black it looked blue. He had a sharp nose and one eyebrow that was cast higher than the other, making him look curious and sly at the same time. His eyes were big and dark and often full of thought, he was cheerful and determined; he was muggins for no one.

Twilight always roamed the streets with a band of Bangladeshi friends, about half a dozen of them, and they stuck together for protection. He only knew Chalotte by sight but he had heard some of the stories that were told about her and her part in the Adventure against the Rumbles. All that didn't matter now; the sight of a Borrible, any Borrible, being taken away by a Woollie was enough to inflame his blood. He called his friends to him and they ran as fast as they could along Whitechapel, on the opposite side to Chalotte, crossing the road eventually some three hundred yards ahead of her, positioning themselves in ambush between the officer of the law and his police station.

There was no time for elaborate schemes. Twilight knew that if he did not rescue Chalotte immediately she would disappear into the cells and never come out again, at least not as a Borrible. Round a corner, where Stanton Street meets the main road, he and his friends waited. When the policeman was only a step or two away Twilight gave the word and he and his gang charged into Whitechapel at top speed with all the energy they could muster. They ran straight at the Woollie, shouting, jeering and yelling.

'Watch out, Woollie; watch out, Woollie!'

Twilight rammed his hard head into the policeman's soft stomach and there it almost disappeared, like a fist punched into a cushion. His mates followed on like a pack of street dogs run wild; tearing, pushing, and laughing too. Everybody went over, the Borribles letting themselves fall forward, using their speed and weight to topple the big policeman to the ground. They stuck to him, jabbed him, butted him and covered his eyes with their hands, and so this strange gyrating lump of noise rolled along the pavement forcing passers-by to leap into the roadway to escape injury. Hands, legs and heads appeared and disappeared as the lump turned once or twice, then whole bodies disengaged themselves. Chalotte felt herself grabbed under the armpits; there was a Bangladeshi Borrible on each side of her, another ran in front to clear the way. The policeman lay groaning on the ground, sorely winded, his mind utterly drained by the suddenness of the attack. It had only taken ten seconds and Chalotte was free.

Once more her feet hardly touched the ground but now she was borne along by friends and there was hope, not despair, in her heart. Nobody said a word, reserving every ounce of breath for flight. They were just a tight knot of brown Borribles carrying a white one to freedom.

The Woollie lurched to his feet and swung round, his arms stiff and straight, and then, with his boots banging the pavement slabs, he set off after the runaways. But he wasn't in the race; by the time he reached the traffic lights the Borribles had disappeared. They had re-crossed the main road and lost themselves deep in the market, hiding like they always did where the crowd was thickest. The policeman knew full well that he had no chance of finding them now; they could be anywhere, under stalls, in their ruined houses, down side alleys, and they would be watching for him. The word would have gone abroad and every Borrible within a radius of ten miles would be taking cover.

The policeman stood and swore at his failure. He had imagined himself walking proudly into the police station with his captive. He had seen himself telephoning Inspector Sussworth and receiving congratulations and thanks; he might even have been invited to join the SBG, a real plum of promotion for anyone in the Metropolitan Police Force. Ah well! It was not to be. He'd best say nothing about the incident; he didn't want to be laughed at. Sadly he turned and retraced his steps. Nothing to report.

*

Back in the hustle of the market the Borribles slowed the pace of their escape, walking at first and then loitering to see if the Woollie was still in pursuit.

'We'd better split up for a while,' said Twilight to his gang. 'I'll take Chalotte back to Spitalfields while you others keep your eyes open for that copper; he may have gone back for help.'

Chalotte thanked the Bangladeshis and walked away from them, following Twilight. She found it hard to believe that she was safe and she smiled, taking pleasure in the business of the market and the feel of human bodies as they pushed past her. The sun, high in the sky, warmed the whole street, and the smells of strange spices drifted on the air. Sandalled Indian women went softly by, enveloped in saris that sparkled with gold. The costers still shouted at the passers-by, their voices vulgar and outrageous and cracking under the strain of many hours of bawling. Chalotte touched Twilight on the arm. The shirt he wore was gaudy, orange, sickly and luminous. His trousers were blue and too big for him, torn in several places; stolen trousers. His feet were bare but in the hot summer that was how he preferred to be. After all, the pavements were warm and cushioned in dust.

'Yes?' he said.

'Thanks for rescuing me,' said Chalotte. 'I was just looking at all this and wondering where I would be now if it hadn't been for you.'

Twilight tried to appear unconcerned. 'Well I heard you call out, didn't I? No Borrible can resist that. Besides, I was sent to look for you.'

'Look for me?' said Chalotte in surprise. 'I never saw you before. I don't even know your name, even if you've got one.'

'Course I have,' said the brown Borrible.

'What is it then?'

'Twilight,' said Twilight.

'Twilight,' said Chalotte. 'That is a good'n and I bet a good adventure lies behind a name like that. You must tell me how you won it some day.'

It was quite normal for Chalotte to speak to Twilight in this manner. Names and how they are won are important to Borribles because for them a name is not given but earned; it is the only way. An adventure of some sort must be completed and out of that deed will grow a name. An adventure of any kind will do. It doesn't have to be stealing or burglary, though it often is because that's what Borribles prefer.

Chalotte studied her companion. 'And while we're on the subject, how come you know my name?'

'I know your name,' said Twilight, 'for the simple reason that everyone knows your name and how you won it. It is one of the greatest Borrible stories ever told but I have never met anyone before who was on the Great Rumble Hunt. When we get home I'd like you to tell me about it. I have heard things that are hard to believe.'

Chalotte's face became stern. 'They were probably true,' she said. 'It all got a bit nasty. Borribles should not have been involved in such things. Five Borribles were killed, five good Borribles. It was a waste. I don't mind telling you the story in return for you rescuing me, but it is not a happy story.'

Twilight smiled and his teeth were bright against his dark skin. Like all Borribles he loved stories, both the telling and the listening, but for the present there was no time and he led Chalotte away from the market into less crowded streets. He took her past rows of shattered houses and dingy blocks of buildings where Bangladeshi families, half-hidden among the bright colours of the week's wash, stood on balconies to keep an eye on their children as they played in the glass-strewn streets. But the Borribles walked on across a derelict stretch of ground that had been bombed flat in the war and not built on since. Here people dumped their rubbish and here the weak sprouts of pale grass fought against the sun and died for lack of water.

On the far side of the bomb-site stood a straggle of terraced houses, leaning one against another as if tired of life and desiring demolition. They were gaunt and reared up against the semicircle of blue sky like an eroded cliff. They had boards nailed over their windows and sheets of corrugated iron over the doors. Their areas were half full of rubbish, their cellars smelt of cats, both alive and dead. The steps of the houses were covered with broken bricks and lumps of plaster; dangerous shards of shattered milk bottles glittered in the sun like silver. The place was a desert of dust and it smelt of excrement and trouble.

It was typical of a Borrible hideout. Borribles are obliged to live where they can and they prefer these abandoned and decaying buildings which are rarely, if ever, in short supply. If a house is already occupied they will sometimes use its cellar; they also camp overnight in schools, especially during the holidays when the buildings are left empty and unused for long periods.

In the middle of the bomb-site Twilight halted. 'I was out looking for you,' he said, 'because we found somebody who said she'd come to see you.'

'See me?'

'Yeah, we came across this girl wandering about on the other side of Spitalfields. White girl, come all the way across London, so she reckons. We checked her ears; she's Borrible all right. We brought her home and then went out to look for you.'

'What's her name?'

'Something funny,' said Twilight, 'but I've forgotten it, something like Harry or Charlie.'

Chalotte drew a breath. 'Was it Sydney?'

'That's it, rings a bell that does, ding-dong.'

'The Great Rumble Hunt,' said Chalotte, 'she was on it too, the Adventure to end all adventures.'

Twilight put a hand on Chalotte's shoulder. 'Let's go and see her then,' he said, and he led the way up the broken and littered stairs of his house.

The front door clanged open, swinging on a loose wooden frame. Inside, half submerged in a litter of bottles, sacks and tattered packages bound with hairy string, lay an old man. His face was unshaven and his shapeless mouth snored. Twilight stepped carefully round the unconscious form and guided Chalotte past a jagged hole in the floorboards.

'I can never understand how he don't fall into the cellar,' said the Bangladeshi, 'but he don't.'

'Who is he?'

'Some meffo,' said Twilight. 'He's harmless, apart from the smell that is.'

The bare wooden stairs were splintered and weak, slippery too with chunks of fallen plaster and slivers of broken windowpanes. At the very top of the house was a small landing with three doors leading from it. Twilight opened one and showed Chalotte into a boxroom which had a sack over the window. On the floor were three old mattresses, darkly stained. A few torn blankets had been thrown across them as well as some newspapers for undersheets and insulation. In a corner, sitting on one of the mattresses, her back against the wall, head in hands, elbows on knees, dressed in worn trousers and a green T-shirt with holes in it, sat Sydney, her eyes closed.

Chalotte crossed the room and crouched to the floor. 'Sydney,' she said. 'Sydney.'

Sydney's eyes flickered once or twice as she tried to come awake. She stared through a heavy glaze of weariness. Chalotte spoke again.

'You haven't walked all the way from Neasden, 'ave yer?'

Sydney yawned and rubbed her face. It was a kind face and Chalotte had always liked it. 'What's up, Sid?' she asked. 'You haven't hiked across London just to say hello, I'll be bound. What's up?'

Sydney looked at Twilight who leant against the door, listening. She hesitated.

'He's all right,' said Chalotte, 'you can speak free.'

'I had a strange message,' said Sydney, 'a Borrible message, passed from hand to hand, you know. I'd never seen the bloke who gave it me, ain't seen him since neither. He said it had come clear across London, but he didn't know where from. Then he ran off.' Sydney reached into a pocket and pulled out a ragged scrap of lined notepaper. She gave it to Chalotte who smoothed it out on her knee and read aloud.

'"Sam is still alive. Last seen in Fulham. Needs help. Signed, A Borrible."' She whistled. 'Well that's good news . . .' She glanced into Sydney's face. 'Well, isn't it?'

'I dunno, it seems a bit mysterious to me. I'm not sure what to make of it.'

'Who's Sam?' said Twilight.

'Sam's a horse,' said Chalotte. 'He saved all our lives when we were in Rumbledom.'

Sydney shifted on the mattress and hoisted herself upright. 'The horse belonged to a Borrible-snatcher,' she explained. 'We had to kill the man before we could get away. I mean Knocker did.'

'Knocker and Adolf,' said Chalotte.

'We had to leave Sam when we went underground on our way home,' continued Sydney. 'I hated doing that, seeing how much we owed him, and I made a promise that if I ever got out of that Adventure alive I would go back to get him . . . And I meant it, but I've never known where he went or what happened to him. This is the first news I've had.'

'So?' said Chalotte.

'Well,' said the Neasden girl, 'I got this message about two weeks ago and I didn't know what to think . . . The best thing seemed to be to come and see you, so we could talk it over. I mean we owe it to Sam to see him all right if we can. Somebody might be working him to death.'

Chalotte stretched out on a mattress and was silent. What Sydney had said had brought the whole terrifying expedition back to her. What had started as a great Adventure to win names had turned sour and five Borribles had died. Borribles weren't supposed to die, but those five had. Knocker, whom Chalotte had especially liked; Orococco, the black boy from Tooting; Torreycanyon, the square-faced Borrible from Hoxton, and most dangerous of all, the twice-turned traitor and Wendle warrior, Napoleon Boot. And there had been Adolf too, a four-named Borrible from Hamburg, burnt alive in the halls of Rumbledom. All of them dead. Chalotte sighed. The Great Rumble Hunt had been madness. Never again would she take part in such an expedition.

'I'm sorry about Sam,' she said at length, 'really sorry, but I tell you straight, I'm not marching all the way to Fulham and back on the strength of a dodgy note that's come out of the dark, not a chance.'

'Yes,' said Sydney, 'but I made a promise, a definite promise to Sam.'

Chalotte shrugged her shoulders and quoted from the *Borrible Book of Proverbs*. '"To keep a bad promise does not make it good",' she said.

Sydney turned her head and stared at the floor. There was silence.

Twilight waited but the girls did not continue the conversation. He unfolded his arms and pushed himself away from the wall. 'Look,' he said, 'Sydney must be very tired, she ought to rest this afternoon, really, and while she's asleep I'll go back to the market with some of my mates. When she wakes up there'll be a feast ready for her.'

'And me too?' asked Chalotte.

'Of course,' said Twilight. 'I'm very good at stealing specialities.' He went to the window and raised the sacking to look out over a jumble of collapsing houses and sloping slate roofs. The whole vista trembled in a heat haze. 'I tell you one thing, Sydney,' he said. 'Chalotte may have had enough adventures, but I haven't. If you ever decide to go looking for your horse, I'll come with you.'

Sydney looked at Chalotte and smiled. 'Thank you, Twilight,' she said, and rolling a blanket to make a pillow she curled her body on the mattress and in a few seconds was fast asleep.

*

'And so,' said Chalotte, 'eight Borribles were chosen, the best runners and fighters and catapult artists in all London.'

Twilight ladled some curry into Chalotte's soup plate and she leant back against the wall. She and Sydney were sitting side by side on two metal milk crates. Twilight and six of his Bangladeshi friends squatted round a large black saucepan. They had come to eat and to hear the story of the Great Rumble Hunt.

Twilight had been as good as his word. While Sydney had slept and Chalotte had waited he had revisited the market. In less than an hour he'd returned with everything he needed to prepare a rich and highly flavoured curry. Cooking it had been no problem; most Borribles are good electrical engineers and Twilight was no exception. In the damp basement of his house was an old electric stove and the Bangladeshis had long ago mended it and tapped into the nearest supply to provide themselves with power. They had all the electricity they wanted.

'Where did they come from,' said Twilight, his mouth crammed, 'these eight Borribles?'

'From all over,' Chalotte went on. She talked slowly, between spoonfuls. The curry was hot; her eyebrows perspired, her forehead shone. Sydney was so busy eating that she hardly bothered to join in the story telling, but she nodded vigorously every now and then.

'There was a Humper from Hoxton, a Totter from Tooting; Sydney is a Nudger from Neasden, there was me and there was a Wendle from Wandsworth. They live underground they do, vicious and sly Wendles are.'

'I've heard about them,' said Twilight, 'never seen one.'

'You ain't missed much,' said Chalotte. 'Anyway, we all met up in Battersea and Knocker trained us. He came along in the end although he shouldn't have done because he had already earned his name, which we hadn't. Spiff wangled that . . . he's double crafty is Spiff.'

Sydney moved her head up and down as fast as she could.

'Spiff?' said Twilight.

'Yeah,' said Chalotte, 'Spiff. A Battersea Borrible and sharp enough to cut yer nails with. I don't like him. Anyway, we nicked a boat and went up the River Thames in it . . . Then we went underground with the Wendles, they're greeny-faced and not a bit friendly. The one we had with us, Napoleon Boot, well we didn't know if we could trust him or not, so we didn't. Later on, when we came out on the other side of Wendle territory we were captured by a Borrible-snatcher and his son. Diabolical that was, he starved us and made us steal for money. We only escaped by killing him. When we left we took Dewdrop's horse and cart, that's how we took Sam to Rumbledom and lucky we did too. There was a terrific battle at the end and we were surrounded by hundreds of Rumbles and we would have died for certain but Sam saved us. Rumbles can't stand horses, you see, horses eat Rumbles, find 'em tasty, reminds 'em of hay and that. But Adolf was killed there; it was a mess all right with Rumbles shouting and waving their spears. We were all wounded and this big entrance came crashing down and Adolf couldn't get out of the way. Great bloke he was . . . We never saw him again, dead, incinerated. Orococco was on fire and Knocker had deep burns across the palms of his hands.'

'That's his second name,' added Sydney, 'Burnthand.'

Chalotte went on. 'We got away and you might have thought that was the end of it, but it wasn't. We were in bad shape and Sam took us down to Wandsworth but Napoleon and Knocker quarrelled and we were betrayed by Napoleon and the Wendles locked us up. They have a leader, not like ordinary Borribles, called Flinthead, greedy and hard. He's the worst Wendle of all the Wendles, and that's saying something. He would have killed us for sure if Napoleon hadn't changed his mind and helped us escape. But we didn't get off lightly, I can tell you. Four of us didn't come back – Knocker, Napoleon Boot, Orococco and Torreycanyon. They stayed behind to guard a tunnel so that we could have time to get away. We never saw them again either, slaughtered by Flinthead they were. You know, I've never wanted to kill anyone but I would him. So only five of us survived to tell the tale: Sydney and me, Bingo from Battersea, Stonks from Peckham and Vulge from just down the road here in Stepney. Afterwards, Borribles called it the Adventure to end all Adventures but I call it madness. We lost five good friends, if you count Napoleon, and nothing's worth that, not the greatest Adventure in the world, not even the best name you could ever earn.'

'I like your story,' said Twilight. 'I have never heard the truth of it before but the rumours say something else, something about a great treasure, a box of Rumble money.'

Chalotte spooned some more curry into her plate and put the lid back on the black saucepan, then she looked at Twilight and her eyes narrowed to a thin line of hardness.

'That was the cause of all the trouble,' she said. 'If it hadn't been for the treasure Adolf wouldn't have been killed, Napoleon wouldn't have betrayed us and Flinthead would have let us pass through the underground citadel of the Wendles without bothering us one bit. Without the money no one would have died, except Rumbles.'

'So Flinthead got the treasure,' said Twilight.

'No, he didn't,' said Sydney. She finished eating and put the empty dish down beside the saucepan.

Chalotte allowed herself an ironic smile. 'We were taking it out in the boat. How we agreed to take the money I don't know; we wanted to get our own back on Flinthead, I suppose. We were crossing the great mudflats of the River Wandle, just after it goes underground. Hundreds of Wendle warriors came at us, frightening they are, carrying Rumble-sticks, catapults, dressed in rubber waders and little orange jackets they nick off the roadmen; they got the treasure away from us. Stonks, the strongest Borrible I've ever seen, he got it back, but in the struggle the box slipped overboard and the money went down into the mud, a quarter of a mile deep it is there, so they say; not even Flinthead can get it out now. The mud is the best place for it, too. Borribles shouldn't have money, they never have had.' Chalotte looked up and quoted her favourite proverb, '"Fruit of the barrow is enough for a Borrible."'

Twilight wiped his mouth with the back of his hand. 'This Vulge,' he said, 'he's a survivor, according to you, and he lives in Stepney. Well, that's not far. Why don't we go and see him tomorrow? You could ask him what he thinks about the horse, about the message.'

Chalotte was silent but Sydney looked her straight in the eye. 'I'd be willing to do that, and anyway it'd be nice to see him again. He was badly wounded in the leg, limps now.'

'What's he like?' asked Twilight.

Sydney laughed. 'Vulge is a bit special. He's small, mousy hair, got a pointed chin; he wags his head sideways, like he knows everything. He looks like he wouldn't say boo to a goose, but he's as tough as nails and never gives in. It was Vulge who killed the Rumble chieftain in his bath . . . and a score or two more. Oh yes, you'll like Vulge.'

2

The next day was just as hot, and the heatwave, which had begun two months earlier in the middle of May, showed no signs of breaking. Twilight woke the two girls early and as they sat up he gave them an orange each.

'Eat these,' he said, 'they're lovely.'

That was breakfast and ten minutes later the three Borribles left the house and made their way towards Whitechapel where they discovered the main road full of the din and uproar of a Monday morning rush hour. Pedestrians hastened along the pavements, running towards work with faces anxious and miserable, as if they had been unhappy and insecure away from their offices and workshops. The tramp of their feet was heavy, raising the dust, and although it was not yet nine o'clock, the sun beat down on the grey macadam of the road and melted it. Each car tyre that passed sounded like a zip unzipping.

Chalotte glanced to right and left, on the lookout for policemen. She saw none. 'Vulge lives down on the Limehouse Fields Estate,' she said, 'I don't know where exactly.'

'It's round the back of the canal,' said Twilight. 'The best thing we can do is go along that way and ask a Borrible.'

They crossed the main road, dodging the traffic, and went away from the noise and exhaust fumes into Fieldgate Street and on down Stepney Way. After walking for a quarter of an hour they came to a large housing estate built in brick of brown and black. Scores of children were already out in the courtyard, loafing in the shade, imprisoned by the rising heat.

'I like the school holidays,' said Sydney, 'there's so many normal kids about the Woollies haven't a chance of spotting us.'

'Don't be so sure,' answered Twilight. He went into the yard of the estate and the girls followed. 'There's got to be a Borrible hiding among all this lot,' he said. 'What about that one in the corner, sitting on the bottom step?'

Chalotte and Sydney looked. The boy on the bottom step was wearing half a mauve stocking on his head, well down over his ears.

'Got to be,' said Sydney, 'no one but a Borrible would wear a hat like that on a day like this.'

'Let's see,' said Twilight, 'but take it easy or he'll run off.'

They crossed the yard and above them faces peered over the balcony walls and someone spat, but the aim was bad and no one was hit. Chalotte saw the gob explode on the ground and without looking upwards she raised two fingers in the air.

The gesture attracted the attention of the mauve-hatted Borrible, who reached behind and pulled a catapult from his back pocket. Borribles are never friendly straight off, even with their own kind. They quarrel frequently, often they fight and they never trust strangers. Quickly and calmly the Borrible loaded a stone, then he gave a piercing whistle between his teeth and the head and hands of a colleague appeared on the first balcony. He too held a catapult.

A yard or two away from the steps Twilight stopped and, his movements deliberate, showed his own catapult and then returned it to his pocket.

What Twilight had done was important. The catapult is the Borribles' traditional weapon and they have used it for generations because of its simplicity and deadliness. It can be made anywhere, and long ago in the nineteenth century, when Borribles endured great hardships, it had become their favourite method of defence. By showing his catapult Twilight had indicated that he was a Borrible and by putting it away he had made it obvious that he came in peace.

'I'm Borrible,' said Twilight, 'and me and these two are looking for a Borrible called Vulge; he lives round here. These girls were on the Great Rumble Hunt with him.'

The Stepney Borrible put his catapult away. He waved a hand and his friend on the balcony disappeared. 'Show us an ear,' he said.

Chalotte lifted her long hair slightly. The Borrible nodded, satisfied.

'Great Rumble Hunt, those two? Don't look as if they could cross the road on their own. Still I'll take your word for it, thousands wouldn't . . . Tell me what Vulge looks like, if you're a friend of his.'

Chalotte described him as Sydney had. 'And he's got a limp now,' she added, 'where he was wounded in Rumbledom.'

The Stepney Borrible nodded. 'All right, go round the back of here, over Halley Street, up by the canal towards Oceans Estate, and opposite the recreation ground you'll see some abandoned houses. The third one down is the one you want . . . I dunno, girls.'

Chalotte glared at him. 'I could take your ear off with my catapult from a hundred yards,' she said.

'And I could put a stone up your nostril from the same distance,' said Sydney.

The Stepney Borrible laughed, a cold sound in the baking square of the black courtyard. 'I heard the story from Vulge,' he said. 'You must be the one who drowned the Rumble in the soup.'

'That's right,' said Chalotte, 'I did.'

'Well it's hard to believe and you can tell Vulge so when you see him.'

'What's your name, then?' asked Twilight.

'Hatrack,' said the Borrible, 'what's your'n?'

'Twilight,' said Twilight.

'Bleedin'-well suits yer,' said Hatrack. It was obvious that he did not like Bangladeshis and he said no more. Twilight forced himself to make a compliment.

'Hatrack is a good name,' he said. 'I would like to hear the story of it, one day.' And then he turned and walked out of the estate with Chalotte and Sydney beside him.

*

They soon found Vulge's house and, making sure they were unobserved, the three Borribles slipped along an alley to the back of the building. There was no sound and the terrace seemed deserted; there was no glass in the windows either and not a door standing. The rubbish from the streets had drifted high into the houses and for the most part the ceilings had collapsed as well; debris was ankle deep and everything smelt of decay.

'I'll go first,' said Chalotte. Cautiously she led the others up a flight of stairs, stairs which shifted a little under the weight of three people. As she went Chalotte whistled, hoping that Vulge, if he was there, would recognize the sound as the signal they had used on the Great Rumble Hunt.

She stopped. Somewhere above them a door opened and a voice said, 'Clear off, you're in the wrong house.'

Chalotte glanced upwards but could see no one.

'I've come to see Vulge,' she said, 'it's Chalotte and Sydney.'

'Well I'll be clipped,' said Vulge, as he moved into view on the landing above. 'Get on up here and let's have a look at yer.'

The two girls ran up the remaining stairs and threw their arms round Vulge's shoulders.

'Gerrorf,' he said. 'Come in my room 'ere, and have a cuppa, bring that friend of yours too, if he is a friend.'

In his room Vulge sat everyone down and brought out a teapot and a packet of tea. Then he switched on an electric kettle. 'I always keep it full,' he explained, 'I drinks a lot of tea.'

Chalotte looked round the room. It was like most other Borrible rooms she'd seen, including her own. The window was covered with an old blanket, there was one bare electric light bulb, a mattress, a few orange boxes for cupboards and a couple of small barrels, upended, to sit on.

Vulge squatted by the kettle and waited for it to boil.

'This is Twilight,' said Sydney.

'A good name,' said Vulge.

'If it hadn't been for Twilight,' explained Chalotte, 'I'd 'ave been clipped by now.' She told the story of her rescue and Sydney's arrival.

Vulge squinted at the Bangladeshi. 'Anyone who saves a friend of mine is a friend of mine,' he said. Then the kettle boiled and he made the tea, pouring it, when ready, into four jam jars, stirring in the sugar with a knife. He limped across the room to distribute them.

'How's the leg?' asked Chalotte.

'Better than nothing,' said Vulge, and he touched the old wound and grinned. 'I don't have too much trouble getting about. I can still run though I looks like a three-legged dog when I do. Still, I stays out of bother. I don't want no more adventures, that Rumble hunt was enough.' Vulge suddenly screwed up his face and a look of suspicion came into his eyes. 'You're a long way from home, Sydney, what you up to?'

'Tell him,' said Chalotte.

Sydney took the scrap of paper from her pocket and handed it to Vulge. 'What do you think of that?' she asked.

Vulge read the message aloud. '"Sam is still alive. Last seen in Fulham. Needs help. Signed, A Borrible."' He handed the paper back and was silent for a moment or two. His face darkened. 'It could be a trap,' he said at last.

'A trap!' said Sydney.

Vulge took a slurp from his jam jar. 'Have you heard of the SBG yet,' he said, 'and Inspector Sussworth?'

Chalotte nodded. 'The Woollie who caught me yesterday said something about him. They're trying to catch all of us.'

'They always are,' said Twilight.

'Yes,' said Vulge, 'but this is different. The law got very upset when they found Dewdrop and Erbie, especially when they found 'em dead. They got this Sussworth to form the Special Borrible Group, mainly to find out who killed Dewdrop but also to catch as many Borribles as they could, clip their ears and turn them back into normal kids. They know all about us, got a book of our proverbs, captured a few Borribles and made them talk. They drive about London all the time, day and night, in blue Transit vans with dark windows. If they see a catapult or a woollen hat or a kid near a house like this one, they're out of their van in a second and it's down the nick and never seen again.'

'We know all that,' said Sydney. 'What's that got to do with this note?'

'Like so,' said Vulge. 'If this Sussworth knows about Dewdrop and Erbie then the chances are he knows about the battle of Rumbledom. He might even know that Sam helped us, so all he has to do is drop a few notes like this one about and, if he knows how Borrible messages are passed from hand to hand, then he knows a message like this stands a fair chance of getting to someone who'd actually been on the Rumble hunt. Now if that person were daft enough to go looking for Sam in Fulham, and if Sussworth caught that person, then the SBG would be pretty sure they'd caught someone who'd had something to do with the Southfields murders, wouldn't they?' And Vulge leant back, wagged his head and supped his tea with the air of a Borrible who could read the mind of a policeman from a distance of half a hemisphere.

Sydney's face creased with disappointment and Chalotte felt sad for her. She knew how much Sam the horse meant to the girl from Neasden.

'I hadn't thought of it like that,' said Sydney. 'But it doesn't *have* to be a trap, does it? I mean Borrible messages do cross London this way; it could have come from a Fulham Borrible who'd seen Sam and knew the story. It could be like that, couldn't it?'

'True,' said Vulge, 'but whoever goes looking for Sam better take a telescope with him because there'll be a copper hiding underneath his tail.'

'I would go with her,' said Twilight. 'I am not frightened.'

Vulge turned on his barrel and smiled. His flat brown hair and his pointed chin gave his face a mischievous look. 'It's not a question of being frightened, it's a question of not getting your ears clipped, of survival, like it always is. If you'd seen half of what we saw on the Rumble hunt you'd be quite happy to stay near your market, live in your house and keep away from the Woollies.'

'But that's just it,' said Twilight raising his shoulders, 'I haven't seen half of what you've seen, and I won't unless I do something.'

'What I feel,' said Sydney, 'is that we owe our lives to Sam. I made a promise to go back for him, I've never forgotten that promise and since I got this note I can't stop worrying about it.'

'Well you're not the only one to have thought about Sam,' said Vulge. 'I have too and I daresay the others have. I felt rotten leaving him there on the banks of the Wandle, but travel is dangerous these days and getting more and more dangerous all the time. We shouldn't go charging about London, getting ourselves caught by the SBG. Sam himself wouldn't want that.'

Sydney stared at the piece of paper in her hand. She wanted to believe in it so much and now Vulge had undermined her confidence. 'Well,' she said, 'I know Chalotte doesn't want to come, but I suppose Twilight and me could go, just to have a look I mean.'

Vulge shook his head. 'I don't want to win any more names; I'm not ambitious like Knocker was. He wanted to win more glory than any other Borrible, and where is he now, dead and deep in Wandle mud. How does the proverb go . . . "One good name is enough if the name is good enough"? Well, my name is.'

No one spoke for a long while after that, they concentrated instead on finishing their tea. Vulge even rose from his seat and made some more, and all the while his guests remained silent. Sydney continued to stare at the message and Chalotte could think of nothing to say that might cheer her friend. Twilight kept his own counsel because it was not his business; it was a matter for three old friends, veterans of a wild and perilous experience that he had not shared.

Ten minutes went by. Chalotte could see that Vulge was thinking intently, resting his top teeth on the edge of his jam jar of tea. At last he got to his feet, limped over to an orange box, took out some apples and handed them round.

'This is my idea,' he began. 'It's the school holidays now, safer for us to travel. I'm not in favour of doing anything dangerous, but what we could do is get the other survivors together, there's only Stonksie in Peckham and Bingo in Battersea, then we could all talk about it. We'll find someone who's going Peckham way and send a note to Stonks and get him to meet us at Bingo's house. On our way to Battersea we'll ask any Borrible we see if they've come across any messages about Sam. If they haven't then the message is likely to be genuine, if they've seen a few then it's probably a trap. That way we don't make any decisions about going to Fulham until we've heard what everyone has to say. How's that strike yer, Sydney, is that better?'

Sydney looked up and smiled, her eyes brightened. 'Oh Vulge,' she said, 'that's marvellous, bloody marvellous.'

*

The four Borribles meant to waste no time and decided to set out the following morning. A message was despatched to Peckham via the Borrible network and Twilight volunteered to make himself responsible for gathering the supplies they would need on the long walk to Battersea. He left Vulge's house that afternoon and promised to return by nightfall.

Vulge checked over his catapult. He also gave Chalotte a spare to replace the one she had lost when captured by the policeman. Later on that day he disappeared for an hour or so, 'To get some good stones,' he said.

That night all four of them slept in Vulge's house and at first light they rose and made a good breakfast.

'We'll get on the streets as soon as it's rush hour,' said Vulge. 'That way we won't be so noticeable. Remember, the slightest sign of trouble and we run. If we get separated we all meet at Bingo's house.'

'This is great,' said Twilight. 'Do you know I've never been out of the East End, let alone across the river.'

'Well,' said Chalotte, 'let's hope it turns out to be just a walk we're going on and nothing more.'

As it happened the walk was a good one. The route lay all along the side of the River Thames and the water glinted and gleamed in the July sunshine. Tugs and barges steamed by on the tide; seagulls swooped down the winding currents of warm air and their long wailing cries made the Embankment sound as exotic as a treasure island. Buses and cars shone and stewed in the heat and the blue smoke of their exhausts floated in a pale stream a yard or so above the bubbling tar of the road surface.

This was central London in summer, and so content were the four Borribles to be a part of their city that they began to sing quietly to themselves as they advanced along the hot pavements, singing a song that told of their way of life and the joy they had in it; one of the most famous Borrible songs ever written:

'Who'd be a hurrying, scurrying slave,
Off to an office, or bound for a bank;
Who'd be a servant from cradle to grave,
Counting his wages and trying to save;
Who'd be a manager, full of his rank,
Or the head of the board at a big corporation?
Ask us the question, we'll tell you to stuff it;
Good steady jobs would make all of us snuff it –
Freedom's a Borrible's one occupation!

'Our kind of liberty's fit for a king;
London's our palace, we reign there supreme.
Broad way and narrow way, what shall we sing –

Alleys as tangled as knotted-up string,
River that winds through the smoke like a dream –
What shall we sing in our own celebration?
Ragged-arsed renegades, never respectable,
Under your noses, but rarely detectable –
Freedom's a Borrible's one occupation!'

And so they marched along the north bank until they reached Albert Bridge; there they crossed. Once over the water they turned right and went past the bus garages, then into Church Road where a great change awaited them. The high black walls of Morgan's Crucible Works, the tall chimneys that had always stood against the clouds, the acres of sooty windows, had all gone. The factory had been demolished.

'Well, look at that,' said Chalotte, 'ain't it strange?'

They went on, halting for a second by St Mary's church and the Old Swan pub.

'This is where we landed after our escape from the Wendles,' said Sydney, 'and we went into some Borrible houses opposite. They've knocked them down too, everything's going.'

At last they came to their destination, turning into the bottom of Battersea High Street and heading towards the market . . . But they did not go unobserved. As they passed the corner of Granfield Street a Borrible, wearing an old Sinjen's School blazer and tattered grey trousers, stepped in front of them and said, 'What are you lot doing here?'

It was Lightfinger, Knocker's friend, and Chalotte recognized him.

'We're Borrible, you know,' she said. 'Three of us were on the Rumble Hunt.'

Lightfinger was not impressed. 'So what?' he said. 'I still want to know what you are doing here; this ain't your manor.'

'Don't give us any bother,' said Vulge. 'We've come to see Bingo, not you. Why don't you get out of our way?'

Lightfinger took a step towards Vulge. 'Long as you haven't come to start some dopey adventure like the last one. Where's Knocker now eh, where's my friend? Dead, ain't he?' Lightfinger clenched his fists and squared his shoulders, ready to take them all on, one against four

'Oh, don't be daft,' said Chalotte. 'We've come for a chat with Bingo, that's all.'

'I'll tell him,' said Lightfinger. 'As for you lot, you'd better go and see Spiff.' With that he spun on his heel and ran off. The four travellers watched him go.

'Friendly little feller, ain't he?' said Twilight. 'Hides it well.'

'He liked Knocker,' said Chalotte, 'so he can't be too bad. Perhaps he hates us because we came back and Knocker didn't.'

'What about Spiff?' Sydney wanted to know. 'It's funny but not one of us had thought about going to see him, had we?'

'What's he got to do with it?' asked Twilight.

'He has the Borrible house where Knocker used to live,' explained Chalotte. 'It was him really who talked everyone into going on the Rumble Hunt. It was him who gave Knocker the secret job of getting the Rumble treasure and bringing it back. If you ask me the money was all he was interested in.'

'We don't know that,' said Vulge, wagging his head.

'No, we don't,' agreed Chalotte, 'but I reckon that Spiff's so crooked you could use him to unblock a sink. Still, if we don't want trouble I suppose we'd better tell him we're here.'

Spiff's house stood halfway up the High Street. It was tall, wide and derelict, all its windows boarded and a heavy sheet of corrugated iron over the main doorway. The front of the building was painted in grimy grey and in black letters along the front was written, 'Bunham's Patent Locks Ltd. Locksmiths to the trade.'

The four Borribles loitered outside for a while and waited until their stretch of street was empty of pedestrians; no Borrible likes to be seen entering an abandoned house. When the coast was clear they went down steep steps into a basement area where they found an open door through which they entered a room that was damp and green and devoid of furniture. Plaster in large quantities had fallen from the ceiling and lay everywhere in lumps.

Vulge looked at the walls and sniffed. 'We left from here,' he said to Twilight, 'this very room, eight of us; Spiff lives upstairs, come on.'

On the first landing Vulge stopped at a paintless door and gave the

Borrible knock: one long, two short, one long. The door opened immediately and Lightfinger appeared. He jerked a thumb over his shoulder as he pushed past.

'He knows you're 'ere,' he said, 'I told him.' Levering his shoulders backwards and forwards as he walked he went down the stairs.

'He's not so bad as he seems,' said a voice. Spiff stood in the doorway.

Chalotte regarded him closely. The little bugger hasn't changed a bit, she said to herself, not a bit. It was his face she remembered: clear and bright like a twelve-year-old's, with eyes that always shone, dark with a fire of deep cunning, a craftiness that might have been ages old. He wore the same orange dressing gown and the same red hat of knitted wool.

'You'd better come in, all of yer,' he said, beckoning them across his threshold.

Inside the room Spiff lowered himself into his old armchair. In spite of the summer's heat his paraffin stove was burning low, and bubbling on top was a large brown enamel teapot. Spiff set four cups on an orange box and poured out a liquid that tasted like gunpowder and needed spoonfuls of sugar to make it drinkable.

'Well, well,' he said after the first sip, 'it really is nice of you to come all this way to say hello. Sydney, Vulge and Chalotte, isn't it? Must be six or seven months since I saw you. Who's this black lad? Don't know him, do I?'

'My name's Twilight,' said the Bangladeshi with some pride.

'That is an unusual name,' said Spiff. 'I hope that while you are here you will find time to tell me your story.'

Spiff then suggested that the four Borribles should take their cups and sit on the barrels arranged along one wall of his room. They did as they were asked and relaxed and drank and perspired in the overheated atmosphere, though they said nothing. This silence was embarrassing and Chalotte wondered if Spiff had been nudged off balance by their arrival. It was always difficult to assess his reactions exactly. There were great echoing corridors of artfulness in that small hard skull.

'Lightfinger said you'd come to see Bingo,' he said eventually across the top of his teacup. The steam strayed upwards over his face and dimmed the light of his eyes. He waited and smiled as if suspecting his guests of knowing something he didn't want them to know and yet wishing, without giving anything away himself, to discover the full extent of their knowledge.

Sydney looked at her three companions, wiped some sweat from her eyebrows, coughed and said, 'We . . . that is me . . . I went to see Chalotte because I was worried about Sam.'

'Sam?' said Spiff, and his brow furrowed as if he didn't know the name. Chalotte tightened her mouth in scorn. She was certain that Spiff remembered every detail of the Rumble expedition and, what was more, spent a great deal of his time thinking about the Rumble Hunt, what had happened on it and what might still happen because of it.

'Sam,' she said, allowing the sarcasm to show, 'was the horse.'

'Oh yes,' said Spiff, 'the horse, of course.' He smiled at the rhyme.

'Well,' continued Sydney, 'I made him a promise that I'd go back for him . . . then the other day I received this.' Sydney handed the message to Spiff, who read it very carefully, examining the piece of paper on both sides.

'Mmm,' he said when his perusal was concluded. 'Fulham; are you going to go?'

Vulge leant forward and settled his elbows on his knees, holding his cup between clasped hands. 'The point is, Spiff, I think the message is a come-on, I think it might be something set up by the SBG.'

Spiff looked at the note again. 'That's a thought,' he said. 'Those Woollies of Sussworth's have become a real pain. I've had this house searched twice, only just got away the second time. We've got Borribles watching each end of the street now. As soon as one of those blue vans arrives, matey, we're off.'

Vulge nodded. 'It would have been dead easy, you know, for the SBG to send that note . . . though I must admit we spoke to a lot of Borribles on the way down here and none of them had seen a message about Sam, so I daresay it's straight. On the other hand, if we do decide it's a trap then we ought to forget about the horse altogether.'

'I should cocoa,' said Spiff. If he had been nervous earlier he was now visibly relaxing. 'What do you think, Chalotte?'

'I don't think anything. I came along for the walk and to see Bingo and Stonks. Sydney made a promise but I didn't.' She shrugged her shoulders.

Twilight interrupted. 'I would go to Fulham like a shot.'

Spiff laughed. 'He's like Knocker, he is.'

'Yeah,' said Chalotte, 'and Knocker's dead and that was your fault. You're so crafty you don't know whether you've been or gone. I say that to your face.'

Spiff's expression darkened. 'I only wanted to share the money out.'

'Borribles should stay away from money,' said Vulge.

Spiff grimaced. 'Well, money certainly stays away from Borribles.' He looked straight into Chalotte's eyes. 'You never liked me, Chalotte, even before Knocker died, but you can't deny that we haven't had a peep out of the Rumbles since we attacked them, not a peep.'

'That's right,' said Chalotte, 'now we've got the SBG instead.'

'The world don't do us no favours,' said Spiff, and then he quoted from the *Borrible Book of Proverbs*. '"The only gift given to a Borrible is the one he takes."' He studied his visitors for a moment. 'What are you going to do?'

'Talk it over with Bingo,' said Vulge, 'and Stonks.'

'Fine,' said Spiff. 'I think you ought to find out where the horse is. If it really is in Fulham and you come to the conclusion that it isn't a trap then we could just wander over there and take a look.'

'We?' exclaimed Sydney.

'Yes, why not me as well? I haven't been on a trip for ages. Don't want to sit here all the time. Besides, it would do me good to get out.'

Sydney and the three others stared at each other. This was a turn of events that flabbergasted them completely. They had never known Spiff leave his room for any length of time.

'I wouldn't walk down the street with you,' said Chalotte.

Spiff raised his eyebrows. 'It doesn't matter, you said you wouldn't be going anyway. Sydney, Twilight and me could manage on our own, even if Bingo and Stonks don't want to come.'

'Wait a minute,' said Vulge, reddening. 'I wouldn't be against going as long as I felt sure that it wasn't an SBG set-up.'

Spiff leant forward. 'It's no good us deciding anything till we get more information. I've got a few friends in Fulham; I'll try to find out if there's any truth in the message.'

Chalotte banged her empty cup on the floor. 'Have you ever had any news out of Wendle country?' she asked.

A gleam of hatred glowed at the back of Spiff's eyes. 'Nah,' he said, 'only rumours, but then not much news comes out of Wendle country at the best of times.'

Chalotte pointed a finger at him. 'You don't even care what happened to Knocker,' she said.

Spiff poured himself another cup of tea. 'I've been a Borrible for years,' he said, 'more years than the rest of you put together. You just watch your lip, Chalotte, or I'll thump you into the middle of next week.'

'Not while I'm here,' said Vulge quietly.

'Nor me,' said Sydney.

'Or even me,' added Twilight.

Spiff raised his cup and bent his head in mockery. 'All right,' he said. 'The top room is empty. There's the market every day of the week; help yourselves, just stay out of trouble and don't upset any Battersea Borribles while you're here.'

'Thanks very much,' said Chalotte, and she went quickly from the room. The others filed after her, only Vulge stopped on the way out.

'Go easy on Chalotte,' he said. 'It upsets her when she remembers the Adventure, Knocker and all that. She thinks it's not right for Borribles to go looking for trouble.'

Spiff smiled his craftiest smile. 'Who has to look for trouble?' he said. 'Trouble knows its way to everyone's house, the trick is to be out when it gets there.' And he threw back his head and his smile broke into pieces and became harsh laughter. Vulge said no more but turned and went away, closing the door quietly behind him before following his friends upstairs.

*

Upstairs was Bingo. 'I saw old misery-guts Lightfinger in the market,' he said, and clapped Vulge on the back. 'Hello, you old cripple, how's the limping, getting better?'

Bingo was slightly built, even for a Borrible. He was about the same size as Twilight but thinner. His skin looked healthy and he had blue eyes that moved all the time though never furtively. His hair was dark and tightly curled, like wire wool. When he talked he smiled; it took a lot of trouble to get him down.

'The limping's very good,' said Vulge, and pushed his mate gently in the face with the palm of his hand.

'Who's the spade?' asked Bingo.

'My name's Twilight,' said the Bangladeshi, drawing himself up to his full height and looking Bingo straight in the eye.

Bingo shouted in delight, 'Twilight is a great and magnificent name. O Borrible from beyond the water, tell me its story.'

'Beyond the water,' said Twilight, becoming angry, 'don't be bloody stupid, this is the first time I've been out of Whitechapel.'

Bingo winked. 'Ah, but you had to cross the river to get here, didn't you?'

'He's having you on, Twilight,' said Chalotte. 'Leave him alone, Bingo. Twilight saved me from a Woollie the other day.'

Bingo went serious for a second. 'Anyone who saves my friend,' he said, 'is my friend,' and he slapped Twilight on the shoulder.

The Bangladeshi was so pleased with this reception that a lump rose in his throat. He found no words to say but just nodded and smiled.

'At any rate,' Bingo continued, 'I won't have you all staying here, it's rotten. I have an empty cellar next door to a supermarket on Lavender Hill. I took a few bricks out of the wall so food is no longer a problem. I offer you a feast and there are mattresses galore. How about it?'

The decision was easily made and the five Borribles clattered down the wooden stairs, halting just for a moment on the ground floor so that Vulge could tell Spiff where they were going and also to leave a messsage for Stonks.

'All right,' said Spiff, 'I'll tell him and if I hear anything about the horse I'll send a runner. Be careful now, and don't get caught.'

'No,' said Vulge, 'we won't,' and he limped away.

*

The period of waiting passed enjoyably. As Bingo had promised there was a ready supply of food in his cellar and most days the five Borribles wandered together round the busy streets of Clapham Junction, talking to other Borribles and joining in the games of ordinary children. Twilight told the story of his name and in return Bingo gave him yet another version of the Great Rumble Hunt, telling of his fight in the library against the best warrior of Rumbledom, a fight to the death with the Rumble-stick, and he told how Napoleon Boot had killed scores of Rumbles and had set fire to the great library.

'That Napoleon Boot,' said Bingo, shaking his head as if he couldn't believe that he had met such a person, 'what a scrapper he was, loved it, he did. I know it was him got us into a mess with the Wendles but I liked him, and you have to remember that it was him that got us out of it in the end. No one else could have, not even Knocker . . . and nobody else could have tricked Flinthead.'

'What was he like, Flinthead?'

'The chief of the Wendles! He's the toughest, coldest, nastiest, cruellest Borrible git in creation,' said Bingo. 'If you ever have the bad luck to meet him, turn and run like hell. Don't try to be brave or anything stupid like that, just run. Flinthead is the kind of person that likes sticking pins in worms and watching 'em wriggle.'

*

Early one morning, after a week of idling and talking, a message, scrawled on a piece of paper, arrived from Spiff. 'Stonks is here,' it read. That was sufficient, Spiff knew, to get the five Borribles down to Battersea High Street in a hurry, and he was right. They left Lavender Hill at a trot and kept it up all the way. They found Stonks waiting for them at the top end of the market, leaning against a traffic light.

Stonks was big for a Borrible, strong-looking with dark heavy eyebrows and a red face which was slow to register his feelings. Stonks never minced his words; he wasn't witty but he was dogged, persistent and dependable. A good friend to have beside you when things turned nasty.

'I've been waiting ages for you bunch of layabouts,' he said, and although he tried to look stern, pleasure forced its way into his expression. 'It's miles from here to Peckham.'

'Shuddup,' said Bingo, 'or I'll let Chalotte push yer face in.'

When these greetings had been exchanged the six friends passed into the market, took some food as they went, and continued along the High

Street until they reached an open area of dusty ground between the railway embankment and a scrapyard where the wrecked bodies of old cars were piled four or five high, slung precariously one on top of another. There the Borribles sat themselves down on the stony dirt in the shade of a plank fence, the hot sky stretched tightly above them. Every ten minutes or so a dark blue electric train rattled by, the noise turning hollow as the wheels clanked over Battersea railway bridge. The Borribles were safe in that spot and they liked it. They ate the fruit they'd stolen and they talked.

'I don't give a monkey's about the SBG,' said Stonks. 'I mean they don't know we're worried about Sam, or that Sydney made a promise. I think we owe that horse at least a try at finding him . . . I've always felt rotten about leaving him behind.'

'That makes four of us,' said Twilight, 'me, Sydney, Bingo and now Stonks.'

'Five, if you count Spiff,' said Chalotte.

At that moment the conversation was interrupted by a scrabbling sound and Spiff himself sprang through a hole in the fence. No longer the tea-swilling Borrible wrapped in an orange dressing gown, but dressed for the road, he looked hard and ready for anything.

'Don't see you out often,' said Bingo.

'I'm out now,' answered Spiff, and he pushed into the group, squatted down and, without any preamble, began to talk, as if continuing the discussion of a week earlier.

'I just heard from a Borrible along York Road; he told me that when Dewdrop was killed there was a bit in the paper about it . . . how the Woollies found all the stolen gear in the house and how they think Borribles did the stealing and then killed Dewdrop in a quarrel over the sharing out. This newspaper also said how the horse was found, cut and bleeding, in King George's Park. It was recognized as belonging to Dewdrop but nobody claimed it. It seems that Dewdrop didn't have any relations except his son and he wasn't much use, seeing as he was dead too, so the horse was given to the RSPCA.'

'That was six months ago,' said Sydney. 'Where's the horse now, I wonder?'

'Well,' said Spiff, 'I looked in a phone book and the RSPCA have got an office in Battersea Bridge Road, by the traffic lights. What I reckon is that a couple of you ought to go down there and say you're distant relatives of Dewdrop. You know, kid them you've just heard about the horse and would like to see it, make sure it's all right. Bingo's good at that kind of thing, with that innocent face of his.'

Bingo, lying full length on his stomach, scratched a pattern in the dirt. 'I wouldn't mind a little run down the road,' he said. 'I could be there and back in half an hour.'

'I'll come with yer, if yer like,' said Stonks.

'And me,' added Twilight.

'OK,' agreed Bingo, 'the rest of you can wait here.' He pushed himself to his feet and Stonks and Twilight did the same.

'You be careful,' said Chalotte, 'we don't want any complications.'

'Don't worry,' said Twilight, 'I move very fast; they call me the black mamba of Whitechapel Road, you know.'

*

Battersea Bridge Road was scorching underfoot, wide and cluttered with hot traffic. The heatwave hung over the city like blue enamel and breathing was like drowning in warm water.

'Strewth,' said Twilight, 'I'm glad I don't live in one of those tropical places abroad.' He backhanded the sweat out of his eyes.

Stonks gazed into the distance. 'You can bet your life,' he said, 'that if you want a number in a road that has a lot of numbers then the number you want is always the number at the other end of the road.'

'Yes, Stonks's Law,' said Bingo.

They trudged on and on for what seemed miles until at last they came to a row of shops by the traffic lights at the corner of Westbridge Road. Here they found, among others, a dull shopfront with its plate glass smeared over with bilious green paint. Above the window was written, in dim yellow letters: RSPCA, Local Office.

'Well, here we are,' said Bingo, 'and in I go. You two better stay out here, in case there's trouble.'

'Trouble, what trouble?' said Twilight. 'They ain't interested in kids, ain't got the time, it's all "puss-puss" and "down Rover" with them.'

Bingo looked at Stonks, who said, 'There's enough of us, we should be all right.'

Bingo opened the door and the three Borribles found themselves in a bleak office furnished only with a cheap desk and a few chairs. There was a typewriter, a telephone, a lady in a brown cardigan and a thick-set man dressed in a shiny black suit. The strange light from the painted window made everything a ghostly green, especially the two adults. They looked like they'd been recently dug up in some damp and mouldy cemetery.

The lady raised her head from the papers on her desk and smiled like a dentist. The man, his buttocks overflowing the small perimeter of his chair, smiled too. Bingo didn't like either of the smiles.

'Yes,' said the lady, 'and how can we help you three nice little boys?' She patted the crust of lacquer on her lifeless hair and her eyes glinted. The man rolled his lips around and said nothing. Inside his heavy suit his body was cooking like a chicken in a microwave and sweat gleamed and trickled across the acres of his pale skin. Bingo looked to the floor expecting to see a puddle of perspiration – he was disappointed. He looked back at the lady, confused. 'Is this the NSPCC?' he asked.

The lady's laugh jangled about the room like an armful of brass bracelets. 'Oh no, my dear,' she said, 'this is the RSPCA. We're the ones with the Royals in front. We look after animals and the ones without the Royals do the children.'

'That's what I meant,' said Bingo. 'I always get them mixed up. My parents sent me . . . to ask about a horse.'

'A horse,' said the man suddenly, 'what kind of horse?'

'Well,' explained Bingo, 'there was this horse found, in King George's Park, about six months ago, and my mum and dad, they are related to the person who owned that horse. Do you know what I mean?'

The lady nodded. 'Of course we do, boys,' she said, purring like an untrustworthy cat.

Bingo went on, 'You see my mum's mad about horses, and I was coming over this way, to visit my friends 'ere, and she said I was to ask you what had happened to the horse, that's if you knew, like.'

'And where do you live, sonny?' asked the man, pushing kindness into his face as hard as he could.

'Clapham Common, South Side,' said Bingo. 'We looked you up in the phone book.'

'I see,' said the man, 'how very enterprising.'

The lady tittered like a toy piano and pulled open a drawer. 'It's not really our part of London,' she said, and her hand appeared holding an address book, 'but I'll phone up Central Records for you, they'll be bound to know something.'

Bingo nodded and shifted his feet. There was something about these two adults he didn't like. Twilight stepped nearer the door, staring at the lady while she composed the telephone number. Her expression went vacant as she put the receiver to her ear and her eyes spun inside out to show only blank whites, though when someone spoke at the other end of the line her face lit up in a series of flashes so that she looked like a fruit machine.

'Ah, hello, Central Records . . . of course you are. This is Battersea here, Battersea. I have three lovely little boys in my office who are very worried about a horse, yes. It was lost in King George's Park about six months ago . . . Yes, certainly.' Her eyelids fluttered and found Bingo. 'They've gone to get the file,' she said, 'we'll have to wait,' and she pursed her lips in a gesture of affection, making her mouth hard and unlovely like a chicken's arse.

'I don't reckon this,' whispered Stonks, 'there's a cop shop just up the road from here, what if that old biddy has tipped 'em the wink?'

'Hello,' said the lady, smiling fiercely into the telephone as if the person at the other end might be improved by it. 'Yes, name, Samson, found in King George's Park, badly cut, now in good health and working for the park keepers on Eel Brook Common . . . Splendid, thank you so much. I'll do my best, bye-bye.'

'I hope you had nothing to do with that poor defenceless creature being wounded,' said the man, still trying to look kind but unable to keep the vicious tone out of his voice. 'I'd horsewhip any child I found hurting a horse.'

'I love animals,' said Bingo, 'and so does my mum, she'll be ever so pleased it's all right. We'll be able to go and visit the horse now, won't we?'

'Of course,' the lady screeched, and then she giggled like a lunatic baby-strangler.

'We'd better get going,' said Stonks, 'we'll be late for our tea.' The Peckham Borrible tugged at Bingo's sleeve and nodded towards the door where Twilight hovered, ready for flight.

'Oh, don't go yet,' cooed the lady. 'I've got some sweeties here somewhere, and I've got more to tell you about the horse.'

'Yes,' snarled the man, 'you wait a minute.' He sprang to his feet and the stiff smile fell from his face like a shutter falling from a shop window. 'I want your addresses,' he said, and, suddenly agile, he took one long stride and folded the flesh of his damp right hand round Bingo's neck and began to squeeze.

Twilight threw open the door and sunshine flooded in. Stonks hesitated, anguished. How could he leave Bingo, but what could he do?

The man squeezed harder at the muscles of Bingo's neck and the Borrible's feet left the floor.

'Run, Stonks,' he yelled in pain, 'run as fast as you can.'

Still Stonks hesitated. The lady began to stand up, still smiling. Stonks charged towards the desk and pushed it at her.

'Oooer,' she said, falling back into her chair, 'you little horror, I'll spank you.'

At that moment a door at the rear of the office opened and a uniformed policeman burst into the room; there was a chequered band circling his hat and SBG in letters of silver on his shoulder.

'Run,' gasped Bingo. 'Run.' The air was scarcely passing through his throat and his limbs were no longer moving. His face was purple.

Stonks hesitated no more. There were three adults already in the office and perhaps more policemen at the back of the building. He shoved Twilight through the doorway and leapt with him onto the pavement. They made as if to turn to their right but the wailing of a police siren stopped them. Three hundred yards away and bearing down in their direction, its blue light whirring round and round like an evil and disembodied eye, was a blue Transit van, a van of the SBG.

'Cripes,' said Twilight, 'time for a touch of the opposite directions.' And he and Stonks turned and ran like they'd never run before, pumping their arms and legs as fast as their hearts could stand, away round the corner and into Westbridge Road.

'We've got a couple of minutes before that van catches up with us,' panted Stonks. 'We've got to get off the street and out of sight, otherwise we've had it for good and proper.'

*

Vulge saw them first and he didn't like the way they were running, fast and panicky. He was sitting by the hole in the fence, on watch; the others were playing fivestones behind him and Spiff was winning. Vulge's face showed worry. 'Oh no,' he said.

The Borribles dropped the stones and got to their feet just as Stonks and Twilight came through the fence. Chalotte was the first to speak and she was angry.

'Where's Bingo,' she snapped, 'what the hell's happened?'

Stonks looked at the ground.

'He's been caught,' said Twilight. 'there was a big RSPCA man there, and a lady, and a Woollie. We only just got away . . . They must have had it set up with the SBG.'

'We couldn't do anything,' said Stonks. 'A van arrived and we had to run for it. We hid in the Somerset Estate.'

'This is terrible,' said Vulge. 'Bingo caught . . . bloody RSPC-bloody-A.'

'Will they clip his ears?' said Twilight in a small voice.

'What else will they damn-well do?' said Spiff, clenching his fists in anger. 'That is they will if we don't get to him quick enough.'

'What do you mean?' asked Vulge. 'Rescue him?'

'We've got to do something,' said Spiff. He looked as unhappy as anyone had ever seen him. Lines of anxiety pulled at his face.

Chalotte rounded on Sydney. 'I told you the horse was a bad idea, now we've gone and lost another Borrible, one of the best too.'

'All right,' cried Sydney, 'so it's my fault, say what yer like, but arguing don't help. We've got to save him if we can.'

'Of course we have,' said Spiff. 'There's no question of adventures or horses now. It's Bingo, Bingo alone, and the sooner the better. Anyone who doesn't want to help should say so.' He looked straight at Chalotte.

'I didn't want any trouble,' she said, 'but this is different. Bingo is Bingo. I'm in.'

'All right,' said Spiff. 'Now this is what I say, anyone who thinks they've got a better plan can say so afterwards . . . Did they tell you where the horse was?'

'They said something about Eel Brook Common,' said Stonks, 'working for the park keepers.'

'Right,' continued Spiff. 'I've got some good catapults indoors, some of those steel ones left over from the Rumble Hunt, one each. Stones we want, food we want, good running shoes. We'll get into Sinjen's School tonight and get a blazer each so we look like proper kids. If we get stopped on the road we'll pretend we're out on some holiday project. We'll leave tonight, as soon as it's dark. We'll break into the RSPCA office on the way, see if we can find out anything about what's happened to Bingo. Failing that we go on to Eel Brook Common, I know where it is, over Fulham way. You see I reckon they'll take Bingo there as soon as they can, show him to the horse and see how the horse reacts. If that horse recognizes him the SBG will know they've caught someone involved in the Southfields murders, and they'll soon make him talk and they'll be on to us in no time. We've got to get there before the law does. A rescue is the last thing they'll be expecting. Anyone got a better idea?'

'No,' said Vulge, 'only get a telescope.'

'A telescope,' said Spiff, 'all right. Get down the market the lot of yer and take what we need before it closes. I'll go back to my house and look out the catapults and see what else I've got. Meet yer back there and we'll rest and eat before we go. And for Pete's sake don't get caught, one rescue a day is enough.'

*

At ten thirty that night a window at the back of Sinjen's School slid open and Spiff's leg came out of it, followed, a second later, by his face. 'It's all right,' he whispered, 'no one about.' He pulled his body across the window ledge, twisted and then dropped to the ground. The others came after, one by one, all of them clothed in stolen blazers and grey flannels, even the two girls. On their feet were trainers, excellent for running. In their pockets were torches, high-grade steel catapults and enough stones to see off an army of coppers. They weren't the best equipped of expeditions but for a trip to Fulham and back they were more than adequately provided for.

Spiff led his five companions into the blackness of the playground and then out into the yellow light of the streets. The Borribles spread out in single file, three yards between each, ready to disperse at the first sign of danger. It was getting late and traffic was heavy; people were driving home from cinemas and bingo halls, the pubs were turning their customers out on to the pavements and everywhere there were drunks stumbling home, lifting their feet high over imaginary kerbstones, tottering backwards down non-existent slopes. Police cars lurked in the dark side roads too, lying low in the gutters like feral cats waiting for carrion.

Resolute and vigilant the Borribles tramped and jogged along and when, after about a quarter of an hour, they reached the traffic lights at Westbridge Road, Spiff slid into the dark entrance of the RSPCA office and tried the door. It was firmly locked. He stepped back and looked at the plate glass window and then up at the two smaller windows on the first floor.

'I won't have any bother getting in here,' he said. 'You others get over to that bus stop and pretend you're in the queue. If you see anything suspicious give a whistle.'

The bus stop was in fact only twenty yards from the office but by the time the Borribles had reached it Spiff had disappeared.

'Look at that,' said Vulge, 'he's inside already. He must be one of the best Borrible burglars ever.'

'The stories say he's got at least twenty names, you know,' said Stonks. 'I've even heard tell that he's been a Borrible for a hundred years, but I find that hard to believe.'

'There's certainly more to Spiff than meets anyone's eye,' agreed Chalotte, 'but nobody knows what it is. I wouldn't trust him further than I could spit upwards. He's got enough neck to look up his own ear'ole, he has.'

'Steady,' said Twilight, 'here he comes now.'

Spiff joined them at the bus stop. 'Not a lot in there,' he said, 'but it looks like an SBG set-up all right. I found a notepad on the desk with Sussworth's address and telephone number written on it. There was also tomorrow's date, and it said Eel Brook Common, nine o'clock.'

'Well,' said Sydney, 'when Sam sees Bingo he's bound to recognize him, and then he's had it.'

'And we'll have had it too,' said Spiff.

'In other words,' said Stonks, 'even if we didn't want to rescue Bingo, which we do, we'd have to try anyway, to save ourselves.'

'Dead bleedin' right,' said Spiff, 'either that or we'd all have to move a long way away from where we live now.'

'It's Hobson's,' said Twilight. 'Hobson's as usual.'

'We'd better get going,' said Spiff looking round. 'It wouldn't be a bad idea to be hidden somewhere near Eel Brook Common before the Woollies arrive tomorrow morning. That way if it looks like a trap we can stay hidden and keep quiet.'

And the Borribles moved on from the bus stop and began to trek up the long slope towards the crest of Battersea Bridge. Once over the bridge they would be in unfamiliar territory and danger would be all around them. They each knew this but they marched on with spirit and determination; they knew very well that they had to rescue Bingo – what they didn't know was that the second great Borrible Adventure had begun.

3

The headquarters of the SBG were not located in a police station and they were not easy to find, which was exactly how Inspector Sussworth liked it. His aim was to pass through life unnoticed by the general public; that was where his strength lay. He wanted to work quietly and secretly. Only the men who took orders from the inspector knew where to find him and their orders were to tell no one.

With concealment as their main objective the SBG had taken over a house in the crumbling hinterland behind Fulham Broadway, an unobtrusive place in Micklethwaite Road, a road that led nowhere. From the outside it looked dilapidated, a ramshackle establishment with varnish peeling from the front door and cracked windows hidden under white paint so that no one could see in and no one could see out. But inside it was different; it was antiseptic, it was smart and it was systematic, Inspector Sussworth saw to that. He liked things to be polished and properly arranged.

Behind the front door, and adorned with thick sick-green linoleum, was a narrow hallway leading to a narrow staircase which climbed steeply to three landings. On each landing were two rooms; each room had a desk, a telephone and a couple of deep, plastic-covered armchairs. At the rear of the ground floor was an enormous stainless-steel kitchen and dining room combined where the men of the SBG cooked meals and made their tea. In the garden a large sports room had been constructed; it contained showers, ludo boards, ping-pong tables and chest expanders. Inspector Sussworth insisted that the constables who formed his group were fit, keen and spotless.

On the first floor the two rooms were occupied by the inspector and his assistant and helpmate, Sergeant Hanks. The inspector had a larger desk than anyone else, a wooden desk that had been varnished and polished so often that its surface shone like a black mirror. He had the softest armchair too, and a colour television. Behind the television, in the corner furthest from the door, was the entrance to the inspector's private lavatory, his pride and joy which he washed and disinfected every day, allowing no other person to use it. The lavatory's every wall was tiled in six-inch squares of white porcelain, so was the ceiling. On the floor was a green carpet of cord and the toilet seat itself was padded and plush-covered; 'just like they are for the Royals,' Sussworth always said, proud and smug. Under an ever-open window, and within arm's reach of the velvet throne, stood a small bamboo table which always carried a pile of tough, water-resistant lavatory paper and several copies of the *Police Gazette*. This was Sussworth's inner sanctum, this was where he retired to think.

In the sergeant's room there was only a small desk but it did have three telephones as well as a radio receiver and transmitter. Hanks did not have a television of his own but he frequently watched programmes with the inspector. In fact, considering how totally different they were, it was amazing how well the two policemen got on. Some people said that Sussworth only kept Hanks in the group to remind himself and his men how gross and unpleasant the world really was. Others, more cruel perhaps, said that the sergeant only maintained his place in the SBG because he knew how to flatter Sussworth to the limit and how to do his bidding, even before it was bidden. Whatever the truth of the matter, they relied on each other a hundred per cent.

On the day of Bingo's capture, and not many hours after that event, Inspector Sussworth sat at his desk in the house in Micklethwaite Road and doodled on a piece of paper, his face lowering in deep concentration while in front of him the vapour rose from a cup of tea: no milk, no sugar, and very strong. The inspector dressed well and his uniform was as splendid as any grenadier's; it was neatly pressed and its buttons shone like stars against the deep blue serge of the material. Sergeant Hanks, always servile, always unctuous, relaxed in an armchair and waited for his leader to speak.

'So,' said the inspector when he had gathered his thoughts, 'we've caught a suspicious Borrible at last, but that's only one, Hanks. This is only the beginning; we've got to do better, much better.'

'We have indeed, sir,' said Hanks, bobbing his head up and down several times, 'and we will, I feel sure.'

The inspector picked up his cup of tea between two delicate fingers and sipped. The beverage was exactly how he liked it and he smiled. He had a strange thin face, made stranger by this smile, and in the face every feature took the wrong direction. His chin, which was sharp, did not go the way it should have gone. His nose bent itself in the middle and tried to aim the end sideways, while his ears threw themselves forward with energy instead of lying back with decorum. Sussworth's face was like a three-fingered signpost, turned by mischievous hands so that everything pointed down the wrong road.

His forehead was narrow, his eyebrows dark and well marked. His hair was lank and oiled and fell over his forehead in a solid lump. His eyes skulked deep in their sockets and, when they could be seen, were the colour of used washing-up water left overnight and found greasy-grey in the morning. Under his nose lived a small black moustache about the size of a jubilee postage stamp; it led a life of its own, that moustache, and twitched whenever it thought it would. Sussworth was only five feet six inches tall, with a slender body. Whether he sat or stood his feet always moved with nervous energy. He kicked the ground when he was annoyed, he did a little three-step dance when he was pleased. He was stubborn and he was proud; his blood bubbled with a lunatic zeal, he was an evangelist for rectitude and decorum, an enforcer of law and order.

By comparison Sergeant Hanks was an enormous man with broad shoulders and hands so big that when he clasped them it looked like he was carrying six pounds of raw pork sausages, unwrapped. His arms were as muscular as other people's thighs and covered all over with curly ginger hair, stiff as wire. He had a belly that surged frontwards; it began just below his neck, it ended just above his knees, but there was nothing flabby about it. It was a powerful belly, and sinew rippled across it all the time and made his uniform move as if he had a large python living underneath his jumper.

His jacket had egg stains down it from collar to hem and from shoulder to shoulder, like the medals on a general's tunic. There was only one thing that Hanks liked more than regular meals and that was the meals in between. His favourite food was four eggs and ten rashers of bacon with as much fried bread as could be stacked on a plate: what he called a 'double-greasy'. His fleshy round face lit up when he smelt such a feast and heard the hot fat sizzling in the frying pan. At such times his pastel blue eyes would shine and glint with greed, but his silver buttons were always dull.

The inspector sipped his tea prudently, like a tea taster. 'Tomorrow morning,' he said, 'we'll take that little malefactor to Eel Brook Common and see what the horse makes of him.'

'We will,' said Hanks, 'indeed we will.'

'And those two little blighters who got away, they'll have run off and told their mates what happened, won't they?'

Sergeant Hanks rolled his head.

'And we know what Borribles do when one of their mates gets caught, don't we?'

'Why,' said Hanks, 'they tries to get their friend uncaught before we clips his ears.'

'Right, Hanks, right. So you can bet your next double-greasy that tomorrow we'll be seeing quite a few Borribles at Eel Brook Common. They'll be there . . . but so will we.' Sussworth jumped to his feet, tipped the remainder of his tea into his mouth and then perched himself neatly on the edge of his desk like a paperweight. 'Get the men down here,' he ordered. 'I want to give them their instructions.'

Sergeant Hanks pressed a button and all round the house bells rang. A moment later there was the sound of heavy boots in the rooms above and in the kitchen below. The noise moved on to the stairs and the door to Sussworth's office opened. Twelve men in blue came to stand in front of their commander, not at attention but relaxed and confident.

'I'm glad to see you section leaders ready,' began Sussworth. 'Now we were lucky today, we caught one. Tomorrow, when we take him to see the horse, I expect a rescue attempt to be mounted. We must be prepared.' He leant forward and stamped twice on the floor. 'During the night I want men from vans two, five and eleven to take over the area surrounding the common. I want some of you to get into the houses, some others up on the roofs. Men from vans three, six and nine will guard all escape roads. You let anyone who looks like a Borrible in, but you don't let anyone who looks even remotely like a Borrible out. At exactly eight thirty I will arrive in van number one with the prisoner.

This is an ambush that must work. You will be in position by midnight tonight. I don't want anyone even to suspect that you are there . . . I have made arrangements for the vans to be hidden in lock-up garages until they are needed. Are there any questions?'

There were none.

'Right, men,' continued Sussworth, 'it only remains for me to commend the work you've done in the past and hope for even better in the future. Remember this is our finest hour. This little blighter we've nobbled knows what we want to know and I'll sweat it out of him just as soon as we've captured his mates.' The inspector slipped from his desk and stretched out both his arms. 'I have only one ambition and I know you men share it with me . . . to rid this city of Borribles. They are a threat to any normal way of life. They say they don't want much and I say that's too much. They say they want to live their way and I say they ought to live the way everyone else does.'

Sussworth's eyes swivelled in his face and he dropped his arms to his side. He stood straight and stiff and he gazed up at his men. 'Go and prepare yourselves,' he said. 'That is all.'

The policemen saluted their officer, nodded at Sergeant Hanks and left the room, shuffling down the stairs one after the other. When they had gone Sussworth fell back into his chair, exhausted by the effort of his speech. He groped for his cup and held it out, at arm's length, to the sergeant. He needed a refill.

'Oh, sir,' said Hanks, taking the cup like it might have been a holy chalice, 'you certainly know how to inspire men. You stir their blood, sir, make their hearts beat the faster. I see it as clear as day.'

The inspector stared dreamily at the surface of his desk. 'It is only because I always tell them the truth,' he said, 'and the truth is what men want to hear.'

*

It was a languid dawn that rose over Eel Brook Common and the Borribles were early awake in it. The night had been warm and sleep difficult. The travellers had arrived in the middle of darkness and hidden themselves in the tiny front garden of a house that faced the common, screened from view by a low wall of brick and a scraggy privet hedge. All night the windows in the street had hung open and gross adults in their beds had snored and blasted their way through sleep, grunting and shouting in their dreams.

'Blimey,' said Twilight, 'if only we could harness all that energy and gas we could obliterate the SBG in five minutes.'

Slowly the sky over London paled and became purple. Traffic started to growl in the main roads like an old monster, the stars glittered one last time and front doors slammed as bus drivers left home for work. Bedroom lights came on brightly and then faded as the day grew stronger; the grunting and snoring softened to nothing. The Borribles rubbed their eyes, sat up and peered through the hedge across the empty yellowness of the flat common.

'Bloody parks,' said Spiff, 'draughty old dumps. Just look at it, nothing to steal for miles. I don't know how anybody can like them.'

It was true that there was little to be seen except, on the far side of the field, a few small wooden huts behind a hedge and an iron railing. It was the sort of place in which park keepers store their tools and eat their sandwiches.

'I bet that's where they keep the horse,' said Sydney.

'Finding the horse,' said Vulge, 'is easy; it's getting it away from keepers and keeping it away from keepers that's tricky.'

'It's difficult to disguise a horse,' said Twilight. 'I mean you can't stick it on wheels and shove it down the street like it was a toy, can you? It might drop a load just as a copper came round the corner.'

'Quiet,' whispered Spiff. 'SBG.'

The others looked where he pointed and they saw a blue Transit van emerge from Wandsworth Bridge Road and come to a halt on the southern side of the common.

'It's full of John Law,' said Stonks.

Spiff shoved a hand in his pocket and pulled out a small collapsible telescope.

'Well I never,' said Vulge, 'you got one.'

'Found it in Sinjen's School,' said Spiff. 'Like you said, very handy.' He raised the telescope and poked it between the leaves of the hedge. He put his eye to it and studied the van. Two policemen emerged.

Spiff grunted. 'Two out, but I reckon there's about eight more inside. Can't see too clearly, they've got mesh across the windows.'

'Look at their shoulders,' said Chalotte. 'What rank are they?'

'Strike a light,' said Spiff, 'that's an inspector, that little squirt. It must be Sussworth 'imself, ugly sod, have a butcher's.' Spiff passed the telescope over to Vulge who stared through it while his companions stared at him.

'Cripes,' he said after a while, 'he's horrid all right, frighten Frankenstein rigid he could, and the sergeant with him ain't a work of art either, strong though, crack yer philbert open as soon as look at yer.' Vulge returned the telescope to Spiff.

The two police officers stood by the side of the van for a minute or two until they were joined by a park keeper wearing a brown uniform and a brown hat. After shaking hands the three officials walked away from the road, heading across the common in the direction of the wooden huts. When they got there the keeper took a key from his pocket, undid a padlock on the iron gate and disappeared behind the hedge. The policemen did not have long to wait. Within minutes the keeper returned leading a small horse behind him, a dingy horse with its head hanging at the rein and its feet dragging over the grass. An unhappy horse.

'Is it Sam?' asked Sydney. 'I can't see from this distance.'

Spiff passed her the telescope. 'Have a look,' he said. 'I wouldn't know your horse from a ham sandwich.'

Sydney raised the instrument to her eye. 'Oh,' she gasped, her face bright with joy, 'it is, it's Sam. The horse who saved our lives.'

'He didn't save my life,' said Spiff.

Chalotte sneered. 'Nor would anyone with any sense,' she said.

'Knock it on the head,' said Stonks, 'something's happening.'

While the Borribles had been talking the keeper had manhandled a small rubbish cart from one of the huts and was buckling Sam into it. At the same time a side door to the Transit van slid open and two more policemen appeared. Between them they held, by the arms, the small and dispirited figure of Bingo Borrible. His hat was gone, his ears were revealed.

Spiff snatched the telescope from Sydney. 'He's still got his ears,' he said, 'there's still a chance.'

'They're taking him over to the horse,' said Chalotte.

The six Borribles crouched behind their hedge and watched. The traffic was thick round the common now and people were striding this way and that towards bus stops and Underground stations. Meanwhile the sun was mounting steeply into the sky, ready to scorch the city for another day.

Bingo was shoved across the common. He did not struggle, neither did he go willingly. His head was down and his feet scuffed over the dry turf. Nearer and nearer to Sam he was dragged, made small and pitiful by the size of the men who escorted him, vulnerable in the middle of that great open space.

'If only he knew we were here,' said Chalotte.

But Bingo did not know. He was hauled up to the horse and made to stand in front of it.

'Don't do anything, Sam,' whispered Sydney, 'don't do anything.'

It was no good. Sam had been lonely and maltreated when he'd toiled for Dewdrop and Erbie and he'd known no love until the Borribles had freed him. He'd never forgotten the great Adventure and he'd not forgotten the face or scent of any one of the Adventurers. He'd dreamed of them many a sad night over the months and months since they'd been obliged to abandon him. Now he raised his head and his nostrils flared and quivered. He saw the uniforms and swung his neck away for he did not like uniforms; then he caught the smell of Bingo and swung his head back. He saw the Borrible – he shook his head and stamped his feet hard into the ground. A huge neighing of happiness burst from him and he strained forward, pulling the cart along with him.

Bingo tried to step backwards, averting his face, but the two big-boned policemen were holding him and they stood firm in their massive boots. Sam came close to Bingo and licked his face and nudged his shoulder, and though the Battersea Borrible tried desperately not to show the slightest emotion it was obvious that the horse knew him and knew him well. In the end Bingo gave up all pretence and threw his arms round the horse's neck. Even though this action placed him in great peril he remembered Sam with gratitude and knew that he owed his life to the horse. He knew also that friendship is never more valuable than when expressed in the deepest danger. Besides, he thought, why should the Woollies make him behave in a manner that was unnatural, in a way that was not like him.

'Sam,' said Bingo to Sam alone, 'there are others who will rescue you. Whatever happens we haven't forgotten our promise.'

From their hiding-place the Adventurers watched as Inspector Sussworth separated Bingo from the horse and they saw too how the police escort seized the captive and frogmarched him away. Sussworth and Hanks shook hands with the park keeper once more and left him. The doors of the Transit van opened and six more policemen came out of the vehicle. They stretched their arms to the sky and smiled.

As soon as Bingo arrived back at the van he was thrown into it and the doors were locked. His white face came to the window immediately and he peered through the grille at Sam who was now obliged to begin his day's work, pacing round the fringes of the common, stopping and starting on command while the keeper loaded the cart with all the litter he could find.

The policemen now stood in an untidy group, congratulating their chief. Sussworth's face became contorted with smiles, his moustache jerked to right and left and his feet stabbed the ground with pleasure. Sergeant Hanks was content too; cradling his magnificent belly in both hands he jiggled it up and down so that he could laugh more easily.

It took some while for the policemen's mirth to subside but when it had the sergeant pointed across the main road to where a man in a dirty white overall was taking down the shutters from the front of a small transport café. The policemen crossed the road in a bunch and the man in the white overall opened the café door and ushered them in. The SBG were going to celebrate success with eggs and bacon and mugs of tea.

'Bingo's alone in the van,' said Sydney. 'Can't we do something now?'

'It looks bloody dangerous,' said Chalotte.

Spiff pushed his telescope through the hedge and peered carefully round the common. 'Of course it's bloody dangerous,' he said, 'and what makes it worse is that I can't see anything the slightest bit suspicious out there, which probably means the opposite.'

'We won't get another chance like this,' said Stonks. 'We've got to have a go, we've got to.'

'Hang about,' interrupted Spiff, 'there's no need for us all to rush over there. Vulge better stay here because of his limp, Sydney too, and Twilight. Chalotte and Stonks come with me. Now, if we get Bingo out we'll head into the back streets between here and the river. I'll open the van on this side, away from the caff, that means you three here will have to watch the park keeper. If he looks up he'll spot us. If he tries to warn the Woollies you'll just have to run out there and clobber 'im. If that happens nick the horse and cart and drive like the clappers, away up the common, make as much noise as you can, create a diversion. After that you'll have to run into the side streets and split up, hide, get into a house, anything.' Spiff drew a deep breath and looked at the circle of frightened faces around him. 'I know it's not much of a plan,' he added, 'but it's all we got.'

'How are you going to pick the lock?' asked Stonks.

Spiff smiled. 'How do you think I did the RSPCA office?' he said, and he drew a small bundle of stiff wire from one pocket and a bunch of filed-down car keys from another. 'I'm a little boy scout,' he explained, 'always prepared.' Spiff smirked then and looked at Twilight from under his eyebrows. 'You'd better take the telescope, and don't look down the wrong end. If you see something you don't like, whistle.' And Spiff thrust his hands into his pockets and sauntered, tough and truculent, out from the garden and on to the pavement. Stonks went too and Chalotte, after grimacing fearfully at Sydney, did the same.

Twilight raised the telescope and studied the keeper for a minute or two. Nothing out of the ordinary there. Next he turned his attention to the café, but the windows were thick with the dirt thrown up by passing juggernauts and the Bangladeshi could see nothing through them. He surveyed the houses opposite, the gardens, the roofs. Everything seemed normal.

Spiff reached the van. Chalotte knelt by its front wheel and watched the café and Stonks stood near the back doors and scanned the common. Spiff, the most casual and courageous burglar in the world, leant on the SBG vehicle and attacked the sliding door with his set of keys. He was a good workman; he didn't rush and he didn't panic, not even when Bingo's face appeared close to his own, separated from it only by half an inch of soundproof security glass. The prisoner moved his mouth but Spiff heard nothing above a murmur. He bent his head and went on with his work, saying, 'Don't worry, Bingo, don't worry, nearly got it.'

'All quiet on the common,' said Stonks, his voice tense.

'All quiet in the caff,' said Chalotte, 'but get a move on.'

Two minutes went by, three. Chalotte continued to keep a sharp eye on the café door, willing it to stay shut. She heard Spiff swear but refused to turn her head, then came the sound of the lock clicking, the door slid open. Bingo was free.

She half rose from her crouching position and turned to see Bingo, pale and bedraggled, leap from the van and into Spiff's arms, shouting, 'You fools, you damn fools, it's a trap, the common's lousy with coppers.'

Chalotte glanced across the road and her mouth dried and her blood congealed into a ball of stone that stuck in her heart. The door of the café had been flung open and the policemen were spreading along the pavement, pushing pedestrians out of their way, cutting off any Borrible escape into the streets that led to the Thames.

'It's coming down harder, now,' said Spiff. 'We'll have to try and get across the common.'

Back behind the hedge Twilight jumped to his feet, dropping the telescope. 'The Woollies are coming out of the caff,' he shouted. 'Sydney, Vulge, come on. It's the cart before the horse now.'

Loading their catapults the three of them ran from their hiding place into the open, making as much noise as they could. The keeper saw them coming and turned to face them, squaring his shoulders as if for an attack he had always expected.

Vulge faltered. 'He knows,' he said, 'he knows.'

'I don't care how much he knows,' shouted Twilight, 'all the knowledge in the world won't stop a catapult.' The Bangladeshi knelt and let fly a stone which flew straight at the keeper and struck him cleanly on the elbow, drawing blood.

'Come on, Sam,' yelled Sydney. 'It's me, Sam, it's me.'

Sam needed no telling. He was a veteran of the Great Rumble Hunt and he could smell danger just as well as he could smell the scent of his Borrible friends. He neighed like a warhorse, eager for battle, swished his tail and ran in the direction of his beloved Sydney, his lips curling back over his teeth in ferocious glee.

There was no time for greeting, not then, not in the middle of such a hue and cry. Sydney sprang on to the cart and seized the reins; Vulge and Twilight leapt up beside her, catapults ready.

'I came back for you, Sam,' cried Sydney breathlessly. 'I told you I would.'

Spiff and his band ran diagonally across a corner of the common. They ran fast and in a fair race would have soon outdistanced their pursuers, but the trap had been well laid. Sweat ran into Spiff's eyes.

'Make for that street over there,' he panted, 'we'll leave 'em behind in no time.' But even as he spoke a blue Transit van skidded round the corner of the road he had indicated. All its doors burst open and another dozen Woollies jumped into the fray. 'Hell,' said Spiff, 'we've been set up.' He swerved in his tracks, the others followed and they ran up the side of the green towards the next street. Another blue van appeared and the Borribles were forced to run on.

'What about the other side of the common?' asked Chalotte.

'Take a look,' said Stonks. Chalotte saw and heard three vans screech into view. They did not stop at the kerbside either, those vans, but drove and bumped and swayed out on to the yellow grass.

'Shit,' said Spiff, 'they're really coming for us today.'

'It was nice to escape,' said Bingo, 'even if it was only for a minute.'

Sydney spied her friends and directed the cart towards them.

'Sam,' she wailed as the horse ran, 'this is not how we meant it to be. Now we're caught for good, now they'll clip us and we'll grow up and hell and dammit.'

The policemen began to advance from three sides, both on foot and in their vans, but Sam's blood came afire with the urge to help his friends and he galloped like he had on Rumbledom. He swerved and slid the cart in front of Spiff and the others and they threw themselves aboard and Sam was away again, heading for the top of the common where the field narrowed to a point and there were no blue vans to be seen.

The seven Borribles, united now, aimed and shot their catapults as rapidly as they could and the policemen on foot fell back under the onslaught of those deadly missiles, but four vans drew alongside the cart and kept pace with the gallant horse.

'Aim at the windscreens,' called Spiff, but it was not that easy. The SBG vans had thicker glass than ordinary cars and the stones rebounded harmlessly into the air.

Sam galloped on, sheering this way and that, trying to reach the streets. More vans drove on to the common, fast at first, then they slowed and circled the cart, drawing closer and closer, forcing Sam away from the edge of the field, into the centre.

Sam wheeled again and looked for a way of escape. There was none. The blue vans slithered to a halt on the dry grass, the doors banged open and scores of policemen rushed into the sunlight – Sussworth's men, his pride and his joy, in full riot gear. They held shields in front of their bodies and on their heads black helmets reflected only a black sunshine. In front of the men's faces were see-behind visors, in the men's hands, long truncheons. The SBG marched towards the cart; the world was theirs and the Borribles were hostages for it.

Sam swerved but he was hemmed in completely and the end soon came. A policeman leapt up and grabbed at Sam's bridle. The horse reared and lifted the man from his feet but he held on. Another policeman ran forward, then another. The Borribles fired stones at their knees, their ankles; many men fell but others ran round them, protecting the injured with their shields. It was a fierce battle but the SBG would not be intimidated and they did not fall back. Sam reared again and the cart crashed into one of the stationary vans. The horse whinnied piteously as he struggled to be free. He bucked, he kicked.

'Leave him alone,' shouted Sydney, and fired a stone at the constable who was punching Sam on the nose.

The cart pitched and tipped and Spiff, drawing back the rubber of his catapult, was thrown to the ground badly stunned. He groaned and rolled on to his back. Chalotte was seized by an ankle and dragged from her feet. Her back cracked against the side of the cart, she was grabbed and chucked from one policeman to another. Someone cuffed her and dropped her down beside the unconscious Spiff. She screamed and covered her ears with her hands.

'Don't clip me,' she yelled, 'don't clip me.'

Stonks was strong. He was held by the leg. He kicked out and the hand let go. He jumped over the edge of the cart and butted someone in the stomach. A way was clear before him, he moved for it but a truncheon struck him across the back and all the wind went from him, sucked from his lungs. He fell to his knees and that was the end of his battle.

Sydney had not thought of fighting. In her heart she was weeping because it had been her idea to look for Sam in the first place and now that idea had brought them all to this defeat. Never had there been such a thing in the whole of Borrible history. Never had so many been caught in one fell swoop.

Vulge sprang from the cart but he was caught in midair by two policemen and they grasped him by the legs and wrists and his skinny body writhed in the air between them. Twilight was on the ground, so was Bingo. Everyone had been taken.

With her heart breaking Sydney jumped on to Sam's back, fell on his neck and clung tightly to him. 'Oh, Sam,' she cried, 'this was all for you and it's all gone wrong, you'll never see us Borribles again.' But there was no time to say more. She was plucked from the horse by brutal hands and flung to the ground.

Spiritless she gazed at the sky. It was blue still and burnt the world. Her body ached and sweat ran over it. The earth was hard in her back and she could feel it spinning, faster and faster. All around her, staring down, was a ring of helmeted heads, moving and motionless, like the rim of a gyroscope. Blank masks: no eyes, no noses, no mouths. Nothing.

Suddenly a section of the circle fell away and into the gap stepped a short man in officer's uniform. He had twisted features and a black moustache. Beside him stood a fat policeman with a shiny face made uneven and bumpy by glowing pearls of perspiration. It was Inspector Sussworth and Sergeant Hanks.

The inspector jeered and clapped his hands and looked at the faceless faces of his men. Sydney saw him do a little jig of happiness, pirouetting from one foot to the other. The sergeant stared lovingly at the prostrate captives and licked his lips as if he were contemplating his favourite food.

'Well, well,' said Sussworth when his dance was over and a smile set crooked on his ugly mouth. 'What a lovely batch of Borribles I've got. Welcome home you little brats, welcome back to the straight and narrow.'

*

After their capture the Borribles were handcuffed together in a long line and locked into one of the Transit vans. Eel Brook Common looked like a no man's land. Two vans had crashed and one of them lay on its side, dented and demolished. Police equipment was strewn over an immense area and many of the SBG, exhausted by the heat of the day and the exertion of the chase, lay where they had fallen, like corpses on a battlefield. On the main road loitered little knots of people, gazing without understanding at the aftermath of the conflict. Some of them questioned the policemen about the cause of the affray but received no answer. They went to leave but halted to witness one last flurry of excitement.

Sam the horse had not finished yet; his body shook all over and his legs trembled, there was froth on his lips. He stood dejected in the shafts of the rubbish cart, his head touching the grass in sorrow, and the park keeper, one elbow bandaged, came up to the horse and caught him violently by the reins.

'Come on, animal,' he said, 'it's back to work for you, and no mistake.'

It is difficult to know what goes on in a horse's mind but something snapped in Sam's. He had tasted freedom for a few minutes, he had seen his friends for a while, knew he was loved, but at the end everything had been taken from him. It was more than he could bear. He lunged and he reared, snorting out a challenge to the man in brown and all that he stood for. His front legs flailed and the park keeper let go the reins and cowered to the ground, shielding his head with his good arm. In the prison van Sydney pressed her face against the wire-meshed window.

'Look,' she said, 'Sam's escaping.'

Sam kicked his hind legs at the cart that he hated. There was a noise of splintering wood and a shaft broke away. Sam reared once more, high and magnificent, and his valiant neighing rang out across the common, defying anyone to enslave him ever again.

The keeper made a last attempt to seize the flying reins but Sam sprang at him, forcing him back, and the second shaft gave and the traces snapped. Now he was free of the cart altogether; now, unhindered and unfettered, he wheeled like a wild stallion, then he chose his direction and galloped off, his neck stretched and his tail and mane and broken leathers streaming behind him.

The exhausted policemen were ordered to their feet and compelled to link arms and form a human chain across the common. Others raced to their vans, but Sam would not be caught. He launched himself at the SBG line as it advanced towards him; he ran faster and faster, his hooves thundered across the turf and the policemen before him faltered; that horse was insane – it was not going to stop. On and on sped Sam and when only a few yards from the human barricade he soared into the air, as high and as handsome as any hunter, and landed gracefully well beyond the reach of those who sought to bring him down. Across the main road he went then and into the freedom of the back streets, like any Borrible would.

'He got away,' said Sydney. 'Imagine that, he got away.'

Vulge kicked the side of the van. 'Well, we didn't,' he said, 'and what will happen to us now?'

He was not kept in suspense for long. The van groaned on its springs and three policemen climbed into the front seat. One of them switched on the engine and his colleagues turned to keep a close watch on the prisoners. The van drove slowly off the common, bumped over the kerbstones and crawled away in the direction of Fulham Road. It was escorted by another van, and another. There was to be no escaping.

It was not a long drive and within a few minutes, sirens howling, the column of blue vehicles swept into a grey yard surrounded by high brick walls; this was Fulham police station. The vans parked and the SBG men bundled out of them to form up in straight ranks while Inspector Sussworth and his sergeant stood happily before them. Just for a little while there was silence, then the inspector raised his arms and opened his mouth.

'Bloody Nora,' said Vulge who had been watching the policemen through the windows of the Black Maria, 'he's going to sing, like some football supporter whose team's won the cup.'

And sing the inspector did, a fine marching song, a song to rouse the blood, and as Sussworth sang his men saluted and marched and tramped on the spot, and every time their leader completed a verse the constables shouted aloud and sang the chorus with verve and energy: but the song sent a chill into the bones of the Borribles as they listened, for the words offered them no hope.

'To make a new society
we must reform the human race;

if all the world were just like me
the world would be a better place.

CHORUS: *'There's law and order in my blood,*
and disobedience makes me mad;
I am the friend of all that's good,
I am the foe of all that's bad.

'I hate the fools who won't obey
the rules we set for them to keep;
it's criminal to err and stray –
good citizens behave like sheep!

'Authority must always win,
dissenters are a mortal blight –
I'll straighten them with discipline,
teach them to put their morals right!

'For we know best what's right and wrong;
we make the laws, we know the form –
I'll come down hard, I'll come down strong
on every sod who won't conform –

'Especially these little brats
the Borribles – the lawless shites
with pointed ears and woolly hats;
I'll crucify the parasites!

CHORUS: *'There's law and order in my blood,*
and disobedience makes me mad;
I am the friend of all that's good,
I am the foe of all that's bad.'

Once the SBG march had been sung no more time was lost. The prisoners were hustled from their van and into the back door of the police station, pushed past some concrete steps leading to the cells, and shoved into the interrogation room. Several policemen went with the Borribles and marshalled them before a large desk. On the desk were piles of paper; behind the desk sat the malignant figure of Inspector Sussworth; beside him, ever subservient, stood Sergeant Hanks.

Inspector Sussworth arranged his papers into squares of neatness and jerked his face into some form of straightness. He cleared his throat. 'I see you're wearing Sinjen's blazers and trousers,' he began, 'some kind of disguise I suppose, pitiful! Well, let's see . . .' He studied a charge sheet. 'I can do you for breaking and entering, damaging police property, resisting arrest, obstructing police officers in the execution of their duty, attacking officers of the law, grievous bodily harm, actual bodily harm, obscene language, horse-stealing – used to be a hanging charge that one, pity – aiding and abetting a prisoner to escape and evade lawful custody . . . I've got enough to put you lot into care until the next millennium, and with your ears clipped I bet you'd grow up into as lovely a bunch of little Lord Fauntleroys as you could wish to see . . . But then I'm not interested in the future, I've got bigger fish to fry.' Sussworth's face twisted and tightened in its anger. 'You lot know something about the Southfields murders; you lot were there and before I've finished with you I'll have you queueing up to tell me about it.'

Spiff looked down the line of prisoners. 'Do you know what he's talking about?' he asked. 'Because I don't.'

Sussworth made a gesture and the policeman standing immediately behind Spiff cuffed the Borrible across the top of the head. Spiff staggered but rode the blow philosophically.

'I've never been to Southfields,' he went on, 'don't even know where it is.'

'I tell you something,' said Sussworth, 'I could clip your ears right now if I wanted to, but I'll give you all a chance. Whosoever gives me the information I want will walk out of here a free Borrible with his, or her, ears unclipped. I can't say fairer than that.'

Vulge stepped forward on the instant. 'I've got something to tell you then,' he cried.

'Yes,' said Sussworth, leaning eagerly over his desk, 'what is it?'

'It's this,' said Vulge, 'I don't know where Southfields is either.'

Inspector Sussworth was not amused. He narrowed his eyes and lengthened his lips. 'A funny man, eh?' he said. 'Well, you won't be laughing long. I'll have your ears done tonight and we'll see how brave you are then.'

Sergeant Hanks propped his belly on the desk and leant into it. 'Perhaps,' he suggested, 'it might be a good idea, sir, if we gave them until tomorrow morning to think it over. They're all a bit full of themselves at the moment but a day and a night in the cells without anything to eat or drink, well, that might help them to see things a bit differently.'

Sussworth's face flared with pleasure. 'Splendid idea, sergeant,' he said. 'You will arrange for the police surgeon to be round here first thing tomorrow morning. We'll soon have these snotty buggers singing a different song.' His eyes moved along the row of Borribles, studying each face, searching for weakness. His scrutiny stopped at Twilight.

'Well, sonny,' said the inspector, 'have you got something you want to tell me? You'd like to save your ears, wouldn't you?'

'Oh, yes,' answered Twilight, 'I would. I wish to announce, categorically, that I am not knowing the whereabouts of Southfields either.'

There was a terrible silence in the room and the tension rose. Under the kneehole desk the Borribles could see the inspector's legs contorting with fury. He drew a breath and held it in his lungs as if to cool his temper. His nose turned in the air like a corkscrew.

'Take 'em down and lock 'em up,' he screamed, 'before I goes berserk. I won't be responsible for my actions if they stays here. I'll see 'em tomorrow; and then, one by one, I'll take their ears off. I'll look forward to that all night.'

The policemen grabbed the Borribles from behind, manhandled them out of the room, and they were taken down a flight of stairs to a corridor along which the cells were situated. A policeman chose one at random and, still handcuffed one to the other, the prisoners were flung inside and the huge steel door clanged shut. A key clattered three times and the SBG men stamped away, their morning's work at last complete.

Left to themselves the Borribles stretched out as best they might on the concrete floor and, for want of pillow or blanket, rested their heads on their nearest friend.

'Well,' said Bingo, 'this is nice. No grub, no hope and after tomorrow, no ears.'

'It stinks of pee down here,' said Vulge.

'Cats?' suggested Twilight.

'No,' said Chalotte, trying to make her head comfortable on Stonks's stomach, 'humans.'

4

The stink came from the prison cubicle next door. Old Ben was in there and Ben was the dirtiest man alive. A retired tramp who no longer tramped, he lived on Feather's Wharf, a huge rubbish dump on the south side of Wandsworth Bridge. He was nightwatchman, rubbish sorter and layabout, and he lived in a ramshackle lean-to in the middle of a wild mountain range of trash. He had only one friend in his life, the stableman at Young's Brewery, and only two occupations, collecting things that other people had thrown away, and drinking beer.

Sometimes Ben drank too much and staggered out of Feather's Wharf and into the streets, weaving along the pavements, rebounding off lamp posts, singing old songs and wagging his finger at everyone who passed. When this happened Ben was arrested and kept in the police cells until he became sober, and that was where he was the day the Borribles were brought in, although he didn't notice their arrival because he was fast asleep, flat on his back on the floor and snoring. The door to his cell was open but then it was always open because no one took Ben seriously enough to lock it. As a general rule the policemen of south London just laughed at Ben and as soon as he had recovered from his bout of drinking they would simply push him on to the streets and tell him to go back to his rubbish dump. 'Keep out of sight,' the coppers told him, 'and you'll keep out of trouble.'

Ben certainly smelt and it was a very special smell: a concotion brewed of body odours, decayed rubbish, dried pee, wood smoke and stagnant Thames water. Ben never washed and the back of his neck was criss-crossed with deep crevices of dirt and pitted with the scars of ancient blackhead volcanoes. Every pore in his body had been clogged with the soot of the smoke that rose from the eternal fires of litter and lumber that he kept burning by the threshold of his shack.

His hair was black and long and gleamed with grease where he had wiped his hands; it had not been cut for years and it grew wild at the ends, tangling into the edges of a huge beard which flourished, abandoned, from one side of his face to the other. Through this hedge stuck an enormous nose, and below, though well hidden, was a large mouth holding prominent brown teeth which had been eroded into wicked shapes by beer and nicotine, saliva and time. Ben's fingernails were jagged too and as broad as shovels, loaded with grime enough, each one, to cultivate potatoes in.

He was tall and gaunt, when he could stand, with hollow shoulders, knobbly hands and eyes tired with wisdom. On his head he always wore a floppy black hat with a wide brim, but he did not wear clothes like other people wore clothes, he inhabited them, layers of them. When his garments became so old or stained that other tramps would have thrown them away, Ben just found another layer and climbed in, discarding nothing. He was like an archaeological dig and somewhere, deep down near his skin, his clothes must have been welded together in an age-old flux of sweat and dust. On top of all his shirts and jackets and trousers Ben wore two or three ancient overcoats, each one of them a labyrinth of tattered linings, poacher's pockets and hidden compartments. In them Ben carried everything he needed: beer, tobacco, bread and matches.

All his belongings came from the rubbish dump where he lived and he wanted for nothing. Ben didn't give a monkey's about the world. He didn't care for work, he didn't care for authority and he didn't care for soap and water. He didn't even care very much for himself.

He had been found the previous night on Wandsworth Bridge, singing 'Shenandoah', his favourite song, and trying to walk along the parapet high above the river. Passers-by had prevented him and had telephoned the police and they had taken him in. Ben didn't mind, he didn't mind anything. 'Might as well do one thing as another,' he used to say. 'All be the same in a hundred years, won't it?'

*

In his cell Ben groaned, opened his eyes, stopped snoring and sat up. He felt sober and he felt terrible. It was time to go home. He was sure that he had a few bottles of Young's Special Brew hidden away in his shack; just what he needed to put him right.

He attempted to focus his eyes on the door and though at first they dived and swooped, eventually they steadied. The door was open and he knew that if he went quietly along the corridor and up the stairs he would come to the ground floor of the police station. There might be someone in the front office, there might not. It would make no difference, they always let him go.

Ben struggled to his feet and felt in his pockets. All his possessions were there. One advantage of being dirty was that no one wanted to search you, not even coppers. Someone in a Salvation Army hostel had tried to give him a bath once but they'd abandoned the experiment after the first pair of sticky trousers.

Ben went into the corridor and shuffled towards the steps. It felt a little cooler though the air was still heavy and oppressive.

'Must be the middle of the night,' he said. 'Cor, I've been asleep all day; it's a wonder I didn't die of thirst.'

He came to the door of the next cell, grabbed at the grille and looked in. He always liked to see who had been arrested when he was put inside but this time he could hardly believe his eyes. In the light of a single electric bulb he saw seven children lying on the concrete floor, huddled together, not for warmth, but for comfort

'That's not right,' said Ben, adjusting his hat with meticulous care, 'kids in here, wonder what they've done, still . . . none of my business is it? None of my business.'

Ben shuffled on and left the Borribles sleeping; their predicament passed from his mind. He climbed the stairs to the corridor above and went to the back door of the police station.

'Hmm,' said Ben. He stared out. It was dark, the darkest part of the night, and a thick white summer mist was rolling up from the River Thames like poisonous gas and lying along the streets like long gobs of cotton waste.

'Hmm,' said Ben once more and leant against the door frame. 'Can't see much, should stay in me cell, really, bound to get lost on my way home . . . Still there's no beer here, leastways not for me there ain't.'

A steady hum of voices and machines came from the busy upper floors of the building. Something stamped in a corner of the yard and Ben tried to look through the soft shreds of mist.

'Can't be,' he said. 'I must be having illuminations.' He looked harder and made out the fuzzy-edged shape of a horse tied to an iron-barred window. 'Well I never, bloody spooky that is, whatever it is.'

He turned immediately and began to slop along the corridor in his broken boots. The door to the interrogation room was open and the front office was also visible. He could see the night sergeant sitting at his desk.

'I'll say goodnight to him,' said the tramp, 'maybe scrounge a couple of bob too. Always good for a touch, he is.'

As Ben advanced the policeman's telephone rang; he picked it up, listened for an instant and then got to his feet. When Ben reached the room it was empty; only the swinging door showed that the sergeant had gone upstairs.

'Hm,' said Ben, 'I'll wait a bit.' He went over to the desk and gazed down at it in wonder; it was not often that he saw such tidiness. Cleanliness and order never failed to bewilder him.

'Ain't they marvellous,' he reflected, 'all that writing things in books, squaring things off, adding things up, underlining things in red . . . Funny way to spend your time.' His eyes wandered to the shelves behind the desk; they carried rows of files and baskets of statements. Ben shook his head. 'And they calls me mad,' he said.

It was then that he saw the keys, hanging on a hook screwed into the side of one of the shelves. He rolled his head on his shoulders, first left, then right; he was alone and there was no sound of alarm from upstairs. Ben's face broke open with pleasure and a big brown smile forced a way through his beard.

'Well,' he said, 'the keys, eh, all numbered and neat, cells and handcuffs, my my. 'Course, it's nothing to do with me, but then nothing is so it won't matter, and even if it did it wouldn't would it? Anyway, it's about time I did something for a lark, haven't had a lark for years, the change will do me good.' Ben raised his right hand and unhooked two lots of keys. 'Don't you jangle now,' he said to them, 'don't you dare jangle.'

He shoved the keys into one of his overcoat pockets so that they would not rattle and retraced his steps as quietly as loose boots and no socks would allow. When he reached the Borribles' cell he peered through the grille for the second time.

'Still there look, it don't seem right, do it? Nice little kids like that.' Ben smacked his lips together, took the keys from his pocket, selected the one that bore the same number as the door and slipped it into the lock. Then he turned it till it would turn no more and the door clicked open, swinging silently on oiled hinges.

Ben entered the cell and began to undo the handcuffs that pinched the skin on the sleeping Borribles' wrists. 'Look at them red marks,' he said when he'd finished, 'terrible really. They'll have to run like the clappers when they get out of here, though. John Law won't like this a smitherin'.'

Chalotte opened her eyes and raised her head, puzzled. She couldn't remember where she was. Slowly her nose wrinkled and her lips tightened into a figure of eight. 'Cripes,' she swore, 'you don't 'arf niff.'

Ben smiled, showed his gothic teeth and held up a fistful of handcuffs. 'Don't mock that smell,' he said theatrically, like an explorer naming a new continent, 'that smell is the smell of freedom.'

Chalotte raised her unshackled hands and stared at them. Then she noticed the open door. 'Who are you?' she asked.

'I'm Ben,' said Ben, 'and I'm on my way home. Coming?'

Chalotte jumped to her feet and shook her friends awake. 'We're getting out,' she whispered. 'Don't ask me how it happened but it has.'

'Who's this bundle of rags?' said Spiff, rubbing his eyes.

'It's Ben,' said Ben again. 'Follow me.'

The old tramp led the Borribles out of the cell and along the corridor. 'Wait here,' he said, 'there may be a copper up above.' Ben climbed the stairs until his eyes were level with the ground floor, then he poked his head round the banister and saw that the office was still empty. He waved a hand behind his back. 'Come on up,' he said.

One by one the runaways crept towards the back door while Ben kept watch for the sergeant.

'What about you?' said Chalotte, who was the last to appear from below. 'Will you be all right?'

'Don't worry about me,' said Ben, 'Those coppers think I'm half drunk all the time; what they don't realize is that I'm only all drunk half the time.'

'Thanks for getting us out, Ben,' said Chalotte. 'I've never known a grown-up do anything like that for a Borrible before.'

'Borribles, eh,' said the tramp, raising his bushy eyebrows, 'I met a few when I lived on the streets, always treated me right they did . . . Why don't you come down to Feather's Wharf, I've got a lovely place down there, plenty of room.'

Chalotte's blood ran cold. She'd been through Feather's Wharf on the Great Rumble Hunt and for her it was just a square mile of desolation where the River Wandle meandered through a moonscape of rubbish before vanishing underground into the sewers – down into the mud of Wendle territory.

'Yes, Ben,' she said, 'we might, one of these days. Right now we'd better run like hell. Goodbye, and thanks.' She left the tramp and went to join her companions in the yard behind the police station.

Outside, but only for a second or two, the Borribles were rooted to the spot in astonishment. There was mist everywhere, damp and warm and clinging to everything it touched, filling the whole world with the smell of the decaying river. Here was a mist that curled and swirled, climbing up into sinister cliffs of dirty white cloud which, as they slowly altered shape, created great canyons of deep darkness below them.

'This'll help us get away from the Woollies,' whispered Chalotte, 'won't it?'

'It won't if we can't find our way home,' said Spiff.

Suddenly Sydney saw the horse on the far side of the yard. 'Look,' she said in great excitement, 'it's Sam; they must have caught him and brought him here.'

'We haven't got the time for that now,' Spiff said. 'We've got to get as far away from Fulham as we can, and you can't do that with a horse.'

'You do what you like,' said Sydney. 'I'm not going to miss a chance like this. I'm not asking any of you to help me. I'd rather you didn't, come to that, then if anything goes wrong you won't be able to blame me if you get caught.' And Sydney tossed her hair, walked over to Sam and began to undo the rope that tied him to the window.

'Let's run while we've got the chance,' said Vulge. 'We'll have to get the horse some other time . . .'

Vulge's comments were cut short by the appearance of Ben, a silhouette in the oblong of light that shone from the back door of the police station.

'You kids ought to buzz off,' he called, 'don't want them coppers running you in twice in a day . . . Shove off home.'

Then things began to happen. It was at this moment that the duty sergeant, returning from his errand, entered the front office. He heard Ben talking and, intrigued by the tramp's behaviour, directed his steps towards the back door to find out what was going on. As he neared the tramp the sergeant heard a horse being led across the yard, then the sound of scampering feet and whispering, and finally Ben's voice chanting, 'Watch out, watch out, there's a Woollie about.'

With a roar of rage the sergeant sprang at Ben and heaved him from the doorway with all his strength. The old man spun on one heel, lost a boot and teetered at high speed along the corridor until he crashed against the iron railing of the banister and slipped slowly to the floor. Ben stared at his bare foot and waggled his grimy toes. 'Me bleedin' boot's come off,' he said.

The sergeant peered into the mist. He saw a child on a horse at the precise moment she saw him. The horse bared its teeth and neighed like some flesh-eating monster; there was a flash of steel-tipped hooves and the animal clattered away through the yard gates, then echoing back from the hollow streets of Fulham came the dull rumble of fast-moving hoofbeats and the triumphant noise of children liberated.

'Strewth,' said the sergeant, 'it's the prisoners,' and he ran back into the building and down the stairs to the cells. He saw the open doors, he saw the pile of handcuffs. 'Oh, my God,' he said, 'Susswroth will have my guts for garters,' and he dashed to the first floor to tell his colleagues of the catastrophe that had befallen.

Left to himself, Ben replaced his boot and slouched back to the office, his hands thrust deep into two of his many pockets. He felt the metal of the keys rap against his knuckles.

'Oh, dear,' he said, 'they'll need those,' and he took out the keys and replaced them on their proper hooks. 'There,' he pronounced with a certain amount of pleasure, 'look at that, nice and tidy, just how they likes it. I'll go home now, all this shennanigans is nothing to do with me.' Staggering slightly, Ben aimed himself with great care across the room, through the main door, down the steps, and into the gloom of Fulham Road, singing as he went his own special song:

'Wot's the point of workin' 'ard?
Wot's the good of gainin' riches?
Money's mean and banks are bitches;
Profit's just a prison yard.

'Sling yer 'ook, an' sling it stealthy;
Gob some grub an' swig some booze,
Find a place ter kip and snooze –
Now *you're 'ealthy, wise an' wealthy!*

'Let the world roll round an' round,
Wiv its hard-worked folk in fetters:
All 'oo think themselves yer betters,
Money-mad and dooty-bound.

'Make yer choice, there ain't so many,
No ambition's worth a fart;
Freedom is a work of art –
Take yer stand with Uncle Benny!'

Not two seconds after the tramp had left the police station the duty sergeant ran down from the first floor and went straight to the telephone.

'Quick,' he said into the receiver, 'this is a general alarm. Alert the SBG and every patrol car in the area, every man on the beat. The Borribles have escaped, every last one of them, yes. How do I know? They're not here, that's all, but I do know we'd better catch 'em. Sussworth will go bananas else.'

The sergeant banged the telephone down and looked at the shelf where the keys were hanging. He refocused his eyes and stared. Was it his imagination or were those keys swinging on the hook? He glanced at the door; there wasn't a breath of air nor a whisper of draught. In spite of the summer's heat he felt a shiver of fear trickle down his spine.

'There's something cock-eyed going on here,' he said, 'something definitely cock-eyed.'

*

Ben sauntered along the Fulham Road and London was silent, just how he liked it; murky and deserted, with no cars and no human beings. Even so he could sense the millions of people all round him, twitching under the weight of bad dreams, their warm toes sticking straight up from beneath wrinkled sheets, groping for the cool air of the night. Ben sighed happily. It was a real luxury, having a city to yourself.

He rubbed his big nose with the back of his hand. Under the street lamps the paving stones gleamed dank and dark yellow and the mist surged across the black tarmac of the road in huge rolling banks. Beyond and between the feeble pools of electric light were deep corridors of gloom that could have led anywhere.

Ben stopped and listened to the quiet. He spat. 'Nah,' he said, 'they don't have those old fogs like they used to, real pea-soupers where you couldn't see your hand in front of your face, people hacking and coughing, dropping dead at bus stops, undertakers working 'emselves to death. Lovely that was.'

As the old tramp went to move on the mist meandered and thinned for a moment and he realized that he was on a corner. At the same time a nameplate showed itself. 'Rumbold Road,' read Ben, 'that'll do nicely, I'll go through there.'

Once he had left the lamps of the main thoroughfare behind him Ben could see nothing and he was obliged to feel his way forward by limping along the gutter, one foot down, one foot up, his body rising and falling as he plodded on. His progress was slow but he persevered until he eventually entered the maze of narrow streets that lie on the north side of the River Thames near Fulham Power Station, there where the great metal containers of the oil depots loom solid and high, like giants petrified.

As Ben approached the river so the mist curdled and its smell became more noxious. Past the Stephendale Works he went, by Pearscroft Court and Parnell House, using instinct to find a way, talking to himself and swearing hard whenever he found that he had strayed into a dead end he did not know.

Finally, after wandering for an hour or more, Ben emerged into Townmead Road, a wide and ghostly place with a dull brick wall that soared into invisibility on the southern side, a brick wall that was pierced with iron gates giving access to the ugly oil wharves. The whole hemisphere seemed asleep and Ben halted yet again to cock an ear. He could hear something. Across the night and down the graveyard streets came the sound of a shod horse walking, hesitant, lost in the river's fog.

The old tramp felt his skin prickle, he had completely forgotten about the animal he'd seen back at the police station. His matted hair shifted on his scalp and some strands of it separated, one from the other.

'Strewth,' he said aloud, 'an 'orse. Is this the ghost of Dewdrop and Erbie, still roaming the streets, looking for lumber?'

Ben raised his hands to his throat and gathered the loose collars about his neck. He had never met the rag-and-bone man from Southfields but he had heard the story of Dewdrop's murder and the tales that told of his restless spirit questing through the streets of south London by night, searching on and on for more and more wealth.

Another wave of mist rolled in from the river and broke in silent slow motion against a row of terraced houses. Ben shivered and shuffled on. 'This is creepy, this is,' he said, 'double creepy.'

The hoofbeats came nearer, insistent, not to be denied. Whichever way Ben turned the noise seemed to be waiting for him. Louder and louder came the sound until, at the place where Townmead Road meets Kilkie Street, a wall of mist rose into the air and without warning Ben came face to face with one of the children he had released earlier. She looked pale and scared and in her hand she held a rope which floated away behind her.

Ben jumped back in surprise, so suddenly that his feet left both his boots behind on the pavement.

'Oh my 'eart,' he cried. 'What the dickens are you doing, creeping about like an evil wish, where'd you spring from?'

'I'm lost,' said Sydney, just as terrified as Ben was. 'I'm not from this part of London, am I? This could be the backside of the moon for all I know about it.'

Ben was on the point of answering when he heard a large beast snort down its nostrils and, though he could not see it, the creature sounded very close.

'My gawd,' he said, 'it's the 'eadless 'orseman, ain't it? The devilish Dewdrop.'

'Don't be daft,' said Sydney, 'that's only Sam, he's with me.' Hearing his name Sam came into sight and gave Ben a friendly nudge in the chest.

The tramp was reassured by this gesture, and flexing his shoulders bravely he slipped his bare feet back into his boots.

'Swipe me,' he said, 'that is a relief. I thought it was one of them bovver beasts what eats 'umans. When you get the dt's as often as I do you never know what yer going to meet.'

'Ain't you the bloke that got us out of the cells?' asked Sydney.

'I am indeed,' said Ben, patting Sam on the neck, 'though I would deny it if called upon.'

'Is there any chance of you getting me across the river?' said Sydney. 'I must be out of sight before daybreak, and I need to find somewhere to hide the horse. Seems like I've been wandering around for hours.'

Ben now laid a hand on Sam's back and although the horse curled a lip at the smell that hovered about the tramp he did not back away.

'If you could just hop me up on to this animal,' said Ben, 'we could travel in style. Our objectives obviously lie in the same direction.'

Sydney did not hesitate; far away on the main roads she could hear the sound of police sirens under the low night sky, and if she did not hurry, her escape route would be blocked and dawn would find her still out on the streets, an easy catch for the SBG.

She backed Sam over to a brick coping about two feet high and helped Ben to climb on to it. Then she shoved and heaved him from behind until he was astride the horse with the reins in his hands.

'Here,' she said, 'hold those, though you won't really need 'em. Sam understands every word you say. Do you think you'll be all right up there?'

'Most certainly,' said Ben proudly. 'I have been a fine horseman in my time,' and as he raised a hand to emphasize the point he swayed alarmingly from the hips, only saving himself from a nasty fall by clutching at Sam's mane. 'Whoa,' cried the tramp fiercely, though the horse had not budged an inch, 'bugger me, but this animal is a lively lad and no mistake.'

Sydney had serious doubts about Ben's ability to find his way out of the back streets at all but she sprang up behind him, drew a deep breath against the dreadful smell and tapped the horse's flanks with her heels.

That slight touch was enough and, taking his orders from Ben, Sam set off at a stately pace in the direction of Wandsworth Bridge.

The old tramp was supremely happy, indeed rarely had he been happier. He sat on Sam's back with his arms loose and his long legs rigid, while his boots hung precariously from his hooked toes and his tattered overcoats floated gently out into the mist like a highwayman's cloak. But, as the outcasts rode along, there came again, and from not so far away, the sound of a police car tearing through the night.

'Sod the law,' said Sydney, 'I hope the others are getting on all right.'

*

The others were not getting on all right. They were trudging, hopeless and lost, through the same muddle of faceless streets as Sydney and Sam, only they did not have Ben to show them the way. They had stuck together and they were following Spiff, mainly because he had assured everyone that he knew the way to Battersea like the back of his hand, but, as time went on, it seemed less and less likely that he did. The Borribles had turned a hundred corners and retraced a thousand steps; now they no longer had any idea where they were. They were tired, dispirited and almost ready to give up.

A siren howled strangely in the night and an SBG van passed nearby. The Borribles ducked behind a low wall but there was no real need. Down there by the river the mist was too dense for light to penetrate. Nothing the police had, neither revolving blue beam nor yellow headlamp, showed up at more than a yard or two. When the van had driven into the distance the runaways resumed their march, and as they did another sound came out of the huge cavern of darkness that surrounded them – the eerie footfalls of an invisible horse stalking along the roadway.

'It must be Sydney,' said Chalotte, 'with Sam. Let's give 'em a whistle.'

She lifted her fingers to her lips but Spiff raised a hand of his own and clasped it over the girl's mouth, jerking her head round roughly so that he could glare into her eyes.

'You bloody fool,' he hissed. 'And it might be a mounted Woollie, and it might be a trap. You whistle and we could be back inside just as sure as eggs is fried. Keep quiet, everyone. Even if it is Sid and Sam the last thing I want is a bleedin' 'orse clip-clopping along behind me telling every copper in London where I am.'

Chalotte struggled but she could not break free of Spiff's grasp and none of the others made a move to interfere. As far as they were concerned Spiff was right. It could be Sam out there but it could be the police too and nobody wanted to be captured a second time. So the Borribles stood without moving, held their breath and listened to the ghostly hoofbeats passing by.

'We'll wait here,' said Spiff, 'till everything's nice and quiet.'

*

Ben was enjoying himself. Sydney was not. Ben sang snatches of his song to while away the time. Sydney was trying to live without breathing. She liked the tramp well enough of course and was grateful to him for the part he had played in her rescue and escape, but riding behind him, arms round his waist and nose bumping into the small of his back, was not a pleasure. Ben's odour, especially at close range, was mature and strong. No one in the history of the world had ever smelt like Ben and he not only carried this smell with him, he added to the strength of it every few seconds, with a great deal of noise.

'I can't help it,' he explained, 'it must be all that beer I drinks.'

Sydney was a brave girl. 'How much further?' she gasped.

Ben glanced to his right and then to his left. He could see nothing. 'Looks like Demorgan Road,' he said, 'we'll be round the corner soon and on to Wandsworth Bridge.'

'Wandsworth Bridge!' Sydney felt frightened. Wandsworth Bridge was right on the eastern frontier of Wendle territory. Beyond it lay the River Wandle and the deep sewers where the most violent and untrustworthy of all Borrible tribes lived: the Wendles.

'Couldn't you take me to Battersea Bridge?' said Sydney. 'Any bridge except Wandsworth.'

Ben twisted round so that he could look at his companion. 'See 'ere, sunshine,' he said, 'you wanted me to bring you to the river, and that's what I'm doing. I'm going to where I knows best, ain't I? I have to; it's pitch dark, see, and I ain't got no radar in me pocket.'

'It's not that,' said Sydney, embarrassed at appearing ungrateful, 'but the Wendles live round here and they don't like us.'

Ben spat and a solid oyster of gob spun once in the air and went splat in the darkness. 'Them Wendles is only bits of kids like you, Borribles, ain't they? I sees one or two of 'em from time to time, on Feather's Wharf. They won't hurt yer, long as you're with me.'

'I hope not,' said Sydney, 'but I don't like it down here.'

Ben took no more notice and faced about. 'Come on, horse,' he said, 'down 'ere a bit and then left.'

Sam stepped out earnestly, thrusting his head into a mist which now grew thicker and warmer at every step, a mist that became so impenetrable by the river that the two riders did not realize they were on a bridge until they felt the ground rising steeply beneath them.

'This is it,' said Ben, 'soon be over the water.'

Up and up went the roadway and Sam stamped his hooves hard upon the tarmac, pacing forward till he reached the high point at the middle of the bridge and there, where the slope began to fall steeply away on the southern side, he stopped for a moment.

All about him was silence, except for the careless slap of a wave or two far below as the black river rolled seawards, forcing itself between the great stone pillars that held the bridge steady in the air. Sydney could see nothing. For a split second she felt that she was soaring, hovering above a sleeping city that was pinned down powerless by the muscular weight of the warm night.

Ben had no such thoughts. 'Come on, Sam,' he urged, 'I'm thirsty, I am. Was born thirsty, wasn't I?'

The horse moved forward once more and soon, though they couldn't see it, Ben and Sydney came to the great modern roundabout which is set at the beginning of the Wandsworth one-way system.

'We'll go right here,' said Ben. 'Wrong side of the road, of course, but us night riders don't have to worry about rules and regulations.'

On they went, under the railway bridge and past a pub or two but not a car overtook them, not a window shone and the street lamps were blind. Only the wail of a police siren occasionally arced through the blackness, faintly and from far, far away across the wide waters. Sam did not falter for an instant; off Armoury Way he strode, right by the splendid entrance of Wandsworth Town Hall and along the High Street, coming at last to the great crossroads at Garratt Lane where the Spread Eagle pub stood locked and silent on the corner.

'Whoa,' said Ben and he swung a leg over Sam's neck and slid his feet to the ground. 'You just sit tight, girl,' he said to Sydney. 'I'll show you somethin', got to hide this 'orse, ain't we?'

In spite of the man's fearful smell Sydney felt her heart go out to him. 'Do you know, Ben,' she said, 'you're almost like a Borrible, but grown-up somehow, and that's impossible.'

'So's most things, sunshine,' said Ben, and he walked on, leading the horse.

At the far side of the road junction Ben came to a high wall of glazed brick; it was dripping with mist. He turned left there and waddled along for a few yards until he reached two enormous wooden gates. Sydney followed him, her mouth open, amazed by the size and magnificence of what she saw; it was like standing before the ceremonial portals of some ancient and fortified city.

Ben's fingers patted at a buttress of the wall until they found a bell-push. He winked at Sydney, then pressed the button, and beyond the gates and on the remoter side of courtyards and warehouses, the bell rang and the sound of it echoed along a river bank and told Sydney where she was. She caught her breath and remembered; she was outside Young's Brewery on the banks of the River Wandle, right in the middle of Wendle territory.

'Dammit,' she exclaimed, leaping from Sam's back to lean against the wall and stare into the darkness. 'Ben,' she asked, 'why have we come here?' She sounded very frightened.

'Come to get a drink, ain't I?' said Ben. 'Young's Brewery this is. Lovely drop of stuff they make here, but over and above that they uses horses to deliver their beer, don't they? And to have horses you have to have stables and to have stables you have to have someone as can look after them, someone who likes horses, and it so happens that the person I means is a mate of mine. On the road together we was in the old days, walking and talking and scrounging, just like the aristocracy. That's the way to live, sunshine, when you're young enough. Sam will be safe here, you'll see, safe as houses, and there's not a copper in Christendom will think of looking for him in a stable, is there?'

While Ben was talking the sound of studded boots started to clang across the uneven stones of a cobbled yard. Nearer and nearer banged the boots until at last they stopped quite close and a dead voice came from nowhere suddenly and the words it spoke suspended themselves in the darkness, like damp tea towels left overnight on a washing line.

'Who is it that wants me at this unearthly hour?'

Sydney shivered as the words touched her, but Ben was unworried. 'It's Ben,' he said, 'and he needs help.'

The voice did not answer but Sydney heard two iron bolts rasp and a small door set into the main gates creaked open and a man's face appeared, floating on its own in the night. It was a face that glowed pale under flat spiky hair. On either side of a hard bony nose two sombre eyes angled up and down. Under the nose grew a moustache.

Sydney pressed her body tight into the warm sweat of the brick wall. The man blinked at Ben as if he'd never seen him before, then he swung his head round to take in Sydney. The expression did not change at first but as the eyes slid beyond the Borrible and saw Sam the face broke into a smile that warmed and transformed the whole countenance. The man spoke through the smile and his tone was no longer loathsome, but friendly and welcoming.

'Well, Ben,' he said, 'and where did you get such an 'orse from, eh? What a beauty. Tired out though, ain't he? Been ill-treated, I'd say.'

Ben wagged his beard. 'He has been, Knibbs, he has been. Name of Sam, this girl's 'orse. Her name is . . .?'

'Sydney,' said Sydney.

'It's like this,' said Ben, ' we got here by way of escaping from police custody and we needs to hide the 'orse while we goes to ground, like.'

Knibbs studied Sydney closely, his eyes keen. 'I'll look after the 'orse,' he began, 'I like 'orses. Can't hide you two though; they'd spot you. Might call the law in, then they'd notice me. Got a bit of form, I have, but they'll never even see an extra 'orse in a stable full of 'orses. Best place to hide church lead is on another church roof, I always say.'

'Ta, Knibbsie,' said Ben, and he went to hand Sam's leading rope to the stableman, but the horse wrenched its head away and sidestepped, frightened by the tall gates and the overhanging walls.

'Now then, come on,' said Knibbs in his kind voice, 'you'll be all right here with me.' Another bolt slid and slowly the big gates opened until there was a gap large enough for Sam to walk through.

Sydney put her arms round the horse's neck. 'You have to hide, Sam,' she said, 'just for a day or two. I'll come back as soon as I can, and I'll never leave you again, honest.'

Knibbs clicked his teeth and stroked Sam gently on the nose. 'It's the life of Riley in here, old son,' he said. 'It's a five-star stable and no mistake.' At last encouraged, the horse stepped through the gap and into the brewery yard.

Once Sam was safely inside Knibbs closed the great gates but the little door he left open. Ben held out his arms, there was a clink of glass against glass and Sydney heard, rather than saw, three pint bottles pass between the two friends.

Ben tucked the beer into the layers of his clothing. 'Ah, thanks, Knibbsie,' he said, licking his lips, 'thirsty work, staying alive, thirsty work.'

Knibbs nodded. 'I'll take care of the 'orse,' he said, shutting the door finally, though they could still hear his voice, 'but in future make sure you come the back way.' And that was all except for the sound of Sam being led away across the cobbles.

'Let's be off,' said Ben, and he began to trudge away into the fog; Sydney walked by his side.

'Are you quite sure that Sam will be all right?' she asked, anxious now that her horse had really gone.

Ben fumbled in his overcoat and brought out one of his bottles and an opener. ''Course I am,' he said. 'Knibbs likes nothing more than an 'orse. He'll look after 'im like a babby, so fat and pampered he'll be, you won't recognize him.'

Ben took the top off his beer and looked at the bottle as if he'd never seen one before. 'My God,' he said, 'I've been waiting a lifetime for this.' He raised the drink to his lips and Sydney watched while he took a deep swig. From miles away over the river came the rise and fall of a police siren, howling through the night like a banshee.

Ben lowered the bottle and expelled a sigh of satisfaction from the middle of his beard. 'That's the stuff,' he said. 'It puts hair on your chest, marrow up your bones and lead in your pencil.'

'Are we going somewhere now?' asked Sydney.

'Somewhere, I say we are,' answered Ben, 'we're going to my place. You can bet yer boots that the Woollies are pounding the streets for you and they won't be full of joy and goodwill if they finds yer, neither.'

Ben laughed at his own joke, tipped the bottle to his mouth again, and still walking, drained it dry. When the beer was finished he gave a fruity belch. 'By gum,' he said, 'I needed that, felt weak and trembly I did.'

'Do you think my mates are all right,' said Sydney, keeping close to the tramp so as not to lose sight of him. 'I hope they all got away.'

Ben looked down at the small Borrible from somewhere beneath the bushes of his eyebrows. 'Them friends of yourn,' he said, 'are alive or dead, free or caught, and all we can do right now is look out for number one.' And with that he plodded off at a fast rate and Sydney kept up with him as best she might, having no wish to be left alone and lost in the middle of dangerous Wendle country.

5

Spiff tiptoed into the garage forecourt. All about him the big petrol pumps, their computer faces half hidden in the shadows, stood like Martians come down to earth. The Borrible halted and looked carefully to right and left. Nothing. Underfoot the oil-stained concrete gleamed in the light that fell from some half a dozen overhead fluorescent tubes; a strange mauvish light it was and one that diffused itself over a million particles of mist and hung in the air like dirty raindrops on a dusty spider's web. It was not yet dawn and the sky beyond the garage was dark and unbroken.

Spiff looked round once more, satisfying himself that the garage was well and truly closed for the night, then he whistled the Borrible whistle and, one by one, his companions stepped out of the blackness.

'Where are we?' asked Vulge.

'Dunno,' answered Spiff, 'but wherever we are we ain't far from the river. Smell.'

Everyone sniffed and the strange odour of the Thames in London, a mixture of varnish and vinegar, was drawn into their nostrils.

'Well,' said Bingo, 'where there's a river there's a bridge and we'd better get across it. If we ain't off the streets by daylight we might as well clip our own ears and save Sussworth the trouble.' He groped his way over to the far side of the forecourt, the rest of the group following.

'Look,' said Twilight, 'ain't that a main road there, anybody know it?'

There was no answer, but after a moment Spiff, who had been staring hard at the ground, said, 'I reckon it's straight on, see how the road rises slightly in that direction, like it was going towards a bridge.'

'Well come on,' said Stonks, 'we don't want to hang about. There's nowhere to hide on a bridge; let's get over before the mist goes.'

But the mist showed no signs at all of going and as the Borribles moved forward it continued to steam up from beneath their feet, growing strangely heavier as it rose, swirling and turning, making it impossible for the runaways to see where they were or where they were walking.

Suddenly Spiff, who was leading, raised a hand and stopped. They had arrived at the highest point on the bridge, where the road began to slant downwards and out of sight as if it had come to an abrupt end on the edge of the world.

'Well, it's definitely a bridge,' said Spiff. 'Look, it goes down this side, over the hump.'

'Yeah,' agreed Stonks, 'but which bridge? I don't recognize it.'

'It ain't Battersea Bridge,' said Bingo.

'And it ain't Albert Bridge or Chelsea Bridge,' said Vulge.

'And it's not Westminster, Lambeth or Vauxhall Bridge,' said Stonks.

'Or Hammersmith Bridge or Putney Bridge,' said Twilight.

Chalotte pushed through the group and put her face, tight with anger, close to Spiff's. 'You know which one it is, don't yer, Spiff?' she said. 'It's the only one it can be . . . You knew you were bringing us here all the time. Go on, tell them.'

Spiff laughed. 'It don't matter which bridge it is,' he said, 'long as we get across it, does it? So it's Wandsworth Bridge, so what?'

'So what,' Chalotte sneered, 'because Wandsworth is Wendle territory. Last time we were here we nearly got killed and four of our mates did. You're up to something, Spiff, and I wish to hell I knew what it was. What's your game?'

'My game,' said Spiff, screwing his face right back at Chalotte's, 'is getting back 'ome with me ears still on.'

As the two of them glared at each other the hoo-ha, hoo-ha of a siren came from somewhere near at hand and there was no more time for argument. All six Borribles ran down the southern slope of the bridge just as fast as they could. If they could make it to the great roundabout they would be able to bear left into York Road and head straight for Battersea; with luck, and in a little while, they would be safe at home, hidden and protected by friends.

It was not to be that easy. Two indistinct and menacing figures, one large and one small, grew out of the mist in the path of the speeding Borribles. Spiff skidded to a halt and the others bumped into him.

'Sussworth and Hanks,' said Spiff, 'and not a catapult between us.'

'A Borrible,' said a voice.

'Cripes,' said Vulge, 'it's Wendles, which is worse.'

'Don't be daft,' said the voice again. 'It's Sydney, and I've got Ben with me; you know, the bloke who got us out of the nick.'

'Oh, it's me all right,' said the tramp, and there was the clink of a bottle in his clothes. 'Small world, ain't it?'

'Wait a minute,' said Spiff suspiciously, 'have you got that bloody horse with yer? We don't want him following us about, clip-clop, clip-clop.'

'Don't you worry,' said the tramp, pulling a bottle of beer from a pocket, 'he's in a safe place.'

'None of that matters now,' said Twilight. 'Look behind you.'

The Borribles did and there, just a little beyond the rim of the bridge, they saw a halo of harsh whiteness reflected on the underneath of the dark sky. It was the beam of a car's headlamps as it got into position on the north side of the bridge, the side the runaways had left only moments before.

As they watched there was more noise behind them: tyres screeching, car doors slamming, men shouting. They turned again; once more a brightness glowed and another arc of silver light clamped itself against the low-lying mist, this time on the southern shore of the Thames and only three hundred yards from where the Borribles stood.

'It's that bloody Sussworth,' said Spiff. 'I bet he's blocked every bridge between Richmond and the sea.'

'We're caught in the open too,' said Bingo. 'Once daylight comes we've had it.'

Ben leant against the balustrade of the bridge and drank from the second of the bottles that Knibbs had given him. 'Well,' he said as soon as the bottle was empty, 'I think you kids better come home with me.'

'Oh, yeah,' said Spiff, 'and what do you think the coppers will do, help us on our way?'

Ben scratched inside his coat and ignored Spiff's sarcasm. 'Behind me,' he said, 'as I stand here, though you can't see it, is the end of the bridge. Behind that is a narrow roadway, next to the river here, and down there is a pub, stands all on its own that pub, in empty ground, called the Ship it is. Behind that pub, about eight feet high and with only a little barbed wire on top is a wall; behind that wall is Feather's Wharf rubbish dump. In the middle of that rubbish dump is my 'ome, a palace with room for everyone.'

'And what's beyond your palace?' asked Spiff.

'The River Wandle,' said Ben, 'where the cranes load the barges with trash before they sails away to export.'

'It's where the Wandle meets the Thames,' said Sydney, 'don't you remember, it's awful.'

'It could be ten times awful,' said Spiff, 'but it's the only way we're getting off this bridge.'

'One thing's certain,' said Chalotte, 'we're getting deeper and deeper into Wendle territory . . . It's almost like someone wanted us to go there.'

Spiff smiled mysteriously. 'Don't blame me,' he said. 'We've got no choice now.'

They did not have far to go. A few paces beyond where they had been standing they came to a slope that dropped steeply away from the bridge; this slope soon became a road and after following it for about a hundred yards, leaving the Ship Inn on their left, they came to a solid brick wall, and as Ben had said, the top of it was looped along with barbed wire.

'We're right on the river now,' explained the tramp, 'so if you climb up this little embankment wall here you can reach round the end of the big wall and you'll feel an iron ring on the other side. Hang on to that, throw your legs out over the water and, lo and be'old, you'll find yourself on Feather's Wharf.'

'And if we falls in the river . . .?' asked Vulge.

Ben snorted. 'I've done it hundreds of times drunk, so I'm sure you bits of kids can do it sober. 'Ere, watch this.' The old man hauled himself on to the low parapet of the embankment, grasped something that was out of sight, kicked his feet, threw himself into space and disappeared. After this exploit there was a second or two of silence, just time enough for the Borribles to look at each other anxiously, then they heard the crash of a body hitting solid earth.

'I hope he's all right,' said Sydney, but at that moment Ben's voice resounded loudly through the night.

'Ouch, ooer, it's me back, bugger it! Come on over, you lot. I'll catch yer this side.'

'I don't want to fall in,' said Twilight, 'I can't swim.'

'Tough,' said Spiff. 'I'm going anyway. I'd rather fall into the Thames than fall into the hands of the SBG.' He sprang on to the wall and leant sideways, an expression of concentration on his face. 'I can reach the ring,' he called down. 'You have to push yourself round here and hang on tight. Like this.' And with that Spiff disappeared as well.

Stonks was next up and he followed Ben and Spiff without the slightest hesitation. Then Sydney went, then the others. Chalotte waited to be last and as she swung her legs out above the rolling darkness of the river she glanced upwards and saw that the sky was becoming pale; she could even see one or two weak stars. The mist was going and dawn was on the way – it was time for the Borribles to be under cover.

Down on the ground there was no light. When Chalotte had pivoted through the air and landed on a patch of hard and dusty dirt she found that the faint glimmer she had seen in the heavens did not penetrate the murk of Feather's Wharf.

Ben's voice came to her from somewhere in the dead atmosphere beside the brick wall. 'Ah . . . what'll we do? Ah yes, best follow me in single file, you lot, and don't take the wrong path, 'cos you'll end up in the rubbish crusher if you do.'

Having given them this warning the old tramp set off into a vast and lightless terrain. This was the wasteland that stretched between Wandsworth Bridge and the River Wandle, an abandoned country which rose in crumbling hillocks and fell in deep valleys of brown and black earth. It was a place of desolation where nothing was visible in the dark but where the Borribles could sense the danger of an emptiness somewhere near, like an unseen cliff beneath their feet.

Silently they trudged, keeping close behind Ben as he went along a narrow track whose surface had been packed firm over many a month and year by the slow scufflings of his broken boots. The path wound this way and that across the land; through wide depressions in which half-squashed tins and rotten cartons were knee-deep, and over hills so precipitous that the Borribles were forced to climb them on all fours, just like the rats that scampered and squealed all around.

There were fearsome smells too, making the air thick as soup as it floated in from the Thames; a foul stench compounded of rancid sewage, mouldering cardboard and the rotting flesh of dead seabirds. The odours pricked at Chalotte's nostrils and as she walked she remembered, from her previous visit, the grotesque ugliness of this strange landscape: a square mile of dullness strewn with the white rectangles of rusty washing machines and gutted gas stoves; a maggoty place.

Chalotte gritted her teeth and followed the shape in front of her, up and down, left and right. Finally the shape and the shapes in front of it stopped, and she heard Ben's voice come from the head of the column.

'We're here,' he said, ''ome, sweet 'ome.'

Staring into the gloom Chalotte could just make out an oblong of shadow that could have been a small building. Ben's tall form merged with it and there was the scraping noise of bone dry hinges grinding on rust. Slowly the Borribles edged through a doorway, step by step, until they stood, seeing nothing, in the unknown space of Ben's hideout, and there they waited, hardly daring to breathe.

For a while they listened to Ben fumbling and swearing in the dark, then they heard the scratch of a match, then another, and a tiny flame sputtered into life. Ben brought the candle to the flame and the light flickered up for a moment, fastening on to the wick and finally growing large and steady. The tramp was strangely silent. He put the candle down and, still without speaking, he went round the room until he had lit every other candle he possessed. When that was done he brought three larger oil lamps from a shelf and lit them too. And now the golden light filled the whole shack and the Borribles gasped and gazed around in wonder. They were in the most remarkable residence they had ever seen; it was a palace, just as Ben had said it would be, but a palace in his own style. Nobody but Ben could have made such a house.

The tramp laughed at the amazement on the faces of the Adventurers and fell into a chair at the head of the long table which occupied the centre of the room. Then he groped under his seat and began to pull bottles of Special Brew into sight, lining them up, one beside the other, until there was enough for everybody.

'Here you are then, mates. You'd better have one of these, celebrate your arrival at Ben's gaff, like.' He looked round the room until he could contain his pride no longer. 'Well,' he asked, 'what do you think of her, eh? I tells yer straight, even ole Queenie ain't got nothing like this; she wouldn't know what to do with it even if she had.'

The Borribles nodded. There was a lot in what Ben said.

They were standing in a large room which had been made by banging tarred planks into the ground and then nailing sheets of corrugated iron across them to form a roof. It was a rickety building and one that seemed liable to collapse at any moment, but it was not the shack itself which astounded the Borribles so much as its contents.

The table, at the head of which Ben now sat drinking his ale like a Viking chieftain, had elegant bulging legs and a chenille tablecloth of a deep burgundy colour. All Ben's candles burned in graceful twirly candlesticks from which the silver plate had worn away to leave the brass gleaming through, brighter than gold.

At one end of the room was an enamelled wood-burning stove with a pot belly and three feet made like lion's claws. Its doors must have fallen off at some time in the past but they had since been re-hung on hinges improvised from the thick wire of a coat hanger. The hut's earthen floor was covered with several layers of carpet, warm and luxurious to the feel of the foot. There was no shortage of armchairs either, all of them threadbare, shapeless and comfortable. Against one of the longer walls leant a huge dresser overloaded with brightly glazed cups and plates; they were chipped and cracked but remained, for the most part, quite serviceable.

Ben had plenty of food too, though it looked as second-hand as the furniture and cascaded out of the front of a large kitchen cabinet: torn packets of cornflakes, broken boxes of dried milk, bags of biscuit pieces, tins of steak and kidney pudding and loaves of sliced bread, mouldy at the edges and spilling out of their waxed paper like grimy playing cards, spreading across the floor, trodden into the carpets.

But that was only a beginning. All round the room at every height were planks of rough wood, loosely bracketed to the walls and sloping precariously. These were Ben's shelves and on them he stacked the things he called useful, the things he had discovered in the mounds of rubbish on Feather's Wharf: old-fashioned valve radios, magazines, knives and forks, sardine cans filled with nuts and bolts and spring washers, bicycle chains, torches, spanners, screwdrivers. The Borribles gazed and gazed. There was even a beer crate under the table stuffed to the brim with dozens of pairs of old shoes and, on a worm-eaten chest of drawers, an ancient wind-up gramophone with a pile of old seventy-eights beside it. Such was Ben's shanty.

The tramp wagged his beard in contentment, pleased at the surprise on the faces around him. He scratched an armpit and opened another bottle of beer.

'I've got something of everything,' he said. 'It's diabolical what people throw away; and that ain't the half of it, just have a look at this.' Ben pulled himself to his feet, seized an oil lamp and went to a curtain that was draped across a corner of the room.

'You see,' he explained, 'this shack we're in now was here when I came so all I had to do was furnish it, but there was so much good rubbish going to waste that I had nowhere to put it all, so I kept adding other shacks to this one. You can come and see if yer like.'

Ben drew the curtain aside, held his lamp high and stepped through a narrow doorway with the Borribles following. Once again they gasped. They were in a lean-to in which pile upon pile of second-hand clothes rose in towers to the roof. There were clothes of all kinds: trousers, coats, shirts, sweaters, cloth caps. There was hardly space enough to move.

'I don't know what to do with it all,' said Ben. 'I swaps some from time to time, just for grub and beer, but people throws their stuff away quicker than I can pick it up . . . There's a damn sight more than this too.'

And there was. Ben had added at least six or seven sheds on to the original one and each construction leant weakly back upon its neighbour for support, looking ready, so it seemed, to fall over at the first puff of wind. It was all dangerously ramshackle but Ben had been obliged to make his house out of the materials that had come to hand: splintered doors, squares of asbestos, bits of broken window, sheets of enamelled iron bearing advertisements, the timber from shattered packing cases, everything nailed and wired together to form a warren of rooms and corridors, and not one of them at right angles to another but sprawled about all higgledy-piggledy, making haphazard corners inside and triangular yards outside, shapes that were ideal for storing the thousands of things that Ben had collected over the years.

In the third room were countless bottles of all colours, stacked row upon row, smelling of stale alcohol and covered in dust and thick black cobwebs: wine bottles, beer bottles, cider bottles and lemonade bottles.

The next lean-to was where Ben kept bits and pieces of hundreds of oil lamps, antique and modern, and between the slanting shelves there were brass hooks and from each one hung a coloured mug or flowered chamber pot. The fifth room had its walls concealed by thousands of tin cans, cleaned and flattened with a hammer and then nailed in position, making the place glitter like a pub at Christmas. Here too were beds and sofas with coverlets, blankets and eiderdowns, enough to sleep an army.

'This is where I snoozes,' said Ben, and he held his lamp up to show a huge brass bedstead adorned with five or six interior-sprung mattresses, making the bed so tall that the tramp needed a stepladder to get into it.

The sixth room was stacked to the height of a man with bundles of newspapers, magazines and books. The seventh was a kind of workshop where Ben stored tools and kept a few deckchairs and sun loungers.

'I like to watch the barges and tugs going by in the summer,' he said, 'and the people rushing over the bridge in their cars on the way to work. It makes you think, that do, all that galloping about so they can throw this stuff away so as I can sit 'ere and watch 'em.' And he shook his hairy head and fell silent, puzzled by this great mystery of life.

When the tour was ended Ben shepherded the Borribles back to the main shanty, sat them down, poured them a mug of beer each and set about making a meal. He began by lighting his stove from a pile of kindling that he kept near the door, and as soon as his fire was burning well he unhooked an iron frying pan, encrusted with grease, and filled it with the ingredients that came to hand.

There was dried milk, dried egg, tinned tomatoes, cornflakes and some cans of beans, all of which the tramp mixed together in a kind of swill and cooked piping hot. When it was ready he laid white soup plates on the table, put out some spoons, and while everyone gathered round he rummaged in the food cabinet and found a couple of sliced loaves that were not too green at the edges.

'You'd better tuck in,' he advised the Borribles. 'In this world you cannot tell what's going to happen tomorrow and you never know where your next meal's coming from.'

The Adventurers did not need to be persuaded of this philosophy and they attacked the food with an appetite. Ben leant his chair against the wall, propped his feet on the table, and watched his guests with pleasure, tipping a bottle of beer into his mouth every time he felt the need. 'Bloody marvellous,' he kept saying, 'bloody marvellous! I ain't never 'ad anyone visit me before.'

In next to no time the plates were empty and the Borribles began to stretch their limbs and relax, forgetting for a moment the dangers that surrounded them. All of them that is except Spiff. He wiped his plate with a slice of bread, licked his fingers clean, left his seat and without a word to anyone went outside.

'Where's he gone?' asked Ben.

Chalotte closed one eye. 'Always on the lookout is our Spiff. Don't trust no one and never leaves anything to chance.'

'Well, he's right, isn't he?' said Vulge. 'If Borribles don't look alive, they're very soon dead.'

Twilight grinned and folded his arms. 'I could live here for ever,' he said. 'this is the best house I've been in . . . All we need now is about twenty-four hours' sleep and we'll be as right as rain.'

'There's enough beds here for yer,' began Ben. 'If you like to go in the other room you can—' but he was interrupted by Spiff who suddenly reappeared, slamming the shack door behind him.

'There'll be no sleeping now,' he said urgently, 'we've got to get out of here, as quick as we can, if we can.'

'How d'yer mean?' asked Stonks.

'The Woollies,' said Spiff. 'It's light outside and I saw them, through the mist, looking over the wall. I had a look the other way too; there's a couple of police cars near the unloading wharf, lights flashing. We're outnumbered and we're surrounded.'

The Borribles stared at each other; the food congealed in their stomachs and went hard like golf balls. Ben hiccuped, took his feet from the table and lowered the front legs of his chair to the floor.

'Let's take a look,' said Vulge. 'There's got to be some way out.'

The Borribles hastened to the door, dropped to their hands and knees and crawled outside to crouch behind the nearest pile of rubbish. It was a silent landscape they saw; not a car could be heard on the streets and no tug hooted on the river. The night had risen halfway into the sky and, though the air was still black on its highest edge, the ground was clearly visible save where the mist formed large pools in the hollows and where white shreds of it twirled upwards like will-o'-the-wisps eager to evaporate.

Spiff pointed to the barrier that divided Feather's Wharf from the Ship Inn. 'Look,' he said, 'along the top of the wall, they must be standing on the roofs of their cars; you can see the heads of about twenty Woollies, just watching.'

'Do you reckon they know we're here?' asked Twilight.

'Could do, easy,' said Bingo. 'They might have been near us in the mist, heard us talking when we came over the bridge.'

'Come round the other side of the shack,' said Spiff, 'it's worse.'

Slowly, so as to make no noise and to attract no notice, the Borribles crept to the other side of Ben's shanty and peered cautiously across no man's land. There was no mistaking the line of sombre figures waiting for the dawn to establish itself along the banks of the Wandle. The police officers stood like shadows, magnified in the last drifts of the early morning haze; behind them were three or four police cars, their whirling blue lights casting a cold and unlovely hue over the whole landscape; it was a colour that drained the life from every living thing. There would be no escape in that direction.

'Let's get under cover,' said Spiff, 'before it gets any lighter.'

Inside the shack there was desperation.

'There's only one way,' said Spiff, 'and that's a run to the river, and the chances are that Sussworth's got boats on it. We might be able to get up the Wandle . . .'

'That bloody Sussworth,' said Chalotte.

'Who's Sussworth?' said Ben, opening another bottle of Special Brew. 'What's he got against yer?'

The Borribles explained.

'Oh,' said Ben, waving his drink in the air. 'SBG eh, don't worry about them. Any friend of mine is a friend of mine.' Ben was getting drunk and once he was on the way he went very quickly.

Bingo called from the door where he had been keeping watch. 'They're coming over the wall. I can see Sergeant Hanks, now

Sussworth and . . . blimey, they're handing a bleedin' great Alsatian dog over.'

Ben swayed upwards out of his chair. He blew into his beard and banged his bottle on the table like a declaration of war. 'That does it,' he snarled. 'I don't often do anything but when I do I do. Dogs, is it? I'll shove so many dogs up this Sussworth's nostril he won't know if he's a Pekinese or a poodle.'

With that the old man fell forward on to his hands and knees and began to pull at the edge of his carpets.

Sydney rushed to him anxiously, thinking that he was overcome by emotion and perhaps dying of a heart attack. 'Are you all right, Ben?' she asked.

Ben turned his head to the light; his red-veined eyes shone with anger. 'Course I'm all right, sunshine, and so will you be in a jiffo. Give a hand here, roll back these carpets.'

When Sydney heard this she bent to the floor and peeled back several layers of carpet to reveal the studded metal cover of a manhole. It was rusty but the words embossed on the edge of it were quite legible: Wandsworth Borough Council.

Spiff chuckled and tapped the cover with his foot. 'The sewers,' he said. 'Well, the Woollies won't follow us down there, that's for sure.' He looked at Bingo. 'What are they doing now?'

'They're waiting for everyone to get over,' answered Bingo. 'There's about ten of them on this side of the wall now, the others are coming. It won't be long before they're in here with us.'

Spiff took a sharp poker from the fireplace and handed it to Stonks. 'Right,' he said, 'let's get it open.'

Stonks forced the point of the poker into the slight crack which ran round the lip of the cover. Spiff knelt by his side and levered upwards with a table knife. They shoved and twisted with all their strength until Spiff made a gap and managed to ram the knife in as far as it would go; then Stonks prodded with the poker and pushed the handle downwards and the great cast iron disc gaped away from the floor. Spiff, with a ready courage, dropped the knife and grabbed at the manhole with his fingers, taking the whole weight of it while Stonks altered his grip and came to Spiff's assistance. Twilight and Vulge took a hand too and on Spiff's word of command the four Borribles heaved together and the lid pivoted upright on two stiff hinges to disclose a large and dangerous-looking hole.

'The Woollies are coming this way,' said Bingo, 'and searching every bit of ground. They're spread out, torches, truncheons, dogs sniffing. Hurry up for Pete's sake.'

Stonks surveyed the steaming blackness at his feet. He wrinkled his nose and then raised a worried face to his companions. 'I recognize that smell, don't you?'

'Not half,' said Vulge. 'It's the stink of Wendles and mud and blood.' As he spoke the smell became noticeably stronger, rising from the depths on a visible curl of green air. The Borribles stared at it, mesmerized with fear until Spiff broke the silence.

'Yeah,' he said, 'and out here it smells of coppers and ear-clippin'. I'm going down. I ain't scared of a few Wendles.'

'You know what Flinthead will do if he catches us,' said Chalotte.

'Then he mustn't catch us,' retorted Spiff. 'Wendle country's big enough, we'll have to hide down there and keep out of the way.'

Ben laughed and his head rolled loosely on his shoulders. He had drunk a lot of beer now. 'You'll be all right, just go down the hole, only don't go far. As soon as the coppers have been and gone I'll let you out again, easy, see.'

'Ben's right,' said Spiff. 'We may only have to stay there half an hour.' He went towards the door and looked over Bingo's shoulder so that he could see what was happening.

Everything had changed outside. The dawn had struggled to the top of the sky and was brightening from grey to blue. The mist had lifted and the line of policemen was plainly to be seen as they walked steadily across the dump, poking at the ground with rods and shining their torches into the dark places. A dog barked, then another. Spiff recognized the small figure of Inspector Sussworth with his long overcoat flapping at his heels; next to him was Sergeant Hanks.

'We'll have to go anyway,' he said between clenched teeth, 'the Woollies will find us in a minute.'

Ben waved his bottle. 'You'd better bugger off, all right; what's the good of me telling this Sussworth feller I don't know you if he walks right in and sees you standing there? Won't look reasonable, will it?'

Spiff elbowed his way past his companions and went to the edge of the black pit. 'Thanks, Ben,' was all he said and then he stepped on to the broad rung of the iron ladder that was built into the side of the manhole and, without sparing a glance for anyone, he climbed rapidly down into the rising steam. In a moment he was gone.

'When I got home from the Rumble hunt,' said Vulge, 'I swore I'd never go within ten miles of a Wendle again . . . Well here we are. I'll be lucky if I'm limping on both legs after this.' And with a sideways jerk of the head he too went down into the stinking vapour.

Just then a police whistle shrilled outside and shouts were heard, the loudest coming from Sergeant Hanks. 'We know you're in there; you'd better come out with your hands on your heads.'

The remaining Borribles waited no longer. Twilight flung himself down the ladder; Sydney followed, so did Bingo and Stonks. Chalotte went last, easing her feet on to the second or third rung so that her head was level with the ground. She looked at Ben. He was sinking lower and lower in his chair. In a few moments he would fall asleep but if he didn't close the manhole behind her it would be obvious to the police where the runaways had gone.

There was another roar: 'You'd better come out, you kids; it'll be the worse for you if you don't.'

Chalotte stretched an arm and grabbed Ben by the ankle and shook his leg. The tramp swung his eyes open with a lurch of the face and stared down at Chalotte. For him she was a disembodied head rolling about on the floor and yet still speaking.

'My God,' said Ben, and he leant forward, his elbows on his knees, 'bloody good stuff this Special Brew.'

'Oh, Ben,' pleaded Chalotte, 'don't be daft, it's me. There's coppers outside. They'll be in here in a twinkling and your only chance is to say you haven't seen us. You've got to close this manhole, roll back the carpet and then move the table over a bit. Do it now Ben, otherwise Sussworth will skin you like a banana. Hurry.'

Ben blinked. The talking head had gone but it had shocked him sober enough to do what was required. He dropped his beer bottle and fell to the carpets, landing on all fours. He took a deep breath to gather strength, and crawled round and round until he got himself behind the manhole cover. Once there he pushed it hard with his shoulder several times, grunting and swearing until it pivoted past its centre of gravity, slamming shut with a muffled thump that echoed through the sewers below but was almost silent above.

Ben was the only person in the world who could move on hands and knees and still stagger. He did it now, wobbling backwards and pulling the carpets after him, smoothing them down as he went. Another shout came from the police cordon. There was a banging of truncheons on the walls of the hut. Ben made one last effort, grabbed hold of a table leg and dragged it towards him. When this was done he smiled and groped for the bottle he had dropped earlier. As soon as he found it he rolled over and gazed at the roof, enjoying the support of the ground in his back.

'I'm weary,' he said, and fell fast asleep.

Sergeant Hanks was the first officer into the shack bashing his way through the door like a fifty-ton tank, his truncheon swinging. Tramping on his heels came half a dozen policemen, heavy and tall, their arms held stiffly by their sides.

'You'd better come quietly,' shouted Hanks, 'the place is surrounded. You can't get away and if you try we'll split yer heads open.'

'There's no one here,' said a policeman after looking carefully into every corner of the room.

Hanks smashed the table with his truncheon. 'Well investigate the other rooms,' he cried, 'they can't get away.'

The sergeant moved round the table and stumbled over Ben's body. 'Here's one,' he said, and while his men searched the lean-tos he sat on a beer crate and gazed into the tramp's dirty face.

More and more policemen stormed into the hut and prodded and stamped their way everywhere. At last Inspector Sussworth came and he stood near the door, lifting himself up on his toes every now and then, stretching his neck like a cockerel. Hanks removed his right index finger from his left nostril and wiped a yellow bogey on to the leg of Ben's table. Then he saluted.

'There's no one here, sir,' he said, 'except this specimen on the floor.' And he kicked Ben in the ribs to show Sussworth where the tramp lay.

The inspector squared his shoulders and sniffed and his little moustache danced under his nose as he tried to identify the various odours imprisoned in the shack.

'There's a malodorous pong in here,' he said, 'a very nasty pong. I suspect it emanates from this recumbent malefactor, alleged.' Sussworth clasped his hands behind his back like royalty and squeezed his fingers till they hurt. He was looking very smart in his flowing overcoat and chequered cap. He took a delicate step round the table and looked at Ben, who still slept contentedly on the floor. 'Wake him up,' said the inspector, 'and ascertain if he can help with enquiries.'

Hanks smiled. This was the kind of job he liked. He grabbed the tramp by the lapels, pulled him into a sitting position and began to shake him vigorously, like a pillow he was knocking the lumps out of. After a few moments of this treatment Ben's eyes blinked, then they opened.

'Oooer,' he said, 'I feel a bit sick.'

Sussworth bent over, tipped the tramp's hat off and seized a fistful of hair, twisting it tight until the tears welled up in Ben's eyes.

'I want to know the present whereabouts of those children you aided and abetted,' cried the inspector. 'Where are those Borribles?'

'Bobbirols,' said Ben, 'whazzem when they's at home? Bobbirols.'

Sussworth pulled Ben's hair tighter and struck him in the face with his free hand. 'Borribles,' was all he said.

'Them kids you saw at Fulham police station,' said Hanks, 'you know who we mean.'

'Oh, them,' said Ben, trying to sniff up his tears, 'them's Bobbirols, are they? Well, I heard 'em in the fog, followed me along they did. I could hear them moving about. Scared stiff, wasn't I? I thought they was going to mug me, you know what kids are like today. Where was the law and order then, I asked myself. I could have been duffed up by them hooligans. I'm an old man, I need protection at my age.'

Sussworth struck Ben once more. 'You will do,' he said.

'I come over the bridge on me way home,' explained the tramp, 'and they went on towards Battersea, I think, down York Road.'

'You're lying,' screamed Hanks, and he jabbed his truncheon deep into Ben's stomach. All the breath he possessed shot out of Ben's lungs and his face was drained of blood in an instant. 'You liar,' shouted Hanks again, 'we had the bridge closed off by then. Our men heard you chatting; don't chat to yourself, do you?'

'Of course I bloody well does,' retorted Ben, trying to look indignant at the same time as having no breath. 'Who the Saint Fairy bleedin' Anne would I talk to else? There ain't no one, is there?'

'For the last time,' said Sussworth quietly, 'those children have absconded from police custody and have stolen government property; item, one horse belonging to the Greater London Council Parks Division. Where are they?' At each word the policeman tried to twist Ben's head from his shoulders, yanking it round and round as if he were unscrewing it.

'Aaagh,' screamed Ben in pain, 'leave off, can't yer? I'd tell yer if I knew, wouldn't I? Can't stand kids, can I?'

The inspector released his grip on Ben's hair and stood up. He stamped his feet angrily on the floor, his body jerking in a spasm of bad temper. 'We're getting nowhere with this imbecile, Hanks,' said Sussworth. 'Those children can't have disappeared, nor the horse. They can't be on the river, they aren't north of us and they can't have got through the cordon back to Battersea. There's only one place they can be, the one place we can't go without getting our noses bloodied.'

Hanks scrambled to his feet in consternation, releasing Ben's lapels with such abruptness that the tramp, who hardly knew what he was doing anyway, fell backwards to the ground, rapping his head so sharply that he rendered himself unconscious.

'You don't mean they've gone below?' the sergeant said.

The inspector looked carefully at his men who, having searched the seven rooms of the shanty, now awaited further orders. 'They'll have dumped the horse and gone down to Wendle country,' he pronounced with finality. 'That much is plain and obvious to the mind of a detective, and if we descended in pursuance of our bounden duty we'd be knee deep in mud and muck, and that I will not tolerate. If the evil vapours did not kill us then there'd be a Wendle behind every corner ready to crack our skulls open with a catapult stone.'

'What are your orders, Inspector?' said Hanks as he crossed his arms and hoisted a fat buttock on to the table to rest it there.

'I know exactly what to do,' said Sussworth twitching his moustache from side to side, delighted with the complication of his own cunning. 'I have a map from the Wandsworth water authority, a map that has every manhole in Wandsworth marked upon it. I'll put a guard on every exit, I'll put a line of men round the whole of this area . . . and then I'll wait. The Wendles won't be able to get out for supplies and will soon conclude and deduce that something amiss is afoot. Wendles are highly averse to strangers; they'll soon find our runaways, and when they do they will boot them straight into our waiting hands.'

At the conclusion of this speech Sussworth stretched his back and made himself as tall as he could. He looked at his men and a black fire burnt in his eyes. He saluted and every officer present returned the salute in a respectful silence which might have lasted quite a long while had not Ben rolled over and farted very loudly in his sleep.

Sussworth blushed and shifted his weight from one foot to the other, embarrassed; his moustache trembled. Hanks touched Ben in the stomach with his boot.

'What shall we do with the prisoner?' he asked.

The inspector narrowed his nostrils against the odours that attacked him from everywhere. 'He's a suspect, he is,' he said, 'accessory after the fact, obstructing a police officer in the pursuance of his duty, drunk and disorderly, carrying an offensive weapon, that bottle for example, obscene behaviour definitely, offending public decency, contravening the health acts, all of them, vagrancy, no fixed abode, squatting, stealing council property . . . My goodness me, there's enough to send him away until the year three thousand and dot. Take him back to Fulham and put him in the cells; only lock him up this time and put him somewhere I can't smell him.'

'Yes sir, certainly sir,' said Hanks, 'but shouldn't we teach him a lesson, sir?'

Sussworth took a step away from the tramp's smell. 'Excellent thinking, Hanks,' he said. 'Get the men to turn the furniture over, break all the bottles, knock down the shelves, rip up the mattresses; let them have a bit of fun, they deserve it after a night like we've had. Next time we ask this slovenly human being for aid and assistance in protecting the *stadium quo* perhaps he'll be a little more disposed to turn Queen's evidence.'

Hanks slipped his bottom from the table and stood firmly planted on his fat legs. He rubbed his hands together with pleasure. 'Oh, yes, sir,' he said, and he gave his orders and two policemen seized the unconscious Ben by the feet and dragged him from his shack. When the tramp's smell had gone Sussworth followed, his legs moving stiffly, his expression cold. As he walked away, along the faint path that wound between the tall piles of rubbish, he heard behind him the sound of falling planks, the crash of crockery and the shouts and laughter of the SBG men. A slow smile crept over the inspector's face. Things were beginning to go well now.

6

The noise of the manhole cover slamming shut sounded terrifyingly loud below ground. Chalotte hung from the iron ladder just under the floor of Ben's palace and listened. She heard a long mumble of voices and she thought she heard someone hitting Ben. Later there came the crashing of furniture and crockery and she felt the earth around her shake with the shock of it. Then there was silence.

Clinging to the ladder still, Chalotte half turned and looked down into the dark. The air was thick about her body and her nose wrinkled at the smell of the sewers. She knew from past experience that it took several days of living underground to get used to it.

'Sounds like they've smashed the place up,' she said, 'pushing Ben about as well.'

'Have they gone?' asked Bingo.

'Seems like,' Chalotte answered.

From further down the tunnel came Spiff's voice: 'Leave it a bit longer.'

They waited a good half-hour, knowing they were near each other but feeling as if miles separated them because they could not see. At last Spiff said, 'Try it now.'

Chalotte placed her ear against the cool metal of the manhole cover. She could hear nothing. She bent her shoulder and pushed, gently at first, then with all her strength. The cover wouldn't budge. Bingo climbed up the ladder and joined his efforts to hers.

'One, two, three,' he said, 'and heave.' They shoved until their eyes bulged white with the effort but the round lump of cast iron would not move. In the end Chalotte made way for Stonks but even he, for all his force and stamina, had no success.

'We need more help,' he said, his breath coming in gasps.

'I know that,' said Bingo, 'but there's only room for two on this top rung.'

Twilight came up then and tried to push Bingo from below in one last despairing attempt but it made no difference. What the runaways did not realize was that Ben's kitchen cabinet, his armchairs and his table lay shattered in a heap over the top of the manhole. There would be no getting out that way. The Borribles were entombed right where they had not wanted to be: in the territory of the Wendles. Slowly Stonks, Bingo and Twilight clambered to the bottom of the ladder and huddled together with their companions in a sad and silent group. They had escaped the men of the SBG, certainly, but they had landed themselves in a predicament that might become far, far worse.

'Oh, hell,' said Sydney, 'I never meant all this to happen.'

'Well it has,' said Vulge, 'and there's no point in moaning. We've got to decide what we're going to do . . . Any ideas?'

'There's nothing we can do, except try to get out some other way,' said Spiff. His voice came from the dark, low and steady. It sounded like he was several yards away in a tunnel. 'The manhole cover is obviously locked or Sussworth has put some effin' great weight on it. We have to go on.'

'Oh, yeah,' said Chalotte, 'and how much food have we got? None. We haven't even got a torch and we don't know where we are. For all we know there are Wendles around us already.'

'That's right,' said Stonks. 'We don't even have a catapult or a Rumble-stick, nothing; our goose is cooked to a cinder.'

After Stonks had spoken there was another long silence as each Borrible considered his fate, but then, when enough time had gone by, Spiff cleared his throat and began to speak, slowly, as if he knew, and had known for a long time, exactly what he was going to say.

'I can get you out of here,' he said, and waited to let the importance of the remark sink in. 'I can see pretty well in the dark,' he added, 'almost like a Wendle.'

'What do you mean?' snapped Chalotte, instantly suspicious. She had never distrusted Spiff more than now and she was convinced that there was a note of triumph in his voice, as if he'd taken a chance on something and it was working out the way he had hoped.

Spiff sighed. 'I have a long, long past,' he said, 'and some of it was here, because, years ago, before any of you were Borribles, I lived here. To cut a long story short, I am a Wendle.'

'I might have known,' said Chalotte, and the words hissed through her teeth. 'I might have known.'

Spiff ignored her. 'I fought against the Rumbles and won more names than I can remember, not many Borribles do that, but I ran away from Wandsworth, ended up in Battersea, been there ever since.'

'Once a Wendle, always a Wendle,' quoted Chalotte.

'The fact remains,' continued Spiff, 'that I can get you out of here easy, if you do as I say. A Wendle never forgets the Wendle ways.'

'That's just what I'm frightened of,' said Chalotte.

'What does it matter?' said Twilight, interrupting the conversation to stop it becoming a quarrel. 'A Wendle's a Borrible after all. If Spiff can get us out then so much the better.'

'Has anyone got any other suggestion?' asked Bingo, 'because I haven't.'

There was no answer, not even from Chalotte.

'Okay,' said Spiff. 'First things first. I reckon Sussworth will block off as many exits from the sewers as he can. We'll have to lie low for twenty-four hours at least, maybe more.'

'But the Wendles will have us,' said Vulge. 'We aren't even dressed like they are.'

'Exactly,' agreed Spiff, 'so the first thing we got to do is find a Wendle storeroom and nick some of their gear, catapults and ammunition too. And we'll need some food.'

'Oh boy, oh boy,' said Twilight, 'this is an adventure at last, just what I wanted.'

'Don't be stupid, Stupid,' said Vulge. 'If I could see you I'd knock your block off.'

'Once we get some Wendle clothes and some weapons,' Spiff went on, 'we'll be able to merge in with the Wendles; they'll never even notice us. We'll watch 'em, see if they go in and out through the various manholes and, if they do, when the time comes we slip out into the streets and back home we go. Does everyone agree?'

'Okay by me,' said Twilight.

'Yes,' said Bingo, 'there's no other way.'

And so the others gave their vote for the plan, even Chalotte, but in her heart she knew that Spiff was up to no good. The triumph in his voice had grown more pronounced, had even developed into a note of pleasure. It seemed to her that Spiff had brought them to Wandsworth Bridge with a purpose, as if he were glad to be back underground where the green slime slid incessantly down the curving walls. She shuddered; there were great dangers ahead. Out there in the darkness some vile horror was uncoiling itself and getting ready to swallow her and her companions one by one. She determined to watch Spiff very closely. He spoke again and she listened.

'Until we get out of here,' he continued, 'you'll have to do as I say, even if it ain't very Borrible. Everyone grab hold of the person in front for now, and don't let go. You get lost down here and the rats'll chew you to nothing, right down to the toenails.'

As they followed Spiff away from the ladder, sightless into the back tunnels, Chalotte found that she was the last in line, clinging on to Bingo's shirt tail. She drew up beside him as she walked.

'I don't like it,' she whispered. 'Spiff's too happy down here. I bet you he's got some scheme up his sleeve. He's so crafty, that one, his right hand's never even seen the left one.'

Spiff suddenly interrupted her, his words curling back along the sewer, brittle with anger. 'Whoever that is, shuddup! Do you want every Wendle in Wandsworth to know where we are? Keep your mouth shut or Flinthead will shut it for you, with mud.'

No one answered Spiff and Chalotte felt her face flush in the gloom. Without another word the little band of Adventurers marched on.

*

Spiff led the way with a cheerful confidence. Stonks, who was behind him, said later, when it was all over, that he was sure he'd heard Spiff quietly whistling between his teeth while he walked – as if he were daring the whole world to come and attack him.

Chalotte of course could hear none of this and her thoughts were taken up with wondering what kind of person it was that could remember the tunnels of his early days with such ease. Had Spiff been back to Wandsworth since his escape all those years ago? Did he have a map in Battersea which he studied secretly in his room at night? She could find no satisfactory answer. Spiff was devious and cunning, even for a Wendle.

All at once the marching stopped and Spiff whispered from the front of the column, 'I can see a light, it might just be the first Wendle crossroads, it might be a guard. You lot stay here and I'll creep up and have a look.'

Spiff left them, and as the Borribles waited they heard only the persistent dripping of the slime all around them and the faraway rush of sludge in the main sewers. They stared at the distant light, watching Spiff's silhouette moving between them and it. At last they saw the tiny figure clasp both arms above its head. That was the signal which meant it was safe to go on.

They found Spiff standing in an open space where three corridors met. In the ceiling, in a recess protected by small metal bars, was a pale electric light.

'This is the beginning,' he said. 'From here on you can expect electric lights at almost every junction, so follow me and be twice as careful.' And he spun on his heel and plunged into another tunnel with no hesitation at all.

On and on went the Borribles and as they marched their eyes became more and more accustomed to the gloom in which they moved. Tunnel after tunnel joined theirs and the sound of sluggish waters came from both right and left. The Adventurers were wending their way across a gigantic maze and those who had been on the Great Rumble Hunt recognized none of it. Spiff was taking them by a roundabout route, purposely avoiding the more populated centres of the underground citadel.

Occasionally they heard the distant voices of Wendle patrols calling to one another, and sometimes Spiff halted, cupping his ear with a hand so that he could listen more intently. Once or twice he stopped by mysterious chalk marks that had been scribbled on the brick walls, studying them and moving his lips soundlessly as if he were reading secret messages left by a friend to guide him in the right direction.

Eventually, after tramping for an hour or so, Spiff brought his companions to an open area where five or six large tunnels met. The arches of the ceiling were high and graceful, built in Victorian times. A main culvert passed here, deep and wide with a ledge on each side of it for the sewer men to walk on. In this channel flowed a solid stream of filth, an oily water that looked as thick as molten lava with strange shapes in it that writhed and struggled just below the surface. Grey chiffons of steam escaped from large and lazy bubbles and smell rose through smell. The air felt rotten and crawled over the skin.

Spiff crouched by the bank and picked up half a brick that had fallen from the roof. 'Care for a swim, Twilight,' he said, and threw the bit of brick into the water. There was no splash, no noise. The brick simply disappeared, hypnotized into the mud like a mouse into a snake.

Twilight did not answer but stared at the sewer and swallowed hard. He began to understand what it was to live in Wendle country.

'Enough of jokes,' said Vulge. 'Why have we walked so far only to get here?'

Before Spiff could answer there came the scrape of a foot scuffing over uneven ground. Spiff looked beyond his friends and smiled. Slowly the Borribles turned, their scalps prickling with fear. In the entrance to one of the tunnels stood two Wendles, one armed with a glinting spear or Rumble-stick, the other with a catapult, its elastic stretched, the stone aimed at Stonks's head.

'Don't move anyone,' said the Wendle with the spear. His voice was as friendly as a broken bottle.

In spite of the warning Chalotte glanced at Spiff, still squatting by the bank of the sewer. He was chuckling, an expression of pleasure on his face. Slowly, very slowly, and showing his hands, he rose to his feet and the Wendles saw him.

'Spiff,' said one of them. 'At last.'

Spiff pushed a way through the group of motionless Borribles and stepped towards his Wandsworth brethren.

'What about this lot?' asked the Wendle with the spear. 'Are they armed?'

Spiff stood between the two Wendles and grinned. 'They're all right,' he said, 'and they are not armed.' Then he explained a little: 'These Wendles are old friends of mine. The one with the spear is called Norrarf, the one with the catapult is called Skug; when the time comes they will tell you how they won their names. They have come to help us.'

Norrarf and Skug lowered their weapons but they didn't take their eyes from the Borribles, weighing them in the balance, wondering, in spite of Spiff's assurances, whether to welcome them.

'What's all this about?' said Vulge. 'What's your game?'

'No talking here,' said Skug, his voice rough and mannerless, 'we've got to get you lot out of sight.' Skug had a square chin that was full of aggression and a right shoulder that jerked every few seconds as if he were dying to throw a punch at someone, or even anyone. His eyes looked into the corners of the world all the time and there wasn't the slightest spark of trust within them.

'That's right,' added Norrarf. 'You won't be safe until you're in Wendle clothes. I don't mind helping you, Spiff, but I ain't going to get myself drowned in mud for no one. Your friends is nothing but trouble.'

Norrarf was short and stocky with a face like a squashed lemon, wider than it was high. His mouth was crowded with teeth and he had a greenish tinge to his skin as did all members of his tribe. He was dressed, like Skug and indeed like all Wendle warriors, in thigh waders of rubber, a metal helmet made from an old six-pint beer can, and a chunky woollen jacket covered in orange plastic to keep out the water; the plastic was luminous like the coats worn by the men who work on motorways.

'All right,' said Spiff, 'you lead, we'll follow.'

The two warriors nodded and backed slowly into a tunnel; Spiff went after them as if prepared to leave his companions on their own if they hesitated for one minute, which they did, looking at each other in doubt and puzzlement.

Twilight, new to Wendles and eager for adventure, was not at all perturbed. 'Well, come on you lot,' he said. 'Don't hang about; we don't stand a chance without their help, do we?'

'Yeah,' said Chalotte, 'and I'm not sure what chance we stand with their help, either.' But she, like the rest, had no choice but to follow Spiff into the tunnel.

This time they did not have far to go, only marching for another fifteen or twenty minutes, though they changed direction a great deal and switched from corridor to corridor until, at last, they were taken through a hole in the wall and came into a small guardroom, long since abandoned it seemed by the regular Wendle patrols.

The walls of the room were built of an ancient brick from which the red dust flaked away at the merest touch, and it was furnished with rough chairs and a table. There was a pile of torn blankets too, but most important of all, thrown down in a corner, was a heap of Wendle clothes and weapons: spears, knives, catapults and a score of bandoliers filled with good round stones for use as ammunition. Chalotte drew in a sharp breath and the blood pounded in her temples; everything had been prepared for them.

She sprang on Spiff and seized him by the front of his shirt. 'Why don't you tell us what you're up to, you crafty little bleeder?' she cried. 'These Wendles knew we were coming, didn't they? And that's more than we did ourselves . . . But you knew, didn't you? You twister.' Chalotte was very angry and she raised her free hand to strike the Battersea Borrible across the head.

Norrarf pushed himself away from the wall where he had been leaning and raised his spear but, quick as he was, Spiff was quicker. With a brutal upward movement of his left arm he freed himself from the grip on his shirt and at the same time shoved the flat of his other hand into Chalotte's face so hard and so fast that the girl stumbled backwards and fell into Bingo's arms. Stonks stepped in front of Spiff, disregarding Norrarf's spear.

'Steady on, sonny,' he said. 'You push me if you want to push someone; see if I fall over.'

Vulge sat Chalotte down on a chair and she fingered her reddened nose and wiped the tears of pain from her eyes. There was quiet as her friends watched her, not knowing what to say, tense, ready to fight.

'You'd better tell us what's up,' said Stonks to Spiff after a while. 'We didn't come here to get ourselves killed just to amuse you.'

'That's right,' said Vulge, 'our adventuring days are over.'

Spiff smiled a smile of contempt to himself and began to sort over the Wendle clothing, looking for garments that would fit him. When he had found what he needed he put them on: the tin hat, the waders, the orange jacket. The costume transformed him utterly and the Borribles stared, forgetting their anger, hardly able to believe their eyes. Now Spiff looked every inch the Wendle warrior: violent, cunning and heartless. He smirked as he chose a catapult and swung a bandolier of stones across his shoulder; he was ready for anything and he looked like he didn't have a scruple in the world.

'You wanted us down here,' said Chalotte, 'and now you've got us. I've known that all along. You've got these friends down here, too. You must have had messages in and messages out for months. You know a lot that we don't, like you always do. What I want to know is what is it that you know?'

Spiff shrugged. 'There's nothing to tell,' he said, 'and anyway you wouldn't believe me whatever I said. If you don't like it here why don't you go up the nearest exit and walk right into the hands of Sussworth an' Co?'

'You will, too,' said Norrarf. 'Our patrols have reported that there's a copper standing on every manhole in Wandsworth.'

'Look,' said Spiff, 'all I want to do is get home, but since we're stuck here for a while we'd better make the most of it. Me and the other two will go and look for some food. While we're gone you'd better change into Wendle gear . . . and keep someone on watch.'

'You'll be all right,' said Skug. 'Hardly anyone comes this far out any more.'

'Let's go,' said Spiff, and his voice had a commanding ring to it. He ducked through the hole in the wall and was gone. The two Wendles obeyed him without question, as if he'd always been their leader and had never been away.

Chalotte shivered and remembered Flinthead, the Wendle chieftain. Suddenly Spiff reminded her of him; he had changed from the sly and lazy rogue she had known in Battersea. Now his eyes were cold and hard in his face, like pale blue marbles stuck in a big blob of raw pastry.

Bingo sighed, fitted a helmet on to his head and pulled a Wendle face. 'That Spiff,' he said, 'never does nothing for nothing. This whole thing smells dodgy.'

Chalotte nodded. 'Do you know what I think . . . I think he's come down here to sniff about after the Rumble treasure box. That's why he's been in contact with Norrarf and Skug, that's why he wanted to come with us in the first place.'

Stonks looked up in surprise. 'He couldn't be that stupid,' he said. 'The treasure box got sunk in the deepest part of the River Wandle. You remember, you were there. It must be covered by miles and miles of mud by now.'

'Yeah,' said Vulge, 'the Wendle legends say that the mud goes right down to the centre of the earth just there.'

'I know what the legends say,' cried Chalotte, 'but Spiff has a way of making his own legends.'

'Oh come on,' interrupted Twilight. 'He can't make us do anything we don't want to, can he?'

Chalotte laughed. 'Spiff can make things happen and then make them look as if they just happened,' she said. 'He's very good at it.'

*

The Borribles waited three hours for Spiff's return and while they waited changed into Wendle uniforms and chose a catapult and a bandolier each. The touch of the weapons reassured them mightily; they felt more confident, more in charge of their own destinies.

It was Bingo who was on guard at the first bend in the tunnel when he heard the noise of footsteps echoing along the brick walls; then there was the trill of the Battersea whistle and a moment later Spiff edged himself into view. He looked tired now and his waders were covered in mud. Over his shoulder was a heavy sack.

'Hello, young feller,' he said. 'Glad someone's on watch.' He went past Bingo and into the guardroom where he dropped his burden on the table. 'Here's some grub,' he said, 'so tuck in.' He upended his bag and stolen food cascaded out: loaves, rolls, bacon, pots of jam, beer and boiled sweets.

'Were you seen?' asked Vulge.

Spiff chuckled. 'Course I was, but with a bit of mud across the face and travelling with Skug and Norrarf no one gave me a second look.'

'And are the SBG still on the manholes?'

'According to Norrarf they are. The Wendles have one or two holes that the coppers don't know about but they're guarded by picked warriors and no one goes in or out except on Flinthead's say-so. We'll have to wait till the coppers have gone.'

'I don't care what Spiff wants us to believe,' said Chalotte, 'I think we ought to go and have a look for ourselves.'

Spiff shrugged. 'Suit yerself,' he said, 'but there's one thing you certainly ought to see . . . over the other side of the citadel, over where you lost the treasure . . . You'll never guess what it is.' He ripped a chunk of white bacon fat with his teeth, rolling it into his mouth and chewing it confidently, like he had all the answers to all the questions.

There was silence. Nobody wanted to ask Spiff anything, except perhaps Twilight, and he kept quiet because he realized there was something going on that he didn't understand, that he wasn't part of. Spiff waited and smiled and smiled in the most provoking manner until at last he said, 'Well, all right then. I ain't proud, I'll tell yer. You've got to hand it to that Flinthead, he never gives up. Right out there, in the middle of all that mud and water he's dug a mine shaft, and above it is a contraption like a North Sea oil rig: a platform made of planks, a treadmill, and a chain of buckets to bring up the mud . . . and down below, slaves to do the digging. Fantastic engineering, real Borrible. I tell yer . . . that Flinthead.'

Stonks snorted. 'He's mad, he can't dig up the treasure box, it's too far gone.'

'He's not mad,' argued Spiff, 'persistent he is, he just never gives up.'

Chalotte rose to her feet and stretched out an arm to point at Spiff. 'And nor do you, you rat,' she said, her voice trembling with rage. 'Now we know why you were so happy to get us down here, it was that treasure all along.'

Spiff's face flushed. 'Don't be idiotic,' he said. 'How could I have known for sure that Sam was a trap, how could I have known that Sussworth was waiting on Eel Brook Common, or that Ben would rescue us? I'm not a magician.'

'Maybe not,' Chalotte went on, looking at her friends for support, 'but you didn't care what you did as long as you got us nearer to Wandsworth. You were too scared to come down here on your own so you made damn sure you got us involved.' She jerked her head at Twilight. 'I told you he had a way of making things happen.'

Stonks rolled a rasher of bacon in his fingers and tucked it into his mouth. 'It don't matter a monkey's, that money has caused enough death and treachery. We came to get a horse, that's all; money's out.'

'Right,' said Vulge. 'That money killed Knocker, Napoleon, Orococco, Torreycanyon and Adolf; it very nearly killed me. It smells of death, always has done.'

Spiff gazed slowly round the room, superior and amused, like an adult watching quarrelling children. He snatched a bottle of beer from the table, opened it and took a long swig. 'Ah, lovely,' was all he said.

'A couple of us ought to go and have a look ourselves,' said Chalotte. 'That way we can make sure Spiff's telling us the truth about the manholes. We've got to get out of here before he gets us mixed up in something.'

Spiff raised his bottle in the air. 'Of course, girl,' he said. 'I'll take you to the Wandle mudflats right away, and I'll show you the exits the Wendles are using; I'll even show you the shaft where Flinthead's digging for treasure. And one day, if you outlive me that is, you'll look back and say, "Old Spiff weren't so bad, he knew a thing or two."' He laughed once more and waved his beer bottle in a circle, embracing everyone in a toast. 'Here's to us,' he said, 'Borribles all.'

*

As soon as they had eaten it was decided that Chalotte, Stonks and Bingo would go with Spiff to check on some of the exits and entrances of Wendle country. They were to inspect as many as possible and weigh the chances of getting out on to the streets again, the chances of getting home.

Spiff led the three towards the centre of the citadel, warning them to keep close at all times if they didn't want to get lost. Again Chalotte wondered how he remembered his way in such an underground labyrinth. Only years and years as a Wendle could have given Spiff his detailed knowledge of the place. Left here, right there, over this sewer, along that one, now in complete darkness, now in the half-light; it was truly amazing and Chalotte came to realize that the more she knew Spiff the more there was to know.

She also saw that in spite of the summer drought and the heat in the city above, the channels and culverts were deep in filth-laden water. Very often, when there were no pathways, the four Borribles were forced to wade along the middle of the sewers themselves, up to their waists in muck and with green slime dripping heavily on to their helmets from high in the vaulted roofs, while all about them they heard whispering voices and the slosh and slurp of Wendles in waders.

As they journeyed on they began to meet the Wendles themselves, though not all of them were warriors, but Spiff knew the ways of that strange subterranean race and did not baulk at pushing his way through the middle of any group he came across. His three companions, fearful of discovery at first, soon learnt that their best procedure was simply to adopt a surly manner and speak to no one. Spiff made them smear their faces with a little mud too, as if they had been on a long march and had crossed many a stream. In that way, and in the gloom of the underworld, there was no danger of the interlopers being identified as strangers.

Spiff was happy. He nudged Chalotte frequently and his teeth shone when he smiled. Each time he passed beneath a manhole cover he stopped and waited for the others to gather round him so he could point upwards, and there, chalked on the underside of each iron lid, the Borribles saw a circle with a 'X' drawn across it: the Wendle sign for danger.

'There you are,' said Spiff, 'and they're all like that.' He smiled at Chalotte's discomfiture. 'I promise you there's a copper's size thirteen boots standing on the topside of that manhole and there's a size thirteen copper standing in 'em too.'

They marched on at a good pace towards the River Wandle and were not far from their destination when two warriors burst out of a branch corridor and ran off, shouting.

'Come on you lot,' they bawled. 'General meeting, Flinthead's orders, haven't you heard?' Their footsteps died away.

'What do we do now?' asked Bingo, his face pale. 'Hide?'

'Not likely,' said Spiff. 'When Flinthead calls a meeting everyone goes except those who are dead or on guard. If we don't do what everyone else does we'll be spotted and dragged out into the light and he'd recognize us for sure. We'll have to go along, and we'll have to sprint too.'

And sprint they did, speeding towards the great hall, and as they ran they were joined by hundreds of Wendles all scurrying in the same direction. The tunnels grew wider and higher and the number of Wendles increased moment by moment until soon there was a solid host of jostling bodies hastening onwards in obedience to Flinthead.

Spiff and the others, their hearts thumping, were borne along in this violent crush for at least half a mile or so, then the pace of the mob around them slackened to a jog, then to a walk and finally to a shuffle.

There were Wendles everywhere now, clamped together, incapable of independent movement. Suddenly they surged forward with a new and frightening power and, caught by an irresistible force, the four Adventurers, their feet no longer touching the ground, were sucked into an immense cavern where the brick roof arched high up and out of sight.

Once, back in the nineteenth century, this hall had been the central chamber for the Wandsworth sewage system until, made obsolete by more modern techniques, it had come under the sway of Flinthead. There he was now, sitting on a tall raised platform, lolling back in a large wooden armchair which served, on all important occasions, as the Wendle chieftain's throne. Beside him was his second-in-command, Tron by name, and within call stood at least fifty members of the bodyguard: hard-fighting warrior Wendles, hand-picked for their loyalty and single-mindedness.

The Adventurers wriggled and pushed through the crowd and made their way to the side of the hall.

'Keep still,' whispered Spiff, 'and don't look up. Whatever happens, don't catch Flinthead's eye; he'll suss you out in no time.'

Chalotte took Spiff's warning seriously and hid herself behind the mass of Wendles who stood between her and the platform, pulling her helmet further down on her head so that she could scrutinize events without fear of being discovered.

Flinthead, she saw, hadn't changed in the slightest since she'd last seen him. Not for him the helmet made from an old beer can; his, and his alone, was fashioned from beaten copper and it had an extra piece that came down the front of his face in order to protect the nose – but that nose was not designed for concealment. It was an evil nose, a big nose, soft and plastic and eager to sniff out anyone who threatened Flinthead or his supremacy. The chieftain's jacket was covered in luminous paint of gold and his waders were soft and of the finest quality, lined with wool to keep his feet warm. But Flinthead's power did not reside in his clothes; it issued from his eyes. They were blank and they did not glint or gleam. Neither did they move unless the head moved; they were opaque and impenetrable, frosted over like smashed windscreens.

Gradually the noise in the great hall died away. Slowly Flinthead raised a hand for silence, but there was no need. The crowd had been stilled by the chieftain's gaze alone. He waited a moment longer before speaking and when he spoke his voice came as a shock. It was a friendly voice and he smiled too, but his mind was a great distance from the smile; his mind was a cold metallic thing, working in silence for its own secret ends.

'Wendles,' began Flinthead, 'I have called you together because there is great danger here. The policemen of the SBG are guarding every exit into Wandsworth . . . I want to know why, I must know why. We have ample provisions of course, but if the blockade goes on too long we will face hardship, starvation even. Why, I ask myself, have we suddenly become the objects of this burst of SBG activity . . .? You will find out for me. You all know of the work I am doing on the Wandle mudflats, it is important work and it must not be interrupted. I do not want policemen down here, I don't even want them to send the sewer men down here. You will remember the dangers we faced before because of outsiders; we do not want any more. The Wandle is for the Wendles. Be vigilant, you warriors, all of you beware strangers. A time of trial is coming, I smell it. The enemy is all around us. Report anything untoward to me or Tron. Be suspicious, be wary, trust no one. Stand guard at every exit, watch over the mine where the work goes on. I am awake for you day and night, brother Wendles; be watchful for me. Something or someone has penetrated our underground citadel, my nose tells me. Sharpen your knives, carry a spear and a catapult always with you. Wendles beware, there will be blood.'

Abruptly Flinthead rose, and the light from the hand torches that almost every Wendle carried shone against his helmet. He stared at the back of the hall, his shapeless nose twitching. No one moved and no one spoke. Slowly Flinthead turned his face, sweeping his dull eyes across Wendle after Wendle, scaring them, sniffing nervously all the while like a city fox. Spiff, Chalotte, Stonks and Bingo stood without stirring, hardly breathing as Flinthead's rigid gaze came to rest near them. It wavered and the nose tilted upwards and flared long and deep. Chalotte's knees trembled and she was thankful that Spiff had made her disguise herself with those streaks of mud.

'There is much amiss,' called Flinthead, but his eyes moved on and searched elsewhere and he did not trouble to look for much longer. Only a moment more went by and then he raised his hand and dismissed the great assembly with a sign. Tron shouted an order and the special bodyguard surrounded their chieftain with a hedge of spears and escorted him away, chanting a kind of hymn as they did so:

'Glory to Flinthead! Praise our lord,
King of the world below!
Sing of his name,
Extol his fame
From which all blessings flow.

'Glory to Flinthead, great and good,
Wendle without a peer!
There are no bold
Heroes of old
To equal his career!

'Glory to Flinthead, saviour true,
Father and guide and friend!
His is the might,
The kindly light
We'll follow round the bend!'

As soon as the four interlopers were free of the cavern and on their own Spiff halted and spoke roughly to Chalotte. 'Now do you believe me?' he hissed. 'There is a copper on every manhole.'

'I believe you,' answered Chalotte, though her mind was preoccupied with other thoughts – the Wendle hymn haunted her. 'Those bodyguards are mad, aren't they?' she said. 'They really believe in that lunatic leader of theirs; Flinthead could do anything with them.'

'Never mind all that,' said Stonks, his voice strained. 'What about that guardroom where we're hiding, won't they find it now?'

'I dunno,' said Spiff, 'lots of Wendles live in old alcoves like that. I think Skug and Norrarf ought to be able to fob them off. I'm more worried about something else.'

'Something else!' cried Bingo. 'What could be worse than this?'

Spiff rubbed his jaw and reached a decision. 'Come with me,' he said. 'I'll show you something you ought to see.'

Chalotte, Stonks and Bingo studied Spiff's expression for a second. He smiled his superior smile.

'All right,' said Chalotte, 'we'll look, but that's all. Don't you go making things happen.'

Spiff shook his head in reassurance and once more he set off into the dark and sloping side tunnels with his companions following. Once more, also, he directed his steps with confidence and precision and it was not long before the small group of Borribles arrived on the banks of the River Wandle.

'Yes,' said Chalotte, 'I recognize this; it was near here that our boat was moored, and it was over the far side somewhere that we left Knocker and the others so that we could escape with the treasure.' And remembering her friends she contemplated the waters of the river and saw that they were still as thick and as foul as fish glue. The Wandle crawled by her feet with a slow and unstoppable strength, only just covering the rolling banks of mud that shifted and rippled beneath its surface.

Spiff gobbed into the water and the spit made no splash or murmur. 'All very touching,' he said, 'but we'd better get going before some Wendle starts asking us what we're up to.'

They pressed on, following the Wandle in the direction of its current, travelling along a well trodden towpath. From time to time they passed small groups of Wendles roaming this way and that, but they were not too closely scrutinized, nor did they receive more than the usual number of suspicious glances.

As they progressed the vault above their heads flung itself higher and wider until it was almost impossible to see the far side of the river. Now the shoals of mud surged into sight above the water and the stream dawdled and meandered through a vast area of black dunes which gleamed wet in the half-light, pulsating like stranded monsters. These were the treacherous swamps of the Wandle mudflats where a relentless suction threatened the life of any creature that lost its way or of any traveller who put a foot wrong.

There were more and more Wendles round the Adventurers every minute, most of them warriors and all of them taking Flinthead's orders seriously, peering into alcoves and tunnels and inspecting each other's faces. But Spiff was not to be put off by this tactic and did likewise, brandishing his catapult in a warlike manner and approaching each Wendle he passed and staring at him offensively, asking who he was and where he came from and what he was doing. Whatever Spiff's faults, there was no doubting his bravery or his audacity.

Chalotte knew this and was on the point of mentioning it to Bingo when she and the others became aware of harsh and unnatural noises in the distance. She heard first a sharp crack repeated at regular intervals, sometimes followed by a cry; then there was a deep rumbling as of wood on wood together with a grinding and a clanking of metal, and all this strident discord was combined with a slurp, slurp, slurp of water and mud. Chalotte felt a finger of ice prodding at her heart and she reached out to touch Stonks's arm, but the face he turned towards her was just as fearful as her own.

The noises pounded on, clanking, rumbling, slurping; louder and louder, oppressive, terrifying. Suddenly, as the four Borribles rounded a bend in the towpath, the noise swelled to a crescendo and the strangest sight met their eyes. Spiff raised an arm and pointed dramatically.

'There,' he said, pleased with himself, 'ain't that wonderful?'

Far away from the spot on which they stood, in between two vast banks of mud and in the middle of the underground river, was moored a floating platform constructed from huge rough planks of stolen timber. In the centre of the platform was a derrick and at the base of the derrick and spliced on to it with a cumbersome wooden axle was a treadmill, large enough for a Borrible, or even two, to walk in. Some poor mud-covered wretch was already toiling in it and, as Chalotte stared, one of the four Wendle guards on the platform cracked a whip and the great wheel revolved and buckets rattled upwards on a long chain, rising to the top of the derrick. There they rolled over to empty their cargo of sludge into the waters of the River Wandle and begin again their long journey down into the deepest depths of the mine.

Spiff sprawled on the ground at the side of the towpath and beamed; the others squatted near him. 'Marvellous bit of engineering, that is,' he said, 'absolutely marvellous.'

Chalotte glanced along the river bank. There were scores of Wendles doing what Spiff was doing; some were chatting, some were just relaxing, but all of them kept a close eye on the activity in midstream, waiting for something to happen.

Stonks spoke to Bingo. 'This is the exact place we lost the treasure.'

Chalotte swore. 'So it is, dammit.'

'But how can you dig down through a river?' asked Bingo.

'Course you can,' said Spiff. 'They do it all the time, engineers. You start on one of those mudbanks, just above the surface of the water, or you wait till the tide's out, and as your hole goes down so you put planking all round you, nice and tight; tongue and groove is best. How do you think they built bridges in the old days? Just the same.'

'Well, it's bloody clever,' said Bingo. 'You've got to admit that.'

'Invented by Flinthead,' said Spiff. 'And whatever else you can say about him he ain't daft.'

'And who's the poor sod in the treadmill?' said Stonks. 'What's he done to deserve that?'

Spiff let his head fall back and looked up into the roof, making his comrades wait for an answer so that their brains had time to work. 'Well,' he said eventually, 'he did just what we are doing, he got on the wrong side of Flinthead, didn't he? Go and have a closer look, Stonks.' Spiff laughed, as cold as death, his laughter mocking the idea that was just beginning to form in the minds of his companions.

Stonks jumped to his feet and a look of understanding, distant as yet, began to spread across the face of the slow Peckham Borrible. He walked along the bank to a point where the land advanced into the river and brought him nearer to the treadmill. For a long while he stared across at the slave who stumbled forward inside the wheel; he winced every time he heard the whip fall. Then Stonks's head fell on his chest in a great sadness; he retraced his steps and sat once more by the others. The blood had drained from his face and his lips were white with rage. He closed his eyes so that he could not see.

'It's my mate out there,' he said. 'It's Torreycanyon, the poor bleeder, he's still alive, after all this time.' Stonks's voice cracked and it seemed that even the strongest of all the Borribles might break down and weep in front of his friends, openly and without shame.

'It's who?' said Bingo, not believing his own ears.

'Torreycanyon,' cried Chalotte. Her voice rose with emotion and it was fortunate for her that the nearby groups of Wendles were talking loudly themselves and did not notice her. She looked at Spiff with hatred, baffled once again by his duplicity, but all he did was narrow his eyes, his face expressionless.

'Don't do anything silly,' he said. 'If you give the game away Flinthead will have us all down the mine.'

'You knew,' continued Chalotte, and her breath shot out of her lungs like steam under pressure. 'You knew all the time.'

'I wasn't sure until I got here,' said Spiff, his eyes flickering a little. 'I couldn't be certain.'

'And the others?' asked Chalotte, ducking her head to brush away the tears. 'What about Knocker?'

'Ah, your special friend Knocker, yes, he's alive too. He's down the bottom of the shaft with Napoleon, and Orococco goes behind 'em, boarding up the sides of the mine to make sure it don't cave in.'

'How do you know all this?' asked Bingo.

'Norrarf and Skug told me, of course,' said Spiff, 'when we arrived.'

'And don't the prisoners ever come out?' said Stonks, holding down his anger with an immense effort.

'They works there, eats there and sleeps there,' explained Spiff. 'The food is lowered down in a dirty old bucket.'

'The bastards,' said Chalotte, 'and so are you, Spiff. You should have told us they were still alive; we'd have come willingly then.'

Spiff sneered. 'Oh, yeah, you wouldn't have believed me for a second. You'da taken it for a trick. I had to get you here some other way.'

'Just so we could get the treasure for you,' said Chalotte. 'Don't try to kid me that you want to rescue Knocker and the rest, I know you too well.'

'There's nothing to stop us doing both,' said Spiff.

No one could speak for a long while after that. Chalotte could only think of the suffering that the prisoners must have undergone during their long months of captivity, and Bingo and Stonks sat gazing at the treadmill as it went round and round. Torreycanyon had been Stonks's mate; they had fought side by side at the Great Door of Rumbledom, and the more Stonks thought of his friend's imprisonment the more he felt a hatred of Spiff rise up in his throat. But there was nothing he could do or say; he dared not give way to his feelings. He was, after all, surrounded by Wendles, Wendles who were now on the watch for the slightest thing out of the ordinary.

At length Stonks came to a decision and he stood up. 'Let's get back to the guardroom now,' he said. 'I think the others will want to ask

Spiff a few questions; they might even want to shove his head through a brick wall.'

The four Borribles walked casually into a side tunnel so as not to attract the attention of any of the watching Wendles. But once out of the sight and hearing of the river bank Stonks raised his arm and caught Spiff a ringing blow across the helmet with his bare hand; the helmet dented under the blow and the sound of it echoed along the damp brick walls. Spiff fell to his knees and shook his head, stunned. A clout from Stonks was no light thing.

Chalotte was excited by the violence; her blood rose and she drew her sharp knife. 'I'm gonna slit his throat,' she said.

'And so could I,' said Stonks, 'but if we do we'll never find our way back . . . It was just that I couldn't resist sloshing him the once.' He stuck the knuckles of his right hand into his mouth and sucked the broken skin.

Bingo helped Spiff to his feet and shoved him forward. 'Come on, Spiff,' he said. 'Take us home and we'll see what the others have to say.'

And so, with his head buzzing from the great swipe he had received, Spiff staggered through the tunnels of Wendle country. Chalotte, Bingo and Stonks followed him, their hearts glad in a way that Knocker and his fellow prisoners were still alive, and yet sad too for the slavery they had endured and the continuing danger of their predicament.

7

Inside the secret house which served as headquarters for the SBG Sergeant Hanks dipped half a bread roll into the pool of egg yolk on his greasy plate and then, when the bread was sufficiently soggy, he folded it into his mouth. The loose flesh on his face wobbled with satisfaction and his blue eyes glinted with pleasure.

'You should eat a bit more, Inspector,' he said, forcing the words through his food so that they sounded moist, 'then you wouldn't worry so much.' Hanks belched fiercely and with an expression of intense concentration began to pick his nose.

Inspector Sussworth lowered his mug of tea to Hanks's desk and set off to the far end of the room. His strides, as always, were nervous and bouncy, like a dancer waiting for his music.

'It's all right for you, Hanks,' he began, 'but mine is the ultimate responsibility. History will look back at this crisis and ask how I handled it. I have the whole of the SBG deployed in Wandsworth you know; my reputation is at stake. The District Assistant Commissioner telephoned me this morning, wanted to know what we were up to.'

'I hope you told him, sir.' Hanks extracted something elastic and green from his nose, examined it closely and stuck it under his chair.

'Of course I did,' said Sussworth, revolving on his right toe like a tin toy. 'I told him that we were on the point of apprehending the dangerous felons whom we suspect of having committed the Southfields murders. "A few more days," I told him, "and the long arm of the SBG would have 'em by the collar."'

'If only we could go underground,' said Hanks, spreading another large roll with butter and honey.

Sussworth stabbed the floor with his heel. 'I know, but the sewer men have told us time and time again how dangerous it is. They only go down if they have to, you know, and even they daren't go everywhere. I ask you, Hanks, what chance would we have? It's a labyrinth. Every time you lift a manhole cover the noise can be heard ten miles away. Wendles can see in everything but pitch dark, we can't. If we went into those tunnels they'd pick us off with their catapults, one by one. There are times for active discretion and this is one of them, we'll have to starve them out.'

Hanks thought and rubbed his nose. 'Why don't we gas 'em?' he said. 'That would work.'

'I'd love to,' said Sussworth, his moustache quivering happily at the idea, 'but imagine the fuss there'd be from all the do-gooders. We'd be pilloried as monsters.'

Hanks squeezed the bread roll between his teeth and honey oozed from it to form a golden waterfall down the front of his tunic. 'Our hands is tied,' he agreed through his half-masticated mouthful. 'Them Borribles kneecap our best officers with their catapults, they steal, they squat in old houses, all that, yet if we so much as lay a finger on 'em there's an outcry.'

'Don't worry, Hanks,' said Sussworth, placing his hands behind his back and raising his body up on his toes, 'I'll get them. Our men will remain on selfless duty at those manhole covers till kingdom come. When those Wendles are starving they'll soon get rid of those malefactors and then we'll snaffle them, every one.'

The two officers were interrupted by footsteps on the landing; there was a knock at the door and it opened to reveal an SBG constable.

'Excuse me, sir,' he said. 'I've got the prisoner.'

'That's right,' said Hanks. 'Bring him in.'

The door was opened a little wider and Ben shuffled into view. He looked tired and hungry, pale under his layers of dirt, frightened too; his shoulders cringed with fear at the sight of Sussworth and his hands trembled in the steel handcuffs he wore.

As soon as he had entered the room the door was shut behind him and Ben leant against it. This was behaviour that Sussworth would not countenance.

'You stand to attention, my friend,' he said, 'out in the middle here.'

'How about some food, guv'nor?' said Ben. 'How about some food, or a nice little drink, eh, what about it, Inspector?'

Sussworth ignored the request. 'For the last time,' he said, screwing his finger into Ben's stomach, 'how did those hooligans get out of Fulham police station? And what's more important, where did they go afterwards?'

Hanks swallowed the last of the honey roll and, using his arms more than his legs, yanked himself from behind his desk, then strolled round it until he stood right up beside the prisoner.

'Listen 'ere, you stinkin' lump of scum,' he said, and he started to push the exhausted tramp with his stomach, edging him back towards the door with every nudge. 'Do you know what we've done to your black 'ole of Calcutta, eh? You don't . . . Well, we've had it cleaned up for you, by order of the council.'

'You see,' said Sussworth, peering up into Ben's face like a short tourist looking at a tall monument, 'you're a living health hazard, you are. All those dirty bottles with spiders hiding in them, gone. All those ancient tins of grub, thrown in the river. All those lamps and tin cans, sent for scrap. All that furniture and all those mattresses, burnt.'

Sussworth did a little tap dance to the window and back again, stepping neatly on to Ben's ruined boots on his return.

'We've left you a bed, a chair and a table,' he continued. 'The social services have disinfected everything; it smells like a Jeyes Fluid factory down there now. My, my, aren't you lucky, Ben?' And with this the inspector grabbed Ben's nose and tweaked it until the tears ran down the old man's beard.

'And I'll tell you what else I'm going to do if you don't tell me what I want to know . . . I'm going to get a health department order on your shack. You shouldn't be living there at all really. Feather's Wharf is a rubbish dump, not a holiday camp. How would you like me to get your place bulldozered to the ground, eh? Answer me that.'

Ben shook his head and wrung his hands. 'Oh, guv'nor, don't do that to me; it's me 'ome. Please don't, I'd have nowhere to go.'

'We've thought of that,' said Hanks, and he seized Ben by the beard and dragged him to an open space so that he could begin nudging him with his stomach all over again. 'You see we're going to be really nice to you. Our police doctor is going to tell us how ill you are, when we tell him to, and that way we'll get you really sorted out. You'll be fumigated, incarcerated and renovated. We'll put you into hospital for months. You'll be washed every week, clean clothes you'll have, there'll be nurses everywhere to make sure you get no beer to drink, and to round it all off we'll have you committed to an old folks' home where there'll be a matron with a moustache to tell you what to do all day. You'd like that, wouldn't you, Ben?'

As the sergeant came to the end of his speech he gave a sharp thrust with his belly and Ben, off balance, fell to his knees. The tramp made no attempt to get up but simply raised his hands in supplication.

'Oh, leave off,' he whined. 'Don't send me away. It's none of my business, all this, straight up it ain't. My cell was open like it always is. Them kids was already outside when I got there; they forced me to help 'em, honest.'

'You were heard talking to a girl on Wandsworth roundabout,' said Sussworth, 'and I swear if you don't tell me what you know I'll ram you into that old folks' home so rapid they'll think you arrived by parachute.'

'All right,' said Ben, 'all right. This is what happened. I came out of the cell and they was out in the yard, see. There was a girl . . . she was leading the horse but I tried to walk past 'em, didn't I? I mean it was none of my business, as usual – you know me – but they wouldn't have it. There was about a dozen of 'em too, tough little bleeders. They don't take no for an answer, kids of today, do they?'

Ben looked up but Sussworth said nothing.

'Well, they saw it was foggy like and said if I didn't take 'em down to the river they'd beat me up. Battersea Bridge was what they wanted but I said I only knew the way to Wandsworth, which is true.'

'Why didn't you call out for help?' Sussworth wanted to know. 'There were plenty of policemen within earshot.'

'Call out!' said Ben, amazed. 'Cor, if I'd so much as opened my mouth there'd 'ave been six boots in it. They don't hang about, them Bobbirols.'

Hanks grabbed Ben's beard and banged his head against the wall.

'Where did they go, you stinkin' old goat?'

'How should I know?' said Ben. 'Once we got across the bridge they pushed me to the ground, gave me a kick and ran off into the fog with that horse. They said something about getting to Battersea before the fuzz arrived.'

Sussworth took a turn round the office, hopping and sidestepping as he went. 'Hmm,' he said. 'Battersea, it keeps coming back to that, but I'm not convinced. I'm a detective, I am. It would have made more sense for them to have found a manhole and gone into hiding with the Wendles. They're all Borribles together after all.'

'I heard something,' said Ben. 'I'll tell yer if you don't put me away . . . I couldn't stand that.'

'Well,' said Sussworth, 'what is it?'

'I heard 'em say something about not going to the Wendles, sounded like they'd had some fight with 'em in the past and didn't trust 'em. I don't think they went down there.'

'It could be true,' said Hanks. 'Remember that Borrible we captured once who told us there'd been some kind of war between the Southfields killers and the Wendles.'

Sussworth rubbed his chin. 'I know that, but I've got a feeling and my feelings are always right. You see I've stationed a couple of SBG men, disguised as costers, on a barrow in Battersea market. I've supplied them with descriptions of our villains and they'll report to me as soon as they're seen.'

'Ah,' said Ben, 'but they'd lie low, wouldn't they, very low?'

He leant against the wall and pushed himself to his feet.

Inspector Sussworth went over to the tramp and sniffed. 'My God,' he said, 'but you do smell.' He walked to the end of the room in order to place himself as far away from Ben as he could. 'Look here,' he went on. 'I'll give you one last chance, you can go back to that slum of yours . . .'

Ben smiled.

'. . . but on one condition only. You've got to render us every possible assistance; you've got to keep your eyes open and report to us every day.'

'I want to help, sir,' said Ben, ducking his head once or twice, 'but how can I?'

Sussworth explained: 'You're always out and about, up and down every street and alley in your part of Wandsworth, scrounging and begging; criminal offences both of them, of course. You see a lot of things that we don't. People clear the streets when they see a copper coming, but not when it's a drunken old tramp, they don't.'

'Oh, yes, sir, they trusts me,' said Ben, nodding sagely. 'I knows and sees a lot of things, I do, that aren't really my business.'

'Well you make it your business, you phone me up and tell me, and we'll give you some lovely money for your trouble, we will. I want to see you alert, Ben. Spying round corners, talking to kids, Borribles especially, and then you report everything to us. You do this and I'll see to it that you are left alone. I can make it easy for you Ben, very easy.'

Sussworth made a sign and Sergeant Hanks fished a key from his pocket and undid the tramp's handcuffs. Ben rubbed his wrists.

'You wouldn't have a few bob on yer, would yer, sir?' he asked Sussworth, giving a little bow. 'For the phone calls and such, and I'm ever so hungry, yer see. I won't get any food till I gets back to the wharf and starts sorting the rubbish.'

Inspector Sussworth laughed and felt in his pocket. 'What a scrounger,' he said, and he gave a few silver coins to Hanks who passed them on into Ben's filthy palm.

'There's one more thing,' said Hanks. 'If you give us the information that leads to the capture of the Southfields killers there'll be a special reward in it for you, Ben, lots of reward.'

Ben's face shone. 'Really, sir, that is good news, oh yes, you can count on me. I'd do anything to get me 'ands on a quid or two.'

Hanks threw open the door. 'Right, get out of here, and remember I'll have someone watching you night and day. You try to slip one over on me and I'll hang you up by your feet and have you put through a hot car wash.'

Ben bobbed his head again. 'My Gawd, yessir,' he said. 'Anything I hears, rely on me,' and he sidled into the corridor.

'They make me sick,' said Sussworth when the tramp had gone. 'Sell their grandmothers for a pint of beer. Swine, animals, that's what they are.'

'I agree, sir,' said Hanks, opening a cupboard and taking out a large tablet of chocolate, 'but it is our task to make use of the materials we have. Care for some fruit and nut?'

Inspector Sussworth took a square and absent-mindedly conveyed it to his mouth. 'I suppose you're right, Hanks,' he said. 'Even that dirty old man may be able to help us in our crusade.'

*

A quarter of an hour later Ben was sticking a fork into a steaming plateful of bangers and mash in a workman's café along the Fulham Road. He sat in a corner, by the window, and talked to himself as he ate.

'He's mad, that inspector,' said the tramp, 'mad. Help him, sunshine? I should cocoa! I wouldn't fart in his face if he was dying of suffocation. Got some money out of him though, didn't I just? Tuck in, Ben, bet you're hungry. I am, yes I am, and that is my business. Wonder 'ow those kids are, wonder 'ow they are? Dying for a drink, ain't I? Don't worry, I'll go and get one in a minute and drink to Sussworth's 'ealth, his bad 'ealth of course.' And laughing, Ben nearly choked on a mouthful of sausage and quickly downed a draught of hot tea to clear his gullet.

*

Spiff, his hands tied, sat on one of the chairs in the guardroom. Five of his fellow Borribles sat or stood near him, undecided. Skug and Norrarf were still absent on business of their own; Sydney was on guard in the tunnel.

'This'll get you nowhere,' said Spiff. 'Tying me up is stupid. You'll get yourselves caught, that's all.' No one answered.

Spiff tried another tack. 'Skug and Norrarf won't put up with this, you know, they'll put a stop to it right away. They won't give you any more grub if I say so, then what will you do?'

'Just think,' said Vulge, 'our four mates working in that mine all these months and he didn't tell us.'

'I didn't know for sure,' answered Spiff, 'and if I'd told you who would have believed me, eh? You didn't even want to rescue Sydney's horse so what chance did Knocker have?'

'And they could have been killed any time,' said Stonks. 'That mud is only held back by bits of wooden scaffolding, it could collapse easy. We've got to get them out as soon as we can.'

'You can't do it without me,' said Spiff. 'You'll make a mess of it.'

'We did for the Rumbles,' said Chalotte, 'without your help.'

'Rumbles, knickers,' said Spiff with contempt. 'This is different; this is Wendles, and Flinthead.'

'You've no right to be a Borrible,' said Chalotte, tossing her wild hair out of her eyes. She paused a moment and went on to say what she had been thinking all along. 'We should clip your ears ourselves.'

Spiff paled and struggled with his bonds. 'You cow,' he said, 'and you say I'm not Borrible. Can't you understand, all I got in the way of messages from here was rumours. First the treasure was saved, then it was lost; then Knocker was dead, then he was alive. I thought that if we went to Fulham to look for the horse we'd get near enough to Wandsworth to pick up some real news, catch a Wendle maybe, ask him questions. Then there was the battle with the SBG and after that what happened, happened, without my help.'

'We're not cutting any ears, Chalotte,' said Stonks. 'Whatever Spiff might have planned, there's enough clipping in the world without us joining in.'

'Flinthead does it,' said Chalotte defensively. She knew her friends were looking at her strangely.

'That's just it,' said Bingo, 'that's why we don't. We're supposed to stick together, even if we do quarrel.'

'This is getting us nowhere,' said Vulge. 'What's certain is that our four friends are alive. Let's get them out of here, and ourselves as well. We've got a reason for being in Wendle country now, that alone makes me feel better. I'll take on a Wendle or two.'

'That's more like it,' said Bingo, 'and we're going to need everyone who can fight.' He took out his knife and held it ready to release the prisoner. 'What do yer say?'

'I say no,' said Chalotte, but she realized as she said it that the others would be against her.

Stonks looked at the faces of his fellow Adventurers and saw their thoughts. 'Okay,' he said, 'cut him free, but he doesn't give orders any more. It's all down to us now.'

Bingo sliced through the cords that bound Spiff to his chair and put the knife back in his belt. Spiff got to his feet and smirked at Chalotte. 'Right,' he said, 'what's yer plan, because you'll need one, a good one.'

Stonks cleared his throat. 'I saw a lot of Wendle skiffs down on the Wandle mudflats,' he said. 'We'll steal one and get over to the derrick, there's only four guards; we'll knock 'em out and throw 'em down the shaft. Some of us can take their places so as not to arouse suspicion. I'll go down the mine and free the others. Then we get in the boats and row down the Wandle until we come out on the Thames. If we do it at night the coppers on the river won't see us. We'll cross to the other bank and get into the streets before daylight, or we'll row all the way down to Battersea, if the tide's right. I don't see any reason why it shouldn't work.'

Spiff leant against the wall and gave a slow hand-clap. 'Oh, great,' he scoffed, 'really great. And while you're doing all this the Wendles on the bank are lolling back with their hands behind their heads saying, "Oh look, our prisoners are escaping, won't Flinthead be pleased?" Ridiculous. What happens if they sink your boats? What happens if you're forced into the tunnels? Are you going to carry Knocker and the others over your shoulders? You saw how weak Torreycanyon was; the other three will be the same, worse even. They won't be able to walk, let alone fight. It won't work.'

'So what would you do?' asked Stonks.

'What would I do? I'd wait till the treasure's found, and then, when the excitement is high and the Wendles are celebrating, I'd move in and take the prisoners. You'd be halfway home before Flinthead realized you'd been here.'

'Oh, no,' cried Chalotte. 'I can see him coming a mile off. He wants to wait till the treasure's found so that he can try and take it with him, and get us to help him fight his way out. Not a chance.'

'Chalotte's right,' said Vulge. 'We got all messed up by the treasure in Rumbledom, let's not do it again.'

'That settles it,' said Stonks. 'We'll attack tomorrow night. We'll row out to the platform as if we were taking a message or changing the guard. I'll try to entice the sentries into the shaft on some pretext and deal with them there. When I come out with the prisoners we'll have to get the boats moving downstream as fast as we can and hope the Wendles on the bank don't notice anything until we run. Vulge, Bingo and Sydney can come with me to the platform. Twilight and Chalotte will stay on the bank. If anything goes wrong, Chalotte, you'll have to create a diversion in the tunnels. Fuse the lights, shout, anything, only make the Wendles chase you.'

'Why leave us behind?' asked Chalotte.

Stonks grinned, not something he did often. 'Obvious,' he said. 'They won't spot Twilight in the dark and you can't stand Spiff so you're the best person to keep an eye on him. We don't know how far we can trust him now.'

'We never could,' said Chalotte, 'only we didn't know it.'

The insults rolled right over Spiff. He smiled ironically and helped himself to some food. 'You lot better eat up,' he said, 'because you're going to need every bit of strength you've got; and get some sleep too, you may not get any more for a day or two. I can tell you one thing though. I shall be watching your rescue attempt with great interest, and I shan't lift a finger to help you.'

*

It was the middle of the night and Bingo couldn't sleep. The ground was hard, but he was used to that. His blanket was grubby and smelt horribly, but he was used to that too. There was a song running round and round in his head and he could not banish it. It was the song the Wendles sang when they were in triumph:

We are the Wendles of Wandsworth Town,
We're always up and the others are down.
We're rough and we're tough and we don't give a damn,
We are the elite of the Borrible clan.
Reach for your Rumble-sticks,
Try all your dirty tricks!
Nothing can beat us
And none shall defeat us.
Say a wrong word and we'll hammer you down,
We are the Wendles of Wandsworth Town!

Bingo sighed and hoped the song wasn't an evil omen. He threw the blanket from his shoulders and sat up. In the pitch darkness he got to his knees, crawled to the doorway and went outside, turned left and immediately bumped his head against the shaft of a spear. There was someone sitting there, on guard. Bingo drew back and stared into nothingness. He could not see a thing; it was like being blind.

'Who's that?' he whispered.

A voice came back at him, a Wendle voice. 'You tell me who you are, mush, or you'll get two yard of spear up yer.'

'I'm Bingo,' said Bingo.

'All right,' said the voice, 'but don't creep about at night, you'll get yourself killed. I'm Norrarf.'

'I couldn't sleep,' said Bingo. 'It's so hot. I thought the air might be a bit cooler in the tunnel.' He leant against the wall, stretched his legs out and looked to where he thought Norrarf was. 'Can I ask you a question?'

Norrarf chuckled and it was no friendly chuckle. 'You can always try . . . Don't go in for idle conversation, us Wendles.'

'Oh, it's not idle,' said Bingo, his tone as cheerful as ever. 'I just wondered how long you've known Spiff. I mean, were you here when he was Borribled?'

Norrarf didn't answer for a while. Bingo began to think he'd gone but then the Wendle spoke.

'He was already here when I came, had been for ages, had more names than anyone else too, including Flinthead. A lot of people liked Spiff in those days, including me and Skug – still do – but Flinthead hated him, which was funny really seeing as the stories told how they were Borribled together, came from the same place and all that.'

'Did they quarrel?'

'All the time,' said Norrarf, 'but Spiff was always too smart so Flinthead started to spread rumours about him. He was jealous, see. Then he got a lot of cronies together and made them into a bodyguard and one day he had Spiff captured and staked him out on the mud and he left him there to drown at high tide. There was a sentry on duty to make sure he didn't get away, and nobody could do a thing about it – too scared, most of 'em.'

'Except maybe you and Skug,' said Bingo, beginning to understand a little of the friendship that existed between the two Wendles and Spiff.

'Me and Skug, we waited till the tide was right in, when Flinthead and the bodyguard thought it was all over . . . Spiff was almost dead, had the mud in his mouth, crawling up his nostrils, over his head. Then as the sentry walked away I did for him and Skug pulled Spiff out of the water; we brought him round and he went to Battersea.'

'And the sentry?'

'Dead. We put his body in Spiff's place and he was eaten by the eels. All that was left at the next tide was a skeleton. Flinthead was as pleased as a dog with two tails . . . There was no one to stop him taking the whole tribe under his control. Later he heard that Spiff was alive after all but he never knew how it was done. That's why he always has at least fifty of the bodyguard round him. He don't know who to trust. Not every Wendle likes Flinthead you know; they're just scared of him. Even Tron, I suppose, and he's pretty brave.'

'Tron doesn't seem to be so bad,' said Bingo.

'He's what he has to be, but what can he do? Flinthead don't trust nobody. He has three men watching Tron and three more men watching each of the men who's watching Tron . . . and so it goes.'

'Has Spiff got a plan, do you think?' Bingo didn't expect Norrarf to answer that question, but he did. Now that he had begun, he seemed to enjoy talking through the watches of the night.

'Well,' he said, 'if you're too thick to work it out for yourself then you must be dopey enough to tell. Spiff hates Flinthead, and perhaps he thinks that if he can get his hands on the treasure then most of the Wendles will go over to his side – that would be the end of Flinthead.'

'Yes, but if Spiff got the treasure he might become as bad as Flinthead,' said Bingo, 'and anyway money's not Borrible.'

'I know that,' said Norrarf, 'but Spiff thinks any method that gets rid of Flinthead is a good method. Spiff's craftier than anyone I've ever known. He can see round corners and tell you what happened tomorrow, he can. That girl with you says he ain't Borrible at all, but he's a damn sight more Borrible than Flinthead. Whichever way you look at it, getting his hands on that treasure is the only way he's going to get your mates out alive. Borrible or not Borrible, that treasure's a powerful weapon.'

'Is that his plan?' asked Bingo, his voice quickening with excitement.

Norrarf clicked his teeth in denial. 'Nah, that's just what I think, ain't it? If you want to know any more you'd better ask him, I've talked too much already. You'd better get back.'

Bingo could feel the Wendle studying him in the dark. He stretched his eyes as wide as he could but saw nothing more than the pulsing of his own blood.

'It takes years to get used to living down here,' said Norrarf. 'That's why we're the way we are, I suppose.'

Bingo got to his hands and knees and turned to crawl back to the guardroom. 'Thanks, Norrarf,' he said as he left, 'thanks a lot.'

Norrarf did not bother to answer.

*

The next evening, when it was time, the Borribles gathered together and made ready to set off. They had checked their catapults; each wore an extra bandolier and carried a Rumble-stick as well. They were indistinguishable from any band of Wendle warriors.

'Right,' said Stonks, 'we'll march along the tunnels as bold as brass; that way we'll be taken for a relief guard on our way to a lookout point.'

Spiff sneered. 'And you'd better get me to walk in front,' he said, 'otherwise you'll get lost.'

'Wait a minute,' said Vulge, 'where's Norrarf and Skug?'

Spiff raised his eyebrows. 'How should I know, they can't nurse us all the time, can they? If we're going, let's go.'

It was a long trek across the underground citadel and the seven Borribles passed many Wendles on their way, but no one asked their business or stopped them to demand their destination. By the time Spiff marched them out on to the banks of the Wandle the Borribles knew their disguise was perfect and they were filled with confidence and determination.

They came to a halt near a small jetty where two skiffs were moored. These were the boats used by the sentries for travelling to and from the derrick. Everywhere, on both sides of the river, sat or stood small groups of Wendles, all of them waiting for the treasure to be unearthed. On the platform itself the great wheel turned and creaked as the buckets clanked and the mud-covered figure of Torreycanyon stumbled forever forward.

'Strike a light,' said Vulge, 'it don't bear thinking about, do it? Our mates working in that shit for months and months. Old Flinthead's got a lot to answer for.'

'That'll do,' said Stonks, walking up and down in front of his companions like a commander inspecting his troops. 'Remember everyone along here is watching us right now, so try to make it look as if you know what you're doing. When I give the order, Bingo, Vulge, Sydney and me will get into this boat here. You other three will make for one of those tunnels. You'll be able to see everything from there, and whatever you do, Chalotte, don't take your eyes off Spiff.'

'I ain't going anywhere,' said Spiff. 'I want to see what a mess you make of it,' and he did a right turn, saluted like a Wendle and stamped off towards the nearest corridor with Chalotte and Twilight following.

Stonks watched them go and then ordered his own contingent into the larger of the two boats. Vulge and Bingo took the oars and, shoving off, they rowed into midstream.

Sydney bit her lip as the water slipped by. 'Have we got a chance, Stonksie?' she said.

Stonks sat in the stern and gazed at the derrick as they approached it. 'Yes,' he said. 'If we're lucky with the four guards and if we can get the prisoners out of the mine before we're noticed, then we'll get away.'

Bingo and Vulge gave a few more strokes of the oars and their skiff arrived at the platform. One of the guards came to the edge of it and Vulge turned in his seat and threw him a rope. 'Tie us up, mate,' he called, and the guard knelt and hooked the painter on to a large nail, but there his friendliness ceased. As soon as Vulge made to climb from the boat the Wendle lowered his spear so that the point of it was only an inch or two away from the Stepney Borrible's face.

'Where do you think you're going, mush? You've got to have a special writing from Flinthead to get on here.'

Vulge hesitated; he didn't know what to say.

Stonks stood up in the stern of the boat, frowning. 'That's exactly it,' he said, 'we're special from Flinthead. It's an emergency. The off-duty guard told him about the shuttering in the shaft, said it was weak, likely to fall in and bury everything; we've got to inspect it.'

'I know nothing about that,' grumbled the guard. 'I've had strict orders.'

Stonks raised both arms. 'You do as yer please, me old china; you know what Flinthead will be like if we go back without having done what we were sent to do. If that treasure gets buried under a thousand tons of mud you can bet your ears you'll be down there with it.'

The guard paled and Stonks reflected, not for the first time, that Flinthead's strength was also his weakness. The Wendles were so scared of him that they had no confidence in themselves. 'It's up to you,' went on Stonks, 'but I wouldn't be in your waders, mate, if you send us off with a flea in our ear.'

'All right,' said the guard, 'but watch yer step or I'll skewer yer.'

Vulge leapt easily on to the platform, in spite of his limp, and held out a hand to pull the three others up to him.

'Thanks,' said Stonks, who came last, and he walked across to the great treadmill. Close to, it was a massive thing and inside it the tortured shape of Torreycanyon shambled along like a drunkard, tumbling forward at a dangerous angle, always on the point of falling over but never quite managing to leave his feet far enough behind. The cumbersome wheel turned, the heavy mud splashed down into the river and the yellow lights above sprayed a dismal colour over everything. As Stonks listened to the rumbling of the treadmill and the banging of the buckets his eyes began to burn with pity and a fearful anger gnawed at the back of his brain.

'I'll kill 'em for this,' he said, under his breath, 'I'll kill 'em, every last one.'

As he stood there one of the guards came up beside him and laughed. 'This is the way to treat 'em,' he said, and he cracked his whip, making it curl across Torreycanyon's shoulders. The captive Borrible lost his balance, tottered for a moment, and then ran on, just a little faster.

Stonks swallowed hard. His friend was a ghost, a shadow. His clothes were in tatters, he was barefoot and covered from heel to head in a dark stickiness, a mixture of sweat, mud and blood. There was slime in his eyes, slime in his hair. He was not far from death, ground down to nothing for the sake of the Rumbles' treasure.

'What's his name?' asked Stonks for something to say.

'Torreycanyon,' said the guard, 'and he's the lucky one. He's a bit like a pet dog to us, running round in his wheel. You should see the others down below, you'd have to see the state they're in to believe it. No fresh air, gasping for breath. If you could see their skin, which you can't 'cos of the mud, you'd find it had all gone green with mildew. I don't reckon they can live much longer, they may not live until they finds the treasure even.'

'Very interesting,' said Bingo, biting back his temper, 'but we're only here to see the shuttering.'

'Yes,' said Stonks, 'we'd better get on with the job.' He went past the treadmill and looked into the mouth of the mine. The chief guard was by his side.

'Well, that's it,' said the Wendle. 'About a quarter of a mile down they reckon they are now, wood planks all the way round the outside with two big beams going across every fifteen feet or so to stop the planks falling inwards, 'cos the weight of the mud and earth behind is enormous, and pushing in all the time. If that lot slipped I don't know what would happen, a bleedin' eruption I should think.'

The rescuers were silent. The shaft was about ten feet in diameter and, as the guard had said, the safety of the diggings depended on the solid beams that crossed at right angles to each other at regular intervals all the way to the bottom. Huge wedges held the first timbers in position; massive they were and rising above the level of the platform. Sydney sidled to the rim and peered down. Below her she saw an electric light and another platform, and below that another and another until they became so small they disappeared.

'Can't see anything moving,' said Sydney.

'And you won't,' said the chief guard, 'they're too deep; they've been out of sight for months. There's two at the bottom digging their hearts out, and another follows behind. Black feller!'

'He's black now all right,' said another guard and he laughed.

'He has to keep the whole shaft in good order,' continued the chief, 'otherwise, if those beams give way, any of 'em, why the whole shebang would collapse and kill 'em all, not to mention losing the treasure.'

'Still getting enough timber?' asked Vulge.

'We're having a bit of trouble since the SBG arrived outside, still we've got enough to be going on with.'

Stonks glanced at the banks of the river. No one seemed particularly interested in what was taking place on the platform. It was time to begin; he had to get rid of the sentries. 'Well,' he said, 'we'd better start our inspection.' He looked at the chief guard. 'Will you come to the first landing with me, I've already seen something there I don't like the look of.'

'Well, all right,' said the Wendle, 'but I'll be buggered if I'll go any further. I can't stand it in there, it gives me the creeps.'

Stonks winked at Vulge and whispered, 'You stay here and send me another one when I asks yer.'

Vulge perched on the coping of the shaft and watched Stonks follow the guard down the ladder. Bingo scrutinized the towpaths and Sydney placed herself near the treadmill. Whatever happened to her, she had decided, the guard with the whip was going into the mud. Her sharp knife was ready.

The moment Stonks arrived below he went to stand by the Wendle and called his attention to a split in the shuttering. The guard leant over to examine the fault and Stonks nudged him gently into space. For a split second the Wendle ran on thin air like a cartoon cat; his spear sprang from his grasp, his eyes bulged and then down he went, surprised, leaving only a small and diminishing scream behind him.

Stonks glanced up at Vulge and raised two fingers; he wanted another one.

'I think your mate's slipped,' said Vulge quietly. 'You'd better have a look.'

The guards who were nearest came to the shaft and bent forward to see.

'He's fallen to the next platform,' called Stonks. 'You'll have to come and help me fetch him up.'

'Dammit,' said the Wendles, but they laid their spears on the planking and climbed down the ladder.

'Blimey,' said Bingo, 'that first guard was a pushover.'

'No jokes,' said Vulge. 'Grab hold of one of them spears and pretend you're on duty. We don't want them Wendles on the shore to get suspicious. I'll watch Stonks.'

But there wasn't much for Vulge to see. The two guards arrived on the landing. Stonks got them to the edge, the Wendles stared downwards and the next thing they knew they were falling fast, rigid with terror, clutching their bodies one to the other in the hope that somehow they could alter the laws of gravity and so save themselves. The noise when it came was solid and sickening. Stonks looked up and raised four fingers; he wanted the guard with the whip.

'Here, mate,' said Vulge. 'Your two chums want you. I can't make out what they're saying, got a speech impediment have they?'

The guard threw his whip on to a pile of tools near the treadmill and ambled over to where Vulge sat. 'They're a bunch of idiots,' he said, and leant over the parapet. Sydney had kept pace with him across the platform and as soon as he halted she hit him very hard in the kidneys, taking the breath out of his body so that he couldn't call or shout, then she bent rapidly to his heels, grasped them securely, and simply upended her victim into the mine. Fortunately he made no sound until his head hit the planks of the landing. There he rolled and groaned until Stonks helped him on his way with a soft touch of the foot, easing the unconscious Wendle into the shaft so that he could join his colleagues.

'My, my,' said Vulge as he watched the body swoop and dive like a swallow, 'he has gone down in the world.'

'Shall we tell Torreycanyon now?' asked Sydney.

Vulge looked at the river banks. All was quiet. 'No,' he said at length. 'He might get excited and give us away. Hurry, let's get on guard, them Wendles on the shore will get suspicious if there ain't someone walking up and down all the time. And keep cracking the whip.'

So the three Borribles seized their spears and stood sternly to attention or marched to and fro across the platform.

'I can hardly believe it,' murmured Sydney. 'It all seems to be going to plan.'

*

Twilight and Chalotte surveyed the river from the safety of a tunnel, staring anxiously across the Wandle to where the wooden derrick floated on the slow rise and fall of the black-green mud. Streams of darkness poured down between the yellow lights that the Wendles had raised and it was a darkness that was at one with the dingy waters of the river. Somewhere behind Chalotte sat Spiff, not watching, strangely melancholy, alone.

'They're going well,' said Twilight. 'Stonks has got three of them into the mine and no one on shore has twigged it yet, and Bingo and Sydney are pretending to be on guard.'

'I know,' said Chalotte, her voice hopeful. 'But it'll be a bit different when they bring the prisoners out; they'll have to go like the clappers then.'

Suddenly Twilight laid hold of Chalotte's arm. 'Listen,' he said. 'What's that whispering in the tunnels?'

Chalotte cocked an ear and the whispering, faint at first, began to grow more definite. It was a threatening and insistent noise, a soft squelching, a noise that brought fear with it. Chalotte was mystified, then she realized what it was; it was the sound of many scores of Wendles in supple waders running at a relentless speed. It was the sound that Flinthead's bodyguard made when it moved – direct, dedicated, unswerving and vicious – and when the bodyguard moved Flinthead moved with it, his shapeless nose sniffing the way.

'Oh, it can't be,' wailed Chalotte, 'it mustn't be.'

Her wishes made no difference. Within a minute or two a mass of heavily armed Wendles poured out of the tunnels on each side of the river, the light glinting on their spears and helmets. Many of them carried lightweight skiffs and their stride did not break as they reached the Wandle and ran on into it, launching themselves, their speed remaining constant as they went from running to rowing so that they flew on to the surface of the mud like black and orange water-bugs. Many more warriors spread out along the banks, prodding ordinary Wendles from the towpaths with the butts of their spears. Then came a clashing of weapons and a huge shout, and in the midst of fifty hand-picked soldiers Flinthead appeared, his golden jacket shining and his eyes brilliantly opaque with the coldness of his triumph.

'Dammit,' swore Chalotte, and she lifted her fingers to her mouth in order to whistle a warning, but strong arms seized her from behind and for a moment she thought she'd been captured – then she remembered Spiff.

'Keep yer mouth shut,' he said. 'It won't do anyone any good to let Flinthead know you're here. Just keep quiet and get ready to run for your life.'

On the platform, Bingo, Vulge and Sydney stood firm and made ready to defend themselves against the advancing warriors. It was pointless; the derrick was too large for three to hold against so many and the Wendle warriors overran the interlopers after the briefest of struggles. They were disarmed, bound and thrown to the floor. When all was secure Flinthead was rowed over and helped on to the platform by Tron, his captain of bodyguards, the stern fighter who had commanded and led the attack.

Then the Wendles waited, silent and patient until, in the end, Stonks climbed into view at the top of the mine shaft, pulling three exhausted and slime-covered slaves behind him. It had taken all his massive strength to bring them up from the bottom of the digging and so engrossed in his task was he that he did not notice the eager faces above him. He raised a hand for assistance and the Wendles grasped it before Stonks realized that things had changed. He was quickly made a prisoner himself, bound with ropes and pushed to the floor to lie by the side of his friends.

'Oh, Twilight,' said Chalotte, the tears flooding her eyes, 'this is awful, all of 'em captured. Look at those three covered in mud, the ones the Wendles are lifting out of the mine, that's Knocker and Napoleon and Orococco. Hell, they're so weak they can hardly stand.'

What Chalotte said was true. The captives swayed and blinked stupidly in the light. They were caked in mud, months of mud, it was ground into their skins like a paste of graphite. Their hearts had filled with joy at Stonks's unexpected arrival and in some unknowable and resolute part of their minds they had discovered strength enough to climb the long ladders upwards, only to find Flinthead waiting for them. It was one of life's rotten jokes and their dejection was total.

The Wendle chieftain laughed like a car-crusher. 'I knew well that something was happening here,' he crowed, 'and look what we have. Another four of them, brought here by greed, trying to steal what is rightfully ours. Well, brother Wendles, they will help us now, help us in our struggle to dig the mine.'

Stonks began to fight against his bonds and he swore at Flinthead. 'You snot-gobblin' little shit-eater,' he cried, 'you no-name pig.'

Flinthead was delighted and one of his guards kicked Stonks in the ribs.

'He's the strongest one, isn't he?' said the chieftain. 'I remember his name from last time . . . Stonks. He's the one who broke open the Great Door of Rumbledom, he'll be just right for the treadmill. Put a good man on the whip. I've waited too long for my treasure, maybe now things will move a little faster.'

'What do you want done with the old ones?' asked Tron. 'Shouldn't we let them go? They don't look as if they could work another day.'

'Send 'em back down,' said Flinthead, 'they can work till they die. Shackle 'em all up and over the top with 'em.'

The new prisoners kicked at their captors as their legs were manacled together with heavy chains, but the others, those they had gone to rescue, had not a word to say. Their muscles had striven beyond pain and their minds were submerged below thought. They knew how to dig and they knew no other thing. When they were ordered to clamber back into the mine they did so in abject silence. Flinthead watched and smiled; that silence was his glory! How were the mighty fallen.

'And let me warn you,' he said. 'If those buckets come up empty of mud I'll make an example of those two in the treadmill. I'll send 'em down to you headfirst, like you did with my guards. I want that treasure and I want it quick. You'll soon learn – no mud coming up, no food going down.'

'We'll get you one day,' shouted Bingo as he was forced on to the ladder with the others, 'and I'll have your nose off and slice it up like a side of bacon.'

Flinthead did not wait to swap insults. 'Double the sentries everywhere,' he shouted, 'twenty on each towpath too.' Then he stepped into his skiff and was conveyed to the river bank, his bodyguard following.

On the shore he was greeted by a multitude of excited Wendles. News of the attempted rescue and its failure had travelled fast. Flinthead was cheered till the roof resounded and there was great confusion as the crowd struggled to approach their leader, to touch him, to look at him.

Chalotte and Twilight had been completely disheartened by the turn of events but now they came out of their tunnel to stare as the bodyguard cleared a path through the mob. Chalotte fingered the knife at her belt and wondered if she should assassinate the Wendle chieftain there and then, but Twilight saw the movement of her hand and guessed what she was thinking.

'It would do no good,' he said, 'and would not help your friends; that is what we must think of now.'

Chalotte was about to answer when a sudden surge in the crowd plucked her from her feet and swung her against the firm flesh of the bodyguard. She looked up and saw that she was only a yard or so from Flinthead, dangerously close to that damp green skin, those lifeless eyes of power and the great shapeless nose. Chalotte shivered in spite of the warm crush of bodies all round her. She turned her head away from the hideous countenance and immediately saw two faces she knew. There, just in front of the chieftain, marched Norrarf and Skug, resplendent in brand new uniforms. They had not seen her; they were too busy smiling with pride.

'March on,' cried Flinthead. 'You did well, Norrarf and Skug; I will remember you when the treasure comes. March on I say, and sing the song of the Wendles.'

Chalotte turned her back to avoid being noticed and pushed her way through the crowd until she reached Twilight. Despair swept through her body and, amidst all the cheering and shouting, the tears ran freely down her cheeks.

'For Pete's sake don't do that,' said Twilight. 'The Wendles will wonder what's wrong with you, this is their celebration.'

Chalotte tried but could not stop her tears and Twilight guided her into a tunnel.

'I saw Norrarf and Skug,' she said miserably, 'in Flinthead's bodyguard. They weren't bodyguards before so that means he must have promoted them . . . It means they must have told Flinthead about us trying to rescue Knocker . . . That can only mean one thing.'

Now it was Twilight's turn to touch his knife. 'Of course,' he said, 'it means that Spiff told them about Stonks's plan, so now there's only the two of us against everyone else.'

A cool voice came to them from the darkness. Spiff's voice. 'If you'd listened to me none of this would have happened. I told you to wait.'

Chalotte wiped her eyes and blinked, trying to locate her enemy; it was impossible. 'You grassed on your friends,' she said, 'and now they're down the bottom of the pit and we'll never get them out.'

'I can get them out,' said Spiff, 'on my own if needs be.'

'Did you tell Norrarf and Skug to tell Flinthead about the rescue?' asked Chalotte. 'Because if you did I swear that I'll kill you the first chance I get.'

Spiff chuckled. 'You scare me to death. Yes, I gave Stonks away and I had good reasons for it. Flinthead knew there was something going on down here, he knew that someone from outside was inside. He'd already doubled the guards on all the exits and all along the Wandle. Stonks had no chance of getting anywhere, with or without the prisoners. He would have been killed; now at least he's alive, and all the others as well.'

'Alive like slaves,' said Chalotte, and she took her catapult from her belt and loaded it.

'Don't you realize,' Spiff continued, 'that I've been planning my revenge against Flinthead for years, every move, every detail. I didn't want it spoiled, so I put a spanner in the works as soon as I could.'

'Yeah,' said Chalotte angrily, 'and it didn't matter about our mates as long as your plan was all right.' She began to stretch the catapult rubber. If she saw Spiff she'd kill him.

'I'll get 'em out of here. Look on the bright side. Sure I had Norrarf and Skug tell Flinthead but now they've been made members of the bodyguard. Now I'll know everything Flinthead knows, but the best thing of all is that Flinthead thinks he's captured everybody. He's stopped sniffing; he doesn't know about us, we're a surprise.'

'What d'yer mean, we?' said Chalotte. She drew the rubber back to her ear and tried to judge Spiff's position from his voice. She'd let fly with the stone, she thought, and then run forward with her knife.

Spiff's voice floated through the darkness again, only now it came from a different part of the tunnel. 'If you put that catapult down, Chalotte, I'll tell you . . . and you too, Twilight.'

Chalotte cursed and lowered her weapon. She looked to her right and caught a glimpse of Twilight doing the same with his.

'You sod,' she said, 'you're about as straightforward as a left-handed corkscrew. Why didn't you trust us?'

'I don't trust anyone,' said Spiff. 'If you so much as pee against the wall down here Flinthead knows about it before you've finished. I'll tell you one thing and one thing only. You want your mates out and you'll have 'em out, that I promise you. What you've got to decide, Chalotte, is this. Do you forget about killing me or do I kill you, right now, because I can. I don't need you, I can do my plan on my own.'

Chalotte squatted on the rough floor, behind her the glow of the river bank and the noise of the Wendles as they dispersed, in front of her the blackness and Spiff's voice. There was no doubt that he could see her whereas she could see nothing. She would have to lie. She was determined to survive if only to make sure that Spiff got his come-uppance. She put her catapult away.

'I'd agree to anything,' she said, 'if I really thought you could still get them out.'

'And me,' said Twilight.

'You'll both have to do exactly as I say,' said Spiff, 'and no questions. I ain't telling anyone what my plan is.'

'Just tell me one thing,' said Chalotte, 'for the sake of curiosity. Was it you who arranged for the Borrible messsage to turn up in Neasden, the one that got Sydney so worried about Sam the horse, the one that made her come to see me at Whitechapel?'

'Yes it was,' said Spiff. 'I wanted to get you all here but I wasn't quite sure how to do it, then Sam and Sussworth and old Ben did it for me.'

'If your plan only needs you why did you need us?' asked Twilight.

Spiff chuckled, but with real mirth this time.

'Twilight,' he said, 'you're as bright as a new bar of soap. It was because my plan needed to lull Flinthead, which ain't easy. I needed someone to be captured, so he'd feel secure. Well he does now; all I've got to do is wait for the right moment.'

'And when's that?'

'I ain't saying. You can come along for the ride if you like or you can go away and hide in a corner till it's all over.'

'And the treasure,' said Chalotte, 'where does that come in?'

'Oh, it comes in,' said Spiff. 'That's power that is, not in a normal Borrible set-up, I know, but down here it is. I'll be honest with you; Flinthead is first, then your mates, then the Rumble treasure chest. All three together would be lovely, but I'll be happy to settle for the first one.'

Chalotte hesitated. She wished she had time to think, wished she had time to talk to Twilight, but there was no time. She sighed in the silence and said, 'All right, Spiff. I've got no choice, have I? It's Hobson's again. I'll go along with you, but when we get out of here, if we do, I might just stick my knife in yer.'

'Me too,' said Twilight.

'I wouldn't expect anything else,' said Spiff, and they heard him roll over and get to his feet.

The sly bugger, thought Chalotte, he's been lying on the floor, and she saw Spiff step into the light, holding a spear across his body.

'What do we do now?' asked Twilight.

'We go back to the guardroom and wait,' said Spiff. 'I'll ask Norrarf to get us a pack of cards. We can play patience.'

'And the others,' said Chalotte. 'I suppose we just leave them in the mine, digging and slaving for Flinthead, until it suits you that is.'

Spiff smiled his most ironic smile. 'Well,' he said, 'at least we know where they are. They can't get lost now, can they?'

8

More than a week went by, a week that for Chalotte was made unbearable by Spiff's confidence and high spirits. It was as if he saw the future with complete clarity and knew that his long-laid plans were at last coming to fruition. But Chalotte had never been so unhappy. Every second she was awake she thought of the captives toiling in the humidity of the mine-shaft, digging their days and nights away, knee-deep in muck. She was homesick, a thousand miles from Whitechapel, and had it not been for the hope of rescuing her friends, she would have made her way to the nearest manhole and gone back into the streets, never mind the SBG; anything to get back to a normal life.

And so she waited with an ill grace. She detested Norrarf and Skug more and more, turning her head away from the sight of them each time they brought provisions and news to the guardroom. That was all she could do; she was helpless and she knew it. She was obliged to accept the situation for as long as it lasted, but she would not acquiesce. She spoke only in grunts to Twilight; Spiff she ignored completely and spent her time either scowling or sleeping. Her usual common sense had deserted her, banished by feelings of frustration and hatred.

Yet deep down, although the waiting seemed endless, Chalotte knew that soon it would have an end and that if there was any chance of freeing her friends then that chance lay with Spiff and the devious workings of his complicated and untrustworthy mind. On the morning of the eighth day after the capture of Stonks, Chalotte at last awoke in good heart; she took a deep sigh and decided only one thing mattered, and that was the deliverance of the enslaved Borribles.

As for Spiff, there was only one thing she could do. She glanced over to where he lay and studied his face, as crafty in sleeping as in waking.

She could not fight him there and then, and anyway if the rescue attempt failed then Flinthead would kill them all. If it succeeded then there would be time enough to settle accounts. She would have to wait and see.

As she thought these thoughts Spiff opened one eye and smiled. He had a way of smiling that convinced Chalotte he could see right through her, and she knew he had realized, with his first second of consciousness, that she had come to a decision.

'It'll be all right,' he said, 'if you leave it to me.'

Whether her tacit acceptance had something to do with it or not Chalotte never knew, but from that day Spiff began to put his plans into operation. From then on they never stopped working. Spiff traipsed Chalotte and Twilight all over Wendle country, familiarizing them with the terrain, stealing systematically and making caches of provisions and weapons in likely and unlikely spots.

'Well,' he said in answer to Chalotte's questions, 'I'm not looking for trouble but when trouble starts it tends to get out of hand. Who knows which way we might have to run; we might have no weapons, no food, we might have to hide for days, weeks even. These supplies could be the difference between life and death.'

'But only if you can remember where they are,' said Twilight. 'That's not much good if we get split up.'

'It's good for me,' said Spiff.

And so he went on working away at his preparations until the fourteenth day and then he declared enough was enough. He and his two companions had just finished hiding their last Wendle skiff when Chalotte became aware of a figure leaning over her in the yellow half-light. She turned quickly in the water where she stood and pulled her catapult from her belt. Spiff waded ashore, laughing to see Chalotte so ready to fight on his side now. 'You still can't see in the dark,' he said. 'That's Norrarf.'

The Wendle threw three brand new orange-coloured jackets on to the ground. 'I'm going to enrol you in the bodyguard today,' he said, 'all three of you, only you'll have to come right now.'

'That's good,' said Spiff. 'Plan A.' And he held out a hand to pull Chalotte from the water to the towpath, but he explained nothing.

'Put the jackets on,' ordered Norrarf, 'and as soon as you get a chance you'd better clean your helmets and waders. If you go round like that Flinthead will suss you for sure. And you'd best invent yourself a Wendle name too, just in case you're asked.'

Spiff slung his old jacket into the river. 'Right,' he said, 'as of now we're in the bodyguard. That means doing what you're told, Chalotte, when you're told, without question. We're walking on a knife's edge. If we get found out it's curtains.'

When Norrarf was satisfied with the look of his recruits he got them into line and marched them upstream until they came to the landing stage, the open space which was level with the mine and its platform. As always the noise of the treadmill and the buckets filled the whole cavern. Chalotte could see Stonks in the wheel with an arm round Torreycanyon, helping him along. Every now and then came the crack of the whip and Chalotte formed her lips to curse, but Spiff was watching and shook his head. 'Not now,' he said, 'not now.'

There were about twenty of Flinthead's bodyguard on duty in the area and their uniforms were spotless and their weapons clean. They leant casually against the brick walls or crouched on their haunches. From time to time, when they considered it necessary, they cleared the towpath of ordinary Wendles so as to make a way for Flinthead should he come. Apart from that they did nothing, though they gave the impression of being ready for anything at a moment's notice. Under the bright helmets their faces were hard; they did what they were told and they did it quickly.

Norrarf marshalled the newcomers on a flat space by the bankside. He clicked his fingers and a warrior brought him an assortment of sharp spears; he gave one each to the three Borribles.

'You have been picked to serve on Flinthead's bodyguard,' he said, loud enough for the nearest Wendles to hear, 'and you know what that means; you will be rewarded for instant obedience, anything less than that and you'll be staked out on the mud. Now dismiss . . . and get your weapons and uniforms clean.'

Spiff saluted and Chalotte and Twilight did as he did, then they turned and walked away to find an uncrowded spot on the towpath not too far from their new colleagues.

'I've seen a few Borrible tribes,' said Twilight, 'but I've never seen anything like Wendles, I mean obeying orders, cleaning clothes . . . How does Flinthead get away with it?'

Spiff spat on the point of his spear and polished it with his sleeve. 'Because he doesn't mind what he does or who he does it to, just as long as he gets his own way. It's also got a lot to do with living so near Rumbledom. Until the Great Rumble Hunt was successful your average Wendle never knew from one minute to the next if he was going to be taken over or not . . . There was always a battle going on along the frontier. That made 'em suspicious of outsiders and always ready for a scrap, but then,' and here Spiff winked, 'so am I.'

*

During the days that followed Chalotte learned more about self-discipline than she had ever thought possible. She steeled herself to ignore the crack of the whip; she pretended to jeer and laugh with others of the bodyguard whenever Stonks or Torreycanyon fell to their knees in the treadmill; and she forced herself not to think of her friends, Knocker in particular, who were still toiling in the deep pit of the mine.

Most of the time she leant against the curved wall of the sewer and looked as ferocious and heartless as she could, or squatted cross-legged on the ground and played fivestones with Twilight, assuming an indifference to all that went on around her, though in reality her blood was seething with anxiety and impatience. Then one day, when she had almost forgotten who she was and why she was in Wendle country at all, Spiff came and sat with her and Twilight, resting his spear across his knees.

'Something's going to happen soon,' he began, 'I have a feeling in my water. Norrarf thinks they'll reach the treasure any day now and when they do he reckons Flinthead will go down to get it because he won't trust anyone to do it for him. He'll come this way, by the landing stage, and be rowed over to the platform, and then down he'll go.'

'Alone?' asked Twilight.

'Not bloody likely, he wouldn't be safe. Bingo, Vulge and Sydney are still pretty fresh, they might wind their leg chains round his neck and strangle him. He'll have to take some bodyguards with him . . . and we're bodyguards. Now whatever happens we've got to get over to the platform with Flinthead. Norrarf and Skug are in charge here and they are going to order us into the rowing detail. We must get to the platform.'

'Supposin' we don't?' said Chalotte.

Spiff dismissed the thought. 'We just have to, even if we take a separate boat. Once we get there you two line up with the Wendles and do as you're told. It's my job to see that I'm chosen as one of the guards to go down the mine with Flinthead.'

'Cripes,' said Twilight, 'you can't do that; it'll be you against all of them.'

Spiff turned his head very slowly and looked at the Bangladeshi, his blue eyes blazing with the bright love of danger. It was a light fuelled by hatred and Chalotte blinked in the glare of it.

'You're mad, Spiff,' she said very quietly, 'you're raving bonkers.' But although she meant it there was a note of admiration in her voice. His bravery burnt like a beacon.

'Maybe I am,' said Spiff, 'but when I get down there I won't let two or three little Wendles come between me and what I've been dreaming of for years.'

'What about when you come back up again?' said Twilight. 'We've got the whole Wendle nation to get past, remember. You said yourself they ain't going to sit back and let us go without a fight.'

'You don't have to know any more than I've told yer at this stage,' said Spiff. 'Just behave like regular bodyguards until I comes with the prisoners, then do as I orders and everything will work out fine.'

There was nothing more to be got out of him and he left them, ignoring them both in the days that followed and spending all his time with the troops of the bodyguard, laughing, joking and making friends. Indeed Spiff became very popular among the warriors, although it was obvious to Chalotte that if it became necessary he would slide his knife into any Wendle who upset his calculations. That was Spiff and he was not to be altered. So Chalotte gave up her contemplation of the strange un-Borrible Borrible and contented herself with counting the days . . . eighteen . . . nineteen . . . twenty . . . twenty-one.

*

An electric light flickered and Chalotte raised her head from between her hands. She was sitting on the towpath and Twilight sat nearby. In spite of her efforts she had lost count of time; there had been something like twenty-four days, she thought, since the capture of Stonks's raiding party.

Chalotte glanced into the roof vault. The light flickered again. Something was wrong in the citadel, there was something missing. Then she realized; there was silence everywhere; the buckets were not clanking, the treadmill was not creaking. Chalotte glanced across the river. Torreycanyon was a collapsed heap and Stonks was kneeling beside him. The guards were as still as stone carvings, their spear points unmoving. Everyone, standing or sitting, was motionless, their ears cocked, their eyes wide open. There had been a noise and they were listening to it. Chalotte herself, preoccupied by her own dreams, had let the sound slip by at first, but then her memory found the noise and brought it back to her and it merged in her ear with a real echo, and Chalotte recognized the sound and the echo for what they were and so did everyone else in the Wendle citadel.

A quarter of a mile below the surface of the River Wandle, at the very bottom of the mine shaft, in a pool of mud and filth, Knocker's spade had struck the steel lid of the Rumble treasure chest and the noise had rung in every Wendle heart, and it still rang and continued to ring as every heart stopped.

Down the corridors and tunnels the bitter noise echoed and no one moved while it passed them, but as it dwindled and died at last there came another sound, as chilling and as frightening as the first. A scream of pleasure rose from Flinthead's throat and rode along the dark passages of his empire. Flinthead had got his way.

Flinthead called again; his duty bodyguard gathered round him and all together they raced towards the river. The chieftain's face was crazed with greed and no one dared to look upon it in those first moments. But from the mouth of every tunnel that Flinthead passed came every Wendle who could move, eager to be with their leader, struggling with each other to be the first to see the box of treasure which they believed would change their lives.

Spiff rushed to Chalotte and Twilight and shook them hard by the shoulders, breaking the spell of fear that bound them. 'Come on,' he yelled. 'Today is the day of all days, follow me and think fast.'

Then Norrarf's voice came over the milling crowds on the towpath. 'Clear the banks,' he shouted,. 'Flinthead is coming.'

'More room,' shouted Skug from somewhere.

'Follow me,' said Spiff, and with the haft of his spear he levered himself through a thick crowd of Wendles and Chalotte and Twilight went with him, shoving and kicking their way.

'Stand back for the guard,' yelled Spiff. Chalotte looked at him; he grinned and she grimaced in return, striking a Wendle with her spear. 'Stand back for the guard,' she shouted.

The three Borribles emerged at last on the landing stage where Norrarf and Skug and their platoon of warriors were fighting hard to keep a space open. Norrarf, who stood in the centre, was nervous, a sickly colour under his greenish skin. He blew his cheeks out with relief when Spiff and his companions arrived.

'You three,' he commanded, 'stand by the big skiff there; you will take Flinthead to the platform.'

Spiff, Chalotte and Twilight ran to the water's edge and stood by the boat. From everywhere came the sound of tramping and shouting, growing louder every moment. Spiff untied the skiff's painter and waded knee-deep into the mud, holding the rope in his hands.

'Stand smart on either side,' he said. 'Don't look at Flinthead; just obey orders and let's hope he's so excited that his nose don't smell us out.'

And then there came an increase in the rush of noise and it swept out of the tunnels like a wind and the Wendle chieftain, running at the head of his men, burst into view and strode to the landing stage, crossing it immediately and heading straight for the river where Spiff held the boat steady against the shore.

'You Wendles,' called Flinthead, addressing his bodyguard, 'you will hold this jetty until my return.' He stared towards the mine, his blank eyes burning. 'Who rows me to the platform?'

'Those three, Flinthead,' said Norrarf, his voice shaking, 'and me.'

'Very well,' said the chieftain. 'I shall need six or seven warriors to come with me to the bottom of the mine to help with the prisoners.'

'There are eight men on the platform now,' said Norrarf, 'ever since you ordered the guard doubled. They are eight of your best.'

Flinthead looked at his rowers and Spiff inclined his head and dragged the boat a little further into the mudbank. Chalotte and Twilight moved a little closer too, their bodies rigid with fear.

Flinthead stepped into the boat and it lurched. He strode over the seats and sat in the prow. Chalotte noticed the long knife in his belt; he kept his hand on it all the time.

'Hurry,' said Flinthead, 'or I'll know the reason why.'

Spiff shouted at Twilight and Chalotte, 'Quickly you two,' and they took their places by the slender oars. Norrarf followed and Spiff pushed the boat out into the flowing mud and leapt aboard expertly, like the Wendle he was.

'Row, you fools,' he shouted, grabbing an oar for himself, 'row, there's not a second to lose.'

The skiff breasted the current and floated slowly round to face the stream. On a word the four rowers leant to their task and the boat shot across the river. Flinthead turned in his seat and stared as the derrick drew near, his eyes steady.

In a moment or two the skiff bumped against the platform and the eight guards crowded forward to help their master disembark. Spiff was only a pace behind him, light-footed and tense like an alley cat.

The boat was firmly moored and Chalotte, Twilight and Norrarf clambered on to the wooden island while Flinthead himself shouted over the river to where Tron and his men stood in an orderly line on the far bank.

'Tron,' called the chieftain, 'while I am down below you will take charge; get over here with your three lieutenants. Anyone who breaks rank or disobeys orders will answer to me as soon as I return, and no one is to move while I am gone, do you understand?'

Tron raised a hand to show that he knew what Flinthead wanted, then he stepped into a boat, three warriors with him, and they began to row towards the platform. Meanwhile, Flinthead directed his attention to the eight guards and gave them their instructions.

'Two of you stay here,' he said, 'the other six will come with me. You won't need your spears, just knives and catapults. Norrarf, you will aid Tron and see that my orders are carried out.' And with one last bleak stare from his blank eyes the chieftain swung a leg over the rim of the shaft and went in search of his treasure.

As soon as Flinthead's face had sunk beneath the level of the planking Spiff pushed himself into the group of Wendle guards.

‘'Ere,' said one, ‘he wanted six of us, not seven.'

‘He gave me my orders earlier,' lied Spiff. ‘I've got something special to do.'

‘Oh that's different,' said the Wendle. ‘You can go first then.'

‘Not a chance,' retorted Spiff. ‘I'm to bring up the rear; I've got to make sure you lot don't get lost.' This sounded so much like one of Flinthead's schemes that the guard believed it entirely and went quickly over the top, his five colleagues following him just as rapidly as they could. Spiff went last of all.

Chalotte watched him go. In that brief moment before he disappeared he glanced at her and she lifted a hand in farewell. She wanted to say something but dared not, for Tron was approaching the platform and coming within earshot. She smiled instead, for, when all was said and done and in spite of her dislike of him, Chalotte wanted Spiff to win, wanted him to conquer Flinthead and free the captives. But there was no need for words, Spiff knew what she was thinking and he returned her smile, his face looking as happy as she'd ever seen it. He was pleased with the danger and overjoyed at the unreasonable odds. That was how he wanted to live; and so he winked just once, ducked his head, and was gone.

Tron climbed on to the platform with his followers and went to stand by the mouth of the mine. On both sides of the river the bodyguards and warriors stood in ranks and kept the tunnel entrances clear. There were many hundreds of Wendles present and over the whole scene the tension tightened. Chalotte held her breath, waiting for the next stroke of her heart, willing it to come, dreading what it might bring. The world had slipped from its axis and was falling all the way down to the end of the universe.

*

Spiff reached the first landing and peered over the edge. Far below he could see the light reflected on Flinthead's copper helmet. The Wendle chieftain was already two or three storeys ahead of his guards and travelling as fast as he could. Spiff swung himself out on to the second ladder and went after him.

The mine was built from rough planks which the Wendles had taken from old packing cases; the black stencilled letters of the original destinations were still visible: Cardiff, New York, Calcutta. Every fifteen feet or so huge beams had been hammered and wedged across the shaft in order to hold the shuttering in place and to support the landings. It was the shuttering, or vertical planking, that kept the mud at bay, straining against terrific pressures. There were hundreds of thousands of tons of that mud on the other side of the planks and Spiff could hear it slide and slither, searching for a way in, the shaft itself shifting and swaying like a great eel in the currents that surrounded it. Every bit of wood in the construction creaked and groaned all the time, every strut and every joist. A thick slime oozed through the cracks and knotholes and trickled everywhere, saturating everything, dripping slowly from one surface to another until it reached the very bottom of that deep, deep hole in the ground.

The air was heavy and it became more and more oppressive as Spiff descended. It was wet too and clung to his limbs like sodden clothing. Sweat trickled down his face and stung his eyes with salt and the mud that covered all began to cover him, making him smell like a cesspool rat. Far above, the tiny blaze of light that marked the top of the pit gradually diminished; then it disappeared.

Spiff spat. 'I've got to overtake them guards,' he said to himself. 'Help them on their way.'

At the next opportunity he rested and stared down into the gloom. Every twenty or thirty feet the Wendle engineers had rigged an electric light and with their aid Spiff could see the figures of Flinthead's bodyguards hastening in pursuit of their master.

'This is no good,' said Spiff. 'I'll have to start moving, I'll have to jump.' Having made the decision he lowered himself over the lip of the landing, to the full extent of his arms, and allowed his body to drop the fifteen feet to the floor below.

He crashed on to the planking and rolled over. The thump of his fall reverberated and fell and made the bodyguards look up in fear. A gobbet of mud slopped and twisted through the air and struck one of the Wendles across the face. He screamed in terror, convinced that the mine was about to cave in and squash him. Then he stood motionless for a long moment, allowing his companions to go on, and as soon as they were out of sight he began to climb upwards, his knees weak and his lips trembling. But Spiff was relentless, thundering from one storey to the next, and the noise and the mud fell again and again; it was like the footfalls of a giant taking great and regular strides.

Spiff was travelling fast and he soon overtook the hindmost of the guards, diving past him as he cringed on the rungs of a ladder, petrified by the appearance of this mud-covered figure rocketing out of nowhere.

There was another crash as Spiff landed and rolled, getting to his feet to beckon at the Wendle in the most friendly manner.

'What you frightened of?' he said. 'We're all chums together, you know.'

'The mine's collapsing, isn't it?' said the Wendle, scrambling down to join Spiff. 'And it's so spooky. I don't care what I do as a rule but I wish I hadn't been picked for this job.'

'You will, certainly,' said Spiff, and with a straight right arm he pushed the bodyguard backwards from the platform.

The Wendle shrieked and the shriek stood across the darkness like a bright light. Even high up on the banks of the Wandle they heard it and there was not one person whose stomach didn't shrivel at the sound. Spiff himself listened to the cry with satisfaction but there was no time for such contentment; there were still five Wendles between him and Flinthead.

He came upon two of those five only a little later. Spiff's first victim, a dead weight plunging at great speed, had fallen on to them like a sack of spuds and had broken their bodies as effectively as any car crash. Now all three lay mangled together, groaning as the blood crept from their wounds to drip between the rough planks, and not far below the remaining guards knew the sticky touch of it on their hands and faces.

They were ready for Spiff when he appeared on the landing above them, and they were suspicious. They had heard strange bumps and bangs and had felt warm blood on their skins; something was wrong, very wrong. They loaded their catapults and aimed at Spiff's head.

'Gerrorf,' said Spiff. 'I'm just a member of the bodyguard, like you lot; you saw me at the top.'

‘What’s all this noise about?’ asked the biggest of the three Wendles. ‘And what’s all this blood?’

‘Ah,’ said Spiff, ‘you see one of your fellows lost his nerve and he’s gone back up again. As for the other two, well, one of them slipped and fell a couple of storeys all in one go and as he went he pulled his mate along with him. They’re a bit the worse for wear, they are, that’s why there’s blood about.’ Spiff grinned and without waiting for the Wendles to come to a decision began to climb down towards them, talking as he went.

‘This game don’t half make your legs ache, don’t it?’ he said cheerfully. ‘How much further do we have to go?’

‘Effin’ miles,’ said the big Wendle when Spiff had joined him, ‘and we’d better get a move on otherwise Flinthead will skin us.’ He studied Spiff closely. ‘Who are you then? You still haven’t said.’

Spiff shut an eye and tilted his head to one side. ‘My name’s Ratrap,’ he said. ‘I’ve only just been made a member of the bodyguard.’

The big Wendle seemed satisfied with this explanation and he and his two colleagues stowed their catapults under their jackets and made ready to continue the journey. Spiff went with them to the top of the next ladder, making sure that he was the last in line as they each awaited their turn to go down. Then, as soon as the big Wendle had begun his descent, Spiff drew his knife, pressed his hand over the mouth of the guard who stood in front of him and quietly slit his throat.

By now the big Wendle had arrived on the floor below and was shouting for the others to follow on. Spiff lowered his victim’s corpse to the planking and allowed the second Wendle to get his foot on the first rung, then he bent over and tapped him on the shoulder.

‘Yes,’ said the Wendle, raising his head. He was caught in an awkward crouching position.

‘Aren’t you the one with the whip,’ asked Spiff politely, ‘the one who’s been bashing Torreycanyon and Stonks about?’

‘Yes,’ answered the Wendle. ‘I’m good with a whip I am.’

‘A-mazing,’ said Spiff. ‘Well, life is full of little surprises and here’s one for you,’ and he lashed out with a fist, striking his enemy hard and knocking him senseless. As the body fell it curved over backwards and dived gracefully on to the head of the big Wendle, smashing open his helmet, splitting his skull and casting him down into the half-darkness.

There were no screams this time; there was nothing but a silent and elegant flight followed by a distant and mortal thud.

Spiff put his knife away. 'Beautiful flyers them two,' he said, 'just like the pigeons that live in Battersea Park . . . And now there's only Flinthead. He's got the treasure and I've got him.'

*

Spiff saw the lights at the end of everything long before he arrived there. He calculated that there must be at least four or five bulbs rigged round the perimeter of the diggings in order to make it easy for the miners to see what they were doing. Wherever the Wendles stole their electric power they certainly stole a lot.

Spiff was travelling slowly now, using the ladders rather than jumping, and all was silent again, except for the bellowing of Flinthead's voice at intervals, ordering his guards to hurry.

At last Spiff saw the chieftain's copper helmet. Flinthead was waiting on the last landing of all, just above the very bottom of the pit, and beyond him Spiff could make out the figures of the Borrible slaves. 'Oh, boy!' said Spiff. 'This is what I've been waiting for.'

Flinthead heard waders scraping across wood and he glanced up. 'Where have you been, you fools,' he cried, but then he saw one guard only and not the expected six. 'Where are the others?' he asked. 'What are you playing at?'

Spiff pulled his tin helmet tight to his head and wiped a muddy hand across his face in an attempt to disguise himself a little more; it was hardly necessary. He was already covered from top to toe in filth.

'I'm sorry, Flinthead,' he said, affecting a harsh Wendle voice, 'I came as quick as I could. One of the others had a nasty accident and that held us up a bit.'

Flinthead swore and looked away and Spiff placed his feet on the rungs of the ladder that alone separated him from the Wendle chieftain. Down he went.

Here, where the shaft petered out, the protective shuttering had a temporary and fragile appearance. The last landing was only half completed, its planks loose and warped, and just one piece of scaffolding board, with rungs nailed to it, led ultimately to the floor of the mine.

Spiff gazed with horror at the scene he had journeyed so far to see.

It was bright with light and black with mud, the end of an abyss, a cruel circle set in the still centre of the earth and dripping with a poisonous heat.

The slaves stood or sat in a slime that was knee-deep and gurgled in from all sides. Spiff's eyes searched for Knocker and then Napoleon and Orococco. They were difficult to distinguish, nearly at one with the mud; their tattered clothes were welded to their limbs, their hair was plastered flat on their skulls and they crouched against the walls, thin and black, bodies drooping. Spiff wrinkled his nose and even his stomach heaved; all the effluent of Wandsworth came here.

Knocker raised his head, stared at Flinthead for a moment, then lowered it again. Spiff bit his lip, shocked for once. Knocker's face was lifeless, there was no blood left in it. Napoleon and Orococco were in the same pitiful state. Bingo and Vulge leant against the shuttering, holding their spades. Sydney sat on a piece of half-submerged wood, trying to keep dry. In the middle of the creeping sludge, gleaming at the corner where it had been cleared, was the brass-banded lid of the Rumble treasure box.

Flinthead squatted at the edge of the landing and pointed.

'You, Vulge, whatever your name is, take your spade and finish digging the box out.'

Vulge moved to a pile of spare timber, sat down and lifted his feet from the water. The iron fetters clashed on his ankles.

'Dig it out yourself,' he said.

Flinthead's voice hardened. 'I've still got two of your friends up top, remember, and I can still make them suffer. What's more I've got reinforcements on the way . . . I'll soon have you doing what you're told, you little rat.'

These threats did not alter Vulge's attitude. He was past fear and he made no attempt to move. It was Bingo, because he knew it would have to be done eventually, who swished his legs through the mud and used his spade to dig the chest free.

Flinthead turned his head from where he crouched and looked at Spiff's face and then up into the shaft. 'Where are those other guards?' he asked. 'They should be here by now.'

'They can't be far,' said Spiff, standing to attention like a good Wendle.

Flinthead lowered his voice to a whisper. 'As soon as they arrive,' he explained, 'I want you all to go down and kill the prisoners. They've done what they had to do, no point in taking them up again.'

'Yessir,' said Spiff. 'What about the two in the treadmill?'

Flinthead laughed. 'I don't need them either; when we get back we'll throw 'em over the top to join their friends.' He went back to watching Bingo and Sydney dragging the box clear of the mud. 'Right,' he said, 'bring it up here, just the two of you, no others.'

'Leave it be,' said Napoleon, 'he's going to kill us anyway.'

Flinthead raised an arm and pointed. 'You will die, Napoleon Boot, certainly, because you are a traitor Wendle. The others I will let free if they do as I say; after all they have dug well and found my treasure for me.'

Napoleon lifted his gaunt face and stared at his chieftain. There was silence for a moment and in that silence a large round drop of rich blood fell from high in the mine shaft and landed on the back of Flinthead's hand, staining it red.

Flinthead brought the hand close to his eyes and stared at that blob of blood. The silence intensified. Slowly every head was raised to look into the darkness, every head except Spiff's. Instead he smiled a seraphic smile and removed his Wendle helmet; a life's work was nearing completion.

'I hate to disappoint you, Napoleon,' said Spiff in his old Battersea voice, 'but Flinthead ain't going to kill no one, I am.'

At these words even Knocker, Napoleon and Orococco found the strength to pull themselves to their feet. Their mouths dropped open with astonishment. Now they recognized Spiff's face: that cocky, crafty face, lined with double-dealing and artful treachery, and life drained back into their hearts.

Flinthead also recognized the face and, crouching as he was, knew himself vulnerable. He snatched for his knife and tried to get to his feet but Spiff was ready; he hooked his foot under Flinthead's behind and then shoved him hard, outward and upward.

The Wendle chieftain made a despairing grab at the air but it was useless. He flew like a bullet across the width of the shaft and his helmeted head rammed against the shuttering on the far side. There was a deep clang, a roar of pain and Flinthead's body jack-knifed and then plunged down the wall into the slop and slurry, crashing heavily across the box of treasure.

Sydney and Bingo toppled over too, diving joyfully to right and left to escape the falling Wendle. Then, in celebration, they slapped the mud with their hands, throwing it at each other and everyone else. Mud splashed over all.

'It's Spiff,' yelled Bingo, 'come from nowhere.'

'About time too,' said Knocker. 'He got us in here, it's only right he should get us out.'

'This is not the end,' screamed a voice, and the Borribles looked and saw that Flinthead had risen and though covered in sludge was standing astride the treasure box, the long knife in his hand.

'Let's get him,' shouted Napoleon. 'Quick.'

'No,' cried Spiff, 'you lot get up here out of the way, he's mine, he is, all mine.'

'My guards will be here soon,' said Flinthead, 'you'll sing a different tune then.' But Flinthead was deceiving himself. At that moment another blob of blood fell from above and slapped on to his dented helmet, and the sound rang in his ears like a death knell.

'Yeah,' said Spiff with a sneer, 'that's a bit of one of 'em dropping in right now.'

More blood fell and Flinthead realized that he was on his own, but he was not afraid. 'Even if you kill me,' he said, 'you'll never get out alive. The whole Wendle nation is waiting for this box of treasure.'

'Let him rant,' said Spiff, 'you Borribles start getting up here out of the way.'

The weakest ones, Knocker, Napoleon and Orococco, were the first to climb from the muck, hauling their bodies painfully from rung to rung, their leg irons banging. Bingo, Vulge and Sydney kept watch on Flinthead in case he should attack with his knife, but Spiff had drawn his catapult and there was a large chunky stone aimed at Flinthead's face.

'I've got him covered, Bingo,' he said. 'You and the other two can come up now.'

When Bingo reached his side Spiff handed him the catapult and his two bandoliers. 'You're a good shot, ain't yer Bingo?' he said. 'If I should lose this fight, kill him.'

Napoleon lifted his head; he lay stretched out and exhausted next to Knocker and Orococco. 'After what I've been through,' he said, 'I could kill him with my teeth.'

Spiff brushed past Bingo and went to Knocker's side. He took the weight of the leg irons in his hand and saw that Knocker's ankles had been rubbed raw by them. He looked into Knocker's tired eyes. 'Sorry mate,' he said, 'really I am . . . Things will be all right now, you'll see.' Then he took a deep breath and, not bothering to use the ladder, sprang from the landing.

The Borribles moved forward to watch, sitting or lying on the loose planking. There could have been no more fitting place for two such enemies to meet; a quarter of a mile of darkness above, the slimy and treacherous mud underfoot, and the walls of the shaft trickling steadily now with black water and red blood under the bleak electric glare.

Spiff fell to his hands and knees, carried there by the impetus of his leap. Flinthead stepped back from the treasure chest, there was a flash of steel at his right hand and his long knife whistled through the air.

Spiff knew the knife was coming and threw himself forward; the dagger missed him and clattered against the side of the mine and disappeared below the surface of the water. Spiff rose, the filth dripping from him.

Flinthead looked round for some other weapon and saw one of the spades, half submerged in sludge. He pulled at it with all his strength and slowly it came away making a long sucking sound.

'Watch out, Spiff,' called Vulge. 'Get the other one, it's just behind yer.'

Spiff turned and grabbed the second spade. He grinned and his teeth flashed white in his dirty face. He backed away, hefting the weapon in his hand.

'So, Flower,' he said, 'at last we're alone, after all these years.'

'Don't you call me Flower,' said Flinthead, and he too tested the weight of his spade.

'He doesn't like being called Flower,' said Spiff, 'that was his nickname when he was a kid, before he was a Borrible even. Everyone's forgotten it, except me, ain't that right, Flower?'

Flinthead leant against the wall and held the spade defensively across his chest. His pale green face glowed with hatred but he showed no fear. 'You're on your own, Spiff,' he said, 'and I've always been the better fighter. Those few up there won't stop me getting out; they're too weak, and their legs is chained. You're going to lose, Spiff, killed by yer own brother.'

'Don't you brother me,' said Spiff.

Knocker pulled himself up on his elbows. 'Brother!' he cried. 'Brother!'

Spiff laughed but he did not take his eyes from Flinthead. 'You might as well know,' he said, 'it don't make no odds now. He's my brother all right . . . We came from the same family, ran away in the time of the old queen we did, became Borribles together. It was hard to stay alive in them days, so we came down here and took over the old tunnels. We did everything together, but then little Flower wanted to take charge of everybody and rule Borribles like they were never meant to be ruled. So they became Wendles and I became a nuisance and he had me staked out on the mudflats, his own flesh and blood, but I got away and now I'm back.'

'Back to be slaughtered,' said Flinthead.

'We'll have to see, won't we,' said Spiff. He lifted his blade and a solid lump of mud slid from it and plopped into the water and the fearsome cutting edge was suddenly revealed, shining with months of digging. The soft sand and mud had worked upon the tool and honed it to the sharpness of a razor.

'Well, brother,' said Spiff, 'I can dig your heart out with this.'

'And mine's as sharp as yours,' answered Flinthead, and the two Borribles moved into the centre of the arena. Spiff held his spade with both hands, his right grasping the handle, the left the shaft, aiming it at Flinthead's throat like a bayonet. He trod carefully, studying his opponent's every move.

The Wendle chieftain held his spade in a different manner, wielding it like a two-handed sword, swinging repeatedly at Spiff's unprotected head. The weapons clanged and clashed. Spiff defended himself well against Flinthead's massive blows, dancing and ducking round his antagonist like a boxer, lunging at him, trying every second to cut and wound. Twice Spiff rang his blade across his enemy's head and twice Flinthead's helmet saved him. Three times Flinthead caught Spiff with the flat of his weapon and three times Spiff rode the onslaught and dodged away before the Wendle could take advantage and go in for the kill.

From the scaffolding the slaves followed every movement of the struggle, their hearts beating against their ribs. Napoleon had scrambled to his knees and he swayed his shoulders in sympathy with every stroke Spiff made. All the months of his captivity rose up in his mind's eye and the hatred he bore his chieftain, for Napoleon had once been a loyal Wendle, was as great as Spiff's.

'Kill 'im,' he shouted. 'Kill 'im.'

Spiff pressed home his attack, beating and bashing, cutting and lunging, and he fought so relentlessly that at last he opened a way through his enemy's guard, and then, using every ounce of strength he possessed, he thrust his spade forward at shoulder height, holding it level, aiming at the heart.

Flinthead shouted and Spiff's weapon struck him fiercely in the chest, making a loud grinding noise like a metal hinge under strain. But it made no difference; the Wendle remained unharmed and Spiff's spade bent and quivered, rebounding from his grasp like a live thing, spinning above his head and splashing down to be lost in the mud. Spiff staggered backwards, dazed, both arms paralysed, his brain shocked.

Flinthead also staggered from the force of the blow but he recovered quickly and came on; he saw that victory was his for the taking.

'The bastard,' cried Vulge, 'he's got some special jacket on, look.'

It was true. Flinthead's golden coat had been cut open where Spiff had swiped him and the onlookers could see that underneath it he wore a garment of closely woven chain mail.

'I've heard about that,' said Napoleon bitterly. 'It's made out of spring washers, all lashed together; it's bullet proof.'

'I'll get him,' Bingo shouted, and he drew the elastic of his catapult tight, but Flinthead was not to be caught that easily. He moved his weapon so that the blade of it covered his face, and what with his legs being deep in the mud and his body protected by armour there was not one part of him that offered Bingo a reasonable target. The Wendle chieftain leered in triumph and went towards the defenceless Spiff whose death now seemed certain.

But Napoleon jumped to his feet. 'No,' he screamed. 'Never!' He ran off the scaffolding and hurled himself down on to Flinthead's shoulders, wrapping arms and legs around the chieftain's body as firmly as he could.

Napoleon was no longer strong. Lack of food had made him almost weightless, but for a second his anger gave him a furious energy and he bore Flinthead into the slurry.

Even so it did not take Flinthead more than a moment to free himself of his burden and he clouted Napoleon hard in the kidneys and thrust him into the mud. He swirled round to face Spiff, eager to finish the fight, but he was just too late. Napoleon's intervention had given the Battersea Borrible time to grope beneath the water, time to find his spade. When Flinthead moved to the offensive he found Spiff ready for him.

'So,' said Spiff, 'wearing a flak jacket, eh? Never take chances, do yer, Flower?' And, with a new determination born of his fortunate escape, Spiff advanced, now catching Flinthead in the teeth with his spade's wooden handle, now stabbing at him with the sharp steel.

The Wendle chieftain retreated round the wall of the pit and Spiff went after him, step for step, cold and deadly, smashing and banging with hatred until at last, in Flinthead's lifeless eyes, a distant red spark of fear began to gleam. The sweat of terror started to trickle under his armpits, his knees faltered and he stumbled. In desperation at last, he lifted his weapon above his head and kept it there. 'Enough,' he cried. 'I surrender.'

Spiff hesitated for a split second and in that second Flinthead whirled his spade in the air, hoping to bring it down on to his opponent's skull with all his might.

It was lucky for Spiff that he knew his man. He had hesitated but in that same moment he'd stepped backwards and sideways and Flinthead's blade ploughed harmlessly into the churned froth of the trampled sludge, the force of the swing yanking the Wendle from his feet and casting him to his knees. There he stayed, beaten, panting.

Spiff leant on his spade like a navvy at the end of a hard day's work. 'There, Flower,' he said, 'you've had too much of the soft life you have; slowed you down it has, and made you untrustworthy. You're going to have to make it up to us, you're going to make sure we get a safe conduct out of here . . . us and the treasure of course.'

Suddenly there was a violent surge in the mud and Napoleon rose from it like an underwater missile. He was unrecognizable. He swayed and scraped layers of filth from his face with the back of his filthy hands. He spat dirt from his mouth.

'Never mind about getting out,' he said, 'kill 'im.'

'Napoleon's right,' said Knocker from the landing. 'I don't care if I don't get away, only killing will do.'

'Wait a minute,' said Sydney. 'There's not only you two to think of, remember there's Stonks and Torreycanyon up top, and Chalotte.'

'Chalotte,' said Knocker, 'is she here?'

'Listen to me,' said Spiff. 'The best chance we have of getting out is to use this twerp as a hostage. If we hold a knife to his throat they can't touch us, can they?'

'Don't be too sure that the Wendles will want him back,' said Napoleon. 'If they see him as a prisoner and realize that they can get rid of him they might just do for the lot of us.'

'On the other hand they might let us go if we hand him over all tied up,' said Sydney. 'How about that?'

'Don't be daft,' said Spiff. 'There's the bodyguard to think of, a couple of hundred of them; without Flinthead they're nothing, they'll want him alive if only to save their own skins, and I can tell you they're all waiting on the platform and along the river banks. No, we need him as a hostage, especially if we're to get away with the treasure as well.'

'The treasure,' said Sydney. 'I say leave the treasure where it is.'

'So do I,' said Vulge.

'Me too,' added Bingo.

'I say kill him,' said Knocker, 'and damn the treasure. I've learnt my lesson about that money.'

Spiff looked up at Knocker. 'I'd like to kill the old sod,' he began, 'but without him and the treasure we don't stand a chance of getting out, and besides—'

Spiff got no further with his explanation; Flinthead gave a loud cry, threw himself forward and with his spade held in his two hands charged at Spiff's throat. He knew that if he could kill his Battersea brother he stood a good chance of fighting his way past the others.

But Spiff was not known as the craftiest of Borribles for nothing. Talking to the others he had not forgotten his adversary; his ears had been cocked and he had heard the movement of the mud as Flinthead had sprung to his feet. Automatically he raised his own spade to protect himself and Flinthead's blow glanced off it, striking a spark as steel clashed against steel. Turning, Spiff saw that Flinthead was only a yard away, pulled off balance by the fierce lunge he had made. Spiff lifted his arms, holding the spade delicately between his hands as if about to throw it gently over a wall. He stood poised, briefly motionless, taking all the time in the world, waiting while Flinthead tottered and tried to draw back out of range – but now it was finished.

Spiff, his expression murderous, balanced his weapon at the level of his eyes and then punched it forward with all his power, guiding it with the left hand and shoving it from the handle with the right so that the bright blade cut into Flinthead's Adam's apple, through his windpipe and jugular, and out through the spine; and as it cut it made the sound of an axe slicing into soggy turf.

And the chieftain's head exploded from his shoulders and stood surprised in the air. Flinthead was slain and yet, for one instant, the opaque eyes of the Wendle shone at last, incandescent with the fire of death, and a red glow illuminated the whole cavern. Then a huge moan issued from the crimson lungs and the body fell, its blood mingling with the mud and water underfoot.

The severed head seemed to hang in the air for an age but at length it dropped into the sludge, facing upwards, staring sightless into the yellow blackness of the mine shaft, staring in such a way that Spiff could not bear the scrutiny. He raised a foot and slowly pushed the face under the mire and the thick and loathsome liquid crept across the eyes and closed them forever. And in his corner, where he swayed and clung in weakness, Napoleon Boot vomited.

But Spiff was aflame with pride, convinced of his magnificence and delirious with his victory. He threw down his spade and shook his fists at his companions and they stepped back in dismay, so terrifying was his face, so distorted with a terrible joy. And Spiff's voice sounded out in a hard and piercing yell of triumph. 'I am Spiff the Spifflicator, killer of Flinthead, stealer of the treasure. I have a hundred names now.'

When the shouting was past there was a great stillness and Napoleon crawled to the ladder and clambered up to join his friends on the scaffolding. While he did so Spiff seized Flinthead's helmet, just visible in the mud, and placed it upon his head.

'Strewth,' said Bingo. 'Brothers were they, and you can see it now he's got that hat on. You wouldn't know who was which, would you?'

Bingo's words made the others take heed and they could not help but see what he meant. The copper headgear made it almost impossible to tell brother from brother, the living from the dead, and Spiff stood like a statue, knowing the effect he was having, knowing how much of Flinthead there was in him. Then he glanced up and slowly the madness left his face.

'It is over,' he said, 'the long battle between us is finished; we must go.'

'How the hell are we to climb out of here?' asked Sydney, 'with Knocker, Napoleon and Orococco so weak they can hardly stand?'

'There's no other way,' said Spiff, 'but we'll go slowly, the stronger ones will pull the weak.'

'We'll make it,' said Knocker. 'We'll have to.'

'Yeah, maybe,' said Orococco, 'but what's to be done when we get to the top, man?'

'You leave that to me,' said Spiff and he groped beneath the mud and turned Flinthead's body over. In a moment he straightened and was seen to be holding the golden jacket, thick with slime. He laughed and threw it up to the landing. 'Here, Bingo,' he said, 'clean it while I get the money.'

'No money,' yelled Knocker. 'When Vulge was wounded in Rumbledom I wanted to leave him behind so that I could bring the treasure. Adolf wouldn't have anything to do with it and carried Vulge on his shoulders and saved his life. I did the opposite; I saved the treasure and got Adolf killed. He was a true Borrible, I wasn't. I won't make that mistake again.'

'We won't help you with that box,' said Bingo.

'All right,' said Spiff, 'have it your own way, but has any one of you smart alecs got a plan for getting out? There's a tribe of Wendles topside, just waiting. And what do you think they'll do when they see us arrive without the treasure . . . give us a round of applause and a free boat trip to Battersea?'

There was silence. The Borribles knew that Spiff was right but no one wished to agree with him.

Spiff laughed. 'Throw down that jacket, Bingo.'

Bingo did as he was told and Spiff slipped the garment over his shoulders. 'Now,' he said triumphantly, 'who am I?'

'You're Spiff,' said Vulge, 'but from here you could be Flinthead, alike as two gobs of spit.'

'Right,' went on Spiff, 'and who do Wendles obey, without question?'

Napoleon looked up. 'All Wendles obey Flinthead, especially if he's got the treasure.'

'Right again,' said Spiff. 'Now to get out of here we've got to give them something to occupy their evil little brains . . . When they see the treasure they'll be so happy they won't even look at me closely, they'll just see what they expect to see.'

'But they'll notice there's no guards; there won't be enough of us,' said Sydney.

'They won't at all,' said Spiff. 'Halfway up the shaft we'll find some bodyguard uniforms, on bodyguards I admit, and a bit damaged. Still, Bingo and Vulge can dress in those, the rest of you will act like captives. The Wendles will be too busy cheering and jumping up and down to start counting how many guards or prisoners there are.'

'Okay,' said Vulge, 'so you're Flinthead. What happens at the top?'

'Easy,' continued Spiff. 'I give orders, everyone else takes 'em. The treasure is locked in my apartments, the prisoners as well, ready for execution. But in reality, as soon as you're rested and got some decent food inside yer, we'll be off.'

'And the money?' asked Sydney.

Spiff grinned. 'Oh, I'll take that with me, there'd be no fun otherwise.'

Napoleon jeered. He might have been a slave for months but his mind had lost none of its Wendle suspicion. 'You expect us to believe that you're going to take Flinthead's place just for a couple of days and then walk away from all that power and take the money back to Battersea, share it out and settle down like a pensioner?'

Spiff shrugged. 'I don't care what you believe, you've got to do as I say or you won't get out at all.'

'Oh, I think you'll get us out,' said Napoleon, 'but I also think you'll stay behind and become Flinthead.'

Spiff ignored the remark and pulled at one of the handles of the treasure chest. It came out of the mud slowly and reluctantly but it came nevertheless. 'I reckon I can make the Wendles into proper

Borribles again,' he said, 'even if I have to kid them along to do it.' He knelt and got the heavy box on to his shoulder and began to climb the ladder. No one moved to help him and Spiff's face grew red with the effort but he would not ask for assistance.

Napoleon and Knocker looked at each other. 'I don't like it much,' said Knocker, 'but he's right, as a plan it's all we've got.' He scraped the dirt from the palms of his hands and found the scars that the red-hot treasure box had scorched there when he had carried it from the burning halls of Rumbledom.

'You were given a second name you know, Knocker,' said Spiff as he arrived on the landing. 'Chalotte chose it, Knocker Burnthand.'

'That's just like her,' said Knocker, 'to give me a name that will always remind me of what an idiot I was.'

'All right,' said Bingo, 'we'll help you with the treasure, as far as the top, but only because it's part of the plan. Nothing after that.'

Spiff nodded and held up something small and bright. 'Good,' he said, 'and in return I'll give you this key. You'll find that it undoes those nasty shackles round your ankles. It won't half make climbing easier.'

'You sod,' said Napoleon, but he laughed.

Orococco laughed too. 'Once a Wendle, always a Wendle,' he said.

When everyone was prepared for the climb Spiff gave his last instructions. 'Let Knocker and Napoleon and Orococco go first,' he said. 'They're the weakest and we'll take their pace. The other four of us will take turn and turn about with the box. When we get to the top the captives will just behave like captives. The two dressed as guards will pretend to be guards. On the last landing I will take the treasure and come up behind you lot, that'll give the Wendles something to wait for, something to cheer. Don't forget at the top I'm Flinthead, so do as you're told. Let's go.'

The seven Borribles bent their heads backwards and looked up into the shaft at the long hard way they had to go. Mud and blood dripped in their faces; the rungs were square and rough.

'I wish,' said Knocker, 'that old Torrey was still working the tread-mill, then we could have ridden up in the buckets like lumps of mud.'

'And why not,' said Napoleon, 'that's just what we look like.'

9

On the derrick platform at the top of the mine Chalotte stood next to Twilight and Norrarf. She was tense, so overwrought she could hardly keep still. Above her in the cavernous arches of the roof hung huge slabs of shadow, solid and black. Nearby Tron strode up and down, only pausing occasionally to look into the mouth of the shaft; time went by and he saw nothing. His three lieutenants leant on their spears and watched him, their faces blank.

On both river banks the bodyguards still held the towpaths clear, controlling the crowds who waited there. Most of the time there was quiet, sometimes there were shouts. Apart from sentries and lookouts every Wendle in creation was present, hundreds of them, all gathered to witness Flinthead's successful return. In the treadmill Chalotte could see Torreycanyon lying on the floor, exhausted and asleep; beside him sat Stonks, his head leaning against one of the rough wooden spokes.

Chalotte sighed. 'Why is it taking so long?' she asked Twilight in a whisper and Tron overheard her.

'Because the shaft is deep,' he said. 'They say a quarter of a mile, though that is hard to believe.' Tron studied her face and Chalotte hoped that he would not recognize her from the time of the Great Rumble Hunt. He didn't, and after a moment he resumed his pacing and the waiting went on; one hour, two, then three.

Once more Tron went to the rim of the shaft and Chalotte and everyone else studied him closely. This time the Wendle stiffened, he had seen something.

'They're coming,' he said quietly, and his three lieutenants straightened and twirled their spears above their heads. A cheer rose from both banks; 'The treasure, the treasure.'

Under orders from Tron every person on the platform was brought to attention and a buzzing quietness was imposed along the river banks, but there was still a while to wait. No doubt, thought Chalotte, they'd be climbing slowly because of the weight of that damn treasure box.

The thought of the treasure made her sick with anguish. She hated it more than anything or anyone in the world. It had ruined the last Adventure; it had killed Adolf and now it was coming back to trouble the Borrible way of life yet again. She bit her lip; who was returning from the bottom of that hellhole, Flinthead or Spiff?

Something stirred at the lip of the mine and Chalotte nudged Twilight's elbow. A black hand, caked in dry slime, grasped the top rung of the ladder and Orococco heaved himself into sight and tumbled out across the platform to collapse, apparently unconscious, by the side of the treadmill.

His arrival brought a mocking cheer from the watching Wendles, and laughter too. They shook their spears and stamped their feet in joy. Now Tron's three men were at the head of the mine shaft and with rough hands they hoisted Sydney from the pit and dropped her down to lie by the side of Orococco.

Next came two members of the bodyguard, their faces smeared with mud and daubed in blood. They strutted to the edge of the platform and gave a thumbs up sign and the crowds along the river went berserk with happiness. Tron's men leant into the shaft once more and when they lifted Napoleon Boot into the light a vicious jeering swelled up and resounded between the mudflats and the high roof, for Napoleon was a renegade Wendle, a traitor. Tron's lieutenants held him high so the crowds could see him and then, when they'd struck him several times, they threw him to the ground.

'Kill him, kill him,' the Wendles cried and shook their spears.

It took more than words to dismay Napoleon Boot; he crawled into an open space, levered himself erect and gave a two-fingered salute to the whole Wendle nation. And when the gesture brought shouts and threats in its turn he ignored them and wobbled back to his friends and collapsed across their bodies. He sighed and closed his eyes, groaning with the pain of extreme fatigue, but there was a hard and wicked smirk upon his face.

Eventually Knocker came and Chalotte's heart leapt, for she liked

Knocker more than any other Borrible she had ever met, but her joy changed to pity in an instant for Knocker was ragged and covered in sludge; his bones protruded through his skin like broken sticks in a sack and the lines of his features were deep enough to lose a finger in.

Tron's lieutenants had no such feelings. They seized Knocker by the hair and hauled him up and beat him to the floor and kicked him. The Wendles under Flinthead had been taught to hate Knocker for he had been brave and unflinching in his conflict with the chieftain and had almost succeeded in stealing the treasure completely away, only failing from ill luck. Again the cry rose from the river banks: 'Kill him, kill him!'

Suddenly Tron held up his hand and all noise stopped. Knocker dragged himself out of the way like a half-smashed cockroach, trailing blood, and Flinthead's copper helmet appeared at the rim of the great pit. At last the whole host of Wendles saw the chieftain climb back into their sight; on his back he carried the great burnt box of Rumble treasure and they lifted their spears high in the air and with one voice they shouted: 'Flinthead, Flinthead, Flinthead!'

The noise was overpowering, Chalotte could hear nothing but noise. She looked at Twilight in confusion. 'It's Flinthead,' she cried, 'he must have done for Spiff. He's got the treasure too; he'll kill us all.'

Twilight could not hear Chalotte's words above the din of the mad rejoicing that rang along the river banks. He pointed to the shore. 'There's too many of them,' he shouted. 'Just keep quiet and hope for the best.'

Chalotte scanned Norrarf's face. Would he betray them now? It certainly seemed likely; he was laughing and shouting with the rest. He half turned towards her. 'It's all right, it's Spiff,' he said, but Chalotte, in that clamour, did not catch his words. She glanced at the treadmill where her friends cowered, beaten and battered. It was heartbreaking. They stared at Flinthead, abject, like slaves about to be sold.

Chalotte gritted her teeth and decided; whatever happened, whether she died or not, she wouldn't allow Flinthead his triumph. The treasure must not return to destroy the Borrible way of life. She and her companions were as good as dead anyway, but if they had to die it was better that Flinthead should die with them.

Another great shout rolled across the river. Flinthead stood on the last rung of the ladder, a crazed smile on his blood-covered visage and smudges of gore on his gold-coloured coat. Chalotte heard him raise his voice.

'I am Flinthead, here is the Rumble treasure and it is mine again . . . Now the prisoners can die.'

'And so can you,' cried Chalotte and, unnoticed in that great commotion, she leapt forward and seized a mallet from among a pile of Wendle tools. Twilight went with her out of a feeling of loyalty, not knowing what she had in mind but eager to help. Tron pivoted on his heel but Chalotte was upon him and he had no opportunity to defend himself. She bashed the mallet against the side of his helmet and Flinthead's second-in-command collapsed, unconscious. Before Tron's lieutenants realized what she intended Chalotte had climbed the parapet of the mine and was hitting out with all her strength, loosening one of the wedges that held the mighty cross-timbers in position. The wedge swivelled, Chalotte clouted it again and the block of wood flew free, clattered against the side of the shaft and then fell away out of sight in a spinning blur.

'Chalotte,' yelled Spiff, 'don't be a fool, it's me.'

For a moment Chalotte did not understand. 'Damn you, Flinthead,' she cried. 'I won't let you bring that money back.' Then she thought that maybe Flinthead was not Flinthead and that perhaps she'd made a mistake, but in the same instant she decided that it was not a mistake and that anything, even Spiff's death, even her own, was better than the recovery of the Rumble treasure. With a cruel determination in her heart she raised the mallet above her head and swung it like a pick to strike at the shifting timbers beneath her feet.

Tron's men sprang at her but Twilight got in front of them and struck out, tugging, tripping and punching. Bingo and Vulge, still acting the part of Flinthead's guard, caught their breath in fright and stretched their arms to pluck Chalotte from where she stood on a cross-beam, shouting for her to stop, dragging her at last to the safety of the platform – but those heavy blows had been enough. The main beam jolted sideways and the tension that had held it in position for months was released and the timbers of the mine shaft lurched, the mud squeezed in and a wild wrenching sob was torn from the heart of the wood. So loud was it that the sound of cheering was stilled and the watchers on the towpaths realized that something had turned their triumph sour; danger had come to take the place of pleasure.

Bingo shook Chalotte as hard as he could, anger and fear mingled in his weary face. 'You damn fool,' he said, 'now we're all dead men.'

Chalotte stared at Bingo like an imbecile, alarmed and fearful. She opened her mouth to speak but now there was no time. Another grinding scream was wrung from the mass of splintering timber, the very grain of it was riven and rent asunder and the great beams at last plunged downwards, their massive weight twisting and gathering momentum to smash and destroy the landings and scaffoldings below.

Spiff called for help but his ladder veered away from the wall of the mine shaft and teetered, becalmed for a second, standing on nothing and near the point of falling. The blood drained from his face, he clung frantically with one hand to a rung, and with the other he grasped the treasure box. It was a long stationary moment; it was almost his last and Spiff knew it.

'Damn you, Chalotte,' he yelled.

Then came another cracking and another rumbling as more scaffolding dropped into the shaft and the shuttering that held the mud back began to slip and great streams of black sludge surged forward. The mud was thick and muscular; it could strangle and it could suffocate, it wanted to drag everything down to the darkness at the centre of the earth.

The top section of the shuttering now collapsed completely and fell inwards, the huge planks coming together like rigid fingers, smashing Spiff's ladder to smithereens and pinning his body in space. Spiff screamed in pain and the treasure box dropped from his grasp, disappearing into the ravenous mouth of mud. Spiff struggled against the timber, trying to push it away, trying to stop it crushing him. His efforts failed; he was held too tightly, like a wireworm in steel tweezers. He raised his head in his agony, but he could not scream. There was no breath. His eyes glazed over until there was no sight left in them and then slowly the timbers slid down into the mud and, inch by inch, they took Spiff with them. He was gone.

Now all around, apart from the soft surging of the thick waters, there was no noise. The Wendles on either towpath stared in disbelief as the

Borrible they believed to be their leader died before them, while the Adventurers knew only too well that it was Spiff who had died there, his eyes blind with terror, his lungs empty of air.

Chalotte shook herself free of Bingo. 'Oh, Spiff,' she cried. 'Oh, Spiff.' And the hot tears ran down her face for what she had done.

'Get back,' warned Vulge. 'Get back, or you'll be dragged in too.'

Bingo pounced on the unconscious Tron and hoisted him to his feet. The Wendle rubbed his eyes.

'Where's Flinthead?' he asked.

'Dead,' said Bingo, 'the way we're all going to be in a minute.'

Tron looked about him and took in the situation. The platform was sinking and the mud was rolling inwards, unstoppable. Only the treadmill seemed solid and even that was beginning to go under.

'Quickly,' Tron shouted. 'The wheel. Get those two prisoners out of it and turn it over, it'll float.'

Suddenly there was another grinding lurch and the platform settled a foot into the mud. Tron's lieutenants and the two Wendle guards threw down their spears and dived into the river in panic, making for the shore.

'Come back you fools,' yelled Norrarf, 'the mud'll swallow yer.'

'Never mind them,' said Tron, 'let's get this wheel over.'

It was no easy matter. By the time Stonks and Torreycanyon had crawled between the spokes the platform had sunk so far that the Borribles were up to their waists in a quicksand that sucked at every movement they made. Yet somehow, and all together, they bent and groped below the surface, grasping the bottom of the treadmill and heaving it upwards with such energy that it rose for an instant above the mud before splashing down on to its side.

'Come on,' shouted Tron again as soon as the wheel was floating. 'Everyone aboard, it's our only chance.' Just as they felt the platform plunge away from beneath their feet the Borribles managed to scramble up on to the solid spars of their makeshift raft. But no sooner had they gained this temporary safety than a new danger threatened them. The mouth of the mine, now clear of debris, had become a mouth indeed; it gaped and pulsated, the centre of a slow whirlpool, a black vortex that waited to devour everything: mud, timber, Borribles and all.

'We must do something,' said Knocker. 'We'll be drowned in a minute.'

'Is there any chance of your blokes getting a boat out to us?' asked Bingo.

Tron stood on the rim of the wheel and looked towards the shore. 'There are no boats,' he said after a while. 'The currents have swept the banks clear, half of my men have gone too.'

'What about a long rope then?' said Stonks. 'Couldn't they pull us in?'

Tron shook his head. 'They don't have a rope that long, and even if they tied several ropes together we'd be at the bottom of the shaft before they'd gone and got them. The river is falling into the mine and we're going with it.'

A muffled scream came from somewhere, then another.

Norrarf pointed. 'That's them bodyguards,' he said. 'They've had it; swimming out there must be like swimming in cement.'

But the Borribles had no time to think of others, their own plight was too desperate. The whirlpool churned on, round and round, and the treadmill went with it. Air bubbles, escaping from below, erupted and threw sludge into the air so that it rained down with a vicious force and made the surface of the Wandle froth and seethe like a volcanic lake. It was a scene from the heart of hell.

And the mud flowed on into the pit, sometimes oozing, sometimes swirling, but at whatever speed it moved one thing was certain: the wheel to which the Borribles clung was steadily dropping into the centre and nothing in the world could reverse its progress.

'We've had it,' said Vulge, 'really had it.' But as he spoke the spate of the torrent eased and in a little while it halted altogether.

'The hole must be full up,' said Bingo, a note of hope in his voice. 'We've stopped moving.'

'It can't be full up,' said Napoleon, 'that mine's a quarter of a mile deep.'

'What is it then?' asked Twilight. He glanced at the shore. There the currents had not stopped and the powerful rise and fall of the waves kept the Wendles high on the banks, watching silently, the warriors resting on their spears.

'This is our only chance,' said Napoleon, 'we oughta swim for it.' But before anyone could move the mouth of the shaft opened again; there was another rush of mud towards it and the treadmill dipped and reared like a switchback.

The Adventurers cried aloud, convinced that their moment of death had come. The great wooden wheel toppled into the very eye of the storm and, half submerged, it tilted sideways and the Borribles were swung above the abyss but, as they swayed there on the brink, a surge came from beneath them and the wheel spun once more, swooped, and finally stuck, wedged across the wide mine shaft.

'What's happened?' asked Twilight, his teeth chattering. 'Are we still alive?'

'Yes,' said Napoleon, 'but the future don't look bright.'

The mud and water raced by like a waterfall, tearing at the Borribles, trying to smash them into the stream. The treadmill was under intense pressure; it cracked and creaked, its timbers began to give and nails and screws loosened and fell away. Then, just as suddenly as it had started, the down-flow ceased. The gaping mouth of the mine became covered and the Wandle drifted over it once more.

'Is it full up now, d'yer reckon?' asked Sydney.

'I told yer before,' said Napoleon, 'it can't be full.'

'I know what it is,' said Knocker, 'it must be an airlock. I think the first lot of mud must have gone down so fast that it trapped a big bubble at the bottom . . . If it stays this way long enough we might have time to get to the shore.'

'We're too weak to swim,' said Orococco. 'It'd be certain death out there.'

'And what do you think it is here,' retorted Napoleon, 'gracious living?'

'I'll tell you something,' said Tron sombrely, 'if there is an airlock down there, sooner or later it's going to explode, and when it does it'll be like a nuclear bomb going off. There'll be shit and slosh going in every direction at once, and bits of us with it.'

No one answered the Wendle; there was no need and no time. From some faraway part of the earth came a great rumbling sound. The vaulted roof of the cavern shook and bricks plummeted from it. The river boiled like hot pitch, faster and faster, releasing a vile gas which from its stench might have been nurtured for months in the reeking flesh of a corpse long dead.

'I can't breathe,' cried Sydney. 'I can't breathe.'

'Don't worry,' said Vulge, wiping the smoky vapour from his eyes, 'in a little while you won't have to.'

The rumbling grew louder. A tidal wave of silt reared up and billowed along the river banks, and the Wendles standing there turned and ran into the tunnels, trampling each other underfoot in their eagerness to be gone; and gone they all were in a few turbulent minutes, leaving only the injured and unconscious behind them, some to crawl away and some to be pulled under by the raging waters.

Still the rushing and the roaring came nearer and the whole world shook and a great explosion hurtled up the mine shaft like a locomotive, and the Borribles crawled towards each other on the wheel and flung their bodies together for protection.

Then the explosion burst out in a mighty upheaval and the treadmill was cast aloft like a pebble, borne upwards on a twisting column of slush that spun and whirled and dipped and swayed like a huge tornado, and the Borribles fought for each breath in the gyrating mud and fought even harder not to be thrown from the wheel and off into the spinning darkness.

Upwards and upwards they went, soaring and gliding a hundred feet high until the wheel was resting lightly on the outermost upthrust of a great pillar of filth. It hovered there for an eternity, balanced between down and up. Then at last, dipping and skimming once more, it swooped away on the crest of a wide and indolent wave that carried it back to the surface of the Wandle flats, where it plunged deep into the river, only to leap into view a moment later with the slime-sodden Borribles still clinging to it; poor black scarecrows coated in muck.

One of the scarecrows weakly raised an arm and tried to shout above the din of the mud storm. It was Knocker and his voice could barely croak. 'Look, look where we are!'

The others scraped the sticky mire from their eye sockets and saw that the wave had brought them more than two hundred yards downstream and near to the north bank. They struck out with their legs and found that their feet could touch the river bottom.

'We're safe,' cried Chalotte, speaking at last, happiness in her tone now that she realized that she had not killed her friends after all.

Napoleon staggered away from the treadmill. 'Don't waste time,' he shouted. 'Get out before the explosion stops.'

He was right. Once the great geyser collapsed the mud would flow back into the mine with even greater power, and everything in the Wandle would flow with it until the shaft was full.

Stonks was still the strongest of the Borribles. One by one he grabbed the most feeble of the Adventurers and dragged them to the shore and shoved them up on to the bank. Napoleon first, then Torreycanyon and Orococco, Knocker last. While he did this the others waded to dry land as best they might, stumbling, floundering, leaning on each other until they all fell together in a heap.

'Never mind resting,' said Napoleon urgently, and finding the strength from somewhere he forced himself to his knees and laid hold of the lump of mud next to him. 'This is Tron, get the other Wendle quick.'

Stonks knew immediately what Napoleon meant but it was impossible to tell one slimy shape from another. It was Norrarf himself who gave the game away, leaping to his feet in panic, and Stonks seized him roughly by the neck and squeezed hard.

'Don't let the Wendles get free,' he yelled, 'or we've had it.'

In spite of Napoleon's efforts to hold him down Tron stood up easily. 'Wait a minute, Napoleon,' he said. 'Flinthead is dead now, there will be no more war between Borrible and Borrible.'

'I'll believe that when I'm out of here, and not before,' said Knocker.

'Don't be idiots,' said Norrarf, struggling in Stonks's grip. 'I was helping Spiff all along wasn't I? Why should I give you away?'

'Everything's changed now,' said Tron. 'Besides, you can be sure that the whole Wendle nation thinks we're dead; nobody stayed to watch exactly, did they?'

Knocker and Napoleon looked at each other. The mud spattered around them and the tornado thundered.

Napoleon shook his head. 'We've been through too much to take any chances . . . Hold 'em fast and keep yer eyes on 'em.'

Tron shrugged. 'I don't blame you,' he said, 'but I can show you that I mean no harm. I'll take you to a safe way out, a secret way out that only Flinthead and I knew.'

'Where is it?' asked Vulge, shouting through the storm.

Tron jerked a thumb over his shoulder. 'That way, along that tunnel; it's a manhole that comes out next to the cranes on Feather's Wharf. It's not far.'

'We'll have a look,' said Stonks, and he began to help his friends to stand, but before they could set out the depths of the mine reverberated and a second air pocket was heard booming its way to the surface. The swirling geyser faltered and dipped for a moment as if about to break, but then it surged upwards with an even greater strength than before and the Borribles fell back, folding their arms over their heads for protection against the mud that pelted them with the force of hailstones.

Chalotte screamed. 'Look,' she gasped, 'look there!'

Her companions peered through the steady barrage of slime and what they saw harrowed their blood and, after all they had endured, warped their sanity to breaking point.

Rising gracefully up the side of the great whirling tornado, turning slowly as if in some grotesque dance of death, the body of Spiff appeared and close by him came the headless trunk of Flinthead, his brother. Languidly they drifted upwards, changing positions unhurriedly, and just below them floated the box of Rumble treasure, so near that at times the two bodies seemed like effigies standing upon it. Spiralling round and round the tableau ascended, moving to the far side of the whirlwind only to reappear a few seconds later, travelling at the speed of the cyclone but seeming uncannily motionless to the eyes of those who watched.

Chalotte touched her face with shaking fingers. 'It's a nightmare,' she said, 'a horrible nightmare.' No one answered her. They stood quite still, all of them, but the horror had not ended. As Flinthead and Spiff revolved in their deathly dance, the lid of the treasure box eased open and, one by one at first and soon in hundreds, bright gold and silver coins began to appear, spread themselves in spangled swathes across the surface of the cyclone and glittered there.

Then the lid of the box opened completely and a thousand banknotes detonated into gaudy streamers and fastened themselves on to this great spinning wall of sewage that turned and turned and drew everything irresistibly towards it. And the paper money shone in all bright colours: green and orange, violet and yellow, amber and pale blue; and the whole whirlwind was festooned with it and so were the bodies of Flinthead and Spiff. It was beautiful.

Chalotte shrieked and the noise shook the Adventurers from their trance.

'It will suck us in if we stay here,' she cried, 'we're too close; run away.' In that instant the mine shaft expelled a long and tumultuous sigh. The last of the imprisoned air escaped from the bottom of the pit and the tornado at last stood still, all power gone. Then its outside skin of slush began to slip and slide until finally it fell with a loud crash back into the depths, burying the bodies and the treasure for ever in the Wandle under countless tons of mud, and huge cowpats came raining down and swamped the Borribles with such a persistent force that they were thrown violently to the ground. Wave after wave reared from the Wandle and threatened to bear them away but they dug their hands into the earth and clung to each other for dear life, and so tightly did they cling that although the river surged and tore and plucked at the Adventurers it could not claim them for all their weakness.

Slowly the clatter ceased and the currents of the river calmed. The tide receded from the banks and the Borribles could raise their heads and look about them. Knocker pushed himself on to his hands and knees; water and slime poured from his limbs.

'I've spent months in this Wandle mud,' he said. 'I've got to get out of it before I go really and truly mad.' He stumbled among the others, looking for Tron.

'Tron, which one are you? Get up.' Tron rose and Knocker went to him. 'Get us out of here, just as quickly as you can.'

The remainder of the Borribles struggled upright and Norrarf went to stand by Tron. 'You can trust us,' he said. 'Honest.'

'Yes,' said Tron. 'Follow me, it is not far.' He put his arm on Norrarf's shoulder and the two Wendles, walking side by side, led the way into a narrow tunnel.

As Tron had said, the secret escape hole was at no great distance. In less than a quarter of an hour's march Tron brought everyone to a halt and pointed at the roof. 'There it is,' he said.

'I don't see no manhole,' said Bingo.

'You won't,' said Tron. 'It's meant to be secret but it's there and it hasn't got an SBG man standing on it, neither.'

'That's as may be,' said Stonks, 'but I'd better go out and have a scout round. If I'm not back in ten minutes you'll know there's something wrong.'

'Suit yerself,' said Tron, 'but be careful, it might be daylight.'

'There's only one way to find out,' said Vulge. 'Let me and Bingo make a step.'

When they were ready Stonks climbed on to their clasped hands and they lifted him into the roof of the tunnel. There was no noise while Stonks groped above his head, but soon his feet shifted and there came the sound of iron grating upon iron.

'Got it,' Stonks grunted, and as he spoke a cool draught carved its way into the stinking atmosphere of the underworld. Each of the Borribles took a long deep breath. It seemed like years since any of them had breathed untainted air.

'Cripes,' said Torreycanyon, 'that's beautiful, like drinking cold water; almost knocks yer unconscious, don't it?'

Stonks's feet disappeared and a second later they heard his voice. 'I'll be back in a few minutes,' he whispered, 'and if I ain't, scarper.'

The Borribles waited and said nothing. Their minds were too full of what they had seen and suffered to allow them to think of talking for the sake of it, but eventually Chalotte did speak and she asked Tron something she thought she ought to know before they parted company, perhaps for ever.

'Why are you letting us go like this, Tron?' she asked. 'Why aren't you calling for your warriors?'

'Well, look at us,' answered the Wendle, 'nearly dead, almost were dead, covered in slime, and for what? The proverb says that fruit of the barrow is enough for a Borrible, yet we seem to have forgotten all that. We've been through something really rotten and it should never have happened, but it did and we were to blame, I suppose, all of us.'

'Funny really,' said Knocker. 'Once it all began it was too late to stop, but I don't mind admitting . . . that mud has taught me a thing or two I won't forget.'

Tron nodded. 'Flinthead wanted power and money, that's where it started, and he made a lot of Wendles think the same, me included . . . Spiff wanted revenge on Flinthead for things that happened long ago, things that we didn't even know about; bloody ridiculous when you think of it.'

'Still,' said Chalotte, 'the Rumble treasure's gone now, and so much the better. That's how it should be with us. It's people like Flinthead who bring trouble, greedy sod, and Spiff was greedy too, in a different way. I don't think it was only revenge he wanted; could have been lots of things, glory, another name. Maybe he did want to take what Flinthead had and keep it. For all we know he really might have wanted to take the money back and share it out equally, but even if he did it wasn't a good idea; it wasn't Borrible.'

'There's enough Rumbles to fight without fighting among ourselves,' said Tron, 'that's plain madness. Anyway, with Flinthead gone I reckon there'll be a lot of Wendles who'll realize they can go back to being Borribles plain and simple, Norrarf here for one, and Skug, and there'll be others.'

'There'll be lots all right,' said Norrarf. 'They didn't dare do anything before because of Flinthead and the bodyguard. You know, just because of the way things were.'

'That's it, though,' said Napoleon. 'I'm a Wendle, remember, or was. I know the bodyguard, they won't let you have everything your own way.'

'We'll have to see,' said Tron, with a sigh. 'We others outnumber them after all. I tell you one thing though, I won't let anyone take over where Flinthead left off, that's for certain.'

And that was the end of it. Stonks's voice dropped down into the darkness and brought the discussion to a close. 'It's nearly dawn,' he said, 'but there doesn't seem to be anyone about. There's a light in Ben's shed. Best thing is to come up quietly; you never know, Sussworth may have a Woollie hidden, waiting for us.'

Tron linked hands with Norrarf to make a step, and one by one the Adventurers said goodbye to the Wendles, friends now, and jumped upwards to grasp the rim of the manhole and haul themselves out into the cool of the summer dawn.

At the very end Knocker stood ready to go. He raised a weary foot and placed it in the Wendles' hands. 'Perhaps,' he said, 'we shall meet again.'

'Sometime,' said Tron, 'when things have gone one way or the other. If I'm still alive I'll come and tell you the story of what I did.'

'Do that,' said Knocker. 'I like a good story.' He turned to Norrarf. 'I didn't get to know you Norrarf, but thanks. Remember, real friends will come when you call . . . and both of you, don't get caught.'

'Nor you,' said Norrarf, and he thrust with his hands and Knocker found himself shoved up through the manhole and pulled over and on to the ground by the strong arms of Stonks. Then he heard a clang and the iron cover slid into its grooves behind him.

10

For a long time the Borribles lay on the uneven and rubbish-strewn dirt. They listened and they heard the sound of the Wandle where it met the River Thames. A tug hooted out on Wandsworth Reach and an early car swished along on Armoury Way. It was warm. The London heatwave had not relented but the outside air felt deliciously cool after the triple-baked temperatures of the underground mine.

Knocker relaxed flat on his back and gazed into the sky; the sky that he had thought never to see again. He smiled and the drying mud cracked on his cheeks. It made him glad to see the pale yellow stars and the deep blue of the night fading into grey on the horizon as the dawn came. His breast swelled with a pleasure he felt he could not endure: the simple pleasure of being alive, of being thankful for it and knowing he was. The tears trickled down the side of his face and into his hair, but nobody could see them, lost as they were in dirt.

He sat up. The mingled odours of river and rubbish were wholesome after the smell of the sewers. He turned his head and saw that he and the others were right by the two steam cranes that guarded Feather's Wharf.

Napoleon sat up too. 'Well, what do you know?' he asked of no one in particular.

'Man,' said Orococco, 'it's like breathing for the very first time.'

The Borribles looked above their heads. In the moments that had elapsed since the closing of the manhole the stars had gone from the sky, a quiet traffic noise was growing and bright squares of electric light were appearing in tall and distant buildings; holes cut from the black sides of Wandsworth. A breeze was riding in on the back of the river and a loose flap of corrugated iron banged on the side of a shed somewhere. In a few minutes the rubbish men would be arriving to work on the dump, digging and delving into the loose mountains of trash and loading the river barges until they almost sank, while the tipper trucks roared in from all over London. It was a new day.

'Let's go to Ben's,' said Sydney. 'I'd like to find out what happened to Sam.'

'Ben?' said Knocker.

'Sam?' said Torreycanyon, who had forgotten all about the horse.

Chalotte pulled Knocker to his feet. 'There's new stuff to tell you – there's Twilight here, and Ben and Sam. There's Susswortth too, and Hanks and the SBG.'

'Sussworth,' Napoleon spat out the word. 'Straight away I don't like the sound of him.'

Stonks swore. 'You won't like the look of 'im either,' he said, 'especially if he catches us out here. Let's get out of sight.' He set off into the mile of space that lay between the Wandle and Wandsworth Bridge, followed by the others along a path that wound between the piles of discarded washing machines and broken refrigerators. They walked quietly in file until they came within sight of Ben's hut, and there they saw a light flickering behind a threadbare sack which hung for a curtain at a lopsided window. They took cover and waited while Stonks went to the door. Carefully he lifted the latch and poked his head inside, then after a moment, he beckoned to his companions, indicating that all was safe.

'This is Ben,' he explained to those who had not been to the shack before, 'and Ben is the only grown-up Borrible in the world.'

The interior of the hut was gloomy, lit only by one oil lamp. Ben was discovered sprawled asleep in a low broken-backed armchair and he looked just the same as he had always looked: covered in many overcoats, his beard spreading over his chest, his long black hair tumbling to his shoulders and his skin pitted and filthy. He smelt just the same too: awful.

'Blimey,' said Orococco, 'he's blacker than I am.'

Sydney closed the door and the slight noise made Ben stir in his sleep. He belched and opened one eye, then the other. Slowly he came awake and shifted in his chair, rubbing his hairy face with a soiled hand.

'Well,' he said, 'strike me purple.' The old tramp shook his head, surprised, but then a broad smile began to grow behind his beard. 'Well, I'll be damned,' he went on. 'I thought Sussworth had got you for sure. Not my business of course, but I didn't like it, didn't like it one bit.' He reached for the beer bottle on the table and took a long swig to reassure himself that the world was still in the same place. 'There's more of you, though,' he said. 'Found some friends ain't yer? What you kids get up to is nobody's business, but whose business is it if it ain't nobody's?'

Sydney, who had spent more time with Ben than any of the others and therefore knew him better, stepped up and touched him on the hand. 'We've had the most terrible time, Ben,' she said. 'Could we hide here for a few days maybe, get some rest? We're dropping on our feet.'

Ben rummaged in his overcoat and began to produce bottles of beer one by one. 'Stay, sunshine,' he bellowed, 'why of course you can,' and he wagged his beard like he was chewing a tough bit of meat. 'Get this sherbet down yer, that'll straighten you out a bit. Strewth, look 'ow muddy you are, and them clothes, waders and orange jackets . . . You've been thieving again.'

Stonks found a bottle opener and passed the bottles round. The Borribles drank and allowed the strong ale to trickle down their throats, but they stood awkwardly in the hut. After all, Ben was an adult, and Knocker and Napoleon kept near the door in case they had to run.

The tramp hoisted himself upright. 'Blimey,' he said, 'you must be tired; I've never known you so quiet. You look dead on yer feet. Why don't yer get into the other rooms and spread out on the mattresses, get some sleep? It'll all be better by the time you wakes up, you'll see.'

Twilight looked around. 'You've changed all the furniture,' he said, 'and all your things are different.'

Ben placed his hands on his hips. 'That was your friend Sussworth,' he said. 'He will have his little joke. The day you left he smashed all me bits and pieces, all me bottles, threw me locks and keys into the barges. It was worth a lot of grub that stuff was. He said he was going to scrub me clean, give me a shave, put me in a home. Bleedin' little Hitler he is. Kept asking me where you'd gone.'

'What happened?' asked Vulge.

'Well, I kept saying it was none of my business and eventually they let me go with a kick up the arse.'

'And all this stuff,' said Chalotte, 'where'd that come from?'

'Oh, that's easy,' said Ben. 'If you live in the middle of the world's biggest rubbish dump you want for nothing, do yer? There's plenty of beds and blankets; I've got more bottles. I'm rich I am, Sussworth can't bother me.'

'Where is he now?' asked Stonks.

'Ah,' answered Ben, 'that's the trouble. He's got the whole of Wandsworth surrounded. He knows you haven't gone home yet. Don't know how he knows, but he knows, but then he makes it his business to know, don't he?'

'Then everything's just as bad as it was before,' said Bingo.

'And so it may be,' said Ben, 'but we've got to look on the bright side, ain't we? Well what is it to be, sleep or eat?'

'Sleep,' said the Borribles.

'Right,' said Ben, 'you know where the beds are, just like before. You show your mates. When you wake up I'll 'ave a feast ready for you, a regular feast. You'll wonder what's hit yer, see if yer don't. Now off you go and get yer heads down.'

The Borribles needed no second bidding. They filed from the room and within a minute or two were all in a deep slumber, dirt, slime and everything. Only Sydney lingered.

'Ben, how's Sam, the horse, is he all right? Has Sussworth found him?'

Ben shook his shoulders loosely by way of a laugh. 'That there horse,' he said, 'is as snug as a bug in a rug. Five-star hotel he's in, first-class oats and hay, fresh water, lots of other horses for company. Saw him only yesterday, hardly recognized him, did I? Knibbsie likes him so much that he never lets him out of his sight, and Sussworth, like I said, never thought of looking for him in a stable; too subtle, that is.'

Sydney sniffed. 'Thanks, Ben,' she said, holding down the lump in her throat with difficulty. 'Thanks.'

Ben spat into a pile of coal. 'I don't often make things my business,' he said wisely, 'but when I does, I does.'

Sydney smiled and went to find somewhere to sleep. Now that the tension of the escape was over she found that she could hardly stand. Ben waited until he was alone and began to feel in his pockets for a pipe. It took him a long time. 'Them bleedin' kids,' he muttered, 'they're something special they are, something really special.'

*

And so the Adventurers slept and slept again. They were to stay with Ben for more than a week and for most of that time they woke only to eat. Every time they opened their eyes Ben was there with more food.

'Eat up,' he kept urging them, 'eat up, you're all so skinny. Plenty more where that came from, all the rubbish in the world here.' And from the depths of his overcoats would come forth packets of this and bottles of that.

During this period the Borribles were quite content to leave their safety in the tramp's hands. 'Sussworth's out there,' he told them, 'him and the SBG, but they don't take no more notice of old Ben.' He'd swig from a bottle and tell them not to worry about the dried mud that was flaking off their bodies and into the blankets. 'I don't care about a touch of dirt,' he insisted. 'A good bit of dirt never hurt anyone except the old lady who broke her back scrubbing the floor.'

Towards the end of the week the Borribles began to recover. Knocker, Napoleon, Torreycanyon and Orococco were the last to get on their feet but then their captivity had been long and arduous. When they finally emerged into the daylight of Feather's Wharf the mud had gone from their skins if not from their clothes. They looked pale and thin but there was a new light in their eyes and the sparks of a new energy could be seen in their movement and thought; they started to exchange their stories, as Borribles love to do.

Vulge told how Sydney had come to Whitechapel, and how Twilight had saved Chalotte from a Woollie that very same day. Sydney spoke of the strange message telling of Sam the horse and how she and the others set out to find him, and Stonks explained to Knocker about the formation of the SBG and who Inspector Sussworth was and how the Adventurers had been captured at the Battle of Eel Brook Common. Then Bingo took up the tale and recounted Ben's rescue of them all and the newcomers looked at Ben with a deep admiration.

'That was the best of it,' said Chalotte, 'but the worst of it was what I discovered when I talked to Spiff while you were all down the mine.

You see he'd planned the whole thing; it was him that sent the message to Sydney, just to start things going, so that he could get back at Flinthead.'

'He was devious all right,' said Knocker, 'double devious.'

'I dunno,' objected Torreycanyon. 'Whatever you say about him he got us out of there alive remember. I don't reckon anyone else could've.'

'That's right,' said Napoleon with respect in his voice. 'He fooled Flinthead all the way, and that's not easy, and what a scrap with the spades. He was Spiff the Spifflicator, there ain't no doubt about that.'

'Wait a minute,' said Knocker darkly. 'If it hadn't been for Spiff we wouldn't have been down the mine in the first place. He owed us a rescue . . . and we might not have got away at all if Chalotte hadn't knocked the wedges out.'

'Of course we would've,' said Napoleon. 'Chalotte nearly got us all killed. All Spiff had to do was pretend to be Flinthead; he could have got us out whenever he liked then.'

'Ah,' said Knocker, 'that's it. Would Spiff have done that? Who knows what he might have done once he found himself in power? He might have let us go, he might not have. There was nothing to stop him kicking us out into the street either and staying behind himself to become Flinthead, swapping identities, like.'

'He wouldn't have, would he?' asked Twilight, his eyes round.

'Spiff was capable of anything,' said Knocker. 'that was part of his strength, that's why he was a danger. What's more that box of treasure did things to people, changed 'em. It made Flinthead worse than he was before, it tempted Napoleon once, it certainly made me ambitious for more and more names. Who knows what it was doing to Spiff, eh, who knows?'

There was so much to think of after what Knocker had said that there was silence for a while. Then Sydney raised her eyes and said quietly, 'So Chalotte was the only one of us all to see it, and when she saw it she destroyed the mine, destroyed the money . . . and killed Spiff.'

Chalotte stared at the floor; her face reddened. 'I didn't know what I was doing,' she began, 'and I don't want to take credit for it. I didn't want to kill Spiff; he was brave, he did save us all in the end, but he never told us what he was doing, you never knew which way he was going to jump. When you came out of the mine I wasn't certain of anything. One moment I thought it was Flinthead climbing out, then I wasn't sure. There was so much noise, so much shouting. I was frightened of what was happening and what might happen. All I know is that I didn't want that money back among Borribles again . . . Knocking out the wedges was the only thing I could do, it seemed like the right thing.'

'I think it was,' said Knocker. 'I think it was, even if it nearly killed the lot of us.'

'She was bloody brave anyway,' said Vulge. 'There was a lot of certain death flying about for a quarter of an hour.'

Chalotte shook her head. 'I wasn't brave,' she said, 'just scared out of my brains.'

'What a great story it will be,' said Twilight. 'It will be the greatest Borrible Adventure ever told, better even than the Great Rumble Hunt, maybe.'

Knocker looked stern. 'I don't know about you others,' he said, 'but there are some things about this Adventure I don't like. Perhaps we shouldn't tell this story, we should keep it secret among ourselves.'

'A secret story,' said Chalotte. 'Well you might be right, you might not. We'd have to think about it.'

Knocker gazed at the scars that were burnt into the palms of his hands. 'You know, Chalotte, I'm glad you gave me that second name, Knocker Burnthand. I'm proud of it in a funny back to front kind of a way . . . but I don't want another. I've had enough adventures to last me a Borrible lifetime.'

And so they talked on and Ben sat and listened with great interest and passed bottles of stout to each speaker in turn so that they could build up their strength, and the Borribles came to accept the tramp as one of their very own. Indeed it was a mark of the confidence they felt in him that the Borribles told their stories in front of an adult at all, for it had never been done before.

It became obvious to them that Ben would have had the Borribles live in his lean-to for ever, but as the Adventurers felt their limbs grow stronger they began to worry about getting home, back to their tumbledown houses in their own areas of London.

'It won't be easy,' said Stonks, when he had explained to Knocker how determined and well trained Inspector Susswort and his men were. 'The SBG know that we had something to do with Dewdrop's death and they won't give up till they've got us and clipped our ears.'

Ben knocked his pipe against the side of his chair and allowed the ash to fall to the floor. 'Every time I go out,' he said, 'I see coppers everywhere; like a bloody coronation it is, except they're searching for you lot, and they look like they're ready to wait for ever, day and night and mainly between here and Battersea, which is where you want to go, ain't it? We'll have to think of something really good this time.'

The discussion went on and on and got nowhere. Some thought it would be a good idea to make a raft and drift down the river in the dark. Others suggested that it would be safer to walk along by the river's edge and get round the police cordon that way. One or two argued that they should stay where they were and wait until Sussworth gave up his task and moved away, but then it was pointed out that there was no guarantee that the SBG would not pay Ben another visit and catch them all there, say, sleeping in the middle of the night. It was dangerous to go and every hour it became more and more dangerous to remain; the situation looked hopeless until one day Ben returned from the outside world, emptied his pockets of provisions, banged a bottle on the table and called for silence.

'I've been thinking,' he said, 'and swipe me if that ain't given me an idea. None of your plans is very good, none of 'em, but I reckon I can get you out of Wandsworth in style and comfort, the horse as well.'

'The horse as well,' said Sydney, her face happy. 'How?'

Ben squinted and filled his eyes with mystery. 'Ha,' he said, 'you'll have to wait and see. Let's say the day after tomorrow, very early in the morning. Get plenty of rest, you may need it.'

For the whole of the intervening time the Borribles could hardly contain themselves. Ben came and went on several occasions and laid in a great stock of rations and swigged from his beer bottles ceaselessly. On one of his appearances he staggered into the lean-to carrying a huge bundle of second-hand children's clothes and threw them down on to the floor.

'Best get out of that Wendle stuff,' he said panting, 'you look like a bunch of bandits. I've got some lovely gear here. Real posh you'll look in this little lot, like bleedin' choir boys . . . and girls o' course.'

Bingo held up a clean shirt that had once been very expensive. 'Where'd yer get it?' he asked.

Ben raised his eyebrows. 'Where'd yer think? It fell off a lorry, just like that. Wonderful thing gravity, I don't reckon we could live without it.'

*

At five in the morning on the day of departure Ben crept into the room where the Borribles were sleeping and shook them gently awake.

'Come on, mates,' he whispered. 'It's time.'

As usual the tramp had sat in his armchair all night with a fire going in spite of the heatwave, drinking and thinking, and although the dawn was warm and sticky he still wore all his overcoats, just like he always did.

The Borribles stretched, rolled from their mattresses, dressed quickly in their new clothes and made their way to the kitchen.

'Got some tea for you,' said Ben as they appeared one by one, 'and there's a kettle on the hob, look, if you want more. Bacon sandwiches on the plate . . . get stuck in.'

It was just light when they left the lean-to a little while later. Two or three seagulls were tearing at piles of offal near the river and Ben looked up at the sky.

'It's going to be as hot as 'ell again today,' he said, and pulled his collars tighter to his neck.

In single file the Borribles followed the tramp over the rough terrain of Feather's Wharf. Across broken and deserted factories, through abandoned houses where glass crunched underfoot and where rotten floors threatened to snap and fall, Ben stepped out, travelling in safety by unmapped and forgotten ways, ways that were known only to himself and which no ordinary adult or policeman had ever seen. Over the railway line they went, along the Causeway by the River Wandle, and finally they stumbled across a dusty field of crumbling bricks and corrugated iron and found themselves on the edge of the broad thoroughfare of Armoury Way.

Ben looked up and down carefully; the Borribles stood behind him. The pavements were grey and empty and stretched for miles. Ben gave the word and he and the Borribles rushed across the road in a gang.

When he was satisfied that no one was watching he grinned and pushed against a plank in the high advertising hoarding beside him. The plank swivelled on a loose nail and the Borribles saw a large hole appear.

'This is how I gets into Young's Brewery,' cackled Ben. 'This is how I goes to see my mate, Knibbsie, and this is how I brings me beer out. In yer go.'

When everyone had passed through Ben replaced the plank and breathed a sigh of relief. 'We're safe now,' he explained. 'We're in the back of the brewery, private property, no Woollies here. Knibbsie and me used to be draymen together once, as well as being on the road. He looks after the horses now, 'cos they still delivers their beer with horses and carts you know; you ever seen 'em?'

'Seen 'em,' said Bingo. 'I should think so. Bloody great animals, big as double-decker buses.'

Ben nodded. 'Come on then, no time to lose.' He shuffled on through the yards and alleys of the brewery and the Borribles went with him. Everywhere they passed stood gigantic wooden drays, high, like carriages for kings, with massive steel-rimmed wheels painted in bright fairground colours.

The tramp stopped by the side of one of these carts and pointed up to the polished seat that must have been a good fifteen feet off the ground.

'That's where the driver and his mate rides,' he said. 'It's like flying, it is. You can see everything for miles up there. You can look into upstairs windows as easy as winking, and see people having their breakfast . . . And all the traffic has to stop for you. The hooves clip-clopping, the leather creaking, the brasses swinging and clanking. I tell you, if you have to work, and I don't wish that on anybody, but if you has to, well that's the best job in the world, and the beer's free too. You just sniff the air in here, for example, and see. Why that air's so heavy with ale that it's good enough to make breathing a crime.' And as if to prove his point Ben sniffed deeply and philosophically before continuing on his way.

They were very nearly at the end of their journey now. Ben took them into a wide stable yard and there, at the far end of it, stood a man in a long leather apron, leaning on a broom. 'That,' said Ben, 'is my mate, Knibbsie.'

Knibbs had obviously been waiting for them for he showed no surprise at their appearance. Sydney, who had last seen him on the misty night of the escape from Fulham police station, looked at him closely.

She remembered the face now: pale, with strange spiky hair sticking out horizontally under a flat greasy cap. His nose was hard and bony, his eyes dark. He wore a big fluffy moustache too and it was stained with brown beer. His face looked glum until he smiled but he smiled now and his face changed and became warm. He beckoned and the Borribles and Ben went towards him.

On either side as they walked were huge yellow doors, divided in half, and the top half of each stall was open and the great shire horses that pulled the drays stood there as solid and heavy as mammoths.

'Swipe me,' said Vulge, 'look at the size of 'em; imagine having one of them step on your toe.'

'And look at their teeth,' added Twilight. 'One mouthful and you'd be gone.' But the horses showed no sign of hostility, they were not interested in a band of insignificant children. They simply shook their heads, snorted, stamped their feet and waited for their early morning feed.

When the Adventurers were standing before Knibbs he leant his broom against the wall and crossed his arms. He looked at Ben and then at the children. 'Borribles, eh? Well I've heard of 'em; never thought I'd see any, knowingly like.'

The Borribles tensed. Knibbs, after all, was an adult.

'Don't worry,' he said. 'Ben's told me all about it. All I want to do is get you out of sight before anyone else gets here. I don't mind helping, but I don't want the sack on account of it, eh, Ben. What would we do for beer then?'

'What indeed?' said Ben sagely. 'What indeed?'

'Wait a minute,' said Sydney, 'don't you remember me? I met you before, that night in the fog. I brought you a horse . . . What's happened to Sam?'

Knibbs looked down at Sydney. 'Sam,' he said, 'why Sam's lovely. You never seen such a horse, not in all your natural you ain't.' He went to a nearby stable door and unbolted the lower section. 'I 'as to open the bottom bit,' he explained. 'Sam isn't big enough to look over it, not like the others.' With that the stableman opened the hatch and there stood Sam. But such a Sam. He was so sleek and well fed. His hooves glittered like anthracite and his coat was so polished that Sydney could see her face in it. No longer the dingy downhearted nag that had once pulled Dewdrop's cart, Sam had been transformed into an aristocrat of a horse, small but distinguished.

The Borribles cried aloud with surprise and pushed forward to stroke and pat the animal and Sam neighed gently and nuzzled them all one by one, recognizing them.

Sydney turned to look at the stableman. 'It's Sam all right,' she said, 'and he looks lovely. But he used to be brown, now he's black.'

'So he is,' said Chalotte. 'I hadn't noticed.'

'Ah,' said Knibbs, 'that's a disguise, that is. We've got to get him past Sussworth today and that's how we're going to do it. If Sussworth recognizes that horse he'll know that you ain't far away; that's it and all about it. Now all of yer, outside and out of sight.'

Back in the yard Knibbs took them to one of the huge drays that stood near the stable office. 'This one's already loaded,' he said, 'and me and Ben are taking it out today because they're short-handed. Now see that ladder, well you lot get up it. Lively!'

The Borribles did as they were told and found themselves on the very top of a mountainous load of wooden barrels that had been piled one on another across the length and breadth of the cart, except that in the middle Knibbs had left a space big enough for the Adventurers to jump down into and hide.

'Don't make a sound,' Ben shouted. 'Don't come out again till I tell yer it's safe.' He threw a square of canvas up to them. 'And cover yourselves with this so yer ain't seen from a buildin' or a bus.'

'Where's this cart going,' said Orococco, 'not Tooting by any chance?'

'No,' said Knibbs. 'Battersea High Street, that's why we're taking you. We're delivering to a pub called the Ancient Woodman. No more noise now.'

The Borribles grinned at each other and scrambled into the centre of the cart and found that they were hidden on all sides by the towering beer barrels. They sat and pulled the tarpaulin over their heads.

'Just think,' whispered Twilight, 'we're on our way home.'

'You ain't home yet,' said Stonks. 'There's still Sussworth and Hanks to get past.'

'Yeah,' said Vulge, 'and just think what they'll do to Ben and Knibbs if they finds 'em smuggling Borribles . . . They'll send 'em to prison for years and years.'

Outside, beyond the barrels, the brewery went about its business and the noises they heard told the Borribles what was happening. First, one of the stable doors was opened and Knibbs and Ben emerged with two shire horses and buckled them into the shafts of the great cart. Then came the light step of Sam as he was brought out too and tied behind. A little later there was more noise as other drivers and draymen arrived to groom their horses and back them into the carts ready for the day's work. Then the foreman came and checked the loads and told the teams which part of London they were to go to, and where they were meant to deliver their barrels. He called out the names of the pubs from his order book: the Fallen Tree, the Old Goat, the Jolly Sailor, the Apple of My Eye, the Garden of Eden, the Charcoal Burner, and many more.

When the foreman had reached the end of his list he rolled out a firkin of beer, lifted it up on to a wooden trestle, broached it and then handed every man present a pint mug of ale so that they could drink to the new day. As soon as their glasses were empty the draymen smacked their lips, shouted goodbye to each other, climbed to the pinnacle of their high carts, cracked their whips in the air and at last allowed the giant horses to move forward.

Now Knibbs cracked his whip and spoke to his horses. 'Come on up, Donner, my beauty; come on up, Blitzen, my girl,' he called, and Ben wrapped his legs in a huge leather apron and the great dray rumbled over the cobbles.

'We're off,' cried Ben, and there was a clashing of horse-brasses as well as a racket of horseshoes and the cart charged down the yard and out through the brewery gates like an engine of war on its way to do battle.

'It's now or never, all right,' said Bingo, jolted so much that his voice shook. 'If we get caught this time there'll be no getting away from in here. It'll be ears clipped for sure.'

Knocker smiled. 'As the proverb says, "There's a time for fingers crossed and mouths shut." This is it.'

It was eight thirty in the morning now and the rush hour traffic in Wandsworth High Street was heavy, not that traffic made any difference to Knibbs. The law of the land gives horse-drawn vehicles right of way over motor cars, and so they were all made to stop and wait as the drays clattered from the brewery to head in different directions, out over London. Knibbs touched on his reins and the great horses strode proudly on, and behind the cart trotted Sam as dainty as a thoroughbred. Into Wandsworth Plain they went, round the one-way system, back into Armoury Way, past the traffic lights and on to the great modern roundabout where Sydney had walked in the mist with Ben, and finally into York Road, towards the line where Wandsworth meets Battersea, where Inspector Sussworth waited in ambush with Sergeant Hanks and the men of the SBG.

And along each road the traffic yielded before the steady progress of the magnificent horses, car drivers leant on their steering wheels and peered up through their windscreens to savour a moment of beauty to take to work with them, and passengers in the hot smoky upstairs of the buses gazed stupidly across at Knibbs and Ben and wondered why they looked so free and piratical, never guessing for a moment that within a secret space, deep among the barrels, lay the Adventurers, escaping across a frontier.

Halfway along York Road the stream of cars and buses slowed to a halt and the horses stopped too. Ben stood on his seat and tried to make out what was happening in the distance. A second later his voice drifted back to the Borribles.

'Steady, mates, I can see a blue van up front . . . It's them all right. They're searching all the cars, they've got a barricade across the road. Keep yer 'eads down.'

Pace by pace the dray advanced and the Borribles bit their lips and waited. They couldn't see and they daren't look but Ben told them that there was a dark blue Transit van parked halfway across the road and two or three policemen were filtering the traffic past it in the direction of the city. Slowly the horses stepped, responding patiently to the commands of Knibbs, until at last they came level with the policemen and there was Inspector Sussworth, standing on the pavement, watching everything with his bright dark eyes. His long coat swept the ground, his buttons shone and the two sides of his square moustache twitched up and down like the wings of a dying moth. Beside him, forever faithful, stood Sergeant Hanks, forever fat, his tunic stained with months of food, greasy layers of it. Sussworth gestured and one of his constables stepped to the side of the cart and gazed up into Knibbs's face.

'Pull that cart over here, out of the way,' said the policeman roughly. 'You're causing an obstruction.'

'Wouldn't be if you didn't have that stupid van of yours halfway across the road,' said Knibbs. 'Broken down, have yer?'

'Watch yer tongue, chummy,' said the policeman, and he made Knibbs bring the cart to the kerb where Sussworth stood, his hands clasped behind his back.

'And where are you going with this lot?' he asked, his manner argumentative and superior, his head pivoting dangerously on his neck.

'We're going to a bottle party,' offered Ben, 'and we don't want to look mean.'

'Don't be smart,' said Sussworth, then he looked again. His expression hardened. 'Well, well,' he said, 'that's old Ben, the tramp. I've had trouble with you before. Didn't think you worked, Ben. I had you down for one of them welfare scroungers. You know, half the year on the dole and the other half in an alcoholic haze.'

'I'm a part-time drayman,' said Ben haughtily, feeling quite safe on his lofty perch. 'It's my trade.'

'Drinks more than you sell, I'll be bound,' said Hanks, and he took a boiled sweet from his pocket, unwrapped it with his teeth and sucked it into his mouth. He licked the paper then let it flutter to the ground, wet with his saliva.

'I asked you where you were going,' persisted Sussworth, 'and if I don't get a proper answer you'll bloody well stay here till your beer goes flat.'

Knibbs said, 'We're delivering in Battersea High Street, the Ancient Woodman, down Church Road to the Swan and then back up Battersea Bridge Road.'

'Hmm,' said Sussworth, not convinced, and the Borribles heard his little dancing steps come nearer to the cart. Behind him thudded Sergeant Hanks, cheeks slobbering noisily at his sweet. It sounded like someone with a bad cold sniffing loose snot.

Suddenly Sussworth took a truncheon from one of his constables and began tapping all the barrels he could reach, one after the other. Fear grasped the Borribles by the heart and they held their breath. Slowly Sussworth worked along the dray, down one side, across the rear, then up to the front. When he'd finished he stood in the roadway, dwarfed by the horses, so small that he could have walked under their bellies without removing his hat.

'What's that horse doing at the back? Stolen is it? Looks familiar to me.'

'Well,' said Knibbs, 'one horse does look very much like another.'

'That's the trouble,' said Ben, looking astute, 'seen one horse, seen 'em all.' And he nodded his head as if he'd been grappling with the problem all his life.

'And why is it so small, then?' asked the inspector. 'Couldn't pull a cart this size, could it? So what's it doing with you?'

'Cor,' said Ben, blowing his cheeks out with indignation, 'give an 'orse a chance. He's little, certainly, but he's learning to be big, ain't he? Still growing, still training. I mean you went to night school, didn't yer?'

'Don't you get uppity with me,' said Sussworth angrily and a dark cloud passed over his face. 'If that horse weren't so black I'd swear it was the little brown job those Borribles nicked.' As he spoke an idea came into his head and he went to the back of the cart again and studied Sam very closely, wiping his hands down the animal's legs. Sam trembled with fear and distaste. He needn't have worried though; the dye that Knibbs had used did not come off on the policeman's hand in spite of the fact that he rubbed as hard as he could. The stableman was a wily old horse-trader and had lived with the gypsies for many years in his younger days. He knew all about disguising horses.

Disappointed and still suspicious Sussworth returned to the front of the cart and stood by the tail of the offside shire horse, the one Knibbs called Blitzen.

'Now listen here, you layabout,' he said to Ben, 'have you seen anything of them kids since I asked you last? There's a reward out for 'em you know, five hundred pounds. Just think what you'd be able to drink with that.'

'Oh,' said Ben, clasping his hands together and lifting his eyes to heaven, 'five hundred pounds, such money. You know I dreams of money, every night, in banknotes mostly. I sees myself stuffing me mattresses with it, and me pillows. I've got my eyes peeled like spuds for them kids, Inspector, sir, honest I have. I'll find 'em out for yer, bet yer boots I will.'

Sussworth thought for a moment and Sergeant Hanks stuck a fingernail into his nose. There was silence as everyone waited for the inspector to come to a decision. The rest of the morning traffic moved slowly past the barrier.

At that moment Blitzen arched her massive tail with an elegant slow grace and a soft wide cable of freshly plaited manure appeared, rolling out of the great body in a heavy lump of steaming brown flecked with straw. It flopped moistly to the ground and exploded over Inspector Sussworth's shoes and trousers.

The inspector cried aloud and jumped backwards immediately, prodding his sergeant in the stomach with a sharp elbow.

'Ouch,' yelled Hanks. His boiled sweet slipped into his throat and stuck there and his fingernail scraped the inside of his nostril and drew blood. Unable to speak a word he staggered to the nearest policeman and, going redder and redder in the face, begged, with gestures, to be thumped hard on the shoulders before he died of a seizure.

Sussworth went frantic; he could not abide dirt. He stamped and scraped his feet on the edge of the kerb, he shook his trouser legs, he shouted and screamed.

'Get those horses away from here, get my car, take me home. I must get changed, I must have a new uniform, I must have a bath. Take those animals away, have them shot. They're disgusting, unhygienic, there ought to be a law against them. I'll have 'em turned into catsmeat, take 'em away.'

Knibbs winked at Ben and shook the reins. Blitzen turned her huge head and gazed with disdain at the prancing figure of Inspector Sussworth and, as the horse moved out into the stream of traffic, she twitched her tail once more and farted loudly, like a cannon.

Sussworth's legs shook in temper, he felt weak with the vulgarity of it all and he covered his face with his hands. 'Hanks,' he moaned. 'Hanks, get my car, take me away. I'll kill that horse if you don't; I won't be responsible for my actions.'

Knibbs held up his whip, the slow traffic stopped and the dray pulled round the SBG van and into the open road beyond. The barrier had been passed, the frontier had been cleared. Down among the beer barrels the Borribles clasped each other in jubilation.

'We've done it,' said Chalotte.

'And with Sam too,' said Sydney. 'We escaped with Sam.'

Knocker grinned and grinned. 'I never felt better in my life,' he said. 'Home, sweet home.' And he threw his head high and sang a song of triumph, not loudly, for he did not want to be heard outside the barrels, but with feeling and gratitude warm in his voice. And his friends closed their eyes, both to concentrate on the words and to keep back the tears of joy. This was Knocker's song.

'Hip hip hooray – we've won the day!
We ride victorious from the fray!
Three cheers for Knibbsie! Three cheers for Ben!
And Donner and Blitzen, three cheers for them!
Defying the odds they've brought us free
Of Sussworth, Hanks and the SBG.
Toast them in beer for all they've done –
Honorary Borribles, every one!'

Donner and Blitzen rattled their brasses as if in answer and trotted on at a fair clip. Past the lights at the end of Plough Road they went, past Price's candle factory and finally into Vicarage Crescent and to the bottom of Battersea High Street. Only then did Knibbs and Ben stop the cart and, to the astonishment of passers-by, they stood on their seat, doffed their hats to each other and gave three cheers.

'You're a gentleman, Ben,' said Knibbs.

'And you're a scholar, my dear Knibbsie,' said Ben.

While the two adults were exchanging these compliments the Borribles climbed out of their hiding place and sat on top of the barrels in order to contemplate their freedom.

'And Ben,' said Sydney, 'you're a real Borrible.'

'And you too, Knibbsie,' said Chalotte, 'a real, real Borrible.'

'Thank you,' said Knibbs. 'I must say I've always felt like one.'

Ben wagged his beard. 'Don't you lot get careless now.' He looked down the street. 'You'd better scarper before you're spotted.'

'But will we ever see you again?' asked Chalotte, her face creased with worry.

Knibbs smiled. 'I should think so. I'll give a whistle every time I come down here with a load, and bring Ben sometimes, when he's sober, that is!'

'Fair enough,' said Napoleon, screwing his face up like a conspirator's. 'And if you two ever need help, no matter what, Napoleon's yer man.'

'And us too,' said the others, and they climbed down the great cartwheels and gathered together on the pavement while Sydney went to Sam the horse, untied him and stroked his neck. The Adventurers looked at one another, suddenly concerned.

'That's a point,' said Vulge. 'What are we going to do with him? We haven't thought of that, have we?'

'That's no problem,' said Bingo, 'there's stacks of empty houses down here. We'll get him into one of those for the time being and then we'll . . .' His voice faltered.

'Exactly,' said Napoleon. 'And then what do we do?'

Sydney tossed her hair. 'Don't you fret,' she said. 'I'm going to take him back to Neasden as soon as I'm ready. I've got a special place all fixed up.'

'Neasden!' shouted Torreycanyon. 'Strike a light, that's right over the other side of London.'

'I know where it is,' said Sydney, 'I live there. Besides I haven't asked you to help, have I?'

Ben called down from the top of the cart, 'Hey you lot, if you've stopped arguing, we're off.'

Knocker waved a hand. 'We've finished and we're going as well. Goodbye you two, and don't get caught.'

Ben hooted with laughter. 'You're the ones as better watch out,' he cried. 'They can't clip my ears any more, only yours. Keep yer eyes skinned for Sussworth, and take good care of Sam, he's a good 'un.'

Knocker looked at Chalotte and smiled. 'Don't worry, Ben,' he said, 'we'll watch out for him.'

Then Knibbs spoke to Donner and Blitzen; the great horses leant into the traces, their hooves struck white scars on the black tarmac and the cart moved up the street to begin its deliveries, leaving the Borribles standing on the pavement with Sam.

'Come on,' said Bingo. 'We have to find somewhere to hide this horse before a Woollie spots us.'

'There used to be an old factory behind the scrapyard,' said Knocker. 'We could get him in there, yards of space there is.'

'But there's a better place up by the market,' objected Bingo. 'It'd be easier for stealing carrots and stuff.'

'It don't matter where we go,' said Stonks, 'as long as we go. I didn't rescue you lot just to get caught by the Woollies again.'

'That's right,' said Napoleon. 'And think what will happen if we try to take a horse to Neasden in broad daylight. It's mad. I thought we were going in for the quiet life now, no more high adventure.'

'You can't desert Sam,' protested Twilight. 'He saved your lives on the Great Rumble Hunt; you owe him. He's a kind of horse-Borrible, and Borribles stick together, that's what we said.'

'A horse-Borrible,' sneered Napoleon. 'Well, I knew Pakis were barmy but—'

'Don't you Paki me,' retorted Twilight. 'I'm a Bangladeshi; and at least I'm brown, not green like a Wendle.'

And so they crossed the High Street in an untidy group and went towards the derelict factory, quarrelling on the way about which was the best building for hiding horses, and how impossible it was to smuggle a horse the length and breadth of London, especially in the teeth of Sussworth and the SBG, not to mention all the other dangers too, like Borrible-snatchers and undiscovered tribes of Rumbles who might be lurking in unexplored parks.

Sydney refused to budge from the pavement. She put her arms round Sam's neck and tears ran down her cheeks. 'I'm not scared,' she said to Chalotte who had stayed by her side. 'I'll take him all the bloody way on my own, you see if I don't'

Chalotte laughed, really laughed. 'You mustn't be daft,' she said. 'You know what they're like, that's just the talk talking.'

'But listen to them – arguing, shouting – they can't agree about anything.'

'But the Borrible who doesn't quarrel is no Borrible,' said Chalotte. 'Look, I wasn't keen on going to look for Sam in the beginning, was I? But now we've got him, well, that's different. Like Twilight said, he's one of us, so we'll just have to do something about him, won't we? It's a rule.' She grinned and nudged Sydney with her elbow. 'Besides, there's no rush mate; it's a long way to Neasden, a very long way.' And without another word she took Sam's halter from her friend's hand and led the horse across the road, following the others.

BOOK THREE

Across the Dark Metropolis

I

Sergeant Hanks of the Metropolitan Police and second in command of the Special Borrible Group sat on a chair outside the office of the District Assistant Commissioner and picked his nose in a state of unalloyed rapture. He had excavated very successfully for ten minutes in the left nostril and he was now delving in the right one. As the curved nail of his index finger dug into something soft and spongy his eyes closed with the joy of an exquisite physical pleasure, and when, at last, the moist and luxuriant bogey was pulled reluctantly away from its tenacious root and coaxed out into the light, Hanks just half opened a single eye and examined his trophy with a close and professional interest.

'Hmm,' he said, 'first class that one, looks like a well-fed whelk.' And he stuck it under his chair and crossed his fat ankles in utter contentment. This was the life.

Inside the office, Sergeant Hanks's superior, Inspector Sussworth, was not enjoying himself. Quite the contrary. He was standing to attention before a large leather-topped desk, his lips tightly clenched and his postage stamp of a moustache humming with indignation. Sussworth was in serious trouble and the District Assistant Commissioner was making sure that he knew it.

'It's not good enough,' said the DAC, 'just not good enough. Two months ago I was assured that you had these Borribles all cooped up in Wandsworth. No way out, eh? That's what you said. And the horse, eh? Where are they now?'

Inspector Sussworth opened his mouth to answer but shut it again immediately as the DAC held up his hand for silence.

'Escaped, that's what, escaped.' The DAC's voice was pointed and half-transparent, like shards of bone china. He was elegantly turned out in a well-cut suit of dark grey and a shirt that was as crisp as newly fallen snow. His tie indicated, discreetly, that he had once been connected with an exclusive regiment, and his shoes shone so brilliantly that it was impossible to tell what colour they were.

He examined one of those shoes for a second, on the end of a stiffly straight leg, and, satisfied with the sheen, he got to his feet, rising easily from his swivel chair. 'You see, Sussworth,' he continued, 'I gave you the command of the finest body of men to be found in any police force in the world, in the world mark you, and all you have managed to achieve is a spectacular failure.' The DAC snorted and began to pace the olive-green carpet that covered the wide expanses of his office floor.

Sussworth gazed out of the window and down on to the jumbled skyline of London. It was wet out there, and cold. It had stopped raining but only so that it could start again presently. Only midway through the afternoon and the office lights were already gleaming across the dark from a thousand windows in a hundred skyscrapers.

Sussworth sighed. London was his patch, all of it. He sighed again. It was the Borribles' patch too; the whole town was lousy with them. At that very moment Borribles were out on the streets stealing stuff like nobody's business; and if they weren't stealing they were idling and lounging about in empty houses; activities that Sussworth had sworn to stop.

The DAC returned from his stroll and stood once again behind the desk, facing the inspector. He was tall and languid, the DAC, and his face was well bred and haughty and pink, like a judge's in a wig. He sighed too, deeply, as if exhausted by being alive; the road of his life had been strewn with fools.

'All you have done, Sussworth,' he said, 'is to smash up some Transit vans on Eel Brook Common, get some twenty of your men injured and invalided out of the force, and then allowed these Borrible ringleaders to escape.' He raised his hand as Sussworth took a breath. '"Safe and sound, sir," you said. "Safe and sound in Wandsworth. They can't get away." Can't get away, eh? Not only did they get away but they got away with a horse. Dash it all man, a horse! It escaped from your own police station. Why, you were the laughin' stock of everyone.'

Sussworth fidgeted on his feet but made no attempt to answer.

'I admit,' went on the DAC, setting off on another stroll, 'that you've captured a few Borribles and clipped their ears, but you couldn't call them important, they aren't the chaps we want. Concentrate on the ringleaders.'

Sussworth twitched his neck. He could not bear to stand still for so long. He needed to be on the go; stamping, turning, marching.

'Don't you realize, Sussworth, that the more you let these Borribles get away with things the more they undermine society? We can't allow it. It is our responsibility to see that society stays where it is. We can't have Borribles doin' what they like, livin' as they like, goin' where they like. You must find this gang of Borribles and eliminate them. Above all you must find their horse, which seems to act as some kind of mascot, and you will turn it into catsmeat. If you fail, Sussworth, then I'm afraid I shall be obliged to hand your job over to Chief Superintendent Birdlime of C Division. He's an up and comin' chap, you know, and as keen as mustard.'

Sussworth was allowed to speak at last: 'I've tried everything sir, but London's such a huge place. It is not plain sailing to apprehend these malcontents.'

The DAC gave Sussworth a pitying smile from the fireplace, where he had propped himself at an angle against the wall. 'My dear Sussworth,' he said, 'it is your duty to apprehend them, and once apprehended to make sure they have no chance to get away again. If the old methods are not successful you must try new methods; you must be crafty, sly and even evil if necessary. Do you think that Caesar and Alexander got to the top by playing the white man? Think, Sussworth, think. You must infiltrate Borrible culture; you need a fifth column, spies, traitors. Do anythin' to achieve your end . . . but don't tell me about it. Inform me of your success, but not how you do it.'

Sussworth's moustache began to twitch in anger but he restrained himself. He nodded vigorously. 'Yes sir, infiltrate, bribe, corrupt. Yes sir.'

The DAC ambled back to his seat and lowered his body into it. He placed his elbows on the desk and laced the fingers of his right hand with those of his left. 'Don't you realize, Sussworth, that life is a game of snakes and ladders? If we are successful, you and I, there is promotion in this. We would both be up the ladder. I could be Commissioner this time next year and you . . . Well, for a man of your energy and intelligence, the sky's the limit, the sky.'

The DAC smiled wisely and rotated his chair at a leisurely speed so that he could look out through the plate glass of his window. The storm clouds, heavy with rain, had lowered themselves down to a dim horizon, and the endless confusion of London roofs and buildings was fading into one dull tone of dark blue.

The DAC stretched his arms. 'Winter's comin',' he said as if the statement were philosophy, 'and that can only help. Not so many people on the streets; the Borribles will be easier to spot. It's up to you, Susswort, complete annihilation of this criminal band of Borribles, nothing else will satisfy me. Don't let me hear anythin' but good news, do you follow? Eh? Or it will be bad news for you. Birdlime is waitin', Birdlime is waitin'.'

'Yes sir,' said Sussworth. 'Of course, sir.' He stood hesitant, not knowing if he had been dismissed or not. He waited for the DAC to swivel round from the window, but the DAC remained gazing into the darkening panorama spread out below him, watching the lights shine ever brighter.

Sussworth decided to leave. His moustache twitched and twirled, and he saluted and turned in one nervous movement and marched quickly over the carpet towards the polished oak door of the office. He opened it and passed through, closing it reverentially behind him, the muscles of his face rigid with hate.

*

Inspector Sussworth seized his hands behind his back and strutted between the door and the window of his office like Admiral Nelson on his quarterdeck. Sergeant Hanks had hooked his large and wobbly buttocks on the desk, folded his arms over his egg-stained tunic and was cocking his fleshy ears to scoop up every word his superior was about to utter. Both men were in the SBG headquarters, Micklethwaite Road, Fulham.

'That was a high-powered conference at Scotland Yard,' Sussworth said, 'very high-powered.'

Hanks loosened his fat lips and smiled blankly. At the same time he pushed his hand into a coat pocket and drew out a bar of chocolate. 'I'm glad to hear it, sir,' he said. 'Care for some fruit and nut?'

Sussworth waved his hand impatiently and spun on his heel through a hundred and eighty degrees, about ninety degrees more than he had intended, and was somewhat surprised to find himself facing the window overlooking the street. 'There is more to life than fruit and nut,' he said, his voice sombre. 'We have problems, Hanks, vast problems.'

Hanks looked at the inspector's back and shoved half the chocolate into his mouth, salivating so freely that the moisture dribbled down his chin. It was a brown colour flecked with chewed raisins.

'The DAC and I,' continued the inspector, 'have decided that the situation, *re* the Borribles, is critical and chronic. A new initiative must be implemented. We are going to concentrate our efforts on the main criminal gang, the gang from Eel Brook Common. Those ragamuffins must be apprehended and their ears clipped without delay. Their hideouts must be demolished. They've got to be made to behave like everyone else, earn money like everyone else and grow up like everyone else. Society is our responsibility, Hanks.'

'It is indeed, sir,' agreed Hanks, masticating slowly, lips smacking.

'There is a slackness in the ranks, Hanks. Both the DAC and I had a long discussion about this. The Borribles are undermining the pillars of society and when that happens those pillars topple. Freedom leads to anarchy. They must conform to law and order.'

'They must conform indeed,' said Hanks. He lifted his weight from the desk and waded to a food cabinet which stood just outside the door of the office. He opened this cupboard and, taking out a roll, he cut it in half, buttered it and then spread it with thick honey.

'I likes this stuff,' he announced, and squeezed the roll between his teeth so that the honey oozed over his chin and on to his tunic.

Sussworth ignored the remark and performed a reverse turn quickstep across the room and around the desk. He sat down and then got up again immediately as if he had sat in something wet and nasty. His expression hardened and his moustache twitched from side to side, matching the movements of his feet.

'The men will have to be reprimanded,' he said, 'and then retrained. We have to get those Borribles and above all that horse. This is a crisis. We must think of something new: bribery, corruption.'

'That's not new, sir.'

'There's promotion in the offing, Hanks. You will become an

inspector; I shall rise to DAC and the DAC will get a knighthood. Imagine the glory, Hanks. Knighthoods. Sir Sergeant Hanks. Lord Sussworth of Fulham. The mind boggles.'

'Boggles,' said Hanks.

Sussworth raised a hand to his forehead and fell into his chair. 'This is our last chance. If we fail we will be demoted to the ranks and Birdlime will be in. We have to think of some means of penetrating the Borrible infrastructure.'

'Super-narks!'

'Exactly.'

'What we need is someone on the inside,' said Hanks. 'That's what we need.'

Sussworth got out of his chair again, stamped both feet at once and strode to the window. His hands, still behind his back, made a determined attempt to strangle one another. 'Precisely,' he said, and emotion steamed out of his ears like there were two kettles boiling in his head.

Hanks stood in the middle of the room, lifted a finger to his nose and screwed it into a nostril just as far as it would go, about the second knuckle. 'What we want,' he said, 'is a regiment of bloody dwarfs.'

Silence slid down over the room like a tipper-truck load of wet cement. Sussworth suddenly crouched and turned from the window very slowly, inch by inch, pointing a rigid finger at his subordinate who continued to stand, all innocent, grappling with a bogey. Sussworth laughed the laugh of contentment.

'Ha! Hanks, ha! I have just had the most brilliant idea.' Sussworth advanced towards his sergeant, still crouching and still pointing. 'Did you know I was top of my year at Hendon Police College? My brain is a computer that never stops computing, taking in information and storing it until the day when, compressed by the white heat of necessity . . . You Reeker! Out comes the desired answer. In other words, what we need is a regiment of dwarfs.'

A look of puzzlement wandered over Hanks's face and he removed the finger from his nose without even looking at it. 'I just said that,' he said. He took a teapot from the cupboard and ladled some tea into it. 'I could have sworn I said that.'

Sussworth straightened his back and dropped his pointing arm. He jigged around to the rear of the desk and sat down. 'Don't be foolish, Hanks,' he said. 'I do not want to see you change the habits of a lifetime, habits that have stood you in good stead. Your job is not inception but implementation.'

'Oh,' said Hanks, and he flicked on the switch that controlled the electric kettle.

'That's why I am in my position and you are in yours, Sergeant,' said Sussworth as prim as a parson. 'Now listen to me. We shall place advertisements, discreetly, in the newspapers, especially the trade papers – *The Stage*, *The Circus and Sideshow*, *Fun-Fair Weekly* – all of them, offering employment to young adult midgets and dwarfs. Got that, Hanks? We only want the young-looking ones.'

Hanks unplugged the boiling kettle and poured its contents into the teapot.

'We want midgets from all walks of life,' said Sussworth. 'We'll train them and get them ready; we'll tell them all about Borrible customs, everything. They'll steal and live in broken houses like Borribles and they'll know all the proverbs, just like Borribles. They will infiltrate, insinuate and penetrate.'

Hanks sucked at his tea and made a noise like water going down a drain in the middle of a storm. 'Dwarfs don't have pointed ears,' he observed. 'Borribles do.' The sergeant smiled like a quicksand smiling at the sound of approaching footsteps; there was no answer to that.

Sussworth banged the desk and stamped the floor. 'You can't beat me,' he said. 'Honours at Hendon, that's what I got. We'll have special plastic ears fabricated, pointed, and we'll clip them on.'

Hanks's vast stomach rolled under his stained tunic like water in a balloon. 'I don't think that will work, sir. If a Borrible gets suspicious of one of your spies and pulls at his ears, why, then the lugholes would come off and bye-bye dwarfs. The Borribles would have their guts for garters.' He handed the inspector a mugful of tea, hot, black and strong.

Sussworth sipped. 'Difficulties,' he said, 'only exist to be overcome by minds like mine. If clips won't achieve our purpose then we shall affix the ears with superglue; nothing gets that off, I can assure you, however a Borrible might pull at it.'

'Superglue,' said Hanks. 'But them dwarfs'd never get the ears unstuck again. I can't see them standing for that . . . I wouldn't.'

'You are not an impoverished midget,' said Sussworth looking closely at his fingernails, 'except in a metaphorical and figurative way, of course. Given enough cash, the human species can be induced to indulge in almost any activity. Everything has been and will be done for money.'

'Not Borribles,' said Hanks. He pursed his lips, peeved.

'That has always been a problem,' agreed Sussworth, 'but the dwarfs we are intending to bribe are not Borribles. I shall train them to a peak of accomplishment, and furthermore I will have one in every market and when those Borribles move I shall know it before they do. We'll have their ears clipped and they'll have to grow up and old like the rest of us . . . and work too. As for that moth-eaten horse of theirs, it will end up as tinned chunks of steak for cats to eat. This time it's curtains, Hanks, curtains.' And the two police officers smirked and raised their tea mugs and clinked them together.

'We'll call it Operation Catsmeat,' went on Sussworth, 'that's what we'll call it,' and he was so pleased with himself that he burst into an impromptu song on the spot. A jaunty little jig it was and the melody of it made the inspector strut and hop in the most energetic fashion.

'It's a catsmeat operation
With a limited objective –
Oh I'd like to tin the nation
But for now we'll be selective.

'Just the horse'll do for starters,
And I'll show you what my wit is
When I have the guts for garters
While its meat is feeding kitties.

'It's a catsmeat operation,
Starting small then growing bigger.
First the horse – and then my mission
I shall prosecute with vigour.

'All the anti-social sinners
Who are ruining Great Britain
I'll have processed into dinners,
Shiny tins for cats and kittens.

'I'll make catsmeat of the shirkers
And malingering midday drinkers,
Of the disobedient workers
And the independent thinkers.

'I'll make catsmeat of the steppers
Out of line, the by-law breakers,
And of all the social lepers
Who are punks and trouble-makers.

'Every dissident defaulter,
Be he Borrible or not,
I shall apprehend and alter –
I'll make catsmeat of the lot!'

At the end of this song Hanks grinned and wagged his head in astonishment. 'Wonderful, sir,' he said, 'absolutely wonderful.' He grinned again and poured tea into his mouth.

As he did so a squall of rain rattled against the walls of the house and Sussworth scuttled to the window. He attempted to peer out into the night but it was as dark as dark in the street and the light from a nearby lamp post hardly fell as far as the pavement.

Sussworth danced with glee. 'Look at that cold rain,' he crowed. 'I wouldn't want to be a Borrible in a broken-down old house right now, Hanks, not right now or ever.'

Hanks laughed. 'Winter's coming,' he said, 'a long hard winter.'

'It will be for the Borribles,' said Sussworth, his moustache moving from side to side like a windscreen wiper. 'A long hard winter for Borribles. I'll drink another cup of tea to that.'

'Certainly, sir,' said the sergeant, and he propelled his huge body across the room in the direction of the kettle.

*

Bingo Borrible pulled his woollen hat down over his ears, turned up the collar of his combat jacket and heaved himself up to the top of the railway embankment. The wind was vicious; the rain stung his face like nails from a catapult. He twisted his head to look behind him. 'Come on, Stonks,' he said. 'There's a couple of trucks in the siding.'

There was a scrabbling noise from below and out of the stormy swirling of the dark rain the head of Stonks appeared. Stonks was big for a Borrible and with a face that was slow to let you know what it was thinking. For all that he was well liked by those who knew him; trusted to the death and as strong as a man. Behind Stonks came Twilight, the Bangladeshi from Whitechapel.

'Well damn me,' he said. 'After that summer, this winter; I need a new raincoat.'

'First thing to do,' interrupted Bingo, 'is to find some food for Sam. He only had a couple of carrots this morning.'

'You think there's anything in those trucks?' asked Stonks. He looked behind and below towards the sparse lighting of Battersea High Street. 'It's a bit exposed up here.'

'Don't worry,' answered Bingo. 'Someone told me there was a load of cattle cake knocking about. I'll go over to the trucks while you keep watch.'

Bingo eased himself over the edge of the embankment and, keeping low, crossed the tracks and went towards the goods siding. Soon Stonks and Twilight had lost sight of their companion, but after a minute or two they heard his call and went to join him.

'What's in there?' asked Stonks. He stood by one of the huge wagon wheels, Twilight beside him.

'Not sure, exactly,' said Bingo. His voice came from inside the truck and his words were ripped apart by the wind. 'There's some stuff in plastic sacks. I had a quick glim with me torch and it seems to be some sort of animal grub.'

'Throw one down,' said Stonks. 'I'll carry it back to the factory.'

'And another,' added Twilight. 'That'll keep Sam going for a few days.'

As the second sack hit the ground there was a loud cry from below them on the far side of the railway line. 'Stay where you are,' roared a man's voice, 'you're under arrest.'

'Railway police,' said Twilight. 'Come on, Bingo, out of that truck.' The Bangladeshi pulled a catapult from his belt, loaded it and fired a shot in the general direction of the shouts. He fired another shot and the voice was raised again. Others joined it.

'You can't get away, we've got men on both sides of the track.'

Bingo jumped to the ground. 'They're lying,' he said, 'otherwise they wouldn't have told us. Come on, into the High Street.'

'What about this cattle cake?' asked Stonks, steadfast as ever. 'The horse is hungry.'

'We can't take it now,' said Twilight, 'it'll slow us down.'

Stonks stooped and picked up a sack and threw it over his shoulder. 'I'll give it a try,' he said.

That was the end of that discussion. The three Borribles turned and ran, stumbling in the dark down their side of the embankment. At the bottom they were brought up against the back wall of the yards that ran behind the shops of Battersea High Street. Bingo had been right; there were no police lying in ambush there. They stood still for a moment listening. The voices were above them now, up by the trucks.

'Over we go,' said Bingo. He joined his hands to make a step and, placing a foot on it, Twilight levered himself to the top of the wall. As soon as he was there Stonks and Bingo slung the sack up to him and Twilight guided it over to the far side where it landed with a gentle thud. Stonks then climbed the wall in his turn, stretched out an arm and pulled Bingo up next to him.

For a while all three of them sat on the wall and held their breath; listening as the shouts and whistles of the police diminished in the distance; listening to make sure that no one lay in wait for them below. They sat with patience, not moving, not speaking. They were used to it; in that kind of darkness you never knew who was near, ready to get you. And while they waited the smell of the back yard rose in their nostrils: cats' pee and concrete, mildew and dead dog.

When ten minutes had passed and the whole area was quiet again the three Borribles slipped off the wall and Stonks hoisted the sack of cattle feed on to his shoulder. 'It's all right,' he said. 'We can get back to the factory now.'

The factory was at the end of Battersea High Street near the junction with Vicarage Crescent, and by keeping to the shadows and climbing over back walls the Borribles arrived without further trouble. To the side of the factory, lying between it and the railway embankment, was a piece of wasteland littered with rubbish and debris. The Borribles crossed this and came to a large door made from wide and heavy planks.

Bingo halted here and gave the Borrible knock: one long, two short, one long, scraping his knuckles. After a moment the door eased open on freshly oiled hinges and a white smudge appeared in the dark. It was the face of Sydney. 'Well,' she said.

'Bingo, Twilight and Stonks,' said Bingo.

Sydney grunted and opened the door just enough for the three Borribles to enter. As soon as they had done so she closed it again. It was darker in than out.

She asked, 'Did you get anything?'

Stonks patted the sack on his shoulder. 'Half hundredweight of cattle cake,' he said. 'That should do it.'

'Good,' said Sydney. 'Go and feed him then.' And they heard her step to the nearest window to resume her watch.

The three Borribles moved away in the blackness, their feet quite accustomed to the uneven floor and its covering of rubble. When they reached the end of the building they went through a hatch in a wall, round a corner and then down a wide ramp which led to a deep cellar.

This cellar was their home. The factory had lain empty for years now and was really too large and draughty for Borribles. Borribles normally prefer small rooms because they are easier to keep warm, easier to furnish. This time the Adventurers had not had a great deal of choice. On their return from Wandsworth some two months before, escaping from Inspector Sussworth and the SBG, they had been obliged to take cover forthwith and also to find a place big enough to hide Sam the horse in. The factory had fitted their bill exactly.

At the bottom of the ramp the Borribles doubled back on themselves and walked to the far end of the cellar, where a solitary electric bulb dangled from a frayed length of flex and gave a weak light. There, in a large space hollowed out under the highest part of the ramp, Stonks threw down the sack and, kneeling beside it, drew his knife and slit the plastic open.

'Looks all right,' he said. 'Come on, Sam, try this.'

A small undistinguished horse, half brown half black as if it didn't really know what colour it wanted to be, stirred in a corner of the cellar and miserably shook its head. This was Sam.

He came forward and dropped his nose into the open sack and chewed upon what lay there. He did not like the taste of it and after only the smallest of samples he blew through his nostrils and backed away.

'Oh, Sam,' said Twilight, anxiety making one of his eyebrows twitch up his forehead, 'you've got to eat; you're not looking well at all.'

Bingo lifted a bucket of clean water. He swirled it round so that it made a sloshing noise. 'Perhaps he's thirsty,' he said.

As Bingo spoke another light was switched on and showed two or three bunks to one side of the cellar and three or four mattresses on the floor as well. Under the archway of the ramp the Borribles had made a kind of rough sitting room with two or three wrecked armchairs, their stuffings and springs visible. There was also a long table made from scaffolding planks supported on saw-horses. Stools had been improvised from orange boxes and barrels. Dirty blankets and torn cushions gave what little comfort there was.

Bingo looked up as the light came on. Faces appeared from the shadows. Knocker threw his blanket back and rose, fully dressed, from his bed on the floor. He came to stand with the others, close to Sam.

'He doesn't look well, does he?' he said.

Chalotte propped herself up on her elbow and looked out from her bunk. 'He's not getting any fresh air,' she said. 'That's what he needs, and exercise.' There was an orange under her pillow. She pulled it out and began to peel it.

There was a loud yawn next and then a burst of swearing and Vulge emerged from under a pile of blankets and sacks. 'Well,' he said, 'as long as the lights are on and you're going to start chatting I might as well make us all a pot of tea.' He filled a kettle from a tap in the wall and plugged it in to boil. 'What time is it, anyway?'

Chalotte looked at her watch. 'It's three o'clock,' she said. 'In the morning.'

Napoleon Boot was next awake. 'Strewth,' he said. 'What the old Mother 'ubbard's going on here?'

'We got some cattle cake for Sam,' said Bingo. 'Do horses like cattle cake?'

There was silence for a while. Everyone watched Vulge make the tea and when it was ready Knocker took a mugful and sat at the table. 'Who's on guard?' he said.

'Sid and Torrey,' answered Vulge. 'I'll take 'em a drink.' He scooped up two mugs and walked off into the darkness, limping slightly.

'I'm worried about that horse,' said Knocker between sips, 'very worried. He looks unhealthy. Look at his coat, half brown and half black; he looks like a carpet.'

'It's the dye that Knibbsie put on him,' said Chalotte. 'The black's wearing out.'

'He eats the carrots we get,' said Bingo, 'and the apples and the cabbages.'

'Course he does,' said Twilight, 'but he's not a bleedin' goat, is he? He needs hay and that.'

'It's the lack of fresh air.' That was Sydney's voice and everyone turned to look at her. She had just come into the light from the bottom of the ramp. Her face was lined with worry. All the Adventurers were fond of the horse but Sydney loved him. For her Sam was something special.

Orococco dropped from a top bunk without a sound, took a cup of tea and went to sit by Knocker. 'How long we been hiding now,' he asked, 'about two or three months?'

'Long enough,' said Napoleon with more than his usual bitterness. 'Long enough for a long summer to turn into a long winter.'

There was another silence as each Adventurer thought his or her own thoughts. Only a few weeks had brought them to this feeling of imprisonment; it was like being under siege. They had returned from Wandsworth in such high spirits too, with Ben the tramp and Knibbsie the stableman. They had only taken refuge in the factory as a temporary measure, hiding until the hue and cry had died down, waiting until it was safe to take Sam to Neasden.

But things had gone wrong, seriously wrong. The search by the SBG had not slackened as the Borribles had hoped and they found their movements terribly restricted. They were hemmed in on every side. There were policemen on every bridge across the River Thames. There were policemen disguised as costermongers. There were policemen guarding every crossroads with their SBG vans circling round and round, like carrion crows. On York Road and at Prince's Head groups of Woollies stopped children at random and inspected their ears. Any stray Borrible who was discovered had his ears clipped as soon as he or she had been questioned. It was even difficult to steal things in the market, the only source of food, and feeding Sam was the biggest problem of all. The Borribles were forced to move about almost entirely at night when there was less food to be had. The danger of capture was always with them and seemed to be increasing every day. They felt they were being strangled. They had become downhearted and homesick for the old Borrible life of independence and freedom; they were too dispirited even to quarrel.

Chalotte swung her legs out of bed and threw her orange-skin into a corner of the cellar; she wiped her mouth with the back of her hand.

'It's been two months too long,' she said. 'We've got to get out of this place and find somewhere quiet to spend the winter. Sussworth knows we're here or hereabouts and the longer we stay the more chance we have of being caught. We won't do Sam any good if we've all had our ears clipped and are growing up like nice little boys and girls in some foster home. After a few months we wouldn't even remember Sam. The memory goes, they say, when you've had your ears done.'

'What if we left Sam just for a while,' suggested Napoleon, 'got out for the winter and then captured him back later?'

No one answered. Knocker looked at Chalotte and then both of them looked at Sydney. It was she who spoke for the horse.

Sydney sat hunched on a barrel; she did not raise her head when she spoke and her voice was low and sad.

'Look,' she said, 'I know you've done more than enough for Sam . . . all that trouble with Spiff and the fighting in the sewers and the digging in the mine. I thought it was all over when we got back here. I thought I would simply take Sam back to Neasden and that would be that. Perhaps Napoleon's right; there is no point in us all getting caught. Perhaps you should all go home until next spring and I'll stay with Sam, keep feeding him and hope I don't get caught.'

'It's not that, Sid,' said Chalotte, 'it's Sam. He's been cooped up in this cellar for two months; it ain't healthy. He'll die if we don't get him out.'

Sydney lowered her head into her hands. 'And so will we, one way or the other. Sussworth's got us on the run.'

Knocker got to his feet and moved from the dark into the light. 'We can't carry on like this,' he said, then he quoted from the *Borrible Book of Proverbs*: '"A Borrible who does not live like a Borrible is not a Borrible." We've got to go somewhere else.'

Orococco poured himself another mug of tea. 'We've got to think positive,' he said. 'First, Sussworth doesn't know where we are, not for sure he don't. Second, it's coming on winter. It'll be dark at three o'clock in the afternoon in another month or so, and it rains most of the time; people keeps their heads down. They won't notice us once we're out of the danger zone.'

'And I suppose,' said Napoleon with the old sneer in his voice, 'they won't notice a thumping great horse walking along behind yer. What you going to tell 'em, eh? It's just a Great Dane with a big head?'

'We owe him our lives,' cried Sydney, 'and don't you forget it, Napoleon Boot Wendle.'

'It won't make sense,' said Twilight, 'if we have to give up our freedom and there's no guarantee of Sam getting his. That would be daft.'

'It would be,' agreed Chalotte. 'That is why we have to be crafty, we have to win this one. That horse is important. We have to get it to Neasden so that Sydney can look after it and so that we can go home and lead normal lives.'

'Neasden,' said Napoleon. 'You realize where that is? It's the other side of the bloody moon, that is. And every inch of the way there'll be Woollies, Rumbles, Borrible-snatchers and Inspector Sussworth and Sergeant Hanks and the boys in blue from the SBG. Why Neasden?'

Sydney stood, put her hands on her hips and faced up to the Wendle. 'I tell you why Neasden,' she said, 'because I live there and I can look after Sam, and because there's an old bloke who lives in these acres and acres of waste ground by the railway line. Adults hardly go there; they think this bloke's daft in the head. They calls him Mad Mick, but he ain't mad, not by a long chalk. He saves horses and donkeys from the knacker's yard, won't let them be slaughtered. There's some people up there who give him grub and hay and straw and stuff. They throw things out the train windows on their way to work. If Sam was there with all the other horses, Sussworth would never find him and I could see him whenever I wanted . . . That's why Neasden, that's why.'

Knocker raised a hand. 'The way I see it is this – the worst thing will be getting out of Battersea because this is the place that Sussworth is watching the hardest. If we could get a few miles away, take it in slow stages, well . . . we might do it. As long as we travelled in the dark we'd only have to hide during the daylight hours and there's only about six or seven of them in the winter.'

'We could head away from the river,' suggested Stonks, 'just at first, because we know old Sussworth has got the bridges guarded; he always does that.'

Twilight jumped to his feet and looked at the circle of faces. 'It's a challenge,' he said. 'It'll be a trek right across London. A second name. I shall call myself Twilight Trekker when I get back from Neasden.'

Knocker wagged a finger at the Bangladeshi. 'We've all had enough adventure and glory to last a Borrible lifetime,' he said. 'You take it easy.'

Chalotte lowered her face so that Knocker should not see her smile. How Knocker had changed since she had first met him. Then he had been nothing more than a brash, self-centred Borrible, wanting to win more names than anyone else in creation. Now he was changed out of all recognition; experience had altered him.

'We'll have to get organized,' said Orococco, 'quick too.'

'Yes,' said Vulge, 'we'll need lots of things for a long trek like this, especially in the cold of winter. Warm clothes, raincoats, boots.

'Torches,' said Twilight.

'New catapults,' added Napoleon, 'and bandoliers; two each, carrying forty stones, times ten, that makes a firepower of four hundred rounds. Ace!'

'And some food for Sam,' said Sydney, looking worried. And with that everyone laughed, stopped, and then laughed again because the laughter was so good to hear.

Knocker tilted his head to attract Napoleon's attention. After the long months they had spent digging together in Flinthead's mine a great friendship had grown up between these two, replacing the ancient hatred and rivalry they had once felt for each other. 'I have an idea,' he said, 'a little scouting expedition to find a safe road out of here, for us and the horse. Will you come with me?'

The Wendle nodded. 'I'll come,' he said.

'I will come too,' said Stonks. 'You might need a hand.'

'That's settled then,' said Vulge. 'While you're doing that we'll get what we need from the shops.'

'You know,' said Orococco, 'it won't be easy, getting to Neasden. I've got a feeling that it will make those other adventures of ours look about as dangerous as a game of tiddlywinks.'

2

After three days and nights Knocker, Napoleon and Stonks returned from their scouting trip feeling dirty and tired but full of optimism.

'We found a way,' explained Knocker, 'dangerous, but at least it's in the opposite direction to where Sussworth will be waiting.'

The others had been busy too. Disguised in stolen Sinjen School uniforms they had managed to avoid the SBG patrols in Falcon Road, and over the same three-day period had brought back to the factory most of the things they needed for the Great Neasden Expedition. There was even a coloured blanket for Sam and Sydney had made a point of stealing some boot polish to rub into the horse's coat to make the brown patches disappear. Once more he was stained a deep glossy black all over.

Orococco banged his thigh with a hand when he saw this. 'I dunno, man,' he said. 'That's the first time I ever saw shoes being polished before they was made.' But he laughed out loud when he'd said it and patted Sam on the neck saying that he couldn't resist a joke, however bad it might be.

It was just as well for the Borribles that they had decided to undertake these preparations quite so soon and it was also fortunate that they were almost ready to leave, because before long events were taken out of their hands.

*

Just before dawn, about a week after Knocker's sortie to find an escape route, Chalotte and Vulge – they had both been on guard – came rushing down the ramp and ran from bed to bed to awaken their sleeping comrades.

'Quick,' said Chalotte, shaking Knocker on to the floor. 'On your feet. There's some workmen coming, they've pushed the fence over, there's a bulldozer, they're going to knock the place down.'

In a few minutes everyone was dressed in their expedition gear, rucksacks of provisions on their backs and bandoliers of stones across their chests. They switched out the lights and gathered together with Sam under the archways of the ramp, waiting, hardly daring to breathe.

From upstairs there came a great deal of noise: the rumble of the bulldozer, the smashing of glass, the banging of sledgehammers and the shouts of men. Two of the workers came stamping down the cellar ramp in hobnail boots, talking loudly. Halfway down they stopped; it was too dark.

'It's as black as a Paki's earhole,' said a voice. 'Wonder if there's anything worthwhile down here?'

'Nah,' came an answer, 'it's just the basement; we'll be filling it up with 'ardcore and then cementing it over a foot thick to make the footings. Won't take us long. They said demolish everything and we're going to.'

The footsteps began to retreat upstairs. The second voice continued issuing instructions. 'But that can wait,' it said. 'Cup of tea first. Get those tiles off and rattle 'em into the back of the lorry, then we'll bash the walls to bits.'

All day the Borribles stood crowded together with Sam beside them and the noise of destruction went on around and above their heads. Huge lumps of concrete and brick toppled to the cellar floor. The beds were smashed into the ground by huge rafters and steel girders. Window frames and door lintels fell thick and fast. Only the sturdiness of the brick ramp saved the Borribles from being crushed to death like the victims of an earthquake. Dust rose and clotted their nostrils and lungs; they coughed and spat; they felt sick in their stomachs with the dirt and some of them vomited on the earthen floor. And all through the day the tide of rubble rose higher and they began to fear that if the work continued much longer they would be buried alive, unable to shift the weight of the debris above them, perishing of thirst and hunger before the expedition had begun.

It was not until the light filtering in from outside grew less that their spirits even dared to lift, and they allowed themselves to hope that the navvies would stop work at dusk and not pursue their activities into the night with the aid of floodlights. Their luck held. Towards the end of the day there was one enormous crash, like a bomb falling, and the cellar and its rubbish shook and the dust swirled up like a tornado. The whole length of the west wall of the factory had been demolished with one blow from a huge iron weight swinging on the arm of a crane. But that destruction was the last of the day; silence settled over the ruins and brought the choking dust down to rest with it.

The Borribles waited for a good hour, until it was fully dark and they were sure that everyone had left the site. Then they moved. It was not easy to free themselves. Under the ramp they had only the little space that had saved their lives. Around them was rubble higher than their shoulders, lumps of it as heavy as a hundredweight or more. Their first task would be to pull bricks and mortar away with their bare hands, making a slope for Sam, enabling the horse to climb to the top of the debris and then on to what was left of the original ramp and so up to ground level.

Stonks whistled through his teeth and rolled up his sleeves. 'Well come on then,' he said. 'There's only one way out of here, and if we don't go tonight we'll be foundations tomorrow.'

It took three hours of hard labour before the Adventurers managed to clear a path for Sam. Once they had pulled and shoved him as far as the ground floor they collected their belongings and then gathered together in the factory yard, a yard which was now full of lorries and mechanical diggers. Light spilled in from Vicarage Crescent and down from the railway embankment. It showed them all that was left of the factory that had been their refuge.

The roof had gone and the first and second floors had been smashed and thrown down to fill the cellar and litter the ground; tiles were scattered everywhere and cracked underfoot like ice on puddles. There was metal piping and electric wire, shattered glass gleaming like precious stones and ragged piles of broken bricks. Of the structure itself nothing remained but three gaunt walls, all punched through with shapeless gaps for windows and doors; a murdered face where mouth and eyes had been.

'Oh what a shame,' said Chalotte. 'Just look at what they've done.'

The Borribles were indeed sad. The factory had only been their home for a couple of months but they had made the cellar comfortable and they had felt reasonably safe there. Now once again they were vagabonds. Who knew where they would sleep that night; who knew where they would sleep for the next hundred nights?

Knocker broke the spell. 'It's no good standing like this,' he said. 'We've got to cover a lot of ground before morning.'

'Which way then?' asked Torreycanyon. 'You haven't told us yet.'

Knocker raised an arm above his head. 'Up there,' he said, 'along the railway. It's the branch line that does Olympia to Clapham Junction. I don't think the SBG are watching it.'

'What about trains, though?' asked Orococco. 'I don't want to be squashed into redcurrant jam.' He threw two tied-together sacks of cow cake across Sam's back.

'There's only four trains a day,' said Napoleon, 'we checked the timetable in the station.' He also threw two bags on to the horse's back.

'Hey,' said Sydney, 'why has he got to carry that? Is it something for him to eat?'

Napoleon smiled in a way that meant he wasn't going to change his mind. 'Sydney,' he said, 'we are about to leave on the greatest trek ever undertaken by Borribles. With or without the horse the odds are nasty. I'm a Wendle, I don't like nasty odds. In those bags are a few hundred more stones for the catapults, I'm sure Sam won't mind.'

There was no more discussion. The Adventurers picked their way across the debris of the factory yard, passed through a gap in a fence and faced the steep slope of the railway embankment. It was not an easy climb and the trip began badly. The sides of the embankment were covered in sharp, slippery shale; stones that cut into the hands and knees of the Borribles as they struggled under their burdens to gain the summit. For Sam it was even worse. He did his best to reach the top with his friends but it was too difficult for his hard shiny hooves and he fell several times and scraped his legs badly as the Borribles tried to push and pull him upwards with their injured hands.

'If we make much more noise,' said Torreycanyon, 'we'll have Sussworth here to help us on our way.'

'Wait,' said Chalotte and she took a thick coil of nylon rope from her shoulder. 'I'll tie one end of this round Sam's chest; the rest of you get on the other end, go to the top and walk down the other side, pull like the dickens, and Sam will walk up this side.'

There was no argument; they tried it and it worked. Five minutes later Sam was standing on the railway line and Chalotte was coiling her rope with hand and elbow, listening as Knocker explained in whispered tones how the first leg of the journey should go.

His plan was simple. The march to Clapham Junction would not take long but once there they would have to wait and hide until the middle of the night. Clapham Junction was a vast railway station where the main lines from both Victoria and Waterloo came together and ran side by side. Hundreds of trains passed through it in a single hour and it would be certain death to cross before the live rails had been switched off and all traffic had ceased; it was the only way to get the horse over without it being killed or injured.

On the far side of the junction they would follow the track that went to Wandsworth Common station. There they would leave the railway line and take cover during the daylight hours. Knocker, Napoleon and Stonks had found just the place while on their three-day reconnaisance run. The next night they would move on, heading eastwards, hoping that they could find a hideout at the dawn of each day; hoping too that they would always find a helpful Borrible tribe to shelter them and one that could, eventually, tell them which, if any, of the bridges across the Thames was not guarded by the SBG.

When Knocker had explained all this the order of march was established. Stonks and Napoleon took the lead, scouting ahead for trouble because they knew the way. Knocker and Bingo brought up the rearguard. Sydney, as always, led the horse, and the other Adventurers were grouped around her for protection should there be an attack. So, with heartfelt wishes of 'Don't get caught,' they took up their positions and set off, catapults at the ready. The Great Neasden Expedition was under way.

*

The railway line curved off into the blustery darkness. The steel lines gleamed only every now and then as a few weak stars shone between low clouds, chivvied along by a hooligan wind. It was a silent march. Few words were spoken for there was no need for them. Everyone knew that the journey they were undertaking was the most dangerous thing they had ever done. It was probably the most dangerous thing any Borrible had ever done in the whole long history of Borribles.

But whatever the dangers they were not going to allow themselves to be disheartened. Lightly they tiptoed over the high-sided iron bridge that crossed Battersea Park Road; below them buses and cars swished along the tarmac. The branch line led them on, sweeping first away from Clapham Junction but then bending back towards it.

The high embankment on which the Borribles marched had now climbed above the topmost level of the rows and rows of terraced houses, soaring over the coal-black slate of the roofs. In the back kitchens of a thousand homes the curtains were not drawn and in the thin electric light the Borribles could see whole families sitting to eat at plastic-covered tables or lounging back in armchairs. But soon the embankment flattened out and the line joined another line and there was a signal box behind some tall hoardings at the entrance to Clapham Junction itself. It was here they must wait until the rattling trains grew silent.

The signal box was a lofty building with a wide wooden staircase climbing one of its walls and, because no traffic used the Olympia line after midday, it was dark and deserted. Its windows were all on the top floor and covered with a plaster of dirt; a nameplate said, 'Clapham Junction, North'.

Sydney led Sam straight into the shelter offered by the staircase. She threw the coloured blanket over his back and she and the rest of the Adventurers crowded round the horse for warmth, keeping themselves out of the wind. While they waited for the long hours to pass they ate and drank from their provisions, squatting against the wall, resting and swapping stories.

Little by little the number of trains passing through the great station diminished and the noise of lorries in the streets grew less and less. The rain came on, gentle and persistent. The Borribles huddled closer together and pulled their waterproofs over their heads. They grew silent and dozed; their heads dropped on to their knees; they slept.

When his luminous watch showed that it was three in the morning, Torreycanyon, whose turn it was to be sentry, shook his sleeping companions awake and once more they got ready to march. This time Knocker took the lead, and in single file, never too close but always in sight of one another, the Adventurers began to cross the dangerous tangle of railway lines that formed the labyrinth of Clapham Junction.

At last, after a passage of painstaking slowness, they arrived on the southern side. They had crossed a stretch of twenty or thirty railway lines without accident and now found themselves on the edge of a steep embankment which gave them a view down on to the crossroads where Falcon Road meets Lavender Hill.

It was eerie to see the place empty like that; not a cat or a dog moved there. Only the light from the towering clock on top of the Arding and Hobbs department store gave life to the scene. It picked out the wrought iron of the public lavatories on the traffic island and shone in the black tarmac of the rainswept road surfaces.

Knocker marched on. He felt the ground rise beneath his feet, smooth and hard. He had reached the sloping concrete of the southernmost platform, platform seventeen. He gestured to the person behind him, then crouched and ran quickly forward, not stopping until he was hidden well away from the slightest scrap of light, under the stairs that took passengers up and over to the other platforms. There he waited for his friends to come up with him and when they did he urged them onward again; for although the station was meant to be deserted at night-time, who could guess at how many policemen or security guards might lurk in the shadows?

*

The route out of Clapham Junction, by way of the railway, lies at the bottom of a deep canyon, the track being carved through a high hill on top of which stands the Granada cinema and bingo hall. Both sides of that canyon are as high as castle walls and held in place with a million bricks which, over the years, have been covered in a grime so thick that even the beating of the harshest rain could not penetrate it nor wash those million bricks clean. There are no roads on the topside of the canyon and no high buildings save the cinema; not one glimmer of light drops down into the chasm of that cutting.

As the Borribles left the western end of platform seventeen they entered this dense blackness. They could not see where to place their feet even. They stumbled and fell, aware only of a curtain of rain an inch from their eyes. They might have been tramping to the centre of the earth but they did not grumble; after all the darkness was their friend, their protector. The longer it lasted the safer they would be.

Because of this darkness the Borribles were forced to keep closer together than was normally considered prudent. None of them wished to go astray and be found, alone and vulnerable, on the main line in the morning with slate-faced commuters staring down at them from halted trains. So each Borrible blindly followed the person in front, and it was only as the sky lightened a little that they noticed the great walls of the embankment were sinking and that the more they advanced the lower became the precipice on either side, until at last, passing below a metal footbridge, they could look to their right and left through wire fences and see the length and breadth of Wandsworth Common.

'Not much further.' Knocker's voice came back through the wind. 'But watch out for the trains, they'll be starting soon.'

Knocker was right. Not long after he had spoken the ground beneath the Borribles' feet began to shake and tremble. The stones lying between the sleepers began to rattle.

'Man,' said Orococco, 'it's an earthquake.'

'Keep well back,' yelled Stonks. 'Hold the horse.'

The Adventurers threw themselves against the slope at the side of the track and pressed themselves into the grass. Sydney held Sam's head and talked to him quickly with soothing words. Stonks stayed close also and stroked the animal's flanks.

The Borribles' actions had not been a moment too soon. There came a terrifying blast on a train hooter; it echoed down the line and all the Adventurers jumped out of their skins, alarmed by the noise. A strong and solid wall of warm air came rushing along the track in front of the train, like an extra carriage, vigorous and invisible. It tore and plucked at the Borribles, tried to seize their bodies and drag them under the wheels, but the Borribles dug their hands into the wet earth and held on.

Then the train itself rose out of nowhere, perilously near, light from the windows pouring all over the fugitives. The ground rocked and the Borribles saw a long line of adult faces pass by in the sky above them, staring like statues into the dark. A regular rhythm beat quick and hard and insistent; and then suddenly the train was gone, wailing, its last carriage wagging helplessly and pathetic, dragging a vacuum behind it that tugged once at the Borribles and then whooshed away, snapping at trees and bushes as it went.

Knocker leant where he was, listening to the disappearing noise with relief. 'This won't do,' he said after a moment. He pushed himself upright and waved an arm at his companions. 'There'll be hundreds of trains along here soon, hundreds, and they'll see us, sure as beans is baked.'

Knocker was right again. The first trains of the morning rush hour began to pass with increasing frequency as the sky grew lighter. Between the passage of each train the Borribles ran forward and the lights of Wandsworth Common station were getting nearer now; so was the outline of the road bridge and when he got there Knocker halted the column.

'Who's got the wire cutters?' he asked.

Napoleon reached into his back pocket. 'I have,' he said. 'I always have wire cutters,' and without waiting for instructions he climbed the embankment and began to cut a hole in the fence large enough for Sam to get through.

One by one the Borribles scrambled upwards and went on to the common. They spread out and took cover behind bushes and trees, sniffing for danger. Once sure that they were unobserved they gave the whistle and Sydney and Stonks appeared with the horse behind them. The Wandsworth fields were silent and empty, silver-green under the falling rain. The streets too were quiet and there were few cars passing. The Borribles and Sam left the common together, running in one tight group across the main road and into a dead end that gave access to the back of the railway station. A tiny but modern trading estate was established here and had been the cause of some older buildings, mainly brick cottages, being abandoned. Stonks and Napoleon halted in front of one of these and Stonks said, 'This was the place, wasn't it?'

The building was long and low with rubbish dumped on three sides of it, rubbish that had been there so long that it had become solid and hard, just one substance. Its windows were all broken though some of them had been boarded up to keep out the weather. In better days the bricks had been painted a cream colour and above the door a sign, hanging from only one nail, bore the words, 'The Wideawake Car Hire Service, "Pouncer" Bedsted, Prop.'

At the rear of the broken cottage was a door large enough to admit Sam. Though locked it was loose on its hinges and Stonks lifted it free with ease. In less than a minute the horse and all the Adventurers were under cover and the door was replaced from inside. Sydney immediately opened a bag of cattle cake for Sam and wiped the rain from his back as he ate.

'There you are,' she said. 'You'll be all right now. I bet that fresh air gave you an appetite, didn't it?' And, as if in answer to the question, the horse neighed quietly, nuzzled the girl in the shoulder and chewed its food with a new-found relish. Meanwhile Sydney's companions removed their haversacks and most of them began to clear a space among the litter and rubble that covered the floor, making just enough room to sit and rest. For his part Stonks pulled some laths from the plaster wall and broke them into small pieces of kindling.

'I'll start a fire,' he said, 'and we'll make some soup. We need it after a night like that.'

'Then we'll need to nick lots of soup as we go,' said Chalotte mournfully, 'because there'll be lots of nights like that one before we're done.'

This remark left the Borribles deeply depressed and it was only later, when they had eaten and rested, that their spirits rose again. Sometime during the middle of the day they awoke and made a saucepan of tea, the leaves bubbling on the boiling water. Then, as they sat there, warming their hands on the steaming enamel mugs, they looked at one another and slowly, one by one, they smiled. They felt proud of what they had achieved that day and what they were setting out to do. They felt strong; felt they could do anything under the sun if only they were true to themselves and what they believed in. Their hearts swelled. It was only a tiny moment of time but, although they knew it would fade, there, in that miserable stinking hut with the rain dripping down its inside walls, they knew the moment was undeniably and irresistibly present; for them it was eternal.

And so, lying in their sleeping bags, eating, drinking, talking and snoozing, the Borribles passed the day away. Nor did they continue their journey as soon as it became dark, for the streets were still busy. They decided instead not to press on until eight or nine o'clock at night. By that time people would have returned from work and settled themselves into their armchairs. It was November now and once home commuters tended to stay home. As for the following morning it would still be dark at seven and the Borribles ought to be able to find a new hideout by then; nine hours' marching every night would be enough for anyone.

But the time for their departure soon came round. The Adventurers rolled up their sleeping bags and packed away their provisions and struggled into their waterproofs. Just before they left Knocker switched on his torch and had one more look at the huge street map of London that he had brought with him.

'This is tonight's march,' he explained, 'just in case we get separated. Through these side streets towards Clapham Common; once on the other side of it we'll go back into the streets and try to get to Brixton.'

'There's a market there,' said Bingo, 'a good one; bound to be Borribles in Brixton.'

'It's not on the way to Neasden,' Sydney objected, looking over Knocker's shoulder.

'I know that,' said Knocker, and he began to fold the map. 'We'll head towards the river after Brixton, up near the City, where Sussworth won't be expecting us to cross. Then we'll cut across the north of London. It's a lot longer but I reckon it's a lot safer too.'

'"The Borrible who keeps his head down keeps his ears on,"' said Stonks, quoting from the *Borrible Book of Proverbs*, and, ending that conversation, he lifted the back door off its hinges and went out into the dark to make sure that the way was clear.

*

No unnecessary word was spoken as the band of Borribles crossed a corner of Wandsworth Common and slunk into the gloomy streets. A cold mist of winter lay along the pavements holding the rain at bay, and only the cracks of light showing from behind thick curtains told the Adventurers that anyone at all was still alive in London.

The Borribles went in pairs now, well separated with at least twenty yards between each pair. Sydney walked with Sam and Stonks somewhere in the middle of the order of march. The leaders and the rearguard were out to spot trouble before it happened. At the slightest hint of danger a whistle was given or a stone thrown, and the Adventurers, and the horse, would disappear into the darkness of a householder's front garden, lowering themselves behind a privet hedge or concealing themselves at the side of a garage.

First down Thurleigh Road they marched, then up the opposite slope, left into Wroughton and right into Chatto, across Alfriston and into Culmstock and finally they crept on to the edge of the windy space called Clapham Common. Advancing into it they gathered together by a stand of trees, merging with the dark.

They were nervous; Borribles always are in open spaces. They miss the protection of the streets, the warmth of crowds. Every now and then a car flashed by on the South Circular Road. Knocker stared. The road was well lit and wide; tricky enough to cross alone without being seen, but with the horse they would be visible from miles away. They would have to choose their moment with great cunning.

As the Borribles took stock of their surroundings they became aware of a low grinding noise coming from far off and sounding like an unoiled machine labouring under a heavy load. The noise came nearer and grew louder.

Suddenly Bingo spoke. 'Duck,' he called. 'Woollies, in a car.'

The next moment there was not a Borrible to be seen. Each one had hidden. Only their voices were to be heard, low whispered voices as they sized up the situation.

'He's going very slow.'

'Too damn slow, he must be looking for us.'

'Bugger! He's stopped.'

'He's started again.'

'Look. Look. He's leading a load of lorries. It must be one of them wide convoys or some'at.'

'Them big convoys have to crawl at night. It's nothing to do with us.'

'It's caravans and lorries.'

'Can anyone see what it is?'

The Borribles watched as the police car crawled along the South Circular, passing only a few yards from their hiding place; but the policemen looked only before and behind, interested in nothing except the passage of the convoy. Behind the police car came several huge lorries riding on monstrous black tyres and, as the first great pantechnicon came level with Bingo, he read out what was painted on the side: 'Buffoni's Circus, Menagerie and Fairground'.

'It's a circus then,' said Chalotte, 'a travelling circus. Blimey! You don't see many of them nowadays.'

'It's quite big,' said Vulge. 'I can already see about seven or eight lorries.'

'Lots of Borribles hang about circuses,' said Orococco. 'I had a cousin who ran away to join a circus.'

The slow procession continued and the police car drove out of sight. The huge circus trucks churned on as if climbing a steep hill and the smoke of their exhausts drifted up into the dark trees above the street lamps. More trailers appeared and there were cages too, though their sides were covered in tarpaulins and no lions or tigers were visible. Between the trailers and cages walked about a dozen figures, their features indistinct. They carried hurricane lamps and had little groups of animals with them. Some camels there were, an elephant and several horses and ponies. A whole village was on the move.

Knocker peered from behind his tree. 'Here,' he said. 'You know what they're doing? They're moving on to the common, over by the Mount Pond. I remember now, that's where the fairs always used to go in the old days.' Knocker ducked back out of the light as the patrol car, its job done, sped by on the road, going fast now, back to the police station on Lavender Hill.

Bingo laughed. 'I've got it,' he said. 'We can get across the road easy now. We'll just tag on to the end of that lot, and then as soon as they're on the other side, we'll shove off. Goodnight and thank you very much.'

The idea appealed to the Borribles. They rose from cover and, surrounding Sam, they led him over the grass and into the bright roadway, taking up places at the rear of the circus column; as it shuffled forward so did they.

Lorry by lorry and trailer by trailer the circus-cum-fairground left the road and established itself in a circle on an open piece of cindery terrain by the side of the Mount Pond. The Borribles, once safely over the road, had at first fully intended to run off into the darkness, but intrigued by the activity going on all around them they hid themselves beneath some trees and watched.

The first thing the men of the circus did was to manhandle the trailers and cages into position and mark out their pitches for the following day.

There were tents to be erected that night and there was plenty of other work to do, too. Huge sledgehammers banged against iron stakes and the wild beasts growled and roared as they were given food and water. At the same time lights were rigged and meals were prepared, smelling delicious.

'I need some more soup,' said Twilight.

As he spoke a caravan was towed into position and deposited only a few yards from where the Adventurers stood. Its door was flung open immediately and about eight small shapes threw themselves down the steps calling and shouting to one another.

'Shove the caravan a bit further in.'

'Who's doing the cooking?'

'Bang in the tent pegs.'

The Borribles huddled back, beneath the trees. 'Let's get going,' said Knocker.

No one answered. The Adventurers were all watching the people in front of them as they toiled in the bright glow of the floodlights. They were so full of energy and enthusiasm, strong and resilient, happy in what they were doing. They bustled and scurried backwards and forwards on strong muscular legs; their shoulders were broad, but not one of these people was over the height of a twelve-year-old child, not one of them was taller than the average Borrible.

'Swipe me,' said Vulge. 'What do you make of them? Are they Borribles?'

'They could be,' answered Orococco. 'Like I said, they have Borribles in circuses, but then they have dwarfs and midgets as well; my cousin told me. But if you look on the caravan it says acrobats, don't it?'

'I don't care what they are,' said Chalotte quietly, 'I've got a feeling we ought to be on the move.'

For many years to come Chalotte was to remember that moment as the turning point in the whole adventure. If only they'd not hesitated, how different things might have been.

3

'Borribles,' began Inspector Sussworth, reading from a prepared speech, 'are the rubbish of our society and as such have got to be swept under the carpet of coercion and stamped upon. You, both men and dwarfs, are to be the agents of this cleansing.'

Sussworth beamed. In front of him stood the group leaders of the SBG, as stiff and as stubborn as a soldier-course of bricks; tall burly men with hair on their knuckles, their necks thick and red, their brows solid with good bone. They listened to Sussworth with wide-eyed devotion.

In front of these men and slightly to one side stood a band of about twenty dwarfs. They were well formed in every respect with strong limbs and fair skins and they had been selected, over and above all the other applicants who had answered Sussworth's advertisements, because of their youthful appearance. What is more they had been thoroughly trained and knew all there was to know about being a Borrible. And they too listened to the inspector with intense concentration. They had been promised good money for the tasks they were to perform and, if they actually managed to capture a Borrible, they would receive a substantial cash bonus.

'You dwarfs,' continued Sussworth taking a turn up and down the main room of the SBG headquarters, 'have been presented and provided with a wonderful opportunity to serve law and order. You will be our advance guard, our intelligence behind the enemy lines. You look like Borribles already, and by the time these specially made pointed ears, covered in human skin, have been stuck to your own ears, why, even Borribles will take you for Borribles.' The inspector smiled and performed a little Spanish dance, stamping his feet and clicking his fingers.

Behind him Sergeant Hanks stepped forward and raised both his hands. In one he held a flesh-coloured Borrible ear and in the other a large container of impact glue.

'Now,' said Sussworth, 'I do not want you auxiliaries to be worried about this superglue. Sergeant Hanks has a special solvent which, when the time comes, we shall apply and, Hay Preston! You'll be back to normal.'

'Please, Inspector,' one of the dwarfs raised his hand. 'If we get caught by one of your men and he can't tell us from the real thing, how do we convince him that we are really adults in disguise?'

Sussworth spun a full turn and nodded like someone who knew the answer to every question ever thought of. 'Simple,' he said. 'Every one of you will be given the password. This password will be known only to you and the members of the SBG.'

'Yessir. What's the password?'

Sussworth jiggled his feet and spoke over his shoulder. 'Yes, indeed. What is the password, Hanks?'

Hanks went very red in the face, lowered his head and looked intently at the ear in his hand. 'Ah,' he said. 'Yes, er . . . Blancmange . . . that's the password. No one will ever guess that.'

Sussworth twitched his moustache, stamped three paces to the right and then three paces to the left. He pointed at the dwarfs like a recruiting poster.

'You have all been thoroughly trained,' he said, 'in anti-Borrible tactics. This is war to the death, no quarter asked, none given. Borribles are all around us; trust no one. You know how Borribles live: empty habitations, stealing in markets, no fixed abodes, petty thievery . . . Well you must do the same. For all intents and purposes you will become Borribles.'

He pirouetted in a swirl of overcoat tails and gazed at a flag-covered map of London which was pinned to the wall. He coughed, and his hands fought with one another behind his back.

'Dozens of dwarfs,' he continued, 'are already in position, idling at street corners and loafing in the markets.' Sussworth placed his hands on his hips and his moustache uncrimped its wings like a moth coming out of a chrysalis. 'This is my greatest idea and it will work like a quartz timepiece. I'm going to get as many of you young dwarfs on the streets as I can. I have a feeling, a strong feeling, that some of my spies are mixed in with that bunch of villains already, pretending to aid and abet them as they make off with that equine animal we wish to apprehend.'

Sussworth stamped his feet one after the other and then turned quickly from the map. His eyes narrowed and his voice grew deeper, taking on a Churchillian ring.

'This time we shall not fail. We shall fight them in the streets and down the alleys, across the labyrinthine ways of the metropolis, every yard, every foot, every inch. Behind each of you dwarfs, remember, are ten men of the SBG. You will overcome and you will never walk alone. This is the big match. I shall bowl the Borribles a death-dealing googly. They shall not pass. We shall be unseen and undetected and the ground will be covered with clipped ears like leaves in autumn.'

Sergeant Hanks grinned and shouted for joy, but Sussworth was not pleased and he held a hand high against the interruption and straightened his back.

'And I shall be right there with you, men. I have made arrangements for a caravan to be placed at my disposal. It will be personal and private with its own bathroom and lavatory. I am going to take up my abode in this caravan and I shall live in it until these scavengers and their horse are captured. There shall I labour, like Monty did in the Western Desert. I shall make our deeds into history.'

Sussworth's moustache revolved slowly now with contained power, like a ship's propeller. 'Epoch-making history! My finest hour! We happy few! The Desert Fox! Never before!'

'Certainly,' said Hanks, taking a digestive biscuit from his pocket and sliding it into his mouth.

Sussworth stood to attention and extended himself to his fullest height and jerked a thumb over his shoulder towards the map. 'Wherever these flags are thickest there shall I be in the thick of it,' he said.

Hanks waved the Borrible ear he held above his head and cheered, spraying the front row of dwarfs with saliva and crumbs. Sussworth inclined his head and the SBG policemen saluted, turned to the right and marched from the room. The dwarfs, after a moment's hesitation, saluted too and then followed them.

The inspector watched them go. His moustache lifted from his top lip like a trapdoor and revealed a smile, the smile of a sharp-toothed rabbit.

'If only the DAC could see us now,' said Hanks, popping another biscuit into his mouth. 'I'd be Sir Sergeant Hanks already with more letters behind my name than a London postal district. Eh?'

Inspector Sussworth sniffed. 'It's just as well he can't see us, Hanks,' he said. 'Using dwarfs is a bit out of order and the DAC wouldn't want to be associated with anything out of order. He wouldn't stop us, you understand, he just wouldn't want to be associated with it. In fact, Hanks, it's all got to be kept very hush-hush. In future, in reports and radio messages and suchlike, make sure the men always refer to the dwarfs as . . . as . . .'

'Lookouts,' suggested Hanks.

'Lookouts,' said Sussworth, 'as I said.' He gazed at the map again and a dreamy expression filled his eyes. 'Somewhere in London, they are, those Borribles . . . somewhere in London. I wonder where. I wonder where.'

*

The Borribles stood under the trees in the darkness. The temperature had risen and the rain was falling again, dripping from the leaves and running down necks. Sam stamped a hoof, impatient to be off.

'We can't stay here,' said Sydney. 'Sam will catch cold; he's shivering already.'

The Borribles were still watching the acrobats erect their tent, fascinated by the speed and expertise with which the operation was performed.

Chalotte touched Knocker. 'Yes,' she said, 'we'd better get a move on.'

Knocker looked at his watch. It was only eleven o'clock. As he raised his head to speak someone bumped into him from the side. It was one of the acrobats, walking backwards and tugging on a length of cable.

'Watch out,' shouted the newcomer. 'Get out the way, can't yer see I'm trying to lash this guy rope?'

Knocker said nothing but reached forward rapidly and grabbed the acrobat by the neck. 'Shuddup,' he said, 'else I'll throttle yer.'

'Leave off,' said the acrobat. 'Stop messing about. Why aren't you getting on with the work? I've a good mind . . .' The acrobat's voice faltered. He had noticed the other Borribles in the darkness under the trees and he was more than a little disconcerted to find such a group on the common in the middle of the night. Stonks came up behind him and took hold of an arm.

‘’Ere,’ said the acrobat, his voice less confident. ‘What’s your game, eh?’

‘Nothing,’ said Knocker. ‘We don’t want nothing, we ain’t doing nothing, we’re just on our way across the common, nice ’n’ quiet like.’

The acrobat moved his face nearer to Knocker’s, looking him straight in the eye. ‘’Ere,’ he said again, ‘you’re the same size as me you are, all of yer. Are you a dwarf too, or are you kids on the run?’

Knocker did not answer for at that moment a voice came from the half-erected tent: ‘Hey Scooter, wake up. Pull on the bloody rope, will yer. The effin’ pole’s waving all over the place.’

‘You’d better let me,’ said the acrobat called Scooter, ‘or they’ll all be over here.’

‘Go on then,’ said Knocker. ‘Don’t try anything funny, there’s ten of us.’

‘Oh is there?’ said Scooter. ‘I’m frightened to death, ain’t I?’ He shook himself away from Knocker and Stonks and passing the rope he held round the trunk of the nearest tree he began to pull on it, and the Borribles could see the centre of the nearby tent rising. When he had finished Scooter tied the end of the rope to a branch and turned to face the Borribles, his hands on his hips, smiling. He made no attempt to escape or call his friends.’

‘You shouldn’t be worried,’ he said, addressing them all. ‘We’re travellers, circus people, fairground gypsies. We’d never give you away to anyone, least of all the law. It’s against our traditions.’

‘Oh yeah,’ said Knocker. ‘How do we know?’

Scooter shrugged his shoulders. ‘Suit yerself,’ he said, ‘but you’ll have to let me go in a minute; I’ve got lots of work to do and the others will start looking for me.’

‘We’re moving on anyway,’ said Napoleon. ‘It’s not safe here. We could take you with us, if we wanted.’

‘Oh yeah,’ said Scooter.

‘We’re on our way to Brixton, that’s all,’ said Knocker at last.

Scooter folded his arms and leant against a tree. ‘So are we,’ he said. ‘In three days’ time we’ll be setting out for Brockwell Park to do a show. You could travel with us. No one would see you in the caravan and they wouldn't notice an extra horse.'

'No,' said Knocker, 'we'll go now,' but it was too late. Six people were suddenly coming close to the Borribles.

'Come on, Scooter,' called one of them. 'Why aren't you doing your share? We all want to go to bed you know.'

The Borribles quickly loaded their catapults and got back to back under the trees. Sydney held the horse ready to run but still Scooter did not move. 'Please,' he said, 'don't be scared. Look.' He turned and raised a hand towards his colleagues. 'Move steady,' he called out. 'I've found some people who could use some help.'

The advancing acrobats halted for a moment and then came on, warily. They spread out under the trees; one of them leant on the handle of a sledgehammer. Against the glare of the circus floodlights the Adventurers could see that although only of Borrible height he was thickset, as big as Stonks. 'Who are they?' he asked. 'What do they want?'

'We don't want anything,' answered Chalotte. 'We're just crossing the common.'

'Look, Ninch,' said Scooter, speaking to the acrobat with the hammer, 'they're just a bunch of kids going to Brixton . . . with a horse.'

'A horse!' retorted Ninch with excitement. 'A horse, eh? Strike a bleedin' light.'

'What about the horse?' said Sydney, immediately on the defensive.

'What about it?' replied Ninch. 'I bet you've nicked one of ours, that's what. Frisby, go and count 'em, quick.'

One of Ninch's companions walked away and the others shuffled their feet, ready for trouble.

'Leave it out, Ninch,' said Scooter, 'they're just bits of kids I tell yer. From what I can see a good meal wouldn't do 'em no harm.'

'The horses are all there.' Frisby's voice came from the other side of the half-erected tent and Ninch's body relaxed.

'That's all right then,' he said. 'They're welcome to come along with us, if they want. Never let it be said that a traveller don't know how to be hospitable.' And with that the chunky figure turned and strode away, his companions following him.

The Borribles breathed a sigh of relief and put their catapults into their back pockets. Scooter laughed. 'I told you,' he said. 'At least come and eat some grub with us before you go. They're cooking up Irish stew tonight. Once we've got the work done, that is.'

'Irish stew,' said Bingo. 'I loves that; with dumplings?'

'Oh yes,' said Scooter, 'with dumplings.'

After that there seemed no good reason for staying out in the rain and the Borribles went slowly towards the tent, which now looked as sturdy as a church. Scooter opened a flap and Sam, followed by the rest of the Adventurers, passed through it.

They found themselves in a space about thirty yards long by twenty wide. Along the shorter side, opposite the entrance, was a plank stage which the acrobats had nearly finished setting up. The Borribles hesitated. These circus people might be small but they were still adults, and Borribles do not like being in an enclosed space with adults.

Scooter had followed them into the tent and he chuckled at their discomfiture. 'You can spend the rest of the night under the stage if you like,' he said, 'the horse as well. Have a good rest. Then you can march along with us when we go. It'll be easier than skulking across the streets at night and less dangerous.'

'Have you got any proper animal food,' asked Sydney, 'for Sam, the horse?'

'Sam, eh?' said Scooter. 'Oh yes, we'll have oats or some'at. What's yer names?'

The Borribles looked at one another, hesitated, and then told him. As each name was given so Scooter's face showed more and more surprise. At the end of the list he smiled hugely. 'My name's Scooter,' he said, 'but I like your names . . .' His eyes narrowed and he looked at Knocker intently. 'I would like to hear the story of them, some day.'

Knocker touched the catapult in his back pocket. Scooter had just spoken the most friendly of Borrible greetings. He looked sideways at the stage. The six or seven of Scooter's companions, who up till then had been working hard, were now silent and still, raised hammers motionless in their hands. They had heard the special words and were waiting for the reply.

The silence continued and then Chalotte said, 'We will tell the stories certainly, and your name is good too, Scooter. There must be a fine tale behind it, you must tell us how you won it before we leave.'

At this a great noise came from the stage as the acrobats threw down their tools and laughed and cheered and jumped to the ground. Scooter smiled again and lifted a hand to his hair, slowly pushing it back to reveal pointed ears, Borrible ears. And the other acrobats approached from the stage and they too showed their ears, all of them Borrible.

Knocker shook his head in amazement. He peered closely at Scooter's ears; they seemed all right.

'You can't be Borrible,' said Napoleon. 'You don't look right.'

Ninch tapped the Wendle on the shoulder. 'Don't look right, what do you mean, don't look right? These are my friends: two girls here, Matzo and Lobda, and then there's Flapjack, Sinbad, Duster and Frisby.'

'They're good names,' said Knocker, 'really, but what Napoleon means is, well, you don't look like Borribles, I mean the ears do but . . .'

'You look too strong,' said Chalotte, 'a bit like short adults.'

Ninch laughed and looked round at his friends. 'Of course we do,' he said, 'it's the circus that does that. The acrobatics, the swinging on ropes, putting up this tent, hauling cages into position. Clowning, you have to be fit for clowning.'

'Anyway,' said Scooter, 'not all Borribles look the same, not by a long chalk. You've got two black ones with you, Napoleon looks green and him, Stonks, he looks more like one of us, doesn't he?'

Stonks gave one of his rare smiles, pleased that his strength had been noticed.

Ninch put his arm round Knocker's shoulders. 'Don't worry so much. Remember we are all Borribles together. We will eat and then you will feel better. Frisby has been doing the cooking in the caravan and he'll be fetching it over in a minute. We'll have a feast, and there's oats for the horse as well.'

And so it was decided. The acrobats made a table with planks from the stage and they improvised a bench too. The Borribles took their places, a huge cauldron of stew was carried across from the caravan by Ninch and Frisby, and soup plates and spoons were placed before each person. Generous portions were ladled into the plates and the Adventurers lost no time in devouring all the food they'd been given, so hungry were they for a hot meal.

Towards the end of it Knocker looked across the table and raised his glass of beer at Chalotte. She returned the glance but her face was serious, expressing doubt. She angled her head at Ninch and shrugged, wondering. Was he a leader or was he just the most forceful personality in the group? The main thing she noticed about him was his strength. Perhaps only Stonks in the band of Adventurers could take him on in a fair fight and stand a chance of winning. All right then, as the proverb said, 'If they won't let you fight a fair fight then don't fight 'em fair.'

Chalotte studied the acrobat carefully, searching his physical appearance for some clue to his personality. His hair was ginger and stuck out sideways like bristles on a chimney sweep's brush. He had a round face, broad as a cabbage, with muscular cheeks and a big adult mouth; one of his eyes seemed wider than the other. His hands were broad and strong; fingers like coach bolts with hexagon nuts for knuckles. He wore a striped jersey of thick wool, cut off jaggedly at the elbows, and his fawn trousers were stained with oil. He made you think of a burglar who'd fallen on hard times. Chalotte shrugged; Borribles were burglars, after all was said and done.

She next turned her attention to Scooter. He was different. He was not so strongly built as Ninch, though he was still broad in the shoulder and beefy in the arm for a Borrible. He looked as tough as a bag of nails but somehow his face was more careless, more open. His black hair shone like tarmac in rain and touched his shoulders. His chin was pointed, his eyes brown and although his expression, like Ninch's, had a touch of the adult, it was not troubled or preoccupied but clear and spontaneous.

Chalotte wiped some stew off her plate with a piece of bread. Something wasn't quite right, but whatever it was eluded her. She looked at all the acrobats in turn. They were all talking and smiling; telling the stories of their names in true Borrible fashion, asking questions about the Great Rumble Hunt and scratching their pointed ears. It must be all right.

And so the eating and talking went on and the acrobats and the Adventurers warmed to each other's company and suspicions fell away. As with all Borribles the stories flew thick and fast. The acrobats told tale after tale of their travels and the strange people they had met in other circuses and fairgrounds. The Adventurers told stories too, of

Rumbledom and Flinthead's mine, but they did not reveal what they were doing crossing Clapham Common at night and why Sam the horse was one of their number.

At last, after every person there had taken his or her part in the story-telling, heads began to droop and the acrobats went to their caravan and the Adventurers crept under the stage, taking Sam with them. Safe and warm in their sleeping bags, their stomachs full, they soon fell asleep and the night was dark and silent all around save only for the sound of a car now and then as it zipped along the rainy road which crossed the common just a hundred yards from where the vagabonds slept.

Only Napoleon Boot was wakeful, his knife under his hand, his catapult by his side. He was puzzled. He and Knocker and Chalotte and all the others had taken a good look at the ears of the acrobats to check that they were what they said they were, but the circus people had not inspected the ears of the Adventurers, and that wasn't Borrible, not a bit Borrible. This thought nagged at Napoleon's mind all night, but then Napoleon Boot had always found it difficult to trust anyone, especially if they were being friendly.

*

Whatever Napoleon's suspicions the night passed without incident. In the morning, at the moment of daybreak, Scooter and Ninch woke the Adventurers with handfuls of fruit and fresh bread rolls and mugs of tea. When this meal was over Ninch went to the back of the tent and, making sure the coast was clear, he lifted the canvas over Sam's head and the horse went out into the open, happy to find there the company of other horses and soft green grass to stand on under the trees. The Adventurers hesitated to follow.

'Won't it be dangerous?' asked Chalotte.

'Swipe me!' answered Ninch. 'No one will have time to notice you. Besides, there's always loads of kids hanging round a circus, a few more won't make any difference.' And so, reassured, the Borribles followed the horse and saw what they had been unable to see the previous evening.

All round them were the trucks and trailers that carried the tons of equipment that Buffoni's circus and fairground needed when it was on the road: tents and guy ropes; generators and miles and miles of heavy, all-weather cable; cages for the animals; containers for their food and of course all the huge four-wheeled caravans where the circus people lived when they travelled.

The noise of diesel engines was overpowering. Burly men in torn and dirty jeans and sweaters were testing the generators and a deep throbbing roar came from everywhere. Voices bawled from several loudspeakers at once; riggers were hammering nails and sawing bits of noggin. It was all chaos; it was all urgency and bustle.

At the centre of all this activity was the big top. Around it, in a semicircle, were arranged the sideshows and the cages of the menagerie, forming rows like the spokes of a wheel so that people could stroll up and down and see all there was to see and enjoy all there was to enjoy.

'It's only a little big top,' explained Ninch as they stood before it, 'but it's big enough for us. We can get four hundred people into it.'

Napoleon sniffed the air as if it smelt of coppers, as suspicious in the morning as he had been the night before. 'All the fairground people,' he said, 'adults, ain't they? Wouldn't they shop you to the SBG if they found out you were Borribles?'

Ninch laughed his laugh, rough like gravel. 'No,' he said. 'First off travellers aren't in love with Woollies, it's a thing that's bred into them.'

'And second?' asked Knocker. He looked up to the roof of the big top and watched a banner unfurling on the tallest flagpole. He read the words on it: BUFFONI'S – THE GREATEST LITTLE CIRCUS IN THE WORLD.

'Second,' said Ninch, 'well, they think we're ordinary dwarfs; that's what we're billed as, that's what it says on the side of our caravan: BUFFONI'S FLYING DWARFS – THE AMAZING ACROBATS. We do trapeze work, slack wire stuff.'

'Then you must be paid money,' said Chalotte. 'That's not Borrible, is it? How do you square that?'

'That's a good 'un,' Ninch said. 'If we had any money, which we haven't, we'd have to give it to Ronaldo Buffoni; he's the guv'nor. It's only because hardly anyone in the circus takes any wages that the whole thing keeps going. All that food to pay for, the animals, vets, costumes, lorries and trailers. Poor old Buffoni.'

'Yes,' said Scooter. 'When Ninch and me first met we just used to follow this circus around. It was as good a way of keeping out the way of the Woollies as any other. There was always food and a place to sleep. Gradually we picked up the other Borribles, became friends with the Buffonis, learnt some circus tricks along the way – years ago that was. Then one day old Ronaldo said we could have our own sideshow as long as we didn't cost him anything. He gave us the tent and the caravan.'

'Working in exchange for food is the thin end of the wedge,' said Chalotte, 'however you look at it.'

Ninch shrugged his shoulders. 'Depends really, doesn't it? Nicking is work too. You have to go out and do it, don't yer? Fruit of the barrow.'

The conversation was ended there and Ninch and Scooter now took the Borribles between the rows of small tents and stalls that housed the sideshows. There was fishing by numbers; a rifle range where moving metal birds and pipes were the targets; a Fat Lady's tent; a Thin Man; a Bearded Lady who, according to Ninch, was really a man; a Siamese Sword Swallower; a One-Man Band who walked round and round the nearby streets and attracted customers with his music. There was Wanda, the One-Wheeled Witch, who performed juggling tricks on a monocycle; a fire-eater; Tanka the Tiger, a maneater from Bengal with his keeper, Amurishi Patadi; a couple of chimpanzees and the only white rhinoceros in captivity. And at the end of it all there were two roundabouts: a slow one for children and a fast one for adults that was called a switchback.

'But where do all these people come from?' asked Torreycanyon, his face creased with puzzlement. 'I mean what with all these riggers and drivers and performers, there can't be room in the caravans.'

Scooter grinned. 'They're all one and the same,' he said. 'They drive the lorries, put up the tents, feed the animals, make the ice creams and popcorn, do the shows and mend the machinery when it breaks down.'

'That's right,' added Ninch, 'and then they'll all change into spangles and cloaks this evening and pretend to have those marvellous names. In fact they're nearly all related to each other, all Buffonis: uncles, aunties, brothers, sisters, cousins. They double up as clowns and all sorts. So do we.'

Vulge shook his head. 'What about that tiger? He looks pretty fierce.'

'Oh he's harmless. He's so well fed that Arthur can hardly get him to climb on a chair.'

'Arthur! I thought he was from Bengal.'

'Bengal,' Ninch hooted. 'He's Arthur Buffoni; that's him over there in the overalls, banging a spike into the ground. He has to black up every night and put a turban on. These Buffonis all come from the Hackney Road, cockneys they are, never mind the name.'

As the Borribles turned away from their contemplation of Arthur Buffoni they came face to face with a well built tubby character dressed in a cloth cap of bright check, a tweed jacket and polished gaiters. He was only a short man but he looked strong and his skin blazed with health and his body looked as if it were bursting with energy and enthusiasm. His cheeks were very round and very red; his honey-coloured moustache bristled and his long and bushy side whiskers spread down the length of his face and nearly reached to his chin. He carried a stick under his arm and walked like a soldier. This was Signor Ronaldo Buffoni and it was obvious to anyone who took the trouble to look at him that he loved his circus with all the strength of a generous heart. His fairground, his sideshows and the people who worked with him were his life. He smiled delightedly when he saw the Adventurers.

'Aha,' he said, slapping his leg with his stick, 'got some more chums, eh? Good. Ever been to Buffoni's before?'

The Adventurers shook their heads but said nothing.

'Thought not. You can all come tonight, for free. You can see to it, Ninch. Never fill the seats, not this weather we won't. Don't be late now, seven thirty, sharp.' And with a cheery wave of his hand Signor Buffoni strode away and climbed the steps to his caravan.

For the rest of the day the Adventurers were left to their own devices. The acrobats were busy helping the Buffonis to prepare for the evening's performance in the big top, and they had also to make sure that all was ready for their own sideshow which took place afterwards.

The Borribles were quite happy with this arrangement. Sydney borrowed a curry-comb and worked until Sam was as well groomed as he possibly could be, and her companions went their own separate ways; some dozing in the warmth of the acrobats' caravan, some drinking tea and chatting in the tent, the remainder strolling among the workers and sightseers.

'You know what?' said Twilight lazily at some point during the afternoon. 'If the rest of the trip is like this it'll be a doddle.'

'Yeah,' answered Vulge, 'and it's always dry until it pisses with rain.'

Slowly the hours passed. The weak daylight faded and the sky went dark. It was evening. Music echoed round the marquees and could be heard from miles away; six different melodies at once. The diesel generators shook and rumbled and kept the lights as bright as gold and as red as rubies. Every now and then the voice of Signor Buffoni boomed through a loudspeaker to announce the main attraction; 'Roll up, roll up, don't miss the greatest show on earth, in the big top at seven thirty. Roll up, roll up.'

The crowds grew thicker and thicker until they formed a solid mob of humanity that could only move in one direction at a time. The grass and cinders underfoot were churned into an ooze of mud and the music blared louder and the switchback turned faster and faster until its riders screamed with fear and excitement.

This excitement of speed and music conveyed itself to the Adventurers and they could barely wait for the performance to begin; all except Napoleon Boot of course. He was tense with something else – suspicion. He went to find Knocker and took him to one side so that they could talk together without being overheard. 'That Ninch,' said the Wendle, his face screwed up tight, 'I haven't seen him all afternoon, and I don't like it.'

Knocker nodded. 'Yes,' he said, 'I noticed it as well. Still, as the proverb says, "Don't scratch where it don't itch." They've been good to us . . . I don't suppose there's anything in it.'

'Huh,' said Napoleon, 'there's an old Wendle proverb too. "Anyone who's that good can't be that good." That's my favourite, that is.'

In spite of all these suspicions Napoleon met his friends at the entrance to the big top and there at last he saw Ninch, standing next to one of the circus men and dressed in bright orange trousers, shoes like barges and sporting a big red nose. Under his arm he held a large bundle of programmes and he gave one to every member of the audience as they entered the tent to take their places. When Napoleon asked the acrobat where he had been all afternoon he just smiled and wiped his forehead with the back of his hand in a mime of exhaustion.

'I haven't stopped all day,' he said. 'Old Buffoni has had me running here, there and everywhere.'

Napoleon accepted this explanation for the time being and passed, with the rest of the Adventurers, into the tent and they were shown to the bench that had been reserved for them in the front row. The audience was increasing minute by minute and notwithstanding what Signor Buffoni had said earlier in the day there was hardly a spare seat to be seen. The noise in the big top grew and in a little while the house lights dimmed and Signor Buffoni himself appeared in a blazing circle of silver light looking gorgeous in a red coat, a bejewelled cummerbund and a black top hat. He carried an enormous whip too and called for silence by cracking it loudly above his head.

'Mee-yer Lorse, Ladies and Gennermen,' he called, his voice resounding all over the tent without benefit of microphone, 'pray be welcome to the ge-reatest show on earth, the Buffoni Circus, Fairground and Menagerie. And-er neow, first tonight, for your pleasure and delectation, Buffoni's er-circus-a proudly preesents . . . the wild horses of the Rushan Steppes. Er-h-until a few short months ago these 'ere 'orses were roaming free in the boundless wastes of Haysha. They 'ave been er-ber-rought 'ere at treemendous hexpense and personally trained by the Magnificent and Marvellous Mazeppa Buffoni and his er-loverly wife, Caterina. Mee-yer Lorse, Ladies and Gennermen, The Magnificent Mazeppa and Caterina.'

At this Signor Buffoni cracked his whip, the lights went out and when they came on again, a second or two later, the ringmaster had disappeared and three horses, two grey and one black, were tearing round the circus ring. Running behind them were a young man and woman dressed in ballet costumes liberally sprinkled with spangles and sequins.

It took hardly any time at all for Mazeppa and Caterina to catch up with the horses, and when they did they jumped upon their backs, performing handstands and leaping from one animal to another at breathtaking speed. At the very last, just to outdo what had gone before, and while still mounted, Caterina stood on her partner's shoulders and faced backwards, waving and smiling. The Borribles and the rest of the audience were spellbound.

Soon the act was over and to an enormous burst of applause the horses disappeared and once again Signor Buffoni took his position at the centre of the ring.

'Er-ran-neow, mee Lorse, Ladies and Gennermen, at no small hexpense

Buffoni's circus would like to er-present for your pleasure, Amurishi Patadi and a fearsome tiger as was h-onlee per-rowling the luxuriant rain forests of hunhexplored Bengawl h-onlee two weeks h-ago. Mee Lorse, Ladies and Gennermen . . . Tanka the Tiger.'

The audience made not a single sound as the lights changed colour and half a dozen clowns pushed a huge cage into the centre of the ring. Arthur Buffoni followed, carrying a small whip and looking like a maharajah with his face properly stained to the hue of strong coffee and his head crowned with a jewel-studded turban.

Arthur bowed to the audience and then began to circle the cage on tiptoe as if approaching a desperate and starving maneater. He kept about six feet from the bars most of the time but occasionally he leapt closer, cracking his whip and then immediately leaping backwards to safety. It didn't look very dangerous and Tanka meanwhile lay unperturbed on the floor of the cage with one eye only watching the audience; the other was firmly closed.

The loudspeakers crackled next and Signor Buffoni spoke from somewhere backstage: 'Mee Lorse, Ladies and Gennermen, I have to point out of course that these Bengawli tigers are at their most dangerous and lethal when they h-appear to be at their most somnolent. We beg the h-audience not to be h-alarmed. All precautions will be taken.'

The sound of the loudspeakers died away and two men in white overalls appeared, both of them carrying rifles, and they went to stand near the bars of the cage. Slowly, to a roll of drums, Arthur opened the cage door and each member of the audience could hear his or her heart thumping. Arthur next seized a chair and poked Tanka with it as he entered the cage. The audience gasped. Then Arthur cracked his whip and with a roar Tanka got to her feet and clambered on to a pedestal, raised a paw and roared again. There was rapturous applause and in response to it Arthur Buffoni did the bravest thing of all and prodded the animal with his whip and insolently turned his back on her, kneeling on the floor.

The audience went delirious but Arthur had not finished with them. He got to his feet and, as a finale, placed both arms around Tanka's neck and kissed the tiger right on the nose. The audience cheered and cheered like madmen but then fell silent in fear as the maneater suddenly bared her teeth and growled with anger. The two men in white overalls cocked their guns and Arthur crept backwards to the door of the cage, slipped through and clanged it shut behind him, securing the lock with a large key which he afterwards placed in his pocket. Smiling, he bowed low several times towards the rear of the tent and wallowed in the generous sound of hundreds of hands clapping. 'Hooray!' shouted the children. 'Bravo!' bawled their parents. 'More, more,' screamed the Adventurers.

After Tanka and Arthur the acts came thick and fast. There were so many that the Borribles could not keep count; and all of them Buffonis. There was Wanda on her one-wheeled bike; Marco the Strong Man with a moustache that looked like a coiled spring; and there was Marmaduke Buffoni too, defying gravity on a high wire.

'You've got to hand it to them,' said Stonks, 'when you think that it's all the same people doubling up most of the time. You wouldn't know unless you knew, would you?'

The interval came all too soon and the Borribles relaxed. The house lights were brought up again and from backstage out rushed six or seven clowns to entertain the audience while it ate ice cream and hot dogs. The clowns were big men, acrobats and tumblers all, and threw each other across the ring, fell over, drove a broken car and sprayed themselves with coloured water from a hosepipe. Everybody watching was helpless – rolling in their seats and holding their sides with the pain of laughter.

'Whatever else you say about this circus,' said Bingo, the tears streaming down his face, 'they certainly make you laugh; I can't stop . . . And look, there's more coming.'

It was true. About a dozen men, dressed as clowns, were coming through the wall of canvas and slipping into the circus ring. But they stood separate from the original clowns and took no part in their hilarious routine. Their make-up was different too. Although they were wearing red noses their faces were all white and their mouths were huge gashes of blue, pointing downwards in expressions of sadness and misery.

The first group of clowns seemed puzzled by these new arrivals and gradually their act faltered and then stopped altogether. They huddled in a group and talked; they looked frightened.

'It's all part of the act,' said Chalotte. 'They'll be having a fight in a minute, I bet.'

'Hang about,' said Napoleon. He half rose to his feet and glanced behind him. 'I don't like this. Look behind you, there's more coming in from the back.'

Bingo twisted in his seat, still laughing. He counted; there were too many. 'This circus ain't got that many clowns,' he said, and his laughter dried like a gob of spit in brickdust.

Knocker sprang to his feet and climbed into the ring. His catapult was in his hand and he loaded it. 'Dammit,' he swore. 'They've got sticks and look at their boots. It's the coppers. Somebody's grassed. We're surrounded.'

There were policemen almost everywhere in the tent now; a long line of them at the back of the ring and several groups advancing in the aisles between the rows of seats. The audience laughed. For them it was all part of the circus, a great battle between the clowns.

'Catapults,' shouted Knocker, and he fired straight at a large policeman, hitting him in the stomach. The policeman grabbed at his midriff and fell to the floor.

'Come on,' shouted Chalotte, 'into the ring. Aim for the lights, it's our only chance.'

Chalotte's idea was a good one. The Adventurers gathered together next to Knocker and the light bulbs above their heads began to shatter as they aimed and fired. The big top grew darker and the laughter of the audience died away as glass fragments began to shower on their heads.

There was a roar from the policemen. 'Borribles,' they cried. 'Stop those Borribles, get 'em.'

Now the audience raised their voices in terror and the adults clasped their children tightly in their arms so that the policemen would make no mistake and drag them away. 'Borribles,' they said to one another, their voices brittle with fear. 'Those kids are Borribles.'

Chalotte was fighting back to back with Knocker. She aimed a stone at the main and central light. She was one of the best with a catapult and she made no mistake this time. There was an explosion and the tent was plunged into darkness. The audience screamed louder than ever and the children wept.

'Don't let 'em get away,' roared a voice and it was a voice that sent shivers down the spine of every Borrible there. It was the voice of

Sergeant Hanks and where Hanks went Sussworth was not far behind. 'Don't let them get away; they're dangerous Borribles.'

Sergeant Hanks had expected perhaps to help his cause by enlisting the aid of the audience but things didn't work out that way. The cry of 'Borribles' was taken up on all sides by the spectators, sure enough, but they panicked and, snatching up their children, they leapt to their feet and began to push their way towards the exits. This confusion assisted the Adventurers for a while. It meant that the policemen, trying to reach their prey from the back of the tent, could not advance against the mass of people trying to leave. All the Borribles had to do now was to evade the policemen actually in the circus ring, get under the canvas and escape into the crowds outside.

This was easier said than done. In the circus ring all was mayhem. Inspector Sussworth, with the intention of keeping the SBG raid totally secret, had not bothered to tell Signor Buffoni or any other of the circus people what he had in fact planned. Consequently the clowns in the ring, the real clowns, once they had recovered from their initial surprise, became very very angry. As far as they were concerned a group of unidentified men, dressed as clowns, had broken into the circus and ruined their performance just when it had been going well. For all they knew they had been attacked by their deadly rivals in the circus trade, Bernardo Mattamori and Sons. Such things had happened before.

Now in total blackness, the police began to grope right and left in an attempt to seize and arrest the elusive Borribles. Unfortunately they only succeeded in catching hold of a number of strong circus men who did not appreciate unknowns handling them in the dark. The circus people started to lay about them with a will, grabbing policemen's truncheons and cracking skulls with all the gusto of men who were used to swinging ten-pound sledgehammers and delighting in it. So the battle was joined in real earnest and although the circus people were outnumbered they more than held their own. They had been trained in the hard school of circus rings up and down the country. They knew all about jumping, falling, tumbling, throwing and ducking; the men of the SBG, for all Sussworth's pride in them, came off second best.

Even in the dark the clowns could find their props and some of them ran to their hosepipe. They turned it on and soaked everybody, policemen and escaping audience alike. They found a fire extinguisher too and covered the men of the SBG in sticky white foam. However hard the Woollies fought back, however loudly they shouted that they were officers of the law on official duty, the clowns would have none of it.

'Don't give us that,' they yelled. 'You're from Mattamori's. You can't keep a good clown down.'

Knocker too was shouting. 'Spread out,' he bawled. 'Separate. We'll meet by the horse if we can and take him with us. Make for Brixton Market and wait there. Go!'

On all sides of the Adventurers adults still fought, pushing and struggling, swearing and stumbling, too busy and too angry to notice the slight bodies of the Borribles as they squirmed and shoved their way to the side of the big top. Knocker found himself thrust against the back wall of canvas with Chalotte next to him. She took a knife and slit the tent open. She put her eye to the gap and stared out.

'Stacks of people,' she said, 'all watching. I can't see any uniforms,' and without saying any more she slipped from the tent and Knocker followed her, hoping that his friends were getting away as easily as he was. Knocker didn't know it but his optimism was misplaced.

As a result of the reprimand he had received from the DAC, Inspector Sussworth was determined not to fail this time. 'Acting on information received', as he put it, he knew for certain that the Adventurers were present at the circus that night and, to avoid alerting them, most of his men were not wearing uniform. He had disguised them as clowns, hot-dog sellers, ordinary citizens and, in case that was not enough, he had an outer ring of officers and police cars all round the outside of the circus, hiding in the trees and bushes, determined to see that no one got away. The crowd into which the Borribles sprinted in such high hopes of safety was laced with members, both male and female, of the SBG. The Adventurers had no chance at all.

Inspector Sussworth himself stood on the roof of his brand new snow-white caravan, a megaphone in his hands. Floodlights lit the whole area as clear as day. Sussworth was happy; he took no notice of the streaks of rain that blew with the wind over everything. He was shouting at the crowds, enjoying his power, his voice rising and falling in the gusty air.

'This is Operation Catsmeat, Operation Catsmeat. No one is to leave the area, repeat, no one. You are all under arrest but anyone apprehending and taking into custody any Borrible or suspicious child will be rewarded. Watch out for Borribles.'

Deep in the crowd Knocker put all his talents to their best uses. He twisted and turned, making for where he believed the horse to be, just beyond the sideshows under the trees. Chalotte followed him, keeping close. She could not understand it; the crowd was not a large lump of thoughtlessness like crowds generally are, this crowd was taking notice. Then Sussworth's announcement came bounding through the night and she knew why; the crowd was not just watching, it was actively looking for Borribles.

Chalotte stopped in her tracks, her heart turning to jelly. Never in her whole life had she been so frightened or felt so hopeless. There was a great roar in front of her and she saw Knocker thrown into the air, high above the heads of the crowd. His face shone in the floodlights; it was drawn and twisted with anger and fear. Knocker was dropped and then thrown up once more. There were shouts of excitement. Chalotte swore and pushed through a forest of legs. She came to the man who was holding Knocker and she sank her teeth into his thigh. The man yelled and grabbed his leg in pain. Knocker fell to the ground next to her but was immediately seized by another man. 'I've got him,' he yelled. Then rough hands caught Chalotte and yanked her up to adult height.

'Bite me would yer,' said a voice, and a fist struck her in the face and she was thrown upwards, dropped, and thrown up again and passed overhead from hand to hand like an unconscious spectator at a football match. She screamed and she kicked and she scratched but it achieved nothing. Rough fingers clutched and tore at her body and she and Knocker were rolled through the air towards the big white caravan on top of which stood Sussworth in his long overcoat, the buttons of it shining like cat's eyes through the wind and the rain.

*

The ground which lay closest to the big top had been trampled into mud by thousands of feet; it was a mud that was deep and stuck like glue. Napoleon crawled into it on his belly, a knife between his teeth, pushing with his hands. Behind him came Bingo.

'Tell you what,' said Napoleon, 'you go that way round the tent, and I'll go this way and meet you the other side. Cut every guy rope as you go and the whole bloody contraption will fall down. That'll keep the fuzz occupied.'

'Right,' said Bingo and drew his knife.

The plan worked well. With no tension to hold it in place the great marquee keeled gracefully over, its huge and heavy folds settling on the still struggling clowns and policemen.

Bingo and Napoleon met as arranged on the far side of the tent and, seeing that the crowd was thinner here, they made a rapid dash towards the obscurity of the nearest stand of trees. They ran fast, dodging this way and that round groups of people who could only stare as the Borribles ran by. Finally in the safety of the dark, under the trees, breathless, they looked back at the dazzle of the police floodlights.

'What a mess,' said Bingo. 'I wonder how the Woollies knew we were there.'

'Easy,' said a voice behind them, 'we knows everything.' And the two Borribles were knocked to the ground by heavy blows. Hands moved over their bodies and relieved them of their knives and catapults. Their arms were forced behind their backs and they were handcuffed. Not until they were hauled to their feet did they see that four or five members of the SBG, in uniform, stood around them. Beyond the trees they could see the indistinct shape of an SBG personnel van.

Bingo could not stand without support. The blow he'd received had knocked the breath from his body.

'You bastard,' said Napoleon. 'He's only a kid.'

The policemen laughed and one of their number leant forward and pulled Napoleon's ear, very hard. 'Oh yes,' he said, 'just a sweet little Borrible kid. Well, you'll be a little kid soon enough, back to normal for you, chummy, and no mistake.'

*

Stonks was strong, the strongest of all the Adventurers. During the confusion inside the big top he had stayed near his friend, Torreycanyon, and pushed a path for the both of them through the mad mob of fighting adults. Once outside they had enjoyed good luck, slipping unnoticed into a group of the audience who had children of their own and had been making their way to the outer ring of tents. The two Borribles had walked with them and when the time was right had ducked into a dark space between two sideshows and stayed there to catch their breath and take stock.

They could hear everything: Sussworth's voice on the loudhailer, and the shouts and jeers of the SBG as they chased and arrested Borribles and any of those circus hands who dared to defend themselves.

'We'll never make it back to the horse,' said Stonks. 'We'll do more good to get out of here and then help anyone who does get off.'

Torreycanyon nodded his agreement and the two friends backed away from the light and went to the rear of the tents. They looked out; darkness stretched for ever, right to the end of the great common.

'Okay,' said Stonks, 'let's run.'

With a sudden burst of speed both Borribles left their hiding place and raced into the open, heading for the trees and bushes they could see in the middle distance. They did not get far. They had covered only about ten or fifteen yards when a dozen shadows rose like trolls from the ground. There was a rapid movement in the air and a finely meshed net dropped over the fugitives and down they went, floundering like stranded fish.

*

Orococco and Vulge got clear of the big top and fought their way through the multitude like explorers hacking their way through jungle. They did not realize that the crowd was full of policemen but they could certainly feel hands snatching at their bodies as they dodged along and they could hear voices above their heads shouting after them.

'We'll have to make for the acrobats' tent,' suggested Orococco. 'It's our only chance; pretend we're with them, working for the circus.'

The two Borribles continued to push forward, kicking and shoving at the legs that barred their way. Somehow they managed to evade capture and got as far as the tent they were looking for. By the side of it was a tiny oasis of calm and they ducked into it. As they recovered their breath Sussworth's voice sounded from close at hand.

'Do not cease your vigilance, all Borribles must be arrested. Any members of the fairground staff who obstruct officers in pursuance of their duty will be imprisoned. The licence for the circus will be revoked.

Mr Buffoni, Mr Buffoni, you will come to the police headquarters caravan immediately. Order all your relations and staff to cooperate with the police. Mr Buffoni, Mr Buffoni.'

'Blimey,' said Vulge, 'the coppers are only just round the back here.'

Orococco nodded. 'That's fine, then they won't be looking for us this close to home. Quick, let's slip into the tent before we're noticed.'

Both Borribles lay on the ground and slithered under the bottom edge of the canvas, pulling themselves along with their elbows. Inside the tent the darkness was thick and there wasn't a sound to be heard.

'We'll make for the stage,' whispered Orococco, 'that'll do nicely.'

The two Borribles were halfway across the tent when there came a loud click; it sounded like a large switch being thrown. It was. Suddenly the whole place was lit from above and twenty light bulbs shone as bright as day. Orococco and Vulge looked at each other and climbed slowly to their feet. There was no point in not doing so.

On each side of the tent stood a row of SBG men and women in uniform, each one holding a truncheon. They smiled sweetly. Vulge nudged Orococco and jerked his head. 'We certainly came to the right place, Coco,' he said. 'Look.'

Orococco did. Laid out before them, at full length on the floor, tightly gagged and handcuffed, were all eight acrobats, arranged in a neat little row. Their hair had been pulled back to disclose their pointed ears and their eyes blinked in the sudden light. They looked full of fear, their bodies sagging, limp and hopeless, like big raw sausages on a grill punctured all over with fork holes and ready for cooking.

'I wonder what it's going to be like, growing up,' said Orococco, but there was no more time for talk. Huge hands seized him and Vulge and they were pinioned and flung to the ground.

*

When the Adventurers had rushed away in different directions from the big top one of their number had hesitated. Crouching low in the darkness just outside the tent she stared at the surging, violent crowd, completely dazed by the shouting and the floodlights.

As the big top began to collapse the circus people tried to come to the aid of their colleagues imprisoned under the falling canvas. Because they knew nothing of the SBG and its plans these circus people were still convinced that their show had been attacked by Mattamori's men, and they could not believe the plain clothes policemen who were insisting that they were indeed officers of the law. The circus people struck out first and asked questions afterwards.

This outburst of hostilities gave Sydney the opportunity she had been waiting for. Making herself as small as she could she passed through the areas of the fairground where the fighting was at its fiercest and managed to arrive at the outer ring of sideshows without calling attention to herself. Once there she crawled under the counter of the coconut shy and bumped into Twilight. Somehow in all that mayhem Sydney had found a friend.

The two Borribles were delighted to be together but there was really only one thought in Sydney's mind: find Sam, cut the rope that tied him to his tree and escape with him out on to the common. The idea that Sussworth might capture the horse and set him to work again filled her with dread and made her heart go cold.

'You're right,' agreed Twilight. 'I'll come along and give you a hand. And anyway,' he added, 'the horse is where we're supposed to meet, isn't it?'

The journey to the acrobats' marquee was accomplished with little trouble, the two friends simply creeping along from tent to tent and keeping on the side furthest from the crowds. Once at their destination they took up a position from which they could observe the marquee and Sussworth too. He was still prancing about on his caravan roof and still shouting into his megaphone for all he was worth. The inspector's staff officers were standing in a group, on the ground, staring at the riotous mob as it swirled past them, screaming in panic. But on the other side of a quiet open space, at the back of the tents and nearer to the Borribles than the policemen, under some trees in the half-dark, was Sam, ignored and unguarded.

Sydney drew her knife. 'I'm going to run over and cut him free,' she said. 'You keep watch, Twilight, and if any of the coppers look round and there's any danger of 'em seeing me, well, you'll just have to attract their attention and make 'em chase you. When I get the horse into the trees, then you come over. Okay?'

The girl did not wait for the Bangladeshi to answer. As light as the wind she ran to the horse, her arms outstretched.

'Oh Sam,' she whispered as she slashed the rope, 'we've got to scarper, like quick.' She pulled at the horse's rein but Sam did not stir. He shook his head like a wild thing, flared his nostrils and Sydney saw that the animal's legs were closely hobbled with tough nylon ropes. He could not move.

'The bullies,' said Sydney, and she knelt to hack at the hobbles, obliged to move fast. She'd been in the open too long. Again the horse shook its head and now it shuffled backwards. 'Oh, Sam,' said Sydney again, 'what's wrong, what have they done to you?'

Sydney had not seen what Sam had seen behind her, the slight form of Twilight dragged into the open, bound and gagged and made prisoner, or the ring of dark figures closing in on the girl from the tents and the trees. But with a glance she saw them and she moaned out loud, throwing her thin arms round the horse's neck, clinging there for dear life.

'Oh, Sam,' she cried, 'I've failed. They've got you again. I'm sorry, I'm sorry, I'm sorry.' And Sydney was downcast and she did not hear the triumphant voice on the megaphone announcing that all Borribles and their allies had been captured and that the battle was lost and won. She did not feel the big hands take the knife from her grasp or the catapult from her pocket, and she did not feel the cold handcuffs snapping on to her wrists like the bite of a dog. All Sydney could do was weep for the end of Sam, the horse she loved, gone for catsmeat.

4

Inspector Sussworth and Sergeant Hanks stood like presidential candidates on the rear balcony of the white SBG caravan. Below them, ankle-deep in mud, washed by a light rain, stood the Adventurers and the acrobats, handcuffed together in one long line, their pointed ears plainly visible. Behind them stood Sam the horse, behind him stood the circus clowns, also handcuffed, their faces bloody and their clothes torn. Surrounding them all stood a solid regiment of policemen, their black macs phosphorescent in the night like wet coal.

The SBG had at last restored order. The general public had been packed off home and the circus people had been locked in their caravans and commanded to remain there until further notice, on pain of arrest. A great quiet reigned where before there had been only riot and pandemonium. Nobody stirred except a few policemen who were wandering through the ruins of the great fight, making sure that no Borrible still lurked under the debris of torn canvas and battered sideshows. The desolation was complete.

Inspector Sussworth beamed over the scene like a lighthouse, striving to contain his pleasure but unable, his smile bursting out intermittently. His hands were grasped tighter than ever behind his back, his right hand trying to dislocate his left shoulder by yanking fiercely on that arm. His heels rose and fell in a persistent tattoo. At last he raised his hand; he was about to speak.

'Men,' he began, 'I offered you blood, sweat and tears but there was no time for weeping. We have won a famous battle, just as I said we would. Here stand the captives and their aiders and abetters, manacled together in shame and disgrace: malcontents and malefactors who would change the world because it doesn't suit them; who would descend to physical violence when the rules of society become inconvenient. Now we have caught the ringleaders and our struggle is almost over. We have caught their mascot too, this moth-eaten, knock-kneed, spindle-shanked, spavin-legged erstwhile equus. This wretched animal has become the symbol and the centre of their revolt. Well, so far and no further. If this horse is their heart, then I shall grasp that heart with both hands and rend it asunder. I hereby order that the aforementioned animal be conveyed from this place to an abattoir or slaughterhouse and there it will be banged on the head until dead and then hung up by its hind legs, from a hook. It will be slit open with a carver and minced into nice neat little tins of food for small kittens. I tell you men, Operation Catsmeat has been a complete success. A campaign medal will be struck.'

Sydney screamd and dropped to her knees in the mud. Because they were handcuffed so tightly together, Chalotte and Twilight were dragged down with her.

'No,' cried the girl as loud as she could. 'Leave Sam alone, it's not his fault. Do our ears if you have to but leave Sam out of it. He's only a horse; he's never done any harm.'

Sussworth laughed and danced contentedly, his hands fluttering up and down his chest like magpies looking for somewhere to land. Hanks's belly wobbled in merriment and he took a sweet from his pocket and shoved it into his mouth.

'Don't take on so,' said Sussworth, tilting his head in a gesture of ironic kindness. 'Sam will be free of all earthly constraints soon, but you and your acrobat friends are the ones in trouble. You will be worked to death once we get them ears of yours clipped. You'll be nice, normal wage-earners for the rest of your lives.'

Now the inspector gestured with his right hand and the regiment of policemen brought their heels together like soldiers.

'Take these Borribles to the special place,' ordered Sussworth, 'and these didicois as well. Lock 'em up and teach them a lesson. In the morning they will be charged with as many offences as I can think of. Take them away.'

As the Borribles were pushed towards the Black Marias parked ready by the side of the SBG caravan, Knocker stepped out of line, the handcuffs forcing his companions to move with him. He got as close to

Sussworth as he could, then he lifted his hands above his head and the chained hands of his friends were lifted too. Knocker shook his manacles till they jangled. There was blood on his cheek, his clothes were torn and his face was wild with anger.

'I'll kill you,' he said, his lips white. 'It's you who's done this violence, not us, Sussworth. I shan't rest till you're dead. I'll—'

Knocker was not allowed to finish. A policeman struck him smartly on the side of the head and he was shoved away with the others, staggering and slipping in the mud. Even the circus clowns were forced into a van and treated no better than the Borribles, but cuffed and prodded and sworn at. At least ten of them were in custody and a sorry sight they were. Some of them had fought long and hard under the big top. The others had been arrested while trying to go to their colleagues' aid. Not for one minute had they understood what had been going on. In the madness of the battle they had thought the circus under attack and had only meant to defend themselves. Now, if found guilty in court they would spend many months in prison, perhaps even a year or two.

Not only that but their circus was in ruins, their costumes had been ripped to shreds and all of them had black eyes, bloody noses and cracked heads. It was more than circus people could take and they too shouted threats at Sussworth and Hanks, but however much they raised their voices it made no difference. They were beaten into the Black Marias and the heavy doors were double-locked behind them. At a sign from Sussworth the vans were driven across the grass to the main road and from there the column turned towards Clapham South, heavily escorted. The Borribles had been caught and Inspector Sussworth was taking no chances.

Clapham South Underground station is only a few hundred yards from that part of Clapham Common where Buffoni's circus had made its pitch. By the time Sussworth's caravan had been towed there the prisoners were standing on the pavement, herded together and guarded by more than twice their number of policemen. The Borribles waited for Sussworth with some apprehension; what had he meant, 'Take them to the special place'? They did not have to wait long for the question to be answered. Near where they stood, on an odd corner of turf that seemed to be neither common nor wasteland, right next to a brick-built set of sour-smelling public lavatories, was a curious cement-covered building, half square, half circular. It was protected by a high wire fence and it was large and windowless, sinister and gloomy.

As soon as the caravan arrived, Sussworth and Hanks marched down its steps and, passing through a gate in the wire fence, went to a large iron door that stood in the square section of this bizarre building. There came the rattle of a key and the sound of a lock opening. The door was pulled outwards, a light was switched on and the prisoners saw a rectangular, unfriendly-looking hallway, quite large and made from concrete blocks.

'Right men,' said Sussworth. 'Bring the prisoners inside; look snappy, we don't want to be noticed.'

The inspector stood by the entrance and watched while his orders were obeyed. 'I want twenty men to lead the way in here,' he said. 'The prisoners will walk in the middle, and twenty more men will bring up the rear with Sergeant Hanks. I also want a guard of six constables on the caravan, and I want two more to take the horse to Wandsworth Prison where it will be incarcerated until the knacker's yard is ready for it. The rest of you will return to headquarters, but report here tomorrow, early. Is that perfectly clear?'

The men saluted and Hanks lost no time in deciding which of them would stay and which would go. These arrangements made, Sussworth ordered the great iron door closed and as the noise of its closing died he locked it with a great key and then put the key in his overcoat pocket, patting it afterwards in self-satisfaction.

Next Sussworth crouched to the ground and took another, smaller key from a different pocket and unlocked a steel flap in a manhole which had been cemented into the floor at the far end of the hallway. He fiddled with a combination lock and when the tumblers had fallen into place he commanded six of his officers to lift the trap. It was not an easy task. The manhole was thick and heavy, but after a great deal of panting and puffing by the policemen it swung back on its hinges.

Sussworth then reached into the hole that had been revealed and pulled a switch. Hundreds of lights came on and an air-conditioning plant began to hum as if from many miles away. The men of the SBG crowded round the opening and stared down. They gasped. They could see a stairway and it seemed to spiral away for ever and ever, disappearing only when it was too small to be seen.

'Yes,' said Sussworth proudly, as if he'd built it all himself, 'this is the eighth wonder of the world. What used to be, during the last war, a mere air raid shelter for the ordinary populace, has been excavated deeper and wider until it stretches halfway under Clapham Common. What we have here is a veritable city that contains all the things that our civilization needs to preserve in the event of a thermo-nuclear homocost: government offices, command posts, food, water, lavatories . . . and a jail, a very large one. If there is total destruction we have to ensure that our administrators survive, and that whatever happens law and order will continue beyond the day of doom. There is always a need for law and order, men, as you know. Sadly, even a thoroughgoing nuclear war won't extinguish villainy.'

'Is it a good strong jail, sir?' asked Sergeant Hanks.

'The best,' answered the inspector, 'that is why we are here tonight. No Borrible, however bright a burglar, can wangle his way out of this one. No clown, however comical, can laugh this off. Now, men,' said Sussworth, bringing his little speech to a close by jumping on to the first step below the trap, 'follow me. It's a long, long way to go, so best foot forward.'

With a flick of his moustache the inspector went out of sight and was followed immediately by the first contingent of his men and then the prisoners. They were followed in turn by Sergeant Hanks and his twenty officers, the very last one of them closing the manhole and locking it from the inside. As Sussworth had said: there was to be no escape.

*

Every step the Borribles took increased their despair. Worse than no escape there was not even the slightest hope of any. There was only one way out and that carefully guarded, and the corridors and passages formed a labyrinth where Sussworth deliberately took the prisoners back and forth, just to confuse them.

On every landing were tunnels leading off in all directions and from those tunnels they saw other tunnels and polished doors without number, each with a notice on it which they could read as they passed: CIGS, M15, M16, Admiralty, Home Office, Foreign Affairs Committee, Cabinet

Room, Squash Court, Security, PM, Swimming Pool, Ministry of Defence. Some of the doors were open and the prisoners caught glimpses of carpeted suites with tables covered in green baize surrounded by comfortable chairs. Many of the rooms had been laid out for relaxation with large sofas, cocktail cabinets and bookcases; and there were some with beds and divans too, all made up with freshly ironed pillowslips in readiness for the great day of Armageddon.

But at last the prisoners, stumbling now from weariness as well as dejection, were brought out into a wide and bare corridor that seemed to form the very base of the underground citadel, and here were more doors, solid steel this time with bolts top and bottom and peepholes for jailers to look through. Sussworth gave his orders and three of the cells with thrown open.

'You'll like this,' said the inspector, 'freezing cold they are.'

'What about some food?' said one of the clowns. 'We must eat.'

'I'm not so sure you must,' said Sussworth, 'certainly not until tomorrow. You'll be a lot more helpful after a couple of days without sustenance. Most people are.' He waved his hand and his policemen shoved the clowns into a couple of the cells and the doors were bolted behind them.

'Ah, Hanks,' said Sussworth, addressing his sergeant who was just bringing up the rearguard, 'I want you to bring those Borrible acrobats along for interrogation; just uncuff them from the others.'

Sergeant Hanks took a key from his pocket and did as he was ordered. 'Wonderful, sir,' he gloated. 'Nothing like a bit of interrogation to sharpen the appetite. I'm quite looking forward to it.'

The acrobats did their best to fight against the power of the policemen but they could not escape their fate. Ninch swore and punched and kicked like a savage, Scooter and Matzo did very much the same, but the rest completely lost their nerve and rolled on the ground, screaming in terror. None of it helped; laughing and jeering the huge, ham-handed policemen dragged the captives away by the feet, bumping their heads along the hard corridors until their cries grew fainter and fainter and were heard no more.

'There,' said Hanks as he prodded the Adventurers into their cell. 'When you see your little chums tomorrow with their ears all bloody and jagged you'll turn as good as gold, you will; tell us all we want to know, you'll see.' The sergeant slammed the metal door and the clang of it echoed along the corridors. Then he shot the bolts and pressed an eye against the peephole. 'There you are,' he said, 'all nice and safely off the streets. We'll have some fun tomorrow, I promise you. A bit of slap and tickle, you won't get bored for a second.' Hanks chuckled loudly to himself and then went away, his flat feet stamping into the distance.

'We're in it now,' said Twilight, 'right in it.'

'Yes man,' said Orococco, 'right in it is right, and we've never been deeper in it than this.'

*

In the most comfortable sitting room of that government command post the DAC poured himself a large gin and tonic, lowered his elegant body into a soft armchair and dangled his leg over the arm of it, swinging his foot gently back and forth. He tilted his glass in celebration. 'Have a drink, Susswort, old boy,' he said. 'My God you deserve it. You've exceeded the PM's wildest expectations.'

'No, thank you, sir,' said Sussworth, fidgeting with his tie. 'I don't drink, sir, ever sir. Certainly not whilst on duty.'

'Whilst, eh?' said the DAC raising an eyebrow. 'Well sit down man, you make the place look tidy.' The DAC smirked at his own joke. He was in a good humour.

Sussworth crossed the room and perched himself on the edge of an armchair which was at least three times too big for him.

'Wonderful place this, eh?' said the DAC, sipping at his drink. 'Such forethought and plannin'.'

'Oh yes sir,' said Sussworth, 'the Medium Operandi has to be protected.'

'Quite so, Sussworth, quite so.'

'You know sir, in a way I would quite welcome this homocost. It would be a way of sweeping things clean sir, getting things in order. Less people to discipline; it would be a fresh start.'

The DAC sipped his drink again. 'Yes,' he said, 'rather. Now I've been discussin' things with Whitehall and they want me to convey to you how pleased they are with the way things are goin' . . .'

Sussworth edged even further forward on his chair. 'Oh really, sir.'

'Yes.' The DAC waved a limp hand. 'Furthermore they want you to hold the prisoners here for as long as you can. They want to see if this Borrible thing collapses under its own weight. Now that you've captured the ringleaders and this blessed horse it might be a good idea for you to slow down.'

Sussworth's moustache drooped in disappointment. 'May I ask who in Whitehall sir, respectfully?'

The DAC sat straighter in his chair. 'Good Lord, Sussworth, go steady. It all comes under the Official Secrets Act. However I can tell you that the Treasury is very worried about the money we're spendin'. They want us to hold fire . . . Now don't look disappointed; it's probably only a temporary measure . . . Whitehall is delighted really, and those other things we talked of the other day, well, it's all on the boil.'

'Boil, sir?'

'Knighthoods, peerages and that, definitely in the offin', maybe even hereditary, none of these short-term life jobs. Any children, Sussworth? No! Eh? Never mind, just as well.'

The DAC emptied his glass and got to his feet. 'Keep up the good work. What have you done with that horse, eh?'

'Sent it to Wandsworth, sir, for the time being. It'll be on its way to the abattoir in a day or two.'

The DAC looked pleased. 'Splendid, Sussworth. Didn't like the way that horse kept poppin' into the picture . . . Odd that. Keep in touch then, on the private line to Scotland Yard. By the way, there'll be nothin' in the newspapers, I've seen to that. Just an affray on Clapham Common; local roughs versus gypsies . . . drunk and disorderly.'

Sussworth got to his feet also and pulled a brown envelope from his pocket. 'My confidential report, sir.'

The DAC reached for his alpaca overcoat; he looked quite shocked. 'Good Lord, no,' he said. 'No written reports, not even secret ones. I don't want to know how you do things, Sussworth, ever. It could be very embarrassin' if things go awry. This Borrible business is all off the record. All I want to know about is success, success. Don't let those children escape now. You'll never make viscount if you do. Keep your wits about you, eh?'

Sussworth twisted his ankles and bent his knees in a movement that was halfway between a curtsy and a bow. 'There'll be no way they can escape from down here,' he said, 'no way. I've got the top entrance guarded.'

The DAC looked at the inspector with distaste and wriggled his fingers into gloves of grey kid. 'No,' he said, and crossed the room to step into the high speed VIP lift that would carry him back to the surface of the earth. The doors closed automatically and Sussworth disappeared from sight. The DAC breathed a sigh of relief. A few seconds later he emerged from a concealed exit by Clapham South Underground station and, turning his collar up against the rain, he walked the few yards to where his black Rolls-Royce waited in the darkness.

The chauffeur was ready and opened a door; the DAC ducked into the car and settled into the soft cushions of the back seat. Then the chauffeur got behind the steering wheel, switched on the ignition and in a second the huge machine slid into the shapeless night, as silent as a cloud of poisonous gas.

*

In that same night and not so very far away the ruins of the circus glistened in the same rain that had fallen so briefly on the DAC. In the yellowness of their emergency lighting the people of Buffoni's travelling circus and fairground took stock and attempted to make good the terrible damage that had been done to them. It seemed hopeless. The big top was a wreck, torn and ripped, its guy ropes cut, its main pole leaning at a crazy angle, its canvas wet and heavy like the sails of a schooner gone aground.

The sideshows had fared no better; their boarding had been splintered, their tented walls unhooked from their moorings, their prizes trampled in the mud. Electric cables had been pulled from sockets and benches had been used as battering rams and lay everywhere in pieces. Lost clothing, hats, scarves and gloves littered the battleground and the ice cream wagon had been overturned, its contents – strawberry, coffee and vanilla – oozing into the mud.

The circus people felt they had been insulted to the depth of their being, brought down and belittled. And what was worse their clowns, all friends and relations, had been arrested and taken away. No amount of begging and pleading with Sussworth and Hanks had helped. The inspector would not even tell Signor Buffoni where the clowns were to be imprisoned and the circus owner had gone to his caravan and hidden his head in his hands.

But Ronaldo Buffoni was not a man easily overcome. For years he had travelled the roads of the world. He had been to India and America, to Australia and the Falkland Islands; many had been the tribulations he had been obliged to overcome. So, although he gave way to sorrow for a little while, ten minutes later he reappeared and gathered his people together in the acrobats' tent – it was the only one left standing – and everyone present could see that Signor Buffoni was in a towering temper. He climbed on to the stage and addressed his audience with words that shook with passion; there was fire in his voice.

'My family and friends,' he began, 'never have we been so insulted. We gave hospitality to some penniless travellers, wanderers like ourselves. We broke no law nor harmed anyone, and yet we were attacked and set upon by the so-called agents of law and order. Our circus and funfair is ruined, our livelihood gone. It will take us many weeks to put things back to where they were.' Signor Buffoni stuck his hands into his pockets; his stomach sagged over his belt unhappily. He thought for a minute and then raised his head. 'But we have survived worse than this, haven't we?'

The circus people looked at one another and began to remember. 'Yes,' yelled several of them. 'Not half.'

Signor Buffoni smiled. 'Remember the New Delhi cricket riots; remember the typhoon in the Java Sea; remember the shipwreck on the Barrier Reef. What is the Battle of Clapham Common to us? A mere bagatelle.'

The circus people cheered, they slapped each other on the back.

Signor Buffoni clenched both his fists and shook them. 'And so, my family and friends, we must get this show back on the road, now, as it is. Mend the timber, mend the canvas and mend the guy ropes. We will work through the night, we will glue it, hammer it, sew it and splice it.'

'Yes,' roared the circus people. 'We'll show 'em. They can't shove us off the road as easy as that.'

'Well said,' shouted Signor Buffoni across the noise, 'but let us not forget that they have imprisoned our clowns and our acrobats. We need our kith and kin, we want our friends to be free. There comes a time when even the law-abiding citizen is forced to break the law . . . and this is it. We must do something and we must do it now.'

The circus people were just about to cheer Signor Buffoni's speech again when there was a movement at the tent flap and Wanda the monocyclist rode headlong through the opening, advanced five yards, retreated three, turned several circles, went into reverse and then jumped to the floor, catching the bike by the saddle as it fell. 'Ta-ra,' she shouted out of force of habit and bowed.

'Neither the time nor the place,' said the Fat Lady. 'We're trying to discuss ways and means, seriously.'

Wanda dismissed the Fat Lady with a wave of the hand. 'You can't discuss ways and means if you don't know the way to the means,' she announced mysteriously.

'Well tell us your story,' said Signor Buffoni, 'and we shall listen.'

Wanda was happy now that she had the undivided attention of her colleagues. She cleared her throat. 'As you know,' she said, 'I am no hero but I am no dope, either. I decided the fighting was not for me and took myself off to the quiet of my caravan and watched the fracas from the window, and some fracas it was and I have seen plenty. When it was all over I see the guardians of law and order loading our clowns and our acrobats into one of their meat wagons like sides of beef. This is not right, I say to myself, so I mount my one-wheeler, slip into a dark-coloured raincoat, wind a scarf around most of my face and set off at a fast rate in the wake of the fuzz.'

'Where did they go?' said Marco, flexing his muscles. 'I'm going to beat them coppers into the ground like tent pegs.'

Wanda held up her hand, palm outwards, demanding patience.

'They are not far, my friends and cousins. But a few yards up this South Circular Road is a strange angular building with a wire fence round it. My guess is that it serves as some kind of long-term lock-up not known to the general public. A secret jail whose hours of visiting are few and not advertised in the morning newspapers.'

'Thinks like that don't happen,' said the Fat Lady. 'How can you tell it is a prison?'

Wanda placed a hand on her hip and sneered. 'Because, chubby-cheeks, for the simple reason I actually see our uniformed friends bending sticks on the heads of our compatriots and pushing them into the aforementioned hoosegow and turning a large key in a small aperture known to all as a lock. For me this is enough. Our chums are inside and maybe will stay there for ever, or until they are deceased which will be quite long enough, for them.'

'Hmm,' said the Sword-Swallower, 'it might be a private entrance to the Underground railway system.'

Wanda shook her head emphatically. 'Since when do the peelers take prisoners to prison by public transport?'

'Well, what are we waiting for?' asked the Fat Lady. 'To the rescue.'

There were shouts of approval from everyone present but Wanda raised her hand again. 'We will need to be cautious,' she said. 'Something like thirty or forty officers of the law went down into the ground with the prisoners, and there are six others on guard outside by the inspector's caravan. A little while later, for I continued to keep my eye on things from behind a tree, a Roller with a chauffeur appeared and from this chariot a toff emerged and he too went below. I fear that something nasty is being cooked up in a kitchen about which we know nothing, and we do not even know what is on the menu.'

'Then,' said Marco, 'the sooner we get our clowns and acrobats out of there the better it will be.'

'Not half,' shouted Vispa the ventriloquist, and he was so excited that he made his voice come from behind everyone and they all turned around to see who was coming and there was confusion and pandemonium.

'Wait a minute, wait a minute,' called Signor Buffoni. 'If we do this—'

'If,' shouted his audience. 'Not if . . . when.'

'When we do this,' continued Signor Buffoni, 'we must first think of the safety of the circus. Let the greater number of us remain behind and load up as quickly as they can all the broken bits, everything . . . Then, when we've rescued our mates we'll be ready to move and take the circus with us, and instead of going on to Brockwell Park, as planned, we'll go back to Hackney and mend everything there. If we move quickly enough we'll be back home and off the streets before the policemen know we've gone.'

There were cheers of agreement at the end of this speech and the circus people left the tent immediately and began to organize themselves; one large group being chosen to get the circus ready for the road, and a smaller one, a kind of commando, being given the responsibility of rescuing their colleagues, the clowns.

'What we must do,' said Signor Buffoni, who had once been in the army although nobody was quite sure which one, 'what we must do is make sure we have a line of retreat. We do not want the police following us back to Hackney; we need a couple of hours' start at least.' And with no more discussion than that the small band of intrepid travellers took leave of their friends and relatives and made off across the dark and silent grass of the common, flitting from tree to tree, heading straight for Clapham South, led there by Wanda on her monocycle.

*

At a distance of twenty yards or so from Sussworth's caravan the circus commando took cover behind two or three large trees. By the light of a distant street lamp they could see three policemen huddled against the wire fence surrounding the mysterious building that was the entrance to the underground citadel. Beyond it the main road curved, empty of all movement, away westwards, down the long hill towards Balham, and a light wind drove the rain from the dark reaches of south London in flurries across the tarmac.

'There were six on guard when I left,' whispered Wanda. 'The other three must be in the caravan . . . and the Roller's gone.'

'What shall we do?' asked Signor Buffoni. 'How shall we proceed?'

'We have a plan,' said Marco, 'Vispa and I. All you have to do is watch.' And at a sign from Marco the ventriloquist threw his voice past the three policemen and against a blank wall so that it rebounded and appeared to be coming from somewhere near the Underground station. The three policemen sprang upright immediately and faced about, turning their backs towards the trees where the circus people were concealed. It was no wonder they moved so quickly. The voice the ventriloquist was using sounded exactly like Sussworth's.

'Have I caught you men napping when you should be on duty?' said the voice. 'I warned you men to be alert; this could mean demotion. Get yourselves over here, you slovenly lot.'

The policemen stared towards the station but they could see no one. Slowly they advanced to the edge of the road, going in the direction they thought the voice was coming from, not daring to ignore the orders of their superior.

No sooner had they begun to move than Marco ran from his hiding place, came up behind them and with his enormous strength banged their heads together so smartly that they fell senseless to the ground.

As soon as this was accomplished the rest of the circus people appeared and dragged the unconscious policemen into the dark by the side of Sussworth's caravan. Here the Sword-Swallower went through their pockets and found a set of keys to the citadel, which he immediately handed over to Signor Buffoni.

'Now,' said the circus owner, 'if we can get our hands on the men in the caravan, we're in business.'

'Don't worry,' said Vispa, and he marched to the caravan steps as bold as brass and began to give more orders, not only in Sussworth's voice this time but in the voice of Sergeant Hanks as well.

'What are those men doing in my caravan, Hanks? I want them out of there. It's a disgrace.'

'Yessir, yessir. Come on now, you constables, let's be 'aving you nice and lively, on the double.'

There were at first only slight sounds from within the caravan but there came more and more as Vispa kept up his stream of orders. In less than a minute or two the door of the caravan was opened and, pushing against each other in their haste not to be last, the three policemen tumbled down the steps.

Once again Marco did his work. His huge fist struck three blows and the guardians of law and order collapsed unconscious.

'Excellent,' said Signor Buffoni. 'Handcuff them all together, gag them too and we'll lock all six of them in the caravan.'

'That's right,' said the Fat Lady. 'We'll take these as well.' She ripped the radios from all six policemen and shoved them under her huge jumper. 'Who knows?' she added. 'They may come in useful.'

The moment all was ready Signor Buffoni used the captured keys to open the gate in the wire fence and then led his troops to the solid steel door which he opened in the same way. Inside they soon found the heavy manhole, and the Sword-Swallower, who was thought to have had a criminal past, made short work of the combination lock. Marco then spat on his hands, rubbed them together and hoisted the trapdoor all on his own. For a second the circus people were stunned, gawping at the staircase that wound down into the infinity beneath their feet.

'Never mind,' said Wanda. 'We can't turn back now.'

'Certainly not,' agreed Signor Buffoni. 'Now follow me, and step quietly. Surprise is everything in these operations.'

It took the Buffonis hours to discover where the policemen were. From each landing led scores of corridors and there were scores of landings – each one needing to be investigated in case the prisoners were overlooked. By the time they had reached the last level of all the circus people had almost given up hope of finding their friends.

'But don't despair,' said the Sword-Swallower, 'there *are* signs of life down here; there are police raincoats hanging up on the wall, there is mud on the floor, there is a helmet on that chair. This is it.'

And it was. Rapidly Signor Buffoni gave his orders. 'The Fat Lady will block the staircase,' he said. 'Let no one pass. The rest of you, follow me.'

There was an uncomfortable feeling in those wide steel corridors, a claustrophobic feeling of lethargy and hopelessness. The circus people could sense it as they tiptoed silently back and forth, looking for a clue that might tell them in which cell the captives lay. But there seemed to be no answer to their problem short of opening all the doors and waking all the policemen; no answer, that was, until Wanda was struck with a brainwave.

'Have you not noticed, you guys,' she said to Signor Buffoni and the others, 'that the fuzz down here is so sure of its security that there's no one on duty? They think no one can find the way in, let alone find the way out. Also, this here is a headquarters for our leaders to live in after the big bang. Now all these doors we have been looking at have spyholes in so that they can double up as prison cells in times of war, revolution and other disturbances. We have not wanted to open these spyholes in case we find a copper staring at us from the other side, but . . . these doors have bolts on the outside, one at the top and one at the bottom.'

'Which means,' said the Sword-Swallower, catching on to the idea, 'our job is relatively easy after all.'

'Too true, friend,' said Wanda, 'too true. All we have to do is open the bolts that are closed and close the bolts that are open, and wrong will be made right and right will be rightly wronged. A philosophical turn-round. Life's problem answered in a nutshell by the sliding of a bolt.'

Very gingerly the circus people went to every steel door on that landing and changed the position of each bolt. At the end of this exercise they found themselves with four doors that they could open. They looked at each other and smiled.

'Well,' said Signor Buffoni. 'I think this must be the time to start the ball rolling.'

Gently, and taking a deep breath, Signor Buffoni eased open the first door. Inside was as brightly lit as outside and a pitiful scene met his eyes. The Adventurers, with no beds, no blankets and no cushions, lay fast asleep on the cold steel floor, curled in each other's arms for warmth. Their clothes were torn, their faces bruised and dirty, furrowed with wandering tracks where tears had run.

Signor Buffoni was speechless with pity. Wanda wasn't. 'Did you ever see such a sight in all your born days?' she said. 'Kids handcuffed.'

'What are we going to do with them?' asked the Sword-Swallower. 'They're not ours.'

'Not ours,' retorted Signor Buffoni, 'of course they are ours. They are friends of our acrobats; they were invited into my big top and what is more they fought on our side. That makes them honorary Buffonis. Wake 'em up and send 'em on their way.'

'Certainly,' said Wanda, and she snatched the bunch of keys from the Sword-Swallower and began to unlock the handcuffs from the wrists of the Adventurers, shaking each one awake as she did so.

Chalotte was the first to open her eyes and she stared at the ceiling, not realizing where she was. She rubbed her hands into her face and then saw that her wrists were free. She looked at Wanda, stupidly.

'I'm dreaming,' she said. 'I'm dreaming.' But she wasn't. There were the others, getting to their feet, massaging their stiff arms, and the cell door was open too and five or six circus people were staring through the opening.

'Hurry,' said Signor Buffoni, 'the way out is clear but there is no time to lose. We have to release the clowns and the acrobats yet. Come on.'

The Adventurers needed no second bidding. Still dazed and confused, and weak from hunger too, they stumbled from their cell and ran along the corridor until they reached the foot of the stairway that would lead them to freedom. Here they found the Fat Lady on guard, wedged into the exit, but she saw them coming and with no need for orders she moved her solid body from their path.

The Borribles hardly said goodbye but raced up the concrete stairs of the citadel as fast as they could go. It seemed to all of them that they would never reach the top, that they would never feel the wind on their faces again, but at long last they saw the trapdoor above them and it was open. Soon they were pushing and pulling each other up the final flight of steps and a moment later they were gulping down huge mouthfuls of the night air.

All was empty around them. No one moved on the spaces of the common or on the high roads. Only the wind and the rain rustled in the trees and not a sound came from Susswortth's caravan. For a second the Borribles looked at each other and touched hands.

'Let's not hang about,' said Napoleon as soon as he'd regained his breath. 'There's no point in staying here to be caught, is there?'

'Yeah,' said Stonks, 'but which way?'

'Any way,' said Knocker, 'but let's go towards Brixton. We know there's a market there, and we need food.'

The Adventurers agreed on this plan of action and set off at a run, cutting across a corner of the common and heading towards the back streets of the South Side. They were bubbling with happiness at being free. It was wonderful to be out in the open – even the rain felt special, like a gift. But in that brilliant moment of happiness they'd forgotten one thing; they'd forgotten the very reason for their journey. Only Sydney remembered it. Only her heart was sad and she could not run at the same speed as the others. Her feet were heavy and the tears streamed down her face. On the very edge of the common, as the Adventurers were about to cross the main road towards the houses, Sydney stopped and leant her forehead against a lamp post.

'I can't,' she said. 'I can't go any further. We've got away but they've got Sam. You heard what Sussworth said. They've taken him to Wandsworth Prison . . . They're going to turn him into catsmeat. Oh Sam!'

The others gathered around Sydney and tried to comfort her. 'What can we do, Sid?' asked Vulge. 'What can anyone do?'

'I don't know,' said Sydney. 'Perhaps I could be near the prison when they bring him out.'

The others did not answer. It seemed that Sam's situation was hopeless. Chalotte sighed and grabbed her friend by the shoulders and there, in the circle of Borribles, under the lamp post, with the rain still soaking them all, she gave Sydney the straight of it.

'It's no good, Sid; you'll have to come with us. We don't stand a chance of getting Sam out of Wandsworth Prison, but we might be able to save him later. Right now our first duty is to save ourselves; we can't help Sam at all if we're in the nick and Wandsworth is the first place Sussworth will look for us. We've got no food, no catapults, no knives, no raincoats, no nothing. We've got to get all those things first, then we can help the horse.'

Sydney sniffed and pushed the wet hair out of her eyes. She looked at the faces of her friends, waiting faithfully for her in the middle of that London night and she tried to smile. 'What you say is right enough; it's just that I hate to think of Sam in the hands of Sussworth and Hanks, let alone him going to the slaughterhouse.'

'We'll get him back,' said Twilight. 'We did it before and we'll do it again, we promise you.' And seizing Sydney by the hands and arms her companions dragged her across the main road at a run and the whole band of Borribles disappeared into those silent side streets where the dawn is always late in coming.

5

Through all that remained of the night, strung out in single file, the Borribles marched and ran. They left the common by way of Narbonne Avenue, Hambalt and Abbeville and it was as they turned into Abbeville that Stonks, who was keeping the rearguard, noticed that he was being followed. He gave a low whistle of warning and it was relayed ahead until everyone in the long line of fugitives had taken cover behind the nearest wall or in the nearest front garden.

Stonks crouched by the side of a dustbin and waited until he saw two small figures run quickly past him. As soon as they'd gone by he emerged from his hiding place and followed. The next in line was Vulge and he did what Stonks had done and when the intruders had overtaken the third Borrible, who was Torreycanyon, they were attacked and brought to the ground, swiftly and silently.

'Give over,' cried a voice. 'We've been trying to catch you up. It's Ninch and Scooter.'

Stonks gave the word and Ninch and Scooter were allowed to get to their feet. 'How did you find us?' he asked.

'The Buffonis let us out right after you,' said Ninch. 'When we got to the top of the stairs we could see you across the common, by a lamp post. We just came after you . . . The others have been clipped.'

Stonks nodded. 'That's tough,' he said, 'but there's no time for talking now. We have to be off the streets by daylight. There'll be Woollies everywhere, so get moving and follow the others.' And then he gave another whistle to denote that all was now well.

In no time at all the Borribles were once more on the move, travelling carefully, keeping away from the main roads and using parked cars to camouflage their movements. In this manner they quickly crossed

Clapham Park Road and entered a maze of tiny alleys which ran through a red-brick estate of little maisonettes and flats; into Triangle Place, into Nelson's Row and out on to Haselrigge Road, running faster and faster now because the heavy clouds of night were lifting and a greyness was creeping down from the sky and into the littered streets.

Knocker glanced upwards. 'Got to find something soon,' he said to himself, and as he did he emerged from a passageway that had led him behind a block of sleeping houses, and found himself looking at a three-storey school with wire over its windows. He read the notice on the high brick wall that protected the playground. 'Aristotle Road School', it said, 'Keep Out'. Knocker smiled. This was just the place, a school that was no longer in use.

*

The Adventurers had no difficulty in making their way into the building and they installed themselves for the day in a small office on the top floor. At first they slept, for they had travelled far and undergone much in the previous forty-eight hours, but they could not sleep for long – their hunger was too acute and the school was without heating. Soon they were shivering with cold.

They were indeed in a sorry plight: they had lost all the equipment they had brought from Battersea; they had no iron rations, no protective clothing, no catapults and no knives. They were defenceless, and what was worse they dared not even venture into the streets to look for food; they knew that Sussworth would have policemen everywhere searching for them. Every suspicious child would be arrested, especially if seen stealing.

'We have to go to ground,' said Stonks. '"Better a day without grub than a life without ears."'

The Borribles heard the wisdom of the proverb and tried not to think of food, snuggling closer together to keep out the cold. Through the day they dozed and coughed and sneezed. Now and then they talked, wondering if the SBG had any idea of their escape route, if Sussworth really intended to have Sam slaughtered; but above all they asked themselves how Sussworth had known that the Borribles had been hiding in a circus on Clapham Common.

'Well it's obvious,' said Napoleon, screwing up his face and looking in turn at everyone in the room. 'Someone told him . . . and more than likely it was someone here. One of us is a traitor.'

'It can't have been,' said Orococco. 'You can't suspect us.'

'I suspect everybody,' said Napoleon proudly and dug his thumb into his chest. '"The Borrible who ain't suspicious long ain't long a Borrible."' He looked at Ninch and Scooter, who sat together on the floor, leaning against the wall. 'What about them?' he said, pronouncing every word with emphasis. 'We don't know them much, do we?'

There was silence and the Borribles stared at the two circus acrobats.

Ninch leapt to his feet. 'I'm as Borrible as you lot,' he cried. 'Leave it out. I'm a Borrible I tell you, look at my ears; you don't get ears like that without being a Borrible. And look at Scooter; you never saw anything more like a Borrible in your life.'

'Yes,' said Scooter, 'we're Borrible all right, else why did we come running after you tonight? To join up with you of course. Borrible should help Borrible.'

'What about the others, then?' asked Napoleon with a sneer in his voice. 'Where are they then? What happened when Sussworth took you away on your own?'

Ninch looked quickly from Napoleon to Knocker and then to Chalotte. 'They interrogated us,' he said. 'Knocked us about. They clipped the ears of the others: Matzo, Sinbad, Duster, Frisby, Flapjack and Lobda . . . all of them. Hanks did it; you can see he likes doing it . . . you can see.'

'It's daft, anyway,' said Torreycanyon. 'How can they be traitors when they got captured with us and nearly lost their ears into the bargain?'

'We can't go back to the circus even if we wanted to,' said Scooter. 'Even if the Buffonis get clean away before Sussworth knows which way they've gone he'll still find them in the end and if he finds us with 'em it'll be snip, snip, snip.'

'Snip, snip, snip is right,' said Ninch. 'I tell you it wasn't us who gave you away.'

Napoleon did not look convinced. 'Someone did,' he said, 'and if I find out who it was I'll skewer him up. I say this: we need a new rule until this is over, the rule of Aristotle Road.'

'What rule?' said Stonks.

Napoleon looked round the room. 'This rule,' he said. 'No one goes anywhere on their own. There's always got to be two or three together.' He straightened his arm and pointed a finger at Ninch and Scooter. 'Especially them two; I don't trust 'em.'

'Don't be daft,' said Scooter, 'we only just missed having our own ears done. Hanks would have too only Susswort was called away to see a bloke from Scotland Yard. Hanks swore he'd clip us in the morning, then he threw us back in the cell.'

'I don't care if they nearly chopped yer head off,' said Napoleon, the anger and impatience getting stronger in his voice. 'You accept the rule or I'll know what to think.' He looked at the others. 'It's better than being shopped again, and whatever you say someone shopped us, you can't deny that. Who agrees?'

Bingo raised his hand immediately. He was Napoleon's special friend. 'I do,' he said.

Then Knocker raised his hand and, slowly, everyone in the room followed suit, even Ninch and Scooter. The Aristotle Rule was adopted.

*

All that day the rain slanted across the sky and fell on the black slate roofs and black tarred roads of the city. It fell on the dead gardens of winter; it fell into the chimneys. It ran down the grimy windows of the shops and across the pavements and into the gutters. The drains and sewers of London were full of rain water and all this time the Borribles rested behind the blank walls of Aristotle Road School. They were starving but they were safe. Not once did they hear a police siren, not once did they hear a caretaker. They just waited for the hours to pass and the daylight to fade. When it was dark again they would journey on towards Brixton and, they hoped, some food, even if it was only the scraps in dustbins.

Then it was night-time. Knocker stood and stretched. He went to the window and looked down at the street lights and the cars passing in Bedford Road. 'We'll give it until the pubs close,' he said, 'and then another hour after that. Might as well be as careful as we can. Sussworth took my map away but if I've got it straight that railway line over there will take us right into Brixton . . . It's only a couple of miles off.'

On the stroke of midnight the Adventurers left the school, crossing the road one by one and moving like shadows into a builder's yard that lay deep in darkness. On the far side of it they came up against a steep embankment which they climbed to the railway line. They halted there and listened; all was quiet and invisible, there was no moon and no stars.

'Tread very careful,' said Knocker, 'and keep yer ears open. I never saw a timetable for this line so if you hear a train coming get off the rails sharpish, and don't step on the live one by mistake; you'll be burnt to a crisp if you do.'

It was not a long march to Brixton, just about two or three miles as Knocker had said. On either side of the railway lay long rows of terraced houses where not one light shone. All was asleep and the weight of sleep bore down on the whole city, and nothing moved in the backyards save for the feral cats stalking mice across the mounds of rubbish.

Halfway through the march the railway line dropped to street level and the Adventurers passed under an old iron footbridge which joined one dead end street to another. It had been scrawled over in white chalk and paint and its side had been covered in wire to prevent children throwing bricks down on to passing trains.

Twilight stopped for a moment to read some of the messages there and discovered a 'Borribles rule, okay' and an arrow pointing towards Brixton. 'That's good,' said the Bangladeshi, 'it means there are some Borribles round here after all.'

'Yeah,' said Bingo, 'and let's hope they turn out sweet and gentle, like the Wendles.'

It was about two in the morning when the Adventurers finally reached Brixton railway station and Knocker climbed on to a parapet to look down into the emptiness of Brixton Road. 'It seems all right,' he whispered. 'Let's get down there and find some food.'

After a short search the Borribles found the station entrance and scrambled without difficulty over the gate that barred it. They then found themselves at the top of two flights of stone stairs and having descended these they saw, by the light of a solitary and dismal lamp, that they were in a low railway arch that led to the streets.

Knocker told his companions to wait and crept to the end of the tunnel and peered out. He could see no one; the street was empty of any human movement. All that remained of that day's market was the deep litter strewn across the pavements. Knocker glanced up and read the road names: Atlantic Road, Electric Avenue. He beckoned to the others and they joined him on the edge of the deserted street. A car went by on the main road but it wasn't a police car.

'What we've got to do,' suggested Knocker, 'is have a quick butcher's at this rubbish and see if we can't find something to eat, just to keep us going.'

There was fruit aplenty in that market and a couple of damaged loaves. Some dented tins of beans had been thrown into a cardboard box and there was a crate of overripe bananas that had not been sold. There was a feast there, almost more than the twelve runaways could carry.

'Come on,' said Bingo, who was now acting as lookout, 'we've got more'n enough. Quick, let's go down here.' Always light on his feet the Battersea Borrible led his friends into Electric Lane, away from the market area and towards what he hoped would be quieter streets, streets with a few derelict houses in them maybe, and a Borrible or two with a cup of tea ready.

Just as he was enjoying these thoughts Bingo suddenly felt his feet kicked away from underneath him. He was tipped heavily to the ground and a dirty cloth went over his mouth. Bingo fought but there were too many holding him now. A knee hit him in the kidneys, hard, and all the breath left his body and he let it go slack.

'You keep real quiet, Honky,' said a West Indian voice, 'otherwise I'll tear your head off.'

Bingo did as he was told; he could do nothing else. He heard the sounds of rushing feet, a few cries and even the noises of a few blows, then there was complete silence again. The voice above Bingo spoke once more.

'I'm going to tie you up now, Honky, and if you struggle I'll strangle you anyway and then rope you to a bus . . . They keeps stopping and starting all day.'

Once his arms had been tightly tied behind his back Bingo was dragged to his feet and pushed forward. He could see that he was surrounded by four or five figures; their faces were black and blended with the night. Beyond them shapes moved indistinctly in the darkness. He heard a cry followed by a blow.

'Why don't you leave us alone?' said Bingo. 'We ain't harming anyone, we're just travelling through.'

'That's right,' said the same voice as before. 'You'll be travelling through so fast your feet won't hit the ground, but every other bit of you will.' Bingo was struck between his shoulder blades. He swore and he stumbled. He heard Napoleon shout, threatening someone with violence. There came the sound of a blow and Napoleon was silent.

The captives were not taken far. Before they reached the end of Electric Lane they were made to turn back into Electric Avenue. Here they passed beneath an arcaded walk of Victorian design, the arcade being held aloft with delicate cast iron columns. About a hundred yards into the arcade, at the centre of a covered market and between two shopfronts, was a narrow entrance, locked, barred and chained. At least it appeared to be. In fact there was a panel in the face of a heavy door and that panel swivelled on hinges to allow the passage of one person at a time, provided he crawled through on his hands and knees.

'Okay, Honky,' said Bingo's guard. 'Follow me.'

It was difficult for Bingo to negotiate the entrance, especially with his arms tied behind his back, but he managed it eventually and found himself in a narrow corridor. That was all he could tell; it was pitch black in there and his captors, though close, were invisible.

One by one the prisoners were gathered together with their guards, and as soon as all were present more orders were given.

'Okay,' said the voice again. 'You'll go upstairs now. I'll switch on one torch . . . but don't try nothing.'

The Adventurers followed the light to the end of the corridor and began to climb some bare wooden stairs. Up they went and on what seemed to be the top floor of the building the stairs widened into an extensive landing with doors leading right and left. Here the prisoners were taken into a room and made to squat in a row, on the floor, their backs against a wall.

The torch beam flickered here and there over the darkness as people came and went and the Borribles waited. Bingo heard people talking in a language he could not understand. He tested the strength of his bonds but they would not shift an inch. Then, without warning, the lights went on.

Now Bingo could see the whole line of his captive friends. They were still together but all of them bore marks of the struggle. Napoleon had a cut over one eye and blood ran down his face. Stonks was covered in traces of market filth where he had rolled on the ground fighting, and Scooter had a black eye.

Bingo next looked at the people who had set the ambush. There were about fifteen in the room, half of them girls. Outside on the landing, Bingo could see many more people staring. They were without exception black, and as far as Bingo could tell, all of them were Borribles.

The Adventurers continued to wait and wonder. Then there was a movement at the door and the Borrible who had spoken to Bingo in the dark came into the room followed by some of his henchmen. He wore an enormous bulging cap, and it drooped to one side of his head; on the other side dreadlocks hung down to his shoulders. The cap was black velvet but the rest of his clothes were in bright and shiny colours: orange trousers with blue leg-warmers over, a plastic jacket of green and a mauve jumper under that. His lips were big and expressive, powerful and generous; his strong teeth protruded slightly. He looked cheerful and when he saw the prisoners he laughed delightedly and slapped hands with his friends. There were about thirty people in the room now and the only whites were among the Adventurers.

Bingo glanced at Knocker and Knocker licked his lips. 'We don't want any trouble,' he said, 'we didn't come looking for it.'

Black-Hat dropped his smile and prodded Knocker in the chest with his foot, hard. 'You can't give us none, Honky, we've got you tied up. You're trespassin' on our manor . . . you're the one in trouble.'

Chalotte jeered at Black-Hat: 'Don't be so bloody stupid,' she said. 'We're Borribles, just the same as you are.'

Before the Brixton Borrible could answer Orococco scrambled to his feet and began to speak, but not in a way the Adventurers had ever heard him speak before. He was using a West Indian dialect which the blacks only spoke among themselves and Black-Hat and all his friends listened to every word, not interrupting once, though they turned to stare occasionally at the captives, sometimes looking serious, sometimes smiling and shaking their heads.

Knocker tried to understand what was being said but all he could manage was to pick out two or three expressions; Rumbledom for one, Sam the horse, Inspector Sussworth and SBG. Orococco was telling most of the story and it took a long while; towards the end of it he reverted to English and looking Black-Hat straight in the eye he said, 'And that's the truth of it, all of it. And you can look at our ears, man, if you want. Knocker Burnthand is there. If you don't believe the story look at his hands, burnt across the palms they are, and his back too if you look at it. I tell you all we want is a few days' rest, some food, and we'll be on the road. You see we just want to get that horse away from Sussworth, that's all, and then go on home. Borrible should help Borrible you know, especially if they are on the run, and we're on the run all right.'

Black-Hat looked at his friends and after the shortest of silences they began to laugh, lightly at first and then louder and louder, slapping their hands all over again. What had been a dangerous situation had now become a highly amusing one.

'My name is Bisto,' said Black-Hat, shouting over the noise, and with a long finger he pushed aside his dreadlocks to reveal a pointed ear, a Borrible ear, one that showed great intelligence and cunning. When this was done he drew a knife and, first inspecting the ears of each and every captive in turn, he cut the ropes that bound them and welcomed them to Brixton.

Orococco, his hands free, rubbed his arms to renew the circulation and introduced each Adventurer, telling of their names and their boroughs.

'I'm a Totter from Tooting,' he explained. 'Twilight's from Spitalfields, Chalotte's from Whitechapel, Vulge from Stepney, Torrey's from Hoxton, Sid's from Neasden, that's Ninch and Scooter from the circus . . . and we've even got a Wendle.'

'A Wendle,' said Bisto, his eyes widening with interest. 'Which one?'

'Me,' said Napoleon Boot, screwing his face up tight to make his hard face look even harder. He looked small against Bisto.

Bisto screamed with laughter and pointed Napoleon out to some of his friends. 'Hey,' he yelled, 'this here's a Wendle. Well, I dunno. I was always told they was the most frightening animals on earth, but you ain't no taller than four-pennyworth of coppers. I've seen more meat on a butcher's pencil.'

Napoleon was not a bit put down. 'You watch it, Marmite,' he said, the old truculent sneer on his face. 'You come up the Wendle with me in a boat, that's all, across the mudflats and we'll see how tough you are then.'

Bisto laughed again. 'Marmite,' he screamed and tears of mirth stood in his eyes. 'That's the best insult I've ever heard, that's wonderful,' and he put his long arm round Napoleon and shook him affectionately and was so amused that Napoleon could no longer be angry or even pretend to be.

*

Once they had been accepted the Adventurers were made to feel very welcome; they felt they had come home. They were fed and clothes were brought for them to choose from. They were given raincoats, sou'westers and also catapults and maps, in fact all the supplies they would need to continue their great trek to Neasden.

They were given the run of Brixton too. 'Don't you worry about the old SBG, man,' Bisto had explained with a generous wave of his arm. 'They don't like coming down here. Wander about where you like; my house is your house.'

The rooms above the market were high and large and it seemed that they had been deserted for years, their windows dark and dirty; only the ground floor being used as shops and warehouses. Adults rarely climbed the stairs, and if they did the Brixton Bumpers, as the West Indian Borribles were called, would simply move from house to house through openings they had made in the dividing walls. The whole three storeys of the long curving Victorian terrace was a honeycomb of rooms and passages, a delight to live in and easy to escape from. There must have been scores of Borribles living there, if not hundreds, and the place had been comfortably furnished too. There were cheerful pictures drawn on the walls; the floorboards were covered in carpets that had been rescued from rubbish dumps and there were old sofas and mattresses, more than were needed. There were dozens of orange boxes as well, standing in corners and brimming over with books and magazines, all of them saved from dustbins and rubbish heaps. It was a Borrible paradise.

Bisto and his band of mates occupied two rooms in this terrace of houses, up on the third floor of Electric Avenue. They were good Borribles, the Bumpers, and some of the friendships made between them and the Adventurers were to last a Borrible lifetime. There was Arfinch, Sherbet and Peelo, they were the girls; as well as Three-Wheels, Butterfly, Tosheroon and Smoky; and every one of them had offered to share their hideout with the Adventurers for however long they wanted to stay.

There was no doubt that the Adventurers did need to rest. Most of the time they were in Brixton they spent indoors, lazing on the mattresses, recovering from their exhaustion. Half sleeping they could hear the sounds of the great crowds in the streets below; thousands of people tramping in and out the shops, wandering round the stalls, and through it all the voices of the costermongers shouting their wares. These were the sounds that made the Adventurers feel very much at home, safe and comfortable.

They did other things of course – swapping stories and telling one another how they had won their names – and they went out on to the streets of Brixton as well, with Bisto and his friends, to be amazed and delighted at the movement and colour they found there.

It was very enjoyable, perhaps too enjoyable. Had there not been the problem of Sam, the Adventurers might have stayed in Brixton for ever. As it was that wouldn't do. A day slipped by, then two, then three. Sydney began to worry about the fate of the horse and reminded her friends of it. The Adventurers, thanks to the kindness of the Bumpers, now had everything they needed for the road; there was no excuse for delay. The only thing they didn't have was a plan. Was Sam still in Wandsworth Prison, or was he already as dead as Sussworth had promised he would be, already minced in shiny tins of catsmeat in some supermarket?

There was much discussion about the problem, and the Bumpers, who had been told in great detail about the Great Rumble Hunt and everything that had happened since, were asked for their advice. It was Arfinch who came up with the best suggestion of all.

'There's a bloke,' she said as they were eating on the third afternoon of the Adventurers' stay. 'He lives down Rattray Road someplace. He's a friend of mine. He ran away from some telecommunications family. Anyway, he's a whizz-kid. He's the one who keeps us in front of the

Woollies. He lives in a cellar and he's dug through to the telephone cable . . . He's plugged into the whole world, he hears everything.'

'That's right,' said Sherbet. 'If anyone knows what the SBG have done with your horse, Stovepipe's yer man.'

'Can we go and see him?' asked Chalotte. 'Would he mind?'

Arfinch opened her mouth wide and laughed. She was a broad-shouldered girl with a big flat face full of life. 'No, he won't mind, as long as you're with me.'

Later that evening Arfinch and Sherbet took Knocker, Chalotte and Vulge to Rattray Road. The two black Borribles were obviously well known in their area and numbers of people spoke to them as they walked by. There were many Borribles too who leant from the windows of their squats to wave a cheery greeting or to invite them into the house. The two Bumper girls returned these greetings with laughs and waves of the hand. 'See you on the way back, man,' they shouted. 'We're going to a place where they got real music.'

Their destination was not far. On the corner of Rattray and Saltoun Road was a beaten-up old Borrible house, with half its roof missing and its windows and doors boarded over. Arfinch led the way to the rear of the house and rapped with her knuckles on the wooden shuttering which covered a back window level with the ground.

The shutter was in fact on hinges and swung open immediately. A black face appeared with a green Borrible hat pulled well down over the ears. This Borrible had a narrow and intent face and his eyes were set well apart, glinting behind wire-rimmed spectacles.

'Ah, Arfinch,' he said. He smiled and then wiped the smile from his face in the same second. He looked at the white Borribles. 'What's this?' he asked. 'What's this lot doing down here?'

'Take it easy, Stovepipe,' said Arfinch. 'They're Borribles and they're on the run from the SBG.'

'Ah,' said Stovepipe again. He stared for a moment at the three Adventurers. 'Yeah, now let me see. This will be Knocker; this will be Sydney, no, Chalotte, and this little nipper with the limp, that's got to be Vulge.'

Knocker threw a quick glance at Chalotte and Vulge and dropped his hand to where his catapault was. This was uncanny. If this fellow

Stovepipe knew so much then something was wrong; he must be working for the Woollies.

Sherbet laughed to see Knocker and his two companions turn so pale and then Stovepipe's intense face broke into a grin. 'Don't be worried,' he said. 'I've been plugged into the SBG headquarters for the last few days and they ain't been talking about nothing else but you and your friends. I've heard your description so many times I could recognize you in the dark, and all the others.'

'Can we come in?' asked Arfinch. 'We want to talk.'

Stovepipe nodded and stepped back from the window. Arfinch led the way over the sill and down a wooden stepladder. In a moment the Borribles were out of sight of the street and the shutter was closed behind them.

They were in a dark room which had been dug out below the ground floor of the abandoned house. It was lit entirely by electric light and the Adventurers could see that the room was crammed with radio equipment, telephones, tape recorders and computers.

'Where's all this come from?' asked Chalotte.

Stovepipe switched on a kettle and emptied a teapot into the sink. 'It's bits and pieces I've put together,' he said. 'I built most of it from stuff that's thrown away; a little bit's nicked of course.' He pulled some folding chairs out from underneath his bed and invited everyone to take a seat. 'Anyway, what do you want?'

As briefly as she could Chalotte told Stovepipe the story of Sam the horse and how she and the others were trying to get him to safety in Neasden. 'We were lucky to get away from Clapham South,' she said when she was rounding off the tale. 'Most of the circus Borribles were clipped but two got away and came with us, Ninch and Scooter.'

'All we want to know,' said Vulge, wagging his head nervously, 'is what Sussworth has done with the horse. Have you heard anything on these machines of yours?'

Stovepipe sat and stretched his legs out in front of him. He jerked a thumb over his shoulder. 'I've got a permanent line to SBG headquarters now,' he explained. 'They've been getting very excited since you got away from Clapham South . . . very.' Stovepipe eased his wheeled chair forward so that he could reach a bank of switches. He touched a button and a tape began to turn. 'I recorded this yesterday,' he said. 'It might be what you're after.'

The tape spun and the Borribles listened. A car went by outside; there was conversation in the street. A voice came from Stovepipe's monitor speaker; it was the voice of the DAC.

'. . . it's bloody stupid, Sussworth. I've had nothin' but flak from the Commissioner and he's gettin' it in the neck from Downin' Street. He wants my head on the block for this, and I warn you, Sussworth, if my head falls you'll be the one goin' for catsmeat, you and that odious Hanks.'

'Yessir,' answered Sussworth, and Knocker glanced at Chalotte. It seemed so strange to hear the inspector close like that, almost as if he were in the same room. The voice continued.

'We'll soon have the culprits who got them out, sir. I know who it is, circus vagabonds, sir . . .'

'Sussworth,' the DAC was shouting, he was very angry. 'You idiot. I don't care who did it. The main thing is that the Borribles have escaped and we are in trouble, both of us. I will have to resign unless you find where those Borribles are, got that? And if I resign I shall make sure that you end up standin' in the dole queue. So, Sussworth, do not bother yourself about who got them out of the shelters, but concentrate all your effort and all your manpower on findin' where they have gone. This is your last chance. After this it's Chief Superintendent Birdlime, understand?'

'Oh yessir,' said Sussworth. 'I understand, sir. I'll find them, I'll get them back into custody. I've dealt with the horse for a start, sir.'

Chalotte covered her face with her hands and the blood left Knocker's face, but before he could say anything the DAC went berserk.

'You've what, you incompetent little cipher? What have you got in your skull, cornflower sauce? What have you done?'

'Sir, you did agree at Clapham South that it should be slaughtered.'

'Your brain is a banana, Sussworth. That was under a different set of circumstances. Tactics alter as and when strategy does. It's elementary Clausewitz. When the horse was alive we at least knew that the Borribles would come lookin' for it . . . it's called a trap, Sussworth . . . an ambush.'

'Ah that's all right then, sir.'

'All right! It's not all right.'

'No, sir. You see, I only sent the horse over to the abattoir this afternoon; they aren't going to slaughter it until tomorrow. I'll telephone and get them to hang on to the horse, sir. They've got plenty of stabling over there.'

There was a long silence on the tape as the DAC digested this news. Vulge jumped to his feet and cheered; Chalotte lifted her face and smiled at Knocker.

'Sussworth,' continued the DAC at last, 'you nearly gave me a coronary. Where have you got this horse?'

'Oh quite safe, sir. In a slaughterhouse in Baynes Street; that's Camden Town, on the canal.'

'Good, good, at least that's somethin'. Put a strong guard on that horse, Sussworth. While we've got it we have a chance of catchin' those Borribles of yours. It seems that they would do anythin' for that horse, anythin'.'

'I know, sir. I can't understand it.'

'Right, anythin' else, Sussworth?'

'No, sir. I've got my men looking in every street in London, sir. Looking into every empty house, sir. Those Borribles won't get far.'

'They'd better not, Sussworth. If you let me down on this I'll see to it that they won't even employ you to collect trolleys in a supermarket car park. Think of that, Sussworth.'

'Yessir, I do, sir. Continually and all the time.'

'Excellent. Now somethin' else. If those Borribles don't know the horse is in Camden Town, how can they attempt a rescue, eh? Answer me that. If they think the horse is just a series of chunks of meat in rows of tins they'll abandon the idea of savin' it, won't they? What are you goin' to do about it, eh?'

'Um,' said Sussworth. 'Ah, that's a good question, sir. Pass.'

'Do your Borribles know you sent the horse to Wandsworth Prison, Sussworth? Do they know that?'

'They do indeed, sir. I made a point of telling them, sir, just to rub it in.'

'Good. We can count on them sendin' a runner as far as that then, just to scout out the lie of the land, but don't set a trap there, Sussworth; we want to catch them all. Put a notice on the prison doors sayin' that the horse has been sent to Camden Town to await execution, and put other notices outside all police stations. That should do it. Make the date of the execution three or four weeks away, give them time to get there, and then watch all the bridges over the river . . . You're bound to catch 'em that way.'

'Oh yessir. A marvellous idea, sir.'

'And don't slaughter that horse until I give the word, do you understand?'

'Yessir!'

'And telephone me with all developments, wherever I am. Where's your caravan?'

'Near Camden, sir. Near the abattoir but not too near.'

'Excellent. Well look lively, Susswoth. Be about your business and no more mistakes. Goodbye.'

The line went dead and Stovepipe switched off the tape machine. 'How's that?' he asked. 'Any good?'

Chalotte banged her hands together. 'Stovepipe,' she said, 'you're a marvel. That machine of yours has told us exactly what we wanted to know. Sam is in Camden Town and alive. Now we have a destination.'

'It sounds dangerous to me,' said Sherbet. 'You heard what they said; it's a trap.'

'Yes,' said Knocker, 'but this time we know it's a trap. That gives us a bit of an edge.'

Stovepipe began flicking through a notebook. 'I write down their radio messages too,' he said, 'and I tell you, if you're going north of the river then you'll have your work cut out. Apart from watching every bridge the SBG seem to have what they're calling "extra lookouts" everywhere.'

'Perhaps,' suggested Vulge, 'that's how they knew we were with the circus. Perhaps these lookouts saw us leaving Wandsworth Common.'

Knocker shook his head. 'If we can't use the bridges, getting across the river will be tricky.' He topped up his tea from the pot and drained his cup. The conference was at an end. With many thanks to Stovepipe for his information and a parting warning that he should not get caught, the two Bumpers and the three Adventurers walked slowly back to Electric Avenue. There would be much to think about and much to discuss over the meal that evening.

*

'The main problem is getting across the river,' said Knocker, leaning back on a broken sofa and spooning some baked beans into his mouth. 'A bridge is the worst place in the world to get caught, no way out but down to the water.'

'We'll be walking into a trap,' said Chalotte, 'when we should be living like these Bumpers live. They've got it right, living in the market, happy with what they've got. Look at us . . . out on the road, fighting for our very existence. It's not Borrible and I know it's not Borrible but at the same time we can't let Sam down. It's a mess.'

Knocker scraped the bottom of his bean can and took a deep breath. 'I reckon I learnt a thing or two down Flinthead's mine, I suppose we all did. When we got out alive I thought how stupid that digging for treasure had been, and yet I came out a better Borrible, I think, and somehow it's all tied up with Sam, getting him away from pulling Dewdrop's cart. He had no life before that, did he? Work, work, work for Dewdrop and then slaving away for the park keepers. Sam has to be kept free, away from Sussworth, away from work.'

Ninch, who was lying on the floor, rolled over on to his stomach. 'Lot of fuss about an old horse,' he said. 'We had better ones in the circus. I didn't notice anything special about him.'

Sydney banged her mug on the floor. 'Not special,' she cried, the anger mounting in her voice. 'He saved all our lives, that's all, but it's not just that. Like Knocker says, you can't describe what it is exactly. We just like him. He is Borrible and he's beautiful too . . . Oh, I don't know how to put it. He's one of us and you have to help him out because he can't help himself.'

Knocker agreed. 'Sid's right,' he said. 'Sam has to go to Neasden; it's more than just getting him there now, it's the beating of Sussworth. Somehow we've got to show that Borrible is Borrible and won't be bullied. For me, being a good Borrible is mixed up with that horse, but now Sussworth has got him prisoner and if he has his way he'll kill Sam and enjoy doing it . . . I'm going to stop him if I can.'

'Are you after a third name?' asked Arfinch, closing one eye. 'Is that what you're after?'

Knocker smiled bitterly. 'Once maybe, not any more. I'm not looking for great adventures; we're just trying to take care of our own, in this case, Sam. I'd want to do that even if he hadn't done us a good turn in

Rumbledom. It's Sussworth who won't let us be Borrible, trying to cut our ears off, demolishing our houses. I hate Sussworth for trying to change us into something we don't want to be. He'd love to have our noses to the grindstone.'

There was a longish silence after this speech. Chalotte studied the carpet in front of her and remembered what Knocker had been like just before the Great Rumble Hunt. He had certainly changed a lot. All he had wanted then was to win more names than any other Borrible. Now his thoughts were a great deal less self-centred. There were obviously more degrees of being Borrible than she had thought possible and Knocker was gradually, but steadily, moving up them.

The silence was broken, strangely enough, by Scooter, who had listened intently to every word that Knocker had spoken. He suddenly leapt to his feet, yelled and threw his empty bean can up to the ceiling. It bounced and fell to the floor with a clatter.

'Horray for Knocker,' he shouted, 'and Sam and Borribles everywhere.' Then he stopped and became self-conscious and sheepish, staring at his feet.

The Adventurers and the Bumpers laughed to see Scooter's red face. It was rare to see a Borrible blush and always caused great mirth among their companions when they did. Only Ninch was not amused.

'Bloody daft, I call it,' he said. 'All that fuss about a horse.'

This time Knocker ignored him. He sat back on the sofa and made himself comfortable. 'All I want to know is,' he said, 'is there anyone who doesn't want to come with me? Because I don't know how I'm going . . . but I'm going.'

Vulge tilted his head sideways. 'We've talked about it enough,' he said. 'Sussworth can't win this one whatever happens.'

Knocker looked at Chalotte and she felt him look at her. 'Who could refuse Knocker?' she said. 'Not that I would anyway because I believe he's right.'

'Okay, okay,' said Bisto suddenly, and he crossed the room so that he could face everyone. 'I've got things to say now, it's an idea. I've been sitting here listening to you talking an' you've got to get across the river, right? Without being seen, right? Well, the answer is staring you in the face. You done it before on the way to Rumbledom. You sails down the river and land between bridges, where it's safe, in the middle of the night.'

'Oh yeah,' said Bingo, 'and where do we get a boat? We're a long way from Battersea Park lake.'

'I thought about all that,' said Bisto. There was a huge smile on his face now, like he was proud to have thought of the idea and delighted to give it away. 'First, you don't need a boat, you have a raft instead; or better still, two rafts because a raft big enough for you all would be too heavy to carry.'

'To carry?' said Bingo.

'Carry,' said Bisto looking pleased with himself. 'Making the raft is no problem. Every night the market streets are covered with old pallets, bits of timber, wire, nails, everything we need to make a good solid craft. The real problem is getting it from here to the river; it's two or three miles.'

'That's too far,' said Knocker. 'By the time we'd carried the rafts we'd be too knackered to paddle, especially if the tide was against us.'

Bisto slapped his hands. 'That's just it, man. Me an' the girls and boys, we had a talk. You don't carry them, we do; you just jog along and carry your own stuff. It'd be our contribution to the war effort.'

'You?' said Chalotte and she shook her head at Arfinch.

The West Indian girl's expression became stern. 'And why not?' she queried. 'It's not only you who can have adventures. There's eight of us, two rafts, four to carry a raft . . . and just in case we'll bring another team of eight to take over when we're tired. They can be lookouts too. We can all run like rockets in Brixton.'

'Run?' said Knocker.

'Yeah,' answered Bisto, 'we'll have to move fast. We daren't set out until after midnight. We've got to cut across to Clapham Road, then down to Wandsworth Road. Over the back of New Covent Garden and across to the river at Nine Elms. You'll need darkness to get over the Thames and we'll need darkness to get back home. We'll have to run. Well, what do you think?'

The Adventurers laughed with pleasure.

'Bisto,' said Chalotte, 'not only is it the best plan we've got, it's the only plan we've got.'

'Okay,' said Sherbet, 'but when?'

Knocker raised an eyebrow. 'Tomorrow night,' he said.

'Tomorrow,' said Arfinch. 'That's soon.

'We've been here three days,' said Napoleon, 'and tomorrow will make four.'

'And every day is more dangerous for Sam,' said Sydney.

'Tomorrow night it is, then,' said Bisto. 'We'll get the stuff tonight and begin making the rafts in the morning.'

*

It became known as the Great Raft Run from Brixton to Nine Elms, one of the most famous chapters in Borrible history. Some of the no-name Bumpers won their names that night; names like Rafto, Pallet and Sweetfeet. It was a real old-fashioned Borrible adventure.

Two large pallets had been taken to construct each raft, one pallet nailed and wired crossways on the top of another. To make them buoyant the insides were stuffed with white polystyrene boarding taken from old packing cases. Everyone was convinced they would float but in Brixton there was no way of testing them.

'It'll be fine,' said Bisto. 'It's just a question of sink or swim.'

The raft run began at one o'clock the next morning. There stood the Adventurers dressed in new warm clothes and raincoats. They had new rucksacks on their back and packed inside them were all the provisions and equipment they needed. The Bumpers had done them proud.

The Bumpers themselves were only lightly dressed, wearing dark clothes and black running shoes. 'Remember,' said Bisto as he gave his final instructions to the Adventurers. 'Half of your lot will spread out in front, running, then comes number one raft, then number two raft, then the rest of your lot. The standby raft team, when not carrying, will run on the wings, keeping watch. If things go wrong, dump the rafts, separate, get into the side streets and make your way back to Brixton. You'll be safe here and we can always try again.'

And so the Great Raft Run set off, slowly at first, with the Borribles crossing the silence of Brixton Road in small groups, gliding like phantoms into the dark patches of the night. But once they had passed under the railway bridge and into the top of Ferndale Road they began to run like they'd never run before. Not once did they halt and luck was with them that night. They ran undiscovered, their hearts beating with a strange excitement and a confidence born of the friendship they felt the one for the other; tribe for tribe, black for white, friend for friend. They were exultant – rulers, if only for an hour or two, of the huge sprawling beast of a city they lived in.

From Ferndale to Kimberley they went and on into Clitheroe. They slowed momentarily to cross Clapham Road, but raced on into Union and turned right at Larkhall Lane, cutting down Priory and Lansdowne until they crossed the Wandsworth Road and went into the gloom of Cowthorpe and the crescent of Crimsworth, and there they halted in an alley made from a dull brick and bounded on the northern side by a high wall where names and oaths were written in aerosol paint and chalk of many colours. Bisto leant against the wall, panting hard. 'This is it,' he said. 'This is the back way into Covent Garden Market; once across it we'll be on Nine Elms Lane, right by the river.'

The pallets had been fashioned so that they could also act as ladders. They were upended, leant against the wall, and one was placed on the side of the other. The slats of the rafts now became rungs and, taking it in turn, the Borribles climbed to the very top of the sheer brick cliff. Once there they sat astride and gripped the coping stones with their legs and pulled the two precious craft up to them with ropes specially brought for the purpose, lowering them down on the market side in the same manner. At the end of the operation the Borribles disappeared from the wall, dropping silently on all fours to the soft grass verge that lay below.

They were now in New Covent Garden, an enormous space full of bustle and business, particularly during the hours of darkness, for it is to Covent Garden that come the great pantechnicons from all over Europe, loaded to overflowing with fruit and vegetables. Here the lamps burn all night so that the great lorries may drive to the warehouse gates, selling and buying, loading and unloading.

For the Borribles it was a place full of danger but they crouched low and their luck stayed with them. It was so busy and crowded that a few kids, carrying what looked like two old pallets for firewood, were barely noticed, and when noticed at all, were completely ignored. The Borribles were glad; they kept to the edge of the adult activity and skirted the blazing lights. In less than a quarter of an hour they had crossed Covent

Garden and emerged, undiscovered, on Nine Elms Lane. On the far side of this thoroughfare they saw an open gateway; passing through it they found themselves in a riverside yard which possessed its own wharf and, what is more, its own iron ladder set into the embankment and leading down to the surface of the water.

The River Thames in this part of London is infinite and evil. In the gloom of the early hours it looks like a black spirit sliding to hell, bearing on its back hapless lumps of rubbish like the souls of the lost and the damned. It moves with a steady surge of muscular power. Nothing can resist it, nothing can fight against it. The Thames is a stream that wants blood; it yearns to suck you down.

That night of the Great Raft Run was no exception. The rain held off but the air was cold and murderous like the blade of an axe, and though there was a moon stealing along behind low wet clouds, only occasionally did the glint of silver touch the water. All was dark, as dark as death. No sky, no skyline, no earth beneath the feet. It was the brink of the world.

But the Adventurers did not falter in their resolve and the confidence they had felt during the long run from Brixton bore them up. So too did the friendship of the Bumpers and, all working together, the Borribles lowered the rafts into the water and the strong smell of the Thames rose into their nostrils, robbing them of their breath. An old smell it was, brewed up from a mixture of toadstool, sewage, sump oil and factory waste.

And now the Adventurers clambered down the metal ladder for there was not a moment to be lost. The river was choppy and snapped at the rafts, but they were buoyant and rode high even when fully laden with their crews, though the tide tugged and heaved as if all the power of the turning world was there under the surface of the Thames, wishing the voyagers ill. It was time to go.

The Adventurers looked up at the wharf, and the excitement that had sustained them that night died like the flame of a little candle; its place was taken by a melancholy as dark and as pernicious as the Thames itself, and because of it the Adventurers could not bring themselves to paddle, only drifting away from the embankment, lacking the courage to say goodbye. And for the same reason the Bumpers themselves said nothing and did not move.

At last Napoleon Boot broke the silence. 'Come on,' he said, and dropped the blade of his paddle into the darkness of the water. 'I'm not scared of the river, and if we don't get a move on the police patrols will find us out here in daylight.'

So the Adventurers left the bank, watching their friends until they were but one black with the black of the night and the Bumpers called goodbye from nowhere.

'You take it easy,' said Bisto in a whispered shout. 'You make sure you come back to see us when it's over . . . and make sure you damn' well don't get bloody well caught. You understand?' And with a sob in his voice that he tried in vain to disguise, Bisto turned away and began the long run back to Brixton, tears blurring his sight, and his friends ran behind him and they exchanged not a single word during the whole long journey.

6

Inspector Sussworth's mobile headquarters was parked in a narrow crescent somewhere between St Pancras Way and the Camden Road. It was a quiet street, ill frequented and little known. In the centre of the crescent was a scrubby and dusty garden where a few pale sprouts of withered grass struggled for life in a rancid and ungenerous soil. The garden was bordered by an iron fence which lurched in all directions at once, like a drunkard. Skirting the perimeter of this cul-de-sac was a line of tall thin houses, squashed one against the other in a tight jumble. Some of the houses had been abandoned, some were inhabited by pensioners whose relatives no longer knew where they lived; their windows were lightless and their doors never opened to visitors.

Sussworth's caravan stood out clearly in the murk of its surroundings. It was painted in white gloss and the four police officers who drove the Range Rover, which pulled the caravan from place to place and guarded the inspector from harm, were under strict orders to wash the caravan once a day, sometimes twice if Sussworth thought it was dirty. In consequence it gleamed all over and the chrome trim on the wheels shone like four moons on a night of frost.

The caravan was a long one, very large and very stable with a balcony at each end so that Sussworth could easily speak to his men. Inside it was spotless. The carpet looked like it had never been trodden on, the walls never leant against and the windows never soiled by anything so vulgar as a glance travelling through them.

At one end of the caravan stood Sussworth's desk and behind that a section had been walled off to provide the inspector with a bathroom and lavatory – for his use only. As at the SBG headquarters in Micklethewaite Road the caravan's facilities were not to be sullied by any presence but the inspector's. No other bum was allowed to lower its weight on to the plush-covered seat of the lavatory pan; no other body was permitted to wallow in the deep pink bath. This was Sussworth's sanctum.

In the middle of the caravan was a comfortable sofa that unfolded to become a double bed, suitable for the inspector's neat and fragile frame. Nearby, on a small table, was a computer terminal that could be plugged in to central criminal records. Beyond that, at the opposite end to Sussworth's lavatory, was the kitchen area and a narrow bunk into which Sergeant Hanks was obliged to squeeze his lumpish body when he needed rest.

In the kitchen there was a stove, a sink and a table where the sergeant could brew his tea and concoct his favourite oily meals: breakfasts of fried bread, bacon, eggs and black pudding. Sergeant Hanks loved eating and the evidence was all too obvious; stains of yellow egg and white lard paraded across the broad bosom of his tunic like the badges of a hundred regiments. Next to eating he loved cooking, and police work had to fit neatly in between those two activities. At the very moment the Adventurers were launching their craft on the dangerous waters of the Thames, Sergeant Hanks was prodding a slice of bacon in his frying pan and waiting for the kettle to boil. Inspector Sussworth sat at his desk, his fingers tapping, his feet clicking, pondering his predicament, impatient for his tea.

'The trouble is,' said Sussworth, 'that since those villains broke out of custody at Clapham South, aided and abetted by those travellers and gypsies, we have lost contact and all knowledge of their whereabouts.'

The kettle boiled and Hanks poured the water into a large brown teapot.

'You see,' went on Sussworth, 'the information received seems to indicate Brixton as their probable and likely destination, but we cannot verify these reports.'

'Tricky,' said Hanks, and poured a mugful of tea for his superior officer, black and strong, no milk, no sugar. 'Brixton's tricky. I mean we don't want to stir 'em up in Brixton, that might be more trouble than it's worth.' Hanks hooked something juicy out of his nose, looked at it from every angle and then stuck it on the underside of the table where it joined the rest of his collection, now nicely crisp.

'Yes,' said Sussworth. 'We can't take chances in Brixton.'

Hanks burped. 'What about the dwarfs? Have they brought in any news?'

Sussworth got to his feet, strutted to the kitchen, seized his mug of tea and sidestepped like a dancer back to his desk where he sat down. He took a deep sip. 'Ah, tea, Hanks, perfect. Yes, the dwarfs. Now there's an idea of mine that worked well.' Sussworth's moustache twitched in glee and trembled like a leaf on the end of a branch. 'But you see, at Clapham South, those circus dwarfs who had done so superbly, they didn't want to do any more, they desisted.'

'Yes,' said Hanks. He put two rashers of bacon on to a piece of thickly buttered bread and watched the butter melt. 'Except two of them, they were keen to go on.'

Sussworth took another sip of tea. 'That is correct, Hanks, and I cannot comprehend why we have heard nothing from them. We should have had a message, a sign, a communication.'

'Perhaps they've had their throats cut,' said Hanks. He placed another piece of bread on the bacon to make a sandwich. 'I mean if the Borribles found out that they were spies, them dwarfs, well, they wouldn't last long, would they?'

Sussworth tapped his fingers on the table and looked stern. 'They wouldn't, Hanks, they wouldn't. Nooch and Scinter, whatever their names were, could well be lying dead in a drain at this very moment. But we knew that was a risk we would have to take; those Borribles will stick at nothing to maintain their so-called independence.'

'They won't, sir, they won't.'

'And that horse, that is a definite flea in the ointment between me and the DAC. I'd like to get rid of it right away, but the DAC won't have it. Got to hang on to the horse, for the time being, at least.'

'Make good steaks, horses do,' said Hanks, and he sat on the kitchen table and shoved half his sandwich into his mouth.

Sussworth's eyes went cloudy and his moustache quivered in ecstasy. 'I have a dream, Hanks, a golden vision of the future. I see it clear. I have captured those Borribles, every one. I starve them for a few days and then I serve them up some delicious stew, really delicious and tasty. They gobble it down, and then, as I clip their ears I tell them they have just eaten their favourite horse, Sam. Isn't that wonderful, Hanks? I'd give up my knighthood for that, I would really.'

Hanks guffawed, and half-masticated bread and bacon splattered down his tunic. 'Oh brilliant, sir, brilliant. You deserve to be commissioner.'

Sussworth raised his mug of tea in a toast. 'I shall be one day, Hanks, I shall be, but only if we can run these vagabonds to earth and deal with them once and for all. Double the rewards, Hanks. Those malingerers will have read the notice on the gates of Wandsworth Prison by now . . . We can expect them to reappear at any moment.'

'We'll get them,' said Hanks. He cuddled his stomach with both arms as he enjoyed the sensation of the bacon sandwich arriving in it. He lit the gas and dropped four more rashers into his frying pan.

Sussworth got to his feet and crossed the caravan to stare into a gilt-framed mirror. He put his face close to the glass and gazed at himself, giving his moustache just the gentlest of twitches. 'We'll get them this time, Hanks, but we'd better hurry. If we don't we'll be back on the beat with Chief Superintendent Birdlime telling us what to do, just imagine that.'

Hanks prodded his bacon with a fork. 'I can't sir,' he said. 'I really can't.'

*

The Adventurers were adrift on a wide and silent sea. To them it was vast, as vast as an ocean. As they floated into the centre of the river the current surged stronger, picking them up and thrusting them along, swirling the rafts round and round, making the Borribles feel sick, forcing them to cling on for all they were worth.

'I want to get off,' said Ninch. 'This is dangerous.'

'Shut yer neck and start paddling,' said Napoleon. 'It's only water.'

The other Borribles said not a word. None of them liked water much, especially when it was cold and they were only a few inches above it, sitting on frail pieces of timber. Luckily for them Napoleon was an exception. He was a Wendle and had been raised along the lower reaches of the River Wandle. He knew about boats and tides. It took more than a river to frighten him.

'Right,' he said, lowering his voice to a whisper, 'the first thing you have to do is take your orders from me and the second is to stop talking. For all we know the SBG may have a boat out, they might be just a few yards away, listening. Next, rope the two rafts together so we don't get separated, and every one of you must use your own bit of rope to tie yourself to the raft. If you fall off in this we won't be able to come back for you, even if we could see you . . . The current's far too strong.'

The Borribles lost no time in doing what Napoleon had told them and when they were ready he spoke again. 'Now remember,' he began, 'a raft isn't a boat. No front, no back, it's just a square. Get it steady and keep paddling. The tide's in our favour and we'll be going at a fair lick, so keep your heads . . . If you panic you'll just send us round and round in circles. Be specially quiet going under the bridges. There'll be coppers on every one, I reckon, but with this dark, even if they're looking straight down they won't see us . . . But if they hear us, they'll switch their floodlights on.'

'Someone should count the bridges,' said Knocker, 'so we don't go too far. Who knows 'em best?'

'I do,' said Vulge. 'Bridges is my hobby.'

'We've got to get off between Blackfriars and Southwark,' said Knocker. 'At Queenhithe Dock, that's what the map said.'

'All right,' said Vulge, 'that makes six bridges, if you count Hungerford. Leave it to me, the first is Vauxhall.'

'Okay, that'll do,' said Napoleon. 'No more talking. Except for my orders and emergencies it's quiet all the way.'

And that was how it was. Once the two rafts were steady, one towed behind the other, they settled into the grip of the current and the crews, paddling with long regular strokes, kept them on a straight course. There in the middle of the river it was all darkness and the lights of the city seemed many miles away. The Adventurers swayed forward and back, digging the paddles deep into nothingness. Spray from the curling waves fell upon them and they were soon soaked to the skin but not one of them was cold; they were toiling too hard for that and their own sweat kept them warm.

And it was darker than blindness on the river, darker than the end of an underground cavern and yet, after travelling for half an hour, a broad shape, even blacker than the water, loomed over the Adventurers. The river writhed and twisted and huge powerful ropes of it came together and were forced between solid stone columns and the water rose like a torrent escaping from the sluices of a dam. A massive wave arched slowly, higher and higher. It hesitated for a second, became motionless and then broke, crashing down against a mighty pillar that soared up and up, into the very roof of the night.

'Vauxhall Bridge,' came Vulge's voice.

Now the rafts burst into slack water; they began to spin, to go out of control. 'Keep paddling, you fairies,' shouted Napoleon, 'or we'll be dragged back in, and you'll drown. Keep paddling.'

And the Borribles did, for all they were worth, until at last, the sweat pouring into their eyes, they passed away from the danger of the first bridge and were able to journey on in silence. They drew breath, their heartbeats slowed and they regained their composure while Napoleon knelt at the front of the leading raft, still paddling as he stared into the gloom, his body swaying gracefully, his face beautiful with excitement. He loved the river.

Sydney, who was next to the Wendle, felt a shiver go down her spine. In spite of all they had been through together Napoleon could still affect her in that manner. He was an odd one, always testing himself against himself at every opportunity.

'What are you looking for?' she asked him.

Napoleon did not turn his head nor did he stop paddling. 'Boats,' he answered. 'If we meet a bunch of barges we'll have to get out of the way sharpish. In this temperature you don't live long in the water, just a few minutes.'

On downriver they went, flying through the bridges on the curling waves, paddling all the time, obeying Napoleon's commands on the instant, through Lambeth and Westminster and Hungerford, until eventually they swept under the spectral arch that was the white bridge of Waterloo.

'We're nearly there,' said Vulge, but as he looked towards Blackfriars he saw a great light blazing up the river, heading straight for the two rafts.

'The fuzz,' said Orococco. 'Must be a police patrol.'

'Worse,' said Napoleon. 'That's a tug with about twenty barges lashed behind. Coming as fast as a train, straight up the middle. Paddle like the clappers for the north side, we've got to get out of the way.'

That was easier said than done. The river had them in the grip of a giant and it bore then irresistibly towards the advancing tug. The Borribles could hear the noise of engines now and bright light began to dazzle their eyes, so long accustomed to the dark. In front of the boat and pushed back by it, churned and tumbled the bow wave; dirty yellow, grinning, splitting the river open and laying bare a deep trough more than large enough to swallow up the tiny rafts and those who rode upon them.

The light towered nearer, as high as the beacon on a castle wall. Under the light was the shape of nothing, the black ship itself. The thump of the engines grew still louder. The bow wave began to race backwards, against the tide, rushing across the surface of the river and travelling faster than the boat that had made it, as if the laws of nature did not exist.

The Borribles wanted to scream with terror but could not. The engines were beating in their ears, robbing them of all thought. The waves rose; the voices of men called to one another through an empty space and behind the tug came a solid mass of barges, a floating town half as wide as the river itself.

With a courage and an energy that were born of desperation the Adventurers worked their paddles faster and faster, but a terrifying force dragged the waters from beneath them and suddenly they were paddling air. The rafts had been flung skywards until they were vertical. Now the Borribles did scream, clinging to one another in panic. The rafts staggered, nearly toppling over backwards, then, with a crash that could hardly be heard in all that din, the bow wave rushed on and the rafts fell deep into a pit and shook and shuddered. Then another wave surged under them and up went the Borribles again and they screamed again, but this time when they fell they were in a calmer place. The bow wave had carried them out of the main current although not out of danger; the barges were still to come.

Napoleon knew this. 'Don't stop,' he shouted. 'Paddle on, paddle on.'

The Borribles did as Napoleon ordered and each blow of their paddles thrust them away from the middle of the river and towards safety. The line of barges was now behind them and the bright lights no longer dazzled their eyes, but the river was still in turmoil. Its waters were moving roughly from side to side and up and down, chopping and slapping. There was a great swishing and swirling of cross-currents too but the noise of the tug itself gradually grew less and less and, at last, like a monster crawling into its lair, the rigid flotilla of boats disappeared under Waterloo Bridge.

'That was a close one,' said Twilight. 'We did well to get out of that.'

Napoleon grunted and then added to the water surrounding him by spitting into it. 'At least no one was seasick,' he said. 'That's something I suppose.'

The very last bridge of all was Blackfriars and the Adventurers navigated it with no more danger or alarm. Then they cut away from the current once more and headed for the north bank where, according to Knocker, they would find the old disused wharf going by the name of Queenhithe Dock.

'We'll have to find it without torches,' said Napoleon, 'in case anyone's watching.'

The Borribles floated right in against the embankment; a sheer wall covered in green slime without a step or ladder. There was no way up that.

'Just paddle along a bit,' said Napoleon. 'It'll be along here.'

It was. Suddenly the cliff of the embankment fell away and there was a shelf of sloping mud running back and up into darkness. The Borribles struck out for it and the rafts ran aground on gravel and sludge.

'Hold steady,' said Napoleon. 'I'll get off and pull yer in.'

He leapt ashore and immediately sank to his waist in cold mud, soft like a sucking jelly. He ignored it; after all he was a Wendle and Wendles were used to mud. He grabbed the ropes, pulled hard and slowly the rafts edged into the beach and stuck there.

The other Adventurers stood, threw their rucksacks towards Napoleon and then jumped after them. Lacking the Wendle's expertise they fell and floundered, covering themselves in a vile and sticky coating of filth.

'Mud,' said Vulge. 'I should cocoa. What a pen and ink!'

Knocker got his arms into the straps of his rucksack and plodded forward. 'Come on,' he said. 'Let's get a move on.'

While Knocker went looking for a way out Napoleon cut the rope that bound the two rafts together and shoved them back into the current. 'Don't want 'em found too near,' he explained. 'Southend would be close enough.'

He sheathed his knife and Knocker's whistle came from above. The Adventurers gathered their belongings and began to squelch up the slope of the shore, no easy task. Their feet slithered and sank at every step, churning the mud into a green slime, and the sewer stench that was everywhere became stronger, escaping as steam from below and crystallizing like hot breath in the cold air. But at least the Borribles left no trace of their passing. As they pulled their legs from the clinging slurry it oozed back in an instant to fill the gaping holes they had made. In no time at all the surface of the shelving bank was as still and as smooth as it had been at any time during the previous hundred years.

So the Adventurers waded forward until they came up with Knocker, who was waiting for them near the bottom of an iron-runged, weed-covered ladder. 'I had a good look at the map before leaving Brixton,' he said. 'I reckon we can make King's Cross before daylight.'

'Why do we have to go to King's Cross anyway?' That was Ninch's voice in the dark.

'Because,' said Napoleon, answering for Knocker, 'King's Cross is a main line station and behind main line stations you always find derelict land, goods yards, empty carriages, old factories, places to hide. Any old Borrible should know that. That's why.'

'Well whatever we're going there for,' interrupted Scooter, 'do you think we could get out of this mud? It's right up to my armpits now and it smells like a dustbin.'

'Okay,' said Knocker, 'but remember, we run fast, single file and we don't stop. This is the City of London we're in and there ain't too many places to hide.'

*

The night was long and arduous. What with the stint from Brixton to Nine Elms and the river trip with its frights and tensions, the Adventurers were exhausted even before leaving Queenhithe Stairs. Now they had to run again and just as far as they had before.

Knocker led them at a cracking pace, leading not because this was his part of London, it wasn't; but simply because he had studied the map and memorized it, and knew which road went where and which would bring them to their destination with the least trouble.

They ran silently and fast, spread out for safety, but they encountered no one. Occasionally a lone car bounded through the emptiness, its headlights dashing the tarmac with gold, or a lorry ground its way to a distant market. But the Borribles kept to the back streets where the lamps were separated by great stretches of nothing and where the pools of gloom were long and deep.

Tall buildings rose on either side of the runners like the hollow cliffs of abandoned cave dewellings, their roofs at one with the endless dark of the sky. Not a light shone in the skyscrapers or in the many-tiered, honeycombed car parks. Almost the only sounds the Borribles heard were the soft footfalls of their own feet and the jingling in the harness of their rucksacks.

They crossed an open piazza under the shadow of St Paul's, up Amen Court where the frost was hard. Down Newgate and Giltspur Street they ran, past Smithfield Market where a thousand slabs of cold beef hung in rows. Along Cowcross and Turnmill, running parallel to Farringdon Road all the time, heading slightly west of north, bending over the top of London as the roads bent.

At Clerkenwell Knocker stopped and the others stopped too, crouching behind him, regaining their breath, looking left and right, forward and back for the slightest sign of danger. At last, reassured, they darted across the open space and raced on through Back Hill and through Rosebery Avenue; flitting black shadows in a town that was as black as they.

As he hastened onward Knocker thought of Sussworth, asleep somewhere, flat on his back, his mouth tightly closed, his moustache like a venomous moth waiting for the dawn, waiting to lay venomous eggs. And Hanks too, his belly spilling out beyond his body, snoring, his spittle dripping on to his pillow and forming an ever-widening stain of thick saliva as he dreamt, smiling, of the breakfasts he had eaten and the breakfasts that were to come.

Somewhere too, in that vast city, was Sam the horse, locked in a stall of some slaughterhouse, the smell of death flooding into his soft nostrils and filling him with dread. Bound by tail and halter to rings in a wall so that he could not move or rest, his eyes wide with fear, expecting only the bullet in the brain and the sharp wide knife that would slit his throat and then spill his entrails on to a sloping concrete ramp, already wet and slippery with the blood of millions gone before to catsmeat.

These thoughts spurred Knocker on and he quickened his pace, always going west of north, across Mount Pleasant and down Phoenix Place; past the Royal Free Hospital, and here in the high windows there were lights shining and nurses moved behind the curtains and lifted people up on their pillows so they might breathe their last breath more easily. People dying and never been Borrible. The thought filled Knocker with terror; he ran harder and his legs ached and the weight of his rucksack chafed his shoulders. But the pain only made him grit his teeth, and his companions, following, ran harder too and cursed Knocker with all their hearts until, glancing up at the sky, they saw the greyness coming and knew why he ran so fast and far. Before daylight they must be well hidden at King's Cross.

The streets went on: Frederick, Acton, Swinton and Wicklow. Finally the Adventurers came out on the Euston Road, just where it meets Pentonville, and they sped towards the awesome pinnacles of St Pancras and those pinnacles towered over the tiny figures like the turrets of an evil castle, a castle inhabited by giants whose only work it is to lie in wait for vagabond children in order to crack their bones and grind them into bread.

One by one the Borribles crossed the main road, heading into the quiet between the two great railway stations, into Pancras Road, aiming at the dead land that lay beyond. Knocker rounded a corner and leant against the wall. The railway arches began here. The road was cobbled, and further on there would be gasworks and rubbish dumps; their smell was heavy on the air.

Knocker could not resist a smile as he pressed his body back against the bricks. They'd done it. How good it was to be alive and to know you were; to feel your own existence as a separate thing, iridescent and jubilant. Yes, they'd done it. The trip from Brixton, across the river and then from Blackfriars to King's Cross, had been accomplished without loss and without disclosing their whereabouts to the SBG. Things were looking up.

It was daylight. Knocker could see clearly the lines between the cobblestones at his feet. He could see too the sooty red colour of the bricks used to build the high arches that kept the railway lines aloft. One by one his companions joined him. One by one they leant against the wall, resting after the long night's exertions.

'We'll follow this line of arches,' said Knocker. 'We might find an empty one; failing that we'll get into the goods yard.'

They set off again in single file, only this time at a walk. At the entrance to each archway, and there were scores of them, Knocker stopped and tried the huge semicircular gates that kept them locked and private.

'Shut,' he said again and again. 'Garages and workshops most of 'em.'

After a hundred yards or so the road bore to the right, near some traffic lights. The arches continued into the distance, some with well painted and heavily barred doors, others with splintered shutters that lay awry and awkward on their hinges. A few cars passed and commuter trains rumbled overhead, more frequently now as the rush hour began to get into its stride. Quickly the Adventurers moved on, Napoleon bringing up the rear, his eyes everywhere. The Borribles had to get off the streets.

As if to add urgency to this thought there came the howl of a police siren from far away on the Euston Road. Then came the sound of another, immediately, almost like an echo, from over on the Caledonian Road.

Knocker bore right again. More arches. He stepped down to one, stumbling on a cobble. He raised an arm to save himself and pushed against the central plank of a door. The plank gave, swivelling on a central pivot as if it were meant to. Behind it was complete darkness. Knocker pushed with more force at the swivel plank and put his head inside the door. He could see nothing. He listened intently but the noise of the trains overhead made it impossible to hear anything else but them.

He pulled his head into the open.

'It's so dark I can't see a thing,' he said. 'Smells like dead rats in there. I'll go in and scout it out.'

At that moment the sound of the police siren came again, closer. Tyres squealed on cobbles. A patrol car had turned into the bottom of Pancras Road.

Napoleon peeped round the edge of the archway. 'It's coming this way,' he said. 'We'll have to get out of sight until it's gone, whatever we do.'

Again Knocker pushed the plank aside and wriggled through the gap while the others followed as quickly as they could. Napoleon went last and shoved the plank back into position. Inside it was as dark as Knocker had said and the racket of the trains, when they passed, was deafening. The only thing the Adventurers could distinguish clearly was the smell. That was too strong to be ignored; a combination of foul breath, dried urine and the gunge that ferments between human toes.

'Blimey,' said Sydney, 'what an Aunt Nell.'

No sooner had the girl spoken than things began to happen. Strong bodies moved behind the Borribles, passing between them and the wooden doors. Shapes pressed against them in the dark and the fearful smell came closer, thick and tangible, suffocating.

The Borribles reached for their catapults but there was no chance of defending themselves. Horny hands held their arms, so tightly that it hurt. A harsh voice cackled and then shouted, 'All right,' and on came a light, a simple bulb on a long flex, high in the arch, swaying as the trains went by.

'Bloody Nora,' said Napoleon, and he stopped struggling. Never had the Adventurers, in all their days, witnessed anything so terrifying.

They were in a huge cave of a place. High above their heads the railway arch rose and fell in a grand sweep; its bricks were dark and damp. Water dripped everywhere; long streaks and stains of musty fungus and mildew ran down the walls. All this was bad enough but it was what the cavern contained that struck a hopeless chill into the hearts of the Borribles.

Close by them were a dozen men, but such men as hardly deserved the name. They looked scarcely human. Their faces were bloated, crimson and purple and blue, a criss-cross of broken veins on the surface of a dead skin, and that skin had black cracks and holes in it, cracks full of a soft grime and holes gouged deep by the action of poisonous alcohol and fiery spirits. Their teeth were isolated black stumps set loosely in spongy gums and their eyes wept in red-rimmed sockets; eyelids corroded, turned inside out, hanging halfway down the cheek, the muscles eaten away. For clothes they wore the bits and pieces they had salvaged from the dustbins and rubbish tips where prouder tramps threw their clothes away. The hands that held the Borribles were ingrained with the dirt of years and the breath of the men's lungs was warm and fetid.

'They're meffos,' said Knocker, stunned.

The Borribles gasped. Knocker was right. They had fallen among some of the most dangerous men and women in London, the drinkers of methylated spirits. These were people who would stop at nothing, whose minds had decayed, whose brains had been eaten alive by booze and drugs. Meffos had no sense of good or bad. They would die without a thought to obtain a bottle of gin, and they would murder anyone just as readily if that would bring them the money to buy a can of beer.

Napoleon swore again. The horror was not over. In front of the Borribles were more meffos, both men and women, dozens of them. Some were resting on the floor under newspapers, crammed together for warmth so closely that there was hardly room to step between them; others sat on beer crates, their hands joined, their heads bowed; and there were yet more who gazed into the distance, their eyes unblinking as the light came on.

The Borribles stared at the rear of the arch, and further, to what seemed to be the entrance of more arches. There were meffos as far as they could see; lying, standing, drinking, eating, peeing against the wall. Most seemed alive, some were perhaps dead. They looked like zombies only half revived. This was the great smell the Borribles had smelt.

All at once there came a great clamour from a doorway to the left of the cavern and a broad-shouldered man appeared with a bottle in his fist. 'Aha!' he bellowed. He waved the bottle above his head and laughed, throwing his head backwards to show a wide wound of a mouth with two or three large teeth in it. He came towards the captives, staggering this way and that, kicking men and women from his path, kicking them hard.

The Borribles huddled closer together. A meffo swivelled an iron bar into position and so locked the cavern doors. Hands fumbled and pawed at the Adventurers. Their knives and catapults were taken away and their rucksacks were ripped from their shoulders.

The shouting man shouted louder and redoubled his kicking. 'Leave the rucksacks,' he yelled, and his face went dark with an instant anger.

'Throw them rucksacks on the floor in a pile; I'll slit the man's throat as dinna. Fair shares for all, you hear. There'll be things in there as is worth money and money is booze and booze is life. Right, pal?'

Still kicking and shouting the man continued his advance until at last he stood before the group of Borribles and the men who held them prisoner. Reluctantly the meffos threw the rucksacks to the floor.

'That's better,' said the man, and he took a swig from his bottle. 'Any one of youse Saxons care to take me on, eh? Any one of youse Saxons wanna take on Hughie MacMungall face to face, eh? Answer me. Face to face, man to man, eh?'

The men shuffled their feet and looked down at the heads of their captives.

'I thought not,' shouted MacMungall. He staggered again. 'He who mocks the kilt must feel the dirk!' With this MacMungall drew a bread knife from his belt and pointed it at the nearest meffo. 'And don't you forget it, pal,' he roared, making the word 'pal' sound like the vilest insult. 'I'll slit yer throat as soon as spit in yer eye, by God I will.' He staggered once more and stared unsteadily in front of him, trying to focus on the Borribles.

'Aye, lads,' he went on, lowering his voice a little, 'you've done well here. Seems to me these bairns might have a few bob on 'em. Things of value in these rucksacks. Share and share alike, pal. Half for you and half for me, that's the way of the clans.' MacMungall took another swig on his bottle. 'Ah,' he said when the liquid hit his stomach. 'Right, lads, go through their pockets, tip out their bags, but remember, anyone trying to slip the goods into their own pockets will have me to deal with.'

At the end of this speech MacMungall swayed backwards and collapsed on to a beer crate that, luckily for him, was waiting in exactly the right position to receive his buttocks as he sat. He shook his head in a vain attempt to clear it, drank again from his bottle and slid his knife out of sight under his coat.

Knocker studied MacMungall with care. He was certainly nowhere near as tough as he pretended but he was still big and brawny, having massive shoulders and long strong arms with hands as big as earth movers at the end of them. He was probably the strongest meffo in the cavern and that was why the others obeyed him so readily, but like them MacMungall was in poor physical shape. His eyes, like theirs, looked like tattered bullet holes shot fresh through his head that morning. His lips were loose, his skin had the texture of a mouldy steak, and for all his brave speech his hands trembled when he raised his bottle so that half of every mouthful he took ran down his chin and neck and disappeared under a filthy old football scarf of green and white.

Knocker also observed that as far as the rest of MacMungall's clothes were concerned they were not one bit better than those of his cronies. He wore a blue anorak stained with oil and ripped at the pockets, and several pairs of trousers to keep out the cold. He had no socks on but sported two odd shoes with the welts gaping away from what was left of the soles, giving a good view of dirty feet, and on his head was jammed a Scottish football fan's tartan trilby. Altogether, thought Knocker, he was a fearsome sight, a coward with no conscience.

But Knocker's time for reflection was over. Without warning, the Borribles were thrust forward. There was a flurry of excitement as the prisoners were searched and their rucksacks upended on the floor. Most of the recumbent meffos got to their feet now and began to press nearer, moaning and shoving at each other with their elbows. All were ragged and dirty, women and men, their clothes torn and tied together. Their eyes were dull with a blank madness relieved only by a glint of greed. Perhaps these children had money, money for drink.

The meffos fought to get near the Borribles, jostling them, tearing at their arms and legs, feeling their bodies and ripping at their clothes to find if money was secreted there. The rucksacks were inspected again, the contents picked up and thrown down, and gradually the meffos grew more and more angry as their disappointment rose. There was no money.

'Hand it over,' they shouted, and those next to the Borribles began to beat them about the head as hard as they could. 'Hand it over, you brats, or we'll rip yer skin off and eat yer alive.'

Sheer weight of numbers separated the Borribles from each other and one by one they were borne to the floor and the meffos came down with them and punched and scratched and spat and bit, and although each Adventurer fought as well as he or she could it made no difference. It seemed likely that they would all perish there, dismembered in that dismal archway behind King's Cross. There was no controlling the meffos any more. MacMungall was drunk and like the Borribles had been pushed to the ground and submerged under a ton or two of mindless flesh.

Suddenly there came a scream which climbed above the tumult of the meffos and even pierced the noise of the trains. The clutching hands dropped away and the offensive smell retreated. The Borribles scrambled to their feet, closed ranks and backhanded the blood from their eyes.

The scream came again and the scream was words. 'Get off,' it cried. 'Get off.' The meffos retreated further, the passion leaving their faces just as quickly as it had come. They stumbled away in haste; some to squat against a wall, most to throw themselves flat upon the ground, all of them surrendering to a deep and habitual despair.

In the middle of the sea of bodies stood a woman, a meffo like the others, but taller and grander though just as dirty and just as savage. She was clothed in a strange and ancient finery, the booty from some suitcase found or stolen in one of the nearby railway stations. It was a long dress she wore, layered pink and silver in taffeta, a dress that had once been the Saturday night adornment of a bronze medallist in ballroom dancing. Now it was stained and torn, ripped at the bosom. Under its tattered skirt were khaki trousers and on the woman's feet was a pair of scuffed, once high-heeled shoes from both of which the heels had been broken. The shoes were blue.

Around her shoulders the woman had slung two or three knitted shawls of black wool, and she held these in place with broad, strong hands. Her face was flat and vulgar, but it was not weak; the nose was a button with open nostrils, the cheeks were pudgy, the chin was round and the mouth a deep slit. Her straw-coloured hair was streaked with black and grey and stood up around her skull like a starched halo. She looked like a witch who had wanted to change herself into a pig and then hesitated halfway. It was immediately obvious to the Borribles that everyone in the cavern went in dread of her.

'Bring them kids over here,' said the woman with a jerk of her head. 'You fools. There might be a reward out for this lot, a big reward, and all you can do is kill 'em. Bring 'em 'ere.'

As soon as he could Hughie MacMungall heaved himself upright, rearranged the trilby on his head and shoved the Borribles across the cavern, eager to claim the glory of capturing such important prisoners. 'Bet their parents would pay a fortune to 'ave 'em back home, eh Madge?' he said, and he looked out craftily from under his eyebrows like a water rat from under a river bank, to make sure he was saying the right thing.

The Borribles could now see that by the doorway from which MacMungall had appeared earlier there stood a rickety table and a couple of plastic-covered armchairs. Madge leant against the table and ran a hand through her stiff hair. She studied the Borribles' faces one by one and as she did so she took MacMungall's bottle from him and poured some of its contents into her slit of a mouth.

Ninch stepped towards her; he was shaking with fright and temper.

'You can't keep me here,' he shouted. 'There's a law against abduction. I'll call the police. I warn you, I'm a—'

Madge's head jerked forward on an arched neck like a snake striking. 'You're nothing here, sonny,' she said, 'but I'm life and death. If I 'adn't woken up just now them animals would have ripped yer to pieces and then eaten yer. They get so drunk they don't know the difference between fish and chips and human flesh. Times is hard, sonny, and cannibals ain't unknown round the back of King's Cross, I can tell yer . . . So now, what are you doing here? The truth I want, or I'll beat it out of yer.'

'We ran away from a home,' said Bingo, who had always been good at lying to adults, 'a foster home.'

'Bloody lot of yer for one home,' said Madge, not convinced.

'It was a big place,' said Bingo, whining and wheedling. 'We decided to run away together, that's why we ain't got any money. We never had any to start with, otherwise we'd give it yer, honest.'

'Honest,' cried Madge, and she spat at the Borribles' feet. 'Honest ain't invented.'

'Throw 'em out,' came a voice from the gloom. 'Let's get some sleep.' A bottle smashed against the wall.

'Shuddup,' roared MacMungall, swaying on his feet, 'or you'll feel my fist, pal. I'm the boss here.'

'You're the what, where?' Madge slowly turned her attention from the Borribles, placed her hands on her hips and glowered at her consort.

'You couldn't scratch yer arse without a book of instructions. Who found this place, eh? Answer me that, you bleeding' haggis. Who keeps the coppers sweet so they turns a blind eye, eh? Answer me that.'

MacMungall evaded the woman's gaze and sank into one of the armchairs. 'Aw, Madge,' he said, 'go easy.'

As MacMungall and Madge began to quarrel the meffos who stood near the Borribles began to lose interest in the captives and shambled away to stretch themselves out on the floor with their mates. This gave the Adventurers a chance to look about them.

For his part Knocker turned his attention to the huge double doors that blocked the exit. A heavy iron bar held them firmly closed. That was not all; between the way out and the place where the Borribles now stood lay row after row of meffos. If the Borribles attempted to make a run for it they would be grabbed by leg or arm before they got anywhere. It would be best to do nothing for the time being; maybe Madge could be persuaded into setting them free.

'Couldn't we go home, please, missus?' said Bingo. 'We didn't mean to come in here but the law was chasing us. Didn't you hear the sirens? We didn't mean no harm.'

'The best thing we can do,' said MacMungall, 'is get shot of 'em. If the cops are looking for 'em they might trace 'em 'ere. We can do without trouble. That little Paki, though, he'd be lovely toasted.'

'Bangladeshi,' said Twilight.

MacMungall threw back his head in a laugh and showed his red mouth again. 'I don't care,' he said. 'I'm not prejudiced. I don't care who I eat, pal.'

'You fool,' said Madge, and she pointed at the rucksacks and catapults which lay scattered on the floor. 'What's that there, eh? That's catapults that is and catapults mean only one thing in this world . . . It means Borribles and Borribles means thievin'. Look under them hats, look at their ears, you fool. We're on easy street, that's what . . . we've got twelve of the little buggers, twelve.'

MacMungall pushed himself to his feet, and seizing the nearest of the captives – it happened to be Torreycanyon – tore his hat from his head and inspected the ears. 'Aha,' he crowed and threw Torreycanyon's hat into the air. 'You're a genius, Madge. You're right. Borribles. A round dozen of Borribles . . . they can thieve for us for the rest of our born naturals. Hooray. Amazin' Grace. Scotland the brave.'

A stream of spittle ran from MacMungall's mouth as his taste buds worked overtime. He stared, dreaming of the future, feeling more booze than he had ever imagined pouring down his throat, warming his stomach. He had never knowingly seen a Borrible but he knew the stories; knew that they were the best thieves and burglars on earth. If you could force a Borrible into stealing for you then you were indeed on easy street.

'Oh no,' said Scooter, his voice shaking with fear. 'I didn't reckon on this. I'm frightened, really frightened.' He moved closer to Chalotte.

Chalotte was frightened herself but she put her arm round Scooter's shoulders and said, 'Don't worry, they ain't real Borrible-snatchers, only amateurs.'

'Amateurs, eh?' said Ninch. 'Well that old cow ain't doing too badly for an amateur.'

Madge crouched and, immensely strong, grabbed Ninch by the hair and bent him backwards over the table; a knife appeared at his throat like magic. 'Keep still, all of yer,' she snarled, 'otherwise his blood'll be all over the floor.'

MacMungall leant closer and looked carefully into Ninch's face. 'What a sly wee devil he looks,' he said, 'don't he?'

'Yes,' said Madge, pressing the knife tighter into Ninch's neck. 'They all are. You can't trust Borribles. They moves fast, runs fast and is as slippery as eels. See the way they looks at yer, Hughie my love, their eyes steady, taking in everything, adding it all up, waiting their chance. Been alive hundreds of years, some of 'em, they say. Wise as mountains, tough as old boots and crafty as curates.'

Stonks raised his arm and pointed at Madge.

'You harm him,' he said, 'you harm that Borrible and I warn you that whatever you do to him, we will do the same to you. We have seen worse than this and survived worse than this. Take care or a message will go out.'

Madge shook her hair and crouched an inch or two lower but did not remove her knife from Ninch's throat. 'You short-arsed little 'ap'orth,' she said. 'You don't frighten me. Do you see how many of us there are in this archway? More than you can handle. You just do as you're told and you might survive. Give me trouble and you'll die, very unpleasant.'

'Borribles, eh,' said MacMungall. 'Why don't we turn them in? There's bound to be a reward posted.'

Madge laughed. 'You've spent your whole life busily avoiding your brains, ain't you? And a first-rate job you've made of it. We might hand 'em over when we're ready, but not before. We've got to get some work out of 'em first.'

'Work?'

'Yeah. From now on we won't have to go out every day, rooting around in dustbins, hanging about the stations, begging, seeing what we can steal, what we can find. From now on these nippers will do it for us.'

Madge pulled Ninch to his feet but she kept the knife at his throat. 'Get some string, Hughie. Tie this one's arms behind his back and then we'll put him in the cage down below.'

'You can't,' shouted Scooter, and he jumped at MacMungall and began to punch him as hard as he could. 'You can't. Leave him alone, he's not even—'

MacMungall was surprised by this onslaught, but only for a second or two. He raised a heavy fist and dropped it on Scooter's face, hard. He hit him again and Scooter fell to the floor, senseless.

'I warned you,' shouted MacMungall. He crouched like a prizefighter and faced the Borribles. 'I strike with speed, pal. The blood of the clans flows in my veins; death to the Campbells.'

Once Ninch's hands were bound behind him, Madge commanded half a dozen of the strongest meffos to take him and Scooter away. 'Put 'em in the cage,' she said. 'I'll see yer all right; booze for all soon.'

'What's the idea, Madge?' asked MacMungall. 'Why the cage?'

Madge laughed. 'Why, Hughie my love? For hostages so the others do as they're told, so they steals hard for us.'

'But they'll only run away, this lot. First chance they gets.'

'Ha!' cried Madge. 'I know about Borribles. They ain't like us. They ain't allowed to leave their mates in the lurch, because they know that if they do I'll hand 'em over to the law and they'd have their ears clipped and that would be the end of 'em.'

'End of 'em?'

'O' course. They'd grow up, just like us, and no sensible kid would want to do that, eh? Grow up like us.'

MacMungall smiled. 'No, they wouldna. What shall we do wi' these others then?'

Madge tossed the end of one of her shawls around her neck and tucked her knife out of sight. 'Send 'em back on the streets,' she said. 'This is the beginning of the good times, Hughie, my love. If they don't come back here with wallets and handbags and suitcases and booze, well then, we just might have to hand their chums over to the law, eh.'

Madge laughed, and as she congratulated herself on her astuteness the half a dozen meffos who had taken Ninch and Scooter to their imprisonment returned and handed her a large key on a length of chain. 'Aha,' she cried, snatching it. 'Now open the doors, I'm going to throw 'em out. They know what they've got to do.'

The big iron bar was swivelled from its sockets and one of the wooden gates was half opened. 'Come on,' said Madge and she and MacMungall began to kick and push the Borribles out of the cavern. 'Just keep bringing stuff back here, you kids, just as soon as you've nicked it, and don't let the law see you. Remember, if they find us we'll hand you over. Go on, off wi' yer.' With a final kick Madge thrust the Adventurers on to the pavement and closed the door behind them.

The Borribles blinked. It was broad daylight outside; the traffic was heavy and it roared by in a solid stream, unceasing.

'Last time we were caught like this,' said Knocker, kicking the ground, 'it was Dewdrop the Borrible-snatcher and we had to kill him to get away.'

'I'd do it again,' said Napoleon, 'if I had to.'

'I'd do it to save Sam,' said Sydney. 'And we may have to if we want to get away in time. It'll be Madge's life against Sam's if she keeps us here too long.'

'Well, what's to stop us going anyway?' said Napoleon. 'Ninch and Scooter are nothing to me. I've always thought there was something fishy about them. Here we are out in the fresh air, halfway to Camden Town. Let's go.'

'We can't, Nap,' said Chalotte. 'We just can't. We've got to think of a way of getting them free.'

'What are we going to do then?' asked Torreycanyon, 'because we've got to think of something.'

Orococco shrugged. 'What can we do?' he said. 'For the time being all we can do is what they say: thieving in the railway stations. Meanwhile we have to think up a plan, a really good plan.'

'Yes,' said Knocker, 'you're right, Coco. But I tell you, this plan will have to be something special, because we'll only get one crack at these meffos, only one crack, and if we get it wrong they'll have our bums for bookends, mark my words.'

7

The days of captivity at King's Cross were very strange. Not that the Borribles were particularly frightened of the meffos, they weren't. It would have been easy for them to have run away at any time, simply leaving Ninch and Scooter to their fate. But they could not; they knew it wasn't right and although discussed as an option it was not seriously considered. Borrible did not leave Borrible in the lurch.

The work of stealing was straightforward and not at all dangerous. There were three stations to choose from: King's Cross, St Pancras and Euston, and each one was crowded from early morning until late at night. Picking pockets was a simple matter and there were unattended suitcases everywhere, providing an endless supply of goods for the meffos to sell or barter in exchange for drink. Food itself was to be had literally for the taking, and during this period the Borribles lived well and put on weight.

To make their job safer, they made themselves look as much like travellers as they could, with suitcases of their own bearing properly addressed labels. When they were questioned by station staff, they always answered that they were waiting for their parents, catching a train to so and so and on their way to such and such. That side of it was all very successful.

In spite of these advantages they were, of course, profoundly unhappy. This was not the way they wanted to live. They were stealing for someone else and stealing for money too. Worse, they were being delayed in their task of rescuing Sam and every day that went by made them more anxious. Sussworth might have disobeyed the DAC's orders and slaughtered Sam out of hand. They had to find out.

But the Borribles did not let the grass grow under their feet. They discovered that the cage where Ninch and Scooter were imprisoned was in an old cellar at the very back of the arch. It was a small brick-lined room dug out of the ground and an iron-barred trapdoor gave access to it. Many years previously it had been used for storing valuable wines and spirits and it was impregnable.

Madge had discovered the key to the trapdoor soon after taking possession of the cavern and she used the cage to lock up any of the meffos who got on the wrong side of her. It had come in just right for the two hostages, and the only way to free them was to steal the key from Madge. That would not be easy. Madge had a secret hiding place somewhere for all her precious things and no one, not even MacMungall, seemed to know where it was. The Borribles watched her closely, day after day, but Madge was too canny to make a mistake.

During most of this time of captivity the Adventurers did not feel like prisoners. They were not beaten as long as they brought home enough stolen goods to keep their hosts intoxicated, and they were free, more or less, to come and go as they pleased. It was only in the evening, when their booty had been delivered and inspected, that the sadness really engulfed them.

Every night they were pushed inside the little alcove which belonged to MacMungall and Madge and bound hand and foot. But even that was no problem. On the very first day the Borribles had stolen new knives and made new catapults; they could free themselves whenever they wanted. That certainly made them feel better but it wasn't enough. They still had to release the hostages and journey on to Camden Town to find the slaughterhouse. They needed a plan and a good plan was not easy to come by. At the very last of all, when they had been forced to conclude that the killing of MacMungall and Madge was the only way for them to get on and rescue the horse, they were saved from murder by the chance arrival of the Queen Mum.

*

One evening, when MacMungall and Madge were inspecting the day's loot and the Borribles themselves were resting and eating by the opening to the alcove, there came a great commotion at the wooden gates of the archway. There was a banging of fists and the sound of someone swearing loudly. The usual noises of the cavern – snoring, coughing, hawking and spitting – suddenly stopped, a wave of movement swept across the bodies lying on the floor and most of the meffos raised their heads.

MacMungall closed the lid of a suitcase and slipped a wallet into his pocket. 'What's this?' he queried, looking wildly about him. 'Is that the law? We don't want to be caught with this little lot of gear. It's them kids, it's theirs. I fought for this country, I did, and in a Highland regiment.' He threw the suitcase towards the Borribles.

'Imbecile,' said Madge. 'Open that door someone before all the coppers in London hears the row. That's the Queen Mum, blast her.'

'The Queen Mum,' said MacMungall. He retrieved the suitcase. 'Trust her to turn up when we've got something bonny organized. Who could have told her?'

Madge sneered. 'Who knows where'll she turn up next? But leastways she don't stop long in one place.'

Intrigued by this conversation the Borribles moved from the shadows and nearer to the light so they could see the arrival of this new personage.

'The Queen Mum,' said Bingo, 'who on earth can they mean?'

Bingo's companions shook their heads, mystified, but they were soon to be enlightened. One of the meffos near the door shambled to his feet and, in obedience to Madge's command, eased open the wooden gates. Out of the darkness and rain, pushing a battered old pram, its wheels squeaking, came the strangest figure.

There was not much to be seen of the Queen Mum to begin with. Her head was wrapped in a large piece of transparent polythene, spotted with raindrops. Her body, which looked as if it might be square and stocky, was made shapeless by a large brown raincoat which reached right down to her black wellington boots. An old potato sack was pinned around her shoulders for added warmth and protection.

The pram, the hood of which had long since been ripped away, was piled high with her possessions; they too were covered with a large sheet of polythene. The Queen Mum was well prepared for the rigours of the road and the cavern was just one of many stops on a never-ending journey that took in all of London, from north to south, from east to west and back again. There wasn't a street, alley or hideout in the whole of the metropolis that the Queen Mum did not know and treat as her own property.

At any rate she pushed straight into the cavern as if she lived there every day of the week and shunted her pram into the bodies that lay in her path. Groans of protest rose from the floor but the Queen Mum took little notice, only yelling at her victims with a rough, toneless bell of a voice the sound of which resounded across the brick archway and clanged from wall to wall.

'Come on, you sods,' she shouted. 'Clear a space for a poor old lady. Clear a space.'

She continued to thrust her way into the centre of the cavern and once she had reached it began to make a clear circle for herself by kicking backwards with her feet and bashing forwards with her pram. When she was convinced she had enough room she removed the sack from her shoulders and then the sheet of plastic from her head. She shook them both free of water.

'Oi, Queenie, give over with that rain,' said a voice from the floor.

'You give over,' retorted the Queen Mum. 'You'd better learn a bit of Christian charity before I boots yer face in. I needs a drink I do, to dissipate the damp.'

During the performance Madge remained slumped low in her armchair, but MacMungall, feeling brave, got to his feet and shook a fist. 'You'll get no drink from us,' he roared. 'We has enough trouble keeping body and soul together for ourselves without you coming round here scrounging.'

The Queen Mum gazed at MacMungall like she had wind in her stomach; she saw Madge and her grin spread even wider. The Borribles saw her face for the first time.

'Man,' said Orococco. 'I knows haunted houses that would get up and run a mile if they saw that.'

The Queen Mum had a nose that was thin and square-tipped like a screwdriver, a suspicious nose that could sniff out any treachery. Her eyes were close together, like the eyes of a ferret and just as sharp; they had been blue once but the colour had faded, worn out with looking on the ground for money and searching for things of value in dustbins.

The dark brown hair was dirty, shiny with grease, drawn back into a straggling bun behind her neck and held in place by a thick elastic band. Her chin was pointed and did its best to rise up to meet her nose while her skin was corrugated all over like the stone of a peach, and there was a shaggy green mould growing deep-rooted in every furrow.

As for her clothes, she wore the jacket of a man's suit and a wide skirt that was made from a double thickness of grey blanket with holes in it. On her hands she wore woollen mittens which showed knobbly fingers with black, bruised nails at the end of them. The Borribles stared.

The Queen Mum took a pipe from her pocket and lit it. Not until she'd puffed out two or three mouthfuls of smoke to join the darkness above her head did she deign to answer MacMungall. She showed no fear.

'Why, Hughie, you ol' fraud,' she began, 'you can take your drink and you can ram it right up your Khyber, and I hope it brings a smile to yer face because there's precious little else I knows of as will. If it wasn't for your old mother, sitting next to yer there, you'd starve. You don't even know which way is up.'

Madge was furious at being called Hughie's mother. She climbed to her feet, burning with a slow rage. 'You old cow,' she said. 'We 'ad enough of you last time, drinkin' all our stuff, shoutin' and fightin', gettin' the police sent for. This ain't the Sally you know.'

The Queen Mum jeered and gave Madge the two-fingered salute. Then she fumbled in her pram and pulled out a bottle of methylated spirits. 'I've got more booze than I need,' she said, lifting the bottle to her lips and swigging down a couple of good mouthfuls. 'I don't need no charity, least of all from you.' And so saying she lowered herself regally to the ground.

For the time being the quarrel seemed over and the cavern settled again after this burst of action, but the blood in the veins of the Borribles raced a little faster. They looked at each other and an idea began to take shape among them. There was an obvious rivalry between these two women, a rivalry that had been going on for many years based, by the look of things, on the disdain that the Queen Mum bore the sedentary Madge and the dread that Madge felt for the itinerant

Queen Mum. Whatever might be the cause of the hatred, it occurred to the prisoners that in the new arrival they might have found an ally.

*

An offer of help came to the Adventurers much sooner than they expected, in fact it came the following day. The prisoners had all met together to eat their midday meal on a bench hidden away behind packing cases in a quiet part of Euston station. They were morose and unsmiling. As always they were preoccupied with planning their escape and the rescue of the two hostages who were still locked in the wine cage at the back of the cavern.

'Well all I can say,' said Napoleon, biting into a stolen cheese sandwich, 'is if we haven't thought of something in a few days I'm going to do a Dewdrop and Erbie on Madge and Hughie. Them other meffos won't give us any trouble . . . their brains is all pickled.'

'I dunno,' said Vulge. 'They give me the creeps.'

'Watch out,' said Twilight who was keeping an eye open for trouble, 'here comes someone we know.'

Sure enough, with the squeak of the pram wheels announcing her presence, the Queen Mum was approaching, once more dressed in her plastic and sacking, shuffling noisily along in her old wellington boots, her eyes fixed on the ground, searching for coins.

Slowly she advanced on the Borribles and they watched, mesmerized. At last the Queen Mum stopped before them, her eyes rising from her scrutiny of the floor. She said nothing. In the distance, trains whistled and passengers scurried along; an announcement came crackling over the loudspeakers. At last the woman spoke. 'Move up,' she said with that metal voice of hers. 'I want to sit down. I've got some'at to say to you, I have, yes, some'at to say.'

Still silent the Borribles squeezed up tight to each other and made room for the Queen Mum to sit. She held her pram near so that it was close enough for her to reach into, which she did, pulling out her bottle. She swigged at it between sentences.

'I found out about you poor little 'ard-done-by children today, I did,' she said. 'Yes, I did, except you ain't poor little 'ard-done-by children, are you? You're 'orrible little Borribles.'

'So what?' said Napoleon. 'You going to tell Old Bill?'

'Old Bill!' hooted the Queen Mum. 'I wouldn't pee in a copper's ear if 'is 'elmet was on fire. Nah, what I want to know is how come you're hand in glove with that ragbag, Madge, and ol' Face-ache, her fancy man. I don't know much about Borribles but from what I 'eard I thought they wouldn't have anything to do with the likes of her.'

'We ain't in with them,' said Knocker. 'We ran into that place the other morning because the law was breathing down our necks. Madge caught us.'

'I see,' said the Queen Mum. She spat between Bingo's feet with great accuracy. 'Well, why don't you shove off?'

'Because,' said Stonks, 'they've got two of our mates locked up round the back and we can't go without them.'

The Queen Mum nodded. 'Hmm,' she said, 'you haven't told me the half of it, 'ave yer? I may be an old tramp, you know, but I ain't stupid. What are you doing on the road? This ain't your manor; I can see that, no one knows London like I do.'

Sydney looked at Chalotte and then at Knocker. Knocker nodded and Sydney told the story of Sam the horse, the trip to Rumbledom, the escape, Inspector Sussworth and Ben the tramp. The whole saga.

The Queen Mum lit her pipe as she listened and smoked it thoughtfully. It was a long story but at the end of it she blew a smoke ring and said, 'Well I'll be filleted . . . It's amazing what goes on behind yer back. What larks! That Ben. Many's the boozy night I've spent with him down on Feather's Wharf. He was good-looking when he was younger, he was. So was I. Used ter be a fashion model before I took to the road. Tall and willowy, I was, with eyes as big as manhole covers.'

The Queen Mum knocked the dead tobacco out of her pipe and tightened the muscles round her mouth. She straighted her back and took on a certain air. She had come to a decision. 'It's easy really,' she said. 'This afternoon, this evening, don't nick anything for 'em but booze . . . no food. The strongest stuff you can get yer hands on, mind: whisky, gin, vodka. They likes vodka, throws it down so fast it don't hit the sides of their throats. That'll put 'em all to sleep, then you can find yer chums and get away.'

'We thought of all that,' said Knocker, 'ages ago, but even if we gets 'em all drunk there's still Madge; she might not fall for it, and she's got the key, remember, and we've no idea where she keeps it. It'll be no good if we don't find that key.'

The Queen Mum put her pipe away and her nose twisted with pleasure like it was doing up an invisible screw. 'You get enough booze,' she said, 'and them meffos will sleep for two or three days. It's a way of life with them. As for Madge, let that be my problem. I've got an old score to settle with her.' The Queen Mum stared dreamily at the station roof and dropped into a reverie, talking now to herself. 'Like to break her spine, I would. I owes her one. She got me six months inside once, sicked the law on to me, didn't she? Do you think I've ever forgotten that? No I haven't. You leave her to me. And those poor little blighters in the cage. Teems with water down there, it does. They'll die of gangrene if they stay there much longer. Have to put them through a mangle just to get the water out of their bones.'

Suddenly the Queen Mum broke off and came back to herself. 'Ha,' she said, 'don't take no notice of me, but I mean it, I tells yer; I ain't letting her get away with nothing.' She settled the clothes on her body and flapped her thick blanket of a skirt so that it fell out of its creases. 'I'll be off now.'

Napoleon stood and put his face close to the tramp's, quite unabashed. 'Do you think you could hang about between the stations with your pram?'

'What the devil for?' said the Queen Mum. 'Why?'

'Well,' said Napoleon, 'just so we can hide some of our bottles in it. It'll save us a lot of time and we can nick more booze and nick it quicker.'

The old lady smiled and her chin moved up to meet her nose. 'My boy,' she said, 'you remind me of me.'

*

The Borribles set to with a will. At last they had a plan. Not a detailed, thoroughgoing plan but at least they were doing something and they had an ally in the enemy camp.

That day they stole an enormous amount of strong drink, and an endless variety. Everything that could be found in shops, off licences and supermarkets they took. There was whisky from Scotland and Ireland, vodka from Russia and Poland, Bulls' Blood from Hungary, white wine from Germany, claret from Bordeaux, advocaat from Holland, bourbon from the USA and slivovitz from Yugoslavia. In a few short hours the Borribles collected enough alcohol to sink a battleship and drown the crew as well.

Very many of these contraband bottles were stowed in the Queen Mum's pram and were to go back with her that evening. She wanted to have some ready, she said, to distribute when she thought the time was right. A certain amount of booze was taken back to the cavern by the Borribles as and when it was stolen, so as to make sure the meffos became well intoxicated during the day, but the bulk of it all was hidden on waste ground and watched over until the Borribles were satisfied they had amassed enough to achieve their purpose.

That evening, when the shops had closed, the Borribles trudged back to the cavern heavily laden, most of them being obliged to make several journeys before their rich haul was delivered. As they entered the archway with the last of their booty, tension rose high; much fine alcohol had already been consumed and appetites were keen. The meffos wanted more and more; they desired only to drink until oblivion relieved them of the strain of living, anything to escape from the heaviness of time. They groaned and stretched out their hands and the Borribles gave them their bottles as fast as they could and the meffos gibbered with happiness and greed; their mouths slavered and their broken red eyelids were brilliant and wet. Never had these down-and-outs seen so much high-quality liquor.

MacMungall and Madge were just as greedy as the others and of course they took the pick of the booty; they always did. The table that stood by the armchairs and just in front of the alcove was stacked with containers of all kinds standing shoulder to shoulder. MacMungall's bloated face burnt like a flare with the heat of gin and whisky indiscriminately mixed. The small smashed veins in his fleshy nose were all bursting afresh, exploding like fireworks in a dark purple sky. His eyes glinted with new blood; the ecstasy of nothingness was approaching.

Madge was suspicious, but she did drink. Even she could not resist an empty bean can full of port and Drambuie; nevertheless she grabbed Knocker by the scruff of his neck and shook him hard.

'There's gallons of it,' she said, 'gallons. What are you up to, eh?

Trying to get us drunk. Well it won't work, Sunbeam. You'll never find the key, never.' And Madge fell backwards across her armchair, her khaki trousers showing under her taffeta dress.

MacMungall, meanwhile, sat bolt upright and snatched a fresh bottle from the table before him. His head rolled loosely on his shoulders as if his neck had been broken; he was halfway drunk already. 'Remember,' he shouted, 'work is the screw of time,' and he undid the top of his bottle and poured a third of its contents into his throat at one go.

Madge swore at him, leant over from her chair to his and clouted him round the head with a fist as hard as a rock. 'Tie them kids up, you drunk,' she screamed. 'Tie 'em up, you hear. I don't trust them.'

'Aw, Madge,' said MacMungall, 'they'll be all right.'

Madge leant over again and swept the bottle from the man's hand with such violence that it hit the wall and smashed. 'You do as I say,' she whispered, her voice trembling with temper, 'or I'll slit yer throat while yer asleep, you beetle-brain, you.'

The Borribles themselves, sitting on the ground within earshot, were not worried in the slightest by this exchange. They heard it, or something like it, every night. At that moment they were much more interested in watching the results of their handiwork, their mouths falling open in disbelief.

There were drunken meffos rolling about the floor everywhere, shouting and screaming with pleasure. Others, a good many of them, were on their feet, kicking their heels up and singing, moving in strange stumbling circles of delight, their cracked voices chanting out in a wild celebration of booze:

'Drink it and sink it and clink it again,
Swill it and kill it and fill it again,
Booze it and lose it and choose it again.
The world is a bad house,
A prison a madhouse,
To hell with all sober respectable men.

'Here we go beer we go blear we go down,
Wine we go fine we go blind we go down,
Flesh we go meths we go death we go down.
This life is a farce,

Of the gods and the arse,
Of the universe wearing the face of a clown.

'Steal the stuff feel the stuff deal the stuff more,
Quaff the stuff laugh the stuff splash the stuff more,
Curse the stuff worse the stuff nurse the stuff more.
There's no good in thinking,
Oblivion's in drinking,
So pickle your brains till you drop to the floor.'

It was an unearthly scene, frightening, a dance of death in the sulphurous glow of a single electric light bulb, a bulb that was made to sway and dance itself as each train passed by overhead; a bulb that made grotesque shadows move over the fungus-covered bricks of that rumbling cavern. It was a graveyard giving up its dead.

The Borribles were not allowed to watch this mournful spectacle for long. Under the constant promptings of Madge, MacMungall eventually lurched out of his armchair, fell round it and began to urge his prisoners to their feet with good strong kicks, but when he spoke there was a note of entreaty in his voice. He was anxious to get back to his drinking. 'Come on you kids, in yer go,' he said. 'Don't give me trouble, you know what us Highlanders are like when we're roused. Highland blood is explosive, you know, like nitroglycerine.'

The Borribles did as they were ordered; they had no intention of doing anything that might interfere with the Queen Mum's plan at this stage. Meekly they allowed themselves to be shepherded into the alcove and remained quiet while MacMungall knelt to bind their arms and legs with rope left there for the purpose, though he made but a pitiful job of it.

'Aw, yer not bad, you kids,' he kept saying, his breath smelling like a drain. 'Salt of the earth, us Scots, rough diamonds. All be the same in a hundred years, so we might as well have a little drink to help us on our road, eh!' And with this said he got to his feet and, staggering, he made his way back to his armchair, falling heavily into it and grabbing a new bottle from the table as he fell. 'Hoots!' he yelled. 'This is the life!'

The moment MacMungall had left them the Borribles freed themselves and crept to the entrance of the alcove. From here they could keep an eye on Madge and also see the Queen Mum sitting by her pram in the middle of the cavern. Now it was just a question of waiting.

There were far fewer meffos on their feet now. Most of them were lying spark out on the ground, rendered legless by the power of alcohol. To those that were still awake the Queen Mum gave bottles from her own secret store. Soon they would all sleep the sleep of overfed swine, only calling out in their dreams now and then as they tried to escape the monsters that pursued and tortured them.

Gradually, as the hours went by, the cavern became still. The trains ceased to pass overhead as the timetable worked its way through to nothing, and the silence deepened. The night dripped away drop by drop, right down to the last empty second, and it was then, and only then, that the Queen Mum decided to move. She rose from her seat, massive like a gasometer.

MacMungall snored. The eyelids of Madge flickered and she lifted her bottle to her lips and swore in a half-sleep. The Queen Mum pulled her shawl of sacking tightly round her shoulders and began to pick her way gently among the unconsciouos meffos, making no sound, but Madge, sensing someone moving, sat bolt upright, her hair stiff in its halo, her head jerking out on its neck.

'What do you want, you old bitch?' she asked when the Queen Mum reached her.

The Queen Mum looked at the bottles on the table, most empty, some full.

'I'm just going to take a bottle,' she said. 'Everyone's had a bottle tonight, save me. That gin'll do. I likes a drop of gin.'

'Listen to her,' said Madge, jeering as if to the assembled company, though there was no one awake to hear her save the Borribles. 'Jus' look at yer,' continued Madge. 'I wouldn't give yer nothin' 'cept a mask. You leave my booze alone, you unnerstan'? If I catch you stealing I'll 'ave you put away again – another six months in Holloway.'

The Queen Mum's face became angry as she was reminded of her shame. She placed her hands on her hips and rolled the top half of her body round in a circle and stuck her curving chin forward as if offering Madge a free swipe at it. 'That's about all you're fit for, grassing and selling one of your own kind down the river.'

'One of my own kind,' retorted Madge scornfully. She crossed her ankles, leant back in her armchair and took another pull at her drink. 'Why, you're hardly human. For two pins I'd snap yer back like a rotten carrot.'

'Oh yeah?' said the Queen Mum and she clenched her fists and took half a step forward. Her brow furrowed as she searched her mind for more insults. It was clear to the watching Borribles that she was trying to goad Madge into a fight. 'You watch yer lip, you tuppenny-ha'penny tart. Your fancy man can't help you now, he's too drunk even to run away.'

Madge looked at MacMungall. He lay deep in his chair, his mouth open, his red eyes spongy and his nose a blazing amethyst. She turned her head again and stared down the cavern. All she saw was an uneven carpet of human bodies stirring only slightly, close, warm and murmuring like fat flies on dead meat.

'I don't need help,' said Madge at length, 'not with the likes of you I don't. Piss off.'

'I will, I will,' said the Queen Mum at the top of her voice. 'I might just piss off to the local nick and tell 'em about all the stolen property they could find here . . . and you'd be the one to spend six months in Holloway, not me. Make you wash they do, Madge. And there's no drink. I'd be revenged then, nicely revenged.'

Now Madge lost her temper. She pushed herself up from the armchair and, although staggering a little, she seized an empty bottle by the neck and smashed it against the edge of the table; the jagged glass made a deadly weapon.

'You ain't telling no one nothing,' she said, 'you bleedin' hyena. I'm going to cut yer throat, you see if I don't.' Madge advanced and raised the bottle out in front of her, eyes mad, hair wild about her face.

The Queen Mum fell back several steps, enticing Madge on, taunting her. 'You drunken old mare, they'll have you for child murder they will, I'll make sure about that. If them two kids in the cage croaks of pneumonia I'll have something to tell Old Bill then.'

Madge could take no more. She screamed with all the power of her lungs and leapt at her enemy, shoving the broken bottle at the Queen Mum's neck. Quick as she was the Queen Mum was quicker. She slipped to one side of the table, avoiding the onslaught, raised her hands to her sacking shawl and pulled it from her shoulders. As Madge turned to renew the fight the Queen Mum whirled the sack above her head and with the end of it she caught Madge a blow across the temple. Madge stumbled and the bottle fell from her hand and smashed to the floor. The Queen Mum whirled the sack again, twice, three times round her head; faster, faster, then thump! The corner of it caught Madge once more on the temple and there was a cracking sound like a coconut splitting. Madge pitched to the floor, face down, and then rolled over on her back to stare blindly up at the light bulb. Her eyes blinked a few times and blood trickled from her nose. Her last breath was expelled from her lungs in a long wheezing rattle. Madge was dead.

A smile slowly grew on the Queen Mum's lips. She replaced the sack on her shoulders and stepped towards the body. She pushed it with her foot, then she kicked it hard, twice. 'You cow,' she said quietly, 'I promised you I'd get you one day and so I have. No one sends the Queen Mum to prison and gets away with it, no one. Now you've had your last drink and fought your last fight. Good riddance.'

One by one the Borribles emerged from the alcove and stood by the table staring down, their mouths dry. MacMungall still snored; an empty bottle rolled from his hands and clinked on to the floor but did not break.

'She's killed her,' said Twilight.

'Course she has,' said Napoleon. 'What did you expect, three clean rounds and a win on points?' He knelt and examined the bruise on the side of Madge's head. 'How did you do it, Queenie?' he asked. 'How did you kill her with an old sack?'

The Queen Mum sniffed professionally and said, 'That old sack has a big lump of lead sewn into the corner. I've killed men twice the size of her before now, mate. I've had to, sometimes.'

Napoleon stood and looked at the Queen Mum with new respect. He also took a catapult from his pocket, just to be on the safe side. 'Where do you think the key is?' he asked.

The Queen Mum inspected every Borrible in turn. Each one of them now had a makeshift catapult in his or her hand. She smiled. 'Saint Fairy Anne,' she said. 'I'm proud of yer; you don't trust no one and that's right, of course, but I ain't going to go back on yer. Come over here.'

She led the way to the brick wall directly behind Madge's armchair and, taking a knife from a pocket in the side of her skirt, she began to scrape away at the mortar. 'I saw her put some stuff in here years ago,' she explained. 'Old Madge thought I was drunk but I'm never that drunk.'

One of the bricks loosened and then another. The Queen Mum levered with the knife blade, the bricks fell to the floor and a black hole appeared. The woman cackled and shoved an arm into the wall, up to the elbow, and felt around for a second or two. At last she turned, triumphant, holding a large iron key. 'Here it is,' she said, but she made no attempt to hand it over.

'Give it us,' said Napoleon. 'We want to be on our way.'

'Yes,' said the Queen Mum. She squinted craftily down at the Wendle. 'Certainly, but first I want you to tell me that you don't want nothing else out of this hole . . . That's in return for me getting the key for you, like.'

'Of course not,' said Chalotte scornfully. 'We don't want anything that Madge had, nothing at all.'

The Queen Mum stared deep into Chalotte's eyes until she was satisfied, then tossed the key into Napoleon's outstretched hands. 'Just as well Borribles ain't interested in money,' she said, 'otherwise this 'ere might not have turned out quite so friendly.'

Napoleon ignored the woman and turned to his companions. 'Some of you better tie old Hughie into his armchair,' he said, 'just in case he wakes up and decides to be brave. Me and Knocker will go and get Ninch and Scooter.' Without waiting for a reply he spun on his heel and, stepping over the still sleeping meffos, he set off for the back of the cavern. Knocker followed him and there, in the blackest corner of all, by the light of a torch, they found an iron ring attached to a wooden hatch. They flung this open and underneath discovered an iron-barred door with a heavy lock in the middle of it. The key fitted, moving easily, and pulling upwards with all their strength the two Borribles managed to lift this door as well, throwing it down with a resounding clang. The meffos stirred in their sleep but did not wake.

Knocker led the way now, descending green slimy steps, his torch shining weakly into a kind of steam, rising thick and white, smelling of mushrooms.

At the bottom of the stairs Knocker and Napoleon found themselves in a cell; there were two bunks and a bucket and that was all. Black water streamed down the walls and gathered in wide puddles on the uneven flagstones. In each bunk, wrapped in a tattered blanket and shivering with cold, lay a cowering and whimpering figure. It was Ninch and Scooter and they lifted their heads when they saw the light; their eyes reflected, full of terror, in the beam of the torch.

'Leave us alone, Madge.' It was Ninch's voice, strained, near to breaking point. 'We ain't done nothing.'

'It's us,' said Knocker. 'We've come to get you out.'

Scooter rolled out of his bunk and his feet splashed on to the floor. 'Oh Knocker, at last. I thought you'd come in the end but it seemed like years.'

'It's been six days,' said Napoleon. 'We've been as quick as we could.'

Knocker went across the room and helped Ninch out of the top bunk. He was surprised to feel how light the acrobat was. He felt like a bag of sticks and he was shaking uncontrollably.

'Come on,' said Knocker. 'We'll have to get you out into the light and get some dry clothes on you. I'm surprised you're still alive.'

'So am I,' said Ninch. 'So am I.'

The two captives were half walked and half carried from the dungeon and taken back to where the rest of the Adventurers, wasting no time, were now searching for their rucksacks. Ninch and Scooter sank to the floor. Warm clothes were found for them and they were given food and drink. The Queen Mum tipped some brandy down their throats and then sprawled at ease in Madge's armchair, staring at the rivulet of blood that crept out of her victim's nose, along the side of her cheek and on to the floor.

'What's that?' cried Ninch, pointing at the body.

The Queen Mum laughed and folded her arms in contentment. 'That's Madge,' she said, 'that is – or was. Quiet ain't she? I had to give her a clout round the brains.'

'That's murder,' said Ninch.

'It most certainly is,' said the Queen Mum. 'It was also justice. It was her or you, you know. You'd have been dead in a couple of weeks down that Black Hole of Calcutta. You should see yourself.'

It was true. Both Ninch and Scooter looked like ghosts, with their faces pale, their cheeks sunken and their skin tinged with lichen. They trembled continually and were too weak to stand for any length of time without help. It was certain that they would not be able to travel very far until they had rested for several days.

'And what's that?' asked Ninch again. He pointed at a large leather holdall that nestled on the Queen Mum's lap.

She laughed once more and unfolded her arms. 'This is Madge's ill-gotten gains,' she said, pulling at the zip and opening the top of the bag. 'There's more money here than they've got in the Bank of England. She must have been salting this away for years. Stealing from meffos, enticing strays off the stations, nicking their stuff when they was drunk or asleep; killing them too I should think.'

'What are you going to do with it?' Ninch said. He glanced over his shoulder, but the Adventurers were still trying to gather together what remained of their possessions.

'Do with it?' echoed the Queen Mum. 'I'm going to save it for me old age, Petal. There's jewellery too, enough to keep me in luxury for the rest of me born natural.'

'Hm,' said Ninch. 'Enough to share out, is there?'

The Queen Mum stared at Ninch and her nose twitched. 'No,' she said, 'there ain't.' She got to her feet and shoved the bag out of sight at the bottom of her pram, covering it over with a square of old blanket. 'I'd better get out of here,' she said. 'There'll be hell to pay when them others wakes up and finds Madge dead and her treasure gone. I want to be far away when that happens, like Australia.'

'And us,' said Knocker. He came up to Ninch and Scooter and threw them a raincoat each. 'Put them on,' he said. 'We've got to get on the road. It's dark out.'

Vulge limped over to Knocker with the other Adventurers behind him all prepared to continue their journey.

'What d'yer reckon, Knocker? What can we do?'

Knocker scratched his head. 'Not much choice,' he said. 'It's Hobson's really. We ain't far from Susswortth's abattoir, but we can't do anything for Sam with Ninch and Scooter in the state they're in. Best thing would be to find some empty house nearby and while they're resting we'll go on a scouting expedition and see what we can find out. I reckon that's best.'

The Queen Mum looked up from packing her pram. She had her

raincoat on now and the strip of polythene was tied round her head. 'I know where you can hide,' she said. 'Not far from here. Ha! No one knows London like me. Inside out I knows it.'

'Where?' asked Napoleon.

'Just turn right out of here, under the railway, you'll come to York Way; there's a big blank wall. You turn right again into Wharfdale Road, back of the canal, then into Balfe Street. You'll see an old block of flats there, huge, due for demolition and boarded up. I've spent many a night in there. Coppers never go in . . . too scared. Some of your lot there, I think. Borribles . . . funny to look at they are. All right though, always left me alone.'

Napoleon hoisted his rucksack on to his shoulders. 'Well, we've got all the food and stuff we're going to find here,' he said. 'We might as well get going.'

The Adventurers went carefully towards the exit, stepping softly round the meffos in their way so as not to waken them. The huge bar that closed the double doors rested in its sockets just above their heads.

'That's no problem,' said Stonks. 'We'll just get underneath it and push upwards one way and it'll swivel down the other.'

The Adventurers did exactly as Stonks suggested and with them all working together the iron bar was easily moved and the gates opened. As was to be expected the thump of the iron bar and the creak of the rusty hinges roused one or two of the meffos from their drunken sleep, but their eyelids only flickered for a moment and if the sight of the escaping Borribles penetrated as far as their tired brains it certainly did not register. They groaned, rolled over and went back to sleep. They would be drunk for days yet.

One person did wake and he discovered himself tightly bound into his own armchair. That person was Hughie MacMungall. Slowly his mind stirred into life. Gradually he became aware of the Queen Mum standing before him, hands on the push bar of her pram, dressed for the road. He licked his lips and said, 'Gi' us a drink, woman, I canna move. My body must be paralysed with thirst.' But then he looked down at his arms and noticed what had happened to him and when he looked up again he saw that the Queen Mum was smiling a smile of triumph. She laughed now and went to the table and picked up a bottle of red wine. The Borribles stood hesitant on the threshold of the open door, the black night behind them, and they watched. MacMungall shook his head and his eyes rolled helplessly as if all the muscles to them had been cut. 'Oh, Madge,' he moaned, his voice pathetic and low. 'Oh, Madge, where are you my love, my life, where are you?'

For a moment the Borribles thought that the Queen Mum might strike the helpless man with her bottle, but that was not her intention. She unscrewed the top, stepped close to MacMungall and simply upended the contents on to his head and face, letting the red liquid splash over him, fill his eyes and run in and out of his mouth, soaking his chest.

MacMungall cried out weakly and struggled to sit upright but could not. 'Oh, where's my Madge,' he whimpered. 'Where's my wee girl, where is she? I canna live without my Madge.'

The Queen Mum threw the empty bottle on to the floor and it smashed. 'You'll have to, me old china,' she said, and stood back, pointing to Madge's body lying half under the table. The blood was now thickly congealed on the corpse's face.

MacMungall, still drunk, could hardly believe what his eyes saw. His mouth dropped open, he blinked several times and began to weep and moan. 'Oh no,' he cried. 'Oh no. Queenie, you've done this; you've killed her and how will I live now? Who will see to me? I canna live without her, Queenie, I canna. This lot here will kill each other without her and they'll kill me too. Oh, Madge, my love, my love, how will I live without you? How will I live now?'

The Queen Mum shrugged her shoulders and pushed her pram away. 'You'll manage, Hughie,' she said. 'Anyway, I'm off.'

MacMungall fought against the string that bound him. 'Damn it, Queenie,' he swore. 'Don't leave me here like this, with her dead. Don't you know what them others'll do when they come to their senses?'

The Queen Mum halted her pram and looked back over her shoulder. 'They'll tear yer to pieces, I should think,' she said, 'or just leave you to starve to death, sitting in that chair.'

MacMungall pulled at his bonds again. 'That would be the best of it,' he said. 'Untie me, untie me!'

The Queen Mum shook her head. 'Sorry, Hughie. I untie you and you might try one of your little tricks. I couldn't have that.'

'Queenie,' MacMungall shouted, 'leaving me in this armchair is as good as slitting me throat.'

'I know,' said the Queen Mum, and she went on pushing her pram towards the door, wheeling it over one or two sleeping meffos and ignoring the cries of MacMungall as he continued to beg for mercy.

At the gates the Borribles stood back to let the old woman pass and she smiled crookedly at them, her nose and chin still trying to touch, like the claws of a crab.

'Where are you going now?' asked Napoleon.

The Queen Mum turned to face the rainy night and sniffed as if a sniff could decide direction. 'North,' she said, 'but I don't know how far.' She turned back to look down at the Wendle. 'But don't worry, Sunshine, I'll be seeing you lot again. I've got a nasty feeling in me water.' And with no more farewell than that the Queen Mum pushed her pram out of the cavern and set off along the street that led to Mornington Crescent.

'No, Queenie, no,' roared MacMungall as she disappeared. 'Don't leave me like this, they'll cut me ter pieces! Oh, Queenie, Queenie, come back!' But the Queen Mum did not come back and all that could be heard from her was the squeaking of her pram wheels growing less and less in the distance.

MacMungall became desperate then and he dribbled at the mouth, rolling his eyes in madness, turning them on the Adventurers, who still stood watching from the doorway. He pleaded with them: 'Don't leave me, kids, don't leave me.' He was weeping now, floods of tears pouring down the canyons of his face. 'I didna do you any real harm. I didna do you any real harm.'

'We can't stand here all night,' said Twilight. 'What we going to do?'

Chalotte glanced at Knocker and he nodded.

Napoleon shook his head. 'Leave it out,' he whispered. 'Who'd miss him anyway?' But Knocker nodded again and Chalotte drew her knife and went back to MacMungall's armchair to stand in front of him.

'I'll let you free,' she said, 'not that you deserve it. You'd have kept us here for ever if you could've.'

'No lassie, no lassie,' said MacMungall. 'I'd have seen you got off, eventual, honest.'

'Honest ain't invented,' said Chalotte, quoting Madge. 'Listen,

Hughie, I'm going to cut your ropes . . . You try anything and we'll sort you out. We're armed, you know.'

MacMungall twisted his head to one side and saw that the Borribles, all of them, were now holding loaded catapults. 'I didna mean no harm,' he said. 'I didna mean no harm. Just cut me loose, eh. Someone's got to look after poor Madge, someone's got to look after her.'

Chalotte bent over the armchair and cut the bonds that held MacMungall prisoner, stepping back smartly so that he could not grab hold of her, but the wretched man was broken and he made no such attempt. He scrambled from his chair and fell to the floor, seizing hold of Madge's body and cradling her head and shoulders in his arms. Then his voice rose in a long moan and rocking to and fro on his heels he began to chant and cry, all at once.

Chalotte rejoined her companions at the door as quickly as she could. 'He's going bonkers,' she said. 'We'd better be on our way.'

There was no more to be said or done. Cautiously, and with never another look at that awful cavern, the Borribles stepped out into what was left of the night. From somewhere away to the north came the sound of the squeaky wheels of the Queen Mum's pram and above it the rough noise of her voice raised in a song of independence and defiance. For a moment the Adventurers listened, picking out the words as they echoed along the hollow arches.

'O give me a slimy alley, mate,
O give me an old canal,
Or pass me in state through Bishopsgate
And I'll call you a pal.
O give me an unused dockland Gents,
Or doss beside the line,
And I'll be content to pay no rent
And make the bugger mine!'

Then the song stopped and the Adventurers turned south, following the broken pavements in the direction of the Caledonian Road, bearing Ninch and Scooter along with them, blotting the sound of the song from their memories.

But one sound they would never forget. It was the sound of Hughie MacMungall keening for his love, holding her bloody, sow-like head in his lap as he nursed his grief backwards and forwards, sobbing out the same words time after time, his voice thick with anguish: 'Oh, Madge, how will I live without you? How will I live without you? How will I live without you? Tell me that Madge. How will I live without you?'

The Borribles closed their ears against this dreadful lament and left the archway of the meffos for ever, just as fast their legs would carry them.

8

The Borribles pressed ahead as fast as the condition of Ninch and Scooter would allow, but they had no intention, that night, of travelling any great distance. They realized that what the two acrobats needed above all else was rest and recuperation. So, with this idea first in their minds, they went quickly forward and came eventually into a wide road named Goods Way, which took them into a main thoroughfare just at the place where it passed over the Grand Union Canal on Maiden Lane Bridge. Here, following the instructions given them by the Queen Mum, they turned right and then left. This brought them through Balfe Street into New Wharf Road which itself runs behind a huge but abandoned section of the canal called Battlebridge Basin. Alongside this basin, fenced in behind a high wooden barrier, was a block of flats, tall and forbidding and dark, their legal inhabitants long since gone to friendlier and cleaner places. Across the road, not a hundred yards distant from this block, the Borribles gathered together in the doorless doorway of a ruined workshop and peered into a deep gloom.

'Can't see any lights,' said Vulge, 'but then you wouldn't if there was any Borribles in there.'

'Borribles, eh?' said a strange voice behind them. 'That's all right then, 'cos we're Borribles too.'

Stonks spun round and switched on his torch. In its broad beam the adventurers saw two figures sitting side by side on an old oil drum only a few yards away. As the light revealed them the two strangers leapt to their feet and crossed the floor. 'We've been looking for you,' they said as they advanced, 'in fact a lot of us have.'

The Adventurers bunched together. 'What do you mean, looking for us?' asked Napoleon suspiciously. His hand felt for his catapult.

Still in the light of Stonks's torch the newcomers halted. They were an odd sight and the Adventurers stared. Both of them girls, they were dressed in a more outlandish way than most Borribles care for. Borribles normally like to pass unnoticed; these two were different. They wore leather jackets – torn in many places and then repaired with dozens of safety pins – baggy khaki trousers, metal belts and cut down welly boots. They both had their hair brilliantly coloured; one had dyed hers scarlet and the other had sprayed hers pale blue with broad golden streaks running through it. The hair itself stuck out stiff and spiky in all directions though there was enough of it combed over the ears to make sure they were well and truly hidden.

'My name's Swish,' said the girl with the scarlet hair, 'and this here's my mate. She's called Treld.'

There was a long silence following this announcement until Chalotte pushed to the front of the group of Adventurers. 'My name's Chalotte,' she said, 'from Whitechapel, and this is Sydney from Neasden. Your names are good names and we hope you will tell us the story of them one day.'

Treld nodded and her hair sparkled with golden glitter in the torchlight. 'And your names have a good story behind them . . . like the Great Rumble Hunt, maybe.'

'How do you know about that?' asked Orococco.

'We've been watching you on our railway stations,' explained Treld. 'We know old Queenie too. She told us that Madge had you, and how you were going to escape. She said something about Wandsworth too, a horse and Ben the tramp. We hear rumours and things you know, even in King's Cross. We want you to tell us the whole business . . . We've been waiting for yer.'

'We'll tell you the story all right,' said Chalotte, 'and a few more, but what we need right now is to get under cover for a few days.'

'Easy,' said Treld. 'That's our block of flats over there and only about half of it is lived in.'

'You can have a room each, if you want,' said Swish. 'We've got plenty of grub too.'

Swish and Treld belonged to a tribe of Borribles who took their name from the Caledonian Road. They called themselves the Caledonian Conkers, or Conkers for short. They ran the whole block of flats among themselves and to the surprise of the Adventurers they were all girls. Most of them wore their hair coloured and their clothes bizarre, but as Chalotte said, 'What does that matter? As long as they're as good as their word.' And the Conkers were.

That night they installed the Adventurers in two joined-together flats on the third floor of the tower block, and Ninch and Scooter were made comfortable on old mattresses and kept warm with piles of old blankets. The food followed almost immediately: stews and soups boiled up on small fires, slices of bread and meat paste and as much fruit as anyone could eat. There were even some tins of beer.

As the Adventurers ate and relaxed, girl after girl from the Conker tribe visited the two flats and brought more and more things to make the travellers feel welcome. Everyone gave a gift, however small. There were orange boxes, old cushions and armchairs, more mattresses and more blankets. In that friendly place the lights gleamed safely behind the blackout curtains and with a fire in every grate it was not long before everyone felt warm and happy and the memories of the hateful Madge and her army of meffos seemed far, far away.

It did not take long for the hideout to become crowded, so keen were the Conkers to hear stories of the Great Rumble Hunt and of the fight between Spiff and Flinthead. They sat cross-legged on the floor and squeezed themselves into every available place; and a fine, exotic sight they were, like visitors from a distant country.

They had hair of all colours and shapes: green, blue, yellow and silver, twisted into spikes, combed into bushes and sprinkled over with sparkle dust like rainbows. Some wore polished bicycle chains round their waists or safety pins on their trousers; some had jackets that were completely covered in badges, both back and front. Others had pale make-up on, their faces marked with brilliant stripes of colour across their foreheads or down their cheeks.

'The stories, the stories,' they yelled, and before the Adventurers were allowed to sleep they were obliged to take it in turn to tell their name stories and the stories of their great adventures. And some of the tales told were humorous and some were sad; some were ancient and some were new, and everyone there laughed and cried and clapped their hands at the telling of such sagas.

And the minds of the Adventurers reeled with all the new names of the people they met, and they could not remember half of them. There were Wazo and Splinters, Mower and Turpentine, Mudguard, Vanilla, Keffa, Batty, Scarpa, Yarmouth, Tintacks, Tramlines and Vendredi and dozens more. But remembering names did not matter too much just then because everyone was so busy talking and listening, shouting and laughing, although, when they spoke of Sam, the Adventurers became melancholy, for his story only reminded them of how many obstacles there still remained to overcome before they could rescue the horse from Sussworth and Hanks and see him safely to Neasden.

After an hour or two it was all over and the Conkers rose at last to leave the Adventurers to their rest. 'Well,' said Swish as she stood at the door, 'we're glad we found you and if you need any help when it comes to getting Sam out of that slaughterhouse you just let us know. That's just up our street that is, blood and guts.' And with a toss of her wild red hair she left the room.

Knocker followed the girl out into the open and from the balcony he could see that dawn was just beginning to spread its light over the endless city and the traffic was coming to life in the streets. Knocker gazed into the distance on the southern side of the river, looking across the jagged outlines of houses and office buildings, right down to infinity at the edge of the horizon where the blue and the grey, the mist and the sky, mingled in rain and smoke. A seagull glided through his line of sight and landed on a piece of waste ground to scratch for offal. An early train rolled along the hollow arches into King's Cross, just beyond the gasometers with the golden tops.

'It's beautiful, isn't it?'

Knocker looked up and saw Chalotte standing a few yards away from him, further along the balcony.

'Yes,' he said, 'most of the time. I was really wondering how things will turn out in the next few days . . . when we go to look for Sussworth and this slaughterhouse.'

'It'll be dangerous,' said Chalotte, 'very dangerous.'

'I know it will,' said Knocker, 'and I ain't mad keen about it, but on the other hand, I can't think of any other way. Can you?'

Chalotte stared at the landscape. 'No,' she said, 'I can't . . . but I wish I could.'

*

When Knocker awoke after a long and restful sleep it was late in the afternoon and almost dark. It was quiet and everyone else except Napoleon was asleep. Napoleon was half on watch, his body stretched across the doorway. Knocker smiled to himself; even when Napoleon trusted someone he didn't trust them. Knocker crawled out of his blankets and went over to the Wendle.

'I'm going to have a chat with Swish and Treld,' he said. 'Coming?'

Napoleon nodded.

One flight lower down the tower block the two Adventurers found the Conkers in the middle of making breakfast.

'Cuppa tea?' asked Treld, and without waiting for an answer she reached into an orange box for two large mugs.

Knocker and Napoleon made themselves comfortable on the floor.

'I've got to go to Camden Town,' said Knocker, 'I've got to find out where Sussworth is and I've got to scout out the slaughterhouse. Find out what their trap looks like without falling into it.'

Treld poured the tea. 'It's easy getting to Camden Town,' she said. 'The rest of it, not so easy.'

'We're pretty sure we know where the slaughterhouse is,' said Napoleon. 'In an alley in Baynes Street near the canal.'

'And Sussworth's caravan can't be too far from there,' added Knocker. 'All we want you to do is show us on the map.' He put his hand into his pocket and brought out his *A to Z*.

Treld looked at Knocker and smiled, then took his map, opened it at the correct page and put her finger right on the spot.

'When do you want to go?' asked Swish.

Knocker sipped his tea. 'I want to go as soon as I've got a bit of food inside me. It'll be a couple of days before Ninch and Scooter are fit to travel. That's why I thought it would be a good idea to do a little recce now.'

Swish and Treld drained their mugs and handed round some bread rolls. 'Come on then,' said Swish. 'We'll have this grub and then be off.'

Knocker choked on his mouthful. 'Not you guys,' he spluttered. 'It's a trap up there; it will be dangerous.'

'It's no trouble,' said Swish. 'We follow the canal. On the west side is St Pancras and King's Cross. On the east side is a goods yard and lots of factories. It's a wasteland more than anything. We go that way to Camden Market all the time. It's a piece of cake.'

Knocker and Napoleon grinned and that decided it. Taking only enough time to pack some provisions and load bandoliers with good stones the four Borribles set off. 'I left a message,' said Swish as they crossed York Way. 'I wouldn't want the others to wonder where we'd got to.'

The journey was as easy as Swish and Treld had said it would be. Once over the high brick wall that ran along one side of the main road the four Borribles were in a land that might have been a million miles from London. It was dark and quiet and they could distinguish nothing, although, according to the girls, in daylight they would have seen the canal striking between disused industrial buildings on one side and empty spaces on the other. A no man's land belonging to no one and in it the Borribles were safe.

After walking for nearly an hour Swish stopped at the bottom of a flight of stone steps. At the top of the flight was an iron gate and the sound of traffic.

'This'll be Royal College Street,' she explained, and climbing the steps she popped her head into the open, level with the pavement. 'The coast is clear,' she said, and the Borribles went out on to the street, turned right and then turned right again to find themselves in a narrow road with only a few lamp posts in it. There was no traffic here.

'How's that for navigation?' said Treld, pleased with herself. 'This is Baynes Street and the slaughterhouse must be along here somewhere. Follow us.'

With no hesitation the two Conker girls took the lead and Knocker and Napoleon came behind. At the end of the road, at the point where it met St Pancras Way, Treld stopped. 'Did you see it?' she said.

'Yes,' said Napoleon. 'A dead end, on the right, seems to run down to the canal. There was a big building there and outside was an SBG van.'

'That's right,' said Treld. 'That's got to be the slaughterhouse. We'll have a look at the back of it on the way home, see if we can get to it from the canal.'

'Keep walking,' said Knocker. 'Don't hang about. It must be lousy with Woollies round here and if we look the slightest bit suspicious they'll have us.'

Swish agreed. 'We'll just walk up and down a few of these back streets,' she said. 'If the slaughterhouse is here then Sussworth's caravan can't be far.'

'Which way?' asked Treld.

Knocker scratched an ear. 'There's a funny place opposite,' he said. 'Let's have a butcher's at that.'

The Borribles crossed over and passed between two huge houses that made a kind of gateway at the beginning of a narrow street. After walking into this street for fifty yards or so they found that it opened into a circular area in the middle of which was a large patch of threadbare grass. Here there was one weak street lamp and beneath it, painted white, its chrome gleaming, its wheels enormous, was a massive caravan, a bright light shining through its windows.

'That's it,' said Knocker. 'That's it.'

Napoleon gazed into the dark corners of the cul-de-sac. 'I don't like this at all,' he said. 'Only one way out and that's behind us.' He stared up at the blackness of the houses. They were faceless and tall, as friendly as glaciers.

The Borribles did not move for a few minutes, made apprehensive by the closeness of Sussworth's caravan and the feeling of copper everywhere. When they had recovered themselves they turned to retreat but it was too late. Four policemen stood behind them, their hands reaching out to grab the runaways by their collars. So surprised were the Borribles that they did not even bother to struggle. In any event such a struggle would have served no purpose; behind these four policemen were four more and beyond those four who knew how many? They had been there in the dark, leaning in the doorways, moving on rubber-soled boots. Knocker's heart died and his knees gave beneath him. Was it to finish as stupidly as this? Sam not saved and the Adventurers not knowing where he and Napoleon were, separated for ever without time to say goodbye, captured without a fight; it was pathetic.

'Well, well, well,' said one of the policemen at last. 'Come to join us have you? That's nice, very nice, very very nice.'

'We were just looking,' said Swish.

'Course you were,' said the policeman, 'and we're pleased to have you looking. Our inspector wants as many of you dwarfs as he can get. You'd better come and wait with the others. I never knew there were so many.'

The Borribles felt themselves propelled towards the caravan and the grip on their collars did not loosen for a moment.

Knocker cursed his luck. It had been his idea to come scouting in such a heavily policed area. He had known it would be dangerous. 'I'm sorry,' he said to Swish. 'This is nothing to do with you. If you get a chance, try and make a break for it.'

As Knocker was speaking he and the others were pushed past the end of the caravan and could now see what had been previously hidden from them. On the far side, between the caravan and the front fence of the nearest houses, stood two unmarked police cars, several policemen in uniform and a line of about twenty Borribles, complete with catapults and woollen hats. In the soft light of the one street lamp everything was quiet and orderly.

'Go and wait in line,' said one of the Woollies, and the four captives felt their collars released and they were each given a shove in the back. With that the four policemen left them and returned round the corner of the caravan so that they might take up, once more, their guard duty at the entrance to the cul-de-sac.

'Do we run for it now?' asked Treld.

'No,' said Knocker. 'Wait till them four coppers are well out of it; there's something going on here. We'll have to—'

But there was no time for Knocker to say more. At that very moment yet another policeman approached the four Borribles with a clipboard in his hand. 'Right,' he said, pen poised above his paper, 'have you thought yourselves up a Borrible name, you lads, because that's how you'll be known by us for purposes of administration and pay?'

'Oh yes,' said Swish, 'it's Swish.'

The policeman wrote it down. 'Swish,' he said. 'I should think so with that red hair. What's this one's name, the one with the 'airstyle like a runny egg?'

'My name's Treld,' said Treld. 'I done my hair special.' She smiled and twisted one of the spikes on her head.

Knocker glanced at Napoleon and they understood each other. They daren't use their own names; they were too well known to the SBG, perhaps the best known of all Borrible names.

'Well,' said the policemen, his pen poised again. 'What's your name?'

'Backander,' said Knocker.

'Sprazi,' said Napoleon.

'Sprazi!' said the policeman. 'Sounds foreign, that does. What's it mean?'

Napoleon placed his hand on his catapult. 'It means a tanner,' he said. 'Sixpence. Before your time I should think.'

The policeman smiled. 'Probably,' he said. 'Cheeky sod. Right that's fine. Over there then and get on the end of the line with the rest of them dwarfs. You'll be going in to see the inspector in a minute, four at a time. He'll give you your orders and tell you all about it. You'll get your plastic ears while you're waiting.'

'Plastic ears?' said Swish.

The policeman put his fists on his hips. 'So you look like Borribles of course. They'd torture you to death if they found out you weren't real. Go on, wait over there.'

Knocker and Napoleon looked dazed as they walked away from the policeman, obeying his orders although their brains were reeling.

'What's it all about?' asked Treld. 'I don't understand. Who are all these people? What are they doing with the Woollies? And plastic ears?'

Napoleon looked at Knocker and Knocker returned the stare evenly, his eyes as cold as a tombstone. A lot of things were becoming clear. Napoleon's face grew spiteful. 'They ain't Borribles,' he said, 'They're something else.'

'But they're the right size,' said Treld.

'They are,' said Napoleon, 'and that's all they are. Apart from that they're adults.'

Knocker swore. That was how they had been captured so easily on Clapham Common and that was how Sam had been taken. The circus Borribles had not been Borribles at all. That must be it. They had been dwarfs or midgets, just like these, working for the SBG and Sussworth. How could he have missed it? Knocker kicked at the ground. 'Dammit!' Even now he'd only made this discovery out of luck. If he'd only known beforehand he could have left Ninch and Scooter behind with the meffos at King's Cross.

'You realize what this means,' said Napoleon, as angry as Knocker was; he hated being taken for a mug. 'It means we spent all that time at King's Cross being loyal to a pair of traitors. We could have left them there.'

'Who?' asked Swish and Treld together, puzzled.

'Those two we brought with us,' said Knocker, 'the ones who'd been locked up by the meffos; well they ain't Borribles they're dwarfs, like these here, spies.'

Napoleon was beside himself with worry. 'And our mates don't know,' he said. 'We must get back to the flats before them midgets do any more harm.'

Another policeman called out at that moment and strolled towards the four Borribles. He was carrying a handful of small paper packages. 'Here you are,' he said. 'These'll fit you a treat. There's some glue as well.' He spun on his heel and returned to the squad cars.

The Borribles waited a second or two and then opened the paper bags they'd been given. Inside each one, nicely wrapped, was a pair of Borrible ears, or rather the top halves of them, made from flesh-coloured plastic, perfect replicas, hollowed out to make them weightless and with special grooves to take the superglue. They were indistinguishable from the real thing.

'Blimey,' said Napoleon, 'how the Mother Hubbard can we wear two pairs of ears at one and the same time? We're for it now.'

'It's risky all right,' agreed Knocker, 'but I get the feeling that if we try to run off we'll get caught, but if we pretend to be dwarfs and go through with it then we'll get away.'

The policeman with the clipboard called out again and the line moved forward.

'There's only one thing we can do,' said Swish. 'We'll have to shove these plastic jobs in our pocket and make out that our real ears are plastic ones.'

'That's it,' said Treld. 'And while we're waiting we'll pretend we're sticking them on, like.'

'Supposing they recognize us, Knocker?' said Napoleon. 'It'll be curtains then, eh?'

Knocker shook his head. 'Not likely,' he said. 'Sussworth only ever saw us once, remember, when we were captured on Clapham Common, but we were all of us covered in mud, all our clothes, our faces. All you have to do, Nap, is just be polite.'

'I don't know about that,' replied Napoleon, 'but I do know that we'll never have a better chance than this for getting rid of Sussworth, like we did Dewdrop. What about it, Knocker? He wouldn't be able to kill Sam then, would he?'

Again Knocker shook his head. 'It wouldn't help,' he answered. 'Somebody else would only kill Sam and we'd get caught and we wouldn't be able to warn the others about the dwarfs. No, the main thing is to make sure we stay alive long enough to get back to King's Cross.'

'And deal with Ninch and Scooter,' said the Wendle.

'Yes,' said Knocker, 'that's for sure.'

As they moved closer to the caravan the four Borribles started to go through the motions of glueing on their ears, making a great show of it. These efforts seemed hardly worthwhile however for not one of the policemen on duty nearby took the slighest notice of them. On the other hand the dwarfs who were standing in front of the Borribles became very interested in the activity.

''Ere,' said one of them to Swish, 'you've done yours a treat. Could you help me stick mine on?'

'And me,' said another. 'Make a good impression on the inspector, that will, I bet.'

Swish agreed readily; she was only too pleased to occupy her nervous hands with some kind of work and Knocker thought it might be a good moment to ask questions. He looked at the dwarf nearest him, not liking what he saw: a face that was neither adult nor childlike, neither old nor young, a strange blank face a bit like Ninch's. Knocker forced a smile.

'How did you get the job,' he asked, 'you're not a copper are you?'

'No fear,' said the dwarf. He was feeling his newly stuck-on ears and

Knocker had to admit that they changed his whole appearance. 'They advertised in the stage papers; we're only in it for the money. You know, cop it and hop it is our motto.'

'Is it much money?' asked Napoleon, sidling up close.

'Aha,' continued the dwarf, 'it all depends on how many Borribles we catch, special bonuses. It's going to be very exciting, sloping round the town at night, spying. They're murderers, you know. Killed a poor old rag-and-bone man and his harmless son in Southfields. They told us.'

'The villains,' said Napoleon.

'Villains is right,' said the dwarf. 'Ain't scared, are you?'

Knocker laughed. 'I think he is. Look, he's gone quite pale.'

Before Knocker could ask any more questions the policeman with the clipboard crouched down beside them all and inspected their ears; dwarfs first, then the Borribles.

'They're very good,' he said, 'some of the best I've seen. My goodness me, if I didn't know you weren't I'd swear you were, in a court of law too. Excellent.' And with that he marshalled the dwarfs into the caravan and the four Borribles were left waiting at the foot of Sussworth's steps on their own.

They did not wait long. In less than ten minutes' time the four dwarfs were sent quickly on their way and it was the turn of Knocker and Napoleon, Swish and Treld, to climb towards the figure of Sergeant Hanks who stood just by the caravan's open door, waving them into the presence of Inspector Sussworth.

The four Borribles stepped bravely forward and were made to stand in a line facing a huge desk. Sussworth sat behind it looking tiny, flicking through his papers. Above him on the wall, a new addition to the decor, were two photos, one of Field Marshal Montgomery, the other of Rommel, both smiling.

Slightly to the side of the Borribles a kettle was bubbling; just in front of them Sergeant Hanks leant against his bunk, his fat arms folded. The double bed had been folded away and a policeman sat in its place at a temporary desk, keeping a record of all that was said.

'These are the last four tonight,' he said, and read out the names. 'Swish, Treld, Backander and Sprazi.'

Without looking up Sussworth suddenly shouted, 'And what do you say when you hear a Borrible name?'

'Er . . . what a good name, I hope that I shall hear the story of the winning of it, one day,' said Knocker, his throat dry.

'Good,' said Sussworth. 'Remember, every one of you from now on and into the future has to live and think like a Borrible. If they so much as guess your true identity your lives won't be worth a second-hand peanut. On the other hand . . . for every ordinary common or garden Borrible you capture I shall pay the sum of two hundred pounds. If by chance any subsequent investigation and questioning of your prisoner should lead us to any one of the Southfields murderers you will receive a further thousand pounds. But if any of you become responsible for the capture of any of that gang of malefactors yourselves, well, there will be a reward of five thousand pounds.' Sussworth leant forward, his moustache quivered. 'Just imagine that. I happen to know that there are approximately ten of these vagrants in the Southfields gang, so it is not beyond the bounds of possibility that you could catch yourself a grand total of fifty thousand pounds. That is enough to retire to Portugal on, several times.'

Knocker did not know how the others were feeling but he had never been so nervous in his whole life. The sweat poured from his brow and into his eyes. He gulped and wiped his face with the sleeve of his jacket, then he clasped his hands behind his back to keep them still. He looked round the caravan, studying it. It was so clean. The wood stank of polish, the chrome fittings were burnished bright and the carpet was spotless; and in the place where he and his companions stood was a plastic sheet, spread there to keep mud from the floor.

'So,' continued Sussworth, twitching his face at Hanks, 'what do you think of them?'

The sergeant pushed himself upright. 'Well, sir, I gave them the once-over as they came in. They certainly look like Borribles,' he said. 'In fact they look more like Borribles than some Borribles do.'

'Excellent,' said the inspector, and he jumped to his feet and dodged round the desk like a matador avoiding a bull, his steps delicate but urgent. He continued his progress and danced towards the Borribles in waltz time, finally teetering to a stop in front of them. There he clenched his hands into fists, stretched his shoulders towards the ceiling and switched his moustache from side to side as if he were trying to scratch his ear lobes with it. All this effort made his eyes bright with a mad fire.

'I want you volunteers to understand,' he said, 'the responsibilities and dangers you are undertaking. Borribles are nasty, Borribles are a social enemy; above all there are these Southfields assassins, and I will have them here, in front of me, their ears littering the floor. I have their names engraved on my heart. I know them all: Knocker, Chalotte, Napoleon Boot, Orococco, Bingo, Stonks, Twilight, Vulge, Torrey-canyon, but, perhaps worst of all . . .' Sussworth's voice rose to a scream, he brandished his fist and leapt up and down, his spittle spraying over the faces of the four Borribles like acid '. . . perhaps the worst of all is that animal-lover, Sydney. Ah, but I have the horse and she'll never see that again. Safe in an abattoir it's kept, roped to a wall at tail and head. And it is your duty, you dwarfs, to patrol the streets and to see that no Borrible gets anywhere near it. That horse is dirty and filthy and the Borribles love it; it's their pride and joy and I have sworn to wipe it from the face of the earth.'

Sussworth drew in a deep breath and pushed his face close to Knocker's. 'Haven't I seen you before, dwarf?'

'I don't think so, sir,' answered Knocker. His mind went blank with fear.

'It's just that we've made ourselves up to look so much like Borribles,' interrupted Treld, touching her gold and blue hair, 'that you think we are Borribles, and that's what's upsetting you.'

'You're the type of thing I mean exactly,' said Sussworth. He switched his attention to the girls. 'I mean you look ghastly and horrid enough to undermine society all on your own. The Borribles will love you, yes, certainly, and the ears! Oh, Hanks, never have I seen such wonderful appendages.' He stared closely at Napoleon. 'Look at that, Hanks, excellent again. With dwarfs like this on the streets the Borribles will not escape me now.' The weakest of smiles flickered on Sussworth's lips for a millisecond before dying like a broken filament in a light bulb. He turned twice on his heels and banged them together, ending up to face the huge map of London which covered part of one wall.

The inspector pointed south of the river. 'These layabouts,' he began, 'were last seen in a definite location somewhere between Clapham Common South Side and Brixton High Road. We have good reason to believe that the aforementioned are making their way in a roundabout fashion towards a certain abattoir, which is here.' Sussworth pointed to Baynes Street. 'It is here also,' he continued, 'that the equus is incarcerated in order to ensure its eventual transformation into mincemeat. It is guarded night and day by twenty men with another fifty within call, and then there's the dwarfs . . . Not quite sure how many there are of them . . . lots anyway.' Sussworth drew a deep breath, bowed at the map as if to a large audience and then pirouetted until he faced his sergeant. 'Have I said everything, Hanks?' he asked.

Hanks leant out from the wall again and his powerful hands stroked his enormous belly and it quivered with pleasure. 'Just the two dwarfs who have disappeared, sir. Worth a mention, sir, I always say. We ought to keep our eyes peeled for their bodies.'

'Quite so,' said Sussworth. 'I was about to remind you to remind me.' He addressed the Borribles once more. 'There were two of your sort sending back tip-top intelligence – disappeared. Haven't had a word from them since they left us at Clapham South . . .'

'Aristotle Rule,' murmured Napoleon.

'Quite,' said Sussworth, not understanding what the Wendle had said. 'I fear that throats may have been cut . . .'

'Soon will be,' murmured Napoleon again.

'Yes,' said Sussworth, 'if you find Scinch and Nooter you must give them every available assistance, get them back to me. They will be in possession of masses of information and I need it.'

'Oh they'll be coming back to you,' said Napoleon. 'I'll see to that myself.'

'Good,' said Sussworth, and he jerked his elbows like a cockerel its wings. 'Well that's it, Hanks, send them on their way. Tell them to report by telephone, emergency services only, secretly, you know.' And with this parting remark the inspector gyrated back to his seat like a man fencing with the three musketeers all at once. Arrived at his chair he fell into it and closed his eyes with exhaustion. Now nothing of him moved save the tiny moustache, which still quivered doubtfully on his upper lip like a swallow undecided about migration.

The constable at the table began to shuffle his papers together and Hanks rolled to the caravan door and opened it.

'Come on you dwarfs,' he said. 'Out. The inspector's had a very busy day, he never stops. He's got to rest and I've got to eat. By the way you'd better have the password . . . it's "Blancmange".'

'Blancmange,' said Knocker. 'What's that for?'

'For us,' said Hanks. 'You see we have to be able to tell who you are or we might take you for real Borribles. You wouldn't like that. So if a policeman thinks you are a Borrible just say "Blancmange" to him and he'll realize you're one of ours and let you go.'

Napoleon smiled a smile of infinite cunning. Knocker had never seen him smile so broadly. 'You mean,' said the Wendle, hardly able to believe what Hanks had told him, 'you mean that all we got to say is "Blancmange" and your coppers will let us go?'

'That's the whole point,' said Hanks, 'the whole point.'

'Well,' said Napoleon, 'that's ace, that is, really ace!'

Hanks nodded, preoccupied, his thoughts turning towards food. He pushed the Borribles through the door and down the steps. 'I know it is,' he said. 'I invented it.' And with that he went back into the caravan to cook his supper, having first closed the door firmly behind him. He was very, very hungry.

9

It was past midnight when Knocker and Napoleon and their two Conker companions arrived at the rough plank hoarding that surrounded the Caledonian tower block. Two guards let them in with hardly a word, and they crossed the lightless yard and climbed silently to the third floor and entered the flat, where the Adventurers waited for them, their faces anxious. Chalotte smiled with relief as the four scouts came into the room; she lost that smile when she saw Knocker's expression. He walked to the table, took his hand from his pocket and threw down two plastic ears. There was a gasp of astonishment from everyone in the room. Swish and Treld threw their plastic ears on the table too and then went into the kitchen to help themselves to some bread. Napoleon closed the front door behind him and leant against it with folded arms. No one was going out that way without his say-so. There was silence. The Adventurers got to their feet and stared.

'Ears,' said Bingo. 'What poor blighter are they off?'

Knocker pointed at them, his face grim. 'They aren't off anyone,' he said, 'but they look real, don't they? It's Sussworth's latest little trick and we've all been fooled by it. Right along the line. It's a wonder we're still alive.'

'That's right,' said Napoleon. 'Sussworth's got these midgets and dwarfs all over London with ears like that stuck on 'em, pretending to be Borribles . . . and what's worse we've had two of 'em with us, all the way, and we risked our necks for 'em.'

Chalotte picked up one of the ears. 'Ninch and Scooter,' she said.

'That's right,' said Napoleon. 'And as far as I'm concerned they're going out that window and down to the ground so fast they'll think they're brick pigeons. Where are they?'

'Gone,' said Stonks. 'One minute they were here, the next gone.'

'We thought they'd just nipped out to get some food,' said Sydney.

Napoleon swore and shook his fist at everyone in the room. 'You idiots,' he shouted. 'And what about the Aristotle Rule, eh? Them dwarfs weren't s'posed to go out on their own . . . Now we're in trouble, you bloody imbeciles.'

'How could we be suspicious when they'd been through all that with Madge?' said Twilight.

'Yes,' said Torreycanyon. 'They followed us after the escape from Clapham South; they came on the river with us even though they were scared.'

'That was their bleedin' job,' screamed Napoleon. 'All they had to do was stay with us and tell Sussworth where we were and what we were doing.'

There was another silence for a while. Vulge went into the kitchen to make some tea and Orococco said, 'What happened with you lot? How did you get on?'

Knocker fell on to a chair with a sigh. 'Okay,' he said. 'We found the slaughterhouse and we're pretty sure Sam's in there, but he's guarded by about twenty coppers with fifty in reserve. We'll have to get past them.'

'And what about Sussworth,' asked Chalotte, 'where's he?'

Knocker looked at her and smiled. 'We got mixed up with a bunch of dwarfs,' he said, 'being recruited. We were taken right into the caravan and there he was. That's how we got the ears.'

'You saw Sussworth?' exclaimed Chalotte.

Knocker nodded. 'And Hanks. We were in there ages. We had to listen to a speech on how to deal with Borribles if we caught ourselves. He knew all about us – names, everything.'

'It was scary,' said Swish, coming back into the room from the kitchen. 'They even inspected our ears . . . I thought it was all over.'

Vulge went round everybody with mugs of tea and Napoleon snatched one from the tray, advancing into the room. 'We can't stand about nattering,' he said. 'We'll have to pack up and be on our way before those two dwarfs get back here with half the Metropolitan Police, because they're going to, you know.'

'Oh no they ain't,' said a strained voice from the door, and the Borribles looked in that direction and saw Scooter leaning there.

Before anyone else could move, Napoleon had thrown down his tea, crossed the room and seized Scooter by the throat. He shook the dwarf, as if to loosen his teeth, and thrust him into a chair. 'I'm going to kill you, Sunbeam,' said the Wendle, 'permanent.' He raised his fist to strike the prisoner but Chalotte jumped forward and laid her hand on Napoleon's arm.

'Wait,' she said. 'He's wounded.' Looking closer the Borribles could indeed see a dark bloodstain at the top of Scooter's left arm and it was spreading. Chalotte removed the dwarf's jacket and then, with her knife, slit the sweater and shirt; both garments were sopping wet with blood. There was a deep gash in the shoulder.

'I'll get some water,' said Sydney. 'We must stop the bleeding.' And she went into the kitchen.

Napoleon sneered. 'Don't bother,' he said. 'When I've finished with him he won't need blood.'

'Let's hear what he has to say,' said Chalotte, 'then we'll decide. Say your say, dwarf.'

Scooter looked at the circle of faces and he saw no friendship. Sydney returned from the kitchen with a kettle full of cold water and bathed the wound. When it was clean she began to wrap it in white rag which she tore in strips from an old shirt. The dwarf winced with the pain but then began: 'Ninch said we had to run,' he said, 'because he thought that you might find out the truth about us if you found Sussworth's caravan . . .'

'We did,' said Knocker.

'But I wanted to wait till you got back, so we hid along by the canal. We saw you all right, and we heard enough to realize that you'd tumbled us.'

'What are we wasting time for?' asked Torreycanyon. 'He's admitting it. Nap's right . . . out the window.'

Knocker held up a hand. 'Scooter, did you shop us on Clapham Common; was it you lot who told the SBG where we were and got Sam captured?'

Scooter dropped his head on to his chest and closed his eyes. 'Yes,' he said.

The Borribles went very very quiet. Chalotte bit her lip and could think of nothing to say. Sydney stopped dressing the dwarf's wound.

'He's got to go,' said Napoleon, lifting his arms and then dropping them. 'He can't be trusted. He's a spy and we know what everybody does with spies.'

'Listen,' said Scooter suddenly. 'I came back to tell you this . . . I didn't have to; I could have been clear away.'

'Go on then,' said Chalotte. 'You'll have to make it good.'

Scooter nodded. 'Ninch got us the job. He saw the advertisement. He went to see Sussworth first and when he told us about it he made it sound really exciting, you know, special training, catching escaped criminals. Ninch stuck our ears on too; told us what Sussworth had said, and all us acrobats believed it, every word. How did we know any different?'

'You shouldn't take anything on trust, that's why,' said Vulge bitterly.

'I know that now,' said Scooter, 'but at the time Ninch convinced us all. He was fed up with being a dwarf in a circus with people laughing at him. He told us there was a huge reward if we captured you. "Nobody laughs at you when you've got pockets full of money," he said.'

'And nobody'll laugh at you when you're dead and buried,' said Napoleon.

Scooter went on with his explanation. '"That's for me," Ninch said. "I ain't going to be no clown no more." And he told us what to do if and when you turned up. So Ninch phoned Sussworth and when the fight was going on he showed the law where Sam was and then afterwards made us pretend to be captured like the rest of you . . . You see Sussworth wanted to use us to find out more things about you, during the interrogation like; that's why he put us back in the cell when we'd had some grub . . . so you'd see us in the morning. But the others wanted to go home and when the Buffonis let us out they did.'

'Oh, Scooter,' said Sydney, her eyes red. 'How could you be so rotten? What harm had Sam ever done to you? To betray him to Sussworth for money to be turned into catsmeat. I don't understand it.'

The dwarf lowered his head, his face scarlet with shame. 'I thought I was working for law and order,' he mumbled.

Napoleon looked round the room. 'I'm happy to take him outside if no one else will. You can find what's left of him in the canal tomorrow morning.'

Scooter raised his head; a tear trickled across the dirt of his skin, blood seeped into his half-tied bandage. 'I didn't know you then. I didn't know how much Sam meant to you, what Sam was. I wasn't your friend then. I am now.'

'Friend!' said Orococco with scorn. 'Some friend!'

'I mean it. I liked being with you lot, even though we were on the run. I felt proud for the first time in my life. I would never have told Sussworth anything if I'd known you right from the beginning, and I don't think Ninch would have either but . . .'

'But what?' asked Napoleon.

'Well, he couldn't think of anything else but the money and how he wouldn't have to work in a sideshow any more, how he wouldn't have people laughing at him.'

Chalotte stepped closer to the dwarf and finished tying the bandage on his shoulder. 'How did you get this wound?' she asked.

'Ninch and I quarrelled tonight. He'd got worse since Madge locked us up in that cellar. He seemed to blame it all on you, on Borribles. All the time he was down there, shivering and swearing, he kept telling me how he was going to make you pay for it; how he was going to live in luxury for the rest of his life thinking of you lot with your ears clipped, growing up, working . . . Adults, just like us.'

'What did you quarrel about,' said Knocker. 'Tell us that.'

'Well, I ran off with him at first because I was frightened of what you'd do when you found out about us. I just wanted to get out of the way, but Ninch wanted to carry on with the job, get you all captured. I said I wouldn't. I said that we'd been through so much with you that we were just like you now . . . You trusted us. I was for coming back to warn you but he drew a knife and stabbed me and pushed me into the canal. He watched me thrash around for a while and then I pretended to go under, drowning. Then he ran away up the towpath, towards Camden Town.'

'Gone to get Sussworth,' said Knocker. 'We must get moving.'

'No,' said Scooter. 'He won't tell the SBG right off; he told me his plans, remember. He thinks that if he tells Sussworth where you are the Woollies will catch you and Sussworth will take all the credit. What he's going to do is go straight over to Camden and round up some of the other dwarfs; there's loads as didn't look young enough for

Sussworth to take on, tough they are. Ninch wants to capture you himself. That way he could screw as much money out of Sussworth as possible. He wants all the glory and all the reward.'

As he finished speaking Scooter's eyes flickered and the light went out of them. He clutched at his stomach, rolled forward and fell from the chair to the floor, unconscious. Fresh blood darkened his bandages.

Chalotte knelt by his side. 'He's probably got a gutful of that canal water,' she said. 'It'll kill him. Pass that mug of tea there.'

'Tea be blowed,' said Napoleon. 'Can't you see that this is all a load of old codswallop? A knife wound, a dip in the canal. Easy. I bet they did this just so they could get a spy back in our camp.' The Wendle's face hardened. He leant over and pushing Chalotte to one side he grabbed at the false plastic ears Scooter was still wearing and ripped them off, one after the other, pulling at them so savagely that the strong glue pulled away the real skin and the tops of the ears began to bleed. 'Look there,' said Napoleon. 'Ordinary ears. He's an adult, a midget, a spy, a traitor.'

Chalotte stepped astride Scooter's body. 'I believe him,' she said. She stood in the middle of her friends and looked at their faces. 'This wound in his shoulder, it wasn't for fun. It's deep and it won't stop bleeding. It's full of dirty canal water. It could kill him. His temperature's low; he's shaking. He couldn't put all that on. He didn't have to come back to warn us.'

'Whatever we do,' said Knocker, 'we can't talk in front of him any more.'

Bingo looked down at the bloodstained figure. 'We won't have to,' he said. 'By the time he comes round we'll be miles away.'

'He couldn't follow us at all from the bottom of the canal,' said Napoleon.

'Hang about,' said Chalotte, and her voice sounded so shocked that the others took notice immediately. She was kneeling again, trying to staunch the blood flowing from the dwarf's ears. 'Look here, under where the false ears were, they've been growing, his ears, see . . . pointed. They're more pointed than a normal's ears but not as pointed as ours. I didn't think it was possible, an adult going Borrible. Perhaps he was telling the truth, after all.'

The Adventurers crowded round Scooter and examined the evidence. Chalotte stood up, amazed, and found Knocker staring at her. 'This is not possible,' he said. 'Adults cannot go Borrible.'

Chalotte tossed her hair over her shoulders. 'I know,' she said, 'but perhaps no adult has ever spent as long with Borribles as Scooter has. Who knows? I don't.' She looked mystified. 'But just think what it could mean.'

'It could mean a lot,' said Torreycanyon, 'but we can't stand around talking all night. What are we going to do with him?'

'Leave him here,' said Knocker, 'like Bingo said. We'll ask the Conkers to keep an eye on him.'

Once this decision had been taken everyone began to move about the two flats with determination and speed. Rucksacks were made ready, catapults and stones were checked and the warmest clothing was chosen. It would be deathly cold along by the Grand Union Canal and the Borribles would need every bit of protection they could get.

During the bustle and activity of these preparations Swish and Treld, who had listened to the arguments about Scooter with great interest, disappeared for a while. When they returned they were carrying as much food as they had been able to find; all of it scrounged from members of the Conker tribe.

'Take it,' they said when the Adventurers objected. 'Hide in one of the empty factories along by the towpath and we'll bring you some more tomorrow.'

'Tomorrow,' said Chalotte, stuffing a raincoat into the top of her rucksack. 'What do you mean, tomorrow?'

Treld grinned and raked her spiky blue and yellow hair with spread fingers. 'We mean,' she said, 'that there's no way you can get Sam out of that slaughterhouse without help. We saw. There's too many Woollies.'

Swish laughed and the safety pins on the front of her jacket jangled. 'You see, us Conkers want to help you get the horse, so we're all coming. We're going to create a diversion for you. It'll be a bit of fun.'

'Some fun,' said Knocker. 'You could get caught. And what about tonight? What if the coppers come here?'

'Don't you worry, Knocker me old china,' said Swish. 'This ain't the only block of flats we got to live in. You just get on your way and we'll catch up with yer tomorrow, just past the gasometers. Find a place with a roof and we'll have a feast.'

Although they were on the run once more and getting closer every minute to the danger of the slaughterhouse, the Adventurers felt relieved; the attitude of the Conkers had cheered them immensely. They pushed their arms through the straps of their rucksacks, doused the lights and crept slowly downstairs, out into the cold and out into the dark.

At the very edge of the tower block the Conkers took their leave and, once more on their own, the Adventurers heaved themselves over the high wall bordering York Way and entered the no man's land that runs uninterrupted from King's Cross to Camden Road.

It was well past midnight now and into the early hours. All was quiet except for the soft lapping of canal water and the sound of the icy wind whistling through the decaying walls of the dead factories. Warily, testing each footstep before the next, the Adventurers struck out into the gloom along the towpath of the Grand Union. Ther were no torches in their hands, only loaded catapults. The Borribles were ready for anything for they knew they might have to be.

*

It was a hard night, cold and cheerless, and the Adventurers spent it in the hollow shell of a huge ruined warehouse. They did not know where they were in that darkness but they could feel the empty space of a drained dock away to the south of them; they could hear the black mud of it noisily sucking at the broken shapes of half-submerged barges and boats.

This part of London was dead, like a place where cholera had killed everything, not only in the water but in the air and on the ground. Even the warehouse had the smell of death about it and it was a smell that kept the Borribles watchful for fear that if they did sleep they might never wake. They sat close together for warmth, side by side against a wall, in the dark, cuddling their knees and staring at nothing, waiting for the dawn of the next day.

When the dawn came it came colder than the night and creaked slowly up over this uninhabited part of London. It was a dawn as pale and as bloodless as a corpse, a corpse that was soiled and cankered. The

Borribles rose and stretched and moved to the holes in the walls that had once been windows. They rubbed their legs and struck each other on the back to warm their bodies, staring out at the landscape that imprisoned them on every side, and all they could see were factories as tall as churches, their girders showing like broken bones, and houses that were rotting into pieces and giving out that stench that was worse than infected flesh.

It was like living on the far side of a lifeless planet, undiscovered and unloved. There was not one creature stirring in it; not a man, not a cat, nor a dog, nor a bird. Only the low grey clouds moved, heavy and clumsy with their burden of dirty water, lurching across the sky with nowhere to go.

Knocker sighed. 'We'd better stay here today,' he said. 'The slaughter-house is only a mile or two further on and we can't make a move until tonight.'

Vulge began to gather kindling wood from the floor, old battens and laths fallen from walls and ceilings. 'I might as well make a brew,' he said. 'There's no one to notice the smoke if I do, and a cup of tea will cheer us all up.'

Bingo crouched down to the plank floor and made a few experimental marks with a lump of plaster. 'The SBG won't find us here,' he said, 'but I think I'd better make a few Borrible signs along the towpath so the Conkers know where we are.' He ducked through a broken doorway and was gone.

'I hope the Conkers do come,' said Chalotte as she watched Bingo disappear. 'We could do with their help. In fact I don't see how we stand a chance without it.'

Silently the other Adventurers agreed and, turning from the windows, they sat down again and watched as Vulge took a saucepan from his haversack and filled it from a standpipe. Then they crouched by the fire he had made to wait while the water boiled. There was nothing else to do.

*

The Borribles stayed under cover all day, there being little to tempt them out into the dreary landscape, but towards dusk, after hours filled with dozing and cups of Vulge's tea, they were roused to their feet by the voice of Bingo calling from the towpath where he was still on watch.

'They're coming,' cried the Battersea Borrible, 'and they look beautiful. Come and see.'

Outside, the edges of the sky had darkened and lowered themselves down to touch the earth. From the clouds the rain slanted, sharp and corrosive like acid, and long squares of shadow had fallen across everything. The surface of the canal was black and the shapes of the stranded barges were once more indistinct, disappearing into the deep mud that would never let them go.

But along the towpath, at a distance of three hundred yards, a long line of human shapes could be seen marching in single file. Each figure bore a golden flashlight and every flashlight scorched a hole as bright as fire across the evening gloom. It was the Conkers, all of them, marching to the aid of the Adventurers so that they could free Sam the horse.

Chalotte came and stood by Knocker's side, and the others too. 'Oh,' she gasped, 'isn't it wonderful?'

Nearer and nearer came the girls of the Conker tribe, their torches held high. Now they were close to the Adventurers, climbing up from the side of the canal, over the broken walls and through the crumbling gateway and into the warehouse itself, whirling the torches above their heads to make circles of light in the air.

They were dressed in the finest gear they had been able to find and the torchlight reflected on their bicycle chains and on their barbarous brooches and bangles. Their strange spiky hair glittered with every colour of the rainbow and scintillated with silver stars. There were aerosol designs sprayed on the backs and fronts of their leather jackets and down their ragged trousers. On their faces were gaudy streaks of paint. Each and every one of them was grinning with the excitement of the moment. Warriors eager for battle, they laughed among themselves at the amazement on the faces of the Adventurers, and from the bags they carried they brought forth an immense amount of food and drink. Eventually, when they had covered the windows of the warehouse with old sacks, they sat down and invited their friends to do the same.

The Adventurers had not felt so happy since leaving Brixton. They had an abundance of food and drink, certainly, but there was something more important than that; here were fifty or sixty friends come to help in that day's attempt at a rescue. It was a celebration of being Borrible.

'Only thing is,' said Napoleon, always wary, 'we'd better not bolt the stable door before we've got away with the horse. Have we got a plan?'

The Adventurers looked at each other, nonplussed. Swish and Treld listened to the silence for a while, smiled, and then Swish spoke: 'The way I see it is this,' she said. 'The best thing us Conkers can do is to create as much noise and mayhem around the slaughterhouse as possible – give the Woollies something to keep them occupied.'

'Exactly,' said Treld. 'And while they are chasing us you others must concentrate on getting the horse out and away.' Treld had dyed her hair a different colour that night. It was now a brilliant orange and in the glow of the torches it looked like a blazing flame. Round her eyes she had drawn circles in green paint.

Napoleon shook his head. 'Don't you realize,' he objected, 'that apart from the coppers guarding the place Sussworth's got carloads of reinforcements just around the corner?'

Swish drank from a can of beer, emptied it and threw it over her shoulder. 'That's where we come in,' she said. 'See, the slaughterhouse backs on to the canal – we made a mark to show you where it is – but at the front there's only a narrow yard. You lot come over the wall from the canal, find your horse, go through the slaughterhouse, down the alley and into the main road. We ought to be able to give you a start, ten minutes maybe, time enough for you to get as far as Camden Town and into Chalk Farm. There's some good Borribles up there, in a scrap-yard. They know you're coming 'cos we sent a runner. They will hide you for a couple of days and meanwhile we'll make sure the Woollies chase us.'

'It won't be that easy,' complained Sydney. 'We'll be spotted before we get anywhere near Sam.'

'No we won't,' cried Knocker, and he slapped his knee. 'I forgot to tell you . . . We know the password that will make the coppers think we're dwarfs.'

'Whoopee!' yelled Vulge. 'What is it?'

'Blancmange,' said Knocker. 'Blancmange, that's what is is.'

'It'll be blancmange for them Woollies all right,' shouted Orococco, and he raised his can of beer and drank from it.

Then all the Borribles shouted and leapt to their feet and held their drinks high, their faces shining with joy.

'Sam the horse!' they cried. 'Sam the horse for ever!' And the cry resounded round the bare brick walls of the abandoned warehouse and made them happy. Nothing could stop them now.

*

As soon as it was well and truly dark the Borribles set about making their final preparations for the assault on the slaughterhouse. At the very last, when everything else had been done, all the catapults and ammunition were checked and all the torches were extinguished. But just as Treld was on the point of leading the Adventurers outside, one of the Conker lookouts, Mudguard by name, slipped quietly into the warehouse and, in a whisper, commanded everyone to throw themselves to the floor and lie as still as they could. No one was to speak or even cough.

So great was the girl's urgency that luckily no one thought for a second of disobeying her. The Adventurers and the Conkers waited, lying face down, without moving, on the dirty planks. Five minutes went by, ten minutes, then came the tramp of marching feet just below on the towpath, and louder than the sound of the marching rang the voice of Ninch the dwarf, bellowing orders.

'Come on,' he roared. 'Left, right; left, right. Come on. They may be still there. We've got to find out where they are and get after them. Think of the reward. Come on. Left, right.'

Gradually the noise faded in the distance but the Borribles did not move or speak until, with another whispered command to remain where they were, Mudguard disappeared through a window. In two or three minutes she returned and spoke to Swish.

'I was up the canal a bit,' she explained. 'Lucky I was listening and going careful, and lucky they were making such a din. They was about our size but I thought they couldn't be Borribles, making that noise, they ain't are they?'

'No,' said Swish.

'Dwarfs,' said Napoleon. 'Nasty little spies and traitors.' In the dark he stretched himself to his full height.

'There must have been about twenty or thirty of them.' Mudguard went on. 'That one who was with you at our place, who ran away, he was leading them. I recognized his voice.'

'So did I,' said Napoleon. 'Which way were they going, back?'

'Yes,' said Mudguard, 'towards the Caledonian Road.'

Knocker looked at Chalotte. 'I hate to think what Ninch'll do to Scooter when he finds him.'

'Ah, but they won't find him,' said Swish. 'The guards will have taken him somewhere else by now.'

Napoleon hitched his rucksack higher on his shoulders to make it sit more comfortably. 'I don't mind what they get up to,' he said. 'If it keeps the dwarfs out of our way for twenty-four hours they can put the little bleeder through a mincer for all I care . . . and so much the better.'

*

As Knocker had said, the slaughterhouse was at no great distance from the hideout, and, after following the towpath for half an hour or so, the Adventurers saw the Conker chalk mark glowing on a crumbling brick wall to their right. This wall had once been high and sturdy, surmounted with shards of broken glass, and had separated the backyard of the slaughterhouse from the canal bank. Over the years it had been worn away by weather and children until now it was little more than knee-high to an adult. Access, over a scrap of wasteland to the sheds and then the streets beyond, was easy. The Adventurers halted and crouched behind the remains of this broken barrier and examined their surroundings. At last they had come to the slaughterhouse; at last they could see it, and smell it too.

Although the winter dark had long since settled over London it was only early evening and the men in the abattoir were still at work. Electric light was blazing out from a huge pair of double doors, flung open in the middle of a long, low-lying, windowless building on the far side of a cobbled yard. A man, just a silhouette against the light, was hosing blood from the cobbles with water that looked thicker than glue and darker than black. Down it went into a gaping drain. He was whistling as he worked, a tuneless melody, and the sound was carried across to the Borribles on damp, death-laden air.

Somewhere a horse whinnied and the whinny became a scream and that scream was ended as a metal bolt was fired through the living bone of a skull and smashed its way into the warm and tender brain. A body fell, legs thrashed. The man in the yard kept hosing and whistling as more steaming blood poured through the double doors and he washed it away. His big leather apron gleamed, moist and shiny his wellington boots squelched. The Borribles stared over the wall, swallowed hard and gritted their teeth. Sydney swore.

'I'll get them for this,' she said. 'Brother, will I get them for this.'

The Borribles continued their scrutiny of the yard. On the left-hand side of it were three juggernaut lorries parked close together in a line. From the first came the bleating of fear-crazed sheep; from the second came the grunting of pigs, scared witless by the smell of blood; and from the third rolled the deep lowing of cows who knew their lives were ended. And out of the rear of each lorry, urine, acrid and foul, dripped steadily to the ground. Near the drivers' cabs – standing, watching, waiting – were two policemen. Three more stood on the right, at the entrance of the lane that led to Baynes Street and the front of the building. Beyond the juggernauts, lining the far side of the yard, was a series of stable doors, about fifteen of them, all bolted on the outside.

Sydney, using the broken wall as cover, crept along until she was close to Knocker and Chalotte. She pointed. 'Those stables,' she whispered. 'I bet that's where they've got Sam.'

Knocker nodded and glanced at his watch. 'We'd better make a start,' he said. 'Chalotte and Nap and me will go and talk to the coppers. Stonks, Torrey, Vulge and Coco can stay behind this wall in reserve. The rest of you creep round behind the lorries and find out if Sam's in them sheds. If you find him just keep quiet until the Conkers start their bit round the front, then we'll go out through the slaughterhouse. Stick together and don't get caught.'

With one last nervous smile for his friends Knocker stood and stepped over the low wall. Napoleon and Chalotte went with him, their hearts knocking like pneumatic drills. As the Borribles came into the light the police officers heard them and turned with a start.

''Allo, what's this?' said policeman number one, recovering from his surprise and folding his arms with an air of ineffable smugness.

'Yes indeed,' said policeman number two. 'And where have you lot sprung from?' He folded his arms likewise and affected a demeanour of insufferable superiority with a touch of no-nonsense-me-lad thrown in for good measure. Both men gazed down from a great height.

'Midgets,' said Napoleon.

'Dwarfs,' said Knocker.

'Blancmange,' added Chalotte.

Both policemen nodded sagely. 'Blancmange,' they repeated.

'We were recruited yesterday,' explained Knocker, 'by Inspector Sussworth, in his caravan in Rochester Gardens.'

'All very well,' said policeman number one. He now began to rock backwards and forwards on his heels like a copper in pantomime, 'but everything's under control. We don't need no dwarfs.'

There was a shout from inside the abattoir, a burst of swearing and laughter, the bleating of sheep and then the sound of small hooves dancing nervously on concrete. More blood surged from the double doors and the man kept whistling and hosing.

Knocker wiped the cold sweat from his forehead with the heel of his hand. He hoped he wasn't going to be sick. The smell was awful and the winter night suddenly seemed hot and sticky. He looked up at the policemen and loaded his voice with sincerity.

'We were ordered to check the canal,' he said. 'We were given instructions to start up at Camden Town and work our way to King's Cross. The inspector thought the Borribles might try to come along the towpath and surprise you.'

'Surprise us?' said number one. He stopped rocking his body, astounded at the effrontery of the remark. 'Take more than a few Borribles to surprise the SBG, chummy. I've got three men over there, and about another twenty round the front, and if that weren't enough we've got another forty in reserve.'

Policeman number two unfolded his arms and put his hands on his hips. 'If those Borribles try to get that horse,' he sneered, 'it'll be them as goes for catsmeat. After all there's only ten of 'em. If they dares to show their faces round here I'll have each and every one hanging up by their chins on meat hooks, all in a row.'

'Too right,' said Chalotte, swallowing hard.

At that moment more noise issued from the slaughterhouse. The sheep were again bleating for their lives. The smell of death was in their nostrils and their instinct told them that soon they would not be smelling anything at all but would be part of the smell themselves. Knocker checked his watch once more. The ten minutes were nearly up. The Conkers would be attacking any time now.

'Oh well,' he said, 'we'll be on our way then. If we see anything between here and King's Cross we'll let you know.'

'You do that, titch,' said number one, drawing his breath over his teeth, 'but you won't see nothing. For my money them Borribles are miles away by now, hiding in another town.'

As Knocker and his two companions went to leave, there came the smash of breaking glass, faintly as in the distance. Then there were shouts, and the radio on policeman number one's lapel began to buzz and speak. 'Stand by, stand by,' said a voice. 'Got some punk dwarfs going berserk round here! Watch out your side. We're calling in the reinforcements. Nothing to worry about.'

Just then, with a perfect sense of timing, Torreycanyon and Stonks jumped up on to the canal wall and fired their catapults at the policemen Knocker had been talking to, aiming to miss.

Napoleon crouched, pointing, half turning. 'Look,' he cried. 'Look at that. Borribles. After them.'

The two policemen, angry at being attacked in this way, ran towards the canal wall and at the same time ordered their three colleagues to stay on guard at the corner of the lane. Firing another stone each Torreycanyon and Stonks leapt out of sight and fled eastwards in the direction of King's Cross, disappearing out of the light and into the darkness. With no hesitation the two men of the SBG jumped the wall and set off in pursuit, close on the heels of the fugitives and calling loudly for them to give themselves up and face arrest.

The officers did not get far. A length of old wire, invisible across the towpath and held tightly in position by Vulge and Orococco, tripped both men. Policeman number one, who was in the lead and running very well, felt his feet pulled from under him while the rest of his body continued forward at an alarming speed. Unable to recover his balance, he found himself curving in a graceful arc over the edge of the canal bank and, shouting with surprise, he splashed into the filthy waters of the Grand Union, his shout changing in a split second from noise to silence as his mouth submerged and took in about two pints of untreated sewage.

Policeman number two, following close behind, made a strenuous effort to avoid his colleague's fate and nearly succeeded. He saw his friend hit the wire and tried to leap high and swerve all at once, but on that narrow towpath there was nowhere for him to swerve to. On his left was a factory wall, on his right the canal.

He kicked his feet against the ground in an attempt to soar upwards, but his body, twisting in mid-flight, struck the wall, bounced off it and then teetered for an age at the very brink of the path, arms outspread, on tiptoe like a dancer. As he swayed there Vulge appeared from his hiding place and, using only one hand, he pushed the rigid policeman into the canal at just the moment when number one was surfacing and vomiting large quantities of water into the air like a fountain. Vulge yelled in triumph and Orococco appeared beside him, a large grin spreading over his face.

The two policemen now struck out with their arms and legs, heading for the canal bank they had just left. Seeing this, Vulge drew his catapult, Orococco too. Vulge fired a stone into the water near number one's face.

'Go for the other side,' Vulge yelled, 'or we'll aim to hit you, and if we do you won't get out of there alive.'

Vulge and Orococco were now joined by Stonks and Torreycanyon, returned from their feigned flight, and all four watched as the policemen swam away to clamber out on the opposite towpath; there they shook their fists and swore at their enemies. But that bravery could not last long. The near-freezing water of the canal had all but stolen the life from the two officers, and shivering violently they left the scene in search of a warm refuge and dry clothing.

As soon as they had disappeared Stonks rallied his companions and led them off in the direction of the slaughterhouse. 'Because it's there,' he said, 'that this battle will be decided.'

At the slaughterhouse everything had changed and everything was chaos. In the right-hand corner of the yard, at the place where the narrow road came from the front, stood the massed ranks of the Conkers, their brilliant mops of hair swaying this way and that as they fought off the dozen or so policemen who were trying to get at them. They were yelling and shouting and firing their catapults as fast as they could. 'A Conker, a Conker,' came their battle cry and they surged backwards and forwards, at least forty of them, always together, always shouting.

Stonks cast his eye across the battleground as he and his three companions climbed over the wall to enter it. The policemen who had been guarding the corner which the Conkers were now defending, had taken up a new position just inside the great double doors of the abattoir. They were pinned down, helpless for the moment, victims of a sustained and accurate fire from the catapults of Knocker, Napoleon and Chalotte. Stonks called to Vulge, Orococco and Torreycanyon and they crossed the yard at a run to add their firepower to the barrage.

Without turning his head Knocker said, 'Where's them two coppers?'

'Very wet,' replied Stonks. 'What's next?'

Knocker tilted his head. Behind the three lorries the stable doors stood wide open, unbolted by Sydney, Bingo and Twilight. Now nineteen or twenty horses wheeled and stamped in freedom, their hooves clashing against the cobbles. They neighed loudly, made frantic by the smell of blood.

One of those horses was indeed Sam, and while Sydney calmed him Bingo and Twilight kept their catapults trained on the lorry drivers who had been fast asleep in their cabs and who now peered, pasty-faced and amazed, through their windscreens at the incomprehensible struggle raging around them; a struggle which they had no wish to join.

'Open up the backs of them lorries, Stonks,' said Knocker. 'The catches were too stiff for us, but you're strong. Set them animals free.'

Stonks nodded and called Torreycanyon, his friend, to go with him. 'I'll need to stand on your shoulders, Torrey,' he explained, 'to reach the handles.'

Knocker watched them run to the rear of the first lorry. He got to his feet. 'Watch them coppers,' he cried to Chalotte. 'I'm going to see Swish. It's time we got out of here.'

Knocker ran to the corner of the yard and elbowed his way into the mob of punks. He found Swish deep in the fray, shouting, singing, directing operations, firing her catapult as quickly as she could load it. 'Blancmange!' she yelled, 'come and get yer blancmange!' Then she saw

Knocker. Her eyes lit up bright, and she even smiled. 'Best fight I've ever been in,' she said.

Knocker peered over the tumultuous ranks of the Conkers. Halfway down the lane he could see a solid line of policemen reeling backwards under the catapult fire but he could also see that behind them reinforcements were arriving and riot shields and helmets were being distributed. That would change everything.

There was a lull in the battle. Knocker pulled Swish to one side; there was a cut on her head and blood was streaming down her face but she was still laughing.

'Swish,' said Knocker, 'what next?'

Swish hooted. 'Don't worry,' she said. 'I sent Treld and the others in at the front of the slaughterhouse. They've let the animals loose and chased the workmen out . . . They've made barricades an' all, and that's the road you're going, through there.'

'Through there?' shouted Knocker, above the noise. 'How?'

'With the animals,' explained Swish. 'We'll get as many together as we can in this street and stampede 'em at the Woollies, just like in a Western. We'll run out behind them; you do the same.'

Knocker glanced over his shoulder. Stonks had opened two of the lorries and sheep and pigs were pouring down the ramps, leaping, squealing and bleating. He and Torreycanyon were now attacking the third lorry containing the cows, big heavy beasts like tanks, lethal with sharp horns. Knocker turned back to Swish. 'How much longer can you hold out?' he asked. 'Stonks will soon have the last lorry open.'

Swish wiped the blood from her face. Her crimson hair was drooping with sweat even on this cold night. 'As long as our ammo lasts,' she said, 'and until they bring in them riot shields.'

'All right,' said Knocker. 'When all the animals are free and we're ready, I'll shoot out this light.' He waved a hand at the electric bulb above his head. 'And you stampede down this street and we'll go through the slaughterhouse, okay?'

A roar came from the lane. Swish and Knocker looked. A fresh rank of SBG men was advancing. Now they had their riot shields and their heads were helmeted in shiny black; there were truncheons in their hands.

'Fire,' screamed Swish. 'Keep firing.' She jerked her head at Knocker. 'Found yer 'orse yet?'

'Yes,' said Knocker, and he left her to get back to the others, but now it wasn't so easy.

While Knocker had been talking Stonks had succeeded in opening the back of the last lorry and dozens of cows had burst out to join their weight to the sheep, pigs and horses already charging in every direction, eager to find a path, any path, that would lead them from this high bedlam and stink of slaughter.

Knocker had to fight for every inch of his way across the yard, kicking, pushing and shoving. It was a terrible struggle. He had never felt so powerless, never had he been so frightened for his life. He stumbled, half fell, seized a handful of fleece and pulled himself to his feet, swayed and nearly fell again. At last, almost riding on a massive ewe, he got back to his friends and found them sheltering by the side of one of the lorries, fighting now to keep themselves from being trampled to pieces on the ground.

The noise was terrifying. The pigs grunted and butted the sheep out of their way, brutally, their hot eyes burning, thick saliva drooling from their mouths. The sheep were brainless with fear; they bashed their heads against anything that got in their way; they clambered over one another, flailing the air with their feet and bleating like imbeciles. The horses neighed and reared like wild stallions and the cows, most dangerous of all, lowered their horns and pranced sideways as desperate as fighting bulls doomed to die in the arena. The Borribles were surrounded by a seething, rolling torrent of flesh and noise; for anyone who went down under those sharp hooves it would be a painful death, a dreadful maiming.

Knocker could see that Sam was sheltering close to the lorry; Sydney sat astride him with Chalotte behind her. The horse was quivering with fear and both girls were trying to soothe the animal with their hands. Knocker pointed to the electric light at the corner of the yard and yelled out his plan, his voice feeble in all that din.

'I'll shoot the light out; that's the signal for Swish and us. Round up as many animals as you can and head them for the double doors. The Conkers will go down the side street at the same time and we'll meet round the front. Keep up close and we'll all crash through and make for the streets. Chalk Farm is the place to go for.'

Chalotte, high on the horse, loaded her catapult. She winked at Knocker, her spirit up with the joy of the fight, and hardly bothering to look at her target, such an excellent shot was she, the girl from Whitechapel released a stone, firing from the hip, and with an explosion of gas and a crash of glass the light on the corner was extinguished.

As soon as this sign was given the Conkers retreated and divided into two groups, forcing their way back into the yard. When they thought they had gone far enough the two groups turned on a shout from Swish and moved towards each other, joining hands to form a long line which enclosed scores of animals. Then they began to shout and to scream, to kick and to walk forward, driving a huge and dangerous herd before them.

The ranks of the SBG, advancing down the narrow lane, were encouraged by the sudden retreat of the Conkers and pressed on quickly, brandishing their truncheons, confident of victory. But so rapid had the Conkers' manoeuvre been that before the policemen could reach the corner where the lane entered the yard they were faced by a solid wall of flesh and bone running amok in their direction. At long last the poor beasts of the slaughterhouse had been shown a way out of the dreadful place where they had been imprisoned and tormented beyond despair. With loud squeals and bellowings they charged, fast on the hoof, driven on by the Conkers who ran behind them still shouting, 'Blancmange! Blancmange!' at the tops of their voices.

The front line of the SBG riot force was not composed of supermen. When those officers of law and order realized that a multitude of animals was bearing down on them, unstoppable and enraged, led by angry, mad-eyed cows with sickle horns upon their heads and followed by forty punk Borribles shooting stones, they turned and ran.

Unfortunately the policemen in the ranks behind could not see what was happening. They were convinced that the first advance had been a sign of victory. 'We've got 'em,' they bawled, and stormed down the lane, swinging their truncheons, banging their shields in celebration.

The two bodies of men, one going, one coming, met head on, and what with the darkness, the plastic visors and the general uproar, blows were struck and great oaths were sworn. There was no time for understanding; neither fire nor bullets would stop these animals, not for a second. Urged on by the Conkers they needed no urging; they needed only this way out.

Down went the second rank of constables under the rushing feet of their escaping comrades. It was a rout. To the rescue dashed a third rank, only to fall across the struggling men already on the ground. And, before they could rise, they were kicked and trampled into the cobbles by the studded boots of the first rank, who were stopping for no one, friend or foe. But even these men lost their footing as they attempted to leap the arms and legs in their path, and over the whole shifting heap of humanity poured the stampede, as irresistible as lava and as murderous as an avalanche. Nothing now lay between the animals and the front of the abattoir or the entrance to Baynes Street. Out of the narrow neck of the lane they thundered, demons on a jaunt from hell.

Standing in front of the slaughterhouse were more policemen, at least twenty or so, grouped round the cars and vans which they had carelessly parked half on and half off the pavements. Here too were Sussworth and Hanks, directing what they thought was to be the final round-up of the Borrible gang they had been pursuing for months.

The inspector and the sergeant were pleased. They had witnessed three ranks of crack SBG troops hastening out of sight on the heels of a band of punk Borribles. There could be no doubt of the outcome. The punks had only got near the slaughterhouse in the first place because they had known the password, but now, whatever happened, there would be no escape. There were reserves of policemen waiting in Royal College Street, and others advancing along the towpath from both directions. Sussworth clapped his gloved hands and looked at his men. 'We'll soon have their ears,' he chanted. 'We'll soon have their ears.'

At this moment he and Hanks and the men standing with them heard a sound that they had never heard before: the sound of more than a hundred animals on the run. That was not all; there came too the shouts of men yelling in pain as they were knocked to the ground and trodden on by sharp heavy hooves. Then, round the corner, bursting into Sussworth's amazed vision and leaning at a racing angle, swept a horde of pig and sheep and horse and cow, their eyes and horns glinting with evil. The inspector's bowels turned to water; the stampede had aimed itself straight at him.

Sussworth was small and agile and Sussworth never wasted time. With not even a second's reflection he pushed past his sergeant and, scrambling like a squirrel, he climbed on to his car roof, hoisting himself away from danger.

Hanks too, for all his bulk, was no slowcoach either when it came to protecting his body from the possibility of injury. He could not climb like the inspector but he tore open the car door and threw himself across the rear seat, covering his head with his arms, his flesh quaking with terror. As for the rest of the policemen, they were not cowards but how could they reason with a stampede? How could they arrest it or even beat it over the head with a truncheon? With admirable common sense they ran, most of them, for the safety of the wider streets.

Sussworth danced on the roof of his car punching the air with rage, his moustache contracting in on itself as if in pain. He could not believe his eyes. There was the cream of the Metropolitan Police turning tail before a pack of animals.

'Come back here!' he screamed. 'Come back here! Arrest those runaways! Send for reinforcements!' Just then the advancing tidal wave reached Sussworth's car and swirled round it on every side, rocking it violently, butting the panels, kicking the paintwork.

'Help me, you men,' roared the inspector, but no one heard him above the clamour and he swayed perilously on top of the car, eventually falling to his hands and knees in order to avoid being thrown to the ground where he would have met his death under the flying hooves. Still the car pitched and bobbed like a tin can at sea. Sussworth's hands scraped at the painted surface, searching for something to grasp. There was nothing. Gradually he slid towards the edge. He raised his narrow twisted face in fear, looking into the heavens for help but all he got in his eye was a sooty drop of water. It was trying to rain again.

*

As soon as Chalotte had smashed the light at the corner of the lane she kicked her heels into Sam's flanks and both she and Sydney urged the horse in the direction of the large entrance at the rear of the abattoir.

Sam resisted these urgings to begin with, alarmed at the prospect of entering such a house of blood, but Sydney leant forward on the horse's neck and spoke words of reassurance to him, and trusting his Borrible friends more than anyone else in the world, he at last advanced with a firm step. On each side of the horse ran the rest of the Adventurers in two wide arcs, whooping and yelling and waving their arms, frightening a huge mob of animals forward, forcing them to pass between the big double doors, squeezing them in.

Once all the animals were crowded inside the slaughterhouse Knocker pulled the huge doors together and shot the bolts. With this done he sprang up on to a butcher's chopping block and with his hands on his hips he surveyed the confusion around him. Never had he witnessed anything like it; it was a madman's fantasy, a bright painting of a nightmare.

The slaughterhouse was thronged with the living and the dead, pressed closely together. From the high hooks of an overhead conveyor hung the skinned and crimson cadavers of cows and pigs, sheep and horses, still steaming with the evaporating warmth of their life's blood; each corpse only a stunted vestige of what it had once been, no head, no feet, no entrails and no skin – catsmeat.

On the same conveyer, hanging by their feet and secured by their own handcuffs, side by side with the dreadful corpses, were the three members of the SBG who had taken refuge just inside the entrance when Swish's Conkers had first charged down the lane at the side of the building. Thinking themselves safe they had been surprised for a second time and taken from the rear when Treld and her band had rushed in through the front doors of the slaughterhouse. Sheer weight of numbers had borne the policemen down and they had been jumped on, stunned, and then trussed like turkeys and hoisted aloft.

Now they twisted round and round, their faces red and their stomachs sick, at the mercy of this sudden rush of animals; animals who were out of their wits at being crushed together in this place with its stench of intestines, its promise of death. As the stampede surged past them the policemen's bodies were battered with bone and struck with horn. Their faces and tunics were glistening with streaks of gob and slavers of snot erupting from the mouths and nostrils of the panic-stricken beasts.

Knocker looked away, searching for Treld. At last he saw her and the rest of her band. The Conkers had taken up positions high in the criss-crossing of the iron girders of the roof space, and there they hung, shouting and waving. Treld herself, as soon as she saw Knocker, dropped on to a catwalk and slid down a ventilation pipe, landing expertly on a girder only a few yards from where Knocker stood. She looked at him and, over the chaos that separated them, she grinned a grin of absolute triumph. 'It's good here,' she shouted above the uproar. Knocker stared. Treld was covered in dirt and grease. Her fine punk clothes were in shreds and it was impossible to see what colour her hair had been; all its spikes were drooping down by the side of her head. The paint too had gone from her face, replaced by grime, and there was a deep cut on her cheek, but her eyes glowed with the fire of life, and her whole body looked charged with power. She shook herself and her bangles and badges jangled.

'Where are the butcher men?' shouted Knocker.

Treld jerked a thumb over her shoulder. 'When we come in they ran into them big fridges over there. All we had to do was lock the doors behind them . . . bleedin' cowards. Still I suppose the sight of twenty punk birds running straight for 'em didn't 'zactly fill 'em with confidence. They'll be catching cold about now.' She laughed at her own joke.

Knocker looked down. He could see that Chalotte and Sydney were still astride Sam but were having difficulty keeping him calm. As for the other Adventurers, they had just managed, like Knocker himself, to find positions off the ground and were clinging to girders, chains and hooks, fearful of falling into the mayhem below. Not one square inch of the abattoir floor was visible. The cows were lunging at the horses, making them rear; the pigs were snapping at the sheep; and the sheep in their turn were wheeling in tight circles or trying to climb walls.

Treld shouted at Knocker again. 'Let's go now. All we have to do is slip down that rope over there and open the door. No copper in the world will stop these animals once they get moving.'

'On yer bike,' yelled Knocker. Treld grinned again, gave a sign to her friends in the roof, and then, totally fearless, ran the length of a girder and slid down the rope she had indicated until she was level with a set of bolts. Leaning over from the rope she drew them back and pushed at the door with a foot.

The sheep found the gap immediately and thrust at it. The pigs felt the pressure grow less in that direction and charged. The horses followed, the cows followed them, and the Conkers shouted and cheered, encouraging the animals forward; the torrent was on the move again and as soon as it was safe to do so the Borribles dropped from their perches to the floor. They gathered near Sam the horse and prepared their catapults for battle. The next few minutes would decide whether or not they would escape; all they had to do was follow on in the wake of their unstoppable war-machine and hope for the best.

*

It was just as this second stampede rolled out of the slaughterhouse that Sussworth fell from the roof of his car, grazing his knees as he landed awkwardly on the cobbles. The inspector clambered to his feet as fast as he could but was immediately thumped in the crotch by an angry pig and the pain took his breath away completely. He hit the ground again and this time he could feel something very wet and soggy under his body, under his hands and, worst of all, under his face.

Whatever it was stank most pungently. Then the realization came to Sussworth in a flash. Of course! With hundreds of animals in a highly excited state the whole area must be covered with a very special mixture of excrement: cows', pigs', sheep's and horses'.

The inspector's hatred of filth made him forget his agony and he sprang to his feet once more. That was a mistake. Although the last of the animals from the first stampede had disappeared round the corner into Baynes Street, the second stampede was now out of the slaughterhouse and, like the first – so it seemed to Sussworth – every single one of these new arrivals had their sights on him. Worse, forty punk girls, emerging from the side lane, had spotted his uniform and were firing their catapults as fast as they could. Stones whizzed past his head; a window of his car shattered; a headlamp exploded.

There was nothing for it. In spite of the muck that covered the cobbles Sussworth dropped to the ground again. He pressed his face closer into it and squeezed his body under the car. The fierce odour made him gag and retch. His hands and face were plastered with slime and slurry. He heard his coat rip on a bracket. The exhaust pipe of the car burnt a hole through his trousers and scorched a leg. Sussworth whimpered. He could not believe that this was happening to him. Where were his men, his proud battalions? Tears welled up in his eyes, tears of rage and frustration. He tried to wipe them away and only got muck in his eye. He sobbed out loud and drummed his feet against the roadway like a child in a tantrum. 'I'll get them for this,' he howled, 'them savages and their horse.'

But in all that hubbub no one, except Hanks, heard the inspector or even knew where he was. The animals charged at the car and battered it severely. The Borribles whooped and yelled and all Sussworth could see from his viewpoint were feet and hooves dancing round him and kicking more muck into his face no matter which way he turned.

Hanks heard the inspector's voice quite clearly but Hanks was not moving. He was safe, he thought, and he cowered on the back seat of the patrol car, his hands covering his tightly closed eyes, hoping to heaven that he was out of danger, but he was not.

As the animals surged round both sides of the motor its bodywork was bashed and dented by their sheer ferocity. So violent was the attack that the chassis of the car must have twisted or snapped at some point, for suddenly, without any warning, the two rear doors fell open, leaving Sergeant Hanks completely unprotected.

The very moment this happened the front runner of the escaping sheep spotted the gap and darted in at one door, to emerge at the other in less than a split second. It was straight away followed by more sheep and then by pigs too, all pushing and shoving and pummelling at Hanks with their vicious hooves.

The sergeant screamed for mercy but it was no use. More and more animals chose that way out, slobbering and slavering and coughing and sneezing to such good effect that at the end of it all Hanks resembled some old round boulder that slugs and snails had crawled over all night, to leave coated with glittering silver in the morning.

*

Treld swung on her rope as the last of the animals left the abattoir, watching her comrades group themselves near Sydney and Chalotte and Sam the horse. Knocker leapt from his chopping block to the floor. 'Come on,' he shouted. 'Quick, let's go.'

The Borribles were fully prepared to do just that but as they moved forward they found their way barred by a line of about twenty policemen, their shields and visors in position, their truncheons at the ready. These men had escaped injury by hiding outside behind the great open doors, swept there by the charge and power of the stampede. They were unharmed, fresh and determined to revenge themselves.

'Oh bugger it!' cried Sydney.

'Catapults,' shouted Chalotte.

Treld, unnoticed in the rafters, took another swing on her rope and, bending as she swung, undid the catch on a huge metal container that was fixed in position above the entrance. She had realized what it was earlier, when undoing the bolts on the front door.

It was a cylinder about twice as high as a man and maybe six feet wide, fed and filled by conveyor belts which rose from the factory floor. The undoing of the catch normally allowed the bottom of the container to open so that its contents might fall into the back of a lorry; only this time there was no lorry and the heavy load dropped straight down and swamped the policemen below entirely, just as they charged. And what fell from above was a ton and a half of viscous offal, bright vermilion lungs and purple livers, gaudy tripes and dark blue intestines, all jumbled together with hearts and kidneys, tails and tongues, trotters and skin, stomachs and bowels, eyes, teeth, bone and brains; and all of it slippery with a fast thickening blood.

The Borribles fell back, sickened and surprised. A soft crimson explosion had engulfed the policemen and they were gone. In their place was a shambles, a rising, heaving quicksand of red sponge. Huge drops of gore pattered down, warm and heavy like a tropical rain. Even the Conkers held up their arms to protect themselves and some of them screamed. So did Treld, but hers was a scream of joy.

Knocker glanced up and understood where this terrible deliverance had come from. As he looked the girl left her rope, ran along a pipe, down a girder and landed near him. She jerked her head at the moving pile of reeking gobbets and rubbed her hands together.

'That should keep 'em quiet for a minute,' she said. 'I think we'd better go now, before they gets annoyed.'

No one laughed and for a brief moment the only sound heard was the sound of Chalotte retching where she sat and swayed on the back of the horse, her face like a broken mask.

But there was no staying there however anyone felt. With a great yell of exultation Treld slapped Sam on the rump and, picking his way round the mass of offal, his nostrils flaring at the thought of freedom, the horse stepped eagerly through the slaughterhouse gates. The Conkers followed, the adventurers too, and outside, so quickly were things happening, they were just in time to meet the advance of Swish and her contingent, rushing along in the wake of the first stampede.

There was a whoop of celebration and friend greeted friend. Knocker stepped aside and took in the scene. The area in front of the abattoir was, as far as he could see, empty of policemen. There were three patrol cars but they were battered wrecks, their tyres flat, their windscreens and headlamps smashed, their doors hanging loose. Beyond them the last few of the animals were leaving the entrance to the yard and galloping into Baynes Street.

Treld pointed. 'We'll have to follow them and keep as close as we can,' she said. 'It's our only chance.'

Knocker nodded and called to the adventurers. 'Try and stay close to Sam,' he said, 'and follow on to Chalk Farm.'

'Blancmange,' shouted Treld.

'Blancmange,' shouted Swish.

'Blancmange,' shouted all the Conkers.

Sydney spoke once more to Sam and the horse neighed like a steed of ancient battles and shook his head and bared his teeth. Ready for anything he moved towards the streets. Sydney grabbed Sam's mane and held on grimly. Behind her Chalotte threw her arms around Sydney's waist and pressed her head against her friend's shoulder. 'I hope I don't fall off,' she said.

It was too late to worry now. Sam began to pick up speed, and the Borribles, all seventy of them, formed a protective hedge around him and swarmed out into Baynes Street and into Royal College Street, lifting their pace to a gallop.

The charge was irresistible and no line of policemen could have stopped it, but there was not the slightest sign of law and order. The SBG had concentrated its efforts in and around the slaughterhouse, little thinking that the Adventurers could break through its defences and not dreaming for a moment that they could break out again even if their first attack were successful. Above all, Inspector Sussworth had not included the Conkers or the animals in his calculations. Under such an unexpected onslaught his troops had run for cover. So the Borribles, following in the wake of the escaping herds and with no one to prevent them, hastened towards the high railway bridges of Royal College Street and Camden Road; and what a sight met their eyes.

It was full rush hour with thousands of people going home by bus and car and on foot. Trains rattled across the sky and it was so dark that the street lamps could hardly shine through the squalls of rain gusting everywhere. Through all this activity the stampede had passed and now everything was in disorder.

Lorries, cars and buses had swerved from the roads, crashing into lamp posts and mounting kerbstones. The drivers, recovering from their shock, were just beginning to climb from their seats and were shouting and arguing with one another. Pedestrians stood dazed, oblivious of the rain, staring after the departing animals as they raced round the corner and down the Camden Road towards Camden Town; the pigs squealing louder than ever, the sheep bleating, the horses neighing and the cows still tossing their dangerous horns.

The people walking up Camden Road could not believe the evidence of their own eyes. Here they were, just up from the Underground, hurrying homeward for tea, their heads bent against the weather and the car lights, when suddenly, out of the black night, came a wave of noise and terror, threatening to engulf them.

Everyone on that crowded street dived for the closest doorway or bolted into the nearest side road or climbed the handiest wall. The traffic stopped immediately and completely, drivers happy to be safe within the protection of their vehicles, never mind the damage. They too could not believe their eyes: sitting in their cars in the middle of one of London's main roads and nothing but animals on all sides just as far as one could see – an ocean of animals. So all the traffic stopped, right back to Kentish Town and beyond; round by Regent's Park and Albany Street and down to Mornington Crescent too. And those at the rear could not understand what was going on and hooted their horns, and got out of their cars and phoned the police and the fire brigade, but that only made matters much worse as more vehicles tried to enter the area and the traffic jam became solid and immovable.

The Conkers were delighted. They sped along the pavements, maintaining their guard around Sam and the Adventurers, hiding them from view, brandishing their catapults ready to warn off any adult who attempted to halt their flight. But no adult dared intervene; they were far too confused and shocked to take an interest. In their very own streets they had witnessed a stampede and then, only seconds later, a horde of mad children had appeared, all of them girls it seemed, their faces begrimed with dirt and spotted with blood, their clothes torn and filthy.

On ran the Borribles, screaming defiance, and they ran where the animals led and the animals led to Camden Town where five wide roads meet to make a star. Here too the traffic was wedged tight, cars and buses locked bumper to bumper, shining under the streaks of light rain where it fell through the lamplight. Commuters, emerging from the Underground station, rushed to shelter from the wet in shop doorways. They gawped, puzzled to see so many headlamps blazing but not moving.

As they stood there they became aware of a noise: a distant shouting and a hallooing, a thundering of feet, a bleating, a squealing and a lowing. They looked at each other nervously. Was this the end of the world as prophesied? Before they could answer the question the question answered itself for into sight came the stampede, heading down the slope of Camden Road straight for the Underground.

There were not quite so many animals now. Some had found their way into the side streets, others had blundered into restaurants or trapped themselves in backyards, but there were still enough to frighten the life out of most of the onlookers, what with the speed they were going and the noise they were making. But that was not all. Behind the herd, riding relentlessly like spirits of the night, were two blood-bespattered girls on a fire-eyed stallion, their hair streaming in the wind, and all round them ran a ragged band of barbarous children.

The horses neighed and galloped on, thrusting the commuters deeper into the doorways, leading the escape into Camden Town itself, and the sheep and pigs and cows followed on without hesitation. Into the entrance of the Underground station they went, cutting a swathe through the evening travellers, breaking down telephone boxes and demolishing the ticket collector's cubicle. Then they wheeled and skidded from the exit, as in a chariot race, changing direction into Chalk Farm Road, hastening north, past the market.

The market stalls were lucky. Most of them were positioned down one side of the road and only three or four were knocked over. Nothing could have suited the Borribles better and as they raced along they bent and scooped up handfuls of fruit; enough food to get them through a week.

'Fruit of the barrow,' yelled Knocker.

'Fruit of the barrow,' yelled the Conkers.

Gradually the market was left behind and the Borribles slowed their pace a little and took stock of their situation. The course they were following would soon take them on over the canal bridge and away in the direction of the LMR goods depot, which lay to the west behind the old locomotive shed that people called the Roundhouse. To the east the side streets were dark and empty, although the main thoroughfare, Chalk Farm Road itself, was still crammed with cars which could not move an inch because of the great traffic jam at Camden Town.

But at least the hubbub of the stampede had grown less, and eventually it disappeared altogether as the animals out-distanced the Borribles and began to climb Haverstock Hill on the road to Hampstead Heath. So Sydney drew rein and Sam the horse eased to a walk and then stopped, and the Adventurers and the Conkers gathered together, recovering their breath, and began to discuss their plight, quickly and urgently. They had to. Once the way was clear the SBG would be on their heels, of that there was no doubt.

Chalotte glanced up and down the road. 'We can't stay here long,' she said to Bingo, who stood by the horse's head. 'It's too open. Too many people.'

The whole band of Borribles was now gathered together on the corner of Ferdinand Street, leaning into the shadows, trying to look inconspicuous, but that was impossible – there were too many of them. Adults were stopping on the far side of the road, wondering. People were staring out of shops. They would be only too eager to tell the SBG what they had seen.

Knocker pushed into the centre of the group, Swish and Treld at his elbow; the rain had plastered their hair to their skulls, the bright dyes had run and were staining their faces.

If we stay here,' said Knocker, 'we'll be caught, sure as fish is fried.'

Swish held up a hand. 'Take it easy,' she said. 'I've got it all worked out. Us Conkers will carry on up to Hampstead. I reckon most of the horses went that way and we'll soon catch up with 'em. As soon as we do we'll split into groups and every group will take a horse and head off in different directions. That way there'll be so many reports going into the SBG about kids and horses old Sussworth won't know his arse from his elbow.'

Chalotte cocked her leg over Sam's back and slid to the ground. 'That's great, but what about us?' she asked. 'We got away and everything but now we must get off the streets, and lively too.'

Treld wiped her nose with the back of her hand. She looked like a savage with the blood on her face. 'We thought o' that,' she said. 'We'll go up the road as far as the Roundhouse. There's a goods depot behind there and a big bit of wasteland. Part of it is a scrapyard, enormous. There's some Borribles in there, Scrappers they're called. You can hide with them.'

'Why don't we just run for it?' suggested Twilight. 'Get as far away from here as we can?'

'Because,' said Swish, 'we'll be doing your running for you. Can't you see, Sussworth will have every copper in London looking for you tonight and all next week. The best thing is for him to be chasing different horses all over London. That'll give you a chance of creeping through to Neasden. It ain't far now, you know . . . Swiss Cottage, Kilburn and Dollis Hill and that's it.'

'We've *almost* done it,' cried Sydney, and she leant along Sam's neck and patted it firmly.

'"If almost was everything fruit would grow on lamp posts,"' said Napoleon, quoting from the *Proverbs*, and he spat on the ground.

'Yes,' said Knocker, '"and a Borrible who lets the grass grow under his feet will soon have it growing over his head."'

Nothing could be added to that and before the eyes of the curious passers-by the Borribles continued their run up to Chalk Farm and Sam galloped with them. When they arrived in front of the Roundhouse the Conkers formed a huge mob across the pavement, blocking it and forcing adults to cross to the other side of the road. Behind the cover of this screen the adventurers levered open an iron gate in the wall at the side of the building, and disappeared from view. At the last minute, as the gate closed, Chalotte remembered something. She halted and grasped the bars with her two hands and pulled her face close to the opening. Swish and Treld waited there, sad but smiling; beyond them were crowded scores of their companions, on the lookout.

'Hang on a mo',' said Chalotte. 'We won't see you again.'

Swish ducked her head, strangely shy. 'Oh, not for a while,' she said, 'but when all this dies down, you'll go home this way and we'll see yer. We'd better.'

Treld placed her hand over Chalotte's. 'Swish is right,' she said. 'Don't be down. You make sure you get Sam to Neasden and don't get caught. You just think of us charging about London with hundreds of horses and poor old Sussworth not knowing whether he's a copper or a cowboy. That'll make you laugh.'

Chalotte nodded, her spirits low. Hours of excitement, exhilaration and danger, and now nothing except an anticlimax and the emptiness and finality of a parting from new but trusted friends. She tried to put a brave face on it and quoted a Borrible proverb. 'Well,' she sighed, '"there's no meeting without leaving."' A whistle sounded from behind her.

'Go on,' said Treld. 'Just remember how it will go down in Borrible history, eh? "The Great Slaughterhouse Rescue of Sam the Horse." I tell you, Camden Town's never seen anything like it.'

'Nor have I,' said Chalotte, and with a melancholy smile she turned and went to catch up with her friends. 'Oh, Swish and Treld and all you Conkers,' she called as she walked away, 'don't you dare get caught, any of you, ever.'

10

After the battle at the abattoir and the headlong flight down Camden Road it was strangely quiet behind the Roundhouse. Not a single sound came from the streets and there was not a light to be seen anywhere, save for a distant shining along some railway lines towards Primrose Hill. It felt odd too, for the Adventurers, to be without the company of the Conkers suddenly. They had been good mates, good Borribles.

But the Adventurers could not allow themselves to dwell on the past, and they advanced with resolution over a rough and unpaved ground, made soggy by the heavy winter rains. Orococco and Twilight were scouting ahead, trying to find the high corrugated iron fence that Swish had told them marked the boundary of the scrapyard, and Sydney led Sam close to the curving brick wall of the Roundhouse while Stonks held a shaded torch to show the way. The rest of the Adventurers followed behind.

It was almost impossible for the fugitives to believe that they were still in London. The black night made them feel weightless, cut off from everything. There was nothing to reach out for and touch, nothing to see.

'It's a bit spooky, ain't it?' said Torreycanyon. 'Like floating through the sky.'

'It'll be worse the other side,' said Knocker. 'Between here and Swiss Cottage the streets get very posh, nowhere to lie low. We need to get right over to Kilburn; it'll be better there.'

As the column approached the railway line a Borrible whistle floated over from the far side. Twilight sprang from the ground.

'That was Coco,' he said. 'He sent me over to tell you we've got to cross the line and the scrapyard's between this line and another one further on. It's a kind of big square of wasteland. He says there's no one about.'

One by one and taking infinite care the Borribles stepped over the rails. When they were sure that everything on the far side was safe Sydney led the horse forward. Here, on the far side of the track, the ground became even soggier, almost like a swamp, and it was impossible to move silently. Every pace they took made a loud squelching noise and the horse made more sound than all the Borribles put together. Knocker swore at the lack of silence, but there was nothing to be done.

After travelling a hundred yards or so they saw, or rather sensed, a huge fence rising up in front of them; guessing it was there only because it was slightly darker than the night sky. A train went by on a distant line. Doors slammed in a station away to the west and Orococco came out of the darkness and grinned.

'This scrapyard goes on for miles,' he said. 'I ain't seen anybody yet but that don't mean they ain't here.'

'It certainly don't,' said an unknown voice, and the Adventurers crouched and made themselves small against the ground, drawing their catapults.

'Catapults, eh?' said the same unknown voice. 'Don't bother. First you're surrounded, second we knew you were coming; them Conkers told us.'

'We're Borribles,' said Chalotte, 'on the run. Are you the Scrappers?'

'Yeah, we're the Scrappers,' said the voice, 'and we know who you are. I expect every Borrible in London knows a bit about you by now.'

'We need somewhere to hide,' said Knocker. 'Only a few hours, then we'll be on our way.'

Two silhouettes moved at the top of the fence. Knocker had an impression of heads and shoulders. There was a sound of people jumping, then the sound of a sheet of corrugated iron being lifted and let fall. Knocker felt someone near him, someone he didn't know. He tensed.

'Take it easy,' said the voice that had already spoken. 'Just follow us along by the fence a bit. There's a bigger gap along there, we'll be able to get the horse in, and don't get any ideas about trying yer catapults. You can't see us but we're all here.'

The Adventurers did exactly as they were told, following the sound of Sam as he plodded along, over his fetlocks in mud.

'Why is it so muddy?' asked Stonks. 'It's nearly up to my throat.'

'Wait till you get inside,' said the Scrapper. 'Mud is a way of life here. They churn it up with machines and lorries. You can swim in it. Have to.'

The noise of walking stopped and another sheet of fencing was pulled back, swinging on hinges, and Sam was taken into the scrapyard. The Adventurers kept close to him.

'Welcome,' said the Scrapper, 'to the largest scrapyard in the world.'

The Adventurers soon discovered that their new companion had not been exaggerating about the mud. Inside the fence it was indeed much worse, and walking was more like wading and the wading released a long imprisoned smell into the air: a stale smell of grease and garbage, all touched over with a whiff of mouldy carpet.

Orococco whistled to himself. 'This must be one of the great niffs of London,' he said, 'but at least it ain't raining.' As he said it the rain began to fall once more, diluting the mud and making it deeper.

The Adventurers trudged on. They were desperately weary now and could only lift their feet with great effort. It was only a few hours since they had left the warehouse and marched to attack the abattoir, yet it seemed like longer – days, weeks. How far away Battersea was. How far Brixton. A lifetime ago.

But although they were weary they were happy. They had recaptured Sam, they were still all together and at last they could see where they were going. At strategic corners electric lights had been set up, rigged on overhead cables by the mechanics who worked in the scrapyard and left burning from dusk till dawn for the benefit of the nightwatchman; a nightwatchman who spent all his nights curled round a hot-water bottle in his wooden shed.

'He never gives us any trouble,' said the Scrapper. 'Never.' He swept an arm out to indicate his vast domain. 'It's like us having our own city here,' he continued, and there was pride in his voice. The Adventurers had to agree with him. The scrapyard certainly was an extraordinary place, laid out like a town but constructed entirely from the ruins of old cars and lorries.

The vehicles, many hundreds of them, all smashed and ruined, were heaped five or six high, one on top of the other, and piled side by side, each pile leaning against the next for support. It was a tidy yard and seemed to stretch on for ever and ever. The Adventurers, once inside, could not see or even guess where it ended. What was obvious was that the Scrapper knew his way round this labyrinth like an ordinary Borrible would his own home town, notwithstanding the scores of streets and the skyscrapers of cars that towered up and out of sight and into the rain.

The most solid of the wrecks had been turned into Borrible houses with sacks or carpets hanging at the windows to keep out the weather and keep in the warmth. In the highest cars were the lookouts, and as the column of Adventurers slogged by, warning whistles sounded out in the dark, echoing like catcalls across the roofs of metal.

At last the Scrapper brought the Adventurers to a dead end which led back to the iron fence. This street was so tall and narrow that here the cars had collapsed against each other on the fifth or sixth level to form a sinister-looking tunnel.

Napoleon Boot halted and grabbed the Scrapper by the arm. 'I don't like this,' he said. '"It's a dead end and dead ends tend to get you dead, in the end." That's a proverb.'

The Scrapper sneered and pointed. 'This is the safest place in the yard,' he said. 'That's why we've given it to you to sleep in. Believe you me, we don't want the Woollies to find you . . . Wouldn't do us any good.'

Napoleon looked where the Scrapper pointed and saw in the gloom – for the nearest light was some distance away – that at the end of the tunnel, parked sideways on, was the remains of a double-decker London bus.

'You see,' went on the Scrapper, 'it looks rough enough from the outside, but inside we've made it very comfortable, and if you have to get away in a hurry, there's an escape hatch at the back which comes out right opposite a hole in the fence. You could be away at the first sign of danger.'

Napoleon fingered his catapult. 'Okay,' he said, but he didn't sound too sure.

Knocker was nervous too. He glanced upwards and saw that a dozen or so Scrappers were on guard above him, catapults at the ready.

The Scrapper smiled. 'We travel through the cars,' he explained, 'from one street to another, along the top . . . You don't want to start anything.'

Knocker nodded. 'Don't want to,' he said. 'All we'd like to do is get in the dry and get some sleep. I feel as wet as the bottom of a drain.'

The Scrapper laughed and led the way to the rear corner of the bus and touched a switch. There was a sound of compressed air being released and a door folded open. 'It's big enough for you to get the horse in,' he said. 'Our lads like horses and nicked some stuff from a pet shop in Chalk Farm. We got some grub for you too.' The Scrapper advanced a little further and there was a fumbling. Then a light came on, though not all at once, only gradually did it glow up to strength.

Sydney took Sam by the leading rein and helped him climb the high step into the vehicle. The horse stumbled in exhaustion, both physical and emotional, and Chalotte was obliged to push him from behind.

'Poor bleeder,' she said. 'He must have thought every moment was his last all the time he was in that slaughterhouse. He must be in a right old state.' Then Chalotte stopped speaking and just stared. The others came and stood close to her, glad to be out of the wind and the damp at last.

'Well I never,' said Bingo. 'Look at that.'

The interior of the bus had been altered completely. All the seats had been unbolted from the floor and rearranged down both sides. There was a kitchen table and one or two kitchen chairs. On the table were plastic shopping bags with food spilling from them. Thick underfoot lay car carpets, and dotted about were small armchairs, rescued from rubbish dumps. What pleased Sydney more than anything else was the huge pile of clean straw and the sack of oats which she could see down at the driver's end.

'Oh,' she said, leading the horse forward. 'Come on, Sam, you're in clover here, real clover.'

The Scrapper placed his hands on his hips and beamed at everybody. He looked very happy with himself. 'The Conkers sent us a runner the other day,' he said, 'so we made it as comfortable as we could. Upstairs you'll find enough mattresses for every one of yer . . . You'll soon be warm and dry.'

The Adventurers fell on to the long upholstered bus seats with groans of fatigue. Now, in the light of the twelve-volt battery lamps, they could see each other.

'Swipe me,' said Torreycanyon. 'Just look at us.'

It was true. Every single one of the Adventurers was covered in thick mud up to the waist and the rest of their bodies were splashed over with it; so were their faces and even their woollen hats. Under the mud was the gore of the slaughterhouse, and under that was the accumulated dirt and grease from the caverns of King's Cross and the towpath of the Grand Union. Their clothes were torn too and their boots and shoes, casualties of the never-ending rains, were gaping along the uppers.

Chalotte removed her raincoat and then touched the Scrapper guide on the shoulder. 'We know your tribe is called Scrappers,' she said, 'but what is your name?'

The Borrible grinned. 'Strikalite,' he said.

Chalotte nodded. 'Well, Strikalite, yours is a very fine name and I hope that while we are here you will have the time to tell us how you won it. My name is Chalotte and this here is—'

'So you're Chalotte,' said Strikalite. 'I thought you might be. I've heard about you. The Great Rumble Hunt, eh? We've heard the tales. That is Sam the horse then; that must be Knocker and that little suspicious bloke, he'll be the Wendle, Napoleon Boot.'

As he spoke Strikalite was joined by two of his friends carrying plastic jerrycans, heavy with liquid. 'Hot broth,' they said. 'We made it with vegetables from Camden Market.' And they began to pour it into some large mugs which they had brought with them for the purpose. The Adventurers held the mugs in their hands and warmed their fingers, scrutinizing the strangers closely as they gave out the food. When Borrible meets Borrible it is the usual thing to do.

In fact the Scrappers were very much like the members of any other tribe, although there were some minor differences due to their strange way of life. They were dirtier, if that were possible, than most other Borribles the Adventurers had met, but that was because they lived in old oily motorcars; their clothing was scruffier too, for the same reason. Not that a great deal of it was visible in wintertime for then the Scrappers always wore over-garments of yellow oilskins, sou'westers and wellington boots. Where they lived mud and water were everywhere.

But these strange Borribles were nothing if not resourceful. As might be expected they were very talented mechanics and could fashion almost anything out of metal, diesel generators included. Some of the cars they lived in were marvels of comfort and design with radios and even television sets in them. Almost everything they needed they put together from junk, using their own clever hands only.

Unfortunately very little of what they made was destined to last long; the very nature of their home saw to that. The yard was there to gather in discarded vehicles, remove anything that was valuable, sell it at the front gate and turn what remained into piles of scrap. Only three or four labourers were needed for the job but they did it thoroughly, working their way round and round the dump and ripping everything to pieces until they were left with only hollow shells of steel. These were eventually shoved into a crusher and squeezed down so hard that each car was, at the last, transformed into a solid lump of metal no larger than an orange box.

Every day the men did their work and every day the Scrappers watched and only when it was necessary did they move their hideouts from one side of the yard to the other. Luckily for them this way of life was not as inconvenient as it might at first seem. The yard was acres wide and no one Scrapper would have to move his home more than once or twice every two or three months. The scrap men ignored the Borribles as long as they kept out of the way and, best of all, the SBG had no idea that anyone was using the place to live in. Given good fortune the Scrappers would never be discovered.

Sunroof and Chevvy, the Scrappers who had carried in the soup, explained all this and the Adventurers began to relax. Gradually the odd oblong room became warmer as a battery-driven heater hummed and hummed. To the Adventurers, that strange bus, lost in London between two railway lines, felt like a palace. Before long they had removed their outer garments and hung them up to dry, and a moment later had all fallen into the deepest of slumbers, lying awkwardly, too tired even to go upstairs to the mattresses that had been prepared for them. Napoleon, the last to succumb, tried to rouse himself before slipping into unconsciousness. He rubbed his eyes and shook his head.

'Someone must go on lookout,' he mumbled.

Strikalite glanced at the Wendle and paused in the act of throwing a rug over Stonks. 'Don't worry,' he said. 'Us three will keep watch . . . All you need to do is kip. Go on, get to sleep.'

Reassured, Napoleon did as he was told, and as soon as all was peaceful Strikalite and his two companions extinguished the lamps and climbed to the bus's upper deck in order to take turns resting and watching, mounting a keen-eyed vigil over the grotesque and silent towers of scrap. All night they kept guard, staring through a rain that fell straight like spikes, a rain that washed the blood from the cobblestones outside the slaughterhouse in Baynes Street and riffled the black waters of the Grand Union Canal.

And in the scrapyard itself that same rain rattled on the tin roofs of a thousand gutted vehicles and half woke the Scrappers who lay curled up beneath them. And the rain fell further, down to the ground, and plucked at the surface of the mud itself, making it look pimpled and blistered all over and yet settling the earth, beating it deeper and denser, effacing the footmarks of all those who had passed through the city of broken motor cars, until at last there was no sign left that Borrible or horse had gone that way that night, or indeed any other night.

*

In the morning the tired light of dawn came only reluctantly to that corner of the scrapyard which sheltered the derelict bus. The rain was still falling from the low sky, but only lightly, swirling without direction in fitful gusts of wind. The Adventurers slept on, their bodies needing to recover after the exertions of the previous twenty-four hours.

They might well have slept for another twenty-four hours had they been allowed to, but eventually the steady silence of the bus was broken by the hiss of the vacuum door and Strikalite appeared carrying a large jug of cold water. He walked over to where Chalotte slept and shook her awake.

The Whitechapel girl sat up immediately and blinked her eyes. 'Cripes,' she swore. 'I aches all over.'

'You'd better wake 'em up,' said the Scrapper. 'It won't be long before the men start work and your mates might have to be ready to move out. You never know.'

'Yes,' said Chalotte. 'Okay. Is it still raining?'

Strikalite swore in his turn. 'Course it is,' he said, 'and the forecast is rain for the next twenty years.'

Chalotte smiled at his remark and began to wake her friends while

Strikalite filled a kettle from his jug and switched it on. 'I'll make some tea,' he said to no one in particular.

As soon as Sydney woke she sat up in the straw where she had spent the night and looked at Sam who was lying next to her. The horse was still fast asleep, his legs stretched out, all his nervousness gone. Sydney smiled and stroked the animal, knocking the dried mud from the horse's flanks with her hand. 'You rest, Sam,' she said. 'It's not far to Neasden now.'

The kettle boiled and Strikalite made the tea in a large metal teapot. There was plenty of food and fruit left over from the previous evening and the Borribles made a good breakfast. Every now and then, as they ate, a Scrapper scout came into the bus and told Strikalite what was happening outside. It was obvious, they said, that the scrap men were working at the other end of the yard that day and the fugitives could relax. Strikalite was delighted. 'You see,' he said, 'it's nice and peaceful here just as long as you keep your eyes open.'

The Adventurers spent the remainder of the day resting and eating, for they were well aware that they would need every bit of strength they had to cover the last miles to Neasden. They dozed, they chatted and they played fivestones, one of their favourite games. They also wondered about their friends the Conkers.

'There was a bit on the wireless this morning,' Strikalite informed them, 'but they never mention Borribles do they? I suppose they don't want to frighten the adults. Anyway, all they said was that a lot of animals had escaped from some lorries in Camden Town and caused a traffic jam, and that most of the animals had been rounded up during the night except some horses that were running wild on Hampstead Heath and beyond.'

'Aha,' said Orococco, 'that'll be Treld and Swish and the others. What a bunch! I sure hope they get away all right.' And with that sentiment everyone present agreed.

And so the hours passed lazily and that evening Strikalite, Sunroof and Chevvy brought the Adventurers even more food from the market at Camden Town, and very many of their Scrapper comrades brought provisions along too, ready to share and enjoy a long and noisy feast.

'You see, they have a hard time during the day,' explained Sunroof, 'always running round, laying in stores. They likes to make themselves comfortable at night.' And make themselves comfortable they did. They stretched out on the seats in the bus, switched up the heating and joined in the banquet with a will. They had all come to hear stories: name stories first and then the story of how the Adventurers had journeyed to this particular part of London, but above all they wanted the story of the Great Rumble Hunt and all that had happened since.

In view of the hospitality they had received it was only right that the Adventurers should tell their tale, especially as it was the most famous Borrible story ever told. So Knocker began, 'Because,' he explained, smiling self-consciously at Chalotte, 'I was supposed to be Historian on that first trip, remember?' And he cleared his throat and took a swig of beer.

He started the saga by telling how the Rumbles went to Battersea Park and how the great expedition had got under way. He told of the trip up the river and the discovery of Adolf, and his companions added to the story as it progressed, and Vulge told how he had killed the chief Rumble and Bingo recounted his great fight in the library. On and on it went, each participant telling his or her own chapter in the way that suited them best, and the Scrappers sat and listened, nodding and asking questions, for there was much to be learnt from the tale and they did not want to miss a bit of it.

In this way the story continued, telling of the leaving of Sam in King George's Park, the expedition to recover him and the saving of the captives in Flinthead's mine, the fight to the death between Flinthead and Spiff and, at last, the bringing of Sam to Battersea with the aid of Ben the tramp and his friend Knibbsie.

By the time it was all told and all the questions had been asked it was very late, but the Scrappers leant back in their seats and clapped their hands and whistled through their teeth and shook their heads. 'Such stories,' said Strikalite. 'I never thought I would hear such stories. You are lucky to be alive.'

'Indeed we are,' agreed Chalotte, her face sad, 'but Adolf isn't and that is not Borrible. It is a great adventure, certainly, but one that we should not have got involved in at the beginning. We should not be risking our ears, we should be living craftily and cleverly like the Bumpers of Brixton, the Conkers of the Caledonian Road and the Scrappers of the Scrapyard, back in our own markets, keeping out of the rain. Somehow it is the Adventure that is dragging us along with it, whatever we try to do.'

'There's no way we could dump Sam,' said Twilight. 'Not now.'

Chalotte nodded at the Bangladeshi. 'What you say is perfectly correct. That is the paradox. To be Borrible we must save Sam; to save Sam we find ourselves doing things that are not really Borrible.'

Vulge wagged his head in his own knowing way. 'I tell you that once Sam's in Neasden, out of Sussworth's way, I swear I'm back to Shoreditch like a dose of salts. It's the complete Borrible life for me then. Quiet and relaxed with stories and just enough nicking to live on.'

'All very nice,' said Napoleon, 'but how do you live like a nice quiet Borrible with Sussworth and Hanks breathing down your neck all the time?'

Orococco sighed. 'Borribles have always been on the run,' he said, 'all through history, and I can't see it ever changing, unless we can turn everyone into Borribles.' He laughed. 'And that would take a few Borrible lifetimes.'

Chalotte tossed her hair and her eyes shone. 'How do we know?' she asked, her tone belligerent. 'There may be more and more Borribles happening all the time, probably is. All we can do is make sure we stay Borrible, don't get caught and turned into adults. Keep out of sight and Borrible must always help Borrible. It's as simple as that.'

There was silence after this while everyone thought their own thoughts, including the Scrappers. The silence lasted for a long while until Chalotte said, 'It's the only way, you know.'

Sydney raised her head. She was sitting next to Sam where he lay at full stretch on his straw. 'It is too,' she said. 'That's why we had to help Sam. He's a Borrible and he helped us once; now we've got to give him what we've got, and all we've got is the chance of getting him away from Sussworth and years of slavery . . . or ending up as catsmeat, one and the same thing really. We owe it to Sam to see that he's looked after, properly, for as long as he lives. It don't matter what lies Sussworth tells about us, that we're murderers and such. We know what he says about us is not true; he'd say anything about anybody who didn't agree with him.'

Sydney drew a deep breath when she'd finished. It was the longest speech she'd ever made in her whole life. She blushed.

'Right,' said Stonks.

'That's why,' added Knocker, 'we have to keep telling our story wherever we go; so that people realize how important it is.'

Sunroof leant back in his bus seat and blew his breath out over his teeth. 'Blimey,' he said. 'That's all too deep for me. I just lives like a Borrible because I am a Borrible.'

'That's it,' said Strikalite. 'Imagine living like a grown-up. Work, work, work; then die, die, die. They must be stone-raving bonkers.'

There were murmurs of approval when Strikalite expressed this sentiment and no doubt the discussion would have continued had it not been for a sudden noise at the door. It hissed, folded open and a gust of wind and rain tore into the warm interior of the Borrible hideout bearing with it two Scrappers dressed in oilskins and streaked with mud. Between them they carried what looked like a bundle of rags, wet and filthy. The two Scrappers dropped this bundle on the floor and one of them prodded it with his foot while the other returned to the roaring night, plunging into the darkness.

'What is it, Clinker?' asked Sunroof. 'Trouble?'

Clinker pulled off his sou'wester to reveal a cunning face, sallow with years of dirt. He sniffed and poured himself a mug of tea from the big brown pot which stood on the floor. He kicked the rags again, not hurrying with his answer.

'We found this creeping about near the Roundhouse,' he said at last. 'We didn't like the look of it so we duffed it up and then brought it in to show you. He's been moaning a lot; must be hurt.'

Twilight, who was nearest, knelt by the unconscious captive and examined him closely. 'I don't recognize the bloke,' he said. 'Give us a wet cloth, someone, and I'll try to wipe a bit of the dirt off his mush.'

Bingo got to his feet and dipped a lump of cotton waste in a bucket of water and then handed it to Twilight who began, gently, to wipe the mud-covered countenance. Knocker and Napoleon came and stood behind the Bangladeshi and gazed down.

Suddenly Napoleon swore: 'Bloody Nora,' he said, 'it's Scooter, that's who that is. This could mean that all the dwarfs in creation are after us . . . and the SBG not far behind. I told you we should have killed him.'

There was consternation in the room and everyone reached for a catapult. One or two of the Borribles even pulled on their waterproofs, ready to run for it.

Chalotte did not panic. She pushed Napoleon aside and bent over the injured dwarf. 'Leave it out, Nap,' she said, 'and just have a butcher's at these ears of his. The plastic ones are gone remember, you pulled 'em off, and the others've stopped bleeding now, see, and they're even more pointed than they were the day before yesterday.'

Even the deep doubts of the untrusting Wendle were tempered a little by this evidence, but he said nothing.

Vulge did: 'Look at that,' he cried. 'His ears are almost as pointed as ours.'

'He looks like a Borrible to me,' said Sunroof, squinting down from the edge of the group that now surrounded the prisoner.

Knocker stared at Chalotte. 'He's right,' he said. 'If he ain't a Borrible quite yet he's certainly becoming one, and we all know that's not possible.'

Napoleon pushed his way forward. 'Plastic surgery,' he said. 'You know Sussworth would stop at nothing to get a spy back in with us.' He knelt and fingered the dwarf's ears. 'I don't know,' he continued eventually. 'How can we tell, we're not medical experts. They can do fantastic things these days. They have heart transplants, kidneys, lungs, even arms . . . all that. Why not ears?'

'Don't be daft,' said Chalotte. 'There'd still be a scar this close to an operation. The ears are changing because he's becoming a Borrible. I'm sure of it.'

'It happened to us all, once, a long time ago,' said Stonks.

'Yeah,' said Napoleon, 'of course it did, but we were kids then; it only happens to kids. This bleeder is a dwarf, a midget, small like us but he's an adult, he's normal.'

'I don't know,' said Knocker, thinking hard, his brow creasing. 'Perhaps what Coco was joking about earlier is possible. Perhaps even normal people, if they want to become Borribles hard enough, will become Borribles. Who knows? Lots of things that we think impossible are possible, I bet.'

'What about Ninch then?' said Napoleon, screwing his face up tight and hard. 'He stayed with us long enough and it don't seem to have made him all sweetness and light, does it?'

'That's because he's interested in money,' said Chalotte. 'That's the difference.'

There was a groan from the figure on the floor, then another, a deeper longer one. Scooter's eyes flickered in his mask of mud and the tip of his tongue tried to moisten his lips. He coughed and his eyes flickered once more and stayed open. He smiled up at Chalotte.

'Hello,' he said. 'I knew I'd find you. Have you seen my ears? I'm one of you now.'

Chalotte nodded. 'We've seen 'em,' she answered. 'In fact we've never seen anything like 'em.'

'Wait a minute,' interrupted Napoleon. 'You should be back on the other side of King's Cross. We told the Conkers to take you with them or keep a guard on you. What happened?'

Scooter lifted himself on one elbow and looked up at the ring of faces above him. 'They did guard me,' he said. 'Took me to some other block of flats just after you left, but they saw my ears changing and said it wasn't their job to guard a Borrible who hadn't done any harm, so they let me go.'

'There,' said Bingo. 'That proves something.'

'Yeah,' sneered Napoleon, 'it proves that them Conker guards have got more trust than sense. "Never trust anyone until you have to and then not much," that's what the proverb says.'

'How's the shoulder?' asked Chalotte.

'Stiff,' said Scooter, 'very stiff, but I'm getting better. I'm well enough to come with you now, honest. Don't leave me behind again . . .' And even as he spoke the dwarf's eyes glazed over and his head dropped backwards to the floor.

Knocker bent and grabbed Scooter under the arms. 'Take his feet, Bingo,' he said, 'and we'll get him warm and dry. He's not well at all, whatever he says.'

Scooter was placed on one of the long bus seats and made comfortable. His wet clothes were exchanged for dry ones and Chalotte examined the dwarf's wound. It was red and badly inflamed. She looked at Strikalite. 'We need some disinfectant.'

Chevvy was in earshot, his raincoat already on. 'I'll get you what you need,' he said. 'There's a first-aid box in the scrap men's lean-to. That'll do nicely.' He jerked his head just once and left.

'Good,' said Chalotte. 'Now we'd better get some food into this bloke. Someone heat the soup while I swab down this gash in his shoulder.'

Scooter opened his eyes again. 'I'd like some food,' he said. 'Don't leave me behind. I promise you I'm really well enough to come with you.'

'Oh yeah,' said Napoleon, who had not left the vicinity of the dwarf since he had been brought into the bus. 'What about your dwarf chums and their reward? Are you sure you weren't followed?'

Scooter answered directly, staring straight at Napoleon, his eyes feverish but the honesty burning through the grime on his face. 'No one followed me,' he said. 'I took damn good care of that. I'm a Borrible now.' And with this remark the dwarf closed his eyes and fell into the deep sleep of exhaustion.

Knocker took Chalotte's elbow and moved her away from the bed. 'What do you think?' he asked.

The girl shrugged. 'We don't know everything, even about Borribles,' she said. 'For the time being I'm going to believe his story.'

'Huh,' snorted Napoleon. 'All right, I admit the ears look kosher, but Aristotle Rule, okay. He's got to be watched and guarded until we're positively sure.'

At this point the door sprang open and another gust from the night blew Chevvy back into the bus. Under his arm he carried a small white first-aid box and he handed it to Chalotte, but he did so automatically. He looked worried.

'I've been talking to some of the lookouts,' he said. 'They say there's something dodgy going on. They're not quite sure what but there's some reports of some little fellers coming into the yard . . . a couple of dozen maybe. Borrible-size they reckon, probably them dwarfs you told us about. They must be looking for you and the horse.'

'The dwarfs,' said Napoleon. 'I told you this bloody Scooter was a traitor. Medicines! There's only one medicine he needs.' The Wendle clenched his fists.

'There's no time for that now,' said Strikalite. 'We can do that after. We'd better get our gear on and find these dwarfs and kick 'em out.'

'It's not the dwarfs so much,' said Napoleon, 'but wherever they are the SBG won't be far behind.'

There was a noise from Scooter's bed at this and he sat up. His eyes were staring straight in front of him and his lips were dry.

'He's delirious,' said Chalotte.

The dwarf ignored her. 'No,' he said. 'Not the SBG, only Ninch. He wants the reward all to himself; he won't tell the police if he thinks he can get the reward all to himself. No SBG this time . . . SBG next time.'

Chalotte rushed over to the dwarf and forced him to lie down. Then she took the disinfectant from the first-aid box and poured some of it over his wound. 'I hope this isn't too late,' she said. 'He looks very ill to me; we'll have to get a doctor to look at him.'

Napoleon put on his waterproofs and made his catapult ready. He jerked a thumb at Scooter. 'Aristotle Rule,' he said. 'Who stays with him?'

'I will,' said Chalotte. 'He needs to be looked after anyway.'

'And I will stay with you,' said Sydney. 'Two is safer than one if we should be attacked. I can get the horse ready as well; we might have to make a break for it.'

'Good,' said Napoleon. He turned to Strikalite. 'This is your patch,' he said. 'How shall we do this?'

The Scrapper counted his troops. 'There's eight of you and about thirty of us not already on watch. You split into three groups and then ten of us will come with each of your groups. We'll spread out, our sentries will point us in the right direction.'

Sunroof buttoned up his coat and tipped his sou'wester down over his eyes. 'We'll get 'em,' he said. 'It's a funny place at night, here.'

Torreycanyon pulled on a borrowed pair of wellies. 'I believe you,' he said. 'I really do.'

*

Outside the night was swirling and pressing down on the earth like a hundred fathoms of ocean. A gritty cloud rolled low over the leaning vehicle stacks and filled the ill lit streets and alleys of the scrapyard with shreds of mist. The wind butted and pushed every way it could, like some ruffian. The high towers of rubbish swayed and groaned like the towers of a drowned city. Black shapes glided across the shadows, their limbs moving in slow motion. Pale fish-like faces floated up at the windows of the broken cars and then disappeared. It would be hard work that night to distinguish friend from foe.

Napoleon blinked the rain from his eyes; the mud sucked at his feet. Behind him marched Knocker, peering to right and left in the gloom; behind came Strikalite and Sunroof and two or three other Scrappers. The rest of the Adventurers and all their groups were somewhere else, out of contact, cut off.

Napoleon swore to himself. 'Where's them midgets?' he said. 'Where are they?'

His question was answered as he rounded a corner and came face to face with five dwarfs, all of whom turned and ran at the very moment the Wendle appeared. 'Follow me,' cried Napoleon without the slightest hesitation, and he rushed after the enemy without even waiting for Knocker to come up with him. Napoleon wanted Ninch.

Knocker was completely taken aback by his friend's sudden departure but set off in close pursuit, shouting a warning as he ran. 'Watch out!' he yelled. 'It may be a trap.'

And so it was.

Napoleon, running with Wendle expertise through the sticking mud, soon began to gain on the dwarfs but in doing so he also began to outdistance Knocker while Strikalite and Sunroof and the rest of the Scrappers were left far behind. In no time at all Napoleon was on his own, way ahead and only dimly perceived by his companions.

When the dwarfs were convinced that Napoleon was isolated they halted their flight, turned and stood their ground, ready to attack their pursuer. They had made a serious mistake. Anyone who knew the Wendle well and knew something of his history, would have known that odds of five to one were the kind of odds that he thought fair, or even slightly weighted in his favour.

Napoleon's pace did not slacken and he fired his catapult as he ran. First one dwarf went down with a stone in his midriff, then another dropped with a smashed cheekbone. Still Napoleon charged, raising his voice in a fearsome Wendle battle cry that rang and echoed round the empty cars. At the last he dived through the air, flying horizontally, butting one dwarf unconscious with his head and punching another in the throat as he dived. The last surviving dwarf, unnerved by this turn of events, made no attempt to assist his allies but was off like a shot. Ten yards was all he covered. Before he could go any further Napoleon was back on his feet and had dropped the fugitive with a well-placed stone in the middle of the shoulder blades. By the time Knocker arrived Napoleon was leaning against a car and scraping the mud from his clothes with the end of his catapult.

'Any trouble?' asked Knocker, panting.

'Nothing much,' said Napoleon. He smiled like a slab of cement. 'Just as well you didn't get here earlier; there wasn't enough for both of us.'

Knocker counted the five casualties. 'I'm glad you're on my side,' he said.

It was then that the trap was sprung; the five dwarfs had done their job admirably. Their role had been to entice Napoleon and Knocker to this spot and they had succeeded. While the two Borribles were deciding what to do next there was a shout above their heads and dwarfs began to appear from all around.

Knocker loaded his catapult and Napoleon followed suit. 'This is more like it,' he said.

'It's no joke,' retorted Knocker. 'They've been waiting for us; there's loads of them up top.'

'Shout for the others,' suggested Napoleon. 'This lot won't be so brave with a few more Borribles here.'

Knocker threw back his head and yelled, but assistance was not quick in coming and Napoleon and Knocker found themselves in deep danger. Worse, they had hardly a target to fire at. In the dark they could catch only glimpses of their enemy, yet all around them they could hear the scrabbling of feet and hands as dwarfs climbed down and through the cars, crawling nearer and nearer.

'Back to back,' said Knocker.

Now hands were pulling and tugging at the Borribles, trying to separate them, trying to drag them away into captivity.

'A Borrible,' shouted Knocker, and fired a stone without aiming and heard a scream of pain. He reached for his torch and switched it on. He saw a face near to him but then his arm was struck with a metal bar and the torch dropped into the mud. Knocker lashed out with his fist and hit nothing; then something struck him a glancing blow on the forehead, something hard.

'They're throwing stuff down from above,' he said and staggered forward, losing contact with Napoleon, but Napoleon grabbed him by the collar and pulled him upright.

More things fell – a rain of junk falling through the real rain – nuts and bolts, steering wheels, clutch pedals, door handles, car seats and even headlight bulbs, exploding like cannon shot.

Knocker staggered again, blood trickling down his face from the wound on his head. Napoleon held him with his arm. He too was struck on the shoulder by something hard and sharp. 'We'll have to get into a car,' said the Wendle, suppressing a cry of pain. 'This is dirty work at the crossroads all right, and no mistake.'

The two Borribles dived into the nearest hulk. Napoleon struck out right, left and centre in the dark and there was the sound of bodies crawling out of the windows. He switched on his torch and shone it in a wide arc and the two Borribles saw faces all round them, in car after car, as far as the torch beam carried.

Napoleon turned the light out. 'Best not to see all that,' he said philosophically. 'You take this side, I'll take the other side. If anything moves, hit it.'

At this moment there was a concerted attack on the Borribles' shelter and more missiles clanked down; a large bolt flew unseen through a window and struck Napoleon in the small of the back. He snatched it up and used it as a weapon, striking into the darkness with very good effect. 'A Wendle! A Wendle!' he yelled at every blow.

At long last the call for help was answered. Torches shone in the roadway outside and the dwarfs retreated. They shouted to one another and climbed upwards, regrouping on the roofs of the topmost cars. A beam of light dazzled Knocker and Napoleon. 'Are you all right?' said a voice. It was Stonks.

'Where've you been?' asked Napoleon. 'We've had to do all the fighting.'

'Oh yeah,' said Stonks, and he lowered the beam. 'I must have been in some other punch-up then.'

Knocker crouched on the floor of the car and wiped the blood from his head. 'How many you brought with you?' he said. 'There's more dwarfs here than we thought.'

Stonks sniffed as a large chunk of metal rebounded off the side of the car. 'There's quite a lot, yeah,' he said, 'but they ain't very good. I mean they keep running away when you get close . . . I've got Torrey with me and Strikalite and some Scrappers outside.'

'Anyone seen Ninch, yet?' asked Napoleon. ''Cos if you do I want him for myself.'

As if in answer to Napoleon's question a voice roared down from a pile of cars on the far side of the roadway. It was the voice of Ninch. Napoleon and Knocker crawled out of their car and looked up, shielding their eyes against the rain. Two or three of the Scrapper torches searched the sky, looking for the chief dwarf. From not too far away, maybe a hundred yards or so, came the sound of more fighting, at least two or three different battles.

Ninch's voice roared again. 'You might as well give up, you lot down there. I've got you surrounded. You won't get out of this one.'

Knocker could feel Napoleon throbbing with anger. The Wendle stepped into the open, leaving the shelter of the overhanging cars. He shook his fist above his head and shouted at the dwarf, even though he was not visible. 'Come down, Ninch,' he bawled. 'Come down here you stunted pygmy, you undersized shrimp. Come down and I'll fillet yer.'

'I don't have to fight with you, mush,' cried Ninch. 'All I have to do is wrap you up and take you to Sussworth and that's what I'm going to do, one way or the other.'

Then another voice sounded from up above, a voice that was weak and twisted on the wind. 'No you won't, Ninch; it's not fair. You always complained at being treated different because you were a dwarf, so why are you treating them different because they're Borrible, eh? Why don't you leave 'em alone?'

Napoleon shone his torch upwards. 'Stroll on,' he said, 'that sounds like Scooter.'

Gradually more torches shone up into the falling rain as Scrapper reinforcements began to arrive on the scene, their battles won. There were other groups of them travelling across the roofs of the cars too, and soon the Borribles would no longer be outnumbered. Orococco, Twilight and Vulge came and stood by Knocker and Napoleon; they also stared into the sky.

Ninch did not answer for a moment. He had thought his fellow acrobat at the bottom of the canal; but he did not remain surprised and silent for long. After a while he spoke and moved into sight, just visible on the edge of a teetering pile of cars. 'So,' sneered the dwarf, 'you're still alive, Borrible-lover. Well I shall have to hand you over to Sussworth as well, won't I? You fool!'

As Ninch finished speaking there was movement in a car at the top of a stack a little further down the road. Some torch beams swung over and showed Scooter climbing, with great difficulty, out of a window and on to the top of the topmost car. Once there he got to his feet and stood in the pelting rain, swaying in the wind and clutching his wounded shoulder. Someone had provided him with a raincoat several sizes too large, and the stubborn wind had almost blown it from his body for it streamed out from his arms like a ragged banner.

'Listen to me,' cried Scooter, shouting against the wind. 'Listen to me, dwarfs. Don't do what you are doing. The Borribles have done you no harm and they mean no harm. They are not murderers like Sussworth says. If only you'd—'

Ninch interrupted this speech with a scream of anger. 'Rubbish!' he yelled. 'Rubbish! Don't believe him. The Borribles are thieves and murderers; the reward for them is enormous. Scooter is a turncoat, a traitor. Don't believe a word he says.'

More torches shone on Ninch now and in the light of them he jumped the gap that separated him from the next pile of cars, and then the next, and the torch beams followed him, and Knocker and the others saw him land close to Scooter and the cars swayed and rocked with the force of his landing.

'Stop him!' cried a voice. 'He'll kill Scooter.' Knocker looked to his right and there was Chalotte with no raincoat, her hair flat to her skull, her clothes drenched, her face drawn with anguish.

As soon as he was within reach Ninch began striking Scooter about the head with all his might, beating him into silence. Scooter was too weak to defend himself. He raised his good arm to ward off the blows and stumbled backwards. He slipped, nearly fell and yet somehow he managed to scramble away from Ninch and on to another pile of cars. But Ninch followed, determined, intent on Scooter's death, trying to push his one-time friend from the heights down to the mud below.

Chalotte pulled her catapult. 'Do something,' she cried, and she fired and fired and Knocker and Napoleon and all the others on the ground did the same. But the shot, though not distant, was a difficult one, the torchlight uncertain, the wind and rain strong, and the stones that reached the dwarf only did so with a feeble power and Ninch did not notice them.

At last a band of Scrappers climbed to the top levels on the opposite side of the road to Ninch and threatened him closely with their catapults and he was struck, once or twice, more forcibly from there.

Ninch realized his danger and leapt back out of harm's way. Scooter collapsed unconscious, incapable of any more resistance. Then Ninch called his dwarfs to him and had them maintain a fierce barrage of junk while he and some others kicked and pushed at the car on which Scooter lay.

This car, only lightly balanced on top of its pile, rocked and began to slip. More dwarfs lent a hand and the whole edifice started shifting. The Adventurers, ignoring the missiles that were falling about their heads and shoulders, began to climb hand over hand through a different stack of cars. They fired their catapults whenever they could but the dwarfs kept under cover, and all the time the tower that bore the defenceless Scooter rocked and swayed more violently.

'Dammit, dammit, dammit,' hissed Napoleon as he clambered upwards, cutting his hands, scraping his knees. 'That bloody Ninch.'

But when Napoleon and the others emerged at the summit a wide canyon still separated them from the enemy, and even those Scrappers who were on the right side of the road were having a hard time getting anywhere near Ninch because he was protected by so many dwarfs.

The Adventurers advanced to the edge of the canyon and stared through the eddying squalls of rain. They could see where Scooter lay, sprawled on his back, the storm beating down on his bloodless face. Napoleon fired his catapult at Ninch but the wind bore the stone away. 'Hey, you,' roared the Wendle. 'You harm that Scooter and I swear I'll kill you, if it's the last thing I ever do.'

Ninch never heard the threat, not only because of the wind but also because at that very moment the car he was pushing slid from the top of its pile, and with an awful grinding and clashing of metal against metal plunged to the ground below, carrying Scooter with it.

Chalotte could not believe what she had seen. She lowered her head into her hands and a cry of dismay rose from deep in her throat. 'Oh the madness,' she moaned, 'the madness of it.'

There was worse to come. With the weight of one vehicle removed, the pile which had supported it lost its equilibrium and began to buckle in the middle, finally toppling over in an avalanche of crumpled steel sheet. The cars in the piles to right and left, no longer held in position, slid sideways, and with more clanging and clatter they collapsed like tower blocks in an earthquake. Windscreens burst and showered diamonds of glass like fountains into the air; exhaust pipes bent and fractured and doors sprang open. A huge section of the scrapyard had slumped over and buried itself in the mud.

The dwarfs cheered and shouted in triumph. Ninch raised his arms and clasped his hands above his head like a heavyweight champion. 'There,' he bellowed into the wind. 'I'm leaving yer now . . . but I'll be back and next time we'll get yer!' With that defiance Ninch began to scramble away over the wet roofs and beneath him, in the citadel of wrecks, his followers crawled from car to car and went after him.

The shock of the avalanche had rippled everywhere and the Adventurers felt the tower where they stood begin to sway and tremble. They moved fast and fled from those treacherous peaks, working their way down to the safety of ground level, where they knew there was much to be done if Scooter was to be rescued. Everything was in chaos and confusion with many cars overturned and others on their sides. It was a dangerous jumble of scrap and every edge of metal was jagged and razor-sharp.

But the Borribles did not falter; there was no time. Strikalite organized the Scrappers immediately, sending most of them in hot pursuit of the dwarfs to make sure they left the yard, but also to put paid to some of them, if possible. The remainder of the tribe, together with the Adventurers, began to look for Scooter, or as Napoleon said, 'What might be left of him.'

The Borribles had a hard time of it. They slipped and slithered over the fallen vehicles, which see-sawed and lurched under their weight. Their torches stabbed the darkness. They pushed their heads through shattered windows and splintered windscreens; they cut their hands on triangles of rust and groped below the surface of the creeping mud where Scooter might lie drowning. The search went on and on, more desperate by the minute, until at last Chalotte found him, his legs sticking out from the underside of a wreck, pathetic, like the legs of a squashed frog.

'Over here,' called Chalotte, and the torches converged on her. 'I hope this is him; I can't be sure.'

Stonks looked down. 'If he's under this car,' he said, 'he'll have suffocated.'

'I recognize his shoes,' said Bingo. 'Hurry!'

'Get along the side of the car, everyone,' Stonks ordered, taking charge. 'Now, get a hold of something and we'll try and lift it. When we do that, Chalotte, you pull him out.'

Stonks bent his knees and took a firm grip on the roof of the upside-down car. His companions did the same and on the word of command they heaved upward with their arms and pushed downward with their legs. The strain was terrifying and the face of every Borrible bulged and turned red with the effort.

'Up, damn you, up!' shouted Stonks, and the strongest Borrible of all heaved and pushed and swore and every Scrapper and every Adventurer there did the same. At last, when it seemed that the car would never move, it did, slowly, just an inch or two with a slow sucking sound as it came free of the mud. Chalotte crouched and eased the body out into the open and a huge bubble of air came up with it.

'I'm in the clear,' she shouted when she was, and after one more second Stonks gave the word and the car was allowed to sink back into position.

Chalotte knelt on the ground and held Scooter's head in one hand and tried to scrape the mud from his face with the other. 'Is he still breathing?' she asked.

Stonks bent and slipped an arm beneath the dwarf's shoulders. 'Take his feet, someone,' he said. 'Let's get him out of the rain.'

The sagging body was half carried and half dragged to the nearest steady car and laid gently along its back seat. Chalotte squeezed into the small space that was left and continued cleaning the battered face with a bit of rag that Stonks had discovered. The rest of the Adventurers poked their heads through the window spaces; the Scrappers kept watch.

'Is it him?' asked Knocker.

'Yes,' answered Chalotte, 'it's him but I think he's dead.' She wiped Scooter's ears with the rag. 'The only adult who ever turned into a Borrible and he has to go and die. Sod's law.'

'Sussworth's,' said Knocker.

Chalotte tipped Scooter's head back and placed her mouth over his mouth; she exhaled and Scooter's chest rose and fell abruptly. His eyelids fluttered.

'He's alive,' said Stonks.

Scooter opened his eyes and looked up at Chalotte. The rain beat down on the roof of the car. 'I'm sorry,' he said. His voice was a broken whisper. 'I thought I could get him to stop, get him to leave the other side and join us . . . but it's the reward . . . It's made him mad.'

'Don't talk,' said Chalotte. 'We'll have to get you out of here, look after you, get you somewhere safe.'

Scooter's eyes closed with pain, blood bubbled on his lips. 'It hurts, Chalotte,' he said, 'inside. I feel bad.'

Chalotte lowered her head to her chest so that Scooter should not see her tears. Napoleon turned his back and stared into the weather. 'What can we do?' he said to Knocker. 'I'm not good at this.'

Knocker shook his head, pale. 'I dunno,' he said. 'I dunno.'

Scooter's eyes opened again. He looked round the windows of the car at the Adventurers, a yellow frieze of austere faces lit from underneath by their own torches. 'How are my ears, eh?' he said, and a pallid smile touched his mouth. A drop of rain fell from the roof and splashed on his face and Chalotte leant her body forward to take the drops on her back. She touched his ears gently.

'They're fine,' she said. 'You have two of the finest ears I have ever seen . . . better than Knocker's, better than Napoleon's even.' She wanted so much to cry but she held back.

Now Scooter's face shone with a bright smile. 'That's good,' he said. 'That's really good.' His breath rattled in his throat. 'I never would have gone in with Ninch, you know, at the beginning, if I'd known about Borribles.'

Suddenly Scooter let out a cry of pain and sat bolt upright, his eyes wide open but seeing nothing. 'I'm glad I'm a Borrible,' he cried with a voice that came from a hundred miles away. 'I'll never grow old now, never!' Then a ball of blood burst at his lips and coloured his teeth bright crimson and he fell into Chalotte's arms like an old limp sack, half full of sand.

Chalotte cradled the head in her arms and wiped the blood from the face. 'Turn out the torches,' she said. 'I don't want to see.' She began to cry then, properly; not with a lot of noise but with a lot of tears.

One by one the torches were extinguished and the Adventurers stood unmoving, their hands by their sides. They said nothing until at last Knocker could bear the sound of weeping no longer, and it was not Chalotte alone who was weeping. Knocker could feel the tears on his own face; Stonks shook his head and his face was wet and not with rain alone. Napoleon, Orococco, Twilight, Bingo, Vulge and Torreycanyon, a great grief had seized them all. A brand new Borrible had died.

Knocker took a deep breath and tried to make his voice firm. 'That Ninch,' he said. 'That Ninch. I promise you by every Borrible oath that ever was, by every adventure we've ever been through, I'll live to see that Ninch dead.'

'And me,' said Napoleon.

'And me,' said Stonks.

'I'm next,' said Twilight.

Chalotte groaned and lifted her head. 'No,' she said. 'Can't you understand? It's what I said. It's this fighting makes us do things which aren't Borrible. If there hadn't been a Rumble hunt we wouldn't be here now. I want to go home. We all want to go home.'

Knocker ducked into the car and eased Scooter's body from Chalotte's grasp and Stonks leant inside and helped him pass it through the window. Then the Adventurers joined hands in pairs and Stonks laid the body along their arms and they bore it away. Knocker remained in the car with Chalotte, next to her on the seat. He touched her shoulder.

'Come on,' he said. 'Let us leave this bloody place. We'll soon be home. Try to remember the good things. Scooter became a Borrible. He showed us something we couldn't have believed if we hadn't seen it with our own eyes . . . That's important, very important. Who knows what it may mean?'

Chalotte shook her head. 'This needn't have happened,' she said. 'It was my fault. If I'd been sensible Scooter would never have got out of the bus. I mean after you left, to look for the dwarfs. You see, he came round, wasn't delirious any more. I told him what had happened and he got up; he seemed all right. He put on a raincoat and said he could talk to Ninch; tell him what was right, tell him what was wrong. How being a Borrible was better than working for Sussworth, or working for anybody.'

'It wasn't your fault,' said Knocker. 'There's no such thing as fault between friends. You couldn't know what was going to happen.'

Chalotte shook her head again; her eyes were swollen but dry now. 'I knew he wasn't well enough to go out. It was just that I believed that if he could stop the fighting, if we could make Ninch change his mind, turn him into a Borrible even, well, I thought it was worth a try . . . Anything to put a stop to this nonsense.'

'It *was* worth a try,' said Knocker. 'Scooter obviously thought so.'

'And when he heard the shouts, "A Borrible, a Borrible," there was no holding him, "I'm a Borrible now," he said. "I'm a Borrible and no Borrible should ignore the call from another Borrible." He wanted to save us all, you see.'

Chalotte's voice faltered and stopped there; she could not go on. At the same time Napoleon Boot returned and thrust his head through a window space.

'We've buried him,' he said, the harshness of his tones belied by the moisture in his eyes. He ducked his head, meaning to go, but stopped and looked at Chalotte.

Napoleon Boot had never been known to apologize to anyone, but he did that night, the first and only time. 'That Scooter,' he said, 'I was wrong about him. He was a true Borrible, one of the best.' And then Napoleon went red in the face and pulled his head from the car.

Knocker scratched his chin. 'I never thought I'd see the day when I'd hear Nap say something like that,' he said. 'It proves you were right, about Scooter changing things I mean.'

This sentiment touched Chalotte and made her smile. 'Yes, Knocker, we've all changed. You have, certainly,' she said. 'We can't stay here, can we? We'd better get a move on.' She half stood and began to edge her way into the open.

Napoleon was waiting for them outside. He jerked a thumb over his shoulder. 'The others have gone to get our stuff together. The Scrappers are making sure that Ninch and his mob have left, but one thing's for sure: Ninch will go for the SBG now. The sooner we're on the road the better I'll like it.'

Chalotte shone her torch and looked around her at the wrecked cars, the trampled mud, the sifting rain. 'I'll never forget this place,' she said. 'It feels like all the roads of London conspired to bring us here.' She shut off her torch and looked at Napoleon. 'Where did you bury him?'

Napoleon blinked. He looked tired, like he hadn't slept for a week. 'We just dug a hole in the ground behind the bus; we put a long bus seat in the bottom to lay him out on, then covered him with an old tarpaulin we found and then we shovelled in the mud. There wasn't anything else we could do.

Chalotte took a deep breath. 'Yes,' she said, 'I know.'

11

The others were waiting at the most westerly of the exits. This was not the main gateway as used by the scrap men; that was more to the south and under a railway line; it was a Borrible exit and only just big enough to lead Sam through.

The Adventurers stood in a huddle by the fence, the horse with them. The encounter with the dwarfs and the killing of Scooter had made them nervous and dispirited. Just when they had been looking forward to a long night of rest they had been called out in the wind and rain to do battle and see death. Now, once again, they were no longer safe; they had to march on, through the night, they knew not where. They glanced up as Knocker, Napoleon and Chalotte approached. Every noise made them jump, every gust of wind made them look over their shoulders.

Strikalite was crouching in the shelter of a car with Sunroof and Chevvy. He whistled at Knocker and the other two and they went over to him.

'I've got your haversacks,' he said, holding them up. 'All your stuff's ready.'

'What are you going to do?' asked Knocker. 'Supposing the SBG come after yer; they're bound to, you know.'

Strikalite shrugged. 'It's very difficult to search a scrapyard,' he said. 'I mean we could hide you easy if it weren't for the horse. We've got emergency shelters underground. If that don't work we'll just take off somewhere for a few days. We can always come back after.'

'Where are all the others?' asked Chalotte. 'I don't see anyone.'

'They're all on lookout,' said Strikalite, 'just in case Old Bill tries to creep up on us. If they comes within two mile of here I'll know it in a second.'

'We're not worried about us,' interrupted Sunroof. 'It's you and the horse that's the problem.'

'Yeah,' said Knocker, glancing to where his friends waited with Sam, 'and once we get off this railway property it starts being posh going westwards; not many empty houses or schools. I don't know what to do.'

'I've got a bit of a plan,' said Strikalite. 'When you get out of this yard you'll find the railway line from Liverpool Street over on your right. Follow that through Primrose Hill station . . .' He glanced at his watch. 'There'll be no one there at four in the morning. After another half-mile the line goes into a tunnel, and when it comes out the other end it goes under another line, northbound, coming up from Marylebone. Follow that and after a while that goes into a tunnel too, then it bears due west, alongside the Metropolitan and Bakerloo lines . . . and guess where it goes?'

'Wandsworth Bridge,' said Napoleon.

'Leave off. No. It goes through West Hampstead, Kilburn, Willesden Green, Dollis Hill and then . . .'

'Yes?' said Knocker.

'Neasden,' said Strikalite. 'It's a pushover. You could probably make Kilburn by morning and find somewhere to hide; it's not posh there.'

Chalotte looked at Knocker. 'I don't see what other chance we've got,' she said. 'Sussworth can't watch all the railways as well as all the roads. Especially if he's still chasing the Conkers and all them horses up on Hampstead Heath.'

'I think you'll do it,' said Strikalite, and he stood up and came out of the car. Sunroof and Chevvy followed him. Once outside Strikalite removed his yellow sou'wester and handed it to Chalotte. 'It's not much,' he said. 'It's just to remind you to come back this way . . . But if I don't see you again, well, have a good life.'

Chalotte dragged her own woollen hat from her head and gave it to Strikalite in return. 'And you take mine,' she said. 'That'll remind you of us and what happened here. We'll be seein' yer.'

Then it was time to go. Hands were shaken, promises made and wishes that no one would ever get caught were exchanged. Sooner than they had wanted the Adventurers found themselves alone and back on the road, a road it seemed they had been tramping for ever. They were weary in their hearts of running away from Sussworth and doubted if they could go much further. Fear of the SBG and loyalty to Sam were the only things that kept them steadfast.

*

Beyond the scrapyard it was murky and the ground was uneven, but at least the rain had stopped for a while. The line of march was decided on and Stonks and Torreycanyon scouted ahead while Napoleon and Bingo brought up the rear. Out on the flanks were Orococco and Twilight, and Sydney led the horse, leaving the rest of the party to walk alongside her.

As they advanced, two main railway lines came from either side and converged to form a single permanent way. The Borribles grouped themselves closer together and followed the track right up to Primrose Hill station.

The station, when they got there, just as Strikalite had said, was utterly deserted. The signals were still, the waiting rooms closed and not a lamp shone anywhere. The Borribles stole by, the platforms higher than their heads, Sam treading delicately between the wooden sleepers.

A little further on, maybe a hundred yards or so, the railway line entered a cutting, dug deep into the ground behind the blind backs of two parallel rows of tall and distinguished houses. Windows loomed high over the Borribles but no lights came on, no one shouted down from the garden walls and not a car moved on the tarmac of the roads nearby.

Now the darkness was strong and terrible, like something malignant that had been growing for a hundred years, undisturbed. It grew stronger too as the Adventurers approached the tunnel which drove into the earth here below Primrose Hill, and it flooded their eyes and brains as if it wanted to make them blind for ever. 'We're not going in there, are we?' asked Twilight, and he removed his hat and ran a nervous hand through his ragged hair. 'Look, even Sam don't like it.'

It was true. Sam's legs had gone stiff and he was tugging back against the rein that Sydney held in her hand. He blew through his nostrils and whinnied with fear and the Adventurers became rooted to the spot.

Fortunately Napoleon Boot suffered from no such apprehensions about dark tunnels and he soon got his friends on the move again, pushing his way through from the rearguard. 'Blimey,' he sneered, 'what's up wi' yer? Are you the same lot who went across the Wandle with me? Come on, you bunch of fairies.' And with this insult the Wendle spat into the air and, without waiting to see if he was being followed, marched into the tunnel and was instantly engulfed in blackness.

Knocker hitched his rucksack higher up on his shoulders. 'Well,' he said, 'we have no option now.' And with a word of encouragement to Sam he advanced in Napoleon's footsteps and the remainder of the Adventurers went after him, Sydney last of all, pulling the reluctant horse behind her.

It was a long march and the Adventurers advanced at a snail's pace. Now that they felt protected from any immediate danger the tension within them lessened, and they began to realize just how weary they were; how scratched and cut they had been by the sharp metal edges on the cars in the scrapyard, how stiff and sore from the battle with Ninch's dwarfs. They rested frequently, the rucksacks became heavier. They stumbled on the rails, they tripped over the sleepers.

This progress was not good enough for Knocker and he tried to hurry everyone along. He became more and more anxious and looked at his watch every few minutes.

'We must hurry,' he kept repeating. 'If we can get to Kilburn before daylight we might find some Borribles to hide us. All the rest of it round here is more Rumble than anything else.'

His bullying and cajoling achieved little. Only Napoleon seemed to have any energy left – forging ahead and returning every now and then to tell his companions that the way was clear – but on one of these occasions his message was different. 'Turn out your torches,' he said. 'There's something odd in the distance and I don't know what it is. Better walk as quietly as you can.'

With the torches extinguished it was possible to see what Napoleon had seen. Far, far in the distance a light was twinkling, a golden light. Not an electric lamp by the look of it, but more like the light of a burning fire.

'I don't reckon this,' the Wendle continued. 'What's a fire doing inside a tunnel, eh? Answer me that.'

Stealthily the Borribles crept forward and the fire grew larger and brighter as they approached it. There was no doubt, finally, that it was a fire, but in the other respect Napoleon had been mistaken. The fire was not in the tunnel at all; it was further on.

As soon as he reached the open air Napoleon stopped and waited for the rest of the Adventurers to come up with him. While he waited he looked into the sky and saw that the solid darkness was fading. What had been black before was now only dark blue. It was not dawn yet, but a new day was rolling in from the far side of the earth and would not be long in coming to Swiss Cottage.

One by one the Borribles gathered together. Just in front of them, above their heads almost, was a huge bridge carrying the northbound track from Marylebone. That was the line that Strikalite had told them to follow next. The lines that issued from the Borribles' tunnel ran directly underneath this bridge and, passing through the brightness of the fire, were swallowed up in the deep shadow that lay in the direction of South Hampstead station. The fire itself was not large, a small campfire only, burning energetically underneath the bridge and to one side, at the mouth of a small alcove. Someone was sitting in that alcove, warming their hands.

'Something nasty there,' said Napoleon, loading his catapult, 'just behind the fire, in the dark.'

'I can't see 'em,' said Twilight.

'Wendle eyes,' said Sydney. 'Is it a trap?'

A harsh cackle broke across the night and clanged about the tunnel entrance. Then a voice the Borribles recognized rose from the gloom in song:

'The fancy and fat-arsed businessmen
Oo thinks they own this town,
'Ave never a clue wot's owning them,
They don't know up from down.
I'll give 'em their office blocks, and stocks,
And all they love the best,
'Cos that isn't London – that's a pox,
It's Queenie owns the rest!'

At the end of the singing the cackle came once more, longer. 'There,' said the voice, 'I told you we'd meet again and ain't I right? Stripe me pink but ain't you the travellers? Real little 'splorers you are. Nearly as good as me, ain't yer? Tunnels and railways lines, learning all the tricks. Too smart for Old Bill you lot, far too smart by half, you are.'

Chalotte gasped. 'It's the Queen Mum,' she said. 'I'd recognize her anywhere.'

Reassured a little by this knowledge the Borribles went towards the light and stood in a half circle around the fire. On the other side of it, cheerfully drunk, reclining on the ground with all the regal aplomb of her namesake, her back against an upright girder and her pram within reach of her right hand, lay the dreadful tramp, the Queen Mum, her eyes reflecting the gold of the flames with an evil amusement.

'Well shiver me knickers,' she said. 'I thought you might turn up again. There ain't many ways across London when you don't want to be seen, is there?' She waved the bottle she held in her right hand and then tipped some of its contents into her throat. 'Ah,' she said, 'good for the bones that is.' She sniffed and then waved the bottle again.

'Well, I'll be paroled,' she went on. 'Is that an 'orse I see before me, or is it the dt's? You won't get far with that, will yer? I mean, the first copper who sees you walking along the street with an 'orse behind yer is likely to get slightly suspicious, ain't he, however daft he is. Unless you pretend it's an Irish Wolfhound or some'at, That 'orse can't bark by any chance, can he? That would be useful.'

The Borribles ignored these remarks, and sitting down near the warmth of the fire they began to eat some of the provisions they carried with them.

'What are you doing here, Queenie?' asked Napoleon, squinting in mistrust at the old woman as she swigged again at her bottle.

'Me?' said the Queen Mum looking down her nose. 'Me? Why shouldn't I be here? It's one of my places this is. Can't be seen from the road, protected from the rain. Been here ages already. Have to hide in this hole in the wall during the day though, seen by the trains else.' Suddenly her quick eyes went suspicious. 'Wait a minute, you can't stay here, nor that horse. No room in this alcove . . . Hang about, there's two of you missing, ain't there? Had their ears clipped 'ave they?'

'One's gone for ever,' said Chalotte.

'And the other's gone for a nark,' said Stonks.

'Swipe me,' said the Queen Mum. 'If that's the way of it I'll be off myself, today. They can't ask you questions if you ain't there, can they? That what I always say. This'll be a good time to nip off to Yorkshire, see me relatives, get me pram loaded with grub and booze . . . And you lot . . . what are you up to?'

'We have to go to Neasden,' answered Knocker. 'We only need to hide one more day; tomorrow night we'll make it, along the railway line.'

'That's right,' said the Queen Mum, scratching her curving chin and chewing with her toothless gums. 'About five or six miles from here, that's all.'

'It could be five hundred,' said Orococco, 'when Old Bill's after you.'

'Ain't that always the same?' said the Queen Mum. 'Someone ought to find them coppers a good hobby, keep them off the streets.'

She pushed her hand under her brown raincoat and pulled out a large round watch. 'Luminous dial,' she said. 'Used to belong to Madge. Well she don't need it now, by crikey she don't. She's got all the time in the world where she is.' The Queen Mum laughed briefly at her joke and stowed the watch away. 'No,' she said, and stopped laughing abruptly. 'You ain't got time to get there tonight. You've only just got time to hide . . . that horse is a problem.' She raised her bottle to her lips and the smell of spirit reached the Borribles. They shifted their feet awkwardly. The dark under the bridge was no longer so dark. They could see the Queen Mum clearly now and not because of the firelight either. They should be going, certainly. But where?

'We're wasting time,' said Knocker. 'We must hide.'

The bottle swished and disappeared into the pram. The Queen Mum wagged her finger at Knocker. 'Don't be so smart, chump,' she said. 'And where do you think you're going, eh?' She got to her feet and adjusted the rags and plastic she called clothes more comfortably around her body, hoisting her skirts and easing the undergarments in her crotch. 'That's better,' she announced and waggled her hips. 'Free and easy, that's me.'

'Come on,' said Napoleon. 'This is useless.'

'Up there,' continued the Queen Mum, ignoring the interruption and pointing above her head, 'is a footpath, by the side of the Marylebone line, as used by the platelayers, and it follows along and takes you right to another tunnel.'

Chalotte nodded. 'That's what Strikalite said.'

'Bugger Strikalite,' said the Queen Mum. 'Listen. That tunnel goes as far as Finchley Road station and also runs alongside the Metropolitan and Bakerloo tunnel, Swiss Cottage down to St John's Wood . . .'

'What's the use of all this?' said Napoloen. He jerked his thumb at the ever-lightening sky. 'We can't hide in a tunnel. We'd get electrocuted or run over.'

'Bugger me,' said the Queen Mum. 'Can't you belt up, you squeaky little fart! You'd get run over if you stayed in the main tunnel, but there's another, see, a connecting tunnel which joins one line to the other, so they can switch trains when there's accidents and blockages. So there.'

'So what?' said Napoleon.

'It ain't ever used, that tunnel,' said the Queen Mum, exasperated. 'And before you asks me how I know, nitwit, I'll tell you. It's another one of my places. I spent the winter of '81 in there, the whole winter. Fierce that winter was, twenty below, and no one bothered me and I never felt a pinch of cold. Like a tick in a rick.'

'All right,' said Knocker. It was his turn to be suspicious. 'Why are you telling us all this? You don't owe us any favours and you're an adult as well.'

'S'easy,' said the old woman. 'Because I don't want you caught by the coppers, do I? You want to get to Neasden and by crikey I want you to get to Neasden, safe and sound, never to be asked a single question by them as asks questions. I mean you know enough about me to have me put away for a year or two. I don't want to go to Holloway lock-up, now, do I? Warder, warder everywhere and never a drop to drink.'

Sydney stepped out from underneath the bridge and looked up at the sky, now a paler shade of blue. 'We haven't got any choice,' she said. 'Let her tell us.'

'I was going to anyway,' said the Queen Mum, and she began gathering her possessions together. 'Go into the tunnel for about half a mile. Then you'll see another tunnel going off to your right. That's it. Follow that a little way and it'll open into a double track; that's the London Transport bit that is. You'll see an old control cabin. They keeps a couple of standby trains there too, just in case like. Behind the control cabin is a kind of big square place in the wall, used to be a workshop or something, warm there. Big enough for you all, and the horse.'

'What happens if you go past the cabin?' asked Napoleon.

'You don't want to do that,' said the Queen Mum, 'or you'll be into Swiss Cottage Underground station, spotted for sure. No, you stay behind that control cabin, hide there during today, and come night you just follow the LMR line as far as Neasden. It's only five mile.'

'Only five mile,' said Sydney, and she stroked the horse's neck. 'Did you hear that, Sam? We'll be there by this time tomorrow.'

'Well,' said Knocker, addressing everyone, 'what shall we do?'

'What can we do,' said Stonks, 'but give it a try? Another half-hour and it'll be broad daylight.'

'Let alone the trains,' said the Queen Mum, 'they'll soon run yer down.' She grabbed her pram by the handle and began to drag it up a steep path that climbed by the side of the bridge up to the Marylebone line. 'Come on, I'll put you on the right road.'

The Borribles needed no more urging and followed the old tramp at once, hurrying under the threat of daylight, pushing the pram from behind. At the top of the path the Queen Mum took a series of deep breaths, wheezing and coughing, making a sound like two bricks being rubbed together. 'It's me lungs,' she explained between gasps. 'I ain't got the puff I used to 'ave.' She placed one hand on her chest while with the other she pointed, and the Borribles looked.

Not more than a hundred yards away they saw a new tunnel; above it rose the tall buildings of a housing estate and there were lights in the windows now. All the rest was in darkness.

'That's it,' said the Queen Mum, 'and count yourselves lucky I told yer. Nobody will find yer there.' She turned and began to push her pram along the path in the direction opposite to the one the Borribles were about to take.

''Ere,' said Napoleon, 'I'd feel safer if you were coming with us.'

The Queen Mum halted and smirked over her shoulder. 'I wouldn't,' she said. 'I want to be as far from you lot as possible. I've no idea how much the coppers know but if they do catch up with yer it won't take them long to get to the truth. On the other hand if they find me on my own I'm in the clear. I'm just a drunk old tramp making for Yorkshire . . . and that's 'ow I want it.' She winked and continued on her way.

The Borribles watched her until she disappeared and then they turned and walked towards the tunnel entrance. They had not slept all night, they were desperately tired and their heads throbbed. Time was running out. They must find the side tunnel that the Queen Mum had described before the first trains came and ran them down, smashing their bodies, and Sam's, to pieces.

Into the darkness they went but with no hesitation this time. Every Adventurer knew that their lives depended on the next few minutes. They marched on as fast as they could go, their ears cocked for the sound of the approaching train that would mean their doom.

The sound never came and things were just as the tramp had said. They found the disused tunnel leading off to their right and once in it they felt out of danger, but it was a dismal place and cast their spirits down. No one but the Queen Mum had passed that way for years.

Their torch beams showed long festoons of black dirt hanging from the arched roof. Their feet trod in six inches of dust, a dust as soft as soot and as fine as graphite. It covered the rusty railway lines making them invisible; it rose in the air as the Borribles marched by and made them sneeze and cough.

Before long the tunnel widened and the Borribles came to the control cabin as promised. Behind it was a wide square area – also thick in dust – that had once been used for a workshop. Nothing had been taken away; there were workbenches, lots of rusty tools, abandoned where they had fallen, piles of brick and sacks of cement, lights and light switches with no current running through them, but best of all there was a water tap that worked.

The control cabin was a solid rectangular hut constructed in the same dirty brick as the surface of the tunnel, and beyond it the cavern was less dilapidated and wider. It was this section that London Transport used, and standing there now, side by side on twin tracks, were two old Underground trains, pensioned off, each one six coaches long. And from beyond them, echoing in the distance, came the deep rumblings of the early morning commuter expresses as they passed through Swiss Cottage on their way to central London on the Stanmore line.

In the old days this emergency link section in which the Borribles had taken refuge had been busy, very busy. The control cabin itself had been a central command post for this part of the railway. Even now its walls were lined with bank upon bank of huge double-handed switches. There was a diagram of the track system of the Bakerloo line and there were telephones and emergency buttons, a table and a dozen chairs. Here too the thick black dust choked everything and made it sinister.

The Borribles peeled off their rucksacks and raincoats and set about making themselves as comfortable as they could behind the cabin, out of sight in the unlikely event of a party of workmen coming by. Most of the Adventurers were so exhausted that they could do no more than throw themselves on to the filthy ground and close their eyes, but there were others who found the chairs and placed them by the workbenches so that they would have somewhere to sit and eat the last of their provisions.

Knocker himself, exhausted, his feet and legs aching, collapsed on to his rucksack and sat with his back against a wall, elbows on knees and face cupped in his hands. He stared at the floor, thinking his own thoughts, nearly fainting with fright when he felt a hand on his shoulder, so taut were his nerves. He looked up to find Chalotte gazing down at him.

'What's the matter, Knocker?' she said.

'Hard to say,' he answered. 'I have this feeling that there's something out there, in the tunnels, something near, doing its best to see that we're caught and turned into catsmeat; and somehow I feel I can't do anything about it. It's a nightmare . . . It must be Scooter dying like that, it's made us all feel rotten.'

Chalotte shivered and looked around but could see nothing. She moved her hand from Knocker's shoulder and touched his hair. 'I hope you're wrong,' she said. 'After all we've been through I really hope you're wrong.'

*

After the great slaughterhouse battle Sussworth's caravan had been moved to a new location in Hampstead – the car park of the GPO sorting office on Rosslyn Hill.

The effect of the stampede on the inspector and his sergeant had been profound. Not only had their bodies been bruised and cut but their self-esteem had also taken a severe battering. Because of what they had undergone both men had become more determined than ever to make the Borribles pay for their audacity.

When dragged from beneath his patrol car, Inspector Sussworth had been insane with anger. At no one time in the whole of his life had so much dirt been so near him. He had trembled with wrath; his hands shaking uncontrollably and his feet banging the cobbles like two pneumatic drills. His men had stood with lowered heads as he berated them. He was unrecognizable; his twisted face twisted itself into straightness so demented was he. He screamed, he danced, he tried to tear the soiled clothes from his body, like a man possessed by devils. His whole being had been taken over by an extravagant fit of infernal ill temper. He frothed with disgust.

It was true that he'd had a great deal to froth about. His clothes had been torn by the sharp edges of the underneath of his car. He had lost his cap in the scrimmage and his hair, hands and face had been befouled with the mess, both solid and liquid, which the fleeing animals had sprayed everywhere. Sussworth had been scratched, buffeted and scared out of his wits.

But worse than all that he had suffered a total defeat. He had been made to look stupid, he was a laughing stock. At least four or five patrol cars had been smashed, their sides dented, their windows and windscreens shattered. The leather seats of his own car, where Hanks had taken refuge, had been torn into filthy rags by the sharp hooves of sheep and pigs. The stench of the dung heap was over everything – on his tunic, up his sleeves, in his trousers. It was more than he could stand, and he knew too that when news of this debacle reached the DAC he would be relieved of his command and Superintendent Birdlime would command the SBG.

With this thought of Birdlime the inspector had raised his voice in anguish, bellowing at his men, 'Get me out of here, you fools; take me away. I must get these clothes off. You idiots. I'll have you all back on push-bikes, every one of you, demoted, sacked, waiting at the job centre. I can't stand it any more. I must have a bath, a shower. Water.'

Hanks, in no better condition than his master, had crawled from his hiding place shaking as if he were in the terminal stages of a lethal nervous disease. He could hardly stand upright so pummelled had he been; he ached in every square inch of his vast body, he was a continent of pain.

Sussworth had swayed and almost swooned when he'd caught a whiff of his second in command, for Hanks had lain directly in the path of scores of terrorized animals for some long period. The sergeant looked like the well trodden and soggy corner of a dirty pasture which had been forever inhabited by flatulent cattle. He smelt like the last shovelful of decayed manure at the bottom of an ancient and fruity compost heap.

Sussworth had staggered under the onslaught of this smell but had been saved from falling by his men and led straight to an ambulance. Once inside he had removed his clothes and then been driven to his caravan. There he had taken a bath, resting in it for hours and changing the water at least three times. Fresh underwear had been brought to him and now, thirty-six hours later, crisply dressed in a brand new uniform and, apart from a bruise on his right cheekbone, bearing no trace of the battle, Sussworth sat at his desk, phone in hand, issuing orders to his new police cars as they patrolled all of north London. By the side of the desk, as admiring as ever and almost as clean as his chief for once – he had been to a police station for his own bath – stood Sergeant Hanks.

*

'Well keep looking,' Sussworth was saying. 'I want every horse you find brought to me. I don't care what colour it is. Those Borribles are capable of dyeing it pink. And any children you find bring them in too. And don't trust any dwarfs . . . They may be Borribles pretending to be dwarfs pretending to be Borribles who are really dwarfs. What? Well I can understand it, you fool.' The inspector snarled and threw the receiver into its cradle with such force that the noise made Hanks jump to attention and salute. Realizing he had made a mistake he walked over to the electric kettle and poured its contents into the teapot.

'How about a nice cup of tea, Inspector?' he asked. 'It'll do your nerves good.'

Sussworth leapt from his seat like a spring bursting out of a sofa. 'Yes, Hanks, yes,' he said, and shaking hands with himself behind his back he began goose-stepping up and down the carpet. 'The trouble is,' he continued, 'the DAC is not happy about that business at the slaughterhouse, and quite right too . . . But how were we to know there was going to be so many Borribles attacking us, eh? How were we to know?'

'It was mass violence and intimidation,' said Hanks, and he waddled across the caravan and deposited Sussworth's mug on the desk. Then he returned to the kitchen cabinet, and picking up a grubby paper bag, brought out a mature bacon sandwich and shoved half of it into his mouth.

Sussworth stopped marching and sipped his tea delicately. 'The DAC has given us one last chance, Hanks. He's in very hot water visavee Downing Street, boiling hot water you might say. He's told me that if I can't wrap everything up in the next two days, neat and clean and tidy, no loose ends, with those ten ringleaders under lock and key, well I might as well try and get a job with Armacor delivering wage packets to building sites. The DAC doesn't care how we do it, Hanks, just as long as we do it quickly.'

Sussworth paused for a moment and flicked an atom of dust from his sleeve then continued to march up and down the caravan. 'What do I look like to the upper echelons with my crack troops covered in giblets and tripe?' The inspector halted and gazed adoringly at the pictures of the two generals on the wall above his desk. 'Did Rommel have this trouble with the Afrika Korps? Or Monty with the Desert Rats? Of course not.' He returned to his tea and took a further sip and his moustache flittered over the surface of the beverage like a water bug on a pond. 'And the complaints from the Camden restaurants, Hanks . . . Animals in every one, knocking over tables, breaking crockery, butting ladies in the . . . well, you know.'

'I have the impression,' interrupted Hanks, licking his lips, 'that a lot of them sheep as strayed into them Turkish and Greek restaurants was kebabs in rosemary before they had time to reach the backyard.'

Sussworth sighed. 'Is everyone dishonest in this sorry society?' he asked, replacing his mug of tea on his desk. 'It is enough to make one despair of ever reforming the world.'

Sussworth might have carried on in this highly moral vein but he was interrupted by a commotion from outside the caravan. There was a bump, the sound of a blow and then a torrent of swearing, first from a man and then from a woman. Hanks put down his tea in turn and rolled, as if on castors, towards the door. Once there he flung it open.

'What's all this going on?' he enquired. 'The inspector is trying to get some research done 'ere.'

'I'm sorry, sir,' said a panting voice, 'but we've got this prisoner, and the inspector said that he was to see everything suspicious, child or dwarf, sheep or horse, fish and fowl . . . though what you'd call this, I dunno.'

Sussworth leant his behind against the edge of his desk and folded his arms as tightly as two strands of a single rope. 'Bring it in,' he called. 'Is it clean?'

'It ain't clean, far from it,' said Hanks, stepping back from the door, 'but it is handcuffed.'

The prisoner was pushed forward and there was a squeal of pain as she stumbled against the caravan steps and fell. 'Ow,' cried a rough female voice. 'Leave us alone, can't yer? I'm a free citizen going about me legal business, ain't I?'

'No such thing,' said Sussworth and went to the rear of his desk. He reached down a large legal volume and placed it on his chair and sat on it, making himself look five inches taller. After that he took his cap from a hook and settled it squarely on his head, composing his features into something resembling a blank wall. 'I'm ready,' he called, and into the room was propelled the dishevelled and grimy figure of the Queen Mum, her rags and scraps of polythene barely hanging on to her limbs. Being handcuffed she was unable to keep her balance and she sprawled across the carpet between the door and the desk.

'Aaaaagh,' cried Sussworth weakly, surprised out of his superior stance for a second. 'Pick her up, Hanks, and get an old newspaper for her to stand on.'

The Queen Mum was dragged to her feet and the inspector's request complied with. The arresting officer entered the caravan and went to stand by the computer, ready to answer questions. The inspector nodded at him. 'You may begin, PC Blume. Tell me what is known.'

The police constable switched on the computer terminal and pumped up the relevant record. 'Susan Palmer,' he read aloud, 'alias the Queen Mum or Queenie, found today wandering north on the Finchley Road, drunk in charge of a pram. Previous convictions include obscene language, behaviour likely to cause a breach of the peace, viz, removing her knickers and waving them under the noses of innocent bystanders—'

'Is there no shame?' said Sussworth quietly. He opened a drawer in his desk and took out a jar of pot-pourri and removed the lid. 'She smells like Camembert,' he added.

Hanks sniffed like a connoisseur. 'Yes,' he observed. 'I bet her armpits are all stuck up with black jam.'

Officer Blume coughed and continued reading. '—causing alarm and despondency on the public highway by singing and dancing in Trafalgar Square, grievous bodily harm, damage to police property and zigzagging down the middle of Fleet Street with her pram during the Lord Mayor's procession, shouting, "I am royalty," thereby causing a breach of the peace.'

Officer Blume raised a hand to his mouth and coughed again. 'The prisoner is also known to all London divisions as a vagrant, a trouble-maker, mentally unstable, and is often found consorting with meths drinkers in the King's Cross area, though she has been known to live in the north for long—'

'Stop,' said Sussworth suddenly, and he leant forward and placed his elbows on his desk, interlacing his fingers and resting his pointed chin on the bridge he had so formed. He had perceived the tiniest flicker of guilt passing across the Queen Mum's countenance.

'King's Cross,' said Sussworth. He smiled sweetly, like deadly nightshade masquerading as a bunch of violets. 'I believe C Division has an unsolved murder at King's Cross,' he said. 'Get it up on the computer, Blume, it might be interesting.'

Blume touched a button on the terminal and the screen glowed with light. His voice sounded out again. 'Right, sir. Murder . . . victim a methylated spirits drinker going by the name of Madge. No witnesses, or rather all witnesses intoxicated out of their brains. A certain Hughie MacMungall held on suspicion but later released. Motive thought to be robbery. Several valuable items, probably stolen goods, missing. General call put out for Susan Palmer, alias the Queen Mum, alias Queenie, a material witness, thought to be implicated. In any case she was accused of the crime by MacMungall during his interrogation. And look here, sir . . . MacMungall also talked about children or Borribles being present on the night of the murder. It looks like they were all in it together!'

Blume finished his reading and a deep and heavy silence settled over the caravan. The Queen Mum began to cry. Sussworth got slowly to his feet and pointed at his prisoner and his finger burnt in the air like an acetylene torch cutting metal.

'I've got you dead to rights, Queenie,' he said, 'because you're going to tell me everything I want to know . . . And one thing is certain, if you don't cooperate I'll see you get weighed off for twice as many years as you've got left to live.'

'I don't know nuffin',' said the old woman. 'I don't know nuffin'. That Hughie MacMungall has it in for me, that's all; he'd say anything to do me down.'

Sussworth crept round his desk and twisted his face sideways. 'There's something you ought to know, Queenie,' he said. 'I hate Borribles and the only thing I hate worse than Borribles are adults who help Borribles. But, Queenie, anyone who helps me in my unending war against those little enemies of society will find herself basking in the sunlight of my pleasure.'

'I had nothing to do with it,' said the Queen Mum. She joined her hands together and dropped to her knees in front of Sussworth and looked up into his face. 'I did see some kids, yes, but I never knew they were Borribles or anything. And I didn't stay at Madge's at all, 'cos her and Hughie were fighting drunk . . . I left.'

'You see,' continued the inspector, 'I don't care, Queenie, whether you perpetrated this murder or not. All I want is information about Borribles. I eat, drink and sleep Borribles; I can smell 'em a mile off and I can smell 'em on you. You've had them round you, Queenie, today, so don't bother to deny it.'

The Queen Mum wrung her hands again and whimpered.

Sussworth rocked on his heels. 'You tell me what you know,' he said, 'and you walk out of this caravan a free woman, but if you persist in your evil ways I'll put you inside, Queenie. You'll do porridge. I'll send you to a criminal asylum, Queenie, with a nice rubber room and plenty of medicines and pills shoved down your throat to make sure you turn into a vegetable. You won't be the Queen Mum any more, the scourge of London, you'll just be a cabbage.'

'Yeah,' agreed Hanks. 'Just a cauliflower.'

'Definitely,' said Officer Blume, 'a cauliflower.' He sighed. 'Imagine, if all the world was cauliflowers, what a garden it would be.'

The Queen Mum raised her hands in supplication. Her straggly hair fell about her wrinkled face and her lips of creased gristle writhed over her gums in a terrible anguish.

'Oh, inspector,' she wailed, 'I don't know nothing about that there murder, I promise you I don't, on my life. But I know you have the power to do what you say and I would die a living death if you took the streets away from me . . . I love them, sir, I do, more than life itself.'

Sussworth sneered with pleasure and thrust his hands behind his back where they clasped each other like long-lost friends. He glanced at Hanks in triumph, performed a smart about-turn and then regained his desk so that he might sit in his chair, leaning forward to eye the kneeling prisoner. His moustache twitched in glee. 'Have you had any truck or converse of any sort or manner with Borribles or any of their allies or accessories? Answer, or it's prison for ever.'

The Queen Mum rose fearfully to her feet. 'I am a weak old lady,' she began, 'unable to get work at my age and unable to get dole money because I am of no fixed abode. I am easily put upon by people younger and stronger, your honour. I did meet up with them Borribles in King's Cross, and they bullied me and beat me something cruel, Inspector, nasty little tykes, and they took what money I had too, though they says they never has anything to do with it . . . but they took mine quick enough, crash, bang and wallop.'

'Yes,' said Sussworth, nodding like a bored child at an oft-repeated tale. 'Go on.'

'And that's why I scarpered out of the arches as soon as I could get away. I took me pram and went, and I never saw 'em again after that, honest. On my life, I didn't.'

Hanks stepped forward at this and cuffed the Queen Mum round the back of her head with all the weight of his mighty arm and she fell on to her hands and knees. Blood dribbled down her chin.

Sussworth leant back in his chair. 'It won't do,' he said gently. 'Do you think we policemen are as unintelligent as common rumour would have it? The smell of the Borribles is on you, I say. It's woven into the rags you are wearing, you guttersnipe. Now listen, you old crone, tell me the truth or it's non-stop to the nuthouse for you. A lifetime of carbolic and bleach, a lifetime of no gin and no vino. Speak up, Queenie, or I will incarcerate you quicker than the speed of light.'

'Yes,' said Hanks. 'Fast.'

The Queen Mum stayed on her hands and knees and stared at the carpet; tears poured down her cheeks and mingled with the blood on her chin. 'Oh help me, someone,' she moaned. 'I don't want this, it ain't what I want to do. I never told the law anything, ever. Why do I have to do it now?'

Sussworth inspected his nails. 'Look at it this way,' he said. 'They're only bits of kids, poor little orphans, and we have their best interests at heart. We are the agents of society, as it were; we pass them on to the proper authority, Queenie, just like we might have to pass you on.'

The Queen Mum lifted her stained face and it was completely drained of hope. 'They're hiding in the old link tunnel between the LMR and the Bakerloo line at Swiss Cottage,' she said. 'Just today, then they're going to—'

Sussworth screamed with delight and scrambled over his desk. He jumped up and down on the floor, his legs stiff and his fists clenched.

'This time, this time,' he yelled. 'I've got them, Hanks. We'll clip their ears.'

'This is wonderful news,' said Officer Blume, and he saluted.

Hanks, by way of celebration, winkled something out of a nostril and held it close to his eye in order to compare it with the hundreds of other soft things he had discovered up his nose in the past. Absent-mindedly he wiped it on the rags that covered the Queen Mum's back. 'Pretty good one that,' said the Sergeant. 'It's amazing where they all come from.' Then he grabbed the old tramp by her hair and dragged her upright. 'What shall I do with the prisoner, sir?' he asked.

Sussworth stopped clicking his heels on the floor and stared at the Queen Mum for a couple of seconds while he made up his mind. 'Why,' he said at length, 'send her down to C Division, of course; she's a murder suspect.'

There was a loud cry and the Queen Mum fainted, slipping from Hank's grasp. She lay on the floor, her old face a solid skull with deep black pits in it.

Officer Blume saluted again. 'Excuse me, sir,' he said. 'C Division? C Division is Birdlime's division, sir. Well, why should we do him any favours? He's going to look very good if he solves that King's Cross murder . . . whereas if we catch the Borribles we'll be unbeatable, sir.'

The constable lowered his voice so that the Queen Mum should not hear though she looked as close to unconsciousness as made no difference. 'We can hold the old bag while we check her story, then, if what she says is true, we can let her go, for a week or two, and then pick her up again. That way we get the Borribles and, after a suitable lapse of time, we'll solve Birdlime's murder for him. We'll be as shiny as a new coin and he'll look about as useful as a cup of yesterday's cocoa.'

Sussworth stopped jerking his body up and down and placed his hands on his hips. He advanced slowly towards the constable.

'Officer,' he said, his face paralysed with wonder, 'you are a mind-reader, a talented mind-reader. I have to admit that you have made an excellent exposition of what was going through my brain at this particular and actual moment in time. My suggestion was merely a test of your powers of thought, a probing of your loyalty to the SBG esbrie de corpse. Mark my verbals, Blume, when all this is over you'll be Sergeant Blume. Hanks could do with an assistant.'

'Thank you, sir.'

The inspector celebrated this latest achievement with a tango step and then trotted over to his map of London. 'Listen carefully,' he said. 'Here are your orders. I want the stations above and below Swiss Cottage blocked off and the exit and entrance to the LMR tunnel as well. Telephone London Transport and tell them that a gang of villains has gone to earth at Swiss Cottage and until we've got them out the power will have to be cut off in that section. Send officers to every station on the Bakerloo and stop commuters using the trains. Telephone the Yard for reinforcements, and, Hanks, round up all the dwarfs you can find at short notice. Get that Nonch fellow here.'

'The dwarfs, sir?'

'Yes, Hanks, why should our men take all the risks? I'll send those dwarfs in as a first wave, that's what Rommel would have done . . . Find out where the Borribles are hiding, flush them into the open. By the time our chaps move in the dwarfs will have done half the work. This time I want no mistakes. This is my finest hour.'

'Of course, sir. Brilliant, sir. Shall I inform the DAC?'

'No, no, no! Certainly not, Hanks. The DAC doesn't want to know how it's done, he just wants to know that it *is* done. Above all he does not want to know about dwarfs . . . Make sure the men realize that, whatever happens. All he wants at the end of the day is a fate accomplice, got that? Now, any questions?'

'Yessir,' said Hanks. 'What shall we do with this prisoner?' He indicated the silent form on the floor.

'Ha, yes,' said Sussworth. In his excitement he had completely forgotten about the Queen Mum. 'Keep her in custody until we know for sure the Borribles are where she said they were, then throw her back on the streets. Right now there is more important work to do.' The inspector smirked at the photographs of Rommel and Monty. 'This time we knock 'em for six,' he said, and quickly pulling on his long overcoat he left the caravan to assemble his men and organize his patrol cars and vans.

The moment the inspector had gone Officer Blume grabbed the Queen Mum by the scruff of the neck, hauled her to her feet and pushed her towards the open door. Sergeant Hanks picked up the telephone and spoke to Scotland Yard, slipping an eager finger into a wide nostril. The Adventurers did not know it but the greatest danger they had ever faced was coming closer and closer.

12

The same darkness as before filled the disused tunnel and the Adventurers were ill at ease in it. Such a darkness was difficult to live with, suffocating and soft, but the fugitives were obliged to make the best of it. They had no option and nowhere else to go. It was daylight now and there would be no hiding place for them or the horse on the streets above. All they could do for the time being was eat what was left of their provisions, drink the tin-tasting water from the old tap, and draw lots to see who should sleep and who should stand guard.

For a long while there was quiet in the lost space behind the old control cabin, a strange prickly quiet, and only the distant thunder of the trains on the Bakerloo line disturbed it, and only occasionally did that same thunder cause a stream of fine dust to pour from the loose bricks of the roof and add itself to the thick carpet of stone dirt already lying deep on the ground.

At last some of the Adventurers went to explore the two deserted trains that stood, rusty, in the sidings. There they soon discovered that the closed doors could be forced open and that in the carriages the long wide seats made comfortable beds, providing them with the best day's sleep they had enjoyed since leaving Battersea.

Those who remained awake sat at the rough workbenches, resting their heads in their hands, talking in low tones, not shining their torches and not daring to think even that Neasden was only a night's march away.

Two Borribles were on sentry-go: Napoleon on the far side of the trains, staring round a bend towards the lights of Swiss Cottage station, and Bingo who watched the back road, peering into the blackness of the tunnel which took the LMR line from Marylebone Road right up to

West Hampstead. It would not do to be caught napping at this late stage in the game; the Adventurers had only to get through the day and then they would be on the final lap. Unfortunately it was not to be that easy; it was not to be that straightforward.

Sometime during the mid-morning of that day Knocker raised his head; he had heard a Borrible whistle coming from Napoleon's direction. He heard someone curse in the dark and the Wendle came round the side of the control cabin at speed. Knocker swivelled on his chair as did the others who sat near him: Chalotte, Vulge and Twilight.

Napoleon flicked his torch on and off, just to show his face. It was angry. 'Have you noticed?' he asked.

'Noticed what?' said Knocker.

'The trains,' retorted Napoleon. 'They've stopped; I haven't heard one for about half an hour.'

'You're right,' said Sydney. She was sitting on the ground by the horse, against the wall.

'I went right up close to the station when I realized,' went on Napoleon, 'right close . . . There's a lot of blokes on the platform, blokes in uniform, Woollies, hundreds of 'em.'

'We've been shopped,' said Chalotte.

'Too bloody right,' agreed Napoleon. 'Queenie! Who else could it be? I said we should have brought her with us, or slit her throat.'

'Perhaps we can get out the way we came in,' said Chalotte, 'before they close the tunnel that end.'

It was the only chance they had but it was scotched at that very moment by the arrival of Bingo, running as fast as he could, his torch beam cutting across the darkness. He halted by the table, gulping for air. 'I went up the tunnel,' he began, 'to explore . . . I heard some noises and back where this tunnel joins the Marylebone one there's lights, a barrier, blokes in uniform. Coppers. What about the other way?'

'We're rats in a trap,' said Napoleon. 'There's just this tunnel and we're in the middle of it and there's Woollies at each end. It's the end of the line all right.'

'Oh no,' cried Sydney. 'Not now, not when we're almost there. They'll get Sam for sure this time. I don't care for me but—'

'I care for me,' said Napoleon. 'I care a lot.'

Vulge struck the workbench with his fist. 'Fancy marching so far and struggling so hard just to end up here . . . in this filthy hole in the ground, just to die in this shitty pit.'

'Well,' said Twilight, 'at least we got Sam away from Sussworth. He's had some freedom, even if it was only for a little while.'

Knocker got to his feet and picked up two bandoliers of stones from the table; he slipped them over his shoulder. 'That's not enough,' he said. 'We shouldn't have to die, we shouldn't have to lose our ears and Sam shouldn't have to be turned into catsmeat, not for any reason at all. It ain't right.'

'One thing's on our side,' said Napoleon. 'They're going to have to fight us in the dark and that won't be too easy for 'em.' And as Napoleon spoke there was a whirring noise in the vaulted roof and a pale and sickly light flickered over the Borribles, disappeared and then flickered again, hesitated and then steadied to become a pallid whiteness that gave no shade. The Adventurers glanced upwards. There in the roof shone long tubes of fluorescent lighting, stretching away as far as the eye could see; tracer bullets along the tunnel.

The Adventurers looked at each other, the blood driven from their faces by this light that had no pity in it. Now they could see the bleakness of the spot to which their fate had directed them: the dirt and the dust, the broken and abandoned tools, the piles of rubbish and the sacks of cement.

There was worse to come, a noise this time, a metallic whining that split the white light in two. The Borribles leapt to their feet and the noise came again, humming and crackling loudly before at last dying away with a plaintive whistling. Someone tapped on a microphone then, and blew and tapped again. A voice resonated through some faraway speakers, counting: 'One, two, three, four; testing, testing. Can you hear me?' It was Sussworth's voice and it skated along the walls of the tunnel, howling and wowing and turning over and over, looping the loop until finally it banged against the eardrums of the Borribles where they stood, rooted to the spot in fear and surprise.

'Can you hear us, Borribles,' Sussworth's voice boomed, 'because we know you're there; your friend Queenie told us. Just goes to show that you can't trust anyone, doesn't it?' A splutter broke in on Sussworth's words; he was laughing and a strange thin laughter it was, whipping through the air like barbed wire uncoiling.

'Now listen,' continued Sussworth when he had recovered himself. 'This time there is no escape. I have men at this end and men behind you, hundreds of men and all the reserves I need. Lay down your catapults and march straight down here to Swiss Cottage and give yourselves up. You will be well looked after and no harm will come to you . . . except of course for the statutory removal of the aural appendages, but that does go without saying.' Sussworth was silent for a moment, as if he expected an answer through the microphone. When he received none he went on.

'You have five minutes to surrender,' he said. 'Walk into this station with your hands on your heads. If you comply with this request your horse will be spared and put out to graze in a special horse hotel and there he will live out the rest of his days in tranquillity. Fortunate horse.'

'Baloney,' said Napoleon.

'But,' the voice resumed, 'if these five minutes of time elapse without your surrender I shall renege on my offer for the horse, and you know what his fate will be then as well as I do. He will end up catsmeat as guaranteed, in tins weighing two hundred and fifty grams, as advertised. Five minutes only or I send in my first wave of shock troops to flush you from your rat holes. Nooch and his dwarfs are ready and eager to come looking for you . . . but, friends, let it not come to that. Surrender and avoid bloodshed.'

There was a silence followed by a click and the speakers went dead.

Knocker took his catapult from his back pocket; the others did the same. 'This is our last battle,' he said. 'Has anyone got a plan, for I haven't. I don't know what to do. I never felt so rotten in my life.'

There was a sound of footsteps by the control cabin and Stonks, Torreycanyon and Orococco arrived. They had been sleeping in the trains but the lights had woken them. They had heard Sussworth's speech too and knew what danger they were in.

'There's nothing to be done,' said Stonks, 'except fight and try to make sure those stinking dwarfs have nothing to crow about.'

'I can't believe this is happening,' said Chalotte, her voice a wail of despair. 'I can't believe it. How did it come to this?'

'It came, that's all,' said Napoleon bitterly. 'I say we get down by the front of the trains and wait for Ninch and his mates. Sydney could stay back here with Sam; that way if anyone tries to take us in the rear she can give us the whistle.'

'It's got to be worth a go, man,' said Orococco.

'A go is all we'll get,' said Knocker. He sounded empty, devoid of hope. 'The dwarfs are only to soften us up. Once the coppers get in they'll have helmets and riot shields and all. Our catapults won't be any good against them.'

'Hide and seek to the death,' said Napoleon.

'And Sam,' said Sydney. 'Is it the end for him too?'

Chalotte sighed. 'A lot of things are going to come to an end today, Sid,' she said. 'All you can do is hide him over there against the wall, behind that big pile of rubbish, then keep a watch on the tunnel for us. At least you'll be with Sam at the very last.'

'Let's go,' said Stonks. 'Get it over with.'

'When it starts going bad,' said Knocker, 'we'll rally round the front of the cabin. That way we'll be able to see 'em coming from both directions and we'll have a wall at our backs.'

There was no better plan than this and it was immediately agreed. Silently the Borribles moved to take up their positions, facing the southbound tunnel from where it was thought the first attack would come. As they walked to the battlefield the nine friends decided to split their forces into three groups as they had done at the scrapyard: Orococco, Twilight and Bingo in the first group, Torreycanyon, Stonks and Vulge in the second; Chalotte, Knocker and Napoleon in the third.

'That'll make sure,' explained the Wendle, 'that them dwarfs don't know where we are exactly.' He glanced beyond the others, looking at the roof of a carriage, his face crafty. 'And we three could hide up there,' he said.

Now that the lights had been switched on there was in fact a good view from the top of the trains. The two sidings were in a wider area than the tunnel itself so there was a kind of open space of about seventy yards square lying just in front of the carriages, though eventually this space narrowed down into a single track which led onwards to Swiss Cottage and the main Bakerloo line.

It was not possible however for the Adventurers to see very far into that Swiss Cottage tunnel. Although it too was lit by the same fluorescent lighting as illuminated the control cabin section, it also curved rather sharply on its way to the station. The enemy, when they came, would not be visible until they turned the corner, about a couple of hundred paces distant from where the Borribles waited.

Knocker and Chalotte followed Napoleon to the roof of the carriage he had chosen and all three lay on their stomachs. Below them and over to one side they could see Twilight, Orococco and Bingo taking cover behind two large packing cases that had been dumped against the wall. Somewhere to the left, Torreycanyon, Stonks and Vulge were hiding behind the wheels of the second train.

'Let them get out into the open before we fire,' Knocker called. 'Don't want to frighten the little bleeders.' Then he settled down to wait, and so did his companions.

Sussworth's five minutes soon elapsed and when the dwarfs came they came quietly, moving cautiously along the tracks, the thick stone dust deadening every footfall. They stepped from sleeper to sleeper, they searched every alcove let into the walls and they peered into every shadow. In their hands they carried long wooden truncheons and they wore green jackets made of luminous plastic so that the police would know them from Borribles in the heat of battle.

The dwarfs – there seemed to be about twenty of them – were led to the end of the tunnel by Ninch himself. When he arrived at the edge of the open space he halted, held up his hand and gazed suspiciously at the two trains that stood before him.

'We know you're there, Borribles,' he shouted. 'You might as well give up, you're outnumbered and surrounded.'

There was no answer. Each Borrible lay motionless in his hiding place, face down, stone and catapult ready. Ninch waited; he shouted again.

'You can't fight all of us, we're stronger than you; you might as well give in.'

Still there was no response so Ninch raised his hand once more and the dwarfs moved into the open, spreading to right and left, heading for the trains and stepping over the criss-cross of the tracks, lifting their feet high over the conductor rail although they all knew there was no power in it. Their truncheons were held at the ready, their eyes were everywhere.

They drew level at last with the packing cases and still everything remained quiet. They came to within ten yards or so of the front carriages and Ninch called out his orders.

'Remember, dwarfs. Get to grips with 'em. Don't let 'em use their catapults.'

'Oh no?' yelled Bingo, and he suddenly appeared from his hiding place, his catapult ready in his hand. 'Well cop this!' And so saying he fired at Ninch and a stone struck the chief dwarf in the chest and he staggered backwards. As Bingo released his shot Twilight and Orococco appeared also and each of their missiles struck a dwarf and knocked some of the bravado out of them.

Before the dwarfs could take cover or even throw themselves to the ground Vulge, Torreycanyon and Stonks emerged from under the trains and fired too, and more dwarfs staggered under the forceful blows of sharp-edged stones. At the same time Knocker, Chalotte and Napoleon got to their feet and fired down on the enemy, striking the dwarfs from above, and yet more of their number fell, seriously stunned, clasping their heads.

'Here's for Scooter,' shouted Chalotte, and she reloaded and fired her catapult as quickly as she could.

The dwarfs faltered and had it not been for Ninch they might have turned tail there and then, but whatever else he was Ninch was no coward. He rallied his troops even under the full fury of the Borrible attack.

'Get to the trains,' he yelled. 'Get under the trains, that's where they are. They can't beat us close to. Remember the reward.' Ninch crouched low and ran forward, diving to safety behind the big carriage wheels. His men followed him but Bingo, Twilight and Orococco fired after them and two more dwarfs stumbled and fell, their knees shattered.

Nor had the other Borribles been idle. Vulge, Torreycanyon and Stonks fired at the enemy as they went to earth and the dwarfs were badly cut and bruised. Knocker and his two companions let fly from above; another dwarf went down. Ninch's troops, who had been told the Borribles would be easy, now knew they had a fight on their hands.

Knocker stood up. 'We've got to keep them at long range,' he said. 'Remember they're adults, stronger than we are.'

Napoleon grinned like the crafty Wendle of old. He closed one eye and the other blazed with the love of battle. 'I dunno about that,' he said. 'I'm going to slip off here and try to get amongst them dwarfs, pretend to surrender maybe, get close to Ninch. With him gone the rest will run like rabbits.' And Napoleon re-opened his eye and lowered himself over the side of the train. Then, catapult between his teeth, he dropped silently to the ground.

Knocker was alarmed. He went to the edge of the roof and looked down. 'Come back, Nap,' he whispered. 'There's too many of them.'

The Wendle did not answer but waved a hand, grinned once more and slipped out of sight under the carriages.

Knocker cursed. 'Dammit,' he said, 'we can't let him go on his own.' He stood on the edge of the roof, perplexed, Chalotte by his side.

'No,' she said, 'we can't.'

Just then the Wendle reappeared from underneath the train, backing slowly, his hands held above his head in a gesture of surrender; after him came two dwarfs, neither of whom was Ninch.

'I surrender,' Napoleon was saying, 'honest. Look, here's my cattie.' He threw the weapon to the ground. 'I've had enough, really. Take me to Sussworth. I want to live a normal life. Don't hurt me, please don't hurt me.'

The dwarfs stepped forward, taking no chances, their truncheons held poised before them, eager to clout Napoleon across the head as soon as they got close enough to him. The Wendle clasped his hands together, dropped to his knees and raised his eyes to heaven, winking when he saw Knocker and Chalotte ready on the roof. 'Oh, please don't hurt me,' he said. 'I couldn't stand it.'

'Here we go,' said Knocker, and seizing Chalotte's arm he leapt into space, pulling the girl with him. As the two dwarfs raised their weapons over the kneeling Napoleon they were suddenly smashed to the ground by the flying weight of the two Borribles landing feet first on their necks. They collapsed completely, demolished like old buildings destroyed with dynamite.

Both Chalotte and Knocker rolled over in the dust and sprang to their feet immediately. Napoleon did likewise, ready for trouble, but the dwarfs lay sprawled across one another in the dirt, one face down, the other gazing blankly into the fluorescent lighting.

'Backs broken,' said Napoleon, and he bent down and retrieved the dwarfs' truncheons, giving one to Knocker. 'You use these for hitting people,' he explained, then he spat. 'I want that Ninch,' he continued, 'more than anything in the whole world.' And with that he ran off alongside the train until he reached the end of the front carriage. Nor did he stop there but ran on into the middle of the open space that lay before the tunnel entrance. Knocker and Chalotte followed the Wendle as far as the front of the train but there they halted and crouched in the shadow of the last wheel.

'He's going bonkers,' said Chalotte.

It certainly looked like it. Napoleon began to run up and down, stooping every now and then to bang a railway line with his truncheon just as hard as he could, making a sound that resonated along the sprung and curving rails for miles and miles. And Napoleon shouted too, a defiant challenge to the arch-betrayer, Ninch.

'Come on out, Ninch,' bellowed the fearless Borrible. 'I want yer, Ninch, don't waste yerself . . . Come and fight with a Wendle.'

And so Ninch came at last. He did not run, nor did he shout, he simply appeared on the far side of the trains to Knocker and Chalotte and with him two of his cronies.

Napoleon stopped his cavorting immediately and twirled his truncheon in delight. 'Hello, Ninch,' he said, and he smiled and his face looked like a rock with a crack in it.

Chalotte whispered into Knocker's ear, 'He is mad; there's three of them.'

'That's all right,' said Knocker. 'There's three of us only they don't know it yet.' He loaded his catapult and Chalotte followed his example. 'You take the one on the right; I'm aiming for Ninch.'

By this time the three dwarfs had approached within a few yards of Napoleon Boot, confident in the knowledge that they outnumbered him. They laughed – the Wendle looked so frail.

'Look what we got here,' said Ninch, leering at his companions. 'A funny little green job.'

Napoleon spat on the floor. 'I'd knock yer brains out,' he said calmly, 'if I knew where you kept 'em. You're a waste of space, Ninch, that's what you are.'

The dwarfs did not answer and moved nearer the Wendle, intending to attack him from three directions at once. They did not get far. Both Knocker and Chalotte stepped into the open and let fly with their catapults. Chalotte's aim was perfect and her target was struck down. Knocker was not so lucky and cursed out loud as he fired. Ninch had crouched and moved forward at the last second and the stone destined for him missed his head by inches though fortunately, at least for the Borribles, the missile wasn't wasted. Behind Ninch stood the third dwarf and Knocker's stone smashed against his temple. With a howl of pain, he fell backwards across the railway lines, unconscious, just like Chalotte's victim.

The chief dwarf half turned, dismayed to see his companions put out of action so effectively. He only took his eyes from Napoleon for a second but that was enough.

'Queensberry rules,' shouted the Wendle, and he lashed out with his captured truncheon and caught Ninch a swinging blow across the side of the head. The dwarf staggered and slipped on the track and sank to one knee.

Napoleon struck again but Ninch was no weakling and he fended the blow away. His muscles had been circus-trained and his reactions were fast and sure. Ninch would never give in and Knocker and Chalotte, watching the struggle from the safety of their hiding place, realized this only too well. One to one in close combat, even Napoleon Boot was no match for the dwarf.

'Over here,' yelled Knocker. 'We'll cover yer. Come on.'

Napoleon, from reasons of pride or out of a simple desire to revenge Scooter's death all on his own, took no heed of his friend's invitation. He twirled his truncheon again, and as Ninch got to his feet he danced around him, making him dizzy, prodding hard into the dwarf's ribs and stomach.

Knocker looked about him. The sounds of battle were moving closer. He spoke to Chalotte. 'We're going to be killed or captured in this fight anyway, Chal, so there's no point in fighting fair. I'm going to drop Ninch from behind before his two chums come round and you'll have to cover me from here.' Knocker started forward, crossing the railway lines to where Napoleon's fight was continuing in the same way it had begun, with the Wendle dodging and fencing and the dwarf striding patiently after him, knowing that once he got his hands on the Borrible he would throttle him.

When Knocker was within twenty yards of the dwarf he came to a halt and drew his catapult rubber back as far as his ear and took very careful aim at the back of Ninch's head. Just then Napoleon, ducking in under his opponent's guard, caught the dwarf a firm blow across the stomach and the sound of that blow was rich and solid like an axe biting into wood.

Ninch dropped to his knees and his truncheon fell from his hand, but even then his tremendous strength stood him in good stead. As he fell he grabbed Napoleon's truncheon from the Wendle's grasp and threw it hard into his face. Napoleon tottered and stumbled, blinded by pain and the blood which spurted from his forehead down into his eyes. He raised a hand to wipe his face clear, tripped on a railway line and fell backwards.

Before Knocker could fire Ninch uttered a roar of triumph and dived forward, throwing his square and chunky body on to Napoleon's. The dwarf landed heavily, pinning the Wendle to the ground. Then, with swift and certain movements, he drew a long-bladed knife from his belt, lifted it high into the air and plunged it down.

Knocker could not believe it. 'No,' he cried. 'No.' He loosed his stone but Ninch and Napoleon were wrestling ferociously and he missed the target. He went to move forward. He must pull Ninch away. Suddenly he heard a noise to his right; he looked. One of Ninch's companions had recovered and he was only a few yards distant, charging at full pelt, intent on Knocker's death. Knocker dared not tear his gaze away from this enemy, but out of the corner of his eye he saw Ninch's knife glint like a long silver tooth as he raised it again. But there was no more time; Knocker dropped his catapult and drew his truncheon.

The charging dwarf was almost upon the Borrible. His mouth was open and his eyes glowed with hatred. Knocker tried to remember all he had ever learnt about close fighting with the Rumble-stick all that time ago; he knew he would need every ounce of cunning he possessed if he were to survive.

Then things happened fast; a stone flew by his face like a bullet, so close that he thought it had grazed his skin. In a second the dwarf was at him. Big and strong and stocky he was not circus-trained, but flat-footed and overconfident.

At the last possible moment Knocker threw himself to one side, stuck out a leg and tripped his enemy as he went past. Quickly Knocker regained his balance and crouched low, ready to fight. There was no need. The dwarf's own momentum had carried him, flying parallel to the ground, across the railway track, and Knocker saw and heard his head clang down on to the solid steel of a rusty rail. The dwarf did not move again. He lay motionless, his head split open like a rotten turnip.

Knocker was next aware of Ninch's second companion climbing slowly to his feet and he turned to face a possible attack, but the dwarf made no attempt to advance. Instead he hesitated, staring stupidly beyond Knocker, then he shouted and ran away towards the train, calling to his friends for help. Knocker looked to where the dwarf had looked though he did not understand what he saw. Ninch still lay across Napoleon, but neither dwarf nor Borrible was moving.

Now Chalotte burst from cover and began leaping across the railway lines to go to Napoleon's aid, her hair streaming behind her, her legs stretched, a catapult in her hand, her face heroic. Knocker never forgot that sight of her and that particular image of the girl remained unchanged in his mind for the rest of his life, like some beautiful sculpture of war and revenge.

But his future memories did not matter then. Chalotte had reached Napoleon, and seizing Ninch by the shoulders she pulled him away from the Wendle, her movements rough and brutal. Ninch rolled on to his back, his right arm flopped out across a railway line and his own knife protruded from his chest. The green jacket he wore was daubed with bright blood and his lifeless eyes stared into the empty vaulting of the Underground. He was as dead as any nail in any door.

Chalotte knelt by Napoleon and Knocker kept watch. No noise came from the Swiss Cottage tunnel, the policemen were still biding their time, but away on the roofs of the two trains Knocker could see dwarfs and Borribles fighting, and from in among the carriages came the sounds of shouting and feet running on the stony tracks.

Chalotte spoke. 'Nap's badly wounded. There's lots of blood coming out of his chest. It's awful, he'll need proper attention.'

'Stabbed twice,' said Knocker. He still kept watch. They were very vulnerable out in the open. The dwarf who had run away would not be long in fetching reinforcements.

Chalotte shook her head. 'No,' she said, 'only once. When you were jumped by the other one I let fly with my catapult and caught Ninch on the back of the head before he could stab Napoleon again. I only just missed you because you were in the way. That allowed Nap to get the knife off him I suppose.'

Knocker bit his lip. 'We can't stay here,' he said, 'out in the open.' He knelt and pulled Ninch's green jacket from the body and put it on, blood and all. The beginnings of a distant idea were stirring in his brain.

'We'll have to carry Nap back to the control cabin,' said Chalotte. 'There's a table there and we can stretch him out on it. Take his legs.'

Knocker did as he was asked and together the two Borribles lifted the wounded and unconscious Wendle between them as gently as they could. They stepped lightly over the rails and passed between the two trains, stopping to hide whenever the sounds of battle came close.

They were lucky and arrived at the control cabin without incident. There, in that strange brick shed, half a mile beneath the streets of London, Napoleon Boot rested from the battle, the blood seeping from his chest.

Chalotte bent over him and tore back the clothing to look at the wound. Napoleon's eyes fluttered open; his greenish skin was pale. He gazed upwards, past Chalotte's troubled face, and stared at the rows of switches and junction boxes and the huge diagrammatic map of the Underground railway system. He looked puzzled and then he remembered.

'Did I get him?' he asked, and when Chalotte nodded the Wendle smiled and closed his eyes again. 'Good,' he said. 'The little sod. Who did he think he was, eh? Who did he think he was?'

The idea of Napoleon dying made Knocker despair of life ever being right again. Never had he thought to be so hurt or so saddened. It was strange that the bond of their friendship, though never mentioned, had grown stronger and stronger over the long months since the two Borribles had first met in mutual dislike and suspicion. Now Knocker could see that if the Wendle died a great part of his own being would be wrenched away like a lump of living flesh, and he would never be the same. He, Knocker, would be altered deep in his very soul. Napoleon Boot, just as he'd boasted on the day of the name-giving before Rumbledom, had covered his name in glory. There was no other Borrible like him. Knocker gulped back a sob. He felt hatred and love rising in his breast; love for the dying Wendle contending with hatred for the causes of death and pain in the world.

Knocker wiped the tears from his eyes and looked at Chalotte. She shook her head and then kissed Napoleon on the mouth, and as she kissed him she felt his lips go cold and she saw the life fade away from him like thin sunlight slipping behind an endless cloud of grey.

Knocker could not stand the watching of this scene and lurched out of the cabin door and leant against the wall and let the tears run unchecked down his face. Napoleon Boot dead. How could he ever live with such a truth? Napoleon Boot dead while dwarfs still sneered and laughed with Sussworth. Napoleon Boot dead, revenging the death of Scooter, the first adult ever to become a Borrible. Napoleon's name would live as long as the world lived. Knocker smiled a grim smile and wiped his face. 'I'd better find a few dwarfs,' he said aloud, but before he could move there was a noise at the corner of the cabin and Sydney appeared, breathless with excitement.

'I've found some old transformer room,' said the girl from Neasden, 'dug into the wall and big enough for us to hide in, horse as well. It's been half built and then left. It might be the answer if we could brick ourselves in.' Sydney was so thrilled with her news that she couldn't get her words out properly. Her eyes were bright with happiness and she was smiling. Knocker did not tell her about Napoleon; she would hear soon enough. Besides he was glad for the hope she brought, glad to have something else to think of.

'Good,' he said. 'Get the horse inside and knock up some cement . . . I saw some trowels . . . Go on, fast. There isn't a moment to lose.'

Sydney nodded and a joy bubbled up in her throat and made her laugh. 'Right,' she said, and was gone.

'Okay,' said Knocker. 'Now for the dwarfs.'

He did not have to go far. As he ran back into the space between the trains he saw four of the enemy in the distance. They saw Knocker too but because of the green jacket he was wearing they stood their ground and gestured for the Borrible to join them.

Knocker smiled as he ran. Kill Napoleon would they? Four against one, eh? That would do nicely . . . Nothing less would satisfy him.

A stone whizzed past his ear as he sped along, missing him narrowly.

He was being foolhardly but he didn't care. His brain failed to register the stone as a danger, failed to realize that stones could kill. Another ricocheted off the train above his head but nothing could stop him now.

The dwarfs waited, glad to add to their strength by one more. Knocker ran faster and the smiles on the faces of his enemies stiffened as they failed to recognize him, but still they hesitated until, with a fearful cry, Knocker leapt upon the nearest opponent and struck out with his truncheon and the unfortunate dwarf fell senseless to the ground.

Knocker did not stop there. His impetus carried him on to the next dwarf and there was another cry, a cry that echoed far along the tunnels, chilling the blood of those who heard it, filling them with despair and reminding them of the nearness of death.

Down went the second dwarf, his head smashed. Knocker whirled round to face the two survivors but they wanted no more of this madman. They threw down their weapons and ran while Knocker leant weakly against a wheel and watched them go. He felt suddenly tired and sick; all his emotion drained from him in a moment. He'd had enough of fighting.

But whatever Knocker felt, the battle was still raging and he must play his part in it. A voice broke into his thoughts and dragged him back to reality; the voice came from the roof of the carriage behind him.

'You want to be a bit more careful, Knocker, running around with a green jacket on. I shot two stones off at you before I realized you weren't a dwarf. You could get yourself killed that way.' Knocker looked up; it was Stonks. Beside him stood Torreycanyon.

Knocker nodded and touched his forehead with the back of his hand. It was then that his two comrades noticed the terrible grief on his face and their own features became lined with anxiety. They dropped quickly and easily to the ground.

'What's up?' asked Torreycanyon. 'You look awful.'

Knocker shook his head. He couldn't bring himself to tell of the death of Napoleon just then. He knew that to tell it would be like causing it again. 'Nothing's up,' he said, his face rigid with misery. 'Look, just take those green jackets off these dwarfs, will you. I think I've got an idea, only I haven't worked it all out yet.'

Stonks knelt and did what was asked, handing the jackets over to Knocker as he regained his feet. 'Where's the rest of us?' he said. 'Are they all right?'

'I dunno,' said Knocker, 'but we'll have to find 'em. I want to get everyone together before the coppers move in. My plan might just work.'

'We'd better go then,' said Stonks. 'They can't be far away, not in this place.'

*

Stonks was right. At that very moment Vulge was standing near the front of the trains and firing his catapult at a group of four dwarfs who were gazing down at the body of Ninch. They were frightened and angry; there lay the corpse of their leader, his eyes white and lifeless, the blood soaking through his shirt.

'Get that murderer,' they shouted, and all four of them, seeing only one skinny Borrible to deal with, brandished their truncheons above their heads and set off in pursuit.

That was exactly what Vulge had wanted. When the dwarfs were near enough to him he turned and ran away, along by the carriages, his pursuers close on his heels and getting closer every second.

Vulge limped along as fast as he could but he had no intention of going far. He was a decoy only and he led the enemy straight to where Bingo, Orococco and Twilight waited, crouching in the shadows beneath the train.

As the dwarfs ran past their hiding place the three Borribles tugged on a length of rope, the other end of which was tied to a junction box fixed to the wall of the tunnel. This rope had been covered over with dust and stones and the two leading dwarfs, running after Vulge at top speed, had no chance of seeing it. Up it came, quick and tight, and down they went, bruising themselves badly on the ground. The following pair, running further to the rear, just managed to slither to a halt in time to see what was happening, then with a cry of dismay they retreated, leaving their companions to their fate.

Vulge turned on his heel and ran back the way he had come. He leapt on the nearest dwarf and, snatching up a truncheon, began to wallop him on the head with it. While this was going on, Bingo,

Orococco and Twilight crawled into the open and dealt with the other dwarf. No prisoners were taken.

The two survivors showed no inclination to join in the fight but continued their retreat. They would probably have run all the way to Swiss Cottage right there and then had not Knocker, Torreycanyon and Stonks chosen that very minute to appear dead ahead, thereby cutting off the road to safety.

With another cry of despair the two dwarfs again skidded to a stop and, seeing an open door above them they clambered up the side of the train and disappeared. Orococco and Twilight went after them.

The dwarfs had in fact taken refuge in a driver's cab and inside it there was very little space. They made feverish attempts to open the door on the far side of the carriage and so escape that way, but in their excitement and fear they could not manage to turn the rusty handle. They would have to dig in and fight, hand to hand.

The advantages should all have been on their side. They were stronger than the two Borribles who had come to attack them and they possessed truncheons whereas Twilight and Orococco did not. The truth was however that the dwarfs had no stomach for the fight. They had seen the dead and bloody body of Ninch, their best warrior; they had seen their comrades go down in the dirt. Their courage had deserted them. They fought only in desperation and terror, lashing out wildly with foot and fist and stick.

Twilight and Orococco lashed out too but there was hardly room to land a blow. Their clothes snagged on levers and switches, tugging the controls backwards and forwards. The dwarfs scrambled up on to the control panel, their feet trampling over the scores of coloured buttons set into the dashboard. They swiped downwards with their truncheons, aiming for the heads of their enemies, and the two Borribles ducked and swore and ducked again.

At last Twilight seized one of the dwarfs by an ankle and pulled hard. The dwarf lost balance and, falling backwards, his truncheon struck the handle of the door that up until then had remained closed. Strangely it sprang open easily, and the dwarf fell through it to land, surprised but standing, on the ground by the track.

Orococco's opponent did not hesitate. The moment he saw the slightest possibility of escape he dropped his weapon and dived over the heads of the two Borribles. He landed beside his companion and the pair of them raced away in the direction of Swiss Cottage, yelling at the tops of their voices for all dwarfs still alive to follow them.

'Let's go after 'em,' said Twilight, eager in the full flush of battle.

Before Orococco could answer, Knocker's voice came from behind. He was standing on the track, only his face visible, level with the floor of the cab. 'There's no one to go after,' he said. 'The dwarfs have had enough, they've all gone. Besides, I think I've got a plan, so come out this side, will yer?'

The Adventurers returned to the front of the trains. There they could keep watch on the tunnel entrance and listen for the advance of the policemen who would soon come to end this, the last battle. Knocker looked at his friends as they clustered around him. Not one of them was unwounded and all of them had blood on their heads. They were covered in dirt, and exhaustion and lack of food had drained their faces of hope and energy. Knocker knew they were brave and would carry on the fight if there were no alternative, but Knocker wanted there to be an alternative; he wanted to make sure they got away and he thought he could do it.

He glanced towards the opening that led to Swiss Cottage. The real fight had not yet begun. Soon the pick of the SBG would march out from the tunnel and it would all be over. Knocker sighed. There were times when physical bravery was stupid and only cunning would do. He could see that now and he was certain that he and his companions had reached that point in their adventure. He dearly wanted to save his friends from the fate that was threatening them. He would sacrifice anything to achieve that end but to do so he would need all the cunning he could summon up from all his experience.

His thoughts went back to Spiff, Spiff the Spifflicator, and a half smile fluttered across his face. Yes, Spiff. That was the kind of cunning he needed now, and it was as if the spirit of that devious Borrible came to inspire Knocker in his hour of need. An idea burgeoned in his mind, and his voice spoke with a certainty that seemed to come from someone else.

'We cannot fight and win,' he began, 'not today, but we owe it to Sam to survive and to make sure we keep on surviving too. The horse can't be sold as catsmeat just because Sussworth says he will, and to save him we have to save ourselves. The two go together. Now listen. Sydney has found a half-bricked-up transformer room, back behind the control cabin. She's got the horse in there already.'

Knocker glanced at the tunnel but there was no sound nor sight of the SBG. 'You lot have to get back there, right away. She'll need help to make the cement and that. I'm going to brick you in. You see, it's important that I make the mortar look old otherwise you'll be found out. Throw dust over it from the outside.'

'Wait a minute,' said Bingo. 'We'll be inside and you'll be outside. That's not right. Susworth will get you.'

'No, he won't,' said Knocker. 'He won't catch me. It's easier for one to hide than all of us and a horse as well.' He glanced at the tunnel opening again. Still nothing. He took a deep breath. Now was the time. He felt his heart breaking within him. 'Napoleon's dead.' He blurted it out. 'Ninch killed him.'

Bingo's faced drained itself bloodless in a second. His eyes contracted into tiny diamonds of pain. His mouth was a hole of horror. He stepped up to Knocker and grabbed him by the neck with both hands and shook him. 'You're lying!' he screamed. 'You're lying! No one could get Napoleon. I love him.'

Stonks put his strong arms gently round Bingo and pulled him away from Knocker. Orococco buried his face in his hands and Twilight turned to look at the tunnel, hiding his tears from eyes that wept as much as his. Vulge's mouth tightened and dropped into an arc of hate; he shook his head in disbelief. Torreycanyon too wept and swore against the world.

Bingo shook uncontrollably and laid his head on Stonks's shoulder. Of all the Adventurers Bingo had been the closest to Napoleon, right from the time they had stolen the boat for the Great Rumble Hunt, and later, when they had fought side by side and had saved each other in the fire of Rumbledom library. And now he was gone. His Wendle wit gone. His toughness gone. His scheming brain gone. His rough Wandsworth voice stilled for ever. For death to come so close it was like all the Adventurers dying in the same instant, their hearts skewered up on sorrow.

Knocker was desolate. As he had known earlier, by telling his friends of Napoleon's death he felt guilty of it; as if he, the bearer of bad news, had been the perpetrator of the deed. But he also realized, now, that he had come to love Napoleon just as much as Bingo did, and that was important because right back at the very beginning he and the Wendle had hated each other much more than any two Borribles ever should have done. And he knew too that Napoleon's death had to serve for something; it must not be wasted. It had to be used to persuade the Adventurers not to fight to the bitter end. They had to be convinced that they must hide. They must save Sam and they must live to fight, perhaps, another day.

'What happened to Ninch?' said Stonks, still with his arms around Bingo. 'What happened? I could take him.'

'Napoleon got him,' said Knocker. 'Chalotte made sure he knew . . . He was still alive afterwards. She was looking after him, in the cabin . . . The wound was terrible.'

'Getting Ninch don't make up for Napoleon,' said Bingo. 'Nothing could.'

'Getting Sussworth might,' said Vulge. He gritted his teeth and shook his head again.

'No,' said Knocker. 'And if we're all dead or clipped and Sam is catsmeat, what good will that do? And what good will it do Napoleon Boot? Who will be alive to tell others all about him and what a Borrible he was? Who will give the lie to Sussworth's lies, eh? Answer me that. Don't you see? He'll be really dead if no one knows what he did; and he'll have died for nothing and we'll have died for nothing and that's exactly what Sussworth wants.'

Stonks lowered his head like a big dog baffled before a locked door. Bingo looked up, his face creased and worn soft like an old paper bag; he wanted to speak but Knocker stopped him, raising a hand and pointing towards the tunnel. 'There is no time for argument,' he said. 'You'll have to trust me. Just this once. I know I'm right . . . There's a feeling of Spiff about it. Sydney's found the perfect hiding place; it's a gift. Dying's no good. Getting your ears clipped is no good, but saving Sam is and saving ourselves is.'

Somehow there was no argument. Knocker looked at the empty faces of his friends. The immense sorrow had beaten the breath out of them, at least for the time being, and by talking he had managed to prevent the distillation of that immense sorrow into an even greater anger. He could feel his mind dancing, like an electronic chip the size of a hillside, restless with the energy of a million million segments.

'Orococco,' said Knocker, and the West Indian turned; Knocker had never seen him so lifeless. 'I want you and Torrey to guard the tunnel until the coppers come. When you see them, fire off a lot of stones and shout. Try to hold them for as long as you can.'

Torreycanyon stepped forward, ready to go.

'But don't let them get near you. Just slow them down. We need time to brick up the wall and things, that's all. As soon as they get close scoot off and join the others.'

'Okay,' said Orococco. 'We'll see if we can't crack a few skulls. Come on Torrey.'

The two Borribles ran lightly over the rails and took up their positions, one on each side of the tunnel entrance. There they drew their catapults and waited.

'So what about us?' said Bingo. 'Have we got to run away and hide now? You can't tell us what to do, Knocker, though you like to think you can.'

Knocker dropped his chin to his chest and stared at the ground. 'Oh, Bingo, you'll be able to do much more out on the streets in a few months' time than you will down here with your ears clipped.'

Stonks came up trumps again. He pushed in front of Bingo and refused to let the argument develop. 'What do you want?' he asked. 'I'll see it gets done.'

'Right,' said Knocker. He raised his head. 'Go back to the control cabin and get Chalotte; she's been there alone with Nap for far too long already. Then go and find Sid. She should have made the cement by now; she may even have the wall half bricked up. If she hasn't finished it off, you do it. Just leave a gap of a few bricks. That's it and all about it. For Pete's sake go.'

Stonks jerked a thumb and Twilight took Bingo away; Vulge followed. As soon as the three of them were out of earshot Stonks looked at Knocker and squinted. 'I may be slow,' he said, 'but I ain't daft. What's the rest of it?'

Knocker returned the look, fair and square. 'I haven't got the time, Stonks, honest, but it will work, believe me. And make sure Chalotte goes with you. If she asks where I am, say I'll be along at the last to brick up the wall. I will come, I promise. Now run, Stonks, run.'

Stonks didn't like it. He really wanted to argue some more, but he trusted Knocker so he nodded and ran off after the others as fast as his legs would carry him. There might be a time for talk some other time, there might not. Right now there certainly wasn't.

The moment he was on his own Knocker sprang into action. He counted the green jackets hooked over his arm; there were two. He ran quickly back to where the victims of the rope trick lay; neither of them moved and he bent and pulled the jackets from their stiffening bodies. That made four. He bent again and heaved the dwarfs along until he had dropped them over the big square rail that had carried the electric current in the old days.

With that accomplished he pulled himself up to an open carriage door, entered the train, crossed a compartment and dropped out on the other side. There he found the bodies of the two dwarfs that he and Chalotte had jumped on and he removed their jackets. That made six.

Still there was more work to do. He must find out if there were any more dwarfs on the battlefield. For his plan to work there had to be the right number; superfluous ones would have to be buried.

Swiftly, with a burst of speed that would have been the envy of any Borrible, Knocker ran up and down between the trains, then alongside one, then alongside the other. He looked underneath, he checked every carriage. There were no more corpses. There was one jacket missing.

Time was getting short. He ran to the front of the trains again. Orococco and Torreycanyon were still at their post, calling out insults and firing their catapults. Beyond them Knocker saw a long hedge of policemen, three or four deep, riot shields at the ready, black helmets on their heads and silver see-behind visors hiding their faces.

'Okay,' shouted Knocker. 'You'd better leg it out of there.'

Orococco waved a hand, and firing a last salvo of stones at the advancing policemen he and Torreycanyon began their retreat. The policemen hardly seemed to notice this alteration and certainly did not bother to change their tactics but continued to walk on at the same steady pace. They did not have to rush and they had no desire to fall into a trap.

Then Knocker saw it, the something that had slipped his mind. Ninch still lay where he had fallen, draped across the power rail. Knocker had already taken his jacket and was in fact wearing it. That made seven. But right close to Ninch was the body of the dwarf that Knocker had tripped, the one who had smashed his head open butting into a rail; his jacket had not been collected.

Knocker laughed. He dashed forward and met Orococco and Torreycanyon by the corpses. He knelt and pulled away the last green garment. That made eight, the magic number.

Orococco jerked a thumb over his shoulder. 'Don't hang about,' he advised. 'There's a hell of a lot of coppers coming, like another bloody royal wedding.'

Knocker stood and removed the jacket he was wearing and handed it, together with the others, to Torreycanyon. 'Take these back to the transformer room and bury 'em deep,' he said. 'They must never be found. Tell the rest I'll be along in a little while. Stonks knows what to do. Now scarper, like lightning.'

Knocker watched them go and a lump rose in his throat. He would never see them again. He pushed the thought from his mind. There in the tunnel, well past the long curve now, the policemen were getting nearer. Knocker licked his lips and looked down at the body of Ninch. 'Dammit,' he said. 'Without you we might have got away and Napoleon would still be alive.' Knocker frowned. 'But then again,' he went on, 'maybe you and yours will see to it that our lot escapes after all, Ninchy-boy. After all there's eight of you dwarfs left for dead and that must be a sign because eight plus me and Napoleon makes ten, and ten Borribles is exactly what Sussworth would expect to find.'

And running lightly on his feet, borne up by the thought that he, Knocker, would win in the end, the Borrible slipped silently away between the trains.

13

Knocker reconnoitred the control cabin from behind the last carriage of the second train. He ducked down suddenly. Had it been his imagination or had someone just darted through the doorway? Knocker bit his lip. He would have to be careful. There might be a Woollie in there, part of an advance guard come in the other way, over from the Marylebone tunnel.

'Damn,' said Knocker. He hadn't expected them so soon. If he couldn't get into the cabin then his plans would be brought to nothing. Knocker crept closer, his feet sliding noiselessly over the stone dust. He edged up to the window but its panes were thick with dirt. He stepped to the door and peered in.

In the light of the one electric light bulb Knocker saw that the body of Napoleon Boot still lay on the table, his arms folded across his chest like those of a warrior king. Beyond the table was another figure raising its hands to the vast control panel, moving its head, reading the labels on the giant switches: Main Lighting, Secondary Lighting, Link Tunnel Power, Emergency Power, Lifts, Main Rail Power North, Main Rail Power South. Knocker recognized the figure immediately. It was Chalotte.

Knocker gasped and went to call out a warning but his throat was dry with fear. Chalotte's hands were on the contacts that once thrown into position would send thousands of volts flowing through every byway of this section of the London Underground.

Knocker tried to speak again but Chalotte allowed him no time. There was a solid clunk as she pulled the first of the switches down and the electric current surged eagerly across the metal that now closed the circuit. Then Chalotte threw another switch, then another and another and so on all along the bank; large switches and small ones, all were swung over.

The lights in the tunnels and the one bulb in the control cabin dipped and dimmed, as if electricity needed to take a deep breath before coming to life. From outside, from the power tracks, there came a humming and a murmuring as the new electric force pushed aside the cold resistance of miles and miles of metal, and the black ropes of cable draped along the curving subterranean walls crackled and swelled with death.

And that mysterious force ran everywhere, searching high and low at a speed that was magical. It was a torrent of bursting sparkling power, irresistible, snaking its way into every corner and cranny. It was strong, it was invisible and it was deadly.

Along the rails of steel it ran, into the ancient motors of the two abandoned trains and into the bodies of the defeated dwarfs, breaking open the soft flesh and lifting it from the bones, searing those bones and baking the marrow black. The bodies jerked and twitched violently as if to escape but there was no escape; the power held them.

Knocker moved at last. 'Chalotte,' he cried, 'don't!'

Chalotte swung round like a wild thing when she heard her name. Her filthy hair fell across her face, her eyes shone with a brilliant madness as if the electricity had jumped the switches, poured through her hands and was now blazing in her brain. All her muscles were tense, ready to spring. 'Knocker,' she cried, 'I thought you were dead.'

The smell of burning corpses came in through the doorway and Knocker felt his gorge rise. He swayed and put out a hand to hold himself steady. 'You idiot,' he gasped, 'you'll spoil everything.'

Chalotte took no notice of what Knocker had said but stretched her arms in front of the control panel, ready to defend it with her life. 'Stonks gave me your message,' she said, 'but the more he said you were coming back the less I believed it. He made it sound as if you were done for already . . . So I swore I'd get Sussworth . . . Sussworth I said, Sussworth for Napoleon; for Scooter and Knocker. I've had enough of running with nowhere to rest. I know there's no chance of us getting away so I came here to fry a few Woollies before they clip our ears . . . and though it's good you're still alive it's all the same really.'

Knocker tried to answer. He wanted to tell Chalotte it was all right. He wanted to turn the power off as well. He must. It had never been part of his plan to kill any member of the SBG. On the contrary, he wanted to make them think they had won an easy victory; anything to stop them searching the battlefield too closely and finding the last hiding place of the Adventurers. All this he tried to say but the only words that came out of his mouth were: 'The power, the power.'

He raised a hand and stumbled further into the cabin. As he did he heard a terrifying noise of groaning and clanking. The fluorescents flickered again and there came the clamour of steel grinding on steel. Lights sprang up in the carriages outside and slowly their great wheels turned. Smoke poured from the brake pads. One of the Underground trains was moving. 'It's the SBG,' screamed Chalotte. 'They've switched on the power too. They must be moving the trains out so they can search the place better.'

This new danger brought Knocker to his senses. 'Quick then,' he said. 'We must get to the others. Hurry! And watch out for the live rail, whatever you do.' And Knocker threw an arm around Chalotte's shoulders and the two weary Borribles passed through the cabin door and made their way across the workshop area, disappearing at last behind one of the huge piles of rubbish.

Knocker could not know it, and nor could anyone else, but there was no one driving the train; it was driving itself, mindless and invincible, the wheels spinning on the tracks.

In the driver's cab where Orococco and Twilight had fought hand to hand with the two dwarfs, fists and feet and truncheons had struck and smashed the buttons and switches; short circuits had been made and terminals joined. As soon as the electric power found itself free it urged the old train to advance, only slowly at first but then faster and faster, and, as the metal brakes worked themselves loose, so the long line of carriages steadily gathered momentum.

*

Inspector Sussworth, Sergeant Hanks and Constable Blume stood on the platform at Swiss Cottage and listened to the shouts and insults of Orococco and Torreycanyon as they came curling out from the tunnel.

'I tell you, Hanks,' said Sussworth, 'it is only the courage of despair. There can't be many of them left alive after that battle with the dwarfs. By the way, Blume, did you pay the dwarfs off and get rid of them?'

'Oh yes, sir, paid them very handsomely too.'

'And did you check very carefully that none of them were Borribles?'

'Of course, sir. Very carefully.'

'Good,' said the inspector. 'I'm very glad to have those dwarfs out of the way at last. They made me very nervous. It would have been the end of my career you know if the DAC had found out we were using auxiliaries in these encounters. Do you hear that, Hanks, Blume? On no account must this classified information come to the ears of the upper echelons. It is far too sensitive and would only upset them.'

'No sir,' said Blume. 'You told us, sir, and we have not forgotten.' He stood to attention and clutched his clipboard more tightly under his arm.

Hanks wrinkled his nose twice in quick succession as if trying to dislodge something juicy and substantial. 'Cost a lot, them dwarfs,' he said. 'I could have sworn some of 'em were going back to the end of the line to get paid twice. Couldn't tell one from the other though with all that dirt and grease and blood on 'em. You could see they'd been in a scrap.'

'Worth every penny we paid them, Hanks,' said Sussworth, rubbing his gloved hands together with contentment. 'They've flushed out the Borribles; killed most of them too, by all accounts. All that remains for our men is to walk in and pick up the pieces . . . There won't be one policeman injured. Our operation will be a complete success. Wonderful!'

'It seems to me,' said Blume, after giving a discreet cough to engage his superior's attention, 'that the noise of shouting has ceased. I should think that our men have completed their task by now and rounded up the survivors, if any. Would you like me to go and see, Inspector? I could put a call through on the radio.'

Sussworth stretched himself to his full height and looked up at Blume as if he were looking down. 'Blume,' he said, twisting his arms behind his back as if he possessed some vital information that he wished to extract from himself by torture, 'Blume, you have captured my very thought as I was about to give it utterance. I have been informed that at the end of that section of loop line which lies before us there is a small marshalling yard where a couple of old trains are kept in reserve. Beyond, they say, it connects with the Marylebone railway tunnel. As you well know I have men guarding that possible escape route and some more advancing along it to join with those that departed from this platform. Our Borribles are in the middle, caught in a pincer movement. The old left hook as Monty used to say when he was jousting with the Desert Fox. Loonieberg Heath, gentlemen. Loonieberg Heath. This is my Loonieberg Heath.'

Hanks stared at the station sign which said Swiss Cottage in letters two feet high. 'It says Swiss Cottage, sir,' he said.

Sussworth ignored this remark and continued his speech while trying to give himself a half nelson at the same time. 'I have no wish to miss my greatest moment of triumph. I want to see this surrender, relish it. I want to see those Borribles grovel in the gravel at my feet. I want to sit in a folding canvas chair whilst I watch the police surgeon remove the pointed tops of their ears. I want to hear the crunch of the world settling back into its normal groove. In a word, Hanks, Blume, I propose to walk along between the rails and go to my men, personally, myself.'

Suiting his actions to his words Sussworth began to pace along the platform, his legs jerking before him, stiff and straight. Hanks rolled forward beside the inspector, right index finger in right nostril, a smile forming on his face. There was something good up there. Blume, still clutching his clipboard, walked a respectful yard behind Sussworth, imitating his superior's manner in every detail. He dearly wanted to succeed.

At the end of the platform, just where it sloped down to the permanent way, Sussworth twirled on his heel, changing direction as abruptly as a dodgem car. His overcoat flared out like a bullfighter's cape and revealed his polished boots, gleaming like gloss paint.

'Constable Blume,' he said, 'when I telephoned to the surface just now I gave instructions that the DAC was at last to be informed of our success. I am expecting his arrival at any time during the next half hour. I want you, Constable, to be here, on this platform, when he arrives. You will inform him of our complete success and, if I am not returned and he is indeed willing, you may bring him to the forward battle zone where he may witness the surrender of the Borribles and the culmination of the magnum octopus of Inspector Francis Sussworth.'

'Francis,' said Hanks. He removed a green bogey from his nostril and studied it. 'Never knew his name was Francis.' Disappointed at the harvest hanging from the end of his finger he shoved it back where it belonged so that it might grow larger and more colourful. As he did so Susswarth performed a rapid about-turn on one foot like a wind-up tin soldier, and faced the other way. 'Come on, Hanks,' he said.

Hanks waddled across to join his master and together the two men descended the short slope that took them down to the level of the track. There was only one line in this link tunnel and so the inspector and the sergeant walked along side by side between the rails. The walls were close together and curved low overhead to form the ceiling. Every word spoken echoed, every footstep sounded like ten, and in spite of the fluorescent lighting there was a morbid feel to the place. The tunnel's glazed bricks were glistening all over with a clammy and poisonous sweat.

This intimidating atmosphere did not inspire conversation and both men walked in silence for some time. After they had covered a quarter of a mile or so, Sussworth spoke. 'Tell me, Hanks,' he said, 'what is the distance appertaining to the points A and B in this case, and how long is this curve? I can no longer see Swiss Cottage behind me, nor our destination in front.'

Hanks was almost breathless by reason of the unaccustomed exercise his body was undergoing; he had never walked a quarter of a mile in his whole life. Nevertheless he managed to pant out an answer for Sussworth's benefit. 'Ah . . . I think it must be . . . ah . . . about half a mile, sir, but I'm not sure . . . But I am sure that I could murder a nice cup of tea and a bacon sandwich.'

'Shush,' ordered Sussworth, and he held up his hand. 'I hear something unusual emanating from point B. Listen and lower your breathing, Sergeant.'

Sussworth and Hanks listened, and as the sound of their breathing diminished and the echo of their footsteps receded the conductor rail on their right flexed itself and spat orange sparks, and the lights in the tunnel roof dimmed and rose and dimmed again. From far away came faint shouts: the shouts of SBG men calling to one another in distress. But behind those desperate calls there was another sound, more frightful and more forbidding. It was the slow rumble of steel wheels advancing, and it was the rumble too of a whole train on the move. Beneath their feet the two policemen felt the sleepers shift and the rails writhe as tons and tons of rolling stock gathered momentum in the distance.

Hanks looked nervously over his shoulder. Sussworth took a sharp step forward, thought better of it and took an even sharper step back.

'There seems to be a train on the move, Hanks,' said the inspector, his voice more clipped than usual as he tried to hide the mounting apprehension in his breast. 'This is out of order, Hanks. I assure you I gave strict orders that no trains were to move from A to B, or even from C to D, until such times as I rescinded the order in person.'

'Yessir,' said Hanks, 'but what to do now, sir?'

'Good question, Hanks. We must take evasive action. Instanto. I have no wish to do a Husskinson.'

'Nor me, sir,' said Hanks, the sweat beginning to trickle in his armpits, 'whatever it is.' The sergeant made as if to turn and he stumbled. 'Oh dear,' he cried. 'May the Lord save us.'

'Back to point A,' said Sussworth. 'That train sounds as if it is moving fairly slowly so we shall move rapidly. In other words, Hanks, run for your life.'

The men set off immediately, their feet stamping down on the loose ballast that lay between the sleepers. Sussworth ran with a single-minded determination, a determination that brooked no obstacle and admitted no alternative. Hanks, on the other hand, already breathless, ran in despair, as if his fate had been decided on the very morning of his birth. His breath ripped through him. He could feel a blunt bowsaw tearing his lungs to shreds. His huge stomach wobbled so violently from side to side that it threatened to pull him off balance at any moment. His knees lost their tension as his fatigue overcame him; his head rolled in panic and his bowels loosened with terror. There was something wet and nasty forming in his trousers, but worst of all, Sussworth was leaving him behind. Twenty yards now separated the two runners.

'Oh, Inspector,' called Hanks, stretching out an arm before him, 'wait for me.'

Sussworth stopped and turned. He placed his hands on his hips and stared in scorn as Hanks continued to pant along behind his stomach.

'I'll wait for you back on the platform, Hanks,' cried the inspector, and he turned again to continue his run. At that moment the driverless train entered the far end of the tunnel, and the vague rumblings of it became a mighty roar as all the separate sounds were squashed together into one sound and pushed along before the front carriage, like a load of broken bricks and clanging iron bars.

The two halves of Sussworth's moustache twitched forward like radio antennae. The message was not good; the train was picking up speed.

Hanks wailed like a banshee and his fear gave him an energy that all the lorry-loads of food he had eaten in the past never had. He became light and tense, his muscles contracted into coils of steel, and before Sussworth could even sense his danger, let alone resume his flight, Hanks was upon him and had grabbed the inspector's right arm with both hands.

Sussworth, who hated being touched at any time and especially by anything as large and ugly as Hanks, tried to pull himself free, using all his strength and pushing against the sleepers with his booted feet.

'Hanks,' he screamed, 'let go! D'you hear? That's an order. Cease this dereliction of duty. I'll have you court-martialled.'

Hanks took no heed. He was beyond listening and his grip was for ever. His whole being was filled with the sound of the advancing train. That one great burst of energy had finished him; he could run no further but he would not be left alone either. He hung on to Sussworth's arm as if to life.

'Don't leave me, sir,' he pleaded. 'Take me home, I need my mother.'

Sussworth lashed out with his feet and kicked his sergeant hard. He pushed and pulled, he cajoled and he shouted. None of it was any good. Hanks held on and the noise of the train rolled round the tunnel's curve and grew and grew, and filled the whole space from side to side and from floor to roof. Sussworth was screaming now to make himself heard above the din but Hanks clung on and begged and pleaded to be saved and yet all the time he was preventing the escape he so dearly desired.

With a sudden surge the wave of sound rose higher and through the curve swept the train itself, tall, long and fiery like some dragon storming from its cave, breathing light and fire from a fearsome head. On it came, imperiously, its windows gleaming in silver and gold.

Hanks raised his voice again and bellowed like a whale, and the cry was so loud that it reached the ears of Officer Blume on the platform at Swiss Cottage and curdled the water in his bladder.

'Oh my God,' sobbed Hanks, wise too late, 'we must get out of here.'

'You moron!' shouted Sussworth, who would gladly have killed his sergeant had he possessed a weapon. 'Get off the track, find an alcove; it's our only chance.'

Having delivered this advice Sussworth attempted to put it into practice by pulling Hanks to the side of the tunnel nearest him. Hanks, his mind working like scrambled egg, thought that his side looked nearer and yanked Sussworth off his feet, dragging him backwards across the railway lines.

Now Sussworth panicked. He knew that Hanks was heading in the direction of the live rail, but Hanks was aware of nothing beyond the animal instinct to survive. 'Hanks, no,' shouted Sussworth.

It was too late. Hanks threw himself out of the way of the charging monster, still holding Sussworth's arm and almost breaking it. He lurched, blinded and confused by the bright lights that were bearing down on him. He saw the conductor rail and recognized it for what it was. He jumped up and over and landed safely on the other side and gave a yell of triumph that never left his throat. Sussworth whimpered and knew his fate. He tried to arch his body up, to levitate himself even, but he could not. Hanks hauled him on and the inspector's leg just brushed the dreaded rail and that was enough.

Electricity loves the human body. In a split second it can romp through every vein and tissue you possess; singe every hair and make the toenails glow like neon signs. Electricity that can drive some sixty tons of train will make a frolic of legs and arms, and so, on that day, it leapt into the inspector's frame with mirth and pleasure, not noticing the obstacle of his flesh and unaware of the tiny life it quenched. It burnt his blood, it broiled his lungs and scorched his heart down to the consistency and shape of a lump of coke. And still it was eager, and swept on looking for more mischief and found the small but proud moustache, and grilled it to a crisp and dirty cinder that curled on Sussworth's charred and blackened upper lip.

And in that same instant the current touched the hand of Hanks, where he still gripped his leader's arm, and it rejoiced and into Hanks it raced and burnt and broiled and scorched all over again, and all his layers of fat seethed and bubbled. And six hundred and thirty volts sought out the flowering bogeys in the dark recesses of the sergeant's nose and cooked them till they coiled and writhed like hot bacon rind.

And when this lark was over the current sped away, searching for yet more space to fill with power, and it left behind it a strange and smoking sculpture: Sussworth and Hanks, desiccated husks, welded together. But the great train came on and smashed the sculpture down. Sussworth and Hanks were dead, nothing more than warm black ashes mingling with an old and worn-out dust.

*

Waiting on the platform at Swiss Cottage, Officer Blume heard the distant grumblings of a moving train. He heard too some high-pitched shouts and screams of terror. He clasped his hands behind his back, in imitation of his inspector, and glanced at the group of SBG officers who were standing near him. Blume hesitated and wondered what to do. Obviously there was something wrong, very wrong. A great deal of noise was coming from the tunnel and it was getting louder every second.

Blume started to walk up the platform towards the opening into which Sussworth and Hanks had disappeared. Perhaps he should go to their assistance after all, despite the orders to wait for the DAC. Blume's brow creased with worry, but he need not have concerned himself. The decision was made for him.

There was an enormous roar and in a cloud of light the driverless train burst out into the open at top speed, swaying madly from side to side. Officer Blume staggered, surprised, and tripped over his feet, tumbling backwards to land heavily on the concrete surface of the platform, damaging his elbows. He lay where he fell, watching helplessly as the train charged past him.

Now liberated from the confines of the narrow tunnel the train began to buck and sway. The carriages bashed against one another and were jostled and nudged from behind, clanging into the tiled wall and bumping along the edge of the platform itself.

In a second or two the front carriages gave way under all this shoving and reared up high. They scraped against the station roof and tore a long section of it down. More carriages left the rails and tried to turn left and right but only smashed harder against the walls or tipped over on to the platform. Their windows shattered into smithereens; their doors bent, and buckled, sprang free. Wheels flew from their mountings and ripped the tracks apart.

The noise was deafening; a tearing and banging and groaning of metal enough to break the eardrums. The din rose like a tornado, a noise that would never stop, a noise to drive men mad, and the officers of the SBG turned and fled, pushing each other out of the way in order to gain the safety of the nearest flight of stairs; anything to escape being crushed to a bloody pulp beneath this splintering, rolling avalanche of iron and steel.

Officer Blume sat where he was and made no attempt to regain his feet. He covered his ears with his hands but it was not over yet. The broken carriages ground their way along to the very end of the platform and, sliding sideways on, crashed against the opening of the far tunnel. Then came an explosion of sound even louder and more terrifying than before and the carriages telescoped one into the other in rapid succession, mounting higher and higher as if trying to climb upwards to freedom, then gradually, finding no way out, they slid backwards and rolled over into stillness, exhausted and demolished, while huge red and yellow flashes of flame made arcs of current across a thick black smoke and gave the station the look and smell of hell.

*

Knocker and Chalotte heard the noise of the crash but to them it was a distant thunder and they could not be sure what it was. They stood behind a large pile of old bricks and other builders' rubbish and listened as the great rolling sounds died away. Chalotte stared in front of her, listless and dejected. She had not spoken since leaving the cabin.

'The law will be along soon,' said Knocker. 'We'd better get inside with the others; let's hope this idea works.'

He advanced a step or two. It was odd here; he was in a wide cavern with a sloping roof and just where the roof met the floor Knocker saw what Sydney had discovered: an old doorway from which the wooden jambs had been torn. Strewn over the ground nearby were all sorts of tools, lengths of rough timber and sacks of cement. One of these sacks had been torn open and a small pile of freshly made mortar, a bricklayer's trowel in the middle of it, gleamed in the fluorescent lighting.

Moving closer to the doorway Knocker was able to see that it had been bricked up, almost to the top, leaving only just enough room for a Borrible to scramble through. The new cement between the bricks glowed wet and bright and showed exactly where the old doorway had been. Something would have to be done about that.

Knocker went up to the wall and made a step with his hands. 'Come on, Chal,' he said, making his voice sound cheerful. 'You go first, I'll follow.'

Chalotte nodded, came forward and placed her right foot in Knocker's hands. He gave a push upwards, she lifted herself high and Stonks appeared behind the gap and pulled her out of sight.

Knocker bent then and placed some spare bricks one upon the other and climbed up on them so that he could look into the hole. The face of Stonks stared at him.

'You'd better get in here,' said Stonks, 'and we'll finish the wall.'

Knocker's heart was heavy. The enormity of what he was about to do suddenly struck home. He felt lonely, very lonely. He lowered his voice. 'I can't come in, Stonks,' he said. 'Just imagine what it would look like out here: a pile of bricks where I'd climbed in, a load of cement, a trowel and fresh mortar between the bricks.'

Bingo's face popped up beside Stonks's. 'I heard that,' he said. 'What are you up to?'

'Someone,' explained Knocker, 'has to hide the evidence out here. It's obvious that the coppers will turn this place inside out. Someone has to hide that cement, finish off the wall from this side, but above all he has to dirty the mortar . . . It's your only chance otherwise they'll find you and it'll be ears clipped before you can say Barnardo's.'

'You'll be took,' said Bingo. 'There's nowhere to hide.'

Knocker tried to laugh in derision. 'Don't say that!' he said. 'I've got more than an even chance. I can lead 'em away from this place, maybe slip past 'em. I'll be in Neasden before you lot. You wait and see if I'm not.'

Knocker could tolerate no more of this conversation. He wasn't too sure how strong his resolve was. He loved his friends as much as life itself and did not want to leave them. He jumped from his pile of bricks and snatched up the trowel, loaded it with cement, took a brick and climbed back up again. He laid the cement on the next course, good and thick, and pushed the brick into position. The faces of Stonks and Bingo stared at him. They said nothing and Knocker got down again for more cement and another brick. He repeated this action several times and little by little the hole at the top of the doorway grew smaller until at last Knocker knew that three or four more bricks would close the gap for ever.

He hesitated. He cocked an ear but from the direction of danger came only silence. He went to smile a goodbye at Stonks and Bingo but suddenly their faces swayed and disappeared; they had been roughly pushed and pulled from whatever perch they had been standing on. In their place stood Chalotte, her green eyes dull, her cheeks still smeared with Napoleon's blood.

'Knocker,' she said, 'what do you think you're doing? Don't try to be a bloody hero.' She began to push at the bricks that Knocker had just laid in place. 'Get in here with us, you fool. Quick.'

Knocker struck with the trowel and cut Chalotte's knuckles. 'Stop her!' he called out. 'Stop her or she'll have the wall down.'

Chalotte was jostled and fell from sight. There was the sound of voices and then she reappeared. 'All right,' she said, looking behind her, 'I'll just talk. Leave me alone.'

Knocker jumped to the floor again, retrieved the bricks that had fallen and put them back in position. He laid another. Three more and the wall would be complete.

Chalotte's voice was toneless, as if she had travelled to the very end of life and found nothing there. 'Why, Knocker?' she asked. 'Why must you stay out there and be caught?'

Knocker flopped some more cement down. 'Because there's no other way, Chalotte. This is a good hiding place but it won't be worth a light unless it's disguised from the outside.' Knocker put another brick up and went for more cement and two bricks. This was it. All he could see through the hole now was half of Chalotte's face. She stared at him and he felt that he could not bear to leave her. At the same time he knew that if he did not everyone in that band of Adventurers, and the horse, would perish. He spread the last trowel of cement and looked at the girl's filthy face.

'It'll be all right, Chal,' he said. 'I'll be there with you, in Neasden.'

'Let me come with you,' said Chalotte. Her face looked smaller, distant even, through the brick-sized hole. 'We could both lead the coppers astray. Do it together.'

Knocker's heart swelled enough to break his ribs. He would have liked nothing better. 'No, Chalotte,' he said. 'I've bricked up the wall now and we haven't got time to knock it down and build it again. The coppers will be here any minute. This way there's a chance of you all escaping. I don't want to get caught, sure I don't, but I'd hate it even more if you were caught with me.'

Chalotte pressed her face close to the hole and looked at Knocker hard. 'You're not getting up to a Spiff trick, are you?' she said. 'You're not after a third name: Knocker Burnthand Slaughterhouse?'

Knocker shook his head. 'I'm past all that, Chalotte. I did a lot of thinking down Flinthead's mine. If it hadn't been for Sussworth after our horse I wouldn't even be here now.'

'Then what is it?' persisted Chalotte. 'I know you inside out. You're up to something and if you expect me to stay in here with the others and do nothing then you'll have to tell me or I'll have this wall down, Stonks or no Stonks, coppers or no coppers.'

Knocker listened. There was no sound of movement in the tunnels. Something must have delayed the police in their advance. He looked at Chalotte again. 'There's eight dead dwarfs out here,' he began, 'and I moved them all so they were touching the power rail. When I came back to the control cabin I just wanted to switch the power on in this section, where the dwarfs were, just for a second or two, burn 'em to cinders. I didn't want the power going all over the place and maybe frying the whole of the SBG. I just wanted it so the coppers wouldn't be able to tell them dead dwarfs from dead Borribles. They'll recognize poor old Napoleon lying there, and they'll recognize me when I show myself in the tunnel, and then I'll lead 'em a dance, see. Eight plus Nap plus me makes ten. That's the number Sussworth will expect to find. I'm hoping he'll think he's done for the lot of us, and once they've had a look round they'll leave. You lot will have to wait in that hole for two or three days maybe; you'll be hungry but you'll be alive. When you think it's safe you just push the wall down and come out. It's only a few hours' march along the tunnel to Neasden and it'll all be over. Lie low for a while and you can all go home.'

'If you're so sure you can give Sussworth the slip in the tunnels,' said Chalotte, 'you can come back here yourself and tell us when it's safe to come out.' The half of her face that Knocker could see had an expression of irony on it.

'Yeah,' said Knocker, 'that's it. Of course.'

'You're lying,' said Chalotte. 'I know you are.'

'When Adolf got burnt to death in Rumbledom,' said Knocker, his voice low, 'I knew it was my fault. It should never have happened, but all I could think of in those days was the treasure and a second name. Compared to Adolf I wasn't even a real Borrible. Remember it was Adolf who carried Vulge to safety and if that wasn't enough he had to go and get himself killed saving me. And Napoleon when you think of it, he had to turn against Flinthead, turn against his own tribe, so that he could save us.'

The despair left Chalotte's eyes but was replaced by the brightness of tears. 'You stayed in the tunnel with the others,' she said, 'so we could get away in the boat.'

Knocker shook his head. 'That was for the Rumble treasure, for a name,' he said, 'just to win. I wasn't doing it for other Borribles. Can't you see, I have to do something? It's no good us all getting caught down here, not if I can get you out of it.'

Chalotte's tears flowed now. 'Oh Knocker,' she said, 'I don't want you to be caught and clipped. I don't want you to grow old and die.'

Knocker blinked and hefted the last brick in his hand. 'I know,' he said, 'but you and the others have to survive and this is the only way I can think of. Sam must get away and you lot must get back to your boroughs so that you can tell this story over and over again so that other Borribles know the truth of things. Just think of the story the SBG will put out. If we don't tell it like it happened no one else will. Borribles must be told to stay Borrible, and above all they must be told about Scooter. If adults can be changed into Borribes . . . well the sky's the limit. Imagine! Can you see Sussworth telling anyone about that, even if he knew? He'd keep as quiet as the grave. Come on, Chalotte, you know it's right; you know it better than me. If there's any possibility of you getting out alive you have to. You know more about being Borrible than anyone.'

Chalotte lowered her head and the visible part of her face disappeared into shadow. 'Oh Knocker,' she said, 'I love you.'

Knocker swallowed hard. 'And I you,' he said, 'and all the others as well. That's why I'm doing this. It may look like we're losing to Sussworth at the moment, but we're not, far from it.'

'I know, Knocker, but what will you do if you get clipped?'

Knocker pretended to laugh. 'There's no chance of me getting caught,' he said, 'not the slightest . . . but if I did I reckon I'd try to write down as much of our story as I could remember before it faded from my mind, before they made me forget it. That would show people what being Borrible is about and how we fought for Sam and that. That's what I'd do.'

There was silence for a while when Knocker finished this speech but Chalotte soon raised her wet face and looked at him, and he could control his sadness no longer and his tears fell and he let them.

'Goodbye, Chalotte,' he said. 'Goodbye. Don't ever get caught.' And his voice cracked and he sobbed and as he sobbed he pushed the last brick into the last gap and, using his thumb, surrounded it with cement and saw Chalotte no more. Then he sank to his knees and rested his forehead against the wall. 'Goodbye, you lot,' he whispered, 'and goodbye, Sam. Stay Borrible, stay Borrible.'

For several long minutes Knocker remained where he was and did not move, although in his heart of hearts he knew that he had no time to indulge his sadness. The police might arrive at any moment and there was still much to be accomplished.

With a deep sigh he stood and wiped his eyes on the cuff of his sleeve. When he could see more clearly he took up the trowel and dug a large hole and scraped what was left of the fresh mortar into it; then he buried the trowel itself, filling the hole with earth and rubbish. Next he scooped up large fistfuls of dirt and dust and threw them at the newly sealed doorway so that gradually the light-coloured wet cement took on the appearance of the black surrounding wall and became indistinguishable from it; just another section of the brick skin lining the London Underground.

Still Knocker was not satisfied. He sank to his haunches and smoothed the ground with his fingers, afterwards scattering handfuls of dust and gravel everywhere so as to obliterate the Adventurers' footprints. When this had been done he found an ancient bench, a broken ladder and lots of old tools and he spread them about in what he hoped would seem to be a random manner. Finally he stepped back to survey his work and he had to admit that even with the full glare of the overhead lighting to aid them, the SBG would have to be very fortunate indeed to discover the whereabouts of the transformer room entrance. Knocker smiled. Yes; with a minimum of luck the Adventurers would get away.

A rough shout from afar broke into these thoughts and with one quick glance around him Knocker ran towards the control cabin, jumped on to the track and looked into the northbound tunnel. Things were certainly happening now. The second half of Sussworth's pincer movement could be seen in the distance: lamps, blue uniforms, helmets and riot shields, stretching across the railway line and advancing slowly.

With no hesitation Knocker leapt into view and waved his arms above his head and shouted, making sure that he was noticed. As soon as he had been he turned and ran back alongside the one train that was left, not halting until he reached the front carriage. There he peeped out to see what was happening by the Swiss Cottage tunnel.

What he saw was puzzling. Before him stood a force of about fifty policemen huddled in groups, talking but not advancing or even searching. They looked scared and worried. A smoky dust curled in the electric air above their heads; it shimmered with the vibration of the great crash.

What was wrong? The policemen were behaving as if some great calamity had struck them. 'Better bring them back to a sense of duty,' he said to himself and he leapt into view again, firing a volley of stones, and without waiting to see what action was taken against him, called out an insult and dashed away at speed.

Strangely there was no pursuit and Knocker slowed his pace, jogged for a while, and then walked until he came to the control cabin. He looked in at the door; the body of Napoleon Boot still lay on the table, alone, his arms still folded. Knocker entered the cabin, sat on a chair and stared at his dead friend. 'I will stay with Napoleon, then,' he said aloud, 'and let them find me.'

And as Knocker waited the fearful loneliness came over him again, and he thought of Chalotte and the others waiting out their time in the hiding place. He hadn't told Chalotte everything, not by a long chalk. There was a weak spot in his plan and it worried him. Sussworth might wonder what had become of the missing dwarfs. Wouldn't he have counted them all out, and counted them all in? Knocker hoped not. On that evening when he, Napoleon and Swish and Treld had gone into the caravan as dwarfs, Sussworth hadn't seemed to take much care over the actual numbers of his auxilaries, or even their names. Perhaps that was still the case.

Knocker had kept this weak spot from Chalotte deliberately. It would have undermined his argument and she would have made even more trouble about letting him go. Knocker leant forward and straightened Napoleon's jacket collar and smoothed it down. He knew that his plan did not have the slightest chance of working unless he, Knocker, were captured and recognized and could, under interrogation, tell Sussworth that the other Borribles were dead. But he must not give the game away immediately. On the contrary he would insist that the Borribles had escaped and Sussworth, being what he was, would be suspicious. Then, as the inspector threatened him, Knocker would pretend to crack and he would say just what the police wanted to hear, but he would say it as if it were the last thing in the world he wanted them to know. It was the only method of convincing Sussworth that the SBG had won. It would be a terrible sacrifice, the ultimate one, delivering himself up like that, and Knocker knew it would be a living death for him in the end, but there was nothing else to do, no other way.

He laid his finger on Napoleon's cold cheek and thought about the past: about the Great Rumble Hunt, about the River Wandle and Flinthead's deep mine and the chief Wendle's fight with Spiff . . . both dead and gone now . . . and Napoleon dead too. Who would have thought it possible after so many adventures, after having so much life in him? 'Damn the SBG,' said Knocker. 'If only they'd left us alone.'

Knocker's head began to droop. 'I must make sure,' he said. 'I must make sure that I remember every detail of these adventures. I must never forget. It mustn't get lost, this story.' And Knocker took Napoleon's hand and laid his head on the Wendle's arm. He closed his eyes, just for a second he meant it, to ease his aching heart and to shut out all the evil things in the world, but exhausted by lack of food and all the fighting and running, he soon fell fast asleep.

*

He was woken by a rough hand shaking him brutally by the shoulder. As he came awake another hand grabbed a fistful of his hair. Knocker was pulled to his feet, and as his eyes opened he saw that the control cabin was crowded with men of the SBG, their visors thrown back over their helmets, their big square teeth grinning and their faces shining with victory.

'Come on you murdering bleeder, let's be having yer,' said a voice, and Knocker's arms were pulled behind his back and he was handcuffed.

'What's yer name?' said the nearest policeman and he twisted his hand harder in Knocker's hair.

'Knocker,' said Knocker, 'and stop pulling my hair.'

'Who's pulling your hair?' said the policeman and he pulled Knocker's hair even harder.

Another policeman moved round the table and shoved his hand under Napoleon's head, lifting it so that he could scrutinize it more carefully. 'Which one's this?' he asked. 'Nasty-looking bit of work, vicious.'

'That's Napoleon Boot,' said Knocker. 'He's dead now, so you needn't be frightened.'

Knocker's head was jerked backwards and he was thrust towards the door. 'Outside, chummy,' said his captor, 'and none of your lip or I'll teach you some manners, personal.'

With this caution Knocker was ejected from the cabin and searched. His catapult and his knife were found and a guard of four men assigned to take him away, frog-marching him alongside the track in the direction of Swiss Cottage. As Knocker was hustled forward he could see groups of police officers everywhere, searching the train and wandering freely over the sidings, safe now that the power in the live rails had been switched off.

The hand tugged at Knocker's hair. 'You'd better tell us where your mates are,' said the policeman who had arrested him.

Knocker twisted his head up and round as far as he could. 'Far away, Woollie, far away where you'll never find 'em.'

‘’Ere,’ said another of the men, stopping Knocker and crouching down in front of him so his face was level with the Borrible’s. ‘It wasn’t you by any chance who turned the power on and made the train go?’

Knocker hesitated and wondered what was the best thing to answer. He could say that Napoloen had been responsible but the SBG would rather have a live captive than a dead one, someone they could bash about a bit. Knocker looked the policeman in the eye; he was chubby, friendly even. There was a bubble of spittle on his lips. ‘I did it,’ said Knocker. ‘I turned the power on and left it on.’

The policeman smiled like a brain tumour and slowly stood, his big knees creaking. The other three constables came closer to him and formed a circle round the small Borrible and Knocker gazed up at their faces.

‘Ho ho,’ said the policeman who had asked the question. ‘You’ll be straight inside you will. They’ll clip your ears and put you to work until you die of exhaustion. You’ll never get out.’ The smile died on the man’s lips and was replaced by an expression of intense anger. ‘I’m glad we caught you alive,’ he said. ‘Your feet won’t touch the ground for a month. We’ll play squash with you. You killed Inspector Sussworth and Sergeant Hanks, you did. Electrocuted them in the tunnel and run ’em over with the train. That’s murder, chummy, murder, and you’ll be paying for it the rest of your life.’

Knocker stared at each large face above him in turn, wondering if they were telling the truth. Fear touched his heart and it missed a beat. They’d certainly do for him now; they’d make him suffer for as long as possible. But then the fear lessened and he thought of Chalotte. By sheer accident, in despair and frustration, she had struck a blow for Borribles everywhere. Knocker smiled; Chalotte had always been guided by some superior wisdom.

A heavy blow wiped the smile from Knocker’s face and felled him to the ground. ‘Smile would yer?’ said one of the guards. ‘You heartless swine. You’ll smile the other side of your face before we’re through with yer. Go on, move!’

Once more Knocker was hauled upright by his hair and led onward. He staggered often and the pain of the blow hurt badly but despite that pain his heart was singing. Wait till the others heard this news. Just wait till the others heard.

At the end of the train Knocker and his four guards emerged into the open space where Napoleon had fought with Ninch. Here were many more members of the SBG and in their midst was a tall man, beautifully dressed in the smartest of clothes and leaning on a furled umbrella. It was the DAC and he wore a wide-brimmed Homburg hat and a dark blue pinstriped suit. Across his shoulders, flung carelessly like a cape, was a navy blue alpaca overcoat.

Beyond the DAC scores of police officers were searching the ground and every nook and cranny they could find. More constables arrived each second and from all directions, bringing reports written on scraps of paper which the DAC scrutinized before handing them on to a constable with a clipboard who stood near him. Knocker could see that a few charred bodies had been assembled near the mouth of the southbound tunnel. That would be the dwarfs.

There was great excitement and talking among the policemen when Knocker and his four guards appeared. The DAC watched attentively as the group approached. When he thought they were close enough he raised his umbrella and pointed at the dishevelled and scruffy Borrible.

'What is that thing there?' he said, his upper crust voice squeezing his vowels flatter than pillowslips in a mangle.

'This is a ringleader, sir,' said one of Knocker's guards. 'Knocker's his name. He's been in it from the very beginning. That business at Southfields, sir. Dewdrop and his son, murder, sir. Escaped from protective custody at Clapham South. Another murder at King's Cross. The list is endless. In capturing this one we have removed the hub from the spokes, sir, as it were. He also admits to throwing the switch that released the current that drove the train . . .' The policeman lowered his voice in respect. '. . . that did for Inspector Sussworth and Sergeant Hanks, sir.'

The DAC raised an eyebrow. 'Did that, did he?' he drawled. 'Well we owe him somethin' and we must see he jolly well gets it, what? And his little friends, where are they?'

Officer Blume glanced at the clipboard in his hand and joined the conversation. 'According to Inspector Sussworth's notes,' he said, 'based on highly secret reports emanating from certain elements of low life, as correlated on our Borrible computer, sir, according to that information we are pursuing ten Borribles, ringleaders from many tribes. This will be Knocker, from Battersea, sir.'

The DAC took the clipboard from Blume's hands and flicked through several sheets of paper for a while before returning it. 'What's the word "Ninch" mean?' he asked. 'Lots of reports from that.'

Knocker felt the policeman next to him go tense; the fingers in his hair tightened.

'Ah, Ninch, sir.' Blume flicked through the report sheets again, making a great show of searching for something. 'Ah, yessir. Here it is. Ninch was the code name for the computer, sir. It was called Ninch.'

The DAC nodded and pushed the matter from his mind. All he had wanted was an answer. He redirected his attention to Knocker and gazed downwards.

'And where are your accomplices, my good man? Serious offences, these you have committed. There's no way out for you, no way at all, but I could search round for reasons for leniency if you are helpful. The ears will have to go of course, but there is such a thing as anaesthetic. We could let you plead manslaughter rather than murder and you'd be out in half the time, but you'd have to turn supergrass and tell us everythin' you know. Could you do that?'

Knocker shook his head. 'The others got away,' he said. 'That's all I'm saying, and you'll never catch them.'

A blow struck the Borrible and he staggered into the body of the constable who still held him by the hair. 'Say "sir" when you answers the DAC,' said a voice.

'Knickers,' said Knocker and took another blow.

The DAC yawned and raised a hand. 'That'll do,' he said. 'Not while I'm here if you chaps don't mind. Now, Blume, what about his accomplices?'

Blume looked at his clipboard again. 'Eight bodies found,' he said, 'but all electrocuted and burnt unrecognizable.'

'Really,' said the DAC and this time he raised both eyebrows. 'They seem to have electrocuted themselves as well as Susssworth. How tidy.' He twirled his umbrella once or twice with satisfaction. 'Eight bodies plus this one makes nine . . . One of 'em's still on the loose then, eh?'

One of Knocker's guard stepped forward. 'Excuse me, sir, but no sir. There's one more body in the control cabin, a little further in. Definitely a Borrible that one. Pointed ears and quite dead. Napoleon Boot by name, a nasty piece of villainy from Wandsworth. What I believe they calls a Wendle. That makes ten.'

'They got away, right away,' said Knocker. 'Them bodies aren't Borribles, you know they ain't; they're something else. I suppose Napoleon died fighting a computer, did he?'

'What is occurin' here?' asked the DAC. He pointed again at Knocker with his umbrella.

Blume glared threateningly at Knocker as if he would kill him on the spot. 'It's nothing, sir,' he said. 'I think this Borrible is a trifle demented, sir, after losing all his friends in such a horrible manner. He probably hasn't eaten for days, either. Borribles can't go without food for long, sir.'

The DAC shot a double cuff of brilliant white sea-island cotton and looked at his watch. 'Nor can I,' he said, 'or claret. Now, can we get a move on? I must say it would suit me to be able to make a nice clear report to the PM as soon as possible. Right, ten Borribles accounted for. Now, about the horse? Isn't the horse important?'

Blume cocked his head to one side. 'Very important, sir, but that was cleared up ages ago,' he explained. 'We are confident that the horse was not brought here from the slaughterhouse. Most of the animals escaped up to Hampstead Heath, sir, though there were some reports of cows and horses as far off as Potter's Bar. In any event they've all been rounded up long since and taken back to the abattoir. And that's it. All been slaughtered sir, and the Borribles' horse was certainly among them. They've lost their mascot for good and the Southfields murders are cleared up once and for all.'

'Excellent,' said the DAC. 'Pity about the horse, but there you are. Every cat must have its catsmeat. It's one of the paradoxes of responsibility: we sometimes have to be cruel to be kind. *Noblesse oblige* and all that, what?'

'Yessir,' said Blume, and he stood on tiptoe once or twice.

The DAC studied Knocker again. 'Well,' he said at last, 'so he seems to be the only survivor. In that case, Blume, see that he is taken off to SBG HQ and interrogated in the usual way, then clip his ears and see that he is put into care. When he's old enough it'll be prison.'

'Yessir, right away, sir.'

'And as far as the media are concerned I expect some pretty nifty footwork there, Blume. There'd be a panic if people knew how many Borribles there really are and what they get up to. The PM is most insistent that this business be kept under wraps, Blume. The story to give out, and make sure you understand this – and the men – is that a bunch of skinhead hooligans, or punks or whatever they call themselves nowadays, got down here and had a pitched battle with an equal number of glue-sniffers. Somethin' like that. Do not breathe a single word of Borribles. Remember, my dear Blume, the best lies are so seemingly reasonable that it would be a gross error of judgement not to believe them. It upsets people to hear things they don't understand. As far as the hoi polloi are concerned Borribles belong in the realm of hobbits, boy-wizards and bunnies, and they must stay there. They must never be believed in.'

Blume made a note on his clipboard. 'I never believed in 'em, sir,' he said. 'My dad used to knock me about the head if I even mentioned Borribles.'

The DAC touched a loose stone with his highly polished shoe. 'Quite,' he said. 'Furthermore I shall be makin' a long statement about Sussworth and Hanks. You know the kind of thing: how proud Sussworth would have been, his life's ambition realized in his finest hour, so few for so many, dyin' valiantly under the streets of London in a successful bid to keep order on those streets, backbone of the nation, an example to us all . . . all that, eh?'

Officer Blume smiled blankly. He looked puzzled and the DAC moved closer to him and lowered his voice.

'Don't look so miffed, Blume. You ought to know that it is always safer to praise a dead fool than pay heed to a live one.' The DAC chuckled loudly at his own wit, twirled his umbrella yet again and winked at Knocker. 'You Borribles aren't the only chaps with proverbs, you know,' he said, and chuckled again before going on.

'You see, Blume, the more we praise Sussworth and Hanks the more we praise ourselves. So the inspector must have a George Medal and an obit in *The Times*, and Hanks will receive a special mention in dispatches and a military funeral on a gun carriage, no expense spared. All nice and tidy, just a secret little report between me and the PM. And of course, later on, it will become exquisitely obvious to the Cabinet that I chose the right men for the job for the simple reason that they were willing to die in the line of duty, and because I manifested such acumen I shall at last receive my knighthood. I was the right man in the right place sayin' the right thing, Blume.'

Blume sniffed and took notes. He looked peeved as well as puzzled now and the DAC noticed it. He laid his hand gently on the constable's elbow.

'My dear Blume,' he said, 'these dicta do not only apply to me but to men of your rank too. You also are in the right place at the right time. As you must know I need a new commander of the SBG and he has already been chosen; Superintendent Birdlime is on his way here at this very moment to take charge of the men. But I know he will need an assistant and I have no doubt that he will take my advice in this matter, especially when I tell him I think I have the very man for the job: a man of energetic discretion. Yes, Blume, you. No, don't try to thank me. I know you will be first class in the position. We have been groomin' you for stardom, you know. It's the first step on the ladder.'

Officer Blume blushed and grew by at least two inches. He looked proudly at the four policemen who still guarded Knocker. 'Oh thank you, sir,' he said. 'Oh thank you.'

'Yes,' said the DAC, 'of course. However, I have to point out that things are goin' to change. Birdlime is a new broom and he must sweep clean. Sussworth was a wasteful man and he spent much too much money on these Borrible operations and you know what the PM is like about money. At any rate, now that we have disposed of the Borrible ringleaders we shall have to make economies; that's your job Blume, and Birdlime's. Understand that. There will be fewer men, fewer patrols, fewer vans. We need to pull our horns in a bit.'

Blume was still beaming. 'That's no problem, sir. I promise you. We've seen the back of any real Borrible trouble, I'm sure of it.'

The DAC nodded and looked content. 'I knew I could count on you, Blume, I knew I could.' His eyes fell on Knocker again. He raised his umbrella and pointed at the four guards. 'Take the prisoner away, you chaps, and be careful with him. I need to show this one to the minister. Whitehall doesn't mind catastrophe and disaster, Blume, as long as there are bodies and prisoners to see at the end of the day. It teaches the nation that calamities are really blessin's in disguise because we get somethin' out of them, even if that somethin' is nothin' more than a self-administered punch on the nose. There! So don't let this urchin escape; he's very important. Now, I'm off to inspect the rest of the corpses, so follow me.' And with another jaunty twirl of his umbrella the DAC walked towards the control cabin, stepping gracefully over the railway lines as he went, Officer Blume at his elbow. On his face was an expression of complete satisfaction; he looked supremely happy.

He might not have felt quite so satisfied with himself had he bothered to observe Knocker being escorted away by the four guards. The Borrible's face also carried a smile of delight and his step had a joyful spring to it. Knocker's heart no longer felt small and shrivelled; on the contrary it was growing larger and larger with happiness at every moment. His plan had worked better than he could have imagined in his wildest dreams. No Sussworth, no Hanks and a smaller SBG; above all an SBG that believed that the Adventurers and Sam were dead when in fact they were alive and safe. Knocker could hardly believe it. He was so happy. His soul soared and he held his head high, and though weary his demeanour did not show it. Indeed he marched forward eagerly, so eagerly that the four policemen with him had to hurry in order to keep pace. On he went, past the spot where Sussworth and Hanks lay under a tarpaulin, one charred boot protruding, and then further, along the tunnel towards Swiss Cottage, until at last he was led up on to the platform and into the beginning of his dreadful captivity – captivity from which only death could free him – and yet not once did his feet stumble, and not once did his determination falter. Knocker knew he had won and he knew too that his friends, the Borribles who loved him, would be free and alive for ever and ever.

14

At about nine in the evening of the third night after Knocker's capture Orococco rolled over in the dark. '"Nothing," according to the proverb,' he said, '"is nowhere near as good as a feast."' He was right. The surviving Borribles were now very weak with hunger and knew that they would have to make a move soon otherwise they would become too ill to continue their journey. And their move, when they made it, would have to be one that was both cautious and quiet. Consequently, to begin with, from the very bottom of the wall they had built, they silently extracted one brick and through the hole they listened for the sounds of men or trains. They heard nothing.

After waiting patiently for a further hour or so, Orococco, who said he was the fastest and the blackest Borrible there, levered some more bricks from the wall and elected to slip out and see the lie of the land. In another hour he returned. It was night, he said, the trains had stopped running and all signs of the battle had been removed. It was time to go.

Even though the Borribles were faint from lack of food and fresh air it did not take them long to demolish the rest of the wall they had built. Sydney led Sam through to the dust of the disused tunnel and her companions followed. Once outside they went straight to the tap and filled an old bucket with water, allowing the horse to drink copiously so that it could both quench its thirst and ward off the pangs of hunger. For the same reasons the Borribles drank deeply themselves, and as soon as they were ready they set out to rejoin the line that would lead them north-westwards: Finchley Road, West Hampstead, Kilburn, Willesden Green, Dollis Hill and, at the very end of the journey, Neasden.

It was not a difficult march, no more than four or five miles to the final destination, and fortunately for the Adventurers, they had all night to get there. 'Just as well,' said Torreycanyon. 'I'm so weak I couldn't run if the whole of the SBG was right behind me.'

Along the empty railway lines and through the deserted stations the eight friends stumbled, creeping forward painfully, every step an effort of will with no energy left for speech. Orococco scouted ahead and Twilight brought up the rear, but they encountered no dangers and fell into no traps. Thanks to Knocker the SBG was certain that the Adventurers and their horse had perished. As far as the police were concerned the Borrible menace was over.

So it was that the fugitives met no enemies and somewhere, before dawn, the narrow tunnel rose to the surface of the city and the Borribles found themselves at last in the open. Instead of the deep close gloom and used-up air of underground there was now the high cathedral darkness of the London night and the soft touch of fresh dampness on the face. Occasionally there was the odd break in the cloud and the silver edge of the moon would gleam bright like a blade for a second, disappear, and then gleam again. Sam pricked up his ears with pleasure, lightened his step and gave a neigh of contentment. He also seemed to know that the end of the long, long journey was close at hand.

'Yes, Sam,' said Sydney when they'd marched a little further. 'Only a little way to go.' And she took the head of the column with Sam beside her, needing neither light nor map to find her road because this was her manor and it was only right that she should go in front.

And on she led until the Adventurers stalked through Neasden station itself, and all the streets and alleys of London lay quiet on every side and a great feeling of achievement came over the Borribles, just for being in that place after everything they'd been through, although nothing was special in the look of it.

'It's just Neasden,' said Sydney, stopping for a moment in the middle of the track. 'It's just like anywhere else, but I love it and I've just the spot for Sam . . . and there'll be some grub there too. Only another half mile.'

Sydney sounded cheerful now and her voice urged her companions to one last effort. It was still dark between the rooftops and the clouds, but high up on the eastern fringes of the sky the stars had faded, and there was a touch of pearl-grey light, growing stronger.

Sydney kept going and took the Adventurers as far as the London

Transport railway works which lie north of the main line, but her destination was not in that direction and instead she headed south, into a part of the city that is white and unmarked on the map, an area unknown and unexplored by normal citizens.

The Borribles did not hesitate to follow. They trusted the Neasden girl and they were well aware that she knew what she was doing. With a sure step she led the horse down a sloping path, through some scrubby grass, and up to an old platelayers' shed built from solid wooden boards. There, out of sight of the track, the runaways lowered themselves to the ground and, side by side, rested their backs against the rough planks of the abandoned hut. 'Wait here,' said Sydney. 'Rest but don't sleep.'

Slowly the day came. A train, the first of that early morning, rushed past as if in a panic to rediscover the long musty tunnels below the earth. The Borribles, only half awake, watched as the weak light grew stronger and stole inch by inch over this sequestered part of their planet. It was such a strange place to have found: so wide, so empty, amputated from the rest of the world, unseen and unimagined.

It was an area that looked like it had been built in fits and starts and then forgotten. A few buildings stood forlorn and half finished, windowless and abandoned, caves for the wind to whistle in, bounded in the east by a sweep of the North Circular Road and to the south and west by the River Brent and Tokyngton Recreation Ground. To the right it was bisected by the Marylebone Railway, and to the left it was divided by a stretch of dull water, a feeder arm supplying the Grand Union Canal; because that canal had journeyed all these miles too, leaving the River Thames at Limehouse Basin and circling north to join it again at Brentford. This is where Sydney had wanted to come, and this is where Sam would be safe; it was perfect, she'd said.

The daylight grew even stronger. About fifty yards away from the platelayers' shed stood an old man dressed in a faded blue anorak, Brent Council overalls and rolled-over wellies. Beside him stood Sam and Sydney. Sam was eating something from the old man's hand. Beyond the man were ten more horses and a score of donkeys grazing on the wild grasses and thistles that grew there. Further back were some dogs and goats, the dogs sleeping.

The wet clouds peeled backwards and showed another layer of sky. The Borribles shivered. In the distance, perhaps a mile away on the other side of this wedge of land, they could see where the ranks of streets and houses took up their march again. Between those streets and the platelayers' hut lay the bleak depots and the piles of equipment that belonged to the council road-men: hoppers for loading grit, rusty rubbish skips and big yellow machines for digging holes and moving earth. From all sides came the roar of motor traffic, grinding to work. From above came the screaming and whining of jet engines as the fat airliners lowered themselves into Heathrow Airport. London was starting a new day.

The man turned and went further into the wasteland, threading his way through his horses and goats and donkeys and dogs. Sydney beckoned to the Borribles, then she followed the man and Sam followed her. The Borribles groaned, hauled themselves to their feet and made themselves go forward, but their journey was a short one. After walking for no more than two or three hundred yards they found themselves outside a long low shed made from corrugated asbestos. Its doors were missing and had been replaced by hanging sacks tied together. There was a bench on the southern side of the shed and some of the Adventurers sat on it while the remainder threw themselves full-length on the ground, unable to take another step. It did not matter too much; they were in a kind of hollow and felt safe. No building overlooked them, no one could see them from road or railway line.

A moment or two after their arrival Sydney emerged from the shed with half a sack of horse feed on her shoulder and poured it on to the ground. Sam began to eat. From inside the hut came the sound of a pan hitting the cooker and then the smell of bacon and bread frying. Sydney disappeared again and in a little while came back, this time bearing a piece of wood sawn from a plank; on the wood she bore eight old bean cans, each one full of steaming tea, and she handed them round.

The hot tea warmed the Adventurers. Sydney sipped from her tin and looked at her friends. Their faces were so begrimed with dirt and oil that it was impossible to see their tiredness, but she could sense it; their movements were rheumatic, no words were spoken, there was no backchat. Sydney stared at the cuts and bruises on the back of her hands; she looked at what remained of her clothing, torn and frayed and smeared with filth.

'He's called Mad Mick,' she said to the others and squatted on the ground, watching Sam eat and stroking his head every now and then, 'and this place is called Mad Mick's; but he ain't mad, not a bit of it. He just likes looking after old horses and donkeys and such. He saves them from the knacker's yard. People bring him food and things he needs, sometimes they throw it over the walls down there. That's how we can help while we stay here, going round the walls picking stuff up. The council know he's here but there's so much space . . .'

Mad Mick shuffled from his shed at this point bearing huge peanut butter sandwiches. 'Bacon's cooking,' he said and went away.

The Borribles fell upon the food like savages, eating and drinking in great gulps. While they ate Sydney talked. It was as though she had to explain everything after what it had cost to get there.

'He's been here years,' she said with her mouth full, 'but nobody cares. He hands out food to us when we're short and when he's short we go and nick some for him.'

'He don't say a lot,' said Torreycanyon.

'He don't need to. He talks to the animals all the time. Still, he told me you could stay here as long as you like, until you've completely recovered and got some really good grub down you.'

'I don't see any markets or shops,' said Torreycanyon. 'We'll need grub all right.'

Sydney waved an arm. 'Willesden and Stonebridge are over there,' she said, 'and Neasden, where I live, over there. I can come here all the time and see Sam, it's no distance.'

As she said this Mad Mick came from his hut with more sandwiches and distributed them, nodding all the while but saying nothing.

'When we're all rested up,' said Stonks, 'and before we leave we ought to make sure Mad Mick has enough grub to last him a twelvemonth. It looks really safe here.'

'Don't talk about leaving yet, man,' said Orococco. 'I'm tired and my legs are aching.'

'I'm not talking about going,' said Chalotte suddenly, broaching the subject that everyone had been thinking of but had not mentioned. 'I'm going to wait for Knocker.'

Stonks took a breath that reached right down to the bottom of his guts. 'Supposing he don't show up?' he said. 'What then?'

'He'll be here,' said Chalotte. 'It'll take more than Sussworth to catch him.'

Stonks was sitting on the bench and he gazed at the ground between his feet, staring past the bean tin he held in both hands. 'You know,' he said, 'when I talked to him the last time it sounded to me like he didn't think he was coming back; like he had a plan . . . like he was going to do for Sussworth but like he might get done himself into the bargain.'

Twilight finished the dregs of his tea and spat a leaf out from between his teeth. 'You talked to him, Chalotte, through the hole in the wall. What did he tell you?'

Chalotte looked behind her and watched the horses as they shook their heads and flicked their graceful tails. They were so beautiful, contrasting strangely with their bleak surroundings, and Sam, his soft brown coat now clean of every trace of Knibbsie's dye and Sydney's polish, was beautiful too. It had been right to bring him here, a good thing for Borribles to have done, worth all the struggle and sacrifice.

Chalotte sniffed. Sam had finished his feed and was moving easily to join the other horses browsing on the rough grass which grew in clumps by the side of a square of tarmac that had once been the floor of a building. The horse was happy now, and safe for ever. He had come home and found friends. Chalotte looked back at Twilight and answered his question: 'He said that there was only one way for him to convince Sussworth that we were all dead. Sussworth had to believe that those dwarf bodies were us, and Knocker reckoned he could do it by leaving Napoleon's body for the Woollies to find and then letting them see him and chase him through the tunnels. "Eight plus two makes ten," he said.'

'It wasn't a bad plan,' said Bingo.

'Suppose he let himself be captured on purpose,' said Vulge, 'so he could be "forced" into telling Sussworth a lie at the same time as making him think it was the truth.'

'He must 'ave,' said Bingo, 'otherwise how did we get away so easily, eh?'

'That must be it,' agreed Twilight. 'The SBG knew we had to come out of the Underground somewhere but we didn't see sight nor sound of 'em. Not one van, not one uniform, not one siren.'

There was silence for a while as everyone thought about what Twilight had said.

Torreycanyon scratched his head. 'What can we do?' he asked. 'We got Sam here all right, we won the battle, but we lost two of the best, two of the very, very best. What can we do?'

Chalotte rubbed her red eyes and got to her feet. She shook her dirty hair free.

'Knocker said we had to get back to our own boroughs – he said it would be easy without the horse – back to being ordinary Borribles. He said we must tell the story of our Adventure, all of it, just as it happened, whenever and wherever, to normal kids as well as Borribles. Look for people like Scooter, he said.'

'Bloody Ninch,' said Orococco.

'We had to stop Sussworth turning Sam into catsmeat, whatever else we did,' Chalotte went on. 'Sam musn't end up as cans on shelves in supermarkets.'

'What else did he say?' asked Stonks.

'He said just to carry on, sharing out what we nick, keeping on running and hiding . . . Don't be bullied. Stay away from work and money, he said, they're the killers for Borribles. Be Borrible and live for ever.'

'We've seen some things,' said Sydney, and she glanced round her friends and they nodded.

Chalotte took a step forward and stretched her arms above her head and looked out across London, many square miles of it visible now where the rain clouds had risen, and the old grey daylight was diffused like silver over a million rooftops, picking out every tile and slate, every brick and chimney. She wiped her eyes clear, a new toughness shining through the grime on her face.

'Knocker said we had to put all this behind us and make a fresh start. Put the grief away, he said, and remember only the good things; and the best things were to enjoy being here, enjoy being alive, enjoy being Borrible.'

Stonks got to his feet and came to stand by Chalotte's side. The others stood also and gathered together in a group around the girl from Whitechapel. They gazed towards Sam and the other horses and beyond them to the furthest rim of the city, right to the edge where it became blue and indistinct.

Stonks put an arm across Chalotte's shoulders. 'Did he say what he'd do if he got caught?' he asked, and his voice broke and he lowered his head and stabbed the ground with his toe.

'Yes,' she answered. 'He said we weren't to go looking for him. If he got away he would find us . . . and if he got caught he . . . There was something he was going to do.'

'Do?' said Vulge. 'Like what?'

'He said he was going to tell our story on the other side; it was the only thing left for him to do. Tell the story before being a Borrible faded completely from his mind . . . You know, when they make him work.'

'Sod it,' said Orococco.

Chalotte shook herself free from Stonks's arm and took a couple of steps away from the group and wept alone for a minute or two; then she swallowed big gulps of air in an attempt to stop the sobs coming. There was so much more she wanted to say.

The Adventurers did not move but stood each with his own tears facing London. The clouds were less dark now and a rough wind was beginning to tear them apart, slashing at them and laying bare the white light beyond, scouring deep tracks of fresh colour across the sky. The air was still damp and heavy but nowhere was it raining on the city, and there was the tiniest patch of deep blue out over the dullness above the River Thames.

'He really was the best of Borribles, that Knocker,' said Sydney. She shook her head furiously to clear her sight. 'He saved Sam and got him here. He was the best of all Borribles.'

Chalotte placed her hands on her hips and slowly turned to face her friends, weary and bedraggled as they stood in that sad scattering by Mad Mick's hut on the wasteland of Neasden. Her eyes were dry at last and alight with a strange and powerful smile.

'Not *was*, Sydney,' she said. '*Is*. Remember that.' She raised a hand and without looking she pointed behind her towards the great ugly mess of London. 'Knocker is,' she said. 'Knocker is.'

Printed in Great Britain
by Amazon

54185019R00435